DALTON AND THE SUNDOWN KID

When Dalton rides into Lonetree looking for work, he finds a town crippled by the local outlaw — the Sundown Kid. Tasked with resolving the Kid's latest kidnapping, Dalton must deliver a ransom to the bandit to secure the safe return of young Sera Culver. However, before he reaches the rendezvous point, the ransom is stolen. Then a fearsome shootout leaves him stranded in the wilderness . . . With the fate of a woman at stake, can Dalton fight the good fight and prevail?

ED LAW

DALTON AND THE SUNDOWN KID

Complete and Unabridged

LINFORD
Leicester

First published in Great Britain in 2014 by
Robert Hale Limited
London

First Linford Edition
published 2015
by arrangement with
Robert Hale Limited
London

A catalogue record for this book is available
from the British Library.

ISBN 978–1–4448–2536–7

Published by
F. A. Thorpe (Publishing)
Anstey, Leicestershire

Set by Words & Graphics Ltd.
Anstey, Leicestershire
Printed and bound in Great Britain by
T. J. International Ltd., Padstow, Cornwall

This book is printed on acid-free paper

1

Beyond the rise, a tendril of smoke was spiralling up into the sky.

Dalton reckoned the town of Lonetree was still an hour downriver and so he rubbed his right leg as he prepared to move quickly. The action eased the tension in a leg he'd broken last month.

The limb was splinted, which created its own problems by forcing him to ride stiffly. When he'd massaged the muscles back into life, he rode at a brisk trot and, after cresting the rise, his worst fears materialized.

Midway between the summit of the rise and Black Creek, a covered wagon lay on its side. Scuff marks on the ground suggested it had rolled too quickly down the slope and toppled, although the smouldering canvas hinted at a more sinister reason for its demise.

The only movement nearby came

from a horse mooching upriver, but as he saw nothing to concern him, he rode openly down the rise and then dismounted.

He stood on his good leg and rocked his splinted leg back and forth, easing the stiffness before he moved on. Although using a hobbling gait was quicker, he usually forced himself to walk as normally as he could and so it took him a minute to walk around the scene.

When he peered inside, nobody was there. The smoke had almost died out suggesting his first impression may have been wrong and this had been an accident after all.

He stood back with an idea taking shape that, after he'd spun the wheels and confirmed they were intact, fully grabbed his attention.

Aside from a broken bow, the wagon was usable, even if he was unsure how he could use it. But he reckoned a man who was looking for work but who had limited mobility might improve his chances if he had a small wagon.

He doubted that on his own he'd normally be able to right it, but the slope gave him a course of action and so he stood at the back and experimentally shoved the base. As it had come to rest in a precarious position, using only one hand he was able to gently rock the wagon.

He put his other hand to the task. He rocked it more strongly until the slope took control of the wagon's motion and let it tip over on to its wheels.

The wagon continued tipping until it stood at an angle looking as if it'd tumble down to the creek, but then it rocked back on to its wheels and shuddered to a halt.

Dalton patted the side and headed around to the front to examine the tongue while he put his mind to the problem of how he could fashion a collar and harness.

'You should have planned this better,' a man said behind him, making Dalton turn.

While he'd been preoccupied, three riders had crested the rise. One man had moved ahead of the others and was considering Dalton sceptically.

'I couldn't plan anything,' Dalton said lightly. 'My name's Dalton and I'm heading to Lonetree. I never expected to come across this.'

'So whose wagon is it?' the man asked after revealing he was Remington Forsyth and his companions were the Broughton brothers, Lawrence and Hamilton. 'Where's the owner gone? What are you — ?'

'I told you: I saw smoke and so I investigated.'

Remington dismissed Dalton's protestations of innocence with a sorry shake of the head before turning to the other two men.

'I haven't got the time to listen to stories. Find out what he was really doing while I head inland.'

As Remington moved off at a gallop, Dalton returned to checking out his lucky find, but following Remington's

4

orders, Lawrence positioned himself between Dalton and the creek while Hamilton rode around the wagon.

With these men being suspicious of his actions, Dalton moved casually towards his horse, but this encouraged the brothers to dismount, ensuring that no matter which way he turned one of them could block him.

'I told you the truth,' Dalton said, backing away while raising his hands. 'I don't want no trouble.'

His movement made Lawrence glance at Dalton's leg for the first time and note the ponderous way he walked. A glimmer of doubt, presumably about Dalton's actions, flashed in his eyes, but it came too late to stop Hamilton from moving in.

Hamilton tried to grab him from behind, but before he could lay a hand on him, Dalton pivoted on his good leg. He used his momentum to slap a straight-armed blow using the flat of his hand against his opponent's cheek, sending him reeling away.

Then he turned to confront Lawrence, but while he'd been tussling, this man had moved out of view. Dalton struggled to turn and seek him out.

So he was looking at Hamilton when a shadow moved on the ground and alerted him a moment before Lawrence leapt out from behind the wagon. He caught Dalton around the shoulders and knocked him over on to his chest.

Quick blows rained down on his back and sides. Then Hamilton joined his brother and knelt on the small of Dalton's back, pinning him to the ground.

It had been a while since Dalton had broken his leg and so jolts no longer pained him, but he still had only limited strength in the leg and so he floundered. After struggling to raise himself with his good leg, he went limp, hoping to make his attackers underestimate him.

This failed as Lawrence dragged his arms behind his back and Hamilton drew him up to a standing position. Dalton didn't fight back, maintaining the subterfuge of being weak.

'We want the truth,' Hamilton said. 'What happened here?'

'I don't know,' Dalton said, with as much calmness as he could muster. 'I was heading to Lonetree when I found this wagon lying on its side.'

Hamilton looked at Lawrence, who snorted.

'I don't believe him,' he said. 'He hasn't got a leg to stand on.'

Both his opponents sniggered and so Dalton uttered a rueful laugh, but that made Hamilton sneer.

'You reckon stealing is funny, do you?' he muttered.

'I only righted it. Without me doing so, it'd have probably rolled down into the water and been lost.'

Hamilton raised an eyebrow, as if something Dalton had said had interested him and he glanced at Lawrence. They both chuckled, confirming they were of the same mind. They made Dalton struggle, but he couldn't dislodge his captors.

He was bent double, turned towards the wagon, and then they ran him towards it. At the last moment he averted his face, but his right cheek and shoulder still mashed into the side of the wagon, making it creak.

He tried to shake off the blow, but that had the unfortunate effect of making him raise his forehead as he was dashed against the side for a second time. The blow cracked a plank and the noise reverberated in Dalton's head as his vision dimmed and his limbs went limp.

He slumped in his captors' grip and, when they dashed him against the side for a third time, it was as if the collision had happened to someone else.

They continued manhandling him roughly; Dalton struggled to focus on what their intentions were as they walked him on and dragged him off the ground while holding only his arms.

He must have blacked out as it came as a shock when he found he was no longer being held. He was lying on his chest with rough wood beneath him and so he flexed his muscles as he gathered his strength before fighting back.

A thud sounded, adding urgency to his need to move. He sat up and found he'd been placed in the wagon. Through the burnt-away section of canvas, the sky was moving and, as he was being jiggled, he struggled to sit upright.

He presumed he was being taken somewhere, but when he shuffled round to face the front, nobody was on the seat. The creek was ahead. And it was getting closer at an alarming rate.

He dragged himself towards the seat, by which time he'd confirmed the men had turned the wagon to the creek and shoved it on its way. The wheels were protesting loudly as they trundled over every rock in their path.

Each obstacle jolted Dalton up into the air making it clear he wouldn't be able to climb on to the seat. So he grabbed the side as he sought to leave by the quickest way possible.

From the corner of his eye he saw only the roiling water as he pulled himself up to the sideboard. Then a crunch sounded, the noise as loud as what Dalton would expect from the wagon hitting the ground rather than water.

He was torn away from the side and, unable to control his motion, he rolled head over heels to the front of the wagon where he tipped over the seat and hit the water flat on his back.

Within moments the creek swallowed him up and, as he'd not had enough time to gather his breath, he waved his arms frantically as he sought to reach the surface.

The strong current tore at him, tipping him over and drawing him along, but to his relief in the water he was less incapacitated than on land and he was able to use both legs.

Two kicks brought him to the surface where he faced the river-bank that seemed to be surging along only a body's length from his hands.

The cold water revived his senses as he kicked towards the bank, but he didn't move any closer and, after another three kicks, he had to admit the bank might as well be a mile away.

Worse, the current dragged him down and he had to use all his energy to thrust his head back above water. While he could still breathe, he gathered a lungful of air and, to rest his previously injured leg, he swam using only his arms as he sought to propel himself to the bank.

He didn't feel he was making any progress, but then darkness swept over him a moment before a prominent length of bank that jutted into the creek looked above him. The current sought to swirl him past the headland, but Dalton reckoned this was his best chance and he dove down through the current.

He managed one forward stroke using his arms. Then his grasping hands clawed against the muddy ground beneath the water.

When he came up, he was pressed flat against the slick bank while the water sluiced over him, threatening to drag him away. Dalton scrambled a hand against the ground and found purchase.

Then he strained to raise his other hand up as far as he was able. His fingers clamped around rotting vegetation and when he tugged, he found enough resistance to let him claw his way higher.

It took him a minute to drag himself only a foot out of the water, but even as his strength gave out, his movements became easier as more of his body emerged from the fierce current. Inch by inch he drew himself on until his legs came free and he was able to flop down on his chest on the ground.

He looked up, seeing his tormentors cresting the rise. They had their backs to him and, to Dalton's relief, they didn't look back as they disappeared from view.

He confirmed he was several feet above water level while the wagon that had started his troubles was a dozen feet out into the creek. Then it slid beneath the surface with a sucking noise that sounded like a sigh.

When Dalton stood up and saw his horse had been run off, he sighed too.

*　*　*

Lights were illuminating the evening sky when Dalton first saw Lonetree. The sight didn't cheer him, though, as his tormentors had ridden this way.

Although the late afternoon sun had dried his clothes, the last few hours had been annoying. He'd not had to walk for any distance on his injured leg before and so it had taken him three hours to catch his spooked horse.

The town overlooked Black Creek and nestled at the base of a hill on which stood a large and solitary dead oak. Dalton rode down the hill and, after passing a saloon, he veered towards a stable, but he stopped when he saw the sign above the door that showed that it was owned by the Broughton brothers.

He was too tired for a confrontation and so he searched for a law office instead, which he located two buildings down from the stable. When he headed into the office, the room was quiet.

The town marshal, Virgil Greeley, sat behind his desk facing the door with his feet up, his arms folded and his hat drawn down over his eyes.

'What do you want?' Greeley asked with bored indifference without raising his hat.

'I'm here to report a crime,' Dalton said.

This declaration did make Greeley raise his hat. He was portly with an unkempt beard that sparsely covered his sagging jowls, but his eyes were lively.

'Now that sure is interesting. What crime are you talking about?'

His raised voice made a man look in

from an adjoining office. For several seconds he and Dalton stared at each other in surprise until with a narrow-eyed glare Dalton acknowledged they'd met upriver.

'I reckon you already know.' Dalton pointed at the newcomer. 'That man Remington told the Broughton brothers to question me, but they attacked me instead.'

While Remington came in and leaned against the wall to consider him, Greeley shook his head.

'Remington's my deputy.' He raised an eyebrow. 'So do you want to take back that accusation or shall I throw you in a cell?'

2

'I'm not accusing Remington,' Dalton said, meeting Greeley's eye. 'I am accusing the Broughton brothers.'

Remington walked across the law office to stand before Dalton.

'You were acting suspiciously and so I left them to question you rigorously,' he said. 'When they returned to town, they told me you'd done nothing wrong. That ought to end the matter.'

'It would, except they decided to have some fun by throwing me in the wagon and rolling it into the creek. I barely got out of the water alive.'

Remington winced, the brothers' actions clearly not being his intent, but he said nothing as he let Greeley adjudicate. The marshal considered Remington, which made his deputy gulp.

'See the brothers and sort this out,' Greeley said, standing up. 'The days when Lonetree tolerated the behaviour of men like Judah Sundown and the Broughton brothers have passed. Any deputy of mine must be seen to uphold the law, not excuse the men who break it.'

Remington was half the marshal's age and a head taller, and so the rebuke made him rock back and forth on his toes until, with an aggrieved grunt, he turned to the door.

'Obliged you believed me,' Dalton said when Remington had slammed the door shut.

'I didn't say that,' Greeley said as he came round his desk. 'That was between me and my deputy.'

'Either way I told the truth.' Dalton watched Greeley raise an eyebrow as if he expected him to say more, and so Dalton shrugged. 'I assume you know whose wagon it was.'

Greeley grunted, suggesting he had wanted to hear that response.

'I do.' He gestured at the door. 'You'll need somewhere to stay tonight. I'll show you to a decent place.'

Dalton didn't press for details and Greeley didn't provide any, but the marshal was as good as his word as the Culver Hotel's rooms were cheap and clean.

Before finding the wagon, Dalton had been undecided whether to cross Black Creek at Harmison's Ford or to move on to Wilson's Crossing. Either way, he had enough money to loiter on the east side of the water for several weeks, even if he couldn't find work.

When Dalton had eaten and rested up in his room, the lively sounds coming from the First Star saloon down the main drag encouraged him to put aside his anger. He stood at the window and, after watching Lonetree at night for half an hour, he saw no reason to change his plan.

Once he'd enjoyed a few nights in the saloon, he doubted he'd find work or anything to occupy his time in such a small settlement.

He was returning to his bed when the

hotel owner Marietta Culver knocked on his door. She was tall with a long neck and a penetrating gaze.

'Marshal Greeley told me,' she said, her voice authoritative but harsh with emotion, 'that you found my daughter Sera's wagon upriver.'

Dalton nodded and offered a smile. 'You don't look old enough to have a daughter.'

'I'm not in the mood for compliments and before you ask, I've yet to be married.'

She gave him a stern look, suggesting she often had to explain this matter and so Dalton returned a concerned expression.

'I hope Sera's fine.'

Marietta frowned, but when he levered himself into a chair awkwardly, she considered his leg. Then, using matter-of-fact movements, she examined his splints before suggesting he should raise his leg. She sat on another chair facing him.

'Nobody has seen her since she left

19

town this morning,' she said, while moving buckles and tightening straps. 'Did you see her?'

'I was heading downriver and I saw nobody.'

'I was told the wagon was on fire.'

She had been making the splints feel more comfortable, but while making her last comment she tugged a strap and so Dalton spoke lightly.

'It was a small fire, and it didn't look as if it had been lit with sinister intent.' He looked her in the eye until she nodded. 'And the fire meant the wagon couldn't have been abandoned for long. So she can't have strayed far.'

'Deputy Forsyth headed upriver and said he saw nobody.' She stopped work to consider. 'With you coming downriver, that means she went inland. I'll make sure tomorrow's search concentrates there.'

Her clipped tone said that despite her comment, she knew Sera could have gone in the only direction they hadn't mentioned.

He gestured at his leg. 'You know what you're doing.'

'I do.'

She leaned back and signalled that he should stand. To his delight, she'd made his splints more supportive than they'd ever been.

'You do.' He smiled, although she didn't return it.

She bustled to the door, but when she'd opened it, she stopped and then turned back.

'I get the impression you know what you're doing too.'

'I'm looking for work, if that's what you mean.' Dalton stood tall, appearing as presentable as he could. 'And I can turn my hand to most things.'

'Would that include finding a missing person?'

'I've never done anything like that before, but I'd like to help in any way I can.'

'I appreciate your honesty, and I was impressed that your summary conveyed more information and concern than

Marshal Greeley managed. If I leave it to him to find Sera, I may never see her again.'

Dalton patted his leg. 'This constrains what I can do.'

'On the other hand, it'll ensure you're thorough. I'll pay a dollar a day plus expenses and each evening I'll help you exercise your leg to aid your recovery. I intend to offer a reward for my daughter's safe return and so if you find her, I'll pay whatever you ask.'

'I accept.' He waited until she nodded and then raised a hand. 'But it sounds as if you expect this search will take a while. So tell me what I need to know.'

She gestured at the window, signifying the whole town.

'I'm a wealthy woman living in a small town with a daughter and no husband, so I wasn't surprised when I received an anonymous, threatening letter demanding money. I didn't let that change my behaviour, so when Sera wanted to go upriver to paint I let her. When she was late back, Deputy Forsyth recruited the Broughton — '

'They'd be the last men I'd turn to for help,' Dalton spluttered, unable to keep his silence.

She frowned. 'I agree, but Deputy Forsyth reckoned he could keep them in line and I trust him.'

Dalton didn't want to mention that the deputy had failed and, when footfalls sounded in the corridor, he provided an encouraging nod.

Deputy Forsyth arrived making Marietta smile for the first time that Dalton had seen. He and Marietta embraced before Marietta left, having promised to see Remington in her quarters when he'd finished speaking with Dalton.

'Did you sort out the Broughton brothers?' Dalton said when her footfalls reached the stairs.

'As best as I could. I need all the assistance I can get, so I can't refuse their help, but I'm sorry for what happened upriver.'

Remington raised an eyebrow and Dalton nodded, accepting his apology.

'I understand. We must all put aside our differences until Sera is safe.'

'And either way, I'm keen to resolve this problem quickly; once I've sorted out this mess Marietta and I are to be wed.'

'I was once a contented married man and so I'll do my best to ensure you're wed quickly.' Dalton gestured at the door. 'She's hired me to find Sera.'

Remington tipped back his hat in surprise.

'Then I hope you won't be employed for long, as I intend to find her before you can hobble out of this room.'

Dalton laughed. 'I hope you can.'

'In case I don't, remember this: despite what I told the brothers, they aren't the sort to listen to advice, so while you're looking for Sera, look out for them.'

★ ★ ★

It was mid-morning when Dalton rode out of town. Earlier, Remington had instructed him to search downriver, even though that might give Marietta the answer she didn't want, while he concentrated his search upriver.

As he rode, Dalton examined the creek for areas where a body might wash up. Remington wanted him to go to Harmison's Ford, as someone there might have seen a body floating by, but after thirty minutes his heart thudded with concern.

Ahead was a bridge that crossed a tributary at Morgan's Gap. The Broughton brothers were at the riverside. They were too far away for him to work out what they were doing, but their hunched postures suggested they were concerned.

He veered down to the water, but his worst fears didn't materialize as they had found a washed-up wagon, presumably the one they'd rolled into the creek the day before. It had become moored in shallow water and they were struggling to draw in a rope they'd wrapped around the anchor.

Their muddied forms suggested they'd been unsuccessful and so Dalton drew to a halt, anticipating entertainment.

His hopes were dashed when the wagon surged clear of the mud and rolled on to dry land. Then Lawrence looked into the wagon and summoned Hamilton's attention.

When Dalton had been bundled into the back, the wagon had been empty, and so he was surprised when they dragged a sack over the side. As they dropped the sack on the ground, he moved closer.

His approach attracted the men's attention. They swung round to face him, their quick reactions making them appear guilty even though Dalton had seen them discover the sack.

They advanced, drawing their guns, making Dalton raise a hand, but they ignored his friendly gesture and fired. The shots were high and intended to warn him off, but unlike yesterday,

Dalton didn't stay to explain himself and he tore the reins to the side and beat a hasty retreat back up the slope.

Two more gunshots hurried him on his way and both shots landed close enough for him to see dirt kick. When he looked over his shoulder, the brothers were gaining their horses.

Dalton didn't look back again as he moved up the rise. They could intercept him if he went for the bridge and so he turned back to town.

Five minutes passed before more high gunfire ripped out, this time accompanied by lively whoops as the brothers enjoyed the chase. When he looked back, his pursuers were cresting the rise, but they were now three hundred yards away.

Dalton concentrated on riding until he was halfway back to town, where irritation at the brothers' behaviour made him stop and then head for a tangle of boulders. Before he reached the rocks, he dismounted and sought refuge behind a mound.

He lay on his chest where he could see for a hundred yards ahead. The sloping terrain kept his pursuers out of sight, but they had been on his tail and so he expected them to appear at any moment.

After two minutes they hadn't arrived and so Dalton raised himself, wondering if they'd carried on to town. When he could see the creek, the two men were still not visible and so, feeling vulnerable, he moved out from the boulders just as he saw movement to his right.

He turned, seeing a shadow flitter on the ground from one of the men having taken a roundabout route to sneak up on him. Dalton had yet to see the other man and so, hobbling as quickly as he was able, he reached the boulder and pressed his back to the rock.

When he heard nothing, he swung round the boulder and met Lawrence edging forward with both hands raised ready to grab him. The two men stared at each other from only two feet apart.

Dalton got over his surprise first and he swung up his fist catching Lawrence with a backhanded blow beneath the chin that cracked his head back and sent him reeling into the boulder. Lawrence rebounded and walked into a punch to the stomach that bent him double before with his good leg, Dalton kicked his legs from under him.

'That's for knocking me into the wagon,' he muttered. He dragged Lawrence to his feet and, while he was still bent double, he turned him to the creek and threw him to the ground. 'And that's for rolling me into the water.'

Lawrence tumbled to the ground and rolled down a slope before he shuddered to a halt in a cloud of dust. He wasted no time in getting up on his haunches to face Dalton.

'You won't collect the reward,' Lawrence muttered.

'I'll get paid no matter who finds Sera.' Dalton watched Lawrence wince, confirming they hadn't been offered the same deal. 'What was in the sack you found?'

Dalton didn't expect an answer, but Lawrence shifted his weight and turned slightly away from him.

'We left it for Remington to examine.'

Dalton nodded, for the first time thinking that these men might have Sera's best interests in mind, even if it was only to claim the reward. But Lawrence used his momentary lapse in concentration to leap aside and roll out of sight.

Dalton backed away and his retreat had a second benefit when a shadow moved and alerted him to the fact that Hamilton had been sneaking up on him.

He hopped aside as Hamilton leapt from the boulder behind him, his action letting Hamilton crash down on his feet without touching him before pitching forward on to his knees. Dalton took advantage and delivered a swiping punch to the back of Hamilton's neck, sending him sprawling on to his chest.

Dalton planted his good foot on Hamilton's right shoulder blade, pinning him down. A moment later Lawrence arrived, his eager grin that anticipated Hamilton's success turning to a scowl when he saw that Dalton was in control.

'We're even now,' Dalton said. He waited, but neither man answered and so he pressed down, making Hamilton grunt. 'We both want Sera's safe return, so I suggest we spend our time finding her instead of feuding.'

Lawrence's right eye twitched, but Hamilton bleated a warning for him to comply, the ground masking his words.

'And I suggest,' Lawrence said, 'the moment we find her you leave town quickly.'

Reckoning this was the best reconciliation they could manage, Dalton raised his foot and Hamilton wasted no time in rolling away and getting up.

Hamilton joined Lawrence and the two men backed away. Dalton let them leave unchallenged while shaking his head in bemusement at their behaviour.

When he was sure they were leaving, he headed to his horse. He resumed his journey downriver except now, with the wagon having washed up, the thought of what else he might find filled him with dread.

★   ★   ★

'You were hungry,' Marietta said.

'It's been a long day,' Dalton said. He pushed his empty plate away and sat back from the table. 'But not a productive one.'

She nodded and drew up a chair to join him in the hotel dining room. She signified he should raise his leg so she could check his straps.

Dalton's journey to Harmison's Ford had been a fruitless one and the return trip had been tiring. He rested his leg on a spare chair and watched Marietta while she worked. Her worried expression confirmed that Sera hadn't been found yet.

32

Dalton searched for the right words to explain what he'd seen earlier, but Remington arrived and resolved his dilemma. He leaned against the doorframe with his expression stern.

'It's too dark to continue searching,' he said to Marietta, his sombre tone providing a summary of his progress and making Marietta lower her head.

'Have you talked with the Broughton brothers yet?' Dalton asked.

Remington headed across the room to face Dalton.

'They showed me the sack they'd found on the wagon, and it makes this situation even worse.'

'How?' Marietta asked with a gulp.

'Sera has been kidnapped,' Remington said, placing a hand on her shoulder. 'A ransom demand was in the sack. You must pay five thousand dollars before sundown tomorrow or Sera dies.'

3

The meeting had lasted for an hour, but so far nobody had offered any good ideas.

Marietta had gathered everyone involved in the search into the hotel dining room to debate what she should do the following day.

Marshal Greeley sat behind a table at the front of the room with Deputy Forsyth who had gone through the incident from the beginning. With the Broughton brothers sitting on one side of the room, Dalton had sat with Marietta on the other side.

Although the marshal's meticulous manner made Lawrence and Hamilton smirk at each other, neither man gave any outward recognition of the incident downriver. So Dalton hoped they'd honour their agreement.

The tales they and Deputy Forsyth

told were similar. They had visited several places without finding any clues as to where Sera had been taken and they had spoken with numerous people without gaining any information on who might have kidnapped her.

Unlike the others, Dalton welcomed hearing the slow relating of events as it filled in the details he'd missed, even if they didn't give him any ideas. Sundown was approaching when the marshal turned to him to explain what he'd discovered that day.

'Nothing,' Hamilton said before Dalton could reply, making Lawrence laugh, although they were silenced when Remington glared at them.

'That sums it up,' Dalton said levelly. 'I know nothing and I found out nothing.'

'Even so,' Greeley persisted, 'take me through what you — '

'We haven't got the time,' Dalton said. 'You have less than a day to find Sera and sitting around here talking won't find her.'

'I agree with Dalton,' Remington said, punching a fist into a palm with a resounding slap. 'We should back our best hunch.'

Greeley considered Remington with irritation.

'So,' Greeley said, sitting back in his chair, 'impress me with your hunch.'

Remington took a deep breath, although his uncertain gaze suggested he couldn't offer a viable course of action, but he didn't get to speak as a steady tapping started up.

The noise continued until everyone turned to Marietta, who was rapping a coin on her chair arm.

'I've heard enough,' she said. 'We won't sit around talking any more, but neither will we back any hunches. I'll pay the ransom.'

'But you can't,' Remington murmured, aghast. 'That'll take every cent you have.'

'The kidnappers are threatening to take every member of family I have.'

Remington opened and closed his

mouth, seemingly lost for words, leaving Marshal Greeley to speak up.

'My deputy's right. If you relent, the future will be bleak for anyone who has money.'

'Dealing with such problems,' Marietta said levelly, 'is your responsibility. As you've failed, I have to do what I feel is right. This discussion is over and we'll now decide how I can fulfil the kidnappers' demand.'

'They've specified the place and the procedure.' Greeley stood up and collected his notes into a pile. 'I suggest you make your own arrangements to comply with them.'

'I thought you'd help.'

'You thought wrong. I won't support a criminal act.' He turned to Remington. 'It's time for us to leave. We've neglected our other duties for too long.'

Remington stood up before with a visible wrench he appeared to register what he'd been ordered to do.

'I can't go,' he said. 'I have to help Marietta sort this out.'

'I can't accept a deputy who doesn't follow my orders.'

Remington glared at Greeley as he considered the obvious ultimatum. Dalton reckoned Remington's firm-set jaw meant he'd defy him, but Marietta spoke up first.

'Go with the marshal,' she said. 'If a lawman gets involved, the kidnappers will react badly.'

'You're right.' Remington sneered at Greeley. 'So I resign, which means I'm free to deal with this.'

Greeley accepted his decision without a flicker of concern. He tucked his notes under his arm and left the room, leaving Remington to gesture at the other men to join him.

While Remington conferred with the brothers, Dalton dallied to speak with Marietta.

'If it helps,' he said, 'I reckon Remington made the right choice.'

'In defying Greeley, yes,' Marietta said, 'but not in accepting assistance from Lawrence and Hamilton. Remington has known them for a long time and so he would never admit it, but he needs help to keep them in line. I'd like you to go with them and watch his back.'

'The brothers are sure to hate that.' Dalton winked. 'So I'd be delighted to go.'

★　★　★

It was dark when the covered wagon that would deliver the ransom was ready to roll out of town. They would use the dried-out and repaired wagon that had been dragged out of the water earlier.

The exchange of money for Marietta's daughter would take place on a ridge in High Pass.

The kidnappers had chosen this location well, as it was a day's journey away, forcing the group to ride for several hours that night before embarking on another long journey the following day to meet the sundown deadline.

The urgency of the situation made

everyone move quickly and without rancour. When Dalton offered to drive the wagon, nobody complained.

He took the wagon behind the hotel, after which Lawrence and Hamilton carried a large box outside and deposited it on the wagon. Dalton was surprised Marietta had raised the money so quickly and Remington was edgy, but with a shrug he appeared to dismiss the matter.

'I don't care about the money,' Marietta said, addressing the four men. 'Sera's life is all that matters. Promise me you'll take no risks.'

She waited until all four men had provided solemn pledges after which she asked them to bow their heads while she murmured a prayer. Then she dismissed them and in short order the men mounted up.

As Dalton moved off, Lawrence and Hamilton flanked the wagon while Remington stayed behind to speak with Marietta before he hurried on to join them. Then, at a steady mile-eating pace, they trundled into the darkness.

Remington rode ahead of the wagon, which was fine with Dalton, as he was unsure of the route. Lawrence and Hamilton dropped back to check nobody had followed them out of town, but after an hour they accepted they hadn't attracted any unwanted attention.

They rode for several more hours without incident until Remington called a halt.

Dalton judged it was about midnight and Remington chose a high point where they could see in all directions. The only shelter they could find from a brisk wind was in a hollow.

Remington didn't want to attract attention with a fire, even if they could find something to burn. So he and Dalton hunched up on one side of the hollow to take the first watch while Lawrence and Hamilton rested.

They aimed to swap watches in the middle of the night and move on at first light.

Despite the need to be vigilant, Dalton struggled to concentrate on the bleak, moonlit landscape and so before long he stood up to stretch his aching leg.

'How did you break your leg?' Remington asked.

'I'd always wondered whether falling fifty feet on to rocky ground would hurt.' Dalton smiled. 'So I tried it. And it did.'

'At least you now know,' Remington laughed before assuming a serious expression. 'It won't stop you taking a full part in tomorrow's exchange, will it?'

Dalton glanced at the Broughton brothers. They were awake and listening to their conversation while sporting smirks that suggested they were waiting for an opportunity to butt in and find fault with him.

'No. I'll do whatever you need me to.'

'That shouldn't be much other than to stay back and look out for deception. I'll complete the transfer.'

'After that, you can't return to your old job, so what will you do?'

'Being a deputy marshal was a temporary position. I only accepted it to prove to Marietta I could do more than tend bar. When we have Sera back, I'll work with Marietta to restore her . . . our fortunes.'

'I'm surprised she raised the money in a few hours.'

Remington frowned at Dalton's obvious attempt to dig for information, confirming that back in town he had been surprised too.

'That's not sinister. She's a wealthy woman.'

'It might not be sinister on her part, but the kidnappers gave her little time to pay up, so they must have known she had the funds available.'

Remington nodded slowly as if he'd not considered this possibility, his silence giving Lawrence a chance to speak up for the first time.

'If we're careful,' he said with a significant glance at the wagon and then his gun, 'you might not have to restore your fortunes.'

Remington pointed a firm finger at Lawrence.

'We promised Marietta we'd take no risks and I don't want to bring Sera back lying in that box.'

Lawrence sneered, but didn't reply. Hamilton stood and took a slow walk around the hollow.

'I know a better way to fill the box,' he said as he stopped behind Dalton, making him turn.

Hamilton's grin was bright in the low moonlight, alerting Dalton to what he intended to do and so he was on guard when Hamilton kicked out.

Dalton caught Hamilton's ankle while the rising boot was still six inches from his face and then twisted it while shoving it aside. His action made Hamilton stumble and, off-balance, he tumbled into the hollow.

Before he could get his wits about him, Dalton shuffled towards him. Then, using his good leg, he kicked off and leapt on Hamilton's back.

He settled his weight on his shoulders and shoved his face into the dirt. Then he looked for Lawrence, but Lawrence had raised his hands while backing away, although that was only because Remington had drawn a gun on him.

'I told you,' Remington muttered, 'I aim to complete this mission without mishaps. I don't want you two slugging it out with Dalton for the next day.'

'Then get rid of the problem,' Lawrence said, his demand making Hamilton stop struggling as he awaited a verdict that, if he could see Remington's stern expression, he would be able to guess.

'I would,' Remington said levelly, 'if I didn't need three men in case tomorrow doesn't go according to plan.'

'We three can deal with anything.'

'I meant that two men won't be enough.'

Lawrence drew in his breath sharply and the two men faced each other until Lawrence relented with a snorted laugh. When Remington glanced at Dalton, he clambered off Hamilton, who joined Lawrence without meeting his eye.

With there being nothing else to say

on the matter, they returned to their previous arrangement of Remington and Dalton sitting on one side of the hollow and the Broughton brothers sitting on the other.

Before long, the brothers dozed and so Dalton and Remington stayed quiet.

Dalton judged the passing of time by the moon's slow passage across the night sky and, when he reckoned half the night had gone, Remington woke up the others.

Nobody spoke as the brothers started their watch, giving Dalton hope that the disagreements had finally been resolved. Either way, he was so tired he went to sleep quickly.

Seemingly, only moments later Remington shook his shoulder. When he stirred and looked around, it was lighter.

'I could have done with a few more minutes,' Dalton said around a yawn before he noted Remington's irritated expression. 'What's wrong?'

'It's the Broughton brothers,' Remington said. 'They've gone. It seems my ultimatum was too . . . '

Remington trailed off and swung round to face the wagon, his concerned expression showing he'd had the same worrying thought that had just hit Dalton.

'No matter how heavily we slept,' Dalton said, as Remington hurried to the wagon and peered into the back, 'they still left quietly. Surely they couldn't have taken the ransom money.'

Remington's eyes narrowed as, with a gulp, he clambered into the wagon.

Dalton reached the back as Remington moved the lid from the box. The ease with which he shoved it aside showed it hadn't been secured well and when he slapped a hand to his brow, Dalton provided a sympathetic groan.

'They've stolen the ransom,' Remington murmured, 'and condemned Sera to death.'

4

'Marietta was worried about the brothers,' Dalton said, 'and she had good cause. You sided with me and they reacted badly.'

Remington nodded and kicked the box, making it tip over, and confirmed it was empty before he jumped down. He looked back towards Lonetree.

'I've known them for years. I gave them the benefit of the doubt and thought I could control them, but clearly I was wrong.'

'You made a mistake, but we can't afford to waste time.' Dalton slapped his arm to encourage him to think positively, but that proved to be the wrong thing to do as Remington bunched a fist. Then, with an angry oath he punched the wood beside Dalton's shoulder before storming away to stand hunched over.

This time Dalton let him calm down naturally.

After a while, his voice still strained, Remington said, 'Go back to town, find them and reclaim the ransom money, or meet the deadline?'

'The exchange is in twelve hours and we face a journey of ten hours, so that's not enough time to find the brothers and, if we go back to town, we'll miss the deadline. But meeting that deadline won't help Sera, so we need another option.'

By way of an explanation Dalton glanced at his gun, but Remington shook his head.

'We do what Marietta would want us to do, which doesn't involve ambushing the kidnappers and risking Sera's life. We meet the deadline and try to explain ourselves so we can buy us enough time to put this right.'

Dalton didn't agree with this plan, but as Remington was in charge, he provided a sharp nod and without further comment, headed to the wagon. Remington mounted up and so, as they had done the previous day, they rode on with Remington leading.

Remington sat in the saddle with his head lowered, clearly lost in thought. So Dalton used the journey to consider plans, but as he couldn't envisage the situation they'd face, he couldn't think of a course of action other than to follow Remington's lead.

At noon they reached the entrance to High Pass. An hour after that they climbed to higher ground, which they spent the rest of the afternoon traversing.

When the sun was approaching the distant horizon, Remington stopped and pointed out the ridge where the transfer would take place.

Even from several miles away, Dalton could see the kidnappers had chosen the location well. The ridge was a narrow passageway between two high points, with the steep sides comprised of loose rocks that would be difficult to climb.

The high point would let the kidnappers see for miles in all directions and ensure it would be hard to sneak up on them unobserved. So they rode openly, reaching the end of the ridge while the sun was still an outstretched hand's width above the horizon.

Both men dismounted and stood back to back to observe all directions from which they could be approached. Fifty yards to Dalton's left the rocky ground sloped away, while to his right an overhang provided cover for anyone who might be watching them.

In this exposed place, he and Remington would struggle to defend themselves and so, with no movement and no noise other than the breeze rustling by, time passed slowly.

'Have you known Marietta long?' Dalton asked after a while.

'I used to tend bar in the First Star and she often visited the owner, Edwidge Star. We got talking and things have gone well from there. I've grown to care for Sera too, which is important.'

Dalton rocked his head from side to side before he asked the question he couldn't help but wonder about.

'Who was Sera's father?'

Remington frowned. 'Marietta made it clear she won't answer that question. I suggest after we've got Sera back, you don't ask her either.'

Dalton nodded after which he was content to remain silent. The sun had grown large and red when Remington got his attention and pointed across the pass. On the high point opposite, people were making their way down towards the ridge.

Dalton counted six people. By the time they were the same distance from the ridge as he and Remington were, he discerned that one person was being secured by two others.

'We're facing five men,' Dalton said, edging closer to Remington.

'Which is too many if you're still thinking about trying something.' Remington gestured at the overhang. 'And others are sure to be hiding up there.'

'Someone could be, but I haven't seen anyone yet.' Dalton raised a hand when Remington started to retort. 'But you're in charge and if you want to argue this out with the kidnappers, that's what we'll do.'

'Obliged. We do nothing that'll jeopardize Sera's life.'

Remington moved away and Dalton fell in behind him. Loose stones covered the ridge ensuring that Dalton found the going slow. So when Remington stopped a third of the way across the ridge he was well ahead of him.

Only then did the people on the opposite side move towards them. In keeping with Dalton's earlier observation, three men walked at the front while the other two walked behind, each man holding the arms of what he could now see was a young woman.

As Remington had done, the lead group stopped a third of a way on to the ridge, arriving at that point as Dalton reached Remington. This left them fifty yards apart where they stood watching each other.

'Do you recognize them?' Dalton asked.

When Remington didn't reply immediately, he repeated his question and that made Remington shake himself before with a gruff voice he replied.

'The lead man is Judah Sundown. He used to sort out trouble in the First Star.'

'And the others?'

'I don't recognize them, but before Edwidge ran him out of town, the saloon attracted plenty of rowdy men. I'd guess he's recruited help from amongst them.'

'Why did Edwidge get rid of him?'

'Judah's method of controlling customers was brutal and so last year Edwidge finally stood up to him, while Marshal Greeley said he'd shoot him on sight if he ever showed his face in Lonetree again.'

'It sounds as if Judah might have a grudge against Edwidge and the marshal, so why has he kidnapped Marietta's daughter?'

'I don't know.' Remington glanced at the low sun and forced a thin smile. 'Perhaps one of us should have realized Judah was behind this, as he used to live up to his name by setting ultimatums that expired at sundown; they used to call him the Sundown Kid.'

'He looks too old to be called that, but it makes this situation even more dangerous.'

Remington nodded and edged from side to side as he waited for Judah to make the first move, but as time dragged on without Judah delivering instructions, he became more agitated and glanced over his shoulder. He winced, making Dalton turn and see that their earlier guess had been correct.

At least five men were clambering down the overhang. When the leading man reached flat ground, he walked purposefully towards their wagon at a pace that within the next minute would uncover that they didn't have the ransom money.

'I guess,' Remington said, 'it's time to explain.'

'Be convincing,' Dalton said, gathering a stern nod from Remington before he moved off.

Dalton had started to move when

Judah raised a hand.

'No further, Remington,' he shouted. 'Until I have the money, you stay where we can all see you.'

Remington kept walking although he spread his hands wide apart, and so Dalton followed.

'We need to discuss the ransom,' Remington shouted. 'There's — '

'No talk. No tricks. No more steps.' Judah gestured at the men behind him. 'Unless you want to take a dead girl back to Lonetree.'

'That's not the deal,' Remington said, still walking. 'We give you money in exchange for Sera. If she's harmed in any way, you don't get your money.'

'It's too late to start making . . . ' Judah trailed off as he clearly noticed Remington's low tone. 'Are you going back on our deal?'

Judah's voice rose as he aimed an accusing finger at Remington, making him stop. Remington lowered his head and kicked at the rocks beneath his feet before he continued in a soft voice.

'There's been a problem. We need to talk.'

Judah gestured at the wagon and a few moments later someone shouted. While still moving on, Dalton glanced back at the man who was standing before the wagon and gesticulating with a clear signal that he'd searched the wagon and it was empty.

'You worked in the First Star and you know what I'm capable of,' Judah muttered. 'Yet still you defied me.'

'Wait!' Remington spluttered.

Judah's sneer said he wouldn't listen to reason and so when Dalton reached Remington, he stopped behind him and whispered urgently in his ear.

'We're exposed out here on the ridge with gunmen ahead of us and behind us,' he said. 'There's no way out of this for any of us unless you're more persuasive.'

Remington gulped as he considered Judah, the gunmen flanking him and the men holding Sera. None of them moved, suggesting he was being given one last chance to state his case.

Remington opened and closed his mouth soundlessly as he clearly struggled to find the right words. Then he gave up trying and dropped to his knees where he raised his hands in a begging gesture.

'Take me as a hostage,' he screeched, his voice echoing in the pass, 'but don't harm her.'

Judah curled his upper lip in disgust and so Dalton decided he would have to do the talking instead. With Remington blocking Judah's view of his lower body, he drew his gun and, when nobody looked at him, he raised his gun arm to aim at Judah.

'Only one thing is certain here,' he declared as he stepped out from behind Remington, 'unless we come to a deal, the Sundown Kid won't see another sundown.'

Judah considered him for the first time.

'Shoot me and the rest will take you alive,' he said calmly. 'Your screams will — '

'Quit with the threats,' Dalton said, still moving forward. 'You gave Marietta only a few hours to gather more money than I've seen in my entire life. So the new deal is: we'll pay the ransom as agreed, but you'll give her enough time to collect it.'

'She has the money. I know.'

Dalton kept walking and didn't reply until he was twenty paces from Judah.

'How do you know that?'

'Edwidge Star never could keep a secret.'

'And how did Edwidge know Marietta had the money?' He walked on and when he didn't get a reply, he persisted. 'What's going on here?'

Judah narrowed his eyes, his clenched fists and hunched posture confirming something about this situation was amiss. But Dalton moved on, figuring he'd taken the initiative and now he had to see it through.

He watched Judah as well as the other gunmen while behind him, Remington finally responded to his actions by murmuring a plea for him to desist. When Dalton didn't stop, scraping sounded as Remington stood up and hurried after him.

Dalton glanced at Sera, offering her encouragement with a confident smile, but she was shaking too much to return his gaze. He stomped to a halt before Judah, who considered him with disdain.

'You've picked the wrong man to try this bluff with,' Judah muttered.

Judah raised his left hand. The action was clearly a pre-arranged signal as one of the men holding Sera swung her forward while the other man released her.

In a moment the man brought his gun up against the side of her head. Dalton saw the fear in the young woman's eyes and the intent in the gunman's posture, and so he jerked his gun arm to the side, but he wasn't quick enough to save her.

Sera struggled and was trying to tear herself free when the gunman fired.

Blood splattered and she staggered away with a hand rising to her forehead.

Behind him Remington screeched in anguish and so Dalton fired, catching the gunman with a high shot to the chest that made him drop to his knees and topple over on to his back.

Dalton could only watch in horror as Sera took a faltering step towards the edge of the ridge before she tipped over to lie on her chest. She landed on loose rocks that shifted and made her slip over the side.

Dalton moved towards her while firing on the run. As the gunmen got their wits about them, he caught the second man who had been holding Sera with a deadly shot to the head.

His other shots were wild, as was the gunfire his opponents returned. When he went down on his good knee and turned at the hip, he saw why they had aimed poorly.

The gunmen were all towering above him. One gunman levelled his gun on him, but then he lowered his arm, as he appeared to rise even higher.

Only then did Dalton realize with a lurch that was both mental and physical that the ground beneath his feet was falling away. As the gunmen disappeared from view above him, he spread his arms, an action that unbalanced him and made him flop down on to his rump.

He landed on a flat rock that was skating down the side of the ridge. So Dalton did the only thing he could: he grabbed the rock with one hand and raised his injured leg high.

Ground level was several hundred feet below, but rising dust soon took that out of view. After sliding along with relative ease for a dozen heartbeats, the rock tipped up and bucked Dalton away.

With desperate lunges he searched for purchase amidst the shifting rocks. He failed to stop himself as everything he touched lacked resistance, leaving him thankful he was riding the cascade. Then, as suddenly as the rocks had moved him, he stopped.

Stones covered his lower body, but as he hadn't stopped due to anything he'd done he lay still, unwilling to risk starting a new cascade. He heard rocks grinding behind him, but the dust blocked his view of what was causing the slippage.

Through the noise, gunfire peppered, but it was some distance away while the crash of rock against rock became louder and closer. Then a wave of shifting stones shoved him aside, landing him on his chest where he slid downwards again.

To his right Remington shouted in panic suggesting he too had taken a tumble down the ridge, but Dalton put Remington's plight from his mind as he dug his hands into the stones and sought to still himself. This time, after sliding for a few dozen yards, he halted.

He rolled on to his back. When he confirmed he was unhurt, gingerly he raised himself to his feet.

As he moved off, he stumbled, but he

was pleased his injured leg had survived the ordeal without incurring any further harm. He worked his way downwards by standing crouched over and walking crablike using short and stiff-legged steps.

With each step the dust cleared and, after a minute, he saw the ground below, which was now only fifty feet away with most of the route down being comprised of larger and more stable-looking stones.

Then he saw movement and when he stopped, the dust settled letting him see that Remington had reached the bottom.

He was coated in dust and he stood awkwardly. His posture was hunched and defeated, and after taking a few more paces, Dalton saw what had concerned him.

At Remington's feet lay the still and bloodied form of Sera, the young woman they'd come here to rescue.

5

'Is she dead?' Dalton asked while he was still ten yards away from Remington.

He didn't get a reply until he'd slid his way down to ground level and then it was accompanied by Remington advancing on him with his expression set in a snarl.

'Yeah,' he muttered. 'But they didn't kill her. You did!'

'I tried to save her.' Dalton backed away for a pace. 'You saw that.'

'I saw what happened. You ignored my order to stay calm and you took over the negotiation. That forced Judah to react.'

Dalton lowered his head, accepting that even if Remington's harsh claim had been spoken in anger to provoke him, he had failed.

'I had to step in because you weren't

explaining the situation well.'

A gunshot blasted, making Dalton look up. Remington was advancing on him and he hadn't fired. When another gunshot rattled, he looked over his shoulder.

This time he saw dust kick from a boulder ten yards away. He looked up at the ridge; at the top the surviving gunmen had grouped together to shoot at them.

From either side other men were hurrying to join them and so Dalton turned back to warn Remington only to walk into a scything blow to the jaw that sent him reeling before he fell over on to his back.

'It was a tough negotiation,' Remington roared, 'and it didn't get any easier after you drew a gun on the Sundown Kid.'

Dalton sighed, reckoning that anything he said would only annoy Remington more and so he pointed upwards.

His action was accompanied by a

fortuitous, in the circumstance, sustained volley of gunfire that made Remington look up. His angry gaze didn't alter as he considered the Sundown Kid and, when Dalton sought cover, he didn't join him.

Dalton shuffled on to a large boulder that was high enough to shield him from the ridge and from where he peered around the side at the kidnappers. They were showing no sign of coming down and so he didn't waste bullets on speculative shots.

'Get over here,' he shouted at Remington. 'We still have a chance to escape.'

Remington stormed over to him and stood in clear view from above with his fists bunched.

'So saving your own hide is all you care about, is it?'

'It's too late to help Marietta's daughter now, but Judah Sundown can't get away with what he did, and that goes for Lawrence and Hamilton too.'

Remington had been rocking back and forth on his toes looking as if he was going to hit him again, but Dalton's last comment made him look aloft. He nodded and looked around before snarling.

'What you did was bad, but what they did was worse.'

He turned on his heel and walked away from the ridge, encouraging the kidnappers to fire at him. Slugs sliced into the ground to either side of Remington, but none of the shots came within five feet of him and neither did they slow him down.

'Wait for me,' Dalton called after him. 'We'll have a better chance together.'

'Just be grateful I'm letting the Sundown Kid deal with you,' Remington shouted with a disdainful wave of the hand before he quickened his pace.

Even if Remington had walked at a normal speed, Dalton doubted he could keep pace with him and so he stayed behind his cover.

When Remington moved out of sight, Dalton considered his own retreat. The sun had set and the terrain was darkening, but if he waited for too long, Judah would be able to make his way down.

As he wasn't prepared to try Remington's anger-fuelled method of just walking away, while he waited for the lull in the firing to become permanent, he planned a route away from the ridge.

He picked out a cluster of boulders as his first target and, after waiting for another fifteen minutes, during which time no more gunfire sounded, he ran on. He adopted a hobbling gait with a short step on his injured leg and a longer leap with the other.

He'd managed twenty paces before he attracted gunfire, but unlike the gunshots that had been aimed at Remington, they were more accurate and the first two shots that rang out kicked dust only a few paces ahead of him.

Dalton looked up the ridge, worried that Judah was coming down, but in fact he was no longer visible and he appeared to have moved on. Then Dalton saw where the shooting had originated.

At the base of the ridge, two men had taken refuge in a hollow after, presumably, following Judah's orders to clamber down and finish him off.

They were too far away and too well embedded for Dalton to take them on and so he hurried on to the cluster of boulders. Several more shots sliced into the ground, each one thankfully landing further away as he gained distance from the shooters.

Dalton only slowed when he'd rounded a large boulder that would hide him from all directions. He considered the rocks until he saw a gap between two sheer-sided boulders, and then moved on.

He figured that if he tried to run, he'd move so slowly he would be hunted down easily and so he had to make a stand. So, when he reached the other side, he went right and tracked along the back of the boulder until he found a place where he could climb.

Even so, by the time he reached the summit, the men had followed him. They were loitering down below and discussing where he'd gone, letting Dalton learn that the two men's names were Ellison and Victor.

A moment after he got his first uninterrupted view of them, his movement caused them to look up at him. So Dalton dropped down on to his chest.

He snaked along to the right and, when he peered down, the men were hurriedly passing below him. Dalton levelled his six-shooter on the nearest man, Ellison, but the men reacted instantly.

Ellison moved towards the boulder and out of Dalton's sight while the trailing Victor drew his gun and fired up at Dalton without raising his head.

The shot still kicked into the lip of the rock a foot from Dalton's right hand making him jerk away. When he moved back, Dalton's chance had been lost as both men were no longer visible.

Dalton slapped the rock in irritation and then shuffled to the left to gain a different angle on the scene below.

He still couldn't see either man and so he craned his neck to peer down the side of the boulder. Ellison was below him and he'd already trained his gun upwards, thankfully at a point several feet to Dalton's side.

In the moment it took Ellison to aim at him Dalton darted back, and the action saved him from a slug that clipped the edge of the rock. He waited for four heartbeats and swung his arm over the edge.

He fired blindly three times, splaying his shots to either side. Then he shuffled along to lie above the last place he'd seen Ellison when he'd glanced over the edge.

Ellison was below him. Again Ellison aimed at him, but this time he didn't fire and so figuring his rapid movement had worried his opponent, Dalton stayed still and listened.

He couldn't work out what Ellison would do next, but he figured the gathering darkness was the more important development. He had only to stay free for a short while before he could hide in the shadows.

The first star was breaking through the darkening sky when he heard scrambling, but he struggled to work out where the noise was coming from. Then with a shocked gulp he worked out that someone was behind him.

He turned as Victor bobbed his head up above the other end of the boulder. They considered each other before Victor dropped down from view.

Earlier, when Dalton had climbed up he had found only one suitable route to the top, but a more mobile man could climb up in numerous places. So he trained his gun from side to side as he waited for Victor to show, but when a minute passed without him appearing Dalton felt vulnerable.

He broke off to look over the side; as he'd feared, Ellison had moved on. Dalton presumed he'd also scale the boulder, perhaps coming at him from a different angle and so he didn't wait for them to combine forces and seize the initiative.

With his right leg thrust out while keeping low he skirted around the edge to a spot where the peak of a second boulder abutted against the one he was leaning on. He hoped this would give him one direction from which he could be sure neither man would approach him unseen.

Sure enough, the side of the second boulder turned out to be too precipitous to climb. And between the boulders there was a drop of twenty-five feet that started with a gap of a few feet and narrowed down to a few inches.

As nobody could slip into the gap without him hearing them, he put his back to the abutting boulder. He looked straight ahead ensuring that no matter where Ellison and Victor appeared, he would see them before they saw him.

Five minutes passed in silence with Dalton sitting calmly as he figured time was his ally. If he had to, he was prepared to wait until nightfall for the gunmen to act.

His opponents weren't so patient, but they were organized as, when they came up, they did so simultaneously, appearing at either corner of the boulder, facing him. Keeping their heads lowered, they slapped their gun hands down on rock and picked out his position with uncanny accuracy.

Dalton was already facing to the left and so he aimed at Victor, but before he could fire two gunshots ripped out. Both shots tore into the rock several yards before him and sliced out a furrow before slamming into the rock at his back.

Dalton kept his cool and fired, but Victor dropped from view and his shot whistled through the air. He moved his arm lower and to the side as he expected him to emerge in a different position, but only a moment later they both bobbed back up again.

This time they had him in their sights and their two shots hammered home only inches from his right boot before they ducked down. Dalton reckoned that before they re-appeared, he needed to move.

With his legs thrust out before him he shuffled to the side. He had moved for several feet without seeing his opponents again when his trailing hand landed on air.

He fell sideways with a jolt, finding to his shock that in the descending darkness he was nearer to the gap than he'd thought he'd been. Using a frantic flailing motion, he sought to right himself, and luckily that let his gun hand land on the edge of the boulder.

Constrained by his stiff leg, he couldn't twist his body and he toppled awkwardly to the right. He landed on his side with his lower body up to his stomach lying on rock and his upper body projecting out over the gap.

Behind him he heard shuffling, making him tense up, which had the unfortunate effect of making him slip. Slowly at first and then speeding up, he slipped inexorably on, travelling downwards headfirst.

With the narrowing gap in the rock below beckoning him forward, he carried out the only action open to him to still his motion and raised his arm to the other side of the gap.

His right palm slapped flat against the rock, but as he was still holding his gun, he didn't gain enough traction to still his fall and he continued sliding downwards.

He grabbed for the rock with his left hand. Thankfully, this hand found purchase on a projection, stopping him with his body angled downwards and with his legs below the knees pointing stiffly up into the air above the edge.

He reckoned that whichever way he moved, he'd unbalance himself. Then he heard movement as Ellison and Victor raised themselves, so he bent his left leg and placed the sole of his boot against the rockface.

As he'd feared, he didn't find traction and he toppled. In desperation, he tightened his grip around the projection while pressing his other hand to the opposite rock face, and so he pivoted round with his legs scraping against rock.

When he came to rest, he was upright with his legs dangling beneath him and his arms splayed across the gap. He looked up, seeing he was only four feet below the edge, but he'd been lucky in swinging beneath the abutting boulder.

Quickly he pressed his legs to either side of the gap. Then he holstered his gun and edged his hands forward.

Three shuffling movements moved him into the shadows beneath the covering boulder. He was pleased he'd acted quickly as footfalls sounded above him as Ellison and Victor approached the edge.

He stopped moving and looked up, finding that the projecting boulder blocked his view of the top and he could work out where the men were only by their shuffling movements.

'I thought,' Victor said, 'I saw him go over the side.'

'I didn't see him at all,' Ellison said. 'But I reckon he's fled.'

Both men muttered oaths. Ellison's rapid footfalls moved by him and receded.

Victor peered down into the gap, but clearly it was too dark for him to see Dalton as he joined Ellison in hurrying away.

All was silent for two minutes and then Dalton heard scrambling as they clambered down to ground level before starting to talk below him.

Dalton relaxed, accepting he'd evaded being found for now, before he turned his thoughts to how he'd extricate himself from the gap.

Above him the rock was smooth and so his only choice was to backtrack along the route he'd taken to get here. With his injured leg constraining his movements, he didn't reckon he could turn safely and so he dragged his right hand backwards, feeling along the projection.

He moved his hand for as far as he was able and repeated the motion with his other hand, but the projection that was supporting his weight broke off.

He fell, albeit slowly, but he couldn't find anything to support his weight and so he pressed his forearms and thighs to either side of the gap to control his descent. He held his right leg high to protect it and he was glad he had as his left foot stilled his motion with a jarring thud.

On either side rock was now only inches from his face, while the top of the boulder was ten feet above him. Worse, he'd only stopped moving downwards because his left ankle was jammed firmly in the narrow gap.

When he looked around, his last sight before the light became too dim to see was that the gap only became narrower further down.

6

Sun-up brought Dalton no respite from his ordeal.

The previous night Ellison and Victor had searched around the boulders until full darkness had descended. Dalton had stayed quiet and they'd not worked out where he'd gone, but by the time he'd been sure they'd moved on, it had been too dark to see his hand when he'd waved it before his face.

Worse, moving for even a few inches was beyond his abilities. His ankle was trapped and the rock to either side was too smooth for him to drag himself upwards.

The only way he could shove himself higher was to put weight on his right leg, but it wasn't strong enough to move him. So he'd found a position in which he could support himself with his elbows and hips while keeping his weight off his trapped ankle.

He'd managed to conserve his strength and so devoted his energies to trying to still his mounting panic through a sleepless night. Now he had enough light to see, he tried moving again, but morning dew had slicked the rock and, when he wriggled, the only motion he made was a few inches downwards.

After that failure, he waited patiently until the rocks were dry while consoling himself with the thought that as he'd slipped downwards, he was still capable of moving. Firstly, he rocked his trapped foot back and forth.

After slipping down earlier, he could now move his foot, but for only an inch in either direction. This was enough to give him hope and so he exerted more pressure.

With his foot arched forward, he was able to strain against the constriction. He pressed for several minutes until, in a shower of crumbling rock, his foot jerked free, making him sigh with relief.

Ahead at his level, the boulders became closer until the gap narrowed to a crack. So while he still had enough strength to move, he decided to shuffle backwards where the boulders spread further apart.

He turned round while supporting as much of his weight as he could with his arms, so that he wouldn't slip downwards again and become trapped. Then he picked his footholds carefully, testing them with the outstretched toe of his boot before he put weight on them.

Over the next thirty minutes, he managed four short steps forward. This moved him for only a yard after which he had to rest his arms, but despite the slow advancement, his success cheered him as he was making progress.

After another thirty minutes of steady movement, he saw that ahead the boulders became further apart until ten yards on the ground became visible.

He moved on, becoming more confident with each step until with a growing desperate urge to extricate himself, he stopped being cautious and scrambled forward. He didn't let his feet rest for more than a few seconds and in the next minute he moved further than he'd managed since the night before.

With each step he dropped down, but that only encouraged him as he was getting closer to the ground. Then his frantic progress provided the inevitable result when he rested his weight on a bump in the rock and it sheared off.

He dropped down and his injured leg wasn't strong enough to stop him, but thankfully his forward momentum kept him moving on. So he went scrabbling down the gap with his hips pressed against the narrowest section and his hands and elbows digging into the rock as he sought to still himself.

Unable to stop his motion, he slid down to ground level where he bent his right leg to avoid jarring it, but that made him land awkwardly and he pitched forward. Constrained on both sides, he couldn't protect himself and his head knocked against the rocky side before he landed on his chest.

He lay, enjoying the feel of the dirt beneath his body after spending so long suspended only a few yards above it while feeling foolish for having hurt himself when he'd been so close to the ground. He dragged a hand out from under his chest and fingered his forehead.

Although he felt only a sore spot, when he got to his knees he felt disorientated. That didn't stop him standing up and, eager now to leave his rocky prison, he made his way along the bottom of the gap.

He emerged in sunlight forcing him to place an arm before his face. The light still made him dizzy and he stumbled before falling to his knees and tipping over on to his side where, with his face shielded, he took deep, calming breaths.

By degrees the pounding in his head receded and he would have gladly lain there for a while, but having survived his perilous situation, the fact he hadn't eaten or drunk for nearly a day gnawed at his stomach.

He looked up at the ridge. Nobody was there, but the sight reminded him that before he put his mind to his own welfare, he had a sad duty to perform.

He stood up and, with a heavy heart and an even heavier tread, he trudged back to the base of the ridge where he looked for Sera's body. She wasn't lying where Remington had found her and so he looked further afield, seeing that her body was now lying beside the boulder where he had taken cover yesterday.

He headed to the boulder while noting the shallow ruts in the ground where she'd been dragged along. The fact that the gunmen, presumably, had moved her but hadn't buried her added to the list of crimes for which they would pay.

She was lying on her chest and so he sat down beside her and murmured a quiet prayer before he turned her over. He judged she was around eighteen, although it was hard to tell as, like her mother, she was lanky; the blood on her face had dried to a thick crust.

Strangely, her eyes were still open and so he moved to close them, but then she exhaled her breath.

He flinched before he got over his shock by telling himself the noise must have come purely from him turning over her body. Then her eyes moved and he couldn't help but speak.

'You're alive?' he murmured.

She didn't reply and so he repeated his question before he leaned over her. With his ear placed above her mouth, he held his breath and he heard and felt her exhale with a gentle wheeze.

He rocked back to give her more air while recalling what he'd seen yesterday. The gunman had shot her, but she'd been moving away from her attacker. Then he'd shot the gunman, who had bled copiously.

This meant she might have avoided serious injury, after all, and the blood that coated her face might not be all her own. As Remington hadn't known this, deeming her to be dead was an easy mistake for him to have made.

Even better, she might have dragged herself to this place.

He located a kerchief and dabbed her cheek. When he'd removed some of the dried blood, his ministrations made her stir and her eyes followed his hand, although they didn't keep up with the movements.

She appeared calm until he dabbed her forehead, which made her murmur in distress, but that helped him to locate a head wound, which when he examined it wasn't as bad as he'd feared. She had incurred a bloody furrow across the temple that suggested the scraping passage of a bullet.

He judged that if the gun had been angled a fraction of an inch nearer to her head when it had been fired it would have killed her. Even so, the shooting of a gun that close to her head had seriously injured her.

'I'm a friend,' Dalton said with a

soothing voice. 'I'll get you to safety. Do you understand?'

Her only reply was to blink rapidly, which confused him until he saw that he'd moved and she was no longer lying in his shadow. He stepped to the side so that her face was shaded again and that made her look at him.

Her lips turned up with a slight smile before she closed her eyes. Dalton reckoned that response was the best he could hope for and so he turned his thoughts to practical matters.

He was a day's ride from Lonetree, a journey that had been across barren terrain without any signs of water, shelter or settlements. Based on how long it'd taken him to secure his horse after the Broughton brothers had accosted him, he judged that the journey would take several days even if he didn't have the girl to look after.

He looked up at the top of ridge, seeking an alternative. He was too close to the slope to see if the wagon was still there, but he figured Judah Sundown would have had no use for it and, even if he'd taken the horses, they'd brought provisions.

'Can you walk?' he asked.

Her only reply was to stir and so Dalton slipped a hand beneath her back and hoisted her up to a standing position. When her feet were planted on the ground, he loosened his grip, but the moment he stopped supporting her, she slumped and so he grabbed her again.

'Perhaps later,' he said.

He rolled his shoulders and, with one arm under her back and the other beneath her legs, he picked her up and clutched her to his chest. He turned to the slope and set off.

He didn't get far.

As he'd feared, the shifting rocks that had caused him to slide down to the bottom of the pass provided no resistance. He managed two upward paces only for the rocks to move and make him slide back down again.

Over the next ten minutes, he tried

several times, but the climb would have been difficult even if he'd been alone and fit. He put Sera down and reconsidered.

Away from the ridge the ascent of the pass was less steep, but that would necessitate a journey of miles followed by the same distance back, all without assurance the wagon would still be there. He was working out which route up was closest to the ridge when his gaze alighted on the junction between the slope and the pass wall.

Here, larger rocks had congregated. Feeling more hopeful he picked up Sera, this time gathering a grateful murmur that suggested she was aware of what he was trying to do, and set off for the wall.

When he faced the slope, the daunting height he would have to ascend made him pause. So he tore his gaze away from the top and concentrated on planning the first dozen steps up.

He located a flat and sloping rock,

which provided him with an easy start. Even better, in crossing the rock he moved into the cooler shadow cast by the ridge and so heartened, he jumped to another flat rock.

For the next fifteen minutes, he made more progress than he'd expected. He had covered a quarter of the route to the top before he had to put Sera down to rest his arms and to stretch his injured leg.

He lay beside her taking deep breaths while avoiding looking up and depressing himself with the enormity of the remaining task.

From his more elevated position, he could see down the pass letting him imagine the arduous journey back to Lonetree if he failed to reach the wagon. This sight forced him to accept he had no choice but to press on.

'How do you feel now?' he asked without much hope of an answer.

She murmured under her breath and, even when he placed an ear over her mouth and asked her to repeat it, he couldn't work out what she was trying to say. He decided to take her responses as positive signs and picked her up again.

As before, he concentrated on the slope he would have to traverse next rather than planning the whole route up. So in short bursts he moved from large rock to large rock, all the time gaining height.

He didn't reckon his luck would hold out for long and, as it turned out, the rocks soon became smaller. Before long he moved between rocks with a single stride, which made his injured leg ache, and so he sat down against the pass wall with Sera propped up beside him.

'Nearly there,' he said optimistically. 'You looking forward to the journey to town in the wagon?'

She grunted dubiously under her breath, making Dalton smile, even though he couldn't be sure she was responding with a note of realism.

'All right,' he said, 'it might not be that easy, but hopefully when we reach the top we'll have some luck. If we do, we'll be most of the way back to town by sundown.'

'Sundown,' she mumbled and rested her head on his shoulder.

They sat like this for a while, but before long the rising sun poked out above the ridge making the temperature soar.

Dalton set off with the wall at his side. Thankfully, his injured leg was beside the wall, letting him swing up his good leg and then lean against the wall while he moved his stiffer leg.

To his relief he made steady progress. Close to the wall the rocks were jammed in tightly and only rarely did one shift when he put a foot on it.

His progress moved him back into shadow and when he next rested, he was nearer to the top than the bottom.

Despite his growing optimism, his journeys became shorter, his breaks became longer and the temperature rose with the rising sun that eliminated all shade.

Every time he stopped to flex his sore leg and tired arms, he talked to Sera using a conversational tone as if he expected an answer. Sometimes she replied with a murmur and so he figured his comments soothed her.

What worried him the most was that she licked her cracked lips constantly, confirming he had to get her water soon. When he next set off, he kept walking even when his arms felt as if they were being dragged from their sockets and his weak leg throbbed with an insistent demand for rest.

This determined policy provided the desired reward when the going became easier. He thought he was walking over a firmer stretch of the slope, but when he looked up, the slope ahead became less steep.

With a sigh, he accepted he'd covered the worst part of the climb. He slumped down to the ground, this time in relief, and lay her down in the shade behind a rock.

'We're almost there,' he said. 'We'll

be able to rest soon.'

'Sundown,' she murmured.

'Long before then, I hope.'

Her only response was to let her chin flop down on to her chest, forcing Dalton to raise her head. He looked into her eyes, but she was struggling to keep her eyelids raised and that was all the encouragement Dalton needed to pick her up again.

This time he held her tightly against his chest as he embarked on a determined walk up the last length of slope. Slowly the scene of yesterday's disastrous encounter with Judah Sundown appeared and Dalton considered the ridge as he searched for the kidnappers.

He couldn't see them and so when the slope petered out and he stood on flat ground again, he turned to the end of the ridge where he and Remington had left the wagon. He groaned.

The wagon wasn't there.

7

'Just a little further,' Dalton said. 'Then we can rest.'

'Sundown,' Sera murmured.

They'd had this brief exchange a hundred times and now it had become an encouraging litany to himself to keep going.

After the disappointment of discovering the wagon wasn't where he and Remington had left it, he had found wagon tracks that headed towards Lonetree. He was following these and, although on the way here the day before he hadn't looked for landmarks, he figured he was broadly traversing the same route.

As he couldn't recall passing running water, he trudged on without hope, but at sundown the cooler temperature provided relief. Even better, when the darkness spread, he saw a glow ahead.

He sped up, eager to reach the light while he could still see the terrain and he soon confirmed the light was from a camp fire. A short while later, the sounds of lively chatter drifted to him and so he placed Sera on the ground to plan his next actions.

'We could have had some luck,' Dalton said.

'Sundown,' she mumbled in distress.

'I had promised we'd be on the wagon by sundown, and we might still be.'

'Sun . . . ' she murmured.

She'd gripped his jacket tightly and so gently he opened her fingers, laid her arm across her chest and moved on. He managed three paces before she started keening.

'I won't ever leave you,' he said, returning to her. He stroked her hand until she quietened and then picked her up. 'But you have to stay quiet.'

She nodded, this being one of the most obvious signs she'd provided so far that she was aware of what he was trying to do. Then she started breathing loudly, as if she'd drifted into an uncomfortable sleep.

So with her condition providing him with a mixture of encouragement that she wasn't beyond help and desperation that he needed to act quickly, he moved on.

When he'd halved the distance to the fire, he saw it had been lit beside a rock formation that provided shelter from the wind. The horses and the wagon were to the side of the rock, confirming he'd found Judah Sundown.

Men were milling around and showing no sign they expected trouble. Even so, Dalton veered away to get behind the rock where he placed Sera on the ground.

As he waited for full darkness, he stretched out with his legs before him. Sera was still breathing deeply as if asleep and so quietly he moved a few feet away from her.

When she didn't display any distress, he moved further away, ensuring he could still hear and see her while being far enough away that he could act decisively when the time was right. That moment came when the light from the fire had become brighter than the dim twilight.

He picked his way around the rock and had yet to see the kidnappers when a low murmuring sounded behind him. For a moment he thought one of the men had found him, but then he realized the noises were coming from Sera.

He hurried back to find her rocking from side to side while reaching out as if searching for him. The moment he grasped her hand she stopped writhing and murmuring.

'I reckon,' he said, 'we should stick together.'

She didn't reply other than to gather a firm hold of his jacket and so they set off, as they had done all day, with him carrying her clutched to his chest. He walked sideways with his back to the rock and he reached his first target of the wagon without mishap.

The kidnappers had left a horse still hitched up as they saw to their own needs first, although he would need some luck to take advantage of their mistake.

He raised her to lie her down in the back and clambered inside where he wasted no time in searching for the food and water Remington had brought. With a sigh of relief he found them lying in the corner, untouched.

He brought the water bottle to Sera's lips, but she turned her head away. So, hoping the sound of running water would encourage her, he supped water until he'd relieved his own thirst before he tried again.

The second time he dabbed her lips and she didn't complain, but other than vaguely licking the moisture, she didn't react. When he poured water into her mouth, she made no effort to swallow and the water dribbled out through her lips.

He rocked back on his haunches, now more concerned than he'd ever been about her condition. He sloshed the water before her face and tried again.

This time she managed a sip and, as if that had triggered an unconscious memory, she wrested the bottle from him and put it to her lips herself.

She gulped down two mouthfuls, but then a spasm shook her body and she dropped the bottle. With her eyes wide and sparkling in the low light, she vomited up the water.

When the spasms had stopped, she lay on her side breathing raggedly making Dalton watch her in horror as if every breath might be her last. But, to his relief, her breathing calmed and she felt around for the bottle.

Dalton placed the bottle in her hands, but this time he kept one hand on it so he could ensure she only sipped the water and, after two small mouthfuls, he lowered the bottle. She lay on her back and her breathing stayed calm with no sign she'd again react adversely to the water.

'Sundown,' she whispered.

Dalton couldn't work out if she'd fixated on this word because it was one of the first things she'd heard him say or because she was recalling who had kidnapped her. But he decided it didn't matter as she'd spoken more strongly than before.

'You make a better Sundown Kid,' he said, patting her arm, 'than the Sundown Kid does.'

She nodded and so Dalton had just started to calm down when footfalls sounded outside. Then Ellison, one of the gunmen who had followed him down the ridge, spoke up.

'I'm sure the noises came from over here,' he said.

'They did,' Victor, the other gunman, said, 'but they sounded like an animal to me.'

A brief muttered conversation took place and so Dalton held his breath to remain as silent as possible. It worked as two disinterested grunts sounded and the men moved away, but then

Judah Sundown's loud and clear voice sounded.

'The noises came from near the wagon,' he ordered. 'Find out what they were before you warm your butts by the fire again.'

Grumbling sounded as the two men returned to the wagon. A thorough search would reveal them and so moving as quietly as possible, Dalton lay down at the back with Sera.

She didn't appear to be aware of the approaching danger and she gestured vaguely, presumably asking for more water. Dalton placed a comforting hand on her shoulder, but she gestured more frantically and murmured, making the shuffling footfalls outside stomp to a halt, so he put a hand over her mouth.

She uttered a low screech of distress from deep in her throat. Dalton pressed his hand down more firmly, which silenced her, but when it made her struggle Dalton winced in annoyance at himself for making the wrong person suffer.

Anger at the way Judah had treated her welled up in his chest, which, as he was breathing shallowly, made him feel as if he was about to choke. Then Judah shouted an order to Ellison and Victor, the sound of his voice making Dalton snarl.

He removed his hand from Sera's mouth and patted her shoulder. Then he drew his gun.

Figuring that if he planned his next move, it would only prove that fighting back against so many men was foolish, he got up on his haunches and vaulted over the backboard, ensuring he landed on his good leg.

Ellison and Victor were coming around the corner of the wagon and his unannounced arrival made them stare at him in surprise.

Before they got their wits about them, Dalton blasted two quick gunshots. The first shot caught Ellison low in the stomach, making him stumble into the wagon where he hung on to the backboard.

The second shot tore into Victor's neck, downing him. So with time to aim carefully Dalton slammed a second shot into Ellison's side that made him slide away from the wagon before he flopped down over Victor's body.

As consternation erupted around the camp-fire, Dalton accepted that to save Sera's life he had to leave her temporarily, even if that distressed her. He moved on and while seeking the protection of the undergrowth, he reloaded.

The scrub was thickest beside the rocks and when he hunkered down amidst decent cover, Judah was directing the kidnappers to spread out into the darkness. The men responded with frantic haste making it clear they were unsure of the nature of the attack.

Dalton added to the confusion by splaying gunfire across the fleeing kidnappers.

With everyone moving quickly, he caught only one man with a glancing shot to the side that made him stumble before he moved out of sight. Then

Dalton looked for a route up the rock.

He located a section that started with a knee-high boulder that he was able to mount before moving across a higher boulder. After clambering over several smaller, flatter boulders, he reached a high rock that even with two strong legs he would struggle to climb and so he made his stand there.

He dropped down on to his chest and wormed his way towards the light finding that he was fifteen feet off the ground and looking down at the wagon. He hoped his absence hadn't upset Sera, but he could do nothing about it as forms were moving in the night.

He couldn't get a clear sighting of any of them and so he stilled his fire. In hushed and urgent tones orders were delivered in the darkness.

Dalton couldn't hear the words, but the concerned tone showed confusion as to the numbers that had attacked them and, confirming his theory, one man ran towards the fire. He kicked dirt over it, extinguishing most of the flames, before running for the horses, where he mounted the nearest steed and moved on.

Dalton let him flee, figuring that if he invited a gunfight, he'd be overcome. Accordingly, two more men appeared from the gloom and they gained horses before galloping away.

The next two men to flee tried to reach the wagon and so Dalton retaliated with rapid shots that made the first man retreat for the horses instead. But the second man went to one knee and, using the light from the spluttering fire, he picked out Dalton's position.

He fired, his gunshot pinging into the rock above Dalton's head. Before the man could get him in his sights, Dalton fired, catching his opponent high in the chest and making him rock backward before he toppled over into the wagon wheel.

Several men appeared together from the undergrowth, but the sight of the shot man appeared to convince them they faced superior numbers and they retreated to the horses. Dalton let them go, saving his gunfire until he saw Judah Sundown scurrying towards a horse.

He couldn't let Judah flee unchallenged and he took aim at him before firing, but the light was poor and the undergrowth blocked his sight so he couldn't see if he had hit his target. Long moments passed in which he failed to see him again, giving him hope that he'd been lucky.

Then he saw Judah again, but he'd mounted up and was riding away. Dalton took a speculative shot at his back, but that didn't slow him before he disappeared into the gloom.

Dalton crawled to the side where he noted that only five horses remained. Having shot three men, it was likely that almost everyone had fled, so he wasted no time in climbing down to ground level where, doubled over, he ran for the wagon.

He reached over the backboard and shook Sera's shoulder, the urgency of the situation not allowing him to alert her gently.

'We're leaving now,' he said. 'Everything will be fine.'

'Sundown,' she murmured and briefly clutched his hand. Then he hurried round to the front and clambered on to the seat.

All his activity of the last few hours had stiffened his sore leg making it feel tight and wooden, and so he struggled to raise himself. He gathered a firmer grip of the seat and tugged, but that failed to move him and it was only when he looked down that he understood his problem.

The man he had shot from up on the rock was still alive and he had used the wheel to drag himself upright and grab his ankle.

Dalton tried to kick out, but he couldn't gain enough traction to force his weak leg backwards and so he grabbed the reins instead. A quick tug encouraged the horse to move and a moment later a pained screech sounded that cut off as the wheel rolled.

The man's grip loosened followed by a bump as the wheel rolled over him, and this movement lifted Dalton into the seat. To his right, the kidnappers shouted as they regrouped, but, with his stiff leg thrust out to the side, he trundled the wagon off into the night.

He moved slowly, not wishing to alert the kidnappers and so it took several minutes before the horse reached a fast trot. Then he looked into the back to check on Sera.

The light was too poor for him to see her, but he heard movement; Sera was more animated than he'd expected her to be. She was moving objects around while shuffling towards him.

'Rest,' he called. 'Everything will be fine now.'

He didn't get a reply, but the movement stopped. As this was an acceptable response, he turned back to the front.

The wagon had trundled along for another minute when a creak sounded behind him, alerting him to a problem a moment before an arm wrapped around his neck from behind and drew him backward. With Dalton being held firmly, someone yanked his gun from its holster and tossed it into the wagon.

'It won't be fine,' Judah Sundown muttered in his ear. 'Your problems have just started.'

8

'How did you get back there?' Dalton asked when he'd followed Judah's instructions by stopping the wagon.

'I doubled back and rode up to your wagon from behind,' Judah said in his ear. 'Now, where's Remington?'

'He's hiding in the dark watching you. He'll — '

Dalton broke off when Judah yanked him backwards, cutting off his windpipe and tilting his head back over the seat. Dalton fought for balance, but only when Judah loosened his grip was he able to sit back down on the seat.

'I'm no fool. Tell me what you and Remington were trying to do on the ridge. Then I'll end this.'

Dalton raised his chin with defiance. 'If you weren't a fool, you'd have the ransom money.'

Judah snorted. 'If you weren't a fool,

you wouldn't have double-crossed me.'

The cold metal of a gun barrel pressed against Dalton's neck. Dalton strained to move away from it, but Judah had a tight grip around his neck and he'd braced himself against the seat.

No matter which way Dalton turned, he could move for only a few inches before Judah dragged him back.

'Spare the girl,' Dalton said when it became clear Judah wouldn't shoot him immediately.

'Shooting her would be kinder than letting her see your fate.' Judah jabbed the gun into his neck. 'You killed trusted friends and my men are eager to make you regret that.'

With this last comment Judah raised his voice and riders came into view on either side of the wagon. The men all glared at Dalton with surly grins and their hands close to their holsters.

'Do what you will with me, but promise me you'll get Sera back to Lonetree quickly.' Dalton heard Judah snort under his breath and so he persisted. 'It's the only way you'll get the ransom money.'

Judah leaned over Dalton's shoulder while keeping the gun held firm. He laughed before looking at his men, some of whom caught on to his mood and provided supportive laughter.

'I knew you'd bargain for your life.' Judah pressed down with the gun, forcing Dalton to hunch over until he was looking at his knees. 'So make your offer a good one and in return I'll make this fast.'

'Two men stole the ransom on the way to High Pass,' Dalton said using as calm a tone as he could manage. 'Remington and I had to meet your deadline, so we came to the ridge and tried to explain what had happened, but you wouldn't listen.'

'I believe you.' Judah relaxed his gun hand, letting a surprised Dalton sit up straight. 'But I'll stop believing you if you claim you can take me to them, so just give me their names and I'll deal with them.'

'First, we take Sera to Lonetree. Then, I give you their names.'

'That's an interesting offer, but it's not interesting enough. Edwidge Star knew about Marietta's money and he often shot his mouth off when he was with those no-account varmints Lawrence and Hamilton. I reckon they took the ransom.' Judah chuckled. 'Am I right?'

Dalton didn't trust himself to lie convincingly, but he reckoned his silence and tenseness provided the answer. He braced his back against the seat and flexed his legs as he prepared to make a last attempt to free himself.

Long moments passed in which Judah did nothing other than breathe deeply. Then Judah tensed before he edged the gun away from Dalton's neck.

'I want them as badly as you do,' Dalton said encouragingly.

'And in return for your help,' Judah said, his voice uncertain, 'you want me to take the poor, defenceless, sweet young lady back to the loving arms of her mother in Lonetree, do you?'

116

'That's the deal.'

'Then tell her you've agreed to it.'

Judah removed his arm from around Dalton's neck and so Dalton turned quickly before Judah changed his mind, which let him see that Judah would honour their deal, as he'd had his mind changed for him.

Sera had made a miraculous recovery. She had found Dalton's gun and turned the tables on him by jabbing it into his back.

This was the most controlled action she'd carried out since Dalton had rescued her, but luckily Judah couldn't see the miracle wasn't as unlikely as it'd first seemed. Sweat beaded her forehead and her eyes were manic as she used all her control just to stay upright.

Before her strength gave out, Dalton seized Judah's gun and clambered into the wagon. He claimed his own gun back from Sera, who closed her eyes before she slumped back on to her haunches and then on to her side.

Dalton squeezed by Judah and

helped her lie on her back as best as he was able while holding two guns. Then he turned to Judah, who considered Sera's weak state with irritation now he could see she probably wouldn't have stayed conscious for long enough to kill him.

'Tell your men,' Dalton said, 'who's in charge now.'

'I'll tell them who's in charge, for now.' Judah shrugged his jacket as he gathered his composure. 'You can't stay awake all the way back to Lonetree and your young helper can't keep her eyes open until I've finished this threat.'

The latter was true, but Dalton provided a confident smile.

'We'll test your theory and when you're proved wrong, I'll hand you over to the law in Lonetree.'

Judah rocked back his head to laugh with mocking confidence.

'That don't concern me none. Virgil Greeley will release me before sundown and then I'll be free to — '

'Quit with the threats. Marshal

Greeley promised to kill you on sight if you ever returned to Lonetree.' Dalton waited for this threat to register, but Judah provided only an unconcerned shrug and so he pointed ahead. 'Now get this wagon rolling back to town.'

With a smile, Judah slipped on to the seat. As soon as he'd shouted instructions to his men to comply with Dalton's wishes, his mocking tone showing he expected nothing of the sort. Dalton sat beside Sera.

'Obliged,' he whispered. 'And this time I mean it when I say you'll be home by the next sundown.'

'Sundown,' she murmured before she provided a wan smile, which was a good enough response for Dalton and he settled down to watch Judah's back while looking out for his inevitable deception.

When Judah moved the wagon on, Sera whimpered restlessly, but she didn't open her eyes and so he let her sleep. He placed her at the back of the wagon where he could check on her condition from the corner of his eye while watching Judah.

Despite his misgivings, as it turned out, they rode on without incident.

Dalton's order that Judah should keep the wagon moving through the night subdued him. So Dalton stayed out of Judah's line of sight, which let him doze for a few moments on numerous occasions so that by first light he felt relatively fresh.

When he peered over Judah's shoulder at the route ahead he felt even more confident as he recognized the high point they were traversing as being the area where the Broughton brothers had stolen the ransom.

Later, Sera awoke and accepted water, but she averted her face from food. Dalton consoled himself with the thought that her condition hadn't worsened since he'd found her, and he settled down with her head resting on his chest and his gun aimed at Judah's back.

Dalton reckoned Judah would act

soon, but when they reached Black Creek and moved upriver over land with which he was familiar, he started believing Judah hadn't lied and that he wasn't worried about returning to Lonetree.

Even so, the closer they got to town, the tighter he gripped his gun.

The only sign that Judah wasn't as confident as he claimed was that only half the men who had left the campsite were still with them, the rest having melted into the night. This didn't worry Dalton as Judah was the leader and he'd settle for seeing him delivered to justice.

It was early afternoon and persistent drizzle was starting up when Dalton first saw Lonetree. Judah's only reaction was to glance into the back and smile, before he carried on into town where, without Dalton asking, he drew up outside the Culver Hotel.

Since the previous night, Dalton had been calm about Sera's condition, but with help only minutes away, he couldn't bear to waste even another moment. He kicked down the backboard and clambered out.

He hurried around the wagon and paused to shoot a warning glare at Judah, who returned a mocking salute, before he hurried into the hotel doorway, shouting for Marietta.

Patrons in the hall took up his call and within moments, a flustered-looking Marietta arrived from a back room where she took one look at Dalton before running towards him.

Dalton turned on his heel and by the time Marietta joined him, he was standing at the back of the wagon.

'You have her?' Marietta said, searching his eyes.

'She's been hurt,' Dalton said with a hopeful smile, 'but I reckon she'll be fine.'

Marietta took a deep breath before looking into the wagon at Sera, who was lying beneath a blanket with another blanket cushioning her head. She was lying at an angle that exposed her head wound and Dalton had become so used to seeing it he hadn't considered how shocking it would appear to anyone else.

Marietta screeched in anguish and the sound made Sera flop her head to the side towards her, although as usual she didn't look directly at the person who had made the noise.

The next ten minutes was a distressing time for everyone as Doctor Thornburgh and Marshal Greeley were called. While Thornburgh and Marietta were in the wagon, Dalton explained the situation to Greeley.

He started from the moment Remington had resigned, which proved to be a bad idea as the marshal scowled and he didn't remove the expression even when Dalton had finished.

'I said giving in to Judah Sundown's demands was wrong,' Greeley said, glaring up at the relaxed Judah. 'But I doubt Remington will have the guts to face me and admit that.'

'He did his best in a difficult

situation and the Sundown Kid was intent on violence.'

Greeley shrugged. 'Judah is my responsibility now. You'll do nothing more, and that includes dealing with the Broughton brothers.'

Greeley gave Dalton a long look before he turned his attention to Judah, who contented himself with a smug wink before he got down off the wagon.

'You know when we'll meet again,' Judah said to Dalton before he moved off down the main drag with the remaining four men flanking him and Greeley following on behind.

By the time they'd disappeared from view, Thornburgh emerged to confirm Sera should be taken to Marietta's quarters in the hotel.

He organized two men to bring a board as a makeshift stretcher, but the moment they tried to move her, Sera whimpered and started shaking. Dalton stepped in and, as he had done through most of yesterday, he picked her up and carried her to the hotel.

Sera quietened and, when Dalton caught Marietta's eye, she was smiling for the first time since he'd returned.

He walked along an aisle created through the watching patrons, who burst into spontaneous applause when they saw that Sera was stirring. Thornburgh and Marietta followed on behind and, once Dalton had placed her on a bed, he backed away.

Sera lapsed into unconsciousness again and so he left to give her space. He sat on a chair in the corridor, although he left the door open in case she panicked about him not being there, and a short while later Marietta joined him.

She was biting her bottom lip and she closed the door carefully behind her.

'She went to sleep the moment she lay on the bed,' Marietta said. 'Doctor Thornburgh says that's a good thing and she needs plenty of rest.'

'I'm relieved,' Dalton said. 'For the last day I've been unsure whether she'd live or die.'

'It looks as if it'll be the latter and that's down to you.'

'Not just me. She's a brave young lady to have coped with what happened and to have fought so hard to survive.' Dalton didn't think Marietta would appreciate hearing how Sera had held a gun on Judah and so he limited himself to a simple explanation. 'She saved my life as much as I saved hers.'

'I already knew she'd make a fine woman and if she can cope with all that's happened to her at fourteen, she'll cope with anything.'

Dalton blinked back his surprise. 'I thought she was older.'

'She's tall, like her mother.'

Dalton shrugged before he described events since he and Remington had left town.

The tale of the Broughton brothers' treachery made Marietta wince. When he described Judah Sundown's involvement, she shook her head sadly.

After this revelation, she stared into the middle distance, seemingly paying only cursory interest to the rest of his tale.

'I haven't seen Remington since he left us,' Dalton said, finishing his story with a suitable version of their argument.

'I hope he comes back soon. Believing that Sera died must have been hard on him.' She sighed. 'I promised I'd pay you whatever you wanted if you brought Sera back and I will, but I have plenty to think about with the Sundown Kid being behind this and with Lawrence and Hamilton stealing the ransom.'

'Perhaps when we get the ransom back, you'll be able to pay me.' He waited until she nodded and then slapped a fist into his palm. 'Which gives me yet another reason to find them.'

9

After the exertions of the previous days, it was several hours after sunup when Dalton awoke, and that was after retiring before sundown.

The rain that had set in the day before had built in ferocity overnight and so the morning presented a dull sight, but it wasn't a depressing one.

When Dalton checked with Marietta, she reported that Sera had enjoyed a restful night. Although she didn't want her daughter to be inundated with visitors and Sera was no longer distressed when Dalton was elsewhere, she let him sit with her.

Sera didn't register his presence, giving Dalton the impression that Marietta was claiming her condition was fine because she was desperate to remain optimistic. Despite this, when Marietta led him aside and asked for his view, he agreed she was making progress.

He asked her if she knew why the Sundown Kid had kidnapped Sera, but she didn't want to talk about him and, after promising to keep Dalton informed of Sera's progress, she left to sit with her daughter.

Despite Greeley's warning to stay away from the Broughton brothers, Dalton wanted to search for the men who had created the crisis. Unfortunately, the intense rain confined him to the hotel.

From the doorway, he watched the few people who ventured out scurry back and forth across the main drag that was rapidly turning to mud while wondering how long he could wait before he checked on Sera's condition again.

As it turned out, Remington Forsyth appeared at the opposite end of town. He was trudging along taking no heed of the pools of water in his path as he was already as wet as Dalton had been when he'd been dunked in the creek.

Dalton expected Remington to go straight to the Culver Hotel, but he veered into the First Star. So Dalton headed outside as fast as he was able.

Despite his speed, when he hurried into the saloon he was drenched and so he sympathized with Remington, who was standing before the pot-bellied stove in a pool of water, clutching a coffee mug to his chest.

'It's a long way back from High Pass afoot,' Dalton said at Remington's shoulder.

Remington swirled round to consider him with surprise. That surprise turned to open-mouthed shock when he saw that Dalton was drier than he was.

'How did you get here first on one good leg?' he said.

'It's a long story and I'll tell you it when you've dried out.'

Remington gave a curt nod. 'I've been dreading breaking the news to Marietta. I assume you've already done that?'

Dalton sat down on a stool and provided a wide smile, preparing Remington for the good news.

'Sera's alive,' he said simply.

Remington flinched, spilling coffee down his chest, although he didn't appear to notice.

'I saw her get shot. Then I found her lying at the bottom of the ridge. She was still and covered in blood.'

'She was unconscious and the blood wasn't all hers. In fact getting shot and nearly being killed was probably the only way she could have — '

'Where is she?'

'She's with Marietta and I'm sure they'll both be pleased to see you, no matter how wet you are.'

Remington closed his eyes for a moment. When he got over his shock, he pointed a stern finger at Dalton.

'If you're lying, I'll punch you all the way back to High Pass.' He slammed his coffee mug on the bar beside Dalton and turned away, but after two paces he stopped. 'If you're not, I'll come back and buy you a drink.'

Dalton didn't reply and, as he was enjoying the warmth from the stove, he settled down at the bar.

Thirty minutes later, Remington returned. He had changed into dry clothing, but he still appeared tense.

'How is she?' Dalton asked.

Remington ordered two whiskeys before he replied.

'Resting.' He fingered his glass. 'I still don't agree with what you did back in the pass, but I owe you a debt for what you did afterwards out there without no help from anyone.'

Dalton nodded and raised his glass in salute. Then they sat in silence for a while, sipping their drinks.

'Have you spoken with Marshal Greeley yet?' Dalton asked, deciding not to add to Remington's obvious guilt about the situation he'd walked away from in High Pass.

'No, and I have nothing to say to him . . .'

Remington trailed off and frowned,

appearing as if he wanted to say more, but instead he gulped down his whiskey and ordered two more. His pensive expression promised he had a story to tell and Dalton had to decide if he wanted to hear it.

As he doubted he'd ever forget the cold-blooded way Judah had ordered Sera to be killed, Dalton asked the obvious question.

'What's going on here, with the Sundown Kid and Edwidge Star and Marshal Greeley and Marietta and, well, everyone?'

Remington sighed and turned his glass round several times as he collected his thoughts.

'They've all lived here for years, but as the town grew, all trouble in Lonetree originated from this saloon, so Judah and Greeley dealt with it in their own ways: Greeley used the law and Judah used fear. Last year Edwidge reckoned Judah was becoming too powerful and he ran him out of town.'

'So why did Judah settle his grudge

with Edwidge by kidnapping Sera? And how did Edwidge know Marietta had money available?'

'I don't know and we can't ask Edwidge. Apparently, nobody has seen him since we left town.'

Dalton sighed. 'Whatever the reason, I reckon we should make the Broughton brothers explain themselves. They can't get away with stealing the ransom money.'

Remington scowled. 'They'll never return here and I can't expect you to help me search for them.'

'Then think of it this way: I won't get paid for helping Sera until we can reclaim the stolen money.'

Remington snorted a laugh before he pushed his glass away.

'When the rain clears,' he said.

Remington was about to turn away, but their debate had gathered the bartender's interest. He caught Remington's eye, winked, and then pointed upwards.

'Some journeys,' he said, 'are shorter than others.'

Five minutes later, Remington and Dalton were walking along the corridor upstairs to the room the Broughton brothers had apparently holed up in at first light. They stopped on either side of the door and listened.

Dalton heard nothing within and so he looked at Remington. With gestures alone he agreed their next actions and raised three fingers.

On the count of one, Remington drew his gun. At two, he moved before the door and on three, he kicked open the door.

As Remington charged in, Dalton swung into the doorway. He picked out Lawrence, who was sitting hunched up on the bed while Remington trained his gun on Hamilton, who was nervously tilting back and forth on his chair.

Both men considered Dalton and Remington with wide-eyed concern.

'We didn't part on good terms,' Lawrence said, 'but we didn't expect to face drawn guns.'

'Get on your feet and reach,'

Remington said. 'Then you'll explain what you did.'

With nervous gulps and several shifty glances at each other, the two men got up and faced them.

'We didn't steal the ransom money,' Hamilton said quickly, making Remington smile.

'Why would you think we want to ask you about that?' Remington waited for an answer neither man appeared eager to provide. 'And why have you returned to town?'

'Because we live here and because we didn't steal nothing,' Hamilton spluttered with his cheeks red with outrage, although to Dalton this made his attempt to appear innocent look as false as it undoubtedly was. 'You shouldn't listen to Dalton's lies.'

'I don't need to listen to anyone. I saw the empty box you left.'

'We didn't leave no empty box.' Hamilton looked at Remington, who responded with a steel-eyed glare that made him sigh and spread his hands wide apart. When he spoke again, his voice was low and honest-sounding. 'We did intend to steal the money, but when we looked in the box it was already empty.'

'How can you expect us to believe that?'

'Because if we'd stolen the money, do you reckon we'd return?'

Remington hunched his shoulders, his gaze appearing uncertain for the first time and when he looked at Dalton, he received a shrug.

'We'll never get to the truth,' Dalton said. 'We have to let Marshal Greeley deal with this. And if he believes them, they'll then only have to convince Judah Sundown they're innocent.'

'The Sundown Kid's back?' Lawrence said, his voice high-pitched with concern.

'He kidnapped Sera.' Dalton smiled. 'And he's got it into his head you two stole the ransom that was meant for him.'

When this revelation made the

brothers cast worried glances at each other, Remington holstered his gun. He pointed at each man in turn.

'Don't go nowhere and before Greeley arrives, get your story straight and come up with an idea about who did take the money.'

He received stern-jawed looks from both men before he moved through the door. Dalton dallied to deliver warning glares to stay where they were and then followed Remington outside.

'If they didn't steal the money,' he said when they were standing at the top of the stairs, 'that means either someone else stole it from us while we were asleep, or it was stolen before we even left town.'

'We talked with Marietta for only a few minutes before we left,' Remington said before he moved down the stairs. 'On the other hand, we didn't sleep that deeply.'

Dalton nodded. He said nothing more until they reached the boardwalk, where he stopped and considered

Remington. Even though Remington's furrowed brow said he couldn't answer his question, he asked it anyhow.

'Clearly the brothers are worried about something, but if the money was stolen while we were in town, who could have . . . ?'

He didn't get to complete his question as a gunshot peeled out. Splinters kicked from the damp boardwalk six inches from his right foot making Dalton go to one knee.

He looked at the buildings opposite, but Remington got his attention and pointed upwards before darting back to the wall.

'The Broughton brothers,' Remington said as another gunshot peeled out from above, 'have given us all the answers we need.'

10

Dalton followed Remington to the hotel wall while glancing up. Moving quickly saved him from a second shot that clattered into the wood where he'd been kneeling a moment before.

With his back pressed to the wall, the saloon sign above his head blocked Lawrence, who was leaning out of the window, but then Hamilton appeared in the window of a different room. Like Lawrence, he was clutching a six-shooter as he peered at the main drag.

It took him only a moment to work out where they'd gone to ground and he swung his gun down to aim at them. Dalton and Remington didn't waste a moment in taking aim, but that didn't perturb Hamilton and he fired rapidly.

His gunshot sliced into the wall above their heads while their shots clattered into the underside of the sill only inches from Hamilton's hand. Hamilton ignored the distraction and he took careful aim at them.

His calm detachment spooked Remington into darting away from the wall, but Lawrence still fired at him. Remington dodged to the left and right before he found the best direction for self-preservation by ducking and fleeing back into the saloon.

When Hamilton fired again and the shot flicked the brim of Dalton's hat, Dalton reckoned Remington had the right idea.

He ran for the door, reaching it as the batwing swung back towards him. It clipped his shoulder unbalancing him, making his retreat inelegant as well as desperate.

He stumbled for a pace, walked into Remington, and both men grabbed each other to stop themselves falling over. When they'd righted themselves, the customers considered them with bemusement making Remington snarl.

'Since I've returned to town I've

wanted to make someone suffer,' Remington muttered. 'It might as well be those two.'

With that, Remington set off for the stairs. Dalton decided to help him by heading to the door.

He gave Remington enough time to reach the first room upstairs before he edged through the batwings. He planned to provide a distraction that would keep Hamilton occupied while Remington burst into his room, but when he looked up, Hamilton was dangling out of the window.

He was hanging on to the sill while looking down as he gathered his confidence to drop. Dalton didn't give him that chance and he stood beneath the sign.

Before he could aim at Hamilton, a shadow flittered on the boardwalk and a scraping sound alerted him to the fact that Hamilton wasn't the only one clambering out of a window. But by then it was too late to stop Lawrence slamming down on his shoulders.

At the last moment Dalton flinched

away and so Lawrence's feet caught him only a glancing blow, but even so, his weight sent him reeling into the wall face first.

He rebounded and staggered away for two paces before he went to his knees. He shook his head as he struggled to regain his senses; then he heard splashes.

By the time his vision had stopped swirling, Hamilton had joined Lawrence in dropping down to the street. Both men had fared better than Dalton had done and they were beating a hasty retreat.

Dalton tried to get up, but his attempt failed and he stumbled. He had to put a hand to the wall for balance and, when he drew himself up for a second time, the Broughton brothers had fled to the bottom of Lonetree Hill.

He moved gingerly away from the wall, gathering his strength with every pace and, when he'd moved off the boardwalk, Remington was looking at him from an upstairs window.

When Remington saw the brothers had reached their horses, he moved away leaving Dalton to walk on. Dalton sped up as the urgency of the situation forced him to shake off the recent blow.

As fast as he was able, he splashed through the puddles that were now forming into a lake and by the time he'd halved the distance to the bottom of the hill, the mounted men were halfway to the top. Then both men turned in the saddle and raised their guns, forcing him to keep his form small as gunshots sliced into the mud around him.

When Remington joined him, the sheets of rain had taken the gunmen from view. He and Remington wasted no time on discussion before they collected their own horses.

Despite both men's earlier reluctance to head into the torrential rain, within five minutes they were galloping through the puddles after the two men.

After cresting the hill, they were able to get close enough to see their quarries, although they stayed at the limit of their vision. Remington and Dalton didn't try to catch up with them as they headed towards the bridge at Morgan's Gap.

When they approached the bridge, the brothers soon disappeared into the undulating ground and low-lying scrub. Once they'd moved over the bridge, they could either hole up and fight them off, or flee to the north or south, so Remington and Dalton agreed that caution was required.

Slowly they approached the bridge head on, but they saw neither man and so at the water's edge, they stopped to discuss tactics. Remington didn't complain when Dalton offered to cross the bridge first leaving Remington to cover him.

The terrain on the other side of the bridge was of low scrub that provided cover if not protection while the bridge had numerous struts. So while Remington hunkered down behind the right-hand corner stanchion, Dalton dismounted and led his horse down the centre.

He moved as quickly as he could on the slippery wood, ensuring he would be visible between each strut for only brief periods while he looked for movement on the land opposite. He saw nothing other than the swollen Black Creek surging by fifty feet below.

At the halfway point, he reckoned that if their quarries planned to attack him, they should have acted by now. So he peered further afield as he looked for clues as to where they'd fled.

He was thirty feet from land when Remington shouted a warning, making him turn. Then Remington fired rapidly.

The bridge blocked Dalton's view of the land and he couldn't see what had concerned Remington. He hurried to the side of the bridge and peered around a strut at the nearby bank, but he saw no movement there and so he moved to the other side.

He saw nothing untoward, but again Remington fired rapidly making him look at the far bank. He then saw movement as two men went to ground making him wince as he accepted the brothers were one step ahead of him.

They had stayed on the near side of the creek to ambush Remington after they'd split up and when they were at their most vulnerable. He broke into a hobbling run and pounded down the bridge with his gun thrust forward.

The struts on either side of the bridge and the driving rain limited his view of what was happening on land, but the cover also gave him confidence to keep running until he reached the end. He stopped beside the final stanchion where he'd left Remington, but he was no longer there.

He worked out where he'd last seen movement and ducked down before he moved into open space. When he reached a pile of mouldering logs, he knelt and slapped his gun hand on the top of the crumbling wood.

He heard a rustling noise, but it came from some distance ahead. Then Remington shouted and several gunshots rang out, the shots so close together they had to have come from gunfire being exchanged.

From the noise he worked out the shooters were to his right and so he hurried into the damp scrub. Within moments, though, his vision was cut down to a few feet and he had to bat wet leaves and twigs aside to make progress, but he figured everyone would be having the same problem and so he battled on.

He'd covered fifty paces when the scrub thinned out giving him a clear view of the scene. Ten yards away Remington was lying on his chest behind a mound, peering over the top at a rill thirty yards away.

Remington flinched when he heard Dalton fight his way clear of the vegetation. Then he swung his gun round to aim at him, making Dalton stop and raise his hands.

He received a nod before Remington gestured, pointing out the spot in the rill where Lawrence and Hamilton were hiding. Remington directed Dalton to head to a point where he could look down on their quarries while he approached their position from a different direction.

Remington didn't wait for Dalton to agree with his plan. He got to his feet and, with his head down, he ran towards a point forty yards away from where the gunmen were hiding.

Dalton skirted around the edge of the scrub. He had halved the distance to the position Remington had ordered him to claim when, from the corner of his eye, he saw Lawrence bob up briefly over the edge.

Lawrence was ten yards away from the place where Remington had thought he'd gone to ground and the sight made Remington throw himself onto his chest. He landed with a splash in the mud and with his arms thrust out to aim his gun at the rill.

Remington rolled to the side twice, and so when Lawrence rose up again in a co-ordinated move with Hamilton, they blasted lead at his previous location.

Before they could aim at his new position, Dalton hammered a quick shot that sliced into the ground between them, sending up a slew of mud and making both men drop down.

Remington hadn't fired, but when the men disappeared from view, he got up and scrambled on to the edge where he vaulted down.

Dalton reckoned Remington was being reckless, but he could do nothing to help him other than keep moving as quickly as he was able while looking out for the gunmen. He was ten paces from the rill and the other side was becoming visible when more gunfire peeled out.

Lawrence stood up with his gun raised and aimed at the unseen Remington, forcing Dalton to fire. His shot caught Lawrence high in the chest and made him drop.

A moment later two rapid shots rattled. Then Hamilton's raised arms appeared before he dropped with a suddenness that suggested he had been fatally wounded.

Dalton kept running, awkwardly, until he reached the edge at which point he hunkered down. Below, Remington was standing up to his knees in water with his shoulders hunched.

Further along in the water, Lawrence lay face down with only the light current making his arms move while Hamilton lay on his chest with his legs in the water and his face mashed up against the side.

As Dalton clambered down, Remington waded down the rill and turned Hamilton over. He knelt by him and although Dalton could see Hamilton's lips moving, he checked on Lawrence first.

By the time he'd confirmed Lawrence was dead and he'd joined Remington, Hamilton had stilled.

'Did he explain why they went loco?' Dalton asked.

'Sure,' Remington said with a scowl. 'And it probably explains everything.'

11

'Who is he?' Dalton asked.

'This is the missing Edwidge Star,' Remington said as he knelt beside the body. 'Hamilton claimed this man stole the ransom, not them, but he wouldn't tell them where he hid it, so they killed him.'

Hamilton had confessed his crimes to Remington before he died and so Remington had led Dalton across the bridge at Morgan's Gap to Edwidge's house. Although the encrusted bloodstains on Edwidge's back said Remington didn't need to check, he turned him over to reveal Hamilton and Lawrence had shot him in the chest and neck.

'The brothers made sure he was dead.' Dalton stood on the other side of the body and glanced around Edwidge's house, noting the open windows and the unsecured door. 'But why didn't they hide his body?'

Remington got up and joined Dalton in looking around. With Dalton taking the right-hand side of the room, they began a systematic search.

'I guess they wanted someone to discover him while they were holed up so their failure to run would make them appear innocent.'

Dalton nodded, but it took another hour before he accepted Hamilton's story. The contents of the house had been strewn around, presumably when the brothers had searched for the money, and so they concentrated their search outside.

Dalton saw that beneath a pile of chopped logs the incessant rain had washed away some of the ground to reveal a sack. Once they'd kicked the logs aside and dragged the sack into the house, Remington wasted no time in opening it up.

He sighed and stood aside to let Dalton see the damp bills, coins and gold that Dalton could imagine amounted to the ransom demand of five thousand dollars.

'So Hamilton was telling the truth,' Dalton said.

'It seems Edwidge stole the money before we left town.' Remington shrugged. 'But I'm thankful we don't have to prove the sequence of events.'

Dalton and Remington directed thin smiles at each other acknowledging they both had no faith Marshal Greeley would be able to confirm the facts either. Then they set about dealing with the situation.

Remington secured the sack while Dalton found a blanket to lay over Edwidge's body, although they left him where he was so the marshal could examine the scene for himself. Then, after securing the door from prying eyes, they left.

* * *

When they returned to town, Marshal Greeley was heading into the Culver

Hotel, saving them a journey. So, acting nonchalantly to avoid drawing attention to what Remington was carrying, they followed him in.

By the time they reached the corridor outside Sera's room, Marietta and Greeley had finished their brief conversation. So Remington spoke with Marietta while Dalton drew Greeley aside to explain what they'd discovered.

'At last,' Marshal Greeley said with a beaming smile as he showed more animation than Dalton had ever seen from him.

'I thought you'd known Edwidge for years,' Dalton said, unable to hide his surprise.

'Sure, but I never liked him and I never drank in the First Star.'

'But you'll have to prove the Broughton brothers killed him to get their hands on the ransom he stole.'

Greeley shrugged. 'That'll be no trouble. Everyone's talking about the brothers shooting up the First Star and riding out of town with guns blazing.

155

You did the town a service by stopping them.'

Dalton nodded and, lost for a reply, he stepped aside, leaving the marshal to wander off with a skip in his step while whistling a contented tune. He turned away, planning to look in on Sera, but to his surprise Marietta blocked his way while Remington avoided looking at him.

'What's wrong?' Dalton asked as he considered her stern expression. 'I thought you'd be pleased we found the money.'

'I'm grateful for what you did for Sera, but not for finding the ransom,' Marietta snapped. 'That money brings nothing but pain and death to whoever has it.'

Dalton couldn't argue with that and so he stood in silence until Remington gestured at the door, signifying the departed marshal.

'Marietta's told Marshal Greeley she doesn't want Judah Sundown charged,' he said. Remington snorted a harsh laugh. 'He'll be free by sundown.'

'You can't do that,' Dalton blurted out, staring at Marietta. 'For Sera's sake, for your safety, for . . . '

Dalton waved his arms as he struggled to think of more reasons why she'd made a bad mistake, but she shook her head.

'You'll be leaving now,' she said in a matter-of-fact manner that sounded like an order.

'I'll leave when the rain stops, which won't be long.'

She bunched her jaw before she went to the sack containing the ransom.

'I told you I'd pay you whatever you asked if you brought my daughter back. You did that. Name your price.'

Dalton shrugged. 'I didn't help your daughter for the money, but my leg still pains me and so I'd like to rest up somewhere for a few weeks. And I'd like to — '

'Is this enough?' she demanded, dragging a mixture of bills and coins out of the sack without considering how much she was offering.

'That's more than generous.'

She emptied the payment into Dalton's hands and gathered another handful, which she waved in his face.

'In that case, for a man like you, this should be enough for you to leave town now, despite the rain.'

Dalton considered the money and then narrowed his eyes as understanding hit him.

'The Sundown Kid will be free shortly. So you want me to leave beforehand in case he comes looking for me.'

She slapped the rest of the money into his hands, and her haste made bills flutter away and coins tinkle to the floor. Then she spoke slowly and with determination, making her cheeks redden.

'I'm grateful you helped Sera, but I don't care what Judah Sundown does to you. I hate having to deal with men like you and the Broughton brothers and the rest. The sooner you're all out of our lives, the sooner we can return to living decently.'

She flared her eyes, defying him to retort, but as he didn't know why she was angry with him, he reckoned anything he said would only anger her more.

He dropped to his knees. When he'd gathered the money, she was heading into Sera's room, leaving Remington edging from foot to foot in confusion as to what he should do.

'Go with her,' Dalton said as she closed the door behind her. 'She's upset and once Judah's free, she'll need your help.'

'But how can I help her when I don't understand what's troubling her?'

'I can see you've never been married before, but I have and so the only advice I can offer you is that you'll have to figure that one out for yourself.' Dalton winked, but Remington frowned. 'Whatever her reasoning, she owes me nothing now and either way, I'm not leaving until the rain clears.'

Remington patted his shoulder before he followed Marietta into Sera's room, leaving Dalton to head to his own room.

Despite his comments and although he tried not to, he couldn't avoid pondering why Marietta had become angry with him.

To take his mind off a problem he doubted he'd ever understand, he counted the money. Marietta had been more generous than he'd expected, having paid him over five hundred dollars.

He sat by the window where he wondered how he could use this windfall while watching for signs of the rain stopping. He saw none and although it was hard to tell on such a murky day, darkness was closing in.

He hoped it'd relent by the morning as, with the ransom returned and with the problems he'd been hired to resolve completed, he could move on. But then he saw movement outside.

He peered down the main drag and although he couldn't see the law office, there was activity nearby with several riders having grouped up.

Presently a man walked into view

with his shoulders hunched against the rain encouraging the riders to direct a spare horse towards him. The man prepared to mount up, but then he stopped and looked at the Culver Hotel: Judah Sundown had been released.

12

Despite Dalton's fears about what the night might bring, Judah Sundown didn't return after riding out of town with his men, both those who had been freed and those who had slipped away earlier.

The morning was no brighter, although the rain wasn't as heavy as it had been, giving Dalton the dilemma of whether to leave town or to put his mind at rest first. He figured that even if Marietta was unlikely to explain her anger, he couldn't leave without seeing Sera, no matter how much it annoyed her mother.

He still dallied, reluctant to have another confrontation with her, but when he saw Marietta hurrying across the main drag to the hardware store, he headed downstairs and knocked on Sera's door.

When he heard shuffling within, he glanced around the door. To his surprise, Remington was inside and fussing around Sera's bed.

Remington was clearly deep in thought, as he didn't register Dalton's presence. When Dalton slipped inside, he flinched and backed away into a chair, toppling it.

'I just wanted to see Sera before I left,' Dalton said.

'I understand,' Remington said quickly, his tone flustered. 'And she's fine, but sleeping, so it'd be best not to disturb her.'

Dalton cocked his head to one side as he considered her, judging she looked healthier than she had the day before, even if she was again asleep. He nodded to Remington and turned to the door, eager now to leave before Marietta returned.

That thought made him realize Remington was probably flustered because he too was hurrying to do something before she returned. He turned back.

'What are you doing?'

'Nothing.' Remington pointed at the door. 'Just go before Marietta gets back and we all have another argument.'

Dalton provided a sympathetic nod and moved to turn away, but then he saw the bag lying beside the bed with clothes poking out of the top.

Remington saw where he was looking and he kicked the bag out of sight before with a shrug he acknowledged he was acting oddly.

That made Dalton note Sera's blankets had been moved aside, while a second door at the end of the room that had always been closed before was now open.

'Are you planning to take her away?'

'I'm . . . I'm taking her somewhere where I can keep her safe. The Sundown Kid will return and I can't assure her safety here.'

'Sundown,' Sera murmured, showing she had yet to shake off this habit.

Dalton narrowed his eyes. 'Marietta doesn't know about this, does she?'

'She doesn't, but then again, she invited him here.' Remington raised a hand when Dalton started to ask one of the many questions on his mind. 'You have to trust me on this.'

'I do trust you.'

'Then let me leave.' Remington shooed him away. 'And keep Marietta talking for as long as possible.'

Remington shot him an imploring look. Dalton was still minded to demand a fuller explanation, but then he heard the main door open forcing him to make a quick decision. He gestured at the other door and turned away.

While Remington bustled, he slipped into the corridor and closed the door behind him. As he expected, Marietta was approaching and she considered him with a harsh glare, but she did at least stop.

Dalton put on the biggest smile he could manage and walked towards her.

'I wanted to look in on Sera before I left,' he said using a placid tone.

'You've done that,' she snapped. 'Now go.'

'I will. I'll head downriver and I doubt I'll ever ride this way again, so you'll probably never see me again, but I hate parting with you ... with anyone, on bad terms.'

'So do I, but you'll have to accept I can't explain.'

She moved to walk by him and so he side-stepped to block her path.

'Why can't you explain?'

'I've thanked you and I've paid you. I don't owe you nothing now. Move aside.' She glared at him, but Dalton returned an equally resolute look that showed he wouldn't move. She sighed and continued in a more conciliatory tone. 'All right, but I don't want my daughter to overhear. I'll check on her and then we'll talk.'

The nature of her unexpected capitulation gave Dalton no choice but to let her pass. He still did so slowly and then he followed her while wincing in anticipation of the inevitable outcry.

Sure enough, within moments of going into Sera's room Marietta came storming out with her fists clenched and her eyes blazing.

'Perhaps you should explain now,' Dalton said, 'and then I'll explain.'

'I'm telling you nothing. Where did Remington take my daughter?'

'He's keeping her safe. He's worried the Sundown Kid will come here.'

'He will do, but that's only so I can make sure Sera will always be safe. I don't want the money, only my daughter.'

Dalton shrugged. 'I've never heard of anyone paying a ransom demand after the hostage has been freed.'

'They might do if they had no use for the money. We'll be better off without it and either way, none of this is your concern.'

Dalton considered her aggrieved gaze and posture, and then frowned.

'It is when the Sundown Kid is around and he's promised to kill me.'

'Then that's all the more reason why

you should leave now.' She flashed a triumphant smile. 'I'll let you guess when he'll be coming here to collect the money.'

Dalton turned away. 'In that case, if I meet Remington, I'll tell him when it'll be safe to bring Sera back.'

'Tell him if he doesn't bring her back immediately, I don't ever want to see him again.'

Dalton headed to the door. 'As you told me, that's not my concern.'

Before she could retort, he slipped outside and stood beneath the board-walk canopy to ponder on where Remington had gone.

He didn't know the area well enough to make a sensible guess, but when Marshal Greeley came scuttling towards him, he decided braving the rain on a fruitless search was preferable to finding out what the marshal wanted.

With a hobbling gait he hurried off making Greeley shout after him, but he didn't look back. He decided to start gathering information about where

Remington might have gone from the well-informed bartender in the First Star, but the moment he went into the saloon he regretted his decision.

The Sundown Kid had taken up residence there.

He, along with the men who had been in High Pass, were splayed out around the saloon room, drinking steadily while casting glares at anyone who came in that were so surly they'd driven most of the customers away.

'I see,' Judah said, 'you've saved me the trouble of coming looking for you.'

'And I'm pleased you're here so I can give you a warning,' Dalton said. 'Everyone knows where you'll be at sundown. Harm nobody or I'll be the one who comes looking for you.'

The eager grins on the faces of Judah's men disappeared and two men scraped back their chairs and stood up, but Judah raised a hand, ordering them to sit down.

'Nobody has forgotten what you did in High Pass, Dalton.'

'And you shouldn't forget you've only just been released from the jailhouse.'

'You reckon I'm worried about Marshal Greeley?'

Dalton tried to reply, but raucous laughter drowned him out. When that petered out, a new voice spoke up from the doorway.

'You should be,' Marshal Greeley said. 'I released you because the charges against you were dropped and because I have no proof about anything else you've ever done in this town.'

Judah turned to face the newcomer. 'You won't do nothing, Greeley. You never had the guts to take me on before and that won't ever change.'

'Except I never wanted to take you on. I kept the peace while you did whatever Edwidge told you to do.'

Judah laughed. 'Not any more he won't after the Broughton brothers filled him with holes.'

'I hated Edwidge, but he was twice the man you or I will ever be.'

'There's only one person who can compare the three of us. Do you want to take back that claim?'

Judah looked around the saloon room. He caught everyone's eye, except for Dalton's, with an obvious encouragement to laugh, and his men took the opportunity.

For his part Greeley stood two paces in from the door with his hands on his hips looking more determined than Dalton had ever seen him, making Dalton wish he knew what they were taunting each other about.

When the laughter died down, Greeley still looked at Judah; silence descended and Judah shuffled uncomfortably on his chair. Then Greeley smiled.

'No,' he said emphatically.

He waited until Judah's right eye twitched before he turned on his heel and walked out of the saloon.

With Dalton seemingly forgotten about, Judah stood up and followed. When he stopped in the doorway his men moved after him, giving Dalton only a limited view of Greeley picking a route between puddles as he made his way down the main drag.

'Hey, Greeley,' Judah shouted, drawing his gun. 'I've got my answer.'

Greeley jumped over a puddle before he turned to face Judah.

'I'm not interested in anything you — ' Greeley trailed off and scrambled for his gun, but before he reached it a gunshot blasted out.

Judah's men snickered as Greeley clutched his chest. Blood seeped through his fingers and dripped into the puddle at his feet, creating a dark patch that swirled and broke up as the rain pattered down.

Greeley fell to his knees in the water before keeling over, face first, into the puddle with a splash that sent the water skating away.

Everyone in the saloon edged forward, but as the water dribbled back to settle around Greeley's body it was clear he wouldn't get back up. It was also clear that with Judah and eight men to face, Dalton couldn't do anything other than get himself killed and so while their attention was on Greeley, he sought a way out.

The bartender saw his problem and beckoned him. So in short order Dalton hurried across the saloon room and slipped over the counter.

The bartender directed Dalton to a back door that he made for without a backward glance. Then he skirted around the backs of the saloon and the three adjacent buildings.

Only when he reached the corner of the stable on the edge of town did he pause for breath. He figured that after shooting the marshal, Judah had nothing to lose and any deals he'd made with Marietta were as irrelevant as Remington clearly reckoned they were.

It was several hours until sundown and so Dalton reckoned he had time to act. Keeping in the shadows of the buildings, he worked his way back to the main drag.

Greeley was lying where he had fallen and nobody had yet to venture outside, but that also meant Judah was still in the saloon. He hurried on and reached the Culver Hotel without incident.

Marietta was pacing the corridor and looking concerned, and unlike before she relaxed when she saw Dalton had returned.

'Judah shot Marshal Greeley,' Dalton said simply. 'You have to leave town now.'

13

Thankfully, when Dalton headed over Morgan's Gap and turned downriver, he saw the small wagon they had taken to High Pass standing outside Edwidge's house.

Marietta didn't know where Remington might have gone and this place had been Dalton's only hunch. Before he drew up, Remington appeared at the door, but when he saw Dalton wasn't alone, he slipped back inside.

'I didn't expect you to follow me,' he said when Dalton hurried inside, 'or to bring her here.'

While Dalton frowned, Marietta brushed past him to check on Sera, finding her lying on folded-over blankets by the wall beside the spot where they'd found Edwidge's body. She was sleeping as quietly as usual, at least proving the journey hadn't caused her undue distress.

'I had no choice,' Dalton said. 'You wouldn't have had a wedding to look forward to if I hadn't let her see her daughter.'

'Wedding or not,' Remington said, 'she's not taking Sera back to Lonetree.'

'I reckon that argument has been won.'

Dalton looked at Marietta, who paused from fussing over her daughter to explain what had happened.

'We have to get as far away as we can,' Remington said when she'd finished. 'Lonetree is no longer safe.'

Remington and Marietta glared at each other with their lips pursed, this clearly being a continuation of their earlier argument that had led to Remington bringing Sera to the cabin.

'As the Sundown Kid wants me dead too,' Dalton said when they'd both been silent for a while, 'can someone explain what's happening?'

'Sundown,' Sera murmured, making Marietta tense.

'All right,' Marietta said with her teeth gritted.

'You've always told me I don't have a right to know,' Remington snapped, 'so why are you going to tell him the truth?'

'His life is in as much danger as ours, so he has a right to know.' Marietta gestured at Dalton. 'Provided he stops referring to Judah by that name.'

Remington nodded. 'And that's why you got annoyed. Sera's hardly spoken and then all she has said is — '

'Sundown,' Dalton said, interrupting as he worked out why Marietta had become angry with him. 'It was the only word she said while I was bringing her back to town and I thought that was accidental, but perhaps it isn't because you don't want her ever using that word.'

Marietta caught both men's eyes and pointed at the door before she headed off. Dalton and Remington followed and outside, Marietta stood on the porch in a position where she could watch Sera, but where the rain pattering on the canopy would drown her voice.

'I don't want her to know that Judah Sundown could be her father,' she said.

Remington raised his hat to brush his fingers through his hair, although his expression didn't change suggesting this explanation wasn't a surprise.

'And is he?' he said after a while.

'Back when I opened the hotel, life wasn't as it is now and people weren't as they are now.' She lowered her head. 'It could be several men.'

'Who else?'

'Judah is the only one who's still alive.'

'Edwidge Star?' He waited until she nodded and slapped his thigh in irritation. 'I knew there was something wrong there.'

'It's worse,' she said, her voice small. 'Marshal Virgil Greeley too.'

Remington winced. 'Any more?'

'Just those,' she declared, her voice becoming indignant now she'd revealed her secret, 'and as it is between those men, you can see why I'd prefer her to never know anything.'

Remington tipped back his hat. 'One man who tried to kill her, one man who didn't care if she lived or died and a man who never wanted anything to do with her.'

'It's not quite as bad as that.'

Her voice had become quieter until she was eventually silent, but Dalton had heard enough to piece together the final element.

'Edwidge Star didn't know about the others and he cared enough to pay for your silence. He paid you small, regular amounts, but you never spent the money. So after fourteen years, it grew into a tidy sum. Then Edwidge found out you'd never used it.'

She nodded. 'I never wanted it, but I thought it'd ensure Edwidge's silence. So I kept it for Sera for when she grew up. But Edwidge was a gossip and he must have told Judah and the Broughton brothers about the money. Judah kidnapped Sera to get revenge against Edwidge, while Edwidge stole the ransom to stop Judah getting his hands on it.'

With the truth revealed the three of them stood in silence. Marietta looked at Remington for his reaction, but when he said nothing and didn't even look at her, she went back in the house.

'What do you think about that?' Dalton asked Remington.

'I understand why she's fought to keep the truth hidden,' Remington said.

'Perhaps she was right and the Sundown . . . Judah will take the ransom and leave, as clearly that's all he cares about.'

'He won't leave.'

With a sorry shake of his head Remington headed inside where he asked Marietta about Sera's condition. As his light tone sounded like they were starting to reconcile, Dalton left them alone and sat on the porch in a dry spot.

He pondered on Remington's final

comment, wondering if Judah would leave after he'd claimed the ransom. Judah probably wouldn't want to run the saloon after Edwidge's demise, but there was a chance he wouldn't find the money she had left at the hotel, which made him wonder if he'd misunderstood Remington.

He considered the wagon. He shook his head, trying to dismiss the wild idea that had occurred to him, but it refused to go away and so he hurried over to it.

He peered in the back and sure enough, the box that had previously contained the ransom was there, the ransom once again intact. Remington had presumably brought it in defiance of Marietta's wishes.

As the light level dropped, this discovery made his assessment of the situation become even gloomier until with a sigh he went inside. Remington and Marietta were sitting together against one wall.

They looked shamefaced with their argument seemingly talked out, which made Dalton recall the times when he too had once enjoyed family life. They were facing Sera and so with a smile, Dalton went over and hunkered down beside her.

Sera was breathing naturally and her colour was strong, so he ran the back of his hand over her cheek, receiving a contented murmur while her eyelids fluttered. He waited and presently she opened her eyes and met his gaze.

Her eyes widened with delight and she smiled, before she closed them again and returned to her previous state.

'It's nice to see how much calmer she is when she knows you're near,' Marietta said.

Dalton nodded, but Remington shook his head.

'A fight's coming our way,' he snapped, seemingly irritated that Sera had enjoyed seeing Dalton. 'We can't sit here kicking our heels.'

'We don't know Judah will come,' Marietta said, 'and even if he does, where can we take her?'

Remington frowned, clearly lost for an answer, but Dalton raised a hand.

'I'll let you work this out,' he said. 'I'll keep lookout.'

When he left, they didn't register his departure as they started discussing options. Outside, Dalton stood on the edge of the porch.

The rain was pelting down on the wagon, sending raindrops bouncing two feet in the air, but the sky was lighter upriver. He judged it was around sundown.

Dalton looked in on the house. He smiled. Then he drew the brim of his hat down low and traipsed into the rain.

Without preamble he gathered up the reins for his horse and Marietta's steed and clambered on to the seat. Working as quietly as he could, he moved the wagon off.

Holding on to two horses while steering a wagon wasn't easy, but to his delight he moved away from the house without anyone appearing.

He presumed the noise of the

pounding rain and the discussion inside was keeping them from noticing his departure, so he was two hundred yards away before Remington came out and looked around.

It took him several seconds to notice Dalton after which he did a double take and hurried away from the house. He splashed through the mud and then found out how slick the ground was when he slipped over and went sliding along on his chest.

Dalton's last sight of Remington before the terrain took him out of view was of him kneeling in a puddle and slapping his hat to the muddy ground.

Then Dalton speeded up and headed for the bridge at Morgan's Gap.

★ ★ ★

When Dalton drew the wagon to a halt on the top of Lonetree Hill, the rain had stopped and Marshal Greeley's body had been taken away.

The townsfolk weren't visible, but the

improvement in the weather had encouraged Judah Sundown and his eight men to loiter outside the saloon. For the first time in days the low cloud was lifting from the horizon and the sun was threatening to poke out, showing it'd be sundown within fifteen minutes.

Judah was looking towards the Culver Hotel. Presumably, he expected Marietta to be waiting for him with the money, but knowing that didn't help Dalton.

Seeing the number of men below brought home to him how foolish he'd been to ride off and face them alone. If he were to prevail, he needed a plan beyond just riding into town and confronting Judah.

He had released the horses after he'd gone over the bridge as holding them was slowing him down. So Remington could be here soon and, as he was doing this to protect him, he needed to act quickly.

He thought back through everything that had happened since he'd first come across the wagon, a thought that made him smile as this old, rickety wagon had been involved in most of the prominent incidents that had happened: the Broughton brothers had pushed him into the creek on it; the ransom had gone missing from it and starting everything; he'd brought Sera back to town on it and Remington had taken Sera away on it.

He'd been pushed into the creek on it . . . That thought gave him an idea, except this time he could use a runaway wagon to his advantage.

Dalton took the wagon away from the crest of the hill to ensure it would be out of view from below and then crawled back to the edge to consider the lie of the land.

He figured the well-worn trail down the hill would ensure the wagon rolled towards the saloon, and this would attract Judah's interest. When it reached the main drag, Judah would recognize it as being Marietta's and investigate.

Hopefully he would see the box on

the back and, guessing what it contained, he would try to reach it, but equally hopefully the wagon would have enough momentum to roll past the saloon. The incline then became steeper and, if Judah didn't get to it first, would ensure the money would plough down into the creek.

This plan had many unknowns and Dalton was unsure how they would play out, but he figured the confusion would let him seize the initiative. As the sun poked out beneath the clouds, he got to work.

He unhitched the wagon, let down the backboard and removed the canopy so the box would be visible from the back, ideally for the first time as it passed the saloon. Then he shoved the wagon towards the edge before moving on to consider what he would do after he released the wagon.

He figured he'd have to act quickly to move the wagon and then mount the horse. Then he'd have to head down the hill unseen to reach a position where he could attack Judah while he was distracted.

Unfortunately, no matter which route he took, he didn't reckon he'd have the time to get into town without being seen even though the light level was dropping as the sun edged towards the horizon. He slapped the wagon in frustration at having wasted time on a plan that probably wouldn't work before he moved to the back and clambered up.

He wondered where he could leave the money while he tried a different plan, but then he saw a rider approaching. He lay down on his front to watch him until he saw that Remington was coming, having clearly located his horse faster than Dalton had anticipated.

Dalton put aside his annoyance and beckoned him on.

'I wanted to avoid this happening,' he called as Remington drew up before the wagon, 'but as it's turned out, I need your help.'

Remington didn't reply as he dismounted and appraised the situation.

He glanced at the route to town and nodded.

'I can see what your plan was,' he said, 'but like your plans at High Pass and Morgan's Gap, it's another poor one.'

'I left you at Morgan's Gap for a good reason.'

'I know. You're a brave and resourceful man, while I'm only fit for floundering in the mud.'

'I didn't do it to make you look bad. I once had a family; you could have what I was denied. I was helping you.'

Remington got up on to the wagon to join Dalton where he kept low to avoid being seen from the town.

'That was your intent, but after you've moved on, how can I be a father to Sera when the only man she's ever looked at with gratitude is you?'

'I can't answer that one now.' Dalton pointed at the red sun. 'We need to act quickly while we still have a chance.'

Still annoyed, Remington slapped his hand away and with Dalton standing in a crouched position, the blow was strong enough to tip him over. He fell against the box and his weak leg gave way sending him sprawling towards the front of the wagon.

'We will,' Remington called as he jumped off the wagon, 'but with Sera's and Marietta's lives at stake, this time you will follow my orders.'

Dalton grunted that he agreed as he moved to follow him, but then he jerked forward.

The movement caught him by surprise and it took him several moments to realize that when he'd fallen heavily, his motion had moved the wagon. He righted himself, but that took some effort as the wheels were still rolling, and when he looked round with concern, he could see down to the town.

Clearly the wagon had crested the top of the hill and it was rolling down the side. He turned back aiming to get off, but already Remington was a dozen yards away and staring at Dalton in horror.

The trundling wheels took Dalton away down the slope. Within moments, the wagon was moving so quickly, he didn't dare jump.

14

Dalton dropped down on to his chest. Then he squirmed to the front of the wagon where he raised himself to look at the path ahead.

As he expected, the wagon was rolling down the main trail, having slipped into wheel ruts that would ensure it reached the main drag through town.

Where it would go then was still uncertain, although Dalton's bigger concern was whether he'd still be on board when it reached the town.

As had happened upriver, the wagon was shaking so much he couldn't keep his balance and the noise of the rattling wheels made it sound as if the wagon would collapse at any moment. The box was rocking from side to side appearing in danger of being bounced off the back and so Dalton clamped a hand on the lid.

That stopped it moving and it also let him brace himself between the box and the side. He looked up the slope, seeing he'd rolled for a hundred yards and Remington had moved out of sight.

Dalton hoped Remington would get over his shock quickly and help him, as the wagon was shaking so much he couldn't do anything to help himself. Even though he kept his head down, every obstacle in the wagon's path bucked him up into the air, letting him see the town ahead.

So in intermittent flashes he saw one of Judah's men get his attention. Judah faced the approaching wagon with his hands on his hips. Then he ordered two men to investigate, but they were wary of what danger the runaway wagon might present and they stayed back.

By the time he was halfway down the hill, he was travelling fast enough to reach the saloon within a minute while Judah and his men had formed a line to watch the wagon approach.

His hopes that the arrival would sow

confusion in their ranks didn't appear to be materializing. Worse, as the trail became less defined with numerous other routes into town becoming available, the wagon found its own route down the hill.

The wagon bounced over two wheel ruts, knocking Dalton to the front. Then he tumbled backwards over the box to leave him lying sprawled over it with his head mashed against a side and his weak leg lying over it.

When he'd righted himself, the main drag was no longer ahead and the wagon was veering to the left to take a new route towards the saloon. Judah was still watching the wagon without apparent concern, but one of his men yelled something and pointed at it.

Dalton presumed he'd been seen and so he clamped a hand on his holster in preparation of defending himself, provided he survived crashing into the saloon. He felt more optimistic about that possibility when the wagon reached smoother ground and it stopped bouncing around.

Even though he was travelling at a

speed that would be nerve-racking when being dragged along by horses, he felt more secure than before. So he risked looking forward again.

The saloon was a hundred yards ahead and he was within a dozen wagon lengths of the bottom of the hill. Judah had spread his men out to take up positions to either side of his potential route and Dalton's best guess was he'd slam into the wall beside the right-hand window.

Dalton hugged the base of the wagon, seeking a handhold, but he couldn't find one on the rain-slicked wood. A few moments later a thud heralded he and the box being bucked into the air before a splash sounded as the wagon ploughed into the mud.

Water sprayed up to create curtains of muddy water on both sides of the wagon that were fifteen feet higher than Dalton's head. With every roll of the wheels through the thick mud the wagon slowed, sending Dalton tumbling up against the front board.

Before, when he'd worked out how fast the wagon would roll through town, he hadn't taken account of how slow the going would be. Now he doubted he'd even reach the saloon, although as he was unable to see through the shower of mud, the only ways to judge his progress were the squelching wheels and his movement in the wagon.

After being thrust up against the front, he slid into a corner, suggesting the wagon was slipping around to slide sideways. Then he suffered a disorientating moment when the wagon tipped to the left before it slopped back down on to its wheels and spun round.

Dalton went careening around the base until, with a lurch, the wagon stopped with him pressed into a corner on his back and with the box tipped up on its edge, lying against his chest. He peered around the side to be faced with the confusing sight of the saloon seemingly standing at an angle.

Then he refocused and accepted the wagon was standing side on to the saloon with two wheels having mounted the boardwalk, leaving him wedged into the lower corner.

'That was lucky,' someone called. 'I thought it'd go rolling into the saloon.'

'Be quiet,' Judah said. 'I'm sure someone was hiding in the back.'

A murmured conversation ensued after which squelching footsteps sounded as two men made their way round the wagon. They both stopped and leaned forward to peer into the back.

Smiles appeared as they saw the box, which rapidly disappeared when they looked past it at Dalton and his drawn gun. Two quick gunshots tore out.

Dalton's first shot took the nearest gunman through the chest making him drop to his knees before he keeled over to lie face down in the mud. The second shot winged the other gunman making him stumble, but he fought off the pain and drew his gun.

Before he could raise it, Dalton planted a slug in his forehead that cracked his head back, making him topple over backwards.

While consternation broke out behind him, Dalton shoved the box aside and sought the other corner of the wagon so he could be in a different position when the gunmen organized themselves.

With the wagon being at an angle, moving while keeping his head down proved to be harder than he thought it'd be and it took Dalton several moments to slide across the base to the other corner. He ended up in a low sitting position with his back against the side and his legs splayed across the wagon floor and braced beside the box.

He waited with his gun thrust forward for the gunmen to make their next move, but as he'd feared that turned out to be wild gunfire.

They must have lined up facing the wagon as round after round tore into the wood; thankfully most of it was aimed at the spot where he'd been sitting previously.

The wood deflected some of the gunfire, but most of it burst through.

Several shots hammered into the box, saving his lower body, but all he could do to protect his upper body was to make himself as small as possible.

Being pressed tightly against the base and side proved to be the right place to be and Dalton assumed he'd inadvertently lain in a position where the seat protected him, as after reloading twice none of the shots came close.

The gunfire must have looked impressive as loud whoops sounded. Then the wagon lurched as a wheel broke, leading to more whoops.

Judah ordered someone to investigate. Despite the encouragement ringing in his ears from the other men, this man moved more cautiously than the previous two gunmen had.

Slurping footfalls sounded as the man approached the seat. Then he moved round to the side, but he didn't come into view, making Dalton realize he was creeping along, crouched over.

He got confirmation of the newcomer's plan when a hand clutched the opposite side of the wagon before the man raised himself. The moment his forehead came into view Dalton fired.

His shot clipped only wood, but it landed inches away from the man's hand and made him rock away, but with his hand clamped down firmly on the side he pushed down and managed to lower the wagon.

The movement made Dalton slide along the slippery base and his redistributed weight made the wagon tip faster. Then a crack sounded as the broken wheel gave way and the already precariously positioned wagon tipped over on to its side.

Dalton went sliding down to the side where his momentum made him fall out of the wagon and go sprawling in the mud on his knees. Laughter sounded until the man who had sneaked up on the wagon cried out.

'I was right,' he shouted. 'That is the box of money.'

'So kill him,' Judah said, 'and get the box.'

Dalton turned on his knees to face a line of seven men, all with guns drawn and all smirking as they took aim.

With a hopeless feeling in his guts, Dalton swung his gun towards Judah while, almost as a harbinger of his impending doom, darkness overcame him.

The gunmen didn't fire; instead they laughed, and Dalton saw the reason for their behaviour when the darkness became deeper. Then he realized what had happened and he prostrated himself in the mud a moment before the wagon tipped over and slammed down over him.

In the darkness Dalton raised a hand to the base of the wagon, finding it had come to rest two feet above his head. He pushed, but the base didn't move and worse, clattering sounded as Judah and his men clambered on to the top.

A moment before they acted, Dalton anticipated what they'd do. With his good leg he pushed himself to the side, the mud letting him slip along with ease.

His quick reaction saved him from a burst of gunfire that tore down through the base making holes of light burst out above the place where he'd been lying.

This time, Dalton reckoned he could use the same tactic.

The moment the gunfire stopped, he aimed at the spot where the men had fired and blasted off two quick rounds before he rolled to the side.

'Get off the wagon,' Judah shouted.

As Dalton reloaded, stomping sounded from the men moving away. Before they got off, Dalton fired at the position where he'd heard Judah.

He was rewarded with a cry of pain and a clattering sound as someone flopped down on the wagon above his head. A second thud sounded as another man got off the wagon, but then fell heavily against the side.

Someone fired down at the wagon, splaying gunfire wildly, but with Dalton lying beneath the body none of the shots came close. His delight was short-lived as Judah ordered the man to get off the wagon, confirming he hadn't hit the leader.

'He can't keep avoiding us,' someone said.

'He won't,' Judah said. 'End this.'

Silence reigned and unlike before, Dalton heard no hints of what the men were doing.

For his part he used the light shining through the bullet holes to locate the box and shuffled closer to it, although he was unsure where the gunmen would be when they fired at him again.

A creak sounded above, giving Dalton a warning of what they planned before a sliver of light appeared along one side of the wagon. When Dalton realized they were righting the wagon, he shuffled behind the box from where he peered at the expanding gap.

When the gap grew to a foot high, Dalton saw three men standing on dry ground in the centre of the drag, suggesting the other two men were righting the wagon.

He could see only their boots, but he reckoned he could still inflict damage and so he aimed at the right ankle of the central man, figuring that man would be Judah.

Unfortunately, Judah must have been aware of the possibility of this response as the men blasted a round apiece at the gap, forcing Dalton to retreat behind the box. But it also made the men who were tilting the wagon shout out in complaint that they were behind the line of fire.

The wagon thudded back down. Then more gunfire erupted.

Dalton cringed, but none of it hit the wagon and even better, rapid footfalls beat a hasty retreat, making him hope that this showed that Remington had made his way down the hill unseen and was helping him.

For several minutes silence dragged on. Then the gap opened up again, and this time nobody was visible.

Dalton judged they'd try the same tactic as before, except they might learn from their mistakes and fire systematically into the wagon from numerous angles. Before they started, Dalton seized the initiative.

He shoved the box towards the nearest corner. The muddy ground helped him move it quickly and as he'd hoped, the box slipped into the expanding gap as it became wide enough to accept it.

This gap was also wide enough to let Dalton slip through and so he snaked under the back of the wagon with his gun thrust out before him. He could see nobody ahead and so as he emerged, he twisted to the side.

His foresight was rewarded when he found himself looking up at one of the men who were tugging the wheels to tilt the wagon. The man released the wheel and threw his hand to his gun, but not before Dalton planted a slug in his chest that made him fall away.

The other man who was tilting the wagon alerted Judah with a strident cry and, when he released the wheel, the edge of the wagon pressed down on Dalton's back leaving only the box to keep the corner elevated.

With his manoeuvring space reduced, Dalton stayed where he was and looked for the other men. Gunfire sounded and so he hugged the ground, but unlike the previous time he didn't hear shots slice into the wagon.

Then at the far corner of the wagon an agonized cry sounded followed by a heavy clatter that had probably been made when the other man who had stayed with the wagon fell over.

He reckoned Remington had shot this man, but Judah's remaining men were closing in on him and so he needed to get out before they trapped him. He squirmed, but the edge was only inches above the small of his back and he struggled to move over the soft ground.

A second burst of gunfire tore out that clattered into the box to his side and the wagon above his back. He stopped trying to slip out and looked up, seeing a man hurrying closer with his gun thrust out.

The man was heading towards Dalton and so he presented a clear target. Dalton fired twice, his first shot being wild while the second shot clipped the running man's shoulder, making him drop.

Dalton kept low while he reloaded, which proved to be a difficult task when constrained and so he had to squirm forward before he could complete the action. Then he looked up to find the wounded man was on his knees and struggling to hold his gun steady.

The man saw that Dalton was ready to take him on and so he splayed lead at him. The shots were wild and clipped the box, and so Dalton took steady aim.

His shot sliced high into the man's chest making him keel over to the side. Then an ominous creak sounded.

The sustained gunfire had clipped the box and it was teetering and no longer looking as if it could support the wagon.

Dalton moved quickly, but he wasn't quick enough and the box tipped to the side making the wagon slam down on his legs. Dalton screeched in pain as both his good and his injured leg were driven into the ground.

The next few moments passed in a blur as he struggled to concentrate.

He gritted his teeth and willed himself to take account of what was happening. When he looked up, through pained eyes he saw Judah Sundown standing before him, considering his predicament with glee and an aimed gun.

15

Dalton held his gun slackly and was lying awkwardly. It would take him several moments to raise the gun and aim, while Judah had already taken aim at him.

'I should have finished you off on the ridge,' Judah said.

'Except you didn't,' Dalton said. 'You were too busy ordering the death of a young girl.'

Judah raised a hand, ordering an unseen man who was standing beyond the wagon to stay back and, presumably, to keep Remington busy. Dalton thought back through the gunfight and he figured that only one of Judah's men was still alive.

'You don't know the full story of why I did that.'

'I'm sure you don't, or you wouldn't have wanted Sera dead.'

Judah shook his head. 'She was Edwidge Star's daughter, not mine; that's why he paid the blackmail money.'

'Marietta told Edwidge that Sera was his, but that was a lie.'

'What does that mean?' Judah muttered, his gun hand tightening as he narrowed his eyes.

Dalton sneered. 'It means you tried to kill your own daughter.'

Judah flinched back in surprise for a half pace, and his gun drifted away from Dalton for a mite.

'I'd never do that, but that doesn't matter as you're lying. Marietta never once spoke to me about Sera.'

Dalton looked Judah up and down, and then snorted with derision.

'Do you think she'd want anyone to know Sera's father is you?'

This comment hit home as Judah's eyes glazed and his gun arm twitched. So with him distracted, Dalton seized what might be his only chance. He twisted the gun in his grip and jerked up the weapon.

Judah saw what Dalton intended to do, but he was still slow to get his wits about him and fire, giving Dalton enough time to blast a shot low into his guts that made him fall forward.

As Judah's gun dropped to the ground, Dalton tried to raise himself to see the other gunman, and his movements became more frantic when gunfire tore out from beyond his vision.

Someone screeched and to his left a man stepped into view. Dalton turned his gun towards him, but with a relieved sigh he stilled his fire and nodded at Remington, who walked on to stand over Judah.

'Is that true?' Judah murmured, clutching his blooded belly. 'Is Sera mine?'

Remington sighted Judah down the barrel of his gun.

'Nah,' he said.

He didn't fire when his taunt took the fight out of Judah and he slumped to lie face down in the mud. Judah didn't move again, but Remington still checked he was dead before he tasked himself with moving the wagon off Dalton's legs.

Remington couldn't help him alone, but with the gunmen dead, customers emerged from the saloon to help tip it over. While Dalton massaged his legs, Remington gathered up the box and set it on the back of the wagon.

Then he straightened the wheel and strained to get the wagon moving. Once it was rolling, to the townsfolk's bemusement, he shoved the wagon on to the corner.

When he'd manoeuvred it past the corner, the slope beyond the saloon took control of the wagon and, as Dalton had planned originally, it rolled from view. It headed down to the creek, the broken wheel making the wagon rattle and scrape along loudly and letting Dalton follow its unseen progress.

When the wagon tipped into the water, the watching townsfolk started murmuring uncertainly and Remington turned away to find Dalton was sitting on the edge of the boardwalk. Dalton flexed his bad leg gingerly and, when he decided it hadn't suffered any further damage, he smiled at Remington.

'I reckon we both did well there,' he said, 'but why did you push the wagon into the water?'

Remington returned the smile and held out a hand to help Dalton to his feet.

'As Marietta said,' he said, 'that money brings nothing but pain and death to whoever has it. So while we still had it, our problems would never end.'

★ ★ ★

'So you're really not concerned about the money?' Dalton asked when he'd eaten the dinner Marietta had provided.

'The money's gone,' Marietta said, not meeting his eye. 'Others might find it, and if they do I hope it brings them as much trouble as it brought me.'

Since Marietta had brought her daughter back to town, Sera had been more animated than Dalton had ever seen, and so Marietta had let her leave her room to sit with them while they ate.

Sera was resting quietly in a chair in the corner, but she had eaten the broth Marietta had fed her and she'd even taken the spoon herself for a few mouthfuls.

Dalton wished he could stay to watch her recovery, but he didn't feel he should as Marietta was still treating him coldly now he knew the secret about Sera's father.

'I hope,' Dalton said, 'not having the money brings you two, as well as Sera, happiness in the future.'

'And I hope,' Remington said, 'having your reward brings you some joy.'

Dalton nodded, but mentioning the future made Marietta frown.

'I do too, and thank you,' she said in her usual matter-of-fact manner, 'but you'll be leaving now.'

This time Dalton accepted her order and stood up.

'I'll stay here tonight,' he said. 'In the

214

morning, I'll leave.'

Then he headed to Sera's chair and knelt down on his good leg. She looked at him and smiled.

'Thank you for everything,' she said, her voice small, but strong. Even better, she was aware she'd spoken softly as she coughed and repeated her comment in a stronger voice.

'I did nothing,' Dalton said, remembering Remington's lament on Lonetree hill. 'I only helped Remington.'

From the corner of his eye, he saw Marietta nod and Remington smiled, but he met Sera's gaze while he had her concentration.

'You carried me from High Pass,' Sera breathed. 'You fought for me. You brought me back here. You saved my life.'

'You're mistaking me for Remington.' Dalton laid a hand on her arm. 'You've been hurt and you're still confused. Rest.'

Sera looked at him with doubt, but her longest conversation since her injury had tired her and she looked away. Her gaze sought out Remington before she closed her eyes and so with that, Dalton stood up and, without looking at the others, he headed to the door.

'Thank you,' Remington said.

Dalton turned and inclined his head, but he couldn't resist asking one final question.

'One matter still troubles me,' he said. 'I moved the box containing the money and which is now in the creek. It was surprisingly light and easy to manoeuvre, almost as if there was never anything in it in the first place.'

Marietta offered him a small smile, as did Remington.

'That matter,' she said, 'will have to continue troubling you.'

THE END

We do hope that you have enjoyed reading this large print book.

Did you know that all of our titles are available for purchase?

We publish a wide range of high quality large print books including:
Romances, Mysteries, Classics
General Fiction
Non Fiction and Westerns

Special interest titles available in large print are:
The Little Oxford Dictionary
Music Book, Song Book
Hymn Book, Service Book

Also available from us courtesy of Oxford University Press:
Young Readers' Dictionary
(large print edition)
Young Readers' Thesaurus
(large print edition)

For further information or a free brochure, please contact us at:
Ulverscroft Large Print Books Ltd.,
The Green, Bradgate Road, Anstey,
Leicester, LE7 7FU, England.
Tel: (00 44) **0116 236 4325**
Fax: (00 44) **0116 234 0205**

GUN STORM

Corba Sunman

Death comes calling on the small mining town of Lodestone when the storekeeper's wife Martha is murdered by a thief. Deputy Jim Donovan pursues and guns down a man witnessed fleeing the scene, but testimony from his brother Joey indicates that the killer is still at large. Elroy Johnson, the stagecoach robber Donovan arrested three years ago, is back in town — could he be involved? Meanwhile, the outlaw Stomp Cullen and his gang have been spotted lurking around Lodestone. All signs point to an upcoming gun storm . . .

THRILLINGLY GOOD BOOKS
FROM CRIMINALLY
GOOD WRITERS

CRIME FILES BRINGS YOU THE LATEST RELEASES FROM
TOP CRIME AND THRILLER AUTHORS.

GN UP ONLINE FOR OUR MONTHLY NEWSLETTER AND BE THE FIRST
TO KNOW ABOUT OUR COMPETITIONS, NEW BOOKS AND MORE.

Also by Mary Torjussen

Gone Without A Trace

Mary Torjuss_____ to televi-
sion in her fai_____ape – she
spent hours reading and writing stories as a child. Mary has an MA
in Creative Writing from Liverpool John Moores University, and
worked as a teacher in___rpool___efore becoming a full-time
writer. She has two adul_ children an___s_n the Wirral. *The Girl
I Used__Pa* is her second novel.

Praise for *Gone Without A Trace:*

'Suspenseful and subtle, this novel plays with all of your expectations. Not to be missed!'
Shari Lapena, author of *The Couple Next Door*

'I practically inhaled this book. A clever and uncompromising
thriller'
Katerina Diamond, author of *The Teacher* and *The Secret*

'A page turner with a cracking ending'
Jenny Blackhurst, author of *How I Lost You* and *Before I Let You In*

'This fast-paced story kept me guessing – great twist at the end'
K.L. Slater, author of *The Mistake* and *Liar*

'A taut, suspenseful debut very much rooted in reality: any one of
us could come home to an empty house and want to find out the
answers. With a twist that will knock your socks off, Torjussen is
one to watch'
Gillian McAllister, author of *Everything But The Truth*

'*Gone Without A Trace* is exactly the kind of book I like to read. It not
only pulls you in, but it also makes the reader think. I loved it!'
Amanda Reynolds, author of *Close To Me*

'Has a twist I really didn't see coming'
Cass Green, author of *The Woman Next Door*

For Rosie and Louis
And for my mother and my late father
And for Ann Perkins in Aberdare
With love

Prologue

Fifteen years ago

Thursday, August 15

When I think of that night now, I remember the heat, clammy and intense on my skin, and the sense of feverish excitement in the air. I think of the taxi ride to the party with my friend Lauren, her body soft and scented against mine as we sat crushed into the back seat with her boyfriend Tom. The radio was on, the windows were open, and 'London Calling' started to play. I remember the surge of happiness I felt then; I'd just been accepted by London University and would be there within a month. Whenever I hear that song now, it takes me straight back to that taxi ride to Alex's house. It's as though I *am* that girl, the girl I used to be.

But I'm not.

I can feel the sandals I was wearing as though I'm wearing them now. I could hardly walk in them; I wore them that night for the first time and within an hour I had blisters. I can remember the feel of my dress, its soft cotton brushing my skin. When I close my eyes I can feel the breeze lifting my

hair. I can smell the perfume I wore, taste the lip gloss on my mouth.

But always, always, when I think of that night, I think of Alex.

It was mid-August, the summer we were eighteen, and over two hundred of us from school were going to celebrate our exam results at Alex Clarke's party. Lauren and I had got ready together at her house, and I'd sneaked in the little pink dress that I'd bought with the money I was supposed to be saving for university. We were tanned from the summer sun; each day we worked until mid-afternoon in the café in our local town, and then we'd strip off our sweaty nylon overalls, pull on our shorts, and spend the rest of the day down at the beach. That afternoon we'd spent an hour or so topping up our tans before going back to her house to get ready for the night ahead. This was the start of the rest of our lives, we told each other. We wanted to look different, like we were ready for our new lives away from home.

We had a few drinks before we went to the party. Lauren's mum came into her room with a bottle of champagne to celebrate our results, and insisted on refilling our glasses whenever they were empty. We didn't tell her we'd already had tequila shots. Lauren had more to drink than I did, but she always did back then. As soon as I was seventeen, I passed my driving test and my dad bought me a runaround so that I didn't have to ask him for lifts. I loved driving and was happy to have soft drinks and ferry everyone about. I suppose that's why it hit me so hard that night.

It was a Thursday in the middle of August and we had to go to the school office first thing that morning to get our results. We felt they were life or death; if they were what we needed, doors would be opened to the top universities, the best courses, and a life full of promise. Just a grade down and we'd be

screwed. The lives we'd hoped for just wouldn't happen. Or so we thought. And while we knew – we'd been told often enough – that everything would work out no matter what, that other universities were still good, we were young enough to believe that no, actually, things wouldn't be okay. We all knew people who'd failed to get into their first-choice university, who'd talked about it for years later.

But that wasn't our fate that summer. It was a stellar year. Everyone seemed to get the results they needed to do what they wanted to do. It was exhilarating, the way we opened our envelopes and screamed, one after the other.

And I remember Alex and his friends, all of them bound for Oxford or Cambridge, trying to hide their elation behind cool exteriors. They were fooling no one. They'd seen themselves as separate from the rest of us – they *knew* they were different – and now they were proven to be right. Or that was how I saw it then. I didn't even know him; I'd only spoken to him once, but that was the impression he and his friends gave.

Lauren and I were standing behind their group that morning in the queue for the exam results and overheard his friend Theo ask, 'The party's on then?'

Alex nodded. 'Spread the word around. People from here only. No one else.'

I'd nudged Lauren and she'd giggled; we'd been looking forward to it for months and had everything planned, right down to the nail varnish we'd wear on our toes.

The local press was there in full force that morning, pre-arranged by the school, and there were photos taken of us all, grouped into sets, our expressions happy and free. Our teachers stood with us, their faces so tanned and relaxed I could hardly recognize them. The relief among all of us was palpable.

Alex's house was in the middle of the countryside, ten miles out of town. We'd guessed it would be bigger, more expensive, but the scale of it surprised us. It was a detached house set in

pristine landscaped gardens on the edge of a village. There were no near neighbours; the garden was surrounded by fields, beyond which we caught glimpses of the river.

He and Theo were standing at the front door when we arrived, making sure that they knew us all. There'd been stories in the news that summer about parties where crowds had gatecrashed and the police had had to be called; it was obvious from the way he checked everyone as they walked up the driveway that he was on guard for that.

'Hi,' he said. 'Come on in!'

Behind Alex was Jack Howard, one of his friends, who was taking photos of everyone as they went into the house. We'd known for a long time that he'd had a crush on Lauren, and when he saw us, he blushed and busied himself with his camera. She slung her arms around Tom and me and we posed there on the doorstep, giddy and excited at the thought of the night ahead. After Tom went through the front door, she turned and blew a kiss at Jack and turned to wink at me.

Whenever I think of Lauren, I think of us giggling. Just about anything could make us laugh. When Alex had greeted us, we giggled and nudged each other and went through the large hallway into the kitchen at the back of the house. It was full of food and alcohol. People had gone overboard and brought spirits and crates of beer and armfuls of wine bottles. I heard Jack say that Alex's parents were away on holiday; they'd agreed that if he got top grades – which meant he'd be accepted by Oxford – and if he paid for a deep clean afterwards, he could have a party to celebrate. They would be back a few days later and didn't want to see any sign there'd even been a party. That was a bit optimistic, I thought.

Everyone in our year was invited to that party and most were there. There were so many I only knew by sight, but we were all on such a high that pretty soon we were kissing everyone and anyone, congratulating people we barely knew,

just grateful that we'd done well and were going to have our chance to get away. You'd think we were living in some sort of hellhole, the way we carried on, as though our only chance of a good life was to leave behind the one we had.

Lauren and I had done well; Tom too. We were all off in a month's time to different universities. She and I had been friends since nursery school, and it would be almost the first time Lauren and Tom would have spent more than twenty-four hours apart in the two years she'd known him. I thought our friendship would last the separation, and guessed she'd stay with Tom, too; there was an ease about them that I envied. That night their arms were entwined and I noticed when she kissed a friend that she'd align herself with Tom, as though they were one person, so they embraced the friend together.

I drank so much that night. All of us did. It was the first time we'd all been together like that and we knew it would be the last time, too. Despite that, people didn't seem drunk. Not really. Nobody was staggering or falling, and apart from my friend Lizzie, who was sick into an ornamental bay tree on the patio before it was even dark, nobody was ill. We were all outside and then the music was turned up and everyone was dancing. I lost Lauren and Tom somewhere along the way. When I saw her later, her dress was buttoned up wrongly and she had a fresh love bite on her neck. She was telling someone she hadn't ever spoken to before that she would always miss them.

Then all of a sudden, past midnight, it hit me. I realized I was more drunk than I'd ever been. I'd been drinking more and more as the night went on, and most of it was punch from a huge bowl that one of Alex's friends had been in charge of. God knew what had been in it – there were bottles of every spirit and liqueur you could think of lying around, and I was sure that most had ended up in that bowl. Lauren and Tom were lying in a hammock nearby by then, and when

I turned to them, clinging onto the back of a garden chair for support, she smiled lazily and closed her eyes. I knew she wouldn't want to go home yet. I was staying at her house that night and we were sharing a taxi home. Her mum had promised to leave the money next to the front door and the key under the doormat, so that we didn't have to take our handbags with us.

My heart sank. It could be hours before Lauren wanted to leave. I started to walk back towards the house and staggered, falling into a bush. I didn't mind; I thought it was funny. One of the girls from school yanked me back up again and asked if I was all right. I nodded. I don't think I could have spoken if I'd wanted to.

When I reached the house I was suddenly desperate for the toilet. There were several portable toilets at the bottom of the garden but I didn't think there was a chance I'd reach them in time. I searched for a cloakroom inside the house and found a door under the stairs, which I thought was probably what I wanted. When I tried to open it, I heard a boy laugh and a girl say 'Shh!' and I realized what was going on. I gave a deep sigh, knowing there was no point in waiting, and went further into the house. I could hardly see by then and was smiling at just about everyone. The mood was high, voices were loud, everyone was happy.

At the foot of the stairs there were a couple of chairs, with a note telling people to keep out. I couldn't wait by then, though, so I squeezed past them and found a bathroom just at the top of the stairs. I stumbled in and sat down so fast I nearly dislodged the toilet seat. I found that funny, and wondered just what was in that punch. I wasn't so drunk that I didn't wash my hands, though, and saw that my face was flushed in the bathroom mirror, my eyes bleary and half closed. I knew I'd suffer the next day; I would have even if I'd stopped after the champagne and the tequila shots at Lauren's

house. I remember grimacing as I thought of the headache I'd have. The following afternoon I was going on holiday to France for two weeks with my family, and already I was dreading the long car journey with a hangover.

As I turned from the basin, I slipped on a towel someone had left on the bathroom floor. I probably should have picked it up, but I realized pretty quickly that if I bent down, I would fall. I doubted I'd be able to get myself back up if that happened, so I kicked the towel to one side and opened the bathroom door. It was quiet upstairs, though I could hear the sounds of the party continuing downstairs and out in the garden. I tripped at the top of the stairs and grabbed the handrail. I didn't think I'd make it down without falling. My head was spinning by then and I had a sudden vision of myself hurtling head first down the stairs.

I backed away from the staircase and stumbled back into a door. It opened behind me. A lamp was lit next to a double bed. From the hockey stick propped up against the wall, I realized it must be Alex's room. He played for the school team; the only time I'd spoken to him was when he dropped his kit when he was hurrying to get to a match. Posters from the Glastonbury music festival he'd gone to that summer were on his bedroom wall. I'd known he was going to it, just after the exams ended. Lauren had heard him talking to Theo about it when they were all queuing up to leave the hall after their last exam. A local band, The Coral, were playing at Glastonbury that year, and Alex was wearing their T-shirt at the party. A drum kit was in the corner of the room next to a guitar and a huge amp. I remember wondering whether he was any good and thinking he wouldn't play if he wasn't.

I sat down on the bed. Suddenly I was so weary, I just wanted to sleep. My head was spinning and everything was blurred. I couldn't summon up the energy to go back downstairs, and I knew that when I did, Lauren would want to stay

longer and wouldn't want to spend time with me. Only that night she'd said that she and Tom had just three weeks left and they were going to spend every single minute together.

So I lay down. The bed was so soft, its covers clean and fragrant. It smelled like my own bed when the linen had just been changed. I loved the scent of clean sheets. And I knew Alex wouldn't know I'd been here – he was a party boy; he'd be outside until dawn.

My head relaxed onto his pillow. I had a fleeting thought that my make-up would be all over the pillowcase, but I couldn't care about that then. The door was half open and I knew that Lauren would come to find me. She'd know I hadn't gone home; how could I? I had no money on me and I wasn't going to go back to my own house as drunk as this. The bedside lamp cast a soft glow over the room and the light from the landing flooded the entrance to the room. *She'll see me here,* I thought. *She'll tell me when it's time to go home.*

I turned to face away from the lamp. I've never liked to sleep with a light shining on my face. As I turned, I felt my dress ride up and I made a half-hearted attempt to pull it down. The scent of the pillow and the alcohol in my bloodstream and the lateness of the hour and the fact that I'd been awake until dawn that morning, worrying about my exam results, meant that when I turned back, my head buried in the pillow, I relaxed completely. I remember sighing as I slipped into sleep.

It had been a great night. A really great night.

Part I

1

Friday, June 16

When I saw him for the first time, I didn't think he'd be trouble. He was tall and broad, built like a rugby player, nice enough, but not the kind of man you'd necessarily look twice at in the street. At first glance he seemed harmless enough. That's how men like him operate, I suppose.

I saw him that morning, looking at the advertising boards in the window of the estate agency I own, but didn't take a lot of notice at first. Over the course of a day maybe a hundred or so people will look at the boards, trying to decide which house they'd buy if they had the chance, and I'd quickly learned that an expression of interest did not mean a sale. He lingered for a while, moving from the cheapest houses to the most expensive. I remember idly wondering what he was looking for.

When he did come in, he hung about in the doorway, as though he were waiting for someone. I glanced around and saw that Rachel, our sales negotiator, was at the photocopier

and Brian, our lettings manager, was busy with a tenant. Usually we leave clients to look around, but he seemed uncertain, so I caught his eye and smiled.

'Good morning,' I said. 'Can I help you with anything?'

'I'm David Sanderson,' he said, coming to sit at my desk. 'I have an appointment.'

'Oh yes,' I said, flustered. He was an hour earlier than I'd expected and I'd planned to run out to meet my friend Grace for coffee for half an hour. 'Hi. I'm Gemma Brogan.' We shook hands. 'Just a moment, I'll call up your details.'

While I did that, I surreptitiously sent Grace a quick e-mail. Sorry, can't meet. Another day?

'So you're looking for somewhere in the city centre,' I said. 'I can see you've selected a number you like the look of.'

'I'm still not sure whether to go for a flat or a house,' he said. He smiled then, a great smile that made his face light up. It transformed him from someone you wouldn't really notice to someone you'd definitely remember. I couldn't help but smile back. 'I'm not sure if I'm ready for a house. I'd rather be near some bars and a gym.'

'Will you be buying on your own?'

I could see Sophie, our junior administrator, who was always on the lookout for a boyfriend, giving a sidelong look at Rachel. I could tell from the way they both became very still that they were waiting for his answer.

'Yes, I'm single,' he said. 'I'm just looking for somewhere for myself.'

I reckoned he was around my age, in his mid-thirties. Now that he was at ease and smiling, it was hard to believe he wasn't snapped up already, though of course he could be divorced.

'Are you from Chester?' I asked. 'I'm trying to place your accent.'

'I grew up in the north-west but I've been working over in

the States for the last ten years or so. Boston. My company's transferred me to the UK for a while. A few years, I guess. I've sold up over there; no point in keeping the old place going.'

'Who're you working for?'

'Barford's. I'm in sales.'

I nodded. Barford's was a large pharmaceutical company that had its headquarters on an industrial estate just outside Chester. I'd found properties for a couple of people there; it was supposed to be a great place to work.

He clarified the amount he was willing to spend; it was in the upper ballpark of properties in Chester, and I started to get excited. We had plenty of properties on our books. Things were moving more slowly than usual and I knew I could find him something. He'd named a great price and he was willing to try out a lot of different areas. I *had* to sell to him. I didn't want to have to come back to the office and tell my staff that he had decided to go elsewhere.

'I'll get some details,' I said. 'I won't be a moment.' I saw that Sophie was busy with a client, so I called over to Rachel, who was putting brochures in the window. 'Rachel, would you make Mr Sanderson a drink, please?' It wasn't her job to do that, but in such a small office we all had to take on that duty if someone else was busy.

She came over to my desk. 'Would you like tea or coffee?'

'I'll have coffee, thanks,' he said.

'How do you like it?'

I glanced at her and had to stop myself from laughing. Her face was pink and she couldn't bring herself to meet his eyes. She and Sophie were always the same when a good-looking guy came into the office. They were both young and single, though Sophie had nerves of steel when it came to dating, while Rachel seemed more shy and nervous.

He smiled at her. 'White, no sugar, thanks.'

She blushed again and disappeared into our tiny kitchen behind the office. Sophie swiftly followed her and I could hear muffled giggles.

We drank the coffee and went through the details of some of the properties I had. He seemed particularly interested in the flats that overlooked the River Dee and others that were in the centre of the city.

I glanced at the office diaries online. I would normally send Rachel out, but she had another appointment that morning. I had a valuation in several hours' time, at four P.M. 'You said in your e-mail you were free until three P.M. I can take you to view some properties now if you like.'

'That would be great,' he said. 'I'd love to look around this area; I don't know it well at all.'

'Just give me a few minutes,' I said. 'I'll make some calls and get my keys.'

'I can drive us if you like.'

'It's fine, thanks,' I said. 'It'll be easier if I drive. I know the quickest routes.'

I asked Sophie to take some details from him and he went over to sit with her. Sophie was only eighteen and fresh from school. She was still learning the ropes; I'd had to weigh up experience versus cost when I'd employed her, and still wasn't sure I'd made the right decision. As I made my calls I saw her, her face bright with excitement, asking David for his details and laboriously entering them into the computer.

I always drive round to the front of the office to pick up clients, so that they don't have to go through the back and into the car park. As soon as he got into my little car I could see I should have let him drive his own. He was over six feet tall, with long legs and broad shoulders, and he looked really cramped in the passenger seat.

'I'm sorry!' I said as he struggled with the seat belt. 'Shall we go in your car? I can direct you.'

'It's fine.' He turned and grinned at me. 'I used to drive a Mini.'

I laughed.

'My mum bought herself one when I was seventeen,' he said. 'I think she thought it would put me off borrowing it.'

'And did it?'

'No, but I saved up for my own car much quicker than I would have if she'd had a bigger one.'

'Clever woman. I'll have to remember that when my son's old enough to drive.'

'How old is he now?'

'Three.' I smiled. Every time I thought of Rory, I smiled. 'Plenty of time to go.'

The first property I took him to was a block of flats set in a gated courtyard within the city walls. As I drove, he asked questions about the area and I talked to him about the old Roman walls that encircled the city.

'Walking around the walls of the city is a great way to get to know Chester,' I said. 'It's a couple of miles and you follow the wall around – it's virtually complete. You get to see the racecourse, the castle, and the cathedral as well as the River Dee. So you can see, it's a pretty small city, but it's got a lot going for it.'

'Have you lived here long?' he asked.

I nodded and told him I'd grown up on the Wirral, twenty-five miles north of Chester. 'I moved down to London to university and then came here.'

'You were in London? I was there too. Imperial. I studied maths. How about you?'

'Queen Mary. Business. I graduated in 2005.'

'Me too!' He grinned at me. 'That's weird. And then you moved back north?'

'I always wanted to work for myself, but it's virtually impossible in London, so I moved here about seven years ago when I decided to open my own business. I love it here.'

'That's your own agency? You've done pretty well.'

'Thanks. I love having my own place.'

I was really proud of myself for running my own business. It had always been my dream. I trained as an estate agent immediately after graduating, and worked down in London for a few years. Sales were high in those days, so my commission was too, and I saved as much as I could, knowing I wanted my own place in the future. When I met Joe, we decided to head north so I could set up on my own. I have a few properties that I've bought to rent out, too. It seemed crazy not to, when there were cheap houses coming up at auction. We're managing agents for a number of landlords, so it's just as easy to manage mine at the same time.

'It's a big responsibility, though, isn't it?'

I nodded. 'It's a lot of work sometimes, but I prefer working for myself.'

'I'd love to do that,' he said. 'I'm in a great job, but there's something about having your own business . . . I'd really like to try it. Did you buy an existing agency?'

'Yes, I bought one that had been running for a few years.'

'What did you do about staff?'

'Brian, the older guy who was in the office when you came in, was someone I inherited. He was a lifesaver; he's worked in lettings for years and knows all the local landlords and tradespeople. I leave the letting side to him, though he's heading for retirement now and works shorter weeks. It won't be too long before I have to look for a replacement for him, I suppose. I hired the women myself.'

We arrived at the first block and took the lift to the fifth floor. The previous owners had already moved, so a sale could go ahead quickly.

'Hmm, this is pretty nice,' he said. 'How long has it been unoccupied?'

'They've just moved out,' I said. 'Last month. May. It's much better that it's empty; you could move in within weeks. You'll probably find there's room to manoeuvre on the price, too. If the vendor's still paying a mortgage, they'll want a fast sale.'

He went over to the window and opened the doors to the balcony that overlooked the central courtyard. There was space out there for a small table and a couple of chairs. He closed the doors without comment, then went into the bathroom. There was nothing to complain about there and he went into the kitchen, pulling out drawers and opening cupboards. Everything there was high spec; it was just the kind of place I thought he'd like.

'What do you think?' He smiled over at me. 'Could you see me here?'

I laughed. 'It's a great city-centre flat. Well, on the edge of the city, which is better, really. You don't get the noise.'

'Oh, I don't know,' he said. 'It's pretty noisy out there, when the French doors are open.'

'Really? It seems quiet to me. Well, it's the middle of the day, so there'll be a lot of tourists and shoppers. At night it'd be much quieter.'

He nodded. 'Let's go. Where's next?'

Next was a house in a popular area a couple of miles from the middle of town. It had its own busy centre, with bars and restaurants, gyms and shops.

'Houses move quickly here,' I said as I showed him around. 'This one's only been on the market for a few days and I'm expecting it to go by the end of the month.'

'Sounds great,' he said. 'I could be living here within a couple of months.'

I smiled, absolutely certain that pretty soon he'd be making an offer on one of our properties.

* * *

By mid-afternoon, though, I'd shown him six places, and although he'd enthused about them all, when I dropped him off at the office he made no suggestion that he'd be taking any of them further.

'I'll be in touch in the next few days,' he said.

'Great!' I smiled at him. 'I'll look forward to it.'

'Any luck?' asked Sophie as I entered the office.

I frowned. A number of people were looking at houses listed on the boards and glanced up in interest when she called out.

'Can I see you for a moment?' I asked, and went into the kitchen to wait for her. She bounced in, but the smile left her face when I reminded her not to call out in the office. 'Just e-mail me or ask me quietly if it's busy out there.'

She squirmed with embarrassment. 'Sorry.'

Rachel came into the kitchen and filled the kettle for tea.

I said, 'That's okay,' to Sophie. I didn't like to reprimand her while anyone else was around.

She was only down for a moment, though, before she nudged me, saying, 'How did it go with that guy? He was nice, wasn't he?'

I laughed. 'I could tell you liked him.'

'Tall, dark, and handsome,' she mused. 'Fit, too. Gorgeous. Rachel thought he was too.'

'I did not!'

'Yes, you did. Pity he's too old for us.'

I raised my eyebrows. 'He's my age, thanks.'

'That's what I mean.'

Rachel, her face scarlet now, nudged her, and I left them to it.

But later, before we closed the office, I called a meeting so we could thrash out some ideas for properties for David. We got together a list of another six that we thought he'd love, and then I e-mailed him to see whether he wanted to view any of them.

He replied immediately.

They sound great. I particularly liked the third one we saw today, the one with the view of the racecourse. I need to get my mortgage sorted out first, though - will be in touch soon.

I sighed. He'd told me he had his mortgage sorted. It seemed he was yet another client messing me around. I'd learned from experience that until someone had got a guaranteed mortgage, they weren't seriously looking. I guessed we wouldn't be seeing him again, but I wrote back saying he should let me know if he wanted me to recommend a financial adviser.

Will do, he replied. See you soon.

2

When I arrived home, I walked through the house towards the happy sounds I could hear in the garden. I stood unnoticed at the patio windows, watching Rory run up the lawn and into the paddling pool, splashing water and shrieking. The hosepipe lay on the grass, filling up the pool, as it emptied every time he jumped into it. Joe sat on the patio, a beer in his hand, wearing just his shorts. He had his Kindle on the table in front of him, one eye on the screen, the other on Rory.

'Hey,' I said, and he jumped. I kissed him on his cheek. 'My two boys.'

'Hi.' He put the bottle down on the patio and I stooped to pick it up again and put it on the table. 'Good day?'

'It was okay.' I sat beside him and sipped his beer. 'I spent hours taking some guy round a load of properties that I don't think he'll be buying.'

'Argh, time-waster,' he said. 'That's the way it is, though, I suppose.'

'You weren't the one wasting your time! Mind you,' I said, looking Joe straight in the eye, 'he was very attractive . . .'

He laughed. 'Perk of the job.'

Joe was a stay-at-home dad. We'd been married for a few

years, but still it was unexpected when I got pregnant with Rory. Joe was working in IT, and though he was paid well, he wasn't enjoying his job much and was looking for a change, whereas I was really happy at work and was bringing in quite a bit more than he was each month. I didn't want to hire a manager and lose control of the place, so when Joe suggested he should stay at home with the baby, I jumped at the chance. My hours were awkward, and I knew I'd never find a childminder or nursery that would keep Rory late at short notice. We were typical prospective parents in that we thought our lives wouldn't change much when our baby was born; Joe had sworn he'd be able to take on part-time jobs while Rory slept, and I'd believed him. That first year had been a massive learning curve for both of us.

And now, well, house sales were down nationally and that was showing no sign of change soon. I had to work longer and longer hours to try to keep clients happy and to keep staffing as low as I could. Any ideas I'd had of taking days off to care for Rory were suddenly blown out of the water. Only two days ago Joe had told me his skills were now three years out of date and he'd suddenly found that he could no longer apply for certain jobs even if he wanted to, as technology had moved on so rapidly. The thought of being the only wage-earner was now making me panic. It wasn't that I minded, just that houses didn't seem to be shifting at the moment and I couldn't think of a way to make more sales. I was worried, too, about the rentals I owned; they were mortgaged up to the hilt and it would only take one defaulter to mean we'd lose hundreds of pounds each month. And if houses weren't selling, I wouldn't be able to sell mine either. Or not unless I made a loss. The thought of that would keep me awake at night. And Joe . . . I had a horrible feeling that he'd stopped looking for work. He changed the subject when I brought it up, and I could never bring myself to press the matter.

Then Rory saw me and all thoughts of that left my mind. He yelled with delight and ran towards me, his arms outstretched.

I leaned down to kiss him, my face buried in his hair. 'Hello, my lovely boy. Have you had a good time?'

'I've been in the paddling pool all day,' he said. 'But I'm starving! What's for tea?'

'It's in the oven,' said Joe. 'Lasagne. It'll just be a few more minutes, so let's get you into the bath and it'll be ready by the time you're out.'

'I'll take him,' I said quickly. 'Come on, Rory; let's go.'

Rory stood between us, indecision on his face. 'I want Dad to take me.'

I felt a familiar prickle of hurt. 'Come on, sweetheart; I haven't seen you all day! You can tell me what you've been up to.'

'Go upstairs with Mum, Rory,' said Joe. 'Come on, be nice!'

My eyes smarted. My own child shouldn't have to be persuaded to spend time with me!

'But . . .' said Rory, and then he looked at my face and I knew he'd seen the hurt there. 'Okay, but will you be a lion? Growl just like Dad does.'

'I'll have a go,' I said, but when I did, it clearly wasn't up to scratch.

He gave me a pitying glance. 'Don't worry, Mum,' he said. 'Dad can do it when we get back downstairs.'

I ran a bath for Rory, and sat next to him as he played and sang and splashed. Hopefully he'd forgotten he was with his second choice. I started to think about the work I still had to do that day. I tried to get home as soon as the office shut at five so that I could spend time with Rory before he went to bed, though often I couldn't manage that because of evening viewings, but the cost of that was that I had to work late. As soon as he was in bed, I'd be on to my e-mails, making calls,

trying to match clients to properties they'd love, keeping track of the finances, and preparing for the meeting we had first thing every morning. The legal work had to be up to date, too, and often I did that at home, as it was easier to concentrate outside the office. Often I'd look up from my laptop late at night to find Joe asleep on the sofa, with something neither of us had been watching muted on the television.

Now that Rory was three, I knew Joe was anxious for us to have another baby, so that the children could grow up together. He loved being at home with Rory, but I was worried that if he was struggling to find work now, he'd find it impossible in another few years' time. And if the property market was still in a slump, what would we do? I tried to forget these problems in the time I had with Rory each evening, but they were always there at the back of my mind.

I took Rory up to bed after he'd had his supper and lay on his bed to read him some stories.

'Do the voices,' he urged. 'Make them scary!'

I tried to do it, but he sighed. 'No, do them like Dad does. Make me shiver!'

I tried again, more forcefully, and he laughed, but said firmly, 'Tell Dad to come up and do it.'

Shamefaced, I called to Joe and he came into Rory's bedroom on all fours, growling and snarling so that Rory screamed with excitement. I stood and watched, and though I loved it, I was hurt, too, that he'd wanted Joe instead of me.

Later, when Rory was asleep, I sat at my laptop, typing up notes for the property valuation I'd seen after I'd dropped David off. I was just about to start to e-mail clients who'd sent me messages that afternoon when Joe came back from the gym.

'You don't mind if I watch this, do you?' he asked, and flicked the television on. A football match was about to start. Wonderful.

There was no way I could concentrate while there was background noise, so I took my laptop into the kitchen and sat at the dining table. Joe came into the room and took a bottle of wine from the fridge. He raised a glass to offer me some, but I shook my head violently.

'Come on, Gem,' he said. 'It's Friday night. Start of the weekend.'

I was so tempted to say, *What weekend? I'm working!* and I think Joe must have recognized the expression on my face, because he put the wine back into the fridge and sat down beside me.

'Give me a job to do,' he said. 'Any job. Come on, I can handle it.'

I laughed and he nudged me, his leg tanned and hard against mine. I nudged him back, feeling a frisson of desire as our bodies touched. 'I've got all the bank statements here,' I said. 'And here's a list of all the fee payments that have come in from solicitors. I need to marry them up and check for outstanding debts. You wouldn't do that for me, would you?'

He moved an inch closer to me. 'Maybe. What's it worth?'

I leaned over and whispered in his ear.

'Pass me that file and my laptop,' he said, 'and give me half an hour, and then I'm going to hold you to that.'

3

'So you'll definitely be able to work on Friday afternoon?' I asked Rachel the following Monday.

She nodded. 'The course is on Saturday, then?'

'Yes, in a hotel in London. Covent Garden. I'll go down late Friday afternoon and come back Saturday night.'

She looked at the rota in front of us. 'And you're at work on Sunday? Are you sure you won't want a day at home?'

'I can't. Brian's off on Sunday. You'll have Wednesday off in exchange for Friday?'

This happened every week. We were short-staffed, but unless the housing situation changed soon, I couldn't afford to take on anyone new. I had to juggle around the rota to keep everyone happy and the place staffed. That was the problem with having a business that had to be open every day of the week. I tended to work most days, taking half-days off where I could, but it was hard and I seemed to be permanently exhausted.

I was happy to work long hours, but I did miss Rory and loved nothing more than to just be on my own with him.

I loved those times we'd spend at the park or having a milk-shake in our local café or at the swimming pool. Joe usually came along too, and I liked that, I really did, but sometimes . . . well, when Joe was there Rory would often turn to him if he was upset and I'd stand there feeling useless, whereas on our own he was totally reliant on me. It sounds selfish but it can be hard for a mum to watch her child run to someone else for help, even if that person is his dad.

Often I'd daydream about the time when Rory was older, when he could walk from school at the end of the day and come to the office and do his homework for an hour while he waited for me to finish. Joe would be out at work, then later, in my daydreams, it would be just Rory and me, in the kitchen, making dinner together while he told me about his day.

It was a strange fantasy, I knew that. It wasn't as though things were bad now, it was just that I felt I'd missed out on that lovely one-to-one time that most mums seemed to have. I shook myself. I loved Joe. I loved Rory. I loved my job, most of the time. There was no reason to live in fantasy land.

I looked up to see Rachel staring at me.

'Sorry!' I said. 'I was miles away.'

'Anywhere nice?'

I shook my head. 'I was thinking of Rory and what he'd be like as a teenager. At secondary school.'

Sophie saw the chance for a gossip and came hurrying over. 'He'll be gorgeous. Totally gorgeous.'

I looked at the photo on my desk. Rory was riding his tricycle in the park, his face serious as he concentrated. His hair was blonde and floppy and glossy, and far, far too long. The photo had been taken a month ago, just as summer started, and already his skin was tanned, his body lithe. Joe and Rory had given me the photo when I got home from work, just as Rory was going to bed, and as soon as he was asleep I'd started to cry at what I was missing.

'He's just like Joe, isn't he?' asked Sophie.

I smiled. 'Yes, beautiful!'

They laughed.

'Would you like another baby?' asked Rachel suddenly. She blushed and I guessed she thought she'd been too forward.

They both looked at me, an eager look in their eyes.

'I'm not sure,' I said slowly. 'I think so. I think Rory would love a baby brother or sister.'

'And they'd love him,' said Sophie, a sentimental look on her face.

'I wasn't going to have another,' I said. 'Not with working full time. It's just something my mum said.' I thought back to Christmas, when she and my dad had come to stay. 'She said the best present I could give Rory was a brother or sister. I've got an older brother and we used to get on really well when we were kids. He's working in Edinburgh now, so I don't see him as much as I'd like, but we're still great friends.'

'She's right!' said Sophie. 'He'd have a friend for life.'

I smiled. 'That's a lovely thought.'

Rachel picked up the coffee mugs. 'I'll get these done,' she said, and went into the kitchen.

'So you decided against going down just for the day, then?' asked Sophie.

'I couldn't face getting the six A.M. train. Joe wanted me to so that he could go to the pub on Friday night, but I couldn't face it.' I left a pause, and then admitted, 'So I told him it wouldn't get me there on time.'

She laughed.

Rachel came back in to put away the biscuit tin. 'What time did you tell him it started?'

'Nine A.M. instead of nine thirty. The train gets in at eight fifty, so I'd have had to rush to be there on time.'

She shook her head in mock disapproval. 'Lies to your husband. What next?'

I laughed along with the others, but I was well aware that I was telling Joe more and more lies lately. Some nights I'd sleep in the spare room, telling him my head was aching, when all I wanted was to be on my own for a while. Or I'd creep in with Rory, just to spend time with him, even though he was asleep. And I knew that Joe suspected I wasn't happy. I'd seen him watching me at times, and when I'd smile at him, he'd seem lost in his thoughts and take a while to respond.

Last night, when we were in bed, I felt he was about to ask me about it and suddenly I thought, *I'll tell him everything, tell him exactly what I'm feeling*, but then he turned away from me and went to sleep. I was still sitting up, putting my face cream on, and I wanted to lean over, to kiss his cheek, to try to regain some of that closeness, but I just couldn't. So I turned away from him too, but I couldn't sleep.

I seemed to have gone from someone who was always honest, always open, to someone who said whatever had to be said for an easy life. I didn't know how that had happened.

4

That night I took Joe up on his offer of wine. It was Monday, that was his excuse, and I realized then that virtually every night lately he'd had an excuse to open a bottle. 'It's Thursday!' he'd shout from the kitchen. 'Nearly the weekend! Come on, let's have a glass.' He was pretty good at having just one or two glasses, though, and so was I, now. I hadn't always been like that.

So that Monday night Joe poured us a glass of wine and we did what I loved best, and lay at either end of the sofa, legs entwined, and talked. We put some music on and I lit some candles and for a while nothing existed but us. Our family. We talked about everything and nothing, as we always did, but the conversation always came back to Rory. It was our favourite topic, guaranteed to put me into a great mood. Joe told me about swimming and the park and how Rory had befriended a dog who lived across the street from us, and I soaked up those stories. I could never hear enough of them.

I told him what the women at work had said about having another child. 'Do you think we should have another?' I asked, suddenly overcome with sentimentality. 'Do you think Rory would like a little brother or sister?'

Joe looked startled. 'Of course! He'd love it. *I'd* love it!' He reached out to pull me to him. 'I thought you didn't want to. You shouted at your mum when she mentioned it, remember?'

I winced as I remembered my mum's shocked expression on Christmas Day when she'd given me her advice and I'd given it back to her with both barrels. She'd instantly looked down at the glass in my hand and I knew she thought I was drinking too much. That had made me even angrier. I couldn't think now why I'd reacted like that. I'd felt so much pressure at work, and the idea of getting pregnant on top of that had seemed just too much.

But now, in the candlelight, with Rory asleep in his bed and my work for the evening all done, I couldn't seem to recapture that feeling of anger and frustration.

'What's changed your mind?' Joe asked.

I shook my head. 'The women at work, I think. Sophie . . . she agreed with my mum. She said he'd have a friend for life, and she's right. Look at you and Caitlin. Mind you, look at you and Brendan.'

Joe laughed. He was probably his elder brother Brendan's greatest fan; he was never happier than when the two of them were together. 'Oh, I wouldn't want one like him. That would be a nightmare.'

Despite the haze of wine and sentimentality, I couldn't help but think how hard I'd have to work to bring in the money needed for a bigger family. Perhaps I could expand the business? But how could I do that when houses weren't moving? My heart sank. I was exhausted as it was, without bringing more pressure on myself.

And then I thought back to when I was pregnant with Rory. It was the first time I'd felt relaxed in my body since . . . well, I could hardly remember. The feeling of a baby inside me, those first tentative movements I'd felt so early on, like a butterfly's kisses. I'd loved him from that moment. Before

then, even. He'd been part of me then; he'd always be part of me. And the thought of going through that again was exhilarating.

'Do you think we could love another child as much?' I asked.

'Of course we could.' Joe's hands were in my hair and I closed my eyes as he kissed me. 'Especially if we have a redhead.' He ran his fingers through my hair and kissed me again. 'A redhead with green eyes, just like you.'

'Maybe we could think about it later in the year,' I said.

'That would be amazing.'

'And maybe I could look at changing my hours so that I can spend more time at home.'

I got caught up in his embrace then, but later, when we were lying in bed and he was sleeping soundly beside me, I lay awake trying to think of ways I could work fewer hours. Joe had kissed me then and I was distracted; it was only later that I realized he hadn't agreed with me.

5

I caught the afternoon train from Chester to London the following Friday and it was packed. As I hurried past the relatively empty first-class compartment, I saw a couple of women relaxing in the large, comfortable seats, glasses of gin and tonic already in their hands, and wished I'd spent the extra money and upgraded my ticket. I couldn't justify it, though; the business wasn't doing well enough for me to throw money away like that.

My heart sank at Euston when I saw hordes of people queuing for the escalator to the underground. There was a notice saying one of the tube lines was out of service, and I knew there'd be bedlam. The station was crammed and stifling with the summer heat, and I felt so hot by the time I reached the escalator that I decided to walk instead.

I stepped outside onto Euston Square. It was early evening by then and I walked down Tottenham Court Road towards my hotel in Covent Garden. Crowds of office workers mingled with tourists, and I thought of the days I'd worked here when I was in my early twenties. I missed those days. I was working

for an estate agent's in North London and it was fast and furious then, before the downturn. Flats and houses would sell quickly for more than the asking price, and the agency could afford to be generous with bonuses and drinks after work.

I'd known it wouldn't be like that when I moved to Chester. And by the time I met Joe I was ready to move on. I was twenty-six then, with five years' experience under my belt, and I was up for the challenge.

We had a great time in those early days. I met Joe when I was in Ireland for Brendan's wedding; Caitlin had invited me and we'd gone to her family's local pub the night we arrived. I'd been over to Ireland to stay with her in the long summer holiday a couple of times before then, but Joe had been off backpacking those summers and I hadn't met him. That night she and I walked into the pub and she stopped in the doorway to talk to an old friend. I went to the bar to get us drinks and watched as a band played, badly, on a makeshift stage. Joe was standing watching them too. We hadn't yet been introduced, but I knew instantly he was related to Caitlin; they had the same tousled blonde hair, the same blue eyes, and besides, his mother had shown me enough photos of the family to recognize him. He winced at every bum note and then saw me looking over at him and laughed.

I said, 'That bad, eh?'

'It's my friend's youngest brother,' he said. 'I don't think he's quite ready for stardom yet.'

I looked at the guitarist, who'd dropped his head so nobody could see his face. I could tell he was aware how badly he was playing.

'Poor guy,' said Joe.

When the band came off stage he went over to the guitarist and clapped him on the shoulder. I could see he was being kind to him, shaking his head as the young man protested. 'It's nerves,' I heard him say. 'Next time you'll be fine.'

He came over to me and said, 'So, you're Gemma.' I remember I blushed then, and he said, 'I've heard a lot about you.'

We stood together at the corner of the bar for hours that night, and it was only when the pub was closing that I turned to see Caitlin smiling at us. She bundled me into the ladies' loo before we left, and as soon as we were alone, she said, 'I knew you'd like him!'

I couldn't deny it. I couldn't stop smiling either. 'Why didn't you introduce me before?'

She hesitated, and immediately I knew what she was about to say. 'Now's the right time,' she said eventually, and I knew she meant she couldn't have risked it before. She was right. I'd been a bit of a mess for years, but she'd helped me get through it.

'You planned this?' I asked.

She grinned at me and refused to answer.

Joe was staying with a local friend, as his parents' home, where I was staying, was full of visiting friends and relations. He offered to walk me back there that night, but we were talking so much by the time we got there that he didn't want to let me go. He said he'd take me on a tour of his old haunts, and we walked for miles around the deserted streets of his neighbourhood. I think I knew that night that he'd always be in my life.

Now, as I approached the hotel, I stopped to send him a text.

`Just walking through Covent Garden. I know it's not Dublin, but it's making me think of the night we met xx`

He replied:

`Oh that was a great night. One of the best nights of my life. Last night was pretty good too xx`

I blushed. It certainly had been.

`For me too. Missing you both xxx`

6

It was a hot night and I felt sticky and horrible from the journey and the walk to the hotel. A big corner bath was calling to me, but when I heard the sound of people talking and laughing out on the terrace below, I decided to have a shower instead and go down to see if there was anyone I knew in the bar. If there wasn't, I planned to come back up, order some food and wine, and have a long bath and an early night.

After a quick shower, I changed into a dark green silk dress with spaghetti straps that I'd brought with me in case I went out to dinner. I put some make-up on, slipped on my sandals, and wondered who'd be there. I had to do these training days every now and then, and often I'd bump into the same crowd. It wasn't that we kept in touch with each other outside the events, but over the years we'd gravitate towards each other whenever we met. Those of us with our own agencies understood each other's problems, and it was always good to talk freely, in a way I didn't like to do with people I met in Chester. I didn't want local people knowing anything about my business worries.

I switched both bedside lamps on, ready for when I returned later, and went down to the bar.

'A gin and tonic, please,' I said to the barman.

'Single? Double?' I hesitated, and he said, 'Why not? Kick-start the weekend!'

I laughed. 'Go on then.'

Drink in hand, I turned to see who was there. The bar was crowded and I could see from the variety of lanyards and badges that there were quite a few events that weekend. I walked around the perimeter of the room but couldn't see anyone I knew. Trying to quell my disappointment, I realized most people would probably just travel down the next morning rather than stay overnight. Usually these training sessions were a two-day event, with everyone staying over on the middle night.

I drank my gin and ordered another, and yes, it was another double. It was a hot summer night, just the right weather for gin and tonic, and I didn't have anyone I was responsible for. I felt if I wanted a drink, I'd damn well have one.

Just as I'd decided to go back up to my room, my phone beeped in my bag. I checked my messages, hoping Rory was ready for a chat before he went to bed. He'd been out to a friend's house earlier, so we'd agreed he'd call at bedtime.

Hey Gem, are you having a good time? Rory's just had a bath and fallen asleep. Sorry, he was going to call you. Fancy a chat? xx

I stared at the phone. That was the one thing I'd asked him to do tonight. He knew how much I missed Rory. I didn't want to talk to Joe now; I'd only get angry. And I'd had a couple of drinks; I knew he'd be able to tell. I didn't want a conversation about that. I was about to ignore his text but knew there'd be a flurry of others and I'd end up snapping at him, so I sent him a message:

In the bath then I'm going to sleep. Will call you tomorrow xx

In seconds he replied:

Oh ok. Night xx

I could sense his disappointment that I couldn't chat and felt bad almost immediately but stopped myself in my tracks. Whenever he went away for the night, I just sent the odd message, but when I went anywhere, he was never off the phone. I ignored the fact that I was usually really glad of this and drank some more gin.

After circuiting the bar, I walked into the lobby. Again, I knew nobody there. Then I saw a group of middle-aged men walk in through the revolving door, and my stomach sank. One of them, Liam Fossett, was one of the most boring people I knew. I should have guessed he'd be here; he worked up in the north-east, so he'd have to stay overnight. When he saw me, his face lit up. He waved and I let my eyes drift past him, as though I hadn't seen him. Out of the corner of my eye, though, I could see that he was pushing his way through the crowd towards me.

In an instant I decided to escape to my room. I turned quickly and bumped into a man standing in a group of other people behind me. He put his hand out to steady me.

'Careful!' he said.

'Oh, I'm so sorry,' I said. 'I didn't see you.'

I looked at his glass, which had spilled red wine onto the floor, then looked up at him.

'It's Gemma, isn't it?' he said. 'Gemma Brogan? David Sanderson. You showed me around some properties in Chester the other day.'

'Oh, of course! I didn't recognize you out of context,' I said, moving back from the spilled wine. 'I'm really sorry I knocked your drink. Let me get you another.'

'Don't worry,' he said. 'What are you doing here?'

'I'm on a training course,' I said. 'It's about new money-laundering regulations. It's easier to come on a course and get all the literature than try to figure it out myself.'

'Nice to get away for the weekend too, I bet?'

I laughed. 'Yes, sometimes it's good to have a break. It's pretty hectic with work and a young child.'

'Is your family down here with you?'

I shook my head. 'No. My son's only three. I didn't dare tell him I was going on a train. He'd have been harassing me for ages to come with me.'

He laughed. 'I was like that when I was a kid. The best part of any holiday was always the journey.'

I felt a tap on my shoulder, and flinched. I knew who that would be.

'Hi, Liam.' I tried to dodge his wet kiss on my cheek but didn't quite manage it. I felt David's arm brush against mine for just a second, and I knew he'd noticed my reaction. 'How are you?'

'Great, thanks, Gem,' he said. 'We're going in to dinner soon. Come and join us?'

I looked at him, at his red face with its slight glaze of sweat. I couldn't think of anything I wanted to do less.

'Oh, I'm sorry,' said David. 'Gemma's having dinner with me.'

I glanced at him. *I am?* I kept my face straight.

Liam looked at David, then at me. 'You want to join us too?'

David shook his head. 'Sorry, it's business. I need to ask her advice. I'm afraid she'll be busy for the next couple of hours.'

Liam nodded reluctantly. 'All right. Maybe a drink later?'

I smiled. 'Maybe.'

David and I watched as he made his way back to his friends. He leaned towards me and whispered in my ear, 'You owe me.'

I laughed. 'You have saved my life.'

He smiled. 'You're lucky I was here.'

'No kidding. But what are you doing here?'

'Oh, I've been in London for business.'

'With Barford's?'

'You've got a good memory! Yes, I'm meeting some suppliers. I've been staying here all week and need to see someone again in the morning. I'll go back north tomorrow.'

'Still looking for a house?' I smiled at him, hoping I didn't sound too cheeky.

He laughed. 'Yeah, sorry I haven't been in touch. There was a hitch on my mortgage because I was waiting for the money from my house sale in Boston, but it's all through now and the bank's ready to go ahead.'

'Well, get in touch whenever you're ready,' I said. 'I'll find you a good deal.' I could feel that my face was hot now and didn't know whether it was the drink. I put my empty glass down on a side table and turned to go. 'Thanks for getting me off the hook with Liam.'

'I don't suppose you *would* have dinner with me, would you?' He saw me hesitate and said quickly, 'You'd be doing me a huge favour. I've been sitting here on my own night after night.' He grinned. 'And I'd hate that guy to think you'd stood me up.'

I paused. I'd been about to go up to my room. I thought of my earlier plans to order room service and have a long bath in peace. I was so tired after this week at work.

And then I thought of the potential sale. Sure, he was a good-looking guy and he did make me laugh, but my business brain was the one I used when I said, 'Okay, but I'll pay.' He started to object, but I said, 'It's a business expense. You're a client.' It wasn't an expense I could afford, but if it led to a sale it would be well worth the money. An investment.

He laughed. 'Well, that would be very nice. Thank you.'

I saw Liam looking over at me. 'Shall we go now?' I gave him a little wave, and David and I walked through the bar to the restaurant.

7

That night seemed to fly by in a flash. It had been a long time since I'd been to dinner with a man on my own, and I was surprised at how comfortable I felt. The waiter came over and asked us about drinks.

I looked at the wine menu. 'You were drinking red wine, weren't you?' I asked David. 'Shall I get a bottle?'

'That would be great, thanks.'

I ordered a bottle of Barolo and David poured us a glass each while he talked me through the menu, telling me which meals he'd had while he was down there. He told me about the places he'd lived abroad: Boston, Dallas, and Hong Kong.

'You're in sales, aren't you?' I asked.

'Yeah. It's not for everyone, but I'm happy in that kind of environment. As long as the company's reputable. You've got to believe in the products.'

'And Barford's is a good company?'

'They've been great. Sent me all over the place. I love that.'

'I wish I'd worked abroad in my twenties,' I said. 'I don't think I realized when I was child-free that I should do as much travelling as I could then.'

'It can be hard work moving around, though. You lose

touch with your old friends and you can be relocated at any time. It's hard to fit in sometimes.'

'I suppose so.'

'Still, you're in a great position now. You have a family and it looks like your business is going well.'

I hesitated, not wanting to admit that in this economy people were avoiding buying property. Of course in any climate people wanted to buy low and sell high, but I was noticing it now more than ever. In the end, he was a potential client, so I just said, 'Yes, it's going well. I'm very lucky.'

'You look tired. Busy week?'

I nodded. 'Always.'

'Why not forget about work for a while? Have a night off.' He picked up the wine we'd ordered. 'Fancy a top-up?'

I looked at the bottle and then back at David. I already had a buzz on and could feel my skin tingling. I'd reached my limit with the drinks I'd already had; I knew better than to drink more, but suddenly the lure of a couple of glasses and some carefree conversation with another adult – okay, another man – was too great.

I pushed my glass towards him. 'Why not?'

We stayed in the restaurant for a few hours, enjoying our meal and some drinks. He was great company, talking about his life overseas and living in London as a student. I felt completely at ease with him; he was entertaining and funny and I felt sure he'd come back to the office in the next couple of weeks to see some more properties. I made a mental note to get everyone at work onto looking for a suitable place; after talking to him I had a good idea of the sort of lifestyle he wanted.

It took a while at the end of the night for our bill to arrive, and then when it did, the waiter stayed at the other side of the restaurant chatting with a waitress and, despite my waves,

didn't meet my eye. I sighed and went over to him to ask him to bring the card machine. When I got back to our table, David was pouring the last of the wine into our glasses.

'Thanks for the meal,' he said. He picked up his glass. 'Cheers!'

Automatically I raised my glass to his. 'You're welcome,' I said, and drank the wine. I looked at my watch. 'I have to go; I've got an early start tomorrow.' I felt unsteady when I stood. 'Gosh, I've drunk far too much!' I looked down at the table and frowned. Two bottles of wine were empty – I didn't think I'd had much more than a couple of glasses. 'Did we drink all that?'

He laughed. 'I'm afraid so. But it's Friday night, time to let our hair down,' he said. 'It's my fault, I think. I drank far more than you did.'

I blinked hard. 'Ugh, I'm going to have such a hangover.'

'Make sure you drink lots of water,' he said. 'Do you have any painkillers? Perhaps take a couple before you go to sleep.'

I nodded. 'I will.'

We walked over to the lift. There were still crowds of people in the bar, and just one elderly couple was waiting for the lift.

David stood next to the lift buttons. 'Which floor would you like?' he asked the couple. He pressed a button for them, then said to me, 'How about you?'

For a moment I couldn't remember, and searched in my bag for the little envelope containing my key card.

He glanced at it and said, 'The ninth? I'm on the tenth.'

The couple got out at their floor, and David and I stood in silence. In the few seconds it took for the lift to take us up to the ninth floor, I felt as though I could sleep for a week. I wondered what would happen if I didn't go to the training. Would it matter? I could hardly remember the name of the training event at that point. Was it in this hotel?

When the doors opened onto the ninth floor, I stumbled out. David grabbed my arm.

'Steady!' he said, laughing. 'Steady on, sweetheart.'

I stared at him, confused.

'What's your room number?' he asked.

I couldn't answer. I tried, I tried to say something, but I couldn't think straight and my tongue felt thick and swollen in my mouth.

He took the key card envelope out of my hand. '912,' he said. He laughed again. 'You've really had too much to drink, haven't you?'

I tried to smile but I couldn't. All I could think about was getting into bed.

He stopped abruptly outside one of the hotel-room doors. I lurched into him. I tried to apologize but nothing came out.

My back was to the door and he reached out and touched my hair. 'Time for bed,' he said, and suddenly the atmosphere seemed to change.

He leaned forward. I twisted my head away and saw a woman standing at the far end of the corridor. She reached out her hand to press the button on the wall to call the lift. I tried to move away from David, to keep the distance between us, but I bumped against the door and then his hand moved to the side of my face and he turned my head towards him. I couldn't take my eyes off him.

And then he kissed me.

8

Saturday, June 24

The next morning I felt as cold as if I'd spent the night sleeping on a stone floor. I opened my eyes to find a beam of sunlight glaring through the gap in the curtains. My eyes hurt just to open them. A glance at my watch told me it was nine A.M. I had to get up; I'd slept through my alarm. I knew I had to go down to the conference room, but my head was pounding mercilessly. My mouth was dry and foul. I needed water.

I hauled myself up out of bed and staggered into the bathroom, kicking aside my dress, which I'd left on the bedroom floor the night before. For a moment I thought I'd be okay, but the sun was shining through the window onto the bathroom tiles and they were such a brilliant, vivid white that they made my head hurt. Immediately I was sick in the toilet. Afterwards my head throbbed so badly I saw stars. I rinsed my face at the basin but avoided looking at my reflection. I knew I'd look awful. There was a minibar in the bedroom, and I took a bottle of water out and drank it down in one, my hands shaking. I brushed my teeth vigorously, but my

mouth still tasted disgusting. I couldn't go downstairs like this.

Outside the door the cleaner's trolley squeaked its way down the corridor, and I winced at the sound. Surely it shouldn't be so loud. I wanted to take some painkillers and go back to bed, but the conference was due to start at nine thirty, and in any case, checkout was ten A.M. so I had to get going.

I had no choice: I had to go down to the conference. I took off my underwear – clearly I hadn't bothered getting fully undressed last night, never mind putting on my pyjamas – and stepped into the shower. Every movement seemed a huge effort, as though my limbs were heavy and weak. Eventually I was clean and dry and dressed, but I knew I looked far from well. I spent longer than usual on my make-up, trying to make myself appear sober and smart, but I doubted I'd be fooling anyone. My eyes were red-rimmed and sore, and I put my sunglasses on to try to hide the fact that I was hungover. I was so furious with myself for drinking like that; it was as though I hadn't had a filter, a gauge to tell me when to stop.

Downstairs I took a cup of coffee from the buffet table and picked up a couple of bottles of water too. There was no way I could eat anything; just the thought made me feel ill. I bought some mints and a newspaper from the kiosk. I had no intention of reading the paper, but I wanted something to hide behind. When a text came through from Joe to wish me a good morning, I winced with shame. When would I ever learn? I hadn't drunk like that for years, not since the old days at university. He'd never known me like that, though he knew I'd been through a tough time there. When I'd met Joe I'd felt comfortable with him immediately and had told him everything about my past. I was ready to move on then, ready to make a new start, and one of my promises to myself was that I wouldn't drink too much. I'd stuck to that promise, too, until now. I flinched. I couldn't tell him I was hungover;

I'd told him earlier in the evening that I was going to bed early.

'Bad night?' Helen, a woman from Cornwall who I met occasionally at these events, sat down next to me. Her expression was sympathetic. 'You look really tired.'

'I feel awful,' I said. 'I had far too much to drink last night. If I have to dash out, will you make my excuses?'

She smiled. 'That bad, eh?'

'Worse.'

'Want some painkillers?'

'Thanks, I've run out.' Grateful, I took them from her. I swallowed a couple with a drink of water; my hand was shaking so much I spilled it on my newspaper.

'Wow, you have got it bad!' she said. 'You can keep the rest of those tablets; you might need them later.'

'Thanks,' I said, embarrassed. 'I don't drink much normally. Haven't for years. I overdid it last night.'

The room started to quieten as Philip Doyle, the tutor, moved to the front of the room and tapped his microphone. The sound made me flinch.

'Were you here overnight, then?' she whispered. 'I was staying with a friend in Surrey. Who else was here?'

My mind went blank. Who had been here? I turned to look around the room and saw a sea of faces. I couldn't recognize anyone at first, and then I saw Liam sitting with his colleagues, laughing at something one of them had said. He looked pretty rough too, though he was managing to eat a huge sandwich. Like me, he must have missed breakfast. I turned away, unable to watch him.

'It was pretty busy,' I said. 'Liam Fossett was here, though. I know I saw him and all his gang.'

'Ugh, you didn't have to spend much time with them, did you?'

'No,' I said. 'One of my clients was here. I had dinner with him. He's been here for meetings all week.'

She smiled at me. 'Nice?'

The thought of David's face as he lowered his mouth to mine came into my mind then. I shuddered. How drunk had I been? I shook my head to try to force the image away. 'Yeah, he's okay. Better than Liam, at any rate. We had too much to drink, though. I'm paying the price now.'

'It's our age,' she said. 'Remember when you could drink whatever you wanted and it didn't make a difference the next day?'

'I don't miss that at all, though. Halfway through a night out I tend to wish I were in my pyjamas, in bed.'

Just then Philip Doyle started to introduce the day's events. I couldn't concentrate on what he was saying; it was like trying to think through fog. I drank more water, then tried to eat a biscuit that was on the coffee cup's saucer, but as soon as I felt the dry, sweet crumbs in my mouth, I had to leap up and run for the nearest cloakroom.

Later, at Euston station, I took one look at the crowds of people waiting for the train back to Chester and upgraded my ticket to first class, where it was quiet. I spoke to the attendant just before the train pulled out and told her that I wasn't well and needed to sleep. She put me at the far end of the carriage, away from the other passengers, and gave me a blanket to wrap around myself. I slept all the way home.

Joe and Rory picked me up at the station.

'Mummy!' Rory shrieked, running towards me and leaping into my arms. 'I've missed you!'

I kissed his head, smelling the fresh scent of his apple shampoo. Just pulling him to me made me feel better.

'I've missed you too,' I said. 'So much.'

47

Joe looked at me oddly. 'Are you okay?'

'I'm not well,' I said. I couldn't bear to tell him I'd had too much to drink. 'I haven't felt well all day.'

He put his arm around me. 'How come, sweetheart? You're not hungover, are you? I thought you had an early night.'

I thought about the text I'd sent him, telling him I was in the bath. Worried in case he smelled alcohol on me, I said, 'I had a couple of drinks in my room. It's probably just that. I drank them too fast and went to sleep. I'm so tired, though.'

'You'll be fine,' he said. 'Have another early night. I'm out with Mike, remember?'

That had been our arrangement when Joe had agreed to stay at home with Rory, that he'd have the chance to see his friends every week. Mike was a guy that Joe used to work with. He lived half a mile from us and often they'd go out for a run or a drink. I'd understood that: I spent all day with other adults and I knew he needed to see his friends. I'd forgotten, though, that he was planning to go out that night.

Rory leaped up and down, pulling at my arm. 'Just you and me, Mum! And you promised you'd play swingball with me before I went to bed!'

My head thumped at the thought of that. I looked up at Joe, hoping against hope that he would offer to stay home, but his eyes were fixed ahead. He knew exactly what I wanted, but he knew I wouldn't ask, either. It was our agreement, after all.

'Swingball it is,' I said weakly, planning already that the moment Rory got into his bed, I would get into mine.

9

Friday, July 21

I was in the office a month later when the post arrived.
We have the same postman every day and of course Sophie
has a crush on him. I don't think I've seen any guy under
twenty-five that she hasn't had a crush on. Fair enough with
this one, though; he's tall and tanned, with a surfer dude
look about him, despite being quite a way from any waves.
She'd been anticipating his visit all morning and I'd noticed
the surreptitious smudge of lipstick and the smell of her new
perfume. She bounced up as he entered the office and passed
me the mail. The day was hot already and a soft breeze came
through the open doorway.

There were no clients in the office. Rachel was working at
her computer and Sophie fetched the postman a bottle of water
from our fridge. She held on to it while she chatted to him, a
ploy to stop him from leaving. It was just an ordinary day.

I glanced through the mail. There were a couple of letters
from solicitors confirming that they were acting for clients.
There was another letter from a solicitor confirming comple-
tion on a sale. A vendor had returned a signed and approved

set of property details. Mostly, though, as usual, it was junk mail and takeaway menus.

'Coffee?' asked Rachel.

'Great, thanks.'

I was just gathering together the junk mail, ready to throw it out, when I saw there was another envelope underneath it. I checked that it was for me, then opened it just as Rachel came over to my desk with a mug of coffee. 'Biscuit?' she asked, and put the tin on the desk beside my coffee.

'No, thanks,' I said. In the envelope was a sheet of paper, folded in half. I opened it up, thinking it was a flyer, but it was a photocopy of a receipt. I looked inside the envelope again to see if there was a compliments slip, but there was nothing.

'What's that?' she asked.

'I don't know,' I said slowly. 'It's a receipt for something.' I squinted at the logo. 'Oh, it's from the Shaftesbury Hotel.'

'The Shaftesbury Hotel?' she said. 'That's not around here, is it?'

I shook my head. 'No, it's the hotel I stayed in when I was in London.'

She picked it up and looked at it closely. 'It's from the restaurant. Steak. Barolo. Two bottles? Very nice.'

I took it back from her, exasperated. There was never any privacy at work. Everyone always wanted to know exactly what was going on.

The postman had left now and Sophie was back with us. She tried to look at the receipt too, but I turned it away from her. She said, 'I thought you were going to have room service and an early night?'

'I was,' I said. 'I changed my mind.'

'There are two meals there,' said Rachel. 'Did you pay for someone else?'

Struggling to keep the irritation out of my voice, I said, 'I met a client there. I paid for the meal.'

Out of the corner of my eye I could see Sophie and Rachel staring at each other and then at me.

'Why have they sent it to you?' asked Sophie.

'Tax reasons,' said Brian. I hadn't even known he was taking an interest. 'You have to keep your receipts so that you can claim the tax back.'

'Well, then,' I said, 'that was very nice of them.' I put the document into the folder I used to store receipts for my tax returns.

But later, when everyone was busy and I had a few moments to myself, I took the receipt out and looked at it again. Why had they sent this to me? And why send a copy? It wasn't as though they needed to keep the original for themselves. They would have a record of it on their system. But in any case, surely if it was just left on the table, they'd throw it away?

I'd tried not to think of that night with David in the restaurant. I'd thought those days where I'd drink too much and get into situations with strange men were over. By the time I hit my mid-twenties and met Joe, I was past all that. But the night I'd met David, I'd drunk so much I couldn't remember much of it. Why had I done that? While Rachel dealt with a client and Sophie spoke on the phone to a solicitor, I forced myself to think about it.

I could remember bumping into David and his drink spilling on the floor. I remember realizing it was him. He'd saved me from talking to someone else, too. I thought hard. Liam, that was it. I was glad he'd done that. And we'd had a meal. I'd had a couple of drinks before the meal, I knew that. I could remember ordering gin and tonics from the barman. Then an image flashed into my mind: two empty bottles of red wine on our table. I never drank more than a couple of glasses, maybe half a bottle, normally, and not as much as that if I'd had gin beforehand. How much had I drunk? I couldn't bear to think about how ill I was the next morning. Being sick from

drinking was something teenagers did, not adults. Surely I hadn't drunk that much? But my head hurt so much the next day . . . I must have been completely out of it. I winced with embarrassment. I hadn't had a drink since that night and planned to keep it that way.

But I kept coming back to the question: why would the hotel send the receipt to me? I'd never known that to happen. Even in a shop, if you walk off without the receipt, the assistant just throws it into the bin. Why spend money and time returning it to me?

Just then the door opened and Joe's sister, Caitlin, came in. I put the receipt back into the folder and stood up to hug her.

'Good holiday?' I asked. The weekend before, she'd come back from a holiday in Italy with her husband, Ben. 'Lovely tan.'

'Thanks. It was tough going to work this week, though.'

'Ben's back in Dubai now?'

'Yes. I won't see him for another couple of weeks.' She looked lost for a moment, then pulled herself together. 'I've just been to Wrexham for a meeting. No point going back to Liverpool now, so I thought I'd call in and see what you're up to.' Caitlin worked in recruitment and was in charge of a number of offices in the north-west of England. 'Are you okay? You looked worried when I came in.'

'I'm fine, thanks. All okay.'

'And Joe? Rory?'

'Yes, they're great.'

'I called in to see them before I went away,' she said. 'You were down in London. Rory and Joe were having a good time.'

'I meant to call you about that,' I said, immediately feeling guilty. 'They said you were there. Did you get roped into cooking for them?'

'Oh, Rory persuaded me to make him an apple pie,' she said. 'He said he hadn't had one for ages.'

'You've been had,' I said. 'Joe makes them for him all the time.'

She laughed. 'He was very convincing. Said it was years since he'd had one.'

I laughed. 'He has no idea of time.'

'I didn't mind, though; it was nice to see them. Did you have a good time?'

I grimaced. 'The course was okay, but I wasn't well on Saturday. I had to keep running out to the loo.' My face burned at the memory of the swift dashes from the room and the knowing looks of some of the guys who must have seen me in the bar the night before.

'Ugh, that sounds horrible. Did you have too much to drink? Weren't you just going to have a quiet night?' We'd talked about it the week before the training day, how I was looking forward to a relaxing night on my own.

I hesitated but luckily she didn't seem to notice. 'I think I just had an upset stomach.'

I don't know why I didn't confide in her. We told each other everything, right from our first night in halls when we were students. We'd always been close, and I loved the fact that she was Joe's sister. His family became mine and mine his; it was perfect for us. But this . . . I couldn't talk to her about this. I hated the thought of her thinking of me drunk and incapable, stumbling and incoherent as I knew I must have been. As she'd seen me so many times before.

10

Caitlin came back to our house with me that night. I knew she was bored and a bit lonely at home since Ben had started to work away. They'd moved up to Liverpool a couple of years after we moved to the north-west and now lived thirty miles from us. We usually saw her at least once a week, particularly when Ben was away.

She came upstairs with me and we sat on the bathroom floor as Rory played in the bath. It was a Friday night and Joe had gone out to pick up some pizzas. I sat with my back against the tiled wall and closed my eyes. The late-summer sun was coming through the coloured-glass window, and the air smelled of Rory's bubble bath. He was singing a little song to himself, one that he'd learned in nursery that week.

I patted Caitlin's hand. 'Watch out for Rory, won't you, if I doze off.'

'Of course I will. He's the one I came here to see! But why don't you go and lie down for a bit? He'll be fine with me.'

I shook my head. 'I don't see enough of him as it is.'

'You look really tired. Are you working tomorrow?'

I grimaced. 'Yeah. Not until the afternoon, though. I've got to be there for twelve.'

'And Sunday?'

'I'm working the morning. Well, until two.'

'So when are you getting time off?'

'I'm not. I can't afford to. But I'm not working nine to five every day. Occasionally I'm working half-days. Well, more like three-quarter-days. I go in mid-morning sometimes, or finish early and then go back to lock up. Or I come home for a longer lunch.' I stopped, confusing myself.

'So you're in work every day?' Her voice softened, and immediately my eyes filled with tears. 'That must be exhausting.'

'It's not that,' I said. 'I am tired. I'm tired all the time. I just miss seeing Rory. Some weeks I'm working until seven for a few nights on a run, if people need to view later on or if I have to value someone's house. He goes to bed at half past, so I hardly see him.'

'Eight o'clock on a Saturday!' piped up Rory.

I hadn't realized he was paying any attention to us and shook my head at Caitlin. *'Pas devant l'enfant.'*

'Did you know I can speak French?' Rory asked Caitlin. 'That means "Not in front of the child."'

She laughed. 'Come on, mister,' she said. 'I've just heard Dad come in; let's go down and have that pizza.'

Later that evening Caitlin and I sat on the patio with Joe. They were drinking wine, but I poured Perrier for myself.

'How come you're not drinking?' asked Caitlin, and then she laughed. 'Oops, sorry, I shouldn't have asked that.'

'What do you mean?' asked Joe.

She shook her head. 'It's none of my business whether she has a drink or not.'

'She's wondering whether I'm pregnant,' I told Joe. 'That's always a clue, if someone refuses a drink on a Friday night. She's being discreet.'

'I was trying to be!'

Joe said, 'You're not, are you?'

I laughed. 'Of course I'm not. Don't you think I would've told you?'

He reached out and put his arm around me. 'I'd hope so!' He kissed my cheek. 'Maybe one day.'

I smiled at him. 'Maybe.' I drank some more Perrier, then said, 'I haven't felt like a drink for the last few weeks. But yes, we've been talking about having another baby, though not yet. Next year might be good. Nothing's guaranteed, though, obviously.'

'You lucky thing,' said Caitlin. For a moment she looked glum. 'No point in my getting pregnant, with Ben being out of the country all the time.'

'You could always go with him.'

'What, and be a trailing spouse? He'd be out of the house for fourteen hours a day and I'd have nothing to do. No thanks.'

Ben was an engineer who worked away for months at a time. On the one hand they were rapidly paying off their mortgage, but on the other I wasn't too sure how long they would last with hardly seeing each other. I was always grateful to have Joe, when I thought of her relationship with Ben. It was so hard for her not being able to spend much time with him.

We talked then about her trip to see him in Dubai in August, and the issue of my not drinking didn't arise again.

When I went up to bed, I thought how different that night was from the Friday I'd spent in London. I hated that feeling of being out of control. I knew I'd drunk those gins that night far too quickly, and again I got a flash of the two empty bottles on the table. I shook my head. I should never drink like that again.

While Joe was in the bathroom, I went back downstairs to find my bag. In the zip compartment was the receipt for the

meal at the hotel that I'd received in the post. I took it out and looked at it again.

Pâté and smoked salmon. Those were the starters. Then steak and chicken.

I closed my eyes. What had I eaten? I had no idea now. How could that happen? No matter how many times I looked at the items on the receipt, I couldn't remember eating any of them.

When I saw the two bottles of Barolo, I winced. Two bottles. What would that be, twenty units? And I'd already had gin. I couldn't remember how many of them I'd drunk. Quickly I took out my phone and found the bill for the hotel. They'd sent an automatic receipt once I'd paid my bill on the Saturday morning. I knew I'd put the bar drinks on my room tab. The receipt showed I'd had a double gin with tonic at seven fifteen P.M. and another at seven forty-five. I'd also had three bottles of water from the minibar. At least I hadn't drunk anything more when I got back to my room.

I frowned.

One thing I could remember was drinking a bottle of water when I woke up that morning. Red wine always makes me so thirsty. I'd taken another bottle downstairs with me and I'd drunk it by the time I got to the conference room. There'd been a table set out with hot and cold drinks and I'd picked up a couple of bottles then to last me the morning.

Had I drunk another in the night? When I woke that morning, light was streaming through the gap in the curtains, so I could see everything quite clearly. I'd been desperate for water then. Surely I would have noticed a bottle of water on the bedside table?

I remembered standing by the door holding my overnight bag as I left the room. There was a waste bin by the door and I remembered throwing the glass bottle into it and flinching as it hit the metal. I'd looked into the bin, to see if it had smashed. There hadn't been another bottle in there.

But then I saw sense. My clothes from the night before had been strewn around the room and my handbag had tipped over. I'd probably had a bottle of water when I got in and left it on the floor.

I switched my phone off and put it in my bag and tucked the receipt back into the inside pocket. I was so glad I hadn't drunk anything since that night. I didn't want to ever get in a state like that again.

11

Saturday, July 22

Caitlin stayed over that night in the spare room, which had virtually become hers since Ben was away so often.

When I woke automatically at seven o'clock, the house was dim and quiet. Joe lay beside me, his body heavy and unresponsive. I knew he'd lie there like that until I got up with Rory; I was well used to that. When I heard the familiar sound of Rory jumping out of bed and coming onto the landing, I sat up to call him into my room, then heard Caitlin say, 'In here, sweetheart. Let's give Mummy a rest, shall we?' and quickly lay back down again.

I love that woman.

Caitlin said, 'Anyone for pancakes?' and the sound of Rory's cheers rang through the house. I snuggled down next to Joe, who hadn't woken at all, and tried not to think about the fact that he hadn't had to wake; he'd known Caitlin or I would take care of Rory. I had to grab whatever time I could with my son.

I forced myself to stop thinking like that. I knew that resentment corroded a marriage. I closed my eyes tight and

made myself think happier thoughts, and the next thing I knew, sunlight was streaming through the curtains and my bedside clock showed it was ten o'clock. I could hear Rory in the garden and the sound of Caitlin calling to him. Joe lay beside me, silent and still, as though he was determined not to be the first to get up. True to my suspicions, when he felt me get out of bed, he yawned and rolled over, stretching out across the bed.

'I won't be long,' he said, and gave me a lazy smile. 'Unless you want to come back?'

'Right,' I said. 'Because ten o'clock isn't late enough?'

'Oh no, is that the time?' He got out of bed and stumbled into the en suite. 'I'm meeting Mike for a run.'

'Don't forget I'm working later.'

He nodded, though I didn't think he was taking much notice, and turned the shower on.

I put my dressing gown on to go downstairs. Caitlin and Rory were in the garden, watering his little patch of vegetables. He was earnestly showing her the pots of herbs he was growing and she was admiring his work.

She looked up and waved as she saw me. 'Good sleep?'

'You're an angel,' I said. 'Thank you so much.'

Rory rushed over to me, planting a huge kiss on my cheek. 'Sit down, Mum, we're making you breakfast!'

I didn't need much persuasion. By the time Joe came downstairs, I was sitting at the patio table eating pancakes with strawberries and drinking coffee and orange juice, all courtesy of Caitlin and Rory.

'Look at you with your servants,' said Joe. He leaned over and kissed me. 'You're a lady of leisure.'

'Yeah,' I said. 'I'm living the dream. You'll be back by eleven thirty, won't you?'

He looked at his watch. 'Why?'

'Because I'm going to work! I said I'd be there before twelve.'

'Oh, for God's sake,' he muttered. 'That only gives me an hour.'

'It's okay,' said Caitlin. 'I can stay with Rory till you get back. I'm not doing anything.'

I bit my lip, determined not to say a word. Caitlin was aware of this and Joe must have been too, because he crashed around the kitchen, getting all his gear together, then gave a brief 'I'm off, then,' before slamming the front door behind him.

'I don't get it,' I said. 'I've got to go to work – it's not as though I'm just off enjoying myself.'

'It's because he's always gone for a run with Mike on a Saturday morning,' said Caitlin tactfully. 'It does him good. You know that.'

'Well, I used to go shopping in town on a Saturday afternoon and have cocktails afterwards,' I said. 'And that did me good, too.'

She grinned. 'I remember. Those were great days.'

'Things change when you have children. And he has plenty of free time when he could go running. Rory's in nursery three afternoons a week.'

'I suppose Mike's not free then,' she said. 'It's different going on your own.'

'I know,' I admitted. I did want to be fair to Joe. 'And it's what we agreed when we had Rory. Joe doesn't know any other stay-at-home dads and he doesn't feel part of the women's groups. He needs to see his friends every now and then.'

Caitlin nodded. 'You do have to stick up for yourself a bit more, though,' she said. 'We've talked about this, Gem. You need to be more assertive with Joe. You can do it at work; you have to make sure you do it at home, too.'

This was something we'd discussed many times. She was right; I had no problem being assertive at work. I knew what had to be done and I did everything I could to make it happen. I felt in control of things there. But at home . . . I still

found it hard to say what I wanted, at times. And I knew why I struggled with it, but that didn't make it any easier to deal with.

She moved her chair closer to me, so that Rory couldn't hear us. 'It's still working for you, isn't it, having Joe at home with Rory? It's much easier than if you had to rush to nursery to pick up Rory every night. Imagine that if you had a client you needed to talk to. If Joe was working in Liverpool or Manchester, the pressure to be there for Rory as well as be in the office would be horrendous.'

I nodded. 'I know, and it does work well. It's just . . . I know it's easier having Joe at home, but it's tough at the moment. I'm working every day and any free time I spend with Rory, but it means I don't have a minute for anything else.'

'What about the evenings? Fancy doing something then? I could stay over. Or I could babysit and you could go out with Joe.'

'I'd love to. It's just I'm usually working till late. I don't think I could cope with going out.' I laughed. 'I don't even know what I'd do if I had some spare time. I don't seem to have any interests or hobbies. I can't remember the last time I finished a book.' I saw the worry on her face. 'Sorry, Caitlin, I don't mean to complain so much. I'm just tired.'

The sun was high now, burning us. I was still in my dressing gown and it was eleven o'clock. Time to go and shower and get ready for the day.

'You weren't this tired before,' she said. 'I know I haven't seen you for a few weeks because I've been away, but you seemed okay then. Is everything all right?'

I looked over at her, at her kind, concerned face. We'd been through so many things together and had always pulled through. She'd been there for me during my darkest time and until now I'd thought I could tell her anything.

I desperately wanted to tell her about the weekend in

London, about how drunk I'd been and how David had kissed me, but something stopped me. When I married Joe, Caitlin and I had become sisters-in-law, and though this had brought us nothing but happiness, I realized with a lurch that her loyalties would be with Joe, not me.

That thought was too much to cope with just then. I jumped out of my seat and started to clear away the plates from the table. 'Everything's fine. Don't worry.'

'Leave this,' said Caitlin. 'I'll do it. You go on up and have a shower. I can keep an eye on Rory while I sort the kitchen out.'

I kissed her cheek.

'And me!' Rory shouted, and he ran down the garden path on his stocky little legs. 'I want a kiss, too!'

I hugged him to me, breathing in the smell of strawberries and grass and milk. I glanced over to see Caitlin looking at me, an expression of yearning on her face.

'You're so lucky, Gem,' she said. She came over to us and put her arms around us. 'I'd give anything to have what you have.' When Rory wriggled away and went back to his tent on the lawn, she said, 'I love you and Joe, you know. And Rory, too, of course. You're my favourite people in the whole world.' She kissed my cheek and whispered, 'I'm so glad you two got together.'

I smiled and hugged her, the guilt of keeping secrets from her and from Joe nearly overwhelming me.

12

Thursday, July 27

The following week was even busier at work. Sophie phoned in sick on Monday morning, and for a day or two I thought we'd manage without her, but after an eight P.M. finish on Tuesday night, I admitted defeat and called Lucy when I got home to ask whether she could help us out. Lucy used to work with us, but after her daughter, Maisie, was born four years ago, she decided to stay at home with her. We remained in touch and over the years Lucy stood in whenever I needed help. We agreed she'd work school hours for the rest of the week.

On Thursday morning I was out with a newly retired couple, showing them properties a little further out of town. We went from house to house and they loved them all. I knew instinctively that they wouldn't be buying anything. They seemed to treat it as a bit of a day out, a chance to have a look around people's homes. They came back to the office to pick up a bunch of other details and went off for lunch, happily chatting about the places they'd seen.

'No luck?' asked Rachel.

I shook my head. 'Sightseers.'

She grimaced. 'Are they selling, too?'

'They are, but not here. They're from Nottingham and their son's up here with his family. I get the feeling this is something they do now and again for a bit of fun.'

'To torment their son, more like.'

'Yes, they took the brochures home to show him and his wife. She's probably threatening divorce right now.'

We laughed.

'Poor things,' said Lucy.

I made some coffee and sat at my desk. I checked my e-mails, then pulled the tray of post that had been delivered to the office towards me.

'I've dealt with most of that,' called Rachel. 'There's something addressed to you personally, though. Obviously I didn't open it.'

I picked up a large white envelope. It had a typed label on it with *Private* written above my name. I ripped it open. Inside was a piece of paper, about four inches by six. It was a photo, glossy and full colour: a photo of David kissing me against the door to my hotel room.

My hand jerked and my mug of coffee went flying over the desk. I grabbed the photo and threw it into a drawer as Rachel and Lucy hurried over with paper towels.

'Are you okay?' asked Rachel. 'You didn't burn yourself, did you?'

'No. I'm fine.' I took the paper towels off her. 'I'll do this, thanks.'

'Did it go on your papers?' asked Lucy.

'No, I got them in time.' I sounded curt but I couldn't help it. I wanted to take the photo out of the drawer and look at it again, but I couldn't do that while they were here. We only had this one office, with a little kitchen behind a partition at

the back. There was no privacy at all; this hadn't been a problem until now, but at that point I would have done anything to have my own room so that I could try to work out what on earth was going on.

That afternoon I sat at my desk and answered the phone and spoke to new clients and arranged appointments, all the while aware of the photo that was sitting in the drawer next to me. Who had taken it? Why would they send it to me?

For the last few weeks I hadn't let myself think about what had happened at the door to my hotel room. It had been both expected and unexpected. If I'd been single, I suppose I would have known he was going to kiss me. It was just the way the conversation was going. We were both drunk, laughing a lot, and very, very relaxed. But he knew I was married. I'd told him about Joe.

I was dying to talk this through with someone. I couldn't talk to Caitlin. Obviously I couldn't talk to Joe. My mum would be horrified I'd kissed someone else.

I looked over at Lucy. She was great fun and a good friend. Very understanding, kind and loyal. But I was her boss. Surely there was a limit to what I could tell her? Sometimes we went running together, and we'd joined a yoga class for a while, but although we had the odd moan about our husbands, it was never anything serious. And I worried that my judgement could be off: I imagined walking into the office and realizing that all the others knew about this and had been talking about it while I was out. My stomach knotted at the thought of that.

'Are you okay?' asked Rachel. 'Are you feeling all right?'

I forced a smile. 'Yes, I'm great, thanks. Just a bit tired.'

'It's nearly time to go home,' she said. 'Not long now.' She'd been to the cloakroom and come back looking as immaculate

as she did when she arrived at work. Her hair was always glossy and pinned back, her make-up always fresh.

'You're looking very nice,' I said. 'Are you going out?'

She blushed. 'No, just going home. Another night in.'

'Me too.' I thought of going home and holding Rory in my arms. Just the thought of it was enough to lower my blood pressure. That was all I wanted to do, to hold him close, to make him laugh. To kiss him until he screamed for mercy. I relaxed at the thought. I looked at my watch. It was ten minutes to closing time. 'Come on, everyone,' I said, 'let's get out of here on time tonight.'

There was a sudden mad dash as people cleared their desks and washed up mugs. While they were in the kitchen I grabbed a folder and threw in the photo and the envelope that had arrived in the post.

'Taking work home?' asked Rachel when she saw the folder on my desk. 'You're tired; you should be relaxing tonight.'

'There's always something to be done.'

She held my bag and folder while I locked the door and pulled down the shutters. The others had walked off in the other direction, and she and I set off to the car park behind our office. In the quiet of the car park I stood next to her as she opened her car door, and for one crazy moment I thought, *Should I ask her what to do?*

Rachel always seemed so capable and sensible. She was quiet; although she'd join in if she was encouraged, she was more likely to sit on the edge of the group. Maybe that meant she'd be less likely to gossip. I desperately needed someone to talk to.

'Rachel?' I said as she got into her car and put her bag on the passenger seat. 'Can I have a word?'

She looked up at me, startled. 'What, now?'

Then common sense prevailed. I couldn't talk to her about David. She was too young and I was her boss.

I shook my head. 'It's okay. Nothing that won't keep until tomorrow.'

She looked relieved and I realized I wasn't the only one who wanted to get home early. I waved goodbye and got into my own car.

13

Although I'd intended to go straight home, I found myself driving in the opposite direction, down towards the River Dee. The car parks there were emptying now and I found a quiet spot in the castle car park. I needed to see the photo on my own.

I pulled it from the folder and looked at it again.

At the bottom of the photograph was the time and date it was taken: June 23 at 22:45. That was the Friday night I was in London. I remembered it had been so hot and humid when I arrived at the hotel that I'd showered and washed my hair before going down to the bar. My hair was gleaming, my make-up still in place. My eyeliner swept my eyes in a smooth line, untouched by the night, but my face was pink and had a sheen that I hoped wasn't normally there. It was easy to tell I'd been drinking.

My eyes were nearly closed and my face was upturned. I was being kissed by a man with dark hair who was touching my face as though we were lovers. His face was in shadow; unrecognizable.

I knew who it was, though. It was David.

And I thought: *What would Joe do if he saw that photo? Would he leave me?*

At the thought of that conversation, of living alone for half the week, of not being able to see Rory every day or to speak to Joe whenever I wanted to, I felt panic course through my body. I could lose everything over this.

I leaned my head against the car seat and closed my eyes. What was going on? Why would anyone take a photo of me that night, and why would they send it to me?

A band tightened around my forehead at the thought of Joe seeing that photo. He'd never believe me if I told him I couldn't remember doing it. He thought I was in bed, asleep, at that time. I'd *told* him I was! And I'd told him by text, too, so I couldn't even deny it. My heart thumped as I thought: *What happened that night? What happened after we kissed?* I was so frustrated. I couldn't remember anything. Had we slept together? Surely not! How would I not remember that? I was furious with myself for drinking so much; I should have learned my lesson by now, but every time I thought of Joe seeing the photo, of hearing what happened that night, I felt sick.

And then I knew I needed to get hold of David and ask him what the hell was going on.

Within minutes I was back at the office. I opened the shutters, unlocked the door, and turned on my computer.

It was nearly six P.M. and I'd told Joe I'd be home early that night. Quickly I logged into the database we kept of all our clients and searched for David Sanderson. I clicked on his name. I pulled my mobile out of my bag and saw I had three missed calls from Joe. I felt a stab of guilt and dialled David's number.

I held my breath as it rang out. I counted eight rings and then it cut dead. It didn't go to voicemail. I tried it again and then again. Why wasn't he answering? Was he monitoring his calls?

Quickly I called from the office phone and withheld the number, so that he wouldn't know it was me. Again it rang out. No reply.

On the database was his e-mail address, and I opened my work e-mail and sent him a quick note.

Hi David, this is Gemma from Chester Homes. Please can you get in touch asap? I need a quick word. Thanks.

I looked at his e-mail address again. It was a Gmail account. What if he didn't see it? I sent him a text with the same message, just in case. I needed to speak to him.

Joe was waiting at the front door when I arrived home.

'You said you'd be back early!' He pushed past me and grabbed his kit bag from the cloakroom. 'I'm late for football.'

'I'm so sorry. I've been at work. You'll be in time if you run now.'

'I called you there and there was no answer!'

'I was halfway home and realized I'd forgotten something,' I said. 'I had to go back. I'm sorry. I forgot about football.'

He snatched my car keys from my hand. 'You've blocked me in. I'll take your car.'

With a bang of the front door he'd gone. It was only when I was bathing Rory that I realized I'd left the folder with the photo of David kissing me on the front seat of my car.

That night Joe came back late, long after I was in bed. I guessed he'd gone to the pub with his friends after playing football. I couldn't sleep when he was out; I always struggled to relax if I knew I'd be woken up.

That night, though, there was no chance of sleep. I lay for hours, rigid with worry. I hadn't expected him to take my car

and couldn't remember whether I'd put everything back into the folder, or whether the photo and envelope were just lying underneath it. Would he see it? Would he come storming in, demanding to know what was going on?

I nearly jumped out of my skin when I heard the front door open. There was a clink as he put my car keys in the bowl on the hall table, then the soft creak of the stairs as he came up to bed. He looked in on Rory first, and by the time he came into our room I realized that of course he hadn't found anything. He never looked at my files at home unless I asked him to. He wasn't very tidy and wouldn't even move them out of the way if I'd left them on the coffee table or pick them up if they were on the floor. There was no way he'd bother to look at one when he was in a hurry to get to football.

'Hey,' he said, and smiled, his earlier temper forgotten. 'Sorry I'm late. I didn't realize the time.'

'Good night?'

'Yeah, it was great. We won, two-nil, then we went to The Crown for a couple of pints.' The Crown is the pub at the end of our road. 'I brought the car back after football and walked down with Mike.'

I could have kicked myself then. I hadn't heard him park the car earlier; if I had, I could have run out to see whether the photo had been moved.

When he eventually got into bed, we chatted about Mike and his family and then Joe said, 'He was telling me about someone he knows who's moving over to Ireland.'

He gave a deep sigh and my heart sank. Joe's from a huge, close Irish family and a couple of his brothers and sisters still live over there. Whenever he has a couple of drinks he talks about moving back home.

'What will he do there?'

'He's transferring his business,' he said. 'He's a plumber

and says he can do that there as well as anywhere. He said there are lots of opportunities in Ireland now.'

One of the things I loved and hated about Joe was his absolute and complete optimism. The trouble was that he was also able to talk all night.

I yawned. 'Can you tell me about it tomorrow? I'm half asleep.'

'Sorry, sweetheart. It's just that I was thinking – we could do that.'

I was losing track. 'Do what?'

'We could go back to Ireland.'

'Back? I've hardly been there!'

'You know what I mean. Everyone goes back home in the end, don't they?'

'But it's not my home.' I wriggled away from him. 'And what about my business? And the rentals?'

'Oh, you could do that anywhere,' he said confidently. 'Everyone needs to buy houses. And you could get someone to manage the rentals. You could even get someone to manage the office and start another one there.' He turned to me, all excited. 'We could make it work, Gem!'

All of me, every cell in my body, told me not to ask the question, but I couldn't resist. 'And what would you do in Ireland?'

'Me?' He sounded puzzled. 'I'd look after Rory, of course. And hopefully we'll have another baby soon. Or more than one.' He stroked my belly. 'Who knows, we could have a football team!'

He snuggled close to me, dreaming his happy dreams. My happy dreams involved being able to take the whole day off for once in my life. Slowly I slid away from him and made a vow not to get pregnant until we were sharing the same dream.

And then, as I lay there feeling the familiar weight of Joe's arm around my waist, his warm breath on my neck, I thought of that photo again and the lies I'd told him. If Joe saw it, he might go to Ireland anyway, without me. He might take Rory with him.

14

Sunday, July 30

On Sunday Sophie was back at work. Her boundless energy made me doubt her illness earlier in the week, which, according to her, had made her think she was dying. I found I couldn't drum up the energy to care. While she managed to type up her notes and kept up a stream-of-consciousness monologue, I sat at my desk and tried to work out what was happening. In the end I couldn't think straight and sent her out to the corner shop for milk, a job that I knew would buy me twenty minutes' peace.

As soon as she'd gone, I called David's number. There was no reply and it didn't go to voicemail. I tried again and again. Frustrated, I sent a few texts, each one more hysterical than the previous one, but then had to stop myself. I was making an idiot of myself.

Sophie returned and made coffee. Surreptitiously I moved my computer monitor slightly so that she wouldn't be able to see what I was doing on my screen, then opened my personal e-mail address. I'd disabled it on my phone the night before, in case a message came in when Joe was with me. I'd felt

75

grubby then, as though I were having an affair. There was no reply to the e-mail I'd sent David. I looked around: the office was quiet. I picked up my phone and car keys and went out to my car. I looked up the hotel where I'd stayed in London and called them.

'Hi,' I said. 'My name's Gemma Brogan. I stayed at your hotel on Friday, the twenty-third of June.'

'Hi,' said the receptionist. 'How can I help you?'

'I met a potential client that night. I believe he was staying with you for a few days around that time. He gave me his business card but unfortunately I've lost it. Would you be able to give me his contact details?'

'I'm sorry,' she said. 'We're not allowed to give out personal details.'

My heart sank. I'd guessed she'd say that. 'I don't suppose you could pass on a message, could you?'

'Yes, of course, I could do that for you as long as he's given us his details,' she said. 'Just let me check. What was his name?'

'David Sanderson.'

'And when did you say you were here? The twenty-third of June?'

'Yes. That was a Friday night; he'd been there all week.'

'I'm sorry,' she said after checking her computer, 'I'd love to help but he must have been staying somewhere else. There's no record of him staying here.'

And then I remembered him saying, *I'm on the tenth floor.*

I thanked her and ended the call, then sat back, confused. I remembered him saying he'd been at the hotel all week. He'd told me he'd tried most things on the menu in the restaurant.

I frowned. I knew he'd said right at the beginning that he was there on his own, that he'd been bored every evening. Did he simply mean he'd been in London? I'd certainly understood him to mean he'd been staying at the SHAFTESBURY.

There was a knock on my car window and I jumped with fright. Rachel stood there.

'Sorry to bother you,' she said when I got out of my car. 'Paula James is on the phone. She says she's thinking of backing out of the purchase. Can you speak to her?'

I went quickly back into the office to reassure Paula, who called nearly every day, that everything was going well and that you couldn't buy a house without the process taking a bit of time. All the time I was working, right at the back of my mind, niggling away, were questions upon questions.

Why did he tell me he was staying at the hotel when he wasn't? Who had taken that photo? Why had they sent it to me? Had the same person sent me the receipt?

I was desperate to talk to someone about it, but who? While Sophie was occupied with clients, I opened the desk drawer and took the folder out. I reached up and took a box file from the shelf behind me and used it to block the folder, then slid the photo out and stared down at it.

I thought back to the times I'd gone out with Caitlin when we were students. She didn't drink much, but I'd keep going as long as we were out. The next day I'd feel 'the shame', as she put it, where I'd lie on the sofa in our student halls and remember stupid things I'd said or done when I was drunk. I seemed to lose all inhibitions at the time, but afterwards I'd curl into a ball, cringing at the memories as they flashed back into my mind, and she'd say how glad she was that she'd stayed relatively sober. She tried to keep me safe, though, keeping tabs on me when we went out, making sure I didn't go off and do something crazy on my own. She didn't always succeed.

And now here I was again, years after I'd calmed down, married to one man and kissing another while I was drunk. I couldn't even remember doing it. David was nice enough, but I hadn't wanted to kiss him when I was sober. Joe was the only man I'd wanted to kiss since the day I met him, and I was

happy with that. He was everything to me. He was my family. I loved him.

But there was no denying it: here was the evidence that I'd betrayed him. When I looked at the photo, I felt a greater shame than I'd experienced before wash over me. I couldn't bear to think of Joe seeing it. It was something we'd agreed on right from the moment we fell in love, that we'd always be faithful. That there would only be him and me. And now it looked as though I'd destroyed our relationship and – worse – done it so casually, too. As though it was worthless.

I looked at the details that had been put onto the system when David had first come into the office. He'd given an address twenty miles south of Chester. I frowned when I saw the location: why would he live there when there were so many rentals in the city centre? I was just about to enter the street into Google Street View when Rachel came back from showing potential buyers around a house nearby, and I took the chance of everything being quiet to go and find out. It was Sunday afternoon; it was likely he'd be home.

'I need to go out for a bit,' I said. 'You're in charge, Rachel, okay? I won't be long. Call if you need anything.'

I had no doubt that as soon as my car had left our car park, Sophie would be at the shop buying magazines and sweets for their leisurely afternoon, and I found I didn't really care. All I could think about was getting hold of David and asking him what he thought he was doing.

As I drove, I thought of what I'd say to him. Would he answer me? Would he deny all knowledge? My stomach clenched at the thought of a confrontation, but I needed to know who'd taken the photo. He'd been with a group of other men when I first met him, but would they have taken a photo of us together? Why would they do that? And had he been at the hotel with them or was it merely casual chat? I just couldn't remember. I hadn't

known them. He hadn't introduced us or even mentioned them; once he turned to talk to me, his focus was on me alone.

I'd always prided myself on my memory. Before we had Rory, Joe and I used to go to The Crown every Thursday night for a pub quiz and he'd laugh as I would remember the most ridiculous facts, things I'd heard once, years before. It was a curse as well as a blessing, of course; some things I really didn't want to remember and I had no choice, so I'd had to learn to block them out. Yet I couldn't remember parts of that night as well as I could remember others from years ago. I was more tired now, though. Maybe that was it.

As I drove to David's house, I remembered that he had said he worked for Barford's on the outskirts of Chester. Just then my phone rang. I saw that it was Rachel and parked in a lay-by to speak to her. She had a quick question about a sale I was involved with, and just before she hung up, I asked, 'Are you busy?'

'No, apart from that query it's fine. Do you want me to do something?'

'Remember that client who came in a couple of weeks ago? David Sanderson. I took him to view the flats down by the river. Can you call his details up for me, please?'

I could hear the click of her mouse as she searched the database.

'Just a second,' she said. 'Oh, I think I remember him. Nice-looking guy?'

I winced. 'I suppose. Dark-haired. Tall.'

'Just a minute, the system's slow,' she said. 'I think I have him now. Do you want his number?'

'No, I've got that. Which company did he work for?'

'It says here he works for Barford's.'

I nodded. That was the name I'd remembered. 'Did he give their address?'

'No.' She was curious now and I could have kicked myself. 'Why do you need his work address?'

'It doesn't matter,' I said. 'I'm just trying to get hold of him. Did he give a number for Barford's?'

She read it out. 'Is there anything I can do, Gemma? Where are you?'

'Don't worry. I'll be back in an hour.' I clicked the phone off before she could ask any more questions. I knew she and Sophie would be talking about me now, wondering what I was up to.

My call went straight through to a recorded message. 'You are through to Thompson and Sons. All of our offices are closed today. Please call back between nine A.M. and five P.M. Monday to Friday.'

I stared at the phone and back down at my notepad. He'd said he worked for Barford's, but this company was called Thompson's. I looked them up online. They were a building company and yes, their number was the same as the one he'd given us.

I checked Google, found the real number for Barford's and called them. Luckily someone was on duty there and answered my call. Nobody by the name of David Sanderson was on their staff list.

15

The street David had said he lived in was a cul-de-sac, arching around a pretty piece of land planted with trees and flowers. The houses were double-fronted, with smart gates and bright, well-tended gardens. I stopped just short of the house and looked around carefully. I thought of what David had said about not being ready to live in a house, preferring a flat instead. These were family houses, exactly the opposite of what he'd wanted.

There was a red Toyota parked outside the garage and I realized I didn't know what car David had been driving when he came to see us. I have CCTV installed in our small private car park, ever since someone had parked there and scratched my car; I took out my notepad and wrote *Check CCTV* so that I wouldn't forget.

My stomach tightened as I rang the doorbell. I didn't know what I would say to him. What could I say? For a moment I thought of leaving, of running back to my car and going back to work, but then a figure appeared through the coloured glass of the porch door and I found I couldn't move.

A woman of about my age opened the door and immediately

I panicked. Was she married to David? How was I going to ask him about the photo if she was there?

She glanced up and down the road as though wondering why I was there and whether I was selling something. 'Hello?'

I pulled myself together and smiled reassuringly at her. 'I'm looking for David Sanderson,' I said. 'Is he at home?'

She frowned. 'Who?'

'David Sanderson.'

'He doesn't live here,' she said. 'I've never heard of him.'

For a second I wondered whether she was lying, but then she leaned into the hallway and shouted, 'Neville!' A few seconds later, a man appeared. He was about my height, fair-haired and stocky. 'This woman wants to find someone called David Sanderson. Do you know him?'

He shook his head. 'Sorry, never heard of him.'

'He gave me this address,' I said weakly. 'He said he lived here.'

They looked at each other, clearly puzzled. 'We've been here for more than ten years,' said the woman. 'And we know all our neighbours. There's no one in this cul-de-sac with that name, I'm afraid.'

The man agreed. 'Sorry. You must have the wrong address.'

They looked so earnest and honest that I didn't feel I could start quizzing them further, so I thanked them and went back to my car. I drove out of the cul-de-sac and back onto the main road, and then parked. I opened Facebook. There were quite a few men with the same name, but those with photos clearly weren't him and those without lived in other countries. I checked Twitter and he wasn't there either.

He'd said he was in sales. Surely he'd be on LinkedIn? I checked, but the only David Sandersons there were clearly not the man I'd met. I entered his name into Google, but it was quite a common one, and even though I scrolled through page after page, I couldn't find anything about him at all. I sat

back and closed my eyes, trying desperately to think. His phone number had rung out; it was impossible to leave a voice-mail. My e-mails to him weren't answered. He didn't live at that address and he didn't work where he said he had, that much was clear.

Just then my phone pinged in my hand, startling me. It was an Instagram message. I only use Instagram with a few people, and on the screen it said the message was from someone I didn't follow. I looked at the sender's name; it was Watch-ingYou. There was a little cartoon figure next to the name, rather than a photo. I frowned and clicked on the message.

There didn't seem to be anything there at first. I was just about to switch off my phone when a video appeared.

It was a video of me.

When I heard my own voice, I nearly jumped out of my skin.

'I don't know. I'm not sure I would have married him if I'd known.' My cheeks were pink and a glance at my eyes made it clear I was drunk. 'It's not that he's lazy,' I heard. My tone was confidential, as though I were telling a secret, and my voice was husky. 'Well, he is lazy sometimes!' On the video I laughed, just a bit too loudly, and covered my mouth to stop myself. 'God, he's so lazy at times.' I sounded irritated now, rather than fond. 'It's just that when he said he'd stay at home with Rory, I didn't think he meant forever! I just wish . . .' My voice became pensive then. 'I just wish I'd been able to stay at home, too. Instead of him. I wish I'd had that chance.' I looked up at the person I was speaking to. 'You only get one chance, don't you?'

On the screen I picked up my glass of wine and drank some. A little wine smile appeared around my mouth. I said, 'What?' and then laughed, using a napkin to wipe it away.

The person I was speaking to said something then. In the car I strained to hear it, but I couldn't. On the screen I replied,

'Well, that's what he wants. And he wants to try for another baby now. I'm just worried that he'll never go back to work.' Again, the other person spoke. I could see my own face in the video, drunkenly focusing on what was being said. Then I replied, 'I don't know. I just don't know if I would marry him again, knowing what it would be like.'

The video stopped there, frozen with my face in a grimace, my glass in my hand.

I stared down at the screen, my mind whirring. What on earth was this? I had no memory of saying it to anyone. I hadn't even thought it, or not for a while, anyway, and only then in a temper. I wanted to play it again, but now the list of messages I'd received appeared, and next to *WatchingYou* it said *Video Unavailable*.

I scrolled through the messages. The last one I'd had, prior to this, was from Caitlin the other day. She'd sent me some photos of toys and clothes that she wanted my opinion on for Rory's birthday. Those photos were still there.

I swiped the Instagram app so that it disappeared from my screen, then reopened it. I could still see that WatchingYou had sent me a video, but that it was unavailable.

I felt like I was about to hyperventilate. Where was the message? Who had sent it to me?

And then I realized. In the video I was wearing that dress I'd worn in London, the night I had a meal with David. Although most of the video showed just my face, there was a moment when I picked up my glass where I'd seen a flash of a dark green shoulder strap. One strap must have slipped down my arm – it was always doing that – and it had almost looked like I was naked.

I drove slowly back to Chester, my mind racing. When I got back into the office, all was quiet. A couple were leaving as

I entered, their hands full of brochures. I forced myself to smile at them, to ask them whether they'd got what they'd come for, and they promised they'd be in touch when they'd looked through the house details. All the time I was thinking about the video, the way I appeared. Drunk. Flirty. Betraying my husband without a second thought.

Brian was on the phone; it sounded as though he was talking to a tenant about rent that was overdue. I looked at him, knowing I should ask him what was going on, but I couldn't concentrate on anything else but my own fears. He gave me a thumbs-up so I let it go. I knew he'd manage without my input.

Rachel was typing on her computer and Sophie was washing up some cups in the kitchen. I took a bottle of water from the fridge, found some painkillers in my drawer, and sank into my office chair.

'You look tired,' said Rachel. 'Is everything okay?' I didn't know where to start. I looked over at her, just dying to confide in someone. She smiled at me. 'Rory okay?'

Rory was about the only thing that was okay, I thought. I wondered what Rachel would say if I said, *Yes, actually, he's fine, but everything else seems to be going wrong*. I pictured her face if I told her what was actually going on and I thought it would only be a matter of seconds before she told Sophie.

I knew that the only people I really trusted were Joe and Caitlin. The only people I wanted to talk to were the ones who mustn't know what was going on.

16

I let everyone at the office leave a few minutes early, saying I would be okay to lock up. I put the *Closed* sign on the door and clicked the latch down, then went through to the back and made sure the door to the small back yard was locked too. When I was certain I was the only person in the office and nobody else could get in, I sat back at my desk and downloaded the CCTV footage for the car park.

I own the tiny car park behind the office. Because of the security systems in place, we have to lock up and leave via the front door, then go round the corner into the car park. There was room for only six cars and the spaces were clearly marked. After the incident last year when my car was damaged, I'd installed a cheap CCTV camera to record vehicles entering and leaving the car park. I wondered whether David had left his car there when he'd come into the office. I couldn't remember whether I'd asked him when we drove off where he'd parked.

I set the CCTV to play. The grainy screen hurt my eyes right from the beginning. I tried to remember what time he'd come in, but decided to put it to run from eight A.M., just in case he'd arrived early and gone for coffee.

Nothing happened at all until eight thirty, when I arrived at the office.

On the screen I could see my car enter the empty car park. I watched myself get out of the car, lock it with my key fob, then leave the car park, turning in the direction of the office. Fifteen minutes later Rachel drove in and neatly reversed into the space next to mine. She sat in the car for a few minutes – I couldn't see what she was doing but guessed she was checking her make-up or on her phone – and then she jumped out and waved at someone on the street. I assumed that was Sophie; they usually arrived at about the same time. Two minutes later, Brian's car entered the car park. He parked nearest to the exit, as he tended to come and go all day.

Nothing happened for the next couple of hours. Then at ten thirty I saw myself walk into view, throw my bag into the back seat of my car, and drive off. It was clear that David hadn't parked there.

I closed down the CCTV and thought about what to do. My office is on a corner, with the car park behind it. We're opposite a restaurant, and I know they don't have cameras there. On the other side of the road is a charity bookshop – no cameras there, either. However, if you walk further up the street to the end of the block, there is a small shop that sells newspapers and groceries. The owner and manager, Michael, was a guy I'd known for a few years through our local small business association. I guessed he'd have a CCTV system because of the problem he'd had with shoplifters at times.

I locked up the office and walked down the street to Michael's shop. I had to wait a while behind people who were picking up groceries, then asked the assistant if Michael was free. When she called him, he came out of his office at the back of the shop and beckoned me over.

'Are your CCTV cameras working?' I asked. I explained that I was concerned about a client of ours but didn't say

anything more than that. I said I wanted to see whether I could see him onscreen, as I wanted to go to the police about him. Michael raised his eyebrows at that, but ushered me into his office and switched on his machine.

'When did you want to check?'

'June the sixteenth,' I said.

Immediately he stopped. 'I'm sorry, Gemma, but we only keep them for a week. It's an old system and we store them on rewritable disks. Every week I erase everything and start again. There's no point in us keeping it any longer if there hasn't been any trouble. What's he been up to?'

I hesitated. I didn't want to tell him the full story, obviously, but I needed him to understand why I wanted to check.

'We had someone come in who was a bit odd,' I said. 'He freaked me out slightly. I checked out his contact details and he was lying about who he was. I wanted to see whether I could find a picture of him.'

'I don't blame you. Remember Suzy Lamplugh?'

I winced. Suzy Lamplugh was an estate agent in London who took a client to view a property and was never seen again. It was discovered later that the client had given a false name when he'd made the appointment. I was only too aware of her whenever I thought of David. The responsibility I had to my staff, sending them into empty properties with people we didn't know, was huge. I decided that the next day I'd tell the staff they had to ask for official ID before showing a client any properties. I'd make them take a photocopy of it, so that at least if something happened, the police would know who was responsible.

'That's why I need to know who he is,' I said. 'I need to protect my staff.'

And protect myself, too.

17

The next morning, I woke with a start. I thought someone had held me by the shoulder and hip and turned me over in my bed. It was the strangest sensation, as though I could still feel hands gripping me tightly and then letting me go as I landed face down on the bed. I couldn't resist, could only do what the hands were making me do. My heart thumped and I gasped.

I opened my eyes and saw that the room was light; it was nearly time to get up. 'Joe?' I touched his shoulder, but he grunted and moved away. 'Joe, did you move me just then?'

'Eh?' Slowly he wakened and turned over to face me. 'What?'

'Did you turn me over in bed?'

He looked bemused. 'I was asleep, Gem. I didn't do anything.'

'That was really weird. Are you sure?'

He closed his eyes. 'You must have been dreaming, honey,' he said. 'I was nowhere near you.'

My heart was pounding still from the sensation of being

moved, and I lay on my side, away from Joe, and tried to calm myself. It was a dream; it had to have been.

The bedroom door opened then and Rory came into the room. I lifted the quilt and he slipped in beside me. I held him to me and kissed his forehead. It was hot and damp.

'Are you all right, sweetheart?' I whispered.

He shook his head and put his hand on his throat. 'It's all sore.'

Just then my alarm went off. I reached out to switch it off, and Rory held on tightly.

'Are you at home today, Mum?'

I hesitated. 'I'm supposed to be going in, pet.' His lip wobbled and he clung tighter. I looked down at him and thought, *What is the point in working for myself if I can't take time off when my child is ill?*

'I'll stay home today,' I whispered. 'I'll stay home until you feel better.'

An hour later, Rory was lying on the sofa, covered in his quilt, with Buffy, his fluffy rabbit, by his side. He was dozing while his favourite cartoon was on television.

'Shall I call the office and tell them you won't be in?' asked Joe.

'I'll give Lucy a call and see if she can come in today.' I groaned. 'She's changed her number and I forgot to put it into my phone. I'll have to go into the office to phone her. I won't be long.'

'I'll go in for you, honey,' he said. 'You stay here with Rory and I'll get the number.' He picked up the keys to his car and the office. 'Where is it? On your desk?'

I froze. Lucy's new number was on a slip of paper in my desk drawer, and in there too was the photo and the receipt. No way was Joe going into that drawer. Luckily it was locked, so none of the staff would be able to get in either.

'It's okay,' I said. 'I need to have a word with them about a couple of things. I'll run in and be back in half an hour.'

Rachel was waiting outside for me. She was holding a cup of coffee from the café up the road and looked at her watch as I approached the door to the office.

'Sorry I'm late,' I said as soon as I reached her. 'Rory's not well. I need to phone Lucy to ask her if she'll stand in for me for a day or two.'

'Oh, the poor boy. But why didn't you call Lucy from home?'

'She wrote her new number down and I forgot to put it into my phone.' I opened the office door and went straight over to my desk to log on to my computer. Rachel stood next to me and I sat there, frustrated, wanting to open the desk drawer but not wanting her to see the photo that was inside it. My mind whirred as I thought of what to do with it. I couldn't risk taking it home, but I didn't want to leave it at work, either. Each of us had our own desk, but Lucy would be using mine that day and there was no reason why I would keep the drawer locked. 'Is everything okay?' I asked Rachel. 'Do you need something?'

She reached over for my computer mouse and clicked on the online diary we all shared. It contained nothing personal; we always checked each other's diaries if we were going to be out. 'I just wanted to see whether you had any appointments today,' she said. 'I don't have any until later this afternoon, so I can share yours with Lucy.'

'Thanks.'

I was so glad it was Rachel in that day instead of Sophie. She had a calm manner that made everything seem okay. I knew she and Lucy could be relied on to do a great job together. Brian would take care of the rentals; he knew exactly what he was doing, and now I felt safe leaving Lucy and Rachel to deal with the sales.

'Do you know how long you'll be off?' she asked. She scrolled through my diary. 'There's an appointment with the accountant that you might want to postpone if you're not going to be in. Lucy's okay to do any valuations, isn't she?'

'I'll be off until he's better. Probably a couple of days.' My dream of having time away from work was coming true, at the expense of poor Rory's tonsils. 'I'll sort out the accountant; I can call her from home. Lucy can do any valuations and you can split the other appointments between you. Let me know if you get stuck; I'll have my laptop with me and I can deal with any problems. I'll probably just be on the sofa all day.'

'Lucky you,' she said, and then added hastily, 'but poor Rory, of course. Have you got Lucy's new number? I can call her for you.'

'It's okay; I'll do it, thanks,' I said. 'I've got it here somewhere.' I unlocked my desk drawer and took out the slip of paper that had her number written on it. Surreptitiously I took out the photo and the receipt and slid them into an envelope. I jumped as I realized Rachel had come back over to my desk, and slipped the envelope under a file. 'That's just something I need to sort out later.'

'Is it for the post?' She held out her hand. 'I'll send it for you.'

I waved her away impatiently. 'No, it's okay. It's private.' And then, because I didn't want her to wonder what it was, I said, 'It's just something I need for the accountant.'

I called Lucy; she'd just dropped Maisie off at school and was only five minutes away. She agreed to come in and said she'd ask her mum to do the school run that afternoon.

I put the envelope into the zip compartment of my handbag, then thought of Joe finding it. Panic rose inside me. I couldn't let him see either the photo or the receipt. I pulled the envelope out of my bag and took it over to the shredder, pushing it in so hard the engine roared.

When I turned to go back to my desk, Rachel's eyebrows were raised, but she said nothing. The door opened and Lucy came in.

'Is Rory okay?' She sounded so concerned that immediately my eyes prickled. 'You go home and stay with him now.' She put her bag into the drawer in my desk – I was able to leave it open now that I'd destroyed the evidence – and said, 'I've just been into the newsagent's. Michael said you wanted to look at his CCTV footage.'

'CCTV footage?' asked Brian, who'd just come in and caught the tail end of the conversation. 'What's up? Has there been a burglary?'

All of them stared at me. I could have kicked myself. Kicked Michael, too. Why did he have to talk about it to my staff?

'There wasn't any sign of something wrong this morning,' said Rachel. 'What do you want to look at CCTV footage for?'

Frustrated, I glanced at Lucy, trying to tell her to shut up without having to say the words aloud. She took absolutely no notice. 'He said something about the car park,' she said. 'He was busy, though, so couldn't tell me much. Have you had trouble here?'

I picked up my bag and headed towards the door. 'No, no trouble. I thought I saw some teenage boys hanging around my car the other night. I was asking if he'd seen them too. He hadn't seen anything, though. It doesn't matter; I doubt they'll be back.'

'I'll keep an eye out for them,' said Brian.

'Me too,' said Rachel. 'If anyone touches my car, I want to know about it.'

I said goodbye, then paused in the doorway and said casually, 'Oh, and by the way, if anything arrives addressed to me personally, just hold on to it, will you? No need to open it; just put it into my drawer and I'll deal with it when I get back.' They would never open personal mail, but I couldn't

take any risks. The thought of them seeing anything incriminating gave me a cold sweat. 'If it's got a company mark on it and it's clearly for a client, then you can open it, otherwise just put it aside for me.' They looked at me, bemused, but I just gave a big smile and said, 'Great, thanks!' and left the office.

18

Tuesday, August 1

I took a couple of days off work, grateful for the rest and the time spent with Rory. He was pretty lethargic, and I stayed on the sofa with him, reading him stories, watching films, and lying with him as he slept. Joe made the most of my being at home and went out for runs or to the gym, leaving me plenty of time to worry. All I could think about was the photo of David kissing me and the video I'd seen of myself criticizing Joe. Why had I done that? I must have been so drunk. And yes, everything I said about him was true, but I loved him. I loved our family. I couldn't bear it if Joe found out what I'd said and done.

My head ached as I wondered who had sent them to me. Was it David? But who had recorded us? How had that happened? I did remember David taking out his phone and checking his messages at one point. Did he film me then? But then I remembered that when he was on his phone, I took out my own and sent Joe a message saying I was in bed, ready for sleep. I winced as I thought of that message. Why had I lied to him? When I put my phone away, David had already slipped his

into his pocket. He couldn't have filmed me then. And he certainly couldn't have photographed me when he was kissing me.

He was definitely involved, though. He'd lied about everything. It was likely he'd even lied about his name. He might not have photographed me, but I was willing to bet he knew who had.

It was only when Rory woke and Joe came into the living room with a tray of cold drinks in his hands, calling, 'Room service!' that I realized the significance of the receipt.

I had told Joe that I was going to order in food that night in the hotel. I remembered saying in the week before I went there, 'I can't wait to have an early night. Room service, something on television and a long sleep. That's all I want.' I'd been so excited at this little treat that I'd talked about it more than most would, but once I was in London I realized I didn't want to hide away in a hot bedroom. The clinking glasses on the terrace below had called to me, and I'd remembered just how long it had been since I'd gone out at night.

That receipt showed I'd lied to Joe. It showed, too, that the sender knew I had.

As I was playing upstairs with Rory on Tuesday afternoon, I heard a text alert ping downstairs, and a minute later Joe came into the room holding his phone.

'My mum wants to know if we want to go and stay for a few days.'

'What, now? Did you tell her that Rory's not well?'

'I'm feeling better,' said Rory.

I looked at him; his skin had certainly lost its earlier clamminess and pallor. 'Not well enough to go to Ireland, sweetheart.'

'I reckon by Thursday he'll be fine. My mum says the weather's beautiful and Brendan will be there with their boys.'

Brendan, Joe's older brother, lived near Glasgow, and we usually saw him two or three times a year.

'Can we go, Dad?' asked Rory.

Joe laughed and ruffled his hair. 'I'd love to. Let's see what Mum says.'

Oh great, make me the miserable one.

'I don't know,' I said. 'I can't take the time off work just like that. Are Sarah or Caitlin going?'

'No, Caitlin's going over to see Ben, remember? And Sarah's got to work. Come on, Gem; it'll be great.'

Frankly, it wouldn't be a great holiday at all. Or it would for Joe, but not for me. When we were at their house, I wouldn't see Rory at all; he'd want to spend every minute with his cousins. I wouldn't see Joe, either, because he'd be with his dad and his brother. I'd be stuck with his mum, who was very nice, but it meant we'd be cooking and cleaning all day for her 'boys'. I think she thought it was an honour to do that for them. If Caitlin or Sarah were going I'd have someone to talk to and go out with, but with just Joe and Brendan there I'd be at a loss for something to do.

Joe looked at me and laughed. 'You don't want to go, do you?'

'Not really. It wouldn't be much fun for me, would it? I'd just be stuck in the middle of nowhere on my own, cleaning up after you lot.'

'Oh, come on now! We'd be there. We could help you.'

I raised my eyebrows at 'help' and he had the grace to look embarrassed. 'You'd be off playing golf with Brendan,' I said. 'You and Rory should go, though. Have a boys' holiday.'

'Would you like that, Rory?' he asked. 'Just you and me on a little holiday?'

Rory looked confused. 'Not Mummy?'

'Just you and me and Brendan and the boys. And Grandad.'

'And Nanny would look after you,' I said. 'She'd love that.'

'Come on, Rory, let's phone Nanny now and tell her.'

He sat down next to Rory on his bed and I heard Joe's mother's excited voice as she realized her boys were going to be back home.

I sent Brendan's wife, Sarah, a text. Seems like the boys will have a nice time at home.

She replied straight away. Mammy will be delighted.

I laughed. We both got on with Joe's mum, but I knew she loved it when she just had her sons home. This would be the first time she'd have sole charge of her sons and grandsons; it was probably the biggest gift we could give her.

Within minutes I got a text from Caitlin. Sarah's just told me. You're not daft, are you? What will you do when they're away?

Work.

She didn't answer for a while, and then I got a text. Sorry, I'll be away visiting Ben in Dubai, otherwise I'd come over and keep you company.

I had mixed feelings about that. If she were here, I knew I would probably tell her everything. I mustn't do that.

That afternoon I went back into work for a couple of hours at the end of the day. All was quiet; Lucy was there still at my desk, and Rachel and Sophie were in the kitchen, chatting, when I walked into the office. Brian was out; they told me he was showing a new tenant around a couple of flats in the city centre.

'How's Rory?' asked Lucy.

'Getting better, thanks. Joe's taking him to Ireland on Thursday for a few days. They'll have a great time there.'

'You didn't want to go?' asked Lucy.

I shot her a look and she laughed.

'Joe's brother will be there with his boys, so Rory will have

a great time playing with them. He loves his cousins. I'll probably have them pressuring me for another baby when they come back.'

'You can't always have what you want,' said Lucy.

I nodded, embarrassed; I knew she would have liked more children. 'I know; if only it were that easy.'

'My sisters drive me mad,' said Sophie. 'I wish I were an only child.'

Rachel got up and collected all the mugs on a tray. 'You don't,' she said.

Lucy and I talked then about the new rota. 'I'll be here full time while Joe and Rory are away,' I said, 'but I'll take a day off when they get back.'

'That's fine. As long as I can take Maisie to and from school, I can work whenever you want.'

We agreed on the shifts for the next week and I booked myself in for all day every day, thinking I might as well make the most of them being away.

Thursday, August 3

In the couple of days before Joe and Rory left, there was a flurry of activity with washing clothes and gathering together everything they needed for the journey, but pretty soon it was Thursday morning, the car was packed up, and I was waving them off. I took a photo of them as they sat in the car ready to go, huge smiles on their faces. We usually went over to see Joe's parents a couple of times a year, but we hadn't visited since New Year and they were both excited about the trip. Rory was fully recovered now and sat strapped into his car seat in the back, diagonally from the driver's seat, so that Joe could check at a glance that he was all right. The front passenger seat was loaded up with a cooler full of drinks and snacks, and Rory had some headphones and Joe's iPad, ready to watch films if he got bored. I knew they'd have a great time; they always did.

Before Joe got into the car, he put his arms around me and kissed me goodbye.

'You have a good rest,' he said, seemingly oblivious to the fact that I'd be going in to work every day and he'd left behind

a house in chaos. 'We'll call you every morning and every night when Rory goes to bed.' He kissed me again and I clung to him, wishing they would stay.

On hearing that Joe had left our house in a state, Sophie was outraged. 'You need to get some cleaners in,' she said. 'There's no way you should be going home and sorting out Joe's mess for him!' She took out her phone and sent her mum a text. 'I'll give you the phone number for our cleaners. They'll do a great job.'

'And,' said Rachel, 'you can tell Joe that you did it yourself.' She laughed. 'Unless you don't believe in lying to your husband.'

'That's a good idea, actually. He's pretty good at feeling guilty. I wouldn't lie normally, but sometimes . . .'

'Sometimes you lie to him?' asked Sophie, wide-eyed.

'No,' I said, impatient now. 'Of course I don't lie to him. But . . .'

'But you don't always tell the whole truth?' said Rachel.

I laughed. 'It's complicated. Marriage is complicated.'

'You're telling me,' said Brian.

Sophie's phone pinged then. 'Here's the number,' she said, 'just in case you want it.' She forwarded it to my phone and I saved it in my contacts list, determined to call them as soon as I could.

Later that day I escaped into the car park and called the cleaning service. They were happy to be recommended and the owner promised to come round to my house later that evening to see what I wanted done. They would be able to fit me in the next day, so I only had one more night of squalor. Before I went back into the office, I sent Joe a text wishing them a happy holiday. While I was waiting for his reply, I scrolled up, looking at the messages we'd sent back and forth

over the months. When I saw the texts I'd sent the night I was in London, I paused.

There it was, clear as anything. At six thirty P.M. I'd written:

Just got to hotel. Going to have a bath and relax! Kiss Rory for me xx

He'd replied: Will do and kisses to you from me. Hope you have a good night xx

I'd replied: Don't worry, I will! I'm going to order a meal and watch TV xx

That had been my intention. That wasn't the problem, though. Anyone can change their mind. I'd looked at the empty room, heard the sounds of people out on the terrace through the open window, and decided to go down for a drink instead of staying alone in my room. That was okay. But then at nine thirty P.M. he'd written:

Hope you've had a good night. What did you watch? xx

And there in black and white was my reply:

I decided to read instead. Ready for sleep now. Night xxx

I felt cold as I looked at the message. Why had I sent that? I remember sitting chatting to David and having a good time when my phone beeped. Often when I'm out with friends, Joe will start to text and want to carry on a text conversation with me. If I'd said I'd gone down to the bar, he would've asked who I was with, what we were talking about ... He wasn't possessive or jealous, he was just interested, but often it would spoil my night out because his texts would fly in while I was trying to talk to someone. And I'd known he'd be bored and lonely in the living room while Rory slept. He loved company, loved to chat. A night on his own after a day looking after Rory wasn't his idea of fun.

I could have gone back to my room and chatted to him, but I hadn't. I'd carried on drinking with someone I hardly knew.

I'd even paid for his dinner. I'd chosen to do that rather than talk to my own husband.

I thought of the photo that I'd received, the photo of me kissing David, or of David kissing me, whichever way it had happened. And I thought of the bill, the proof that I'd been for a meal with someone else when I'd said I was alone in my room. Then I realized: that was a photocopy.

Where was the original?

20

That night, Janet Boyd, the manager of the cleaning company recommended by Sophie's mum, came round and we had a bonding session over the state of my house. She was a quiet, efficient woman and I was immediately won over.

'We'll sort this out for you,' she said. 'Don't worry about it. Go to work in the morning and when you come back it'll be as good as new. If you give me a spare key now, I'll make sure it's left with the bill.'

It cheered me up to hear that. It was bad enough clearing up my own mess, but everywhere I looked I could see where Joe had been over the last couple of days. Everything was half finished, half eaten, half drunk. He had great intentions, but as far as housework was concerned, he seemed to have the attention span of a gnat.

Rory phoned me and told me about meeting his cousins; he was breathless with excitement as he described their adventures, and he said his dad would call me later that night.

I worked into the evening at home, then dialled out for a pizza and, feeling guilty about eating badly, took a vitamin

pill. While I waited for the food to arrive, I lay on the sofa just staring at the television; I couldn't have said what was on.

The landline rang. Startled, I jumped off the sofa and picked up the receiver.

'Mum?' I said. She was the only person who called on the landline.

There was silence. I said, 'Hello?' but there was still no reply. I looked at the handset and saw that it was a withheld number. I sighed. It was likely to be from a claims company, trying to persuade me to claim for an accident I hadn't had. For a second I listened for the background sounds of a call centre, but there was no sound at all. Frowning, I put the phone down. Immediately it rang again. I picked it up and said, 'Hello?' again, but no one answered.

I glanced at the clock. It was after nine P.M. Surely call centres weren't allowed to ring at this time of night? Then the doorbell went, making me jump. I looked through the peephole to check who it was, something I rarely did when Joe was home, and saw it was just the pizza delivery guy. I took the box into the living room and turned back to the television again, but I was no longer hungry. Despite the fact that it was still early, I wanted to sleep, so I put the rest of the pizza into the fridge, filled a glass with water, and went upstairs.

The house felt weird without Joe or Rory in it. I stood in Rory's room and looked at his toys, at his little wooden bed, and his bookcase overflowing with the books I remembered from my own childhood. I would have given anything to have him there then, to kiss him as he slept, to feel him wriggle and then settle under my touch. I sat for a moment on his bed and held his pillow to my face, breathing in the familiar smell, holding it close in lieu of him. When I stood to put it back and straighten his quilt, I saw that his little toy rabbit, Buffy, was still there, stuffed down between the bed

and the wall. Rory had slept with that rabbit every night of his life; I thought Joe must have had a nightmare putting him to bed without it tonight.

After I'd had a quick shower and was ready for bed, I switched on the lamps on either side of my bed and curled up under the quilt with Buffy in my arms. I called Joe but he didn't pick up, and I guessed he'd be down at the local pub with Brendan and his dad by now, his happy mum left with all the children. I took a photo of myself holding Buffy close and sent it to Joe via text, with a message saying, Tell Rory I'm taking good care of Buffy and we can't wait until you're both back home xxx

I wasn't expecting a reply that night. He hadn't seen Brendan for months and they'd be talking all night. I opened my Kindle and started to read, knowing I'd be asleep within minutes.

I was just on the brink of sleep when my phone gave a loud beep, making me jerk back to consciousness. Thinking it was Joe replying to my text, I reached over to grab the phone, hoping he'd sent a photo back.

He hadn't.

On my screen was another Instagram message. As soon as I saw the name, my stomach sank. *WatchingYou*. Again it said the person messaging would only know I'd seen their request if I chose Allow.

I sat up in bed, my stomach tight with panic. I held my breath as I selected Allow. I couldn't *not* see the message.

An image appeared on the screen. It was a photo of me, lying on a bed. My eyes were shut and I looked as though I was asleep.

I had a sheet wrapped loosely around my waist and legs, and I was wearing no clothes – nothing at all.

*   *   *

I think the photo must have been on my screen for about five seconds before it disappeared. All that was left was *Watching You* and *Photo Unavailable*.

My hands started to shake. When had that photo been taken? It wasn't my bed at home, I knew that. We have a white wrought-iron bedstead and the bed in the photo was completely different.

And then I knew. I think I knew right from the moment I saw it, really, but had tried not to believe it. I lay back down on the bed and buried my face in the pillow. It was the hotel room I'd stayed in while I was in London, I was sure of it. That bed had had a brown suede headboard, and I knew the one in the photo was the same.

I had no memory of that photo being taken. How much had I drunk? How much would I have had to drink to expose myself to another man? Fidelity was so important to Joe and me. We'd both been burned by people in the past; it was the one thing we agreed on.

Once that's happened, the relationship's over anyway, whether the other person knows or not, Joe had said, and I had agreed.

Did this mean my marriage was over?

The thought of that whipped me into action. I wasn't going to let my marriage die without putting up a fight. I needed to go down there. I needed to go back to that hotel room and see what I could remember.

21

Friday, August 4

The next day I was at work early. I'd been awake most of the night worrying about what was going on. Everything that had happened kept rolling around my head. The photocopy of the receipt. The photo of David kissing me. The video of me saying horrible things about Joe. And now the naked photo. I felt like screaming.

I'd called Lucy at eight A.M.

'Lucy, it's me, Gemma. I need to ask a huge favour. Are you free today?'

'Do you want me to come in? I can ask my mum to have Maisie after school. I can be there by ten if that's any good.'

'Would you? That would be great. Brian will be in, but Sophie's off today and I don't want to leave Rachel on her own with sales.'

She agreed to that and sure enough she was there just after ten, ready to start the day.

'I've got to go back home,' I told them once everyone was

in. 'My mum's got a hospital appointment so I said I'd go with her. I'd forgotten all about it.'

'Back to the Wirral?' asked Rachel. 'Which hospital?'

Rachel and I had grown up in the same town, though I hadn't known her as I was eight years older and we'd attended different schools. When she'd come for interview six months ago, I'd read her application form and recognized the school she'd gone to. We'd talked for a while about the area. She'd gone on to university in Liverpool but I'd been desperate to leave, and only went back on occasional visits.

'Arrowe Park.' I couldn't think of another one offhand.

'Do you know that area, Rachel?' asked Lucy.

Rachel nodded. 'We're both from New Brighton.'

'Really? I didn't know that. Did you know each other before you started work here?'

'No,' I said. 'Obviously I'm older and we went to different schools.'

'Do you go back often?' she asked Rachel. 'Are your mum and dad still there?'

'No, my mum . . .' All of a sudden Rachel's face was bright red and she looked as though she was going to cry. 'My mum died a few months ago.'

'It wasn't long after Rachel's mum died that she came to work down here,' I said to Lucy. I didn't want Rachel to have to say anything about it if she didn't want to. 'It's still so recent.' I looked at Rachel sympathetically. 'It must have been really tough.'

'It was.' She met my eye, looking proud and vulnerable at the same time. 'Nobody knows what it's like.'

Lucy made a move as though she was going to hug her, but Rachel dashed off to the cloakroom.

'What about her dad?' Lucy asked in a low voice.

'Her mum and dad divorced and he's living abroad with his

new wife now,' I whispered. 'He's in New Zealand, I think. She doesn't see him.'

Lucy winced. 'I don't know how a parent could do that. Poor Rachel, she's only in her twenties.'

I nodded. 'She told me at the interview. I don't think she was going to say anything but when we were chatting afterwards, I asked her what it was like living at home when she was a student. She told me she had been a caregiver to her mum, who'd died a couple of months before.' I thought of Rachel that day. She was so young, only twenty-four, and was all dressed up in a business suit and heels, and I could tell she was frightened of breaking down. My heart had ached for her then, having to cope without her parents. She was a great fit for the job and I offered it to her there and then. I felt really guilty now that I hadn't talked to her more about her family life, but she was so reserved that it had never seemed appropriate. 'I have to go, Lucy. Will you make sure she's okay?'

She nodded. 'Don't worry, you can go now. I'll deal with it.'

I called goodbye to the others and left, feeling guilty that I'd lied to them about where I was going. Once I was in my car, on my way to the railway station, however, I forgot about them immediately. I had a job to do.

22

It was like a repeat of the day six weeks earlier when I'd taken the train from Chester to London. The train to Euston was just as crowded and I was squashed alongside a mother with two children. Those children wriggled more than any child I'd known. Looking at the mother read a book to them, watching them cling onto her arms so she could hardly turn the page, made me long for Rory. I needed him to see him.

I sent Joe a text. Missing you both. Are you having a good time? Take a photo of Rory for me, will you? xx

Immediately he responded. Miss you too. Just about to go out with Brendan. Mum's minding the kids. She's taken them into town and then to a café for lunch. Will send a photo later xx

I looked at my watch. I wouldn't be back home until seven P.M. or so. I'd call his mum when the children were in bed. I didn't want to disturb her while she was having some time alone with them. I tried to quell the thought that I seemed to be the only person who wasn't having time alone with Rory.

Tears pricking my eyes, I sent another message: Is Rory OK? Is he happy? Did he sleep last night? xx

In a few seconds my phone vibrated. Happy? He's ecstatic. Have to run, talk tonight xx

I closed my eyes and thought of Rory running around with his older cousins. Joe was right: Rory would be in his element.

And then I thought of Joe's face if he knew what had happened to me in London. Panic raced through me at the thought of his expression if he saw that photo from last night. I couldn't let that happen.

From Euston I went straight to the hotel, walking down Tottenham Court Road again just as I had weeks before. This time my mood was different. I knew that whatever happened today, I was going to have to do something with the information I had. I knew I should talk to the police, but then Joe would hear about it. That was inevitable. I'd do anything to avoid that.

The hotel reception was busy when I got there. I hovered by the entrance, then decided to look into the bar before speaking to the receptionist on duty.

The bar was open to the public. There was no table service, just one huge mahogany counter lining one wall. I looked to see whether there were any staff I recognized but couldn't see anyone, and besides, they wouldn't have recognized me anyway. There must have been a couple of hundred people crammed into the bar when I was last there; there was no reason why they should remember me.

Today there was plenty of space, with small groups of business people and tourists dotted around the room. I ordered an orange juice and sat at a table by the wall. I remembered that night I'd come downstairs to see whether there was anyone I knew. I'd already bought a couple of drinks by the time I saw Liam, and I remembered trying to hide away from him. I wished now I'd talked to him, stood with his colleagues and

listened to them brag about sales, rather than get drunk with David. What was I thinking?

When I'd finished my drink, I walked over to the restaurant, which was on the other side of the hotel's reception area. I stood in the doorway and looked in. I thought I could remember where I'd sat but realized I couldn't be too sure. I frowned. How could I not remember that? Clients could come into the office and I'd remember which house I'd sold them and for what price even several years later. How could I not remember which table I'd sat at just six weeks ago?

I picked up a menu from a vacant table next to me and read it. It was as though I hadn't seen it before. I thought of the meals on the receipt, the chicken and the steak. I couldn't remember which I'd eaten and which David had had. I felt like ordering both just to see if I could remember when I saw them, but the thought of seeing them made me feel sick.

I left the restaurant and waited at the reception desk until the receptionist was free.

'Please may I have a word with your manager in private?' I asked.

She raised her eyebrows but went through a door at the back of the reception and came out a few minutes later with a woman with an elegant silver pixie cut and a harassed look on her face. She greeted me and ushered me into a small office to the side of the desk.

'How can I help you?'

'I've got an unusual request, I'm afraid. I wondered whether it would be possible to view your CCTV. I stayed here a while ago and I need to identify a man I had dinner with.'

She looked surprised. 'Identify him?'

I swallowed. I couldn't think of any way around this. 'I thought I knew who he was, but it seems I don't.'

She looked completely confused by now.

'I was here for a training conference on the twenty-fourth of June,' I said. 'I stayed here the night of the twenty-third and I bumped into a man I knew from home. I'm an estate agent and he's a client.' I hesitated. My face was burning. 'And I think something happened that night. I think he was in my room.'

'Without your permission?'

'The thing is, I was very drunk. I don't usually drink much but I was really, really drunk. I felt terrible the next day.'

She winced. 'And you think he came back to your room afterwards? Were you hurt?'

'No, not hurt. I just had a hangover the next day. It's just . . .' Suddenly I wanted to tell her. I wanted to tell someone. I was sick to death of having these thoughts racing around my head. 'He sent me photos,' I said quickly. 'I need to contact him to tell him to delete them.'

'Photos?' She saw my face then, and understood. 'Incriminating photos?'

I nodded, humiliated. 'I was naked.'

'And you didn't consent to that?'

'God, no,' I said. 'I can't even remember him taking them.'

She looked horrified. 'You know he's broken the law? You should go to the police.'

'I can't. I can't do that.'

She glanced down at my wedding ring. 'They can be discreet, you know.'

'It would be different if I could show them a picture of the man. Everything he told me was a lie – his name, address, phone number . . . If I had a photo of him it would really help. And that's when I wondered – do you have CCTV from that night?'

'From the twenty-third of June?' She shook her head. 'I'm sorry, but that's over a month ago. We keep records for thirty-one days, and then they're destroyed. That's what we're

advised to do by the police. Our system's automatically set up to delete anything after that time.'

My mind raced. He'd sent me the photo and the video over a month after I came back from London. He must have hoped I wouldn't be able to find CCTV records by then.

'I'm so sorry,' she said. 'Really I am. What he's done is shocking. Illegal. I can understand your reluctance not to get the police involved, but really I think you should.'

'I'll think about it.' I stood up to go. 'Thanks anyway.' I picked up my bag, then remembered something. 'I'm not sure you'd know about this. I paid for a meal in the restaurant here and must have forgotten to pick up the receipt. I was sent a photocopy of the receipt four weeks after I was here.'

As soon as I heard myself say that, I knew that of course the hotel hadn't sent it. Why would they wait four weeks to send a receipt to a guest they didn't even know?

She frowned. 'Who sent you that?'

'I assumed you had,' I said, feeling foolish.

'The restaurant is a franchise,' she said. 'It doesn't belong to us. We simply rent them the space here. We have no connection to them. If someone left their receipt behind in the restaurant, we wouldn't know anything about it. And besides, the restaurant's open to the public. The staff wouldn't know if you were staying here or not. We certainly wouldn't pass on your address.'

So he *sent it to me. Why would he do that?*

I stood in silence for a moment, trying to work out what was going on.

'I know this sounds odd,' I said, 'but if the room I stayed in is empty, would I be able to have a look at it?'

She looked a bit surprised, but clicked her mouse at the computer on the desk and said, 'Which room were you staying in?'

'I don't know. I'm sorry; I can't remember.' I frowned. 'My memory's been really bad lately.'

She looked up, a concerned expression on her face.

'It's just work,' I said. 'I run my own business and it's stressful at the moment.'

'Oh, that must be tough.' She asked for my name and scrolled down the screen, searching the database. 'The room's empty, though someone's booked into it for tonight. They're not due in until late as they're coming in to Heathrow on an evening flight.' She picked up her keys. 'Come on, I'll show you around. You were in room 912.'

As soon as she said that, I remembered. We went up to the ninth floor in the lift, and as we came out, I had a sudden jolt of memory.

I tripped here, didn't I? I remembered reaching out and grabbing the rail. I flushed, embarrassed at the thought of making a fool of myself. Then, as though he were here with us now, I heard David's voice as he laughed and said, 'Steady on, sweetheart.'

Sweetheart? *Sweetheart?*

We walked down the corridor towards my room. Memories were coming back, though they were of my arrival there earlier in the evening rather than later that night. I felt distinctly uneasy as we approached the room.

The manager touched the door plate with her card, then, as a green light flashed, she turned to me. 'Okay?'

I nodded reluctantly.

She opened the door. I stood in the doorway and looked at the room. The curtains were half drawn and it was dark and cool. She flicked on the light switch and I stepped inside. It did look familiar. I saw the brown suede surround of the bed and winced.

'Are you all right?'

I nodded again. 'It's the same bed that was in the photo.' The bed was a divan; there was no room for anything to roll underneath it. I walked over to it, then turned, looking

at the rest of the room. The minibar sat underneath the desk. 'I was charged for three bottles of water but I'm sure I only had two.'

'Oh, I'm sorry. You should have told us and we would have adjusted your bill.'

'It's not that. I'm just trying to figure out what happened. Can a mistake be made with that sort of thing?'

'It shouldn't happen,' she said. 'It's an automated system, but we ask the staff cleaning the room to check, too.'

'I must have made a mistake,' I said, but I knew I hadn't. I turned towards the door. 'Thanks for showing me the room. I really appreciate it.' I stopped in the doorway and looked around again.

'Everything okay?' she asked.

There was something at the corner of my mind, nudging me, that didn't seem right, but I couldn't work out what it was. The room was clean, tidy, and neutral, just like any other hotel room. I shrugged and said, 'Yes, it's fine, thanks,' and she switched off the lights and we left.

23

It seemed a long train journey home. Luckily the seat next to me was empty, so I was able to sit quietly and look out of the window and think about what had happened since I was last in London. It had been good to talk to the manager, but it made me realize how alone I was now. Joe would find out straight away if the police got involved. I really wanted to talk to Caitlin, but she was away visiting Ben, and besides, she might feel she had to tell Joe. And I couldn't tell my mum. I shuddered. I couldn't think how she'd react if I told her.

I drove back home from the station feeling so weary. I was desperate to know what David was up to, but frightened too. Part of me thought of telling Joe, of calling him while he was safely in Ireland and just telling him everything. It wasn't the kind of thing I should tell him over the phone, but how could I do it face to face? My throat burned as I thought of the video where I'd said I wouldn't have married him. I couldn't let him hear that. I was so ashamed of myself. Everyone loses their patience with their partner from time to time, but I wouldn't normally talk like that about him.

By the time I reached my house, I was so exhausted I didn't

know what to do with myself. I opened the front door and stopped dead.

The house smelled different; there was an artificial lemony smell that would have had Joe reaching for his inhaler if he'd been here. And then I saw my spare key and a bill on the dresser in the hall and remembered the cleaners had been.

I walked from room to room, opening windows to get rid of the smell but admiring how lovely it looked. The house was polished and cleaned to a much higher standard than Joe or I did it. The kitchen was spotless, the dishwasher emptied. In the bedrooms the drawers were tidied, and clean laundry had been put away.

I wanted to marry those women. I glanced at the receipt and blanched. I'd asked them to do whatever it took and they had, but it had cost me. When I looked around at the scrubbed kitchen, the spotless living room, and the vases on the windowsills full of flowers from the garden, though, I knew they were worth every penny.

My phone pinged with a message from Joe. He'd sent a photo that his brother had taken, of Joe on a sun lounger with a glass of beer and a huge plate of sandwiches, his mother in the background playing tennis with Rory. How're things? We're missing you. Can't wait to see you again.

I couldn't wait either.

After locking up the house and making a quick snack, I went straight up to bed. It was so lovely to see the house clean and tidy, like being given a huge present. I got under the freshly laundered quilt determined to have an early night and called Joe and Rory from my bed. Rory was in bed too, as he told me all the things he'd been up to. It seemed strange to be going to bed at the same time as my three-year-old son, but it felt wonderful, too, to think of a long night's sleep. I switched the lamps on, though the room wasn't yet dark, then settled

down with my Kindle. I sent Lucy a text to say that I should be okay to work in the morning, set my alarm for seven A.M., and soon I was asleep.

I woke in the early hours with a terrific jolt. My heart banged and for a moment I didn't know where I was. It wasn't a dream; it was as though a memory had come back to me when I was asleep.

I remembered then that I'd switched the lamps on in the hotel room before I went down to the bar, so that the room would be lit when I came back. I could remember it clearly. Each lamp was on a built-in bedside table, either side of the bed, and had a little silver chain that I'd pulled to switch them on. I could actually remember that physical act of reaching over and pulling each chain. One of them stuck a bit and I had to hold the lamp steady so that I could tug it sharply. The main light switch next to the door only controlled the overhead light. I'd noticed that again when I was shown the room the day before.

When I woke in the hotel bed that morning in June, with a crashing hangover and a thirst worse than I'd ever had before, those lamps were switched off. I hadn't done that. I would never do that. It was the one thing I couldn't help. I just can't sleep in the dark, no matter where I am. It was something Joe and Rory had had to get used to, though of course I'd never told Rory why.

I looked around my room. The two bedside lamps were lit and the door to the en suite was ajar; I always left the light above the mirror switched on there. On the landing outside the light was permanently on at night, even though I slept with my door shut tight when Rory was away from home.

It was the way it always was. It was the way it had to be.

24

Back at work the next morning, it was hard to keep up the pretence that everything was all right.

'You look tired,' said Rachel as soon as she arrived. 'Was everything okay with your mum?'

For a second or two I wondered what she was talking about, then I remembered the lie I'd told the day before. 'I'm fine, thanks. She's okay.'

I saw her give me a sidelong look but I ignored her, busying myself at my computer. She came over to my desk and I thought for a second she was going to ask more questions, but she just said, 'Can you add Mr and Mrs Hudson to the viewing requests? I've put their details in the system.'

I'd just started to answer when my phone vibrated in my handbag in the desk drawer. 'Sorry,' I said. 'I need to check it's not Joe.'

She went back to her desk and I took out my phone.

My heart sank. On the screen was an Instagram message from WatchingYou. I closed my eyes for a second. That name was so apt. I struggled to think about anything else.

I glanced over at Rachel. 'Won't be a minute.' I touched the Allow button.

Our Internet connection was always pretty slow, and it seemed to take ages for the photo to download onto my phone. I held my breath. Slowly, almost a pixel at a time, the full photo was revealed.

I was lying on the hotel bed again and this time I was completely naked. There wasn't even a sheet or blanket to cover me. There was no expression on my face; I wasn't smiling or frowning, just staring straight at the person taking the photo.

As I looked at it in disbelief, it disappeared from view and immediately another message came up, causing the phone to vibrate again.

It was a screenshot of my Facebook page, just as it was when I'd seen it earlier that day. Within a couple of seconds, that too had disappeared.

I slammed the phone into my drawer.

'What's up?' asked Brian. He came over to my desk. 'Gemma, are you all right?'

I couldn't answer. All I could think of was how I would feel if someone put that photo of me on Facebook for all my friends to see. For my mum and dad to see. For Joe to see.

'You're shaking,' said Rachel. 'What's the matter?'

I shook my head. 'It's okay. It's just . . .'

They looked at me expectantly, but I couldn't think of a thing to say. What could I say? And I remembered they were friends with me on Facebook too. I took my phone from my drawer. 'Just give me a few minutes, will you?' I went out the back door to the car park and checked Facebook. I breathed a sigh of relief. The photo wasn't there. Quickly I looked through all the notifications; there was nothing unusual there. I deactivated my account. I started to come back into the office but then went back outside and deactivated my Twitter and

LinkedIn accounts, too. I hesitated over the Instagram account. I didn't know what to do; should I get rid of it and have him find another way of getting in touch? I hovered over the screen, trying to work out what to do, but then Brian called my name, asking again whether I was okay, and I slid the phone back in my pocket. I'd decide later.

When I got back to my desk, Rachel went to the fridge and took out a bottle of water. She passed it to me but didn't say anything. I was grateful for that; I couldn't tell her why I'd reacted so badly. My head thumped and I realized I was stupid to take it all on myself.

'Rachel,' I said suddenly, 'will you take over the meeting?'

'Me?' She looked dumbfounded.

'It will be good experience for you. You could stand in for me then, whenever I'm off work.'

She blushed, and I could tell she was feeling proud. 'Yes, of course.' She called over to the others, 'We'll have our meeting in ten minutes.'

She sat at my desk with me and I went through the viewing requests. I talked her through the order in which we should work, then suggested who should take which lead. She photocopied the documents and made quick notes.

'Okay, everyone,' I said, when all of my staff were gathered around the table. 'Apologies for the late start. From now on Rachel's going to be in charge of these meetings. Rachel, it's over to you.'

I sat back and drank my bottle of water. I could hear Rachel reviewing activities from the day before and setting targets for the day with the staff, but all I could think about was the messages I'd received.

I've never, ever had a photo taken like that before. I've always thought that women who send men intimate photos of themselves are crazy; those pictures could appear anywhere, long after the relationship finishes. I couldn't imagine

how drunk I must have been to let someone do that. My stomach curled up in fear at the thought of it appearing on Facebook. I was so glad I'd deactivated my account, even though I knew some of my friends would question why. I'd have to think of some reason; I'd been on there for years.

I don't know how I did it, but I kept my face expressionless throughout the meeting, and all the while I was thinking, *I need to tell the police*.

As soon as the meeting ended, I thanked Rachel and quickly went back to my desk. I took my phone out of my pocket and looked at it again. The contents of both messages had gone. Disappeared into thin air. All that remained was the name *WatchingYou* and the notification for each: *Photo Unavailable*.

And then I realized, of course, I could send a message back. I hadn't thought of that before, because the actual messages had disappeared. I clicked on the Message button and typed, What is it you want?

I turned the sound on my phone up high and put it into my desk drawer. My heart still racing, I tried to work, though I was alert for the ringtone all morning.

There was no reply.

25

Joe called later on in the afternoon. I was in the middle of speaking to a couple of first-time buyers and had to ignore his call. He didn't leave a voicemail, just a text that said, All OK; he knew how I panicked if he called and I couldn't get to the phone, in case something was wrong with Rory. When I left the office, I sat in my car and thought I'd call him then instead of waiting until I got home.

'Hey, sweetheart,' he said, and my heart softened.

'I've really missed you.' I could hear my voice wobble.

He laughed. 'I've missed you too. It's been great seeing Brendan, though. And hey, guess what? He's planning to move back over here.'

'To Ireland? Really? With Sarah?'

'Of course with Sarah! All of them. They want to come back to the old country.'

'Sarah's not Irish.'

'I know, but since her mum and dad emigrated to Spain when they retired, she's not got the ties in England any more.'

My heart sank. I knew the pressure would be on me now.

'So, I've been okay,' I said, in a passive-aggressive attempt to stave off the inevitable discussion about moving to Ireland.

'Sorry, Gem! It isn't that I'd forgotten you. I just wanted to tell you the news about Brendan. So what have you been up to? How are you feeling?'

'Oh, okay. It's been busy here.'

'You poor thing. Make sure you get an early night.'

My mind flashed to the night before when I'd woken at midnight to remember the lamps in the hotel room. I'd hardly slept afterwards, my mind racing about what was going on. 'I will,' I said.

'Anything interesting happen?'

I was silent for a moment. How on earth could I begin to tell him I thought I was being blackmailed? 'Oh, not much,' I said instead, and scrabbled around for something I'd done that I could tell him about. There wasn't anything. 'Just sorting out the house.'

'Oh, I'm sorry, sweetie. It was a bit of a mess before I left, wasn't it? We were in a rush.'

I knew it was grossly unfair, but there was no way I was going to admit to the cleaning service. Not yet at any rate. I reckoned that was worth a good few months of ammunition.

'So you'll be back in a couple of days?' I asked.

'We will. What is it now, Saturday? We'll be back on Wednesday.'

'Okay. I'll miss you.' I could hear someone saying something in the background, and then Joe said, 'My mum says why aren't you on Facebook? She wanted to send you a message there but you'd disappeared.'

'Oh,' I said, frantically trying to think up an excuse. 'I was reading an article about how social media uses up too much of our time, and I thought I'd get rid of it for a few weeks.'

'Good idea. I know it's easy to waste hours on there. I'd better go, sweetheart.'

'Call me tonight, will you, if you get the chance? And is Rory there?'

'He is. Hold on; I'll call him. I love you.'

I heard him call Rory's name, and then my boy was on the phone to me, breathless with excitement about a game he was playing with his cousins that involved chasing and water and Nanny's dog.

I sat in the car for a few minutes after the call ended. I wanted to feel happy for them – I *did* feel happy for them – but I really missed them. I wanted to be the one running around the garden with Rory, or drinking beer and flipping burgers with my family. I started the car, feeling really sorry for myself.

And then my phone beeped and I switched the engine off again. A new e-mail had come through to my Gmail account. I opened the app and saw a message from WatchingYou. My stomach tightened. How had he found my e-mail address?

The message heading was *Soon*.

My fingers shook as I opened it. At first I thought it was junk mail, the kind that usually goes automatically to my spam box, where you're sent a link to a website and asked to enter your bank details and password for a prince in a kingdom far, far away. But the link in this e-mail, the only thing in the message, wasn't to a fake bank and it wasn't asking for a password or my life savings. It was a link to a website and it was clear from the URL that it was a site for voyeurs.

I leaned back, unable to believe my eyes. What did it mean? And then it dawned on me. I'd closed my Facebook account; had he tried to post the photos there? And now, finding that he couldn't, was he going to post those photos of me naked, identifiable, on that website?

Immediately I tapped out a response, What do you want? Is it money? and waited ten minutes, my heart pounding and my mind reeling, but of course the only reply was to tell me that the e-mail address did not exist.

I had no choice. I had to speak to the police.

26

I decided to go to the police first thing the next morning, rather than on a Saturday night. I knew they wouldn't have time to talk to me then.

I waited outside the police station, trying to gather my nerves, then took my phone out of my bag and looked at it again. I scrolled through the messages I'd sent Joe, telling him that I'd had room service. I looked at the Instagram screen with the blank messages, all from the same person. And then I looked at the e-mail with the web address of a voyeur site, and my own pathetic attempts to get in touch with this person. Clearly he'd shut down his account immediately after e-mailing me.

It was so hard to control my anger towards David. How dare he treat me like this? No matter what had happened that night, no matter what I'd done, he had no reason to send me those messages.

At the police station I asked to speak to a female officer. When I was asked for my name, I said I was Gemma but didn't want to give my surname. I also didn't want to tell the

guy at the desk why I was there. He looked at my face; I knew it showed signs I'd been crying, and he said that was all right, that the female officer could take details. I sat down to wait, automatically feeling I'd done something wrong just because I was there.

Ten minutes later a woman came to the desk and ushered me into a small interview room. She introduced herself as Stella Barclay and was a bit older than me. I was nervous enough before I went in there, but that room, well, I thought I was going to have a panic attack. I think she saw that, because she fetched me a glass of water and told me to sit there and drink it and not speak until I felt better.

'How are you feeling?' she said. 'Are you all right to talk?'

I nodded. 'Sorry. I'm a bit nervous.'

'That's okay. Now can you tell me what you're here about?' She had a notebook and pen on the desk, and somehow it helped that she was writing it in there and not staring at me as I spoke.

'I'm an estate agent,' I said. 'I have my own office.'

'What's the address?' she asked.

I hesitated. 'I'd really rather not at the moment. Is that okay? I'm just looking for some advice.'

She closed her notebook. 'That's fine. What's troubling you?'

I nodded. 'A while ago, on the sixteenth of June, a man came in. He wanted me to show him around a few properties.'

'He just walked in off the street? No booking?'

'No, he'd e-mailed us about some properties. I check all the e-mails and voicemail messages and allocate the jobs between us. With the amount he was prepared to spend, I decided to take on the job myself, rather than give it to one of my staff.'

'And do you have that e-mail address?'

I nodded. 'I do, but I've written to him there since and the e-mails have just bounced back.'

She grimaced. 'Go on.'

'So I spent a few hours driving him around. He seemed fine. Very chatty. Charming.'

I think she thought I was going to say he'd assaulted me. She became very sympathetic. 'What happened then?'

'Nothing happened. Not then. I drove back to the office and he went off somewhere after that.'

'And then?'

'A week later, I was in London at a training conference. I was staying in a hotel in Covent Garden and went down to the bar for a drink in the evening. And I bumped into the same man again. It was completely coincidental. We had a meal together. A nice conversation.'

'And then? Did something happen?'

I shook my head. 'I don't know. I just don't know.' I looked up into the officer's eyes and saw nothing but kindness there. I knew she was used to hearing a hell of a lot worse than I was going to tell her. 'But since that night, I keep being sent things. Photos. A video.'

'Can I see them?'

I shook my head again.

'Honestly, Gemma, you wouldn't believe the things we see. There's really no need to worry.'

'It's not that. He's using Instagram and withdrawing the messages immediately afterwards.'

'So they're not there now? How's he doing that?'

I showed her Instagram on my phone. 'All you can see now is the names he used and the fact that the message has been withdrawn. And he sent a screenshot of my Facebook page, too. I've got rid of Facebook now. I deactivated it as soon as he sent that screenshot. And yesterday I received an e-mail. I know it's from him.'

'What does it say?'

'Nothing. There's just a link there to a voyeur website.'

I opened his e-mail on my phone. 'Look.' I passed it to her, and when I saw the expression on her face, I felt my eyes prickle with tears. 'I think he's going to post my photos to the site.'

'Have you opened this link?'

I shook my head. 'I was worried in case it contained a virus.'

'You're right not to open any attachment he sends you,' she said. 'Unfortunately, this is a real site. If you do want to look at it, just type in the address manually, though, rather than clicking on the link he gave you.'

I couldn't imagine wanting to look at it, but agreed that was what I'd do.

'But how is it legal for a website to show photos like that?'

She said patiently, 'Well, no one can police the Internet. If they've set up a site in another country then they have to abide by their laws, even though the site can be viewed anywhere in the world. You can imagine the problems it's caused us. But you can usually get a photo pulled down off a site if you make a complaint; most webmasters will do that. They're not usually after a lot of aggravation, and if you ask, they'll oblige. You can also ask Google to prevent a page appearing in their search results if you are nude or shown in a sexual act, so anyone searching for images of you online wouldn't see the pictures of you naked. They'll do that as long as the act was intended to be private and you didn't consent to the photo being publicly available.' It was clear she was used to reciting this. 'The most important thing, though, is to ask the webmaster to remove the image from the site as soon as you see it.' She must have noticed the stricken look on my face. 'If you see it,' she added hastily.

'But if someone sees it before me,' I said, 'the damage is done then, isn't it?'

She nodded sympathetically. 'We'll do as much damage

limitation as we can. Don't forget to delete all your social media – Twitter, LinkedIn, that sort of thing. Don't give him a platform for posting images that your friends could see.'

'I've done that already. I did it as soon as he sent the screenshot of my Facebook page. But what about Instagram? Should I delete my account?'

'I would. I'd cut off all the ways he can reach you.'

I did it there and then. She asked more questions about David, and I told her how I'd called the numbers he'd given me, and discovered he didn't work for Barford's or live at the address he'd given us. I was getting more and more agitated as I told her everything I knew.

'Look, he's given you a false name,' she said. 'When he came to your office, he knew in advance that he was going to do something. Whether he knew exactly what, who can say now? But he created a fake e-mail address to book an appointment before even seeing you. I don't think he was targeting you at that point. You have a number of staff. Any one of them could have become his victim.'

I shuddered at the thought of the other women in the office being put in this position.

'So you need to increase your precautions,' she said. 'And speak to the other estate agents in your area. No house visits with anyone unless they've shown photo ID. I'll get our community police officers onto it too.' She looked at me sympathetically. 'So when you had a meal with him, you didn't get an inkling anything was wrong with him? No red flags?'

'No, nothing jarred at all. He was really nice. Great company. I drank far too much, though, and had a terrible hangover the next day.' I grimaced. 'I don't usually drink more than a glass or two. I have a three-year-old son and I have to keep my wits about me. But that night I was away from home and I drank more than I usually did.'

'Do you remember going to bed?'

'I remember going down the corridor to my room. I remember stumbling.' I winced. 'I'm mortified now, just thinking about it.'

'And was David with you then, do you remember?'

'Yes. Yes, he was. He pulled me upright.'

'And did you invite him into your room?'

'No,' I said. 'I wouldn't do that. I'm married. Happily married.'

All the while I was insisting on this, the thought was there, though. How did he take a photo of me on my bed? Had I actually invited him in?

'Do you remember brushing your teeth that night? Washing your face? Or did you decide not to bother?'

I stared at her uncertainly. 'I can't remember. I'm sure I did. I always do – it's automatic, isn't it?'

'But can you remember doing it?'

No matter how hard I tried to remember, I just couldn't. I shook my head.

'Think about those moments before you first went into your room,' she said. 'You were walking down the corridor. How would you normally open the door to the hotel room, do you remember? With a card?'

'Yes,' I said. 'It was one of those contactless cards that you hold next to a metal plate on the door. It was a white card, no markings on it. The room number was on a little envelope.'

'And later on Friday night, when you were going back to your room . . . do you remember opening the door then? Putting the card next to the door?'

I closed my eyes and tried to remember, but I couldn't. I shook my head, frustrated with myself. 'I don't know. I must have done.'

'What about your clothes? What were you wearing?'

I described my green silk dress.

'And when you woke up the next morning, what were you wearing?'

I frowned. 'I was wearing my underwear. Bra and knickers.'

She was quiet for a while then, before she said, 'Were they the same ones that you'd worn the night before?'

I stared at her. 'What do you mean?'

'Well, when you arrived at the hotel, did you change before going downstairs?'

I nodded. 'It was a really hot day, so I had a shower and changed my clothes.'

'And do you remember which underwear you put on after your shower?'

I thought hard. 'Yes, I can remember. I bought it when we were in Italy last summer. It's black silk. I always wore that set with my green dress.'

She leaned forward. 'Gemma, when you woke up, can you remember which underwear you were wearing then? Was it the same set?'

I closed my eyes, panic coursing through me.

She spoke gently and I knew she was used to coaxing hidden truths from women in situations like mine. 'What did you do when you first got up? Did you go into the bathroom?'

'I went into the bathroom,' I said. 'I was sick. It was the drink.'

'And did you look in the mirror? What colour was your underwear?'

I felt the blood drain from my face as I remembered seeing my reflection in the mirror as I dashed over to the toilet. My face had been pale and sweaty. The mirror was about three feet square, placed at waist height. In my mind's eye I could see myself as I passed through the room. My underwear was white.

27

As soon as I got home, I raced upstairs to find the underwear I'd been wearing the night I'd had dinner with David in London. I'd come home and tipped all my clothes from my overnight bag into the laundry basket on the landing. That was empty now, thanks to the cleaners, and all of the clothes there had been washed and put back into drawers. I searched my bedroom looking for the set, but knew I wouldn't find it.

I checked the utility room, hoping against hope that they would be there, left in the dryer by mistake, but no, all was spotless, not a thing out of place.

'You told me that you were naked in those photos,' Stella had said. 'So your underwear was obviously off at one point. This sort of man often likes to keep something. A kind of trophy. I wonder whether he took it with him and put your other set on you so that you wouldn't notice.'

Or so that I would notice. So that I'd remember one day, later, after he'd gone.

I sat at the dining table and tried to control my breathing. I couldn't let myself think about this. I just couldn't.

All of a sudden I was overwhelmed with the desire to talk to Joe. I sent him a text to ask if he was free, but I didn't get

a reply. I could phone their house, of course, but guessed his mum would answer, and I just couldn't bear to talk to her now. She'd know something was wrong and she really, *really* mustn't find out what I'd done.

What *had* I done, though? I just couldn't remember a thing. Something had happened and I was being punished for it. I thought again of those photos appearing on social media and sites for voyeurs and just wanted to collapse in a heap.

I picked up my laptop and opened Chrome in Incognito mode. There was no way I wanted Joe to see this. I typed in the address of the site. As soon as I saw the content, I started to cry.

The whole site was devoted to images and videos of women who were unaware they were being recorded. It showed them in the shower, in the street, asleep in bed. There were unsuspecting women on crowded trains, unaware that some creep was holding a camera up their skirt. There were even women on the toilet, completely oblivious to the fact that they were being filmed. I clicked on link after link, feeling more sick by the minute. Most pictures had a stream of comments underneath, congratulating the bastards who'd filmed these women. I felt dirty just reading those messages. There were Like buttons, too; any idea I'd had that this was a niche market was quickly quashed by the sheer number of people who liked these photos.

Tears pricked my eyes as I realized that could be me on there. Next time I looked, there could be comments next to my photo, telling other men what they'd like to do to me. And it was no comfort to think the men I knew wouldn't go on there, wouldn't dream of looking at photos taken by a hidden camera in a woman's bathroom; I knew these things had ways of getting out.

It didn't take long to get a full grasp of what the site was about, and then I started to look for someone to e-mail. There

were thousands of photos posted there since the date I was in London, and I couldn't face looking at them all. I wanted to ask someone what I could do if I found a photo of myself there, but try as I might, I just couldn't find any contact details. I suppose that on a normal site the owners are keen to be identified with it, whereas here they weren't. Then I realized that there was a Report button next to each of the photos and videos. Perhaps I could leave a message that way?

Still in Incognito mode, I created a new e-mail address for myself, using a fictitious name, then reported one of the posts:

Hi, I need to talk to someone about privacy and can't find an e-mail address. Someone is threatening to post explicit photos of me on this site. Obviously I don't give permission for that. If I see a photo of myself and report it, will it be taken down? Thanks.

I added my new e-mail address to the end of the message and clicked Send. I doubted I'd get a reply, but I couldn't think what else to do.

Stella had asked me if I wanted them to take things further but confirmed I shouldn't hold out too much hope. 'What with throwaway phones being so cheap, and as it's more than a month after you met him in London, I really doubt whether there's anything we can do now. I do want you to keep in touch with us, though.' She gave me a contact number and I put it into my phone. 'If you think of anything else, you must tell me straight away. Don't try to contact this man.'

I nodded but she wasn't convinced.

'I mean it,' she said. 'If you want us to investigate, come back and I'll do what I can. But in the meantime, don't try to find him.'

'Right.'

We sat for a second while I got myself together, and then she said, 'I need to ask you something but I don't want to upset you further. Is it possible that you had sex that night?'

'No,' I said immediately. 'No, it's not possible. I would know, wouldn't I?' She said nothing and so I said again, 'No. I would know if I had. I would have noticed.'

28

Monday, August 7

By Monday morning I was desperate for Joe to come back,
if only because I was taking a couple of days off when he
returned.

'Are you feeling all right?' asked Sophie. She startled me; I
must have been miles away, thinking about seeing Joe and
Rory again. I looked up and saw her standing by my desk, a
look of concern on her face.

'I'm fine, thanks.'

'Can I get you some water?'

'I'd love some.'

She fetched a bottle out of the fridge and passed it to me. It
was only when I went to the cloakroom afterwards that I saw
why she was worried: my face looked pale and tense, my eyes
showing the strain of staying up late searching the voyeur
site for naked photos of myself.

At the morning meeting I sat back while Rachel took control. She'd clearly watched me closely at those meetings and
followed the same routine that I did. She seemed so much
more confident now. I had a notebook on my knee to make

notes to go through with her later, but I was too distracted and worried. While I made a pretence of listening to her, I made note after note of what had been done to me and what I had to do to make things right.

Lucy came into the office just as the meeting was about to end. I'd sent her a message asking her to call in when she dropped her daughter off at school. She sat down at the meeting table with us.

'Now that we're all here,' I said, 'I want to bring up the issue of safety. I don't want anyone to meet a client outside the office unless we have seen some form of ID. Check it carefully, then photocopy it and keep it with your files in the office. If you're unsure, ask me.'

'Why's that?' asked Rachel. 'Has something happened?'

'I'm just looking out for you,' I said. 'You've all heard about Suzy Lamplugh disappearing. In those days they just had to write the client's name in the diary. We do more than that since we collect their address, e-mail, phone number, et cetera, but it's still not enough. If we're taking clients to a property, we need to make sure we're safe. And if you have any doubts about a client – any at all – then make sure you don't go anywhere with them. I'll deal with them myself. If I'm not in, tell them they have to wait until I'm back. And when I'm not here, I want two of you to lock up together. If that's not possible, I'll come back to the office or send Joe to do it.'

They looked a bit subdued.

'Everyone still remembers the code word, don't they?'

'Anne-Marie Thomson,' said Sophie.

'That's right,' I said. Anne-Marie had been a friend of mine when I was in school and I'd chosen her name as our code word, which acted as a distress signal. If any one of us used it in a call, it was a signal that we needed help. 'Don't forget, it doesn't matter what you say, as long as you mention her name. You can say she'll be coming into the office later than

planned or that you need to meet with her. Anything at all. Rachel, can you remind us what happens when Anne-Marie's name is mentioned?'

'We have to ask questions where the answer's yes or no,' she said promptly. 'Like "Are you where it says you are in your diary?" If the answer is no, we have to phone 999.'

'And don't forget, you must never go out without your panic alarm. If you leave it at home, let me know. There are spares in the cupboard, but I need to know if someone's taken them out. Do you remember the rule about always walking behind the client?'

Lucy said, 'That's quite a hard one to stick to. Some people are quite insistent that I go into the house first.'

'If you get any bad feeling about that, as though they're trying to make you do something you don't want to do, then don't go into the house with them. Always have an excuse prepared, like you need to get something from your car.'

They were in a pretty sombre mood by then.

'Has something happened?' asked Sophie. 'You've told us all this before, but . . .' She looked up at me and her face appeared so young and scared. 'I know I'm here in the office all the time, but it frightens me to think that someone might attack one of you. I'd hate to get a call where someone spoke about Anne-Marie.'

I could see that Rachel looked pale and scared too, as though she were panicking about what she'd do if someone frightened her when she was on her own. Lucy seemed more confident, though she was much more experienced and more likely to see trouble coming. I knew, though, how easily something could come out of the blue and destroy your sense of self.

'No, there's nothing for you to worry about,' I said. 'I was reading an article about personal safety the other day. A woman in Bolton is running courses; I'll get in touch with her later and ask for some advice.'

After the meeting Rachel and I sat together and I went through some points she hadn't raised in the meeting.

'Thanks for not bringing them up in front of the others,' she said. She sounded a bit embarrassed and relieved. 'That was really nice of you.'

'It's okay,' I said. 'I remember what it was like when I first started holding the morning meetings.'

She looked at me, curious now. 'What, you were scared?'

I laughed. 'I was petrified. I used to work in London when I first left university. It was so competitive there, especially in the estate agency business.'

'I would have thought you'd like that. You're pretty competitive, though, aren't you?'

I shook my head. 'Not really. I just wanted to run my own business. In London . . . well, it got a bit cut-throat. All sorts of tricks were pulled. You used to work for Bailey and Harding back home, didn't you? That's the sort of place I want here.'

She nodded. 'I worked for them every weekend when I was at university, and then for about a year afterwards.'

'They gave you a great reference.'

She blushed. 'How was your mum when you went back the other day?' she asked. 'Did everything go well? She was at Arrowe Park, wasn't she?'

'What?' I'd completely forgotten that I'd told them I'd been up to see my mum when I'd really been in London. 'Oh yes, she was fine, thanks. It was just a checkup.'

We sat for a few more minutes. I could hear Sophie busy with the photocopier in the back office, and Brian was washing up the cups from our meeting.

'Do you ever go back there?' I asked Rachel.

She started. 'Back where?'

'Back home.' I smiled. 'I don't know why I call it home. I haven't lived there since I was eighteen.'

'There's nothing for me to go back for,' she said. 'And I was glad to get away. It doesn't hold very good memories for me.'

'Me neither.'

Rachel put all her papers back into her file and stood up. For a moment I saw her mouth tremble, and I felt guilty. Her mother had only died last year; it was obviously still raw. I watched her as she sat at her computer and drank some water. She was soon typing really fast, focused on her work, and I hoped she'd be all right.

Before I started work, I e-mailed the personal safety adviser and asked her to contact me. A reply bounced back saying she was on holiday until August 18 but that she'd be in touch, so I set up a reminder on my diary to make sure I contacted her then if I hadn't heard from her.

The morning went quickly, with a sudden rush of clients calling in around lunchtime, so we all had to abandon any hope of lunch. At three P.M., as usual, the office grew quieter. Everyone set about their routine jobs so that everything was arranged for the next morning. Sophie was in the window, stocking up the brochures, while Brian was on the phone to a plumber to fix a leak in a tenant's flat.

'Sophie, do you fancy running out for some cakes for everyone?' I asked. 'My treat.'

'Cakes? It's not your birthday, is it?'

'No, I just wanted to treat everyone. We need a sugar hit.'

While Sophie went off happily to the shops, I went over to Rachel's desk. 'I wanted to talk to you alone for a minute,' I said. 'How long have you been here now? Six months?'

Rachel nodded, her expression wary.

'You've worked really well. I've had this place for over seven years now and you've picked things up quicker than anyone else who's worked here.'

She blushed and looked down. Her hands played with the

rings on her fingers. 'I'd been working for Bailey and Harding, don't forget. I learned a lot there too.'

'Don't undervalue yourself. You've done really well here. And I've realized that I need someone who can stand in for me. I want to cut down my hours a bit; I want to spend more time with Rory. So, I thought I'd promote you to senior negotiator and look for someone new for your role. What do you think?'

She looked up, astonished. 'But you can't do that!'

I laughed. 'Why not?'

'But . . .' Her face was pink with embarrassment. 'What about Lucy? I thought she'd be coming back soon. I don't want her to think I'm taking her job.'

'Lucy's great, really great, but she only wants casual work for the next couple of years. Even then I think she'll just want part time. Anyway, I'm offering you a promotion; you shouldn't say someone else would be more suitable!'

She looked awkward and I realized just how young she was. She dressed older than her years and always looked well groomed, as though she wanted to be taken seriously at work, but she was still very young. I knew I'd done the right thing; she deserved this promotion.

Just then Sophie returned with the cakes and I stood to go back to my desk.

'Please would you make us some coffee, Sophie? We've got something to celebrate.'

29

There was just one day to go before Joe and Rory returned, and the house was lonelier than ever without them. As soon as I got home from work that night, I put the chicken and salad I'd picked up from the local deli into the fridge and went upstairs to have a bath. I poured bath oil into the running water and found my Kindle. I locked the bathroom door firmly behind me – something I rarely did when Joe and Rory were at home – and put my phone by the side of the bath. I wasn't going to take any chances.

I lay in the bath and thought of Rachel and her pride in her promotion – she seemed embarrassed that her skills had been noticed and hardly met my eye after I told the others. Sophie was the opposite: she was very keen that I should know she was progressing well, and I half expected her to ask whether she could have Rachel's job, despite the fact that her only experience was a year in administration, but luckily she didn't.

I sent Joe a text asking when Rory would be free for a chat, and he replied immediately, asking me to call in an hour. Perfect. I picked up my Kindle and started to read. The room

was steamy now and the late-summer sun shone through the window, making it hard to see the screen. I jumped out of the bath to open the window, then sank back into the warm water to read some more.

I was just drifting into a nap when I heard a ping from my Kindle and jolted awake. My phone pinged then too, a second later. I clicked on the notification on my Kindle and my e-mail box opened.

I didn't recognize the sender's address. I frowned. Was this junk mail? The heading was *Are you ready?*

My stomach fell. I knew this was meant for me. I clicked on the e-mail. There seemed to be nothing there and then I saw a link. Should I click it? I thought of what Stella had said, that I shouldn't open any attachments or links, but I couldn't resist. I touched it lightly and held my breath.

An image appeared. A gif. It was a timer and it was counting down in seconds. The time left on the image was five hours and forty minutes. I stared at it as the numbers clicked over, then looked up at the clock on the bathroom shelf. It was now six twenty P.M.

It was counting down to midnight.

In a panic I clambered out of the bath, pulled a towel around me, and sat on the chair in the bathroom with my Kindle and phone. The same message was left unopened on my phone; it hadn't yet registered that I'd opened it on my Kindle.

My heart was thumping hard. What was going to happen at midnight? I would be here alone. Suddenly I was so scared I just didn't know what to do.

As quietly as I could, I slid open the lock on the bathroom door and peeped out into the bedroom. Everything looked the same as when I'd left it to have my bath. I pushed a chair against the bedroom door and dressed hurriedly. My mind worked frantically – what was going to happen? I couldn't stay here, that much I knew. I had to get out.

I checked my messages to see what Caitlin had said about when she was returning home. It was as I thought: she wouldn't be back for another week, so I couldn't go to her house. My mind raced as I tried to think where I could go. I thought of my other friends, but quickly abandoned that idea. Freya was a friend I'd made while I was on maternity leave with Rory; we still met up every now and again, but she'd had twins a year after her son was born and her life was really hectic now. Besides, she didn't have a spare room; I knew she wouldn't be able to put me up. It was only until tomorrow, when Joe was back, but even so I couldn't just turn up there; I hadn't even seen her for a few months, though we'd kept in touch on Facebook. And my friend Grace's husband had been unfaithful last year and had walked out when he was confronted; he'd been meeting the other woman in hotels all over the place, so I didn't want to tell her what I might have done in case she thought I was the same as him. Really, I wanted Caitlin, but she was Joe's sister – how could I tell her I might have been unfaithful to her brother? I'd lose her. I'd lose him.

I started to panic. If I lost Joe, I could lose Rory too. Joe was the one who took care of him each day, and yes, he could only do that because I worked all the hours I did, but the fact remained that he was Rory's primary caregiver. If Joe left me, he might take Rory with him. They might go and live in Ireland.

I felt dizzy at the thought of that. I was not going to lose my son. I wouldn't do anything that would put me in that position. But what could I do?

I had no choice. I grabbed an overnight bag from under the bed and crammed some clothes and toiletries in it for the next day, then picked up my handbag and car keys and left the house.

30

An hour later, I was in a hotel five miles from home and on the phone to Joe. It was only when I was safely in the room that I remembered I was supposed to be calling to speak to Rory. I'd decided not to say anything to Joe while he was away, and still couldn't figure out whether to *tell* him, or even what to tell him.

'Is Rory there?'

'I'm so sorry, Gem. He's flaked out already. I gave him a bath and brushed his teeth and went downstairs for his cup of water and by the time I came back up he was flat out.'

'Can you take a photo of him? I really want to see him.'

'Okay.' I could hear him smiling and my heart just reached out to him. I wanted to be near him, to hold him. Both of them. I shouldn't have agreed to them going away without me. I could hear Joe walking upstairs, then heard his mother's voice. He said, 'Won't be long,' and I didn't know whether he was talking to her or to me, but then a few seconds later my text alert sounded and Rory was on the screen. He was lying in a double bed with his two little cousins, his blonde hair tousled, his Spider-Man pyjamas pulled up to show his plump

belly. All of them were asleep, snuggled up against each other, their faces pink and scrubbed after their bath.

I enlarged the photo so that I could see only Rory's face. Tears welled in my eyes and I brushed them away. 'He's grown since I saw him,' I said. 'He looks more like a boy than a toddler.'

'Oh now, we've only been gone a few days!'

'So you'll be back tomorrow?'

He laughed. 'Have you missed me?'

'Put it this way, you're not going away without me again.'

'What, ever?'

'No,' I said. 'I miss you too much. I need you here.'

'I promise. How's work?'

'I've decided to promote Rachel to senior negotiator. She's going to take over some of my jobs and in a while I'll take on a junior. It'll mean I can get some time off in the week.'

There was a silence, and then he said, 'That was a very quick decision.' He sounded hurt; we usually talked over staffing issues together. 'Won't it be expensive?'

'Would you prefer me to work every day?'

'No, no, of course not.' He sounded defensive. 'Stop putting words into my mouth. You know I didn't mean that.'

'There's no alternative.' Anger surged through me. He was on his holidays with his mum looking after him and he wanted me to carry on without any help! 'Either I work every single day or I take on someone new. One or the other.'

He was quiet and I guessed he was figuring out whether the business could afford more staff.

'I need to go,' I said, though actually there was nothing I needed to do. I hadn't brought any work home with me for a change, and I only had my Kindle for company. 'I'll see you tomorrow. Send me a text when the ferry arrives in Holyhead and I'll make sure I'm home to meet you.'

I sounded subdued, I knew, and he hated that.

'Oh, okay then, if that's how it is,' he said. 'I'll give your love to Rory.' He ended the call and I knew that if he could have slammed down his phone, he would have.

I didn't know what to do then. I couldn't go home. I could not be in my bed at home at midnight, waiting for something to happen. What if someone came into my house? I broke into a cold sweat at the thought of that. I put the television on and flicked mindlessly through the channels. I couldn't concentrate. I couldn't think straight. What on earth was I doing alone in a hotel? I was being chased out of my own house. I thought of calling the policewoman, Stella, but by now it was eight o'clock and I guessed she wouldn't be at work. And what could I tell her?

I looked at the e-mail again. What if Stella said that it was just junk mail? I knew it wasn't, but how could I prove it?

Quickly I sent a reply:

Why are you doing this? What is it you want?

Just typing that message made me feel pathetic. That didn't stop me from sending it, though. Thirty seconds later it bounced back: there was no such e-mail address. Of course there wasn't. He'd closed it now.

At nine that night my phone beeped with a message. My heart leaped as I thought it was Joe, apologizing for our argument earlier. No such luck. An e-mail had arrived from the voyeur site in response to my query.

We operate under DMCA law, it said. There was a link to Wikipedia's Digital Millennium Copyright Act. If someone makes an abuse request we process it and remove content from the site.

Well, that was a relief. Now all I had to do was to find the photos. I switched my iPad on and started to search the site again, trying desperately to find any photos David had taken of me. I dreaded seeing them, but at least I knew now I could have them taken off the site. As I scrolled through pages and pages of images of women – yes, all women – being photographed in intimate situations, without a clue they were going to end up on a site like that, I started to cry. What kind of person was I dealing with here?

I tried to sleep but couldn't. The hotel bed was comfortable, the room was warm, and I felt safe there, but I lay in bed wondering what on earth I was going to do. I had to admit

everything to Joe, I knew that. Part of me thought I should sell up, move to Ireland as Joe wanted, and leave all my problems behind. I could change my e-mail addresses and contact numbers, go back to my maiden name, even, and just run away. And part of me really did think that was what I should do; it was the only thing I could do. But then I got furious, with David and with myself. Why should I do that? Why should I have to hide when I hadn't done anything wrong? Even if I'd invited him back to my hotel room in London, even if I'd *asked* him to take those photos, there was still no reason for him to torment me like that.

And then, just before eleven P.M., I thought again of the countdown gif. I opened the e-mail again and the timer was still ticking down. Seventy minutes to go now. Suddenly I was in a blind panic, wondering what would happen then. He would assume I was in my house, wouldn't he? What was he planning?

I jumped out of bed and got dressed. If something was going to happen, I needed to know about it.

I spent an hour driving around my neighbourhood. All was quiet; it always was late at night in that part of town. I didn't know what I was looking for or what I'd do if I found it. I drove past my house and watched as the neighbours' lights popped off for the night. The road was quiet; the only cars around were ones I recognized.

When it was nearly midnight, I parked near my house and took out my phone. I opened the e-mail and clicked on the timer gif and watched as the digits clicked nearer to their goal. In another window I opened the voyeur site and clicked frantically on the Latest Pickings section. Just the name of that made me feel sick. That last minute to midnight seemed to last an hour; I held my breath as the figures changed. What was going to happen? I had visions of my phone ringing, of a

photo appearing online, of seeing someone approach my house.

Nothing happened.

I sat and watched the street, my hand clutching my phone, feverishly refreshing the screen, reassuring myself that if someone went into my house I'd see them and if something appeared online I'd see it. Nothing stirred on the street and the screen remained full of strangers. At half past twelve, I started the car. There were some parked cars by the side of the road, but nobody sat in them. The street was empty, the alleyways were clear, but still I drove quietly up and down, my eyes straining to see if anyone was around.

Finally, exhausted, I headed back towards the hotel. The receptionist greeted me and asked if I had my key card. I nodded, unable to speak, and took the lift to my room, where I collapsed into bed wondering what the hell that had been about.

32

I overslept the next morning and reached the office ten minutes after Rachel and Sophie, though as I'd given Rachel the spare key, they didn't have to wait around outside. When I walked in, I felt Rachel's eyes on me.

'What's up?' I asked.

'You look tired. Are you okay?'

I said, 'I'm fine,' but when I went into the cloakroom I grimaced as I saw what she meant. I always prided myself on looking groomed, but that day my skin was dry and patchy, its usual response to stress, and my make-up was all over the place. My eyes were red from lack of sleep and I quickly put on glasses to hide them. I locked myself in the cloakroom and spent a while tidying myself up, but I could still see everyone staring at me when I came out.

'We'll have the meeting in five minutes, shall we?' asked Rachel, sorting out the files on her desk.

I looked up, startled. Even though I'd happily promoted her, it was odd to realize that responsibility for that task would no longer be solely mine. 'Yes, just give me a moment.'

'It's just that it's now nine fifteen and I've a few things I need to get through,' she said. 'I got here early so I've made a list of all the overnight enquiries.'

That put me in my place. I bit hard on my lip and tried to stop myself from making a sharp comment.

'Okay. Let's start,' I said.

Rachel sat at the head of the table, just where I'd sat from the first day I opened the office seven years ago. I didn't mind; I wanted to pass it all on, but it felt strange and I could tell that Sophie and Brian were uneasy. They kept glancing over at me as I sat in Rachel's old seat, as though I was going to object, to oust her from her place.

I reached into my bag and pulled out my iPad, so that I could make a few notes on the meeting. When I switched it on, it opened at the voyeur site; I must have fallen asleep with it still open. Hastily I switched it off again, then picked up a pen and a notepad from the nearest desk. My face was hot with embarrassment. Had anyone seen the screen? I glanced up at the others. Sophie's expression was as plain as daylight; all she was thinking about was whether to have a cake with her morning coffee. I looked at Brian – was he averting his eyes? Oh God, what if he thought I was looking at porn?

Then I realized Rachel was looking at me closely. She was the one I really hoped hadn't seen my screen. She noticed everything; while that was great at work, I really, really didn't want her to know my private business. I gave her a questioning look and she avoided my eyes, then started the meeting.

We had a number of things to get through in a short time, and I watched Rachel organize everything that needed to be done that day. She was very efficient, and fair, too, I thought; in the past I'd worked with people who, once they were promoted, refused to take on any of the boring or awkward jobs themselves, but she wasn't like that.

'You did a good job today,' I told her, once the meeting was over.

She blushed. 'Thanks.'

'It'll be easier on the days when I'm not here,' I said. 'The last thing you want is me watching you.'

'Oh, that's okay,' she said, but I knew I was right.

Joe sent me a text at three P.M. telling me they'd just arrived at Holyhead. Within minutes I'd packed up my things, ready to go home.

'You're in a rush!' said Sophie.

'I'm just desperate to see them.'

She smiled. 'Have a lovely evening. See you on Friday.'

I'd picked up groceries in the supermarket at lunchtime, so I was able to dash back home to get dinner ready for Joe and Rory. It would take them a couple of hours to get home from Holyhead if the traffic was good, so I had time to cook for them. At the front door I took the post from the letter box and put it on the hall table. Everywhere still looked lovely after the cleaners had been there, and I wondered how long I'd be able to fool Joe that I'd done it.

They arrived home at five P.M. I heard the car pull into the driveway and ran out of the house to greet them. Rory gave a shriek of joy when he saw me and flung himself into my arms when I opened the car door. I held him close to me, rocking him as though he were a baby. I breathed in the sweet scent of his shampoo, felt his T-shirt rise up as my arms held him, so I could feel his skin, soft and warm and damp from the heat of the car.

And then Joe was behind him, his arms around both of us.

'We've missed you.'

My throat tightened. 'I've missed you too.' I thought of the loneliness I'd felt since he'd gone, the worries I'd had. *I'll tell*

him, I thought. *I'll tell him tonight. Everything will be all right. He'll help me sort it out.* He hugged me tighter, and for that moment I truly believed it would all be okay. He was on my side.

In the house, dinner was ready for them. I took the roast lamb out of the oven and put it onto the counter ready to be carved. The gratin dauphinois was bubbling and golden and the air smelled of garlic and rosemary. The patio doors were open and the table was set for dinner, with roses in bud vases and our special-occasion glasses and cutlery shining on the crisp white linen tablecloth.

'Wow, this place is clean!' said Joe. He turned to me, a guilty expression on his face. 'I'm really sorry it was such a mess when we left. How long did it take you to clean up?'

'Oh, you know,' I said. 'I did it as I went along.'

'It looks brand new!' Rory said, and promptly tipped his biggest box of Lego onto the rug.

'How are you?' asked Joe. He held me tightly and kissed the side of my neck. 'Anything been happening while we were away?'

I hesitated. 'There'll be lots to talk about. Let's get Rory fed and bathed first, eh?'

We sat at the dining table to eat our dinner. Joe lit candles around the room, though it wasn't yet dark, and poured us a glass of wine and a cup of juice for Rory, and they told me what they'd been up to in Ireland.

After dinner I let them go upstairs ahead of me, as I wanted to hear their reaction to the rooms up there. The cleaners must have spent hours putting everything back in drawers – my husband and son were so messy and favoured the floor for everything. As they walked upstairs I noticed the mail that had arrived earlier in the day. There was a bowl of white roses on the hall table and a couple of petals had fallen onto the envelopes. I picked up the mail and gave it a cursory

glance. A renewal for our car insurance. A takeaway food leaflet. A letter from a credit card company we'd never used; I assumed it was junk mail. At the bottom of the pile was a padded envelope addressed to me. I was just about to open it when something about it made me stop in my tracks. I knew I hadn't ordered anything lately. Was he sending something to my home? But how would he know where I lived?

Even as I raised that question, the answer was there. I knew that if I Googled myself, my home address could be easily discovered.

I heard Joe's exclamations as he saw how tidy and clean everything was upstairs and his footsteps as he came to the top of the stairs. Before he could come down, I shoved the envelope into my handbag and zipped it shut.

'Yes!' I called as I ran upstairs towards them. 'I've been really busy!'

33

It was hours before I could check the envelope. I left my handbag downstairs by the front door when I went up to Joe and Rory. I knew that otherwise I'd be looking at it all the time, willing them to go away so that I could open it. We stayed upstairs all evening. Rory had his bath; I'd so missed doing that each night, missed his warm, sweet body as he'd stand up in the bath ready to come out, his skin slippery with bubbles. As usual he soaked me as he leaped out, but that night there were no recriminations, just gratitude that he was back home. A little voice at the back of my mind kept saying, *This is how it would be, not seeing him for days at a time*, and the fear of that just kept me frozen, stopped me from saying anything to Joe. After I'd read Rory a record-breaking number of stories, he finally dozed off. By then I'd changed into my pyjamas as I was so wet after his bath, and Joe had had a shower.

'Shall we go downstairs?' he asked. 'Watch some television?'

I groaned at the thought. 'I'm going to stay up here, I think.'

'Good idea,' he said. 'You look like you need a rest. You must have been working so hard, cleaning the whole house.'

We lay on the bed, his arm around me, and chatted about his trip to Ireland.

'So Brendan and Sarah are moving back there?'

'Yes, they're planning to be there within the next few months. They'll rent their house out over here, to keep their options open. He's trying to persuade his boss to give him a leave of absence for a year, so they have the freedom to come back if they want.'

'Good idea. But what happens if one wants to stay and the other wants to leave?' I couldn't see Sarah putting up with her in-laws getting as involved in their lives as they'd like to be. 'Are they going to live near your mum and dad?'

He ignored the first question I'd asked. 'Yes, they're looking for houses now.'

My heart sank. I could tell from the longing in his voice that it was something he was really keen to do as well.

We were quiet then and I knew he wanted to talk about us going there. I was desperate to sleep, but I knew that if I didn't say something he'd be awake for ages thinking about it.

'You do know we couldn't do that, don't you?' I asked. 'My job's here. My business. I couldn't just pack up and leave here and start again in another country.'

He squeezed me tight. 'Nothing's impossible, sweetheart.'

'Seriously, Joe. We couldn't do it. I don't know the first thing about the property market in Ireland.'

'Oh, you'd be fine,' he said. 'Okay, so the laws are different, but essentially it'd be the same, wouldn't it?'

'Do you have a time in mind?' I asked, my voice tight with irritation. 'When would you like to go?'

He squeezed me tighter. I didn't know how he hadn't noticed my body was rigid. 'I was thinking maybe the end of the year?'

'What? You want me to close down my business, arrange management for the rentals, sell this house, move to Ireland,

buy another house, and set up another company in the next four months?'

'We wouldn't have to do it all at once. We could get a manager in to do your job.'

'One manager?' I asked. 'I'm at work every day of the week!'

'Perhaps two, then, job sharing. We could rent out this house, too. Brian would look after it. And there's no rush with setting up over there. We could settle in and you could get used to the area.'

'But where would we live?'

'If we were renting this place out, we could rent somewhere over there,' he said. 'Just take a short contract at first till we found somewhere we liked.'

I was quiet. I hadn't realized he'd thought this through, and I wondered now whether he and his brother had cooked it up between them.

'Nothing's impossible,' he said again. 'You just have to want it enough.'

'But I *don't* want it enough!' I shouted, unable to hold back any longer. 'I don't want it at all!'

'You'd see more of Sarah,' he said. 'You like her.'

'And I wouldn't see as much of Caitlin,' I said. 'If I wanted to see more of Sarah, I would. It's my own son I want to see more of.' I could hear my voice wobble now. 'I need to spend time with him. I don't want to be left behind while you take him on holiday.' I could feel Joe's hostility; he was always like that when he felt guilty. 'And I especially don't want to have to clean up after you while you go on holiday.'

As I said this I knew there was no going back and I would never be able to admit to having the cleaning service. I felt so angry in that moment, it was as though I *had* scrubbed the house from top to toe.

We lay in silence. I was full of things I wanted to say, but I just didn't feel that I could. I never had; I could only

say what I wanted, what I needed, when we were fighting, and then afterwards, when we'd made up, Joe would think the problem was resolved. I hated it; I hated being unable to assert myself. I lay there simmering, thinking of things I should have said to make him see my point of view, and then I realized his breathing had slowed down and that he was asleep.

I slid out of bed and took my dressing gown from its hook. At the door I paused. Joe didn't move; his breathing didn't alter. I pulled the door closed and went downstairs to get a glass of water.

Once Joe got hold of an idea, he found it hard to let it go. Obviously he'd guessed I wouldn't want to go to Ireland to live, but if his brother and sister-in-law were going, then he must have thought he'd have a bigger chance of persuading me. It wasn't Ireland that bothered me. It wasn't as though I had an emotional connection to Chester. My friends now were mainly from university and were scattered all over the world. My mum and dad were still on the Wirral and I saw them every few weeks, but the flights to Ireland were cheap and they had just retired, so were young enough to travel.

It was work that was the problem. How could I set up a business over there? It was a completely different country! I felt a surge of anger at the thought of his suggestion. I knew, too, that I'd struggle to talk this through with him in the cold light of day.

And then I remembered the padded envelope. The argument forgotten now, I sat at the table and opened my bag. I took out the envelope and looked at the label. It was neatly typed and addressed to me, and it reminded me then of the envelope that had arrived containing the photo. Suddenly I was scared. I didn't want to open it. I didn't want to see what else this nutcase had sent me. But I had to. I had to know. He'd upped his game now, sending something to me at home.

My hands shook as I ripped it open. I kept hoping that it would be nothing.

When I saw what was inside, it took me a minute or two to comprehend it. It was a piece of black silk. Black silk with pink embroidered roses on it. I blinked hard. Those were my knickers. What the hell were they doing here?

There was a thud from upstairs and I leaped up from my seat. Was that Joe? I stood in the doorway, my heart pounding, then heard Rory give a little wail. I shoved the knickers into my dressing gown pocket and put the envelope back into my bag, then ran upstairs to my boy, who was wondering where I was.

34

The next day was pretty quiet. Joe seemed to find plenty of excuses to leave me alone with Rory, which suited me just fine. Rory was tired after his trip and was happy to potter around with me. We spent the morning doing some gardening, and in the afternoon I took him swimming and to the park. Later we had a barbecue in the garden and invited one of his friends from nursery; they played on the lawn in a little tent, while I relaxed on the sun lounger. This was as close as I was going to get to a summer holiday, and the jealousy I felt as Joe planned what he was going to do over the next few weeks with Rory was overwhelming. I felt a band tightening around my head at the thought of having this conversation with Joe again.

He hadn't talked any more about going to Ireland but had seemed pretty distant. Normally he'd be all over me after a trip away, but now he seemed cautious, as though he was tiptoeing around me. That wasn't what I wanted, but it gave me an excuse not to confide in him about David. I didn't know where I'd stand with that now. Ever since I'd found my underwear in the mail I'd had trouble breathing whenever I thought of David.

That evening, after Rory's friend had gone home, I was going from the garden into the house to get the bath ready for Rory, and as I walked into the hallway, I saw the shadow of someone through the coloured-glass panels of the front door. The figure seemed to hesitate, and then slowly something was pushed through the door.

Without time for the thought to process, I'd collapsed onto the bottom stair. It was as though I were underwater; all I could hear was the sound of my own blood thrumming through my veins. Black splodges appeared in front of my eyes and whatever I looked at seemed to be moving.

'Gemma? What is it?' Joe ran through the kitchen to the hallway where I sat. 'Are you all right?'

I turned to look at him. It seemed to take hours. I couldn't see his face properly; it was blurred. Out of focus.

'Put your head between your knees,' he said sharply. 'Breathe in slowly. Come on, Gem, you can do this.' He crouched down beside me and put his hand on my shoulder.

I tried to focus, to breathe, but I had to see what had come through the door. If it was another envelope, I had to get hold of it before Joe saw it.

I pushed him away. 'Give me some space.'

He moved back and I could see a brightly coloured sheet of paper lying on the doormat. I felt weak with relief; it was just a pizza delivery leaflet.

Slowly my breathing returned to normal. Joe stood beside me, his face pale and concerned. 'What is it, sweetheart? I haven't seen you like that for years. Has this happened while I've been away?'

I looked up at him, feeling lonelier in that moment than I'd ever felt. Who could help me?

'It's okay,' I said, struggling to my feet. 'I don't know what happened. I felt a bit faint, that's all.'

He helped me upstairs, then insisted I lie on our bed while he went back down to get Rory.

'I'll sort his bath out,' he said. 'Just lie there and try to relax. And I don't think you should be going in to work tomorrow, either. Or not in the morning, at any rate. You need to rest. You've been working too hard, what with the office and cleaning the house.' He had the grace to look shamefaced at that. I knew I should have told him the truth; I knew he would normally find it funny, but I didn't want to. I felt he was in the wrong, leaving the place a mess. If he felt guilty now, there was a chance he'd up his game a bit.

'I can't stay off work tomorrow. Rachel's got a couple of days off. She's going with some friends to Amsterdam for a hen weekend and won't be in until Monday afternoon. She's been going on about it for months.' It showed how little Joe and I had talked lately that he didn't know this.

'What about Lucy?'

I shook my head. 'She can only do school hours. I need to be there to open and close if Rachel's not there.'

'Couldn't Brian do it?'

'It's his day off tomorrow. I'll be fine. Don't worry.'

He sat down on the bed next to me. 'I'm worried about you, Gem.' He reached out to put his arm around me, but I flinched. I don't know why, it was automatic, and the hurt on his face was plain to see. He went out of the room, closing our bedroom door tightly. I heard him in the family bathroom, calling Rory in to him.

'I want Mummy to do it,' I heard Rory say.

I couldn't hear Joe's reply, but a moment later Rory shrieked with laughter. I didn't think he was missing me.

An hour after Rory got into the bath, he came tumbling into my room, holding a big fluffy towel around him.

'You must be waterlogged,' I said, getting off the bed to dry him. 'I'll get your pyjamas. Just wait a minute.'

As I took his pyjamas from his chest of drawers, he shouted, 'Can I wear your dressing gown, Mummy?'

I laughed. 'Put your pyjamas on first, then.' I helped him into them, then said, 'Which one do you want tonight?'

'The blue one,' he said. 'The one with the flowers on.'

He climbed onto my bed and I draped my Chinese robe around his shoulders, just as he liked it, and he rubbed his face against the silk. I asked him which books he wanted me to read and went into his room to find them. When I took them back into my bedroom, I got onto the bed beside him and opened one of the books. Before I could read a word, he started to laugh.

'What's up, poppet?' asked Joe from the doorway.

Rory laughed. 'Mummy's knickers are in her pocket!'

My head shot round. 'What?'

Rory held up my black silk knickers, the ones that had arrived through the post yesterday. I'd completely forgotten that I'd shoved them into my dressing gown pocket. He waved them in the air. 'Look!'

I grabbed them off him and threw them into the laundry basket on the landing.

'Why were they in your pocket?' Joe's voice was both curious and wary.

I shrugged. 'I found them on the floor downstairs yesterday and put them in my pocket so I could put them in the laundry basket.'

'But there was nothing on the floor yesterday,' he said. 'Everywhere was pristine.' He tried to joke. 'I would have noticed a pair of knickers, believe me!'

I shrugged. 'They must have fallen out of the basket when I took it downstairs.' I didn't think I was going to be able to keep this up. 'Anyway, gentlemen' – I poked Rory in his

tummy – 'never ask a lady about her knickers!' Rory shrieked with laughter. I could see that Joe was still looking confused, but I just said, 'I'll read to Rory now, then.'

'Okay.' He stood looking at me for a few seconds longer. I shot him a bright smile and opened Rory's book. The door closed gently behind Joe and I heard his footsteps as he ran downstairs. I breathed a sigh of relief. What an idiot I'd been, leaving them in my pocket like that. All the time I was reading to Rory, I thought of Joe and the lies I'd told over the last few weeks.

I could hardly recognize myself.

35

Friday, August 11

Work was quiet the next day, with just Sophie and Lucy around. Brian had taken a day's holiday and Lucy was covering for him. Rachel was on the seven A.M. flight to Amsterdam; she'd sent Sophie a text just before the plane took off to say a big crowd of men on a stag weekend had got onto the plane, all drinking cans of beer and causing general disruption.

After lunch, when Sophie was out and Lucy was busy with a client, a call came through on Brian's line. He had a dedicated line for rentals and I scooted across the office to pick it up.

'It's Zoe Hodge here,' said the caller. 'I'm a tenant at 50 Globe Street.'

'Oh yes,' I said, quickly checking our database. 'You're in flat three?'

'Yes. I've given in my notice and I'm leaving this weekend. Brian said he'd come round and do the inventory before I left.'

Those flats weren't furnished but were carpeted and came with a fully fitted kitchen. We had to check carefully when a tenant left, so that we could repair or replace anything for the next tenant. I looked up the property on

170

our system; Zoe had been living there for four years. Then I looked at Brian's diary online and saw that he'd made a note to carry out the inventory the following afternoon.

When I told Zoe this, she said, 'I wondered whether it could be done today? I'd rather he did it while I was here, just in case there are any queries.'

'Just a moment,' I said. 'I need to look at my own diary.' I went back to my desk and checked. 'I'm not free until five P.M.,' I said, 'but I could come then, on my way home from work, if you like.'

'That'd be great,' she said. 'I'm moving my stuff all afternoon, but I'll try to make sure I'm back then. If you're there before me, do you want to just let yourself in and make a start on it?'

'As long as you're all right with that. Keep your phone with you so I can contact you.'

I made a note in Brian's diary and then in my own. When Lucy got off the phone, I asked her if she and Sophie could lock up so that I could make a head start on the inventory.

'That's where Rachel lives, isn't it?' she said. 'She's on the ground floor.'

'Yes, Brian was asking her if she knew anyone who wanted to move in to Zoe's flat, but she didn't. It's a shame she's away. She could have come with me and learned how to do an inventory.'

'You made the right choice promoting her,' said Lucy. 'She's a good worker, isn't she? Picks things up really quickly.'

'And calm, too,' I said. We watched Sophie hurry across the road to the office. She was ten minutes late back from lunch. There was no need for us to say a word.

Globe Street was very narrow, with only residents' parking, so I parked in a small car park off the nearby main road and walked around the corner to the property. At the entrance to the street there were workmen repairing a pothole, but apart

from them there was nobody else about. There were six flats in the block, two on each floor. Zoe lived upstairs, on the same side of the building as Rachel. I remembered Rachel coming back to the office with Brian after he'd shown her around, her face lit up with happiness and relief. In that afternoon she'd got herself a job and a flat nearby and she looked a different woman from the nervous one who'd turned up to the interview.

'Did you like it?' I'd asked.

'I love it!' she said. 'I was expecting something like student accommodation, but it's great.'

'The landlady for that building is really good,' I said. 'She takes excellent care of it, but if you have any problems, you must let Brian know and he'll get it sorted. We're the managing agent, so everything comes through us.'

'And I can move in straight away?'

'Yes,' said Brian. 'It's empty now. Move in whenever you like and we'll start the tenancy from there. And if you go to work somewhere else,' he added, 'then of course that won't affect your tenancy at all, though you'll still have to come through us if there are any problems.'

'I hope that won't be for a while!' I said.

'Me too.'

She'd been in the flat for several months now and seemed happy there. As far as I was aware she hadn't complained about anything at all; I knew Brian would have told me if she had. Her living room faced the front garden and the street, and I could see she had photo frames and vases on the deep windowsill there. There were blinds at all the windows in the block, and hers were half drawn.

I stopped at the entrance to the building. There were six bells on the wall and an intercom grille next to them. I rang the bell for Zoe's flat, but there was no answer. I guessed she was taking her things to her new home, so I used

the keys I'd brought with me and let myself in. Inside, the staircase and hallway were carpeted with a warm thick-pile carpet and the only furniture was a small table with a flowering azalea on it. The landlady paid for the shared area to be cleaned every week and I could smell polish in the air; presumably the cleaners had been in that day.

I ran upstairs to Zoe's flat and knocked at the door. When there was no answer, I opened it. I called, 'Hello,' just in case she was in the bathroom, but there was no reply. In the living room were a couple of suitcases and a pair of bedside lamps, and apart from a few boxes in the kitchen, nothing else was left there. She'd clearly been busy all day. I moved one of the suitcases to wedge the door open, so that she wouldn't panic if she heard someone in the flat when she returned.

The inventory she'd signed when she moved in was on my clipboard, and I searched for a pen in my bag. Just then I heard the sound of the front door downstairs opening. For a moment I heard the dull roar of the road drill outside, and then the door clicked shut and all was quiet again. I went out onto the landing and was just about to call out Zoe's name when I heard a cough. I leaned forward to look through the banisters into the hallway below and froze.

A man stood outside the door to Rachel's flat. In his arms were several carrier bags. He put his key in the lock and pushed the door open.

I held my breath.

I heard him dump the bags on the floor, and then he went back to the front door and opened the mailbox with a key.

Just then a mobile phone rang downstairs, making me jump almost through the ceiling. Instinctively I scrabbled in my pocket to find my own phone and muted it.

'Hey, babe,' the man said, and in that instant my head started to buzz. I took a step back from the banisters. 'Everything okay?'

There was silence while he listened to the caller, and then he said, 'Yeah, I've just got home.' He laughed. 'No, just going to get changed, then I'm off out.' Silence again. I couldn't breathe. 'Not sure. No, of course I won't. I'm meeting Danny in Liverpool.' More silence, and then he said, 'Hold on, just let me get in and you can tell me all about it.' I heard him walk into the flat and slam the door shut.

For a moment, I stood like a fool, unable to believe what I'd heard.

Why was David in Rachel's flat?

Part II

Part II

36

Rachel

Friday, August 11

It was so good to be sitting in a bar in Amsterdam with my old friends from university that first afternoon. We'd had lunch and then it started to rain, so we'd found the nearest cocktail bar and were steadily making our way through the menu. I was a lightweight compared to them, though, and had to alternate cocktails with soft drinks so that I didn't make a fool of myself.

I hadn't seen the other girls for three years, since leaving university, though it was clear they'd kept in touch all that time. They all lived in London now, had gone through graduate training, and were earning more than twice my salary. I was still friends with them on Facebook and kept up with their lives there, but I used private messaging to chat to them and never posted anything about myself.

There were six of us that weekend. I met them at the airport; they'd flown in from Gatwick and had waited around for my flight from Liverpool to come in. I know this sounds weird, but I felt like a normal person, meeting them. I'd had my hair and nails done, just as I knew they would have. I'd bought

clothes and shoes and bags specially for the weekend, and spent a fortune on a cabin bag for the flight. I'd scoured Facebook for details of where they'd shopped and I made sure I went to the same places. I looked just like them when I arrived, and saw a couple of them glance at each other in surprise. I'd always been a bit of a mouse at university; I had so many responsibilities at home, making sure the bills were paid and my mum was fed and looked after, and I neglected myself a bit. I couldn't see the point in wearing make-up or fashionable clothes when all I did was sit in lectures and go straight home again. I was depressed – I can see that now – and it showed in the way I looked. Now, now that everything's going well, I look better. I spend a lot of time on my clothes, my hair. I go to the gym regularly. I feel great, really I do.

At university I'd never felt part of their gang; at least now I looked as though I was. I made so much effort to fit in that weekend, but by the time I came back, my face was strained with smiling too much, my head pounded with jokes I didn't quite get, and I knew that now, just as then, I didn't fit in. And I knew why – it was my secrets that kept me apart.

I'd never told them a thing about my mum when I was at university, and I didn't mention her now. They had no idea she'd died or even how she lived. I don't know why I said nothing; I knew they would have supported me, come to the funeral, helped me with the house. I couldn't bear them to set foot in my house, though, to see it as it was now. I couldn't bear to tell them about my mum and why she was the way she was. Our lives were too different and their pity would have been too much for me. It was easier to be alone, I'd found.

In those days at university, while they trooped off to a house party at the end of the night, I'd leave them to it and look for a taxi that would take me through the tunnel to the Wirral – not easy when the driver knew he wouldn't get a return fare. I'd tell them I was tired, that I had to go home,

and they'd lose interest, sometimes going off without even saying goodbye. I got nervous if I stayed out too long; I had to check that my mum was all right, that she hadn't set the house on fire or done some drunk-dialling.

Now, when I look at it objectively, I can see that I have to take some responsibility. I could have forced her to see a doctor. I could have moved away and left her to it. I could have told my friends about her. Instead I got used to living two lives; one in public and one in private. That was good preparation for now, really.

My mum would always be awake when I got back. Not waiting up for me, nothing like that. We'd switched the mother and daughter roles long ago. She'd be awake because she was drinking. She'd go out to the taxi to pay my fare, no matter what time of night it was, and would try to spark up a conversation with the poor taxi driver, who just wanted to get back on the road. I'd hover around her, trying to usher her back into the house.

'It's a miserable night for you,' she'd say, and I'd hear the guy say, 'What?' and I'd realize that by now she was so far gone that nobody else knew what she was saying. And of course taxi drivers are used to drunks; it was a sign of how bad she was that they couldn't understand a word she said.

She'd stumble back into the house, having given the guy a huge tip or, once, a penny, and she'd look at me and my heart would sink. It would go one of two ways, then: either she'd cry and talk about the past, or she'd turn on me.

I don't know which I hated more.

But all that was over now and I knew I shouldn't dwell on it. That afternoon, as agreed, I called David and spent ten minutes giggling on the phone. I missed him so much; it was hardly worth my going away. I was sharing a hotel room with my friend Emma, so I wasn't sure how much I'd be able to talk to him at night. He and I had never been apart since the

day we met. I wasn't sure how it would feel to be alone now, after being with him.

I must have looked miserable at that thought, then, because the bride-to-be, Laura, nudged me and whispered, 'Are you okay?'

I smiled at her. 'Yes, I'm fine. Having a great time.'

'Me too,' she said. 'I'm sorry you can't make the wedding.' This had been a bit of a sore topic within the group; we'd had over a year's notice, after all, but as David said, there was no way we wanted our photos on social media.

'Oh I am, too!' I said. 'I would have loved to be there. I'd already paid for the holiday, though.'

'That's okay. And thanks so much for the wedding gift. It arrived last week.' She looked so pleased, then, her irritation at my pulling out of the wedding assuaged by my choosing one of the more expensive presents she'd registered at a top department store. She put her hand on my arm and the diamonds in her engagement ring twinkled. 'It's so good to see you again. You look great. So much happier.'

I really didn't want to go into how I'd been in the past. As David said, there was no point in thinking about that now. So I shifted the attention back to her.

'That's a lovely ring,' I said. 'What's your wedding ring like?'

She curled up next to me and I was treated to a long, long description of her shopping trip with her fiancé for wedding rings. When she'd finished, she squeezed my arm and said, 'It'll be your turn soon. Maybe that guy you were calling just now?' She winked at me. 'Don't think I didn't notice.'

I laughed. 'Maybe.'

I'd never told any of them about David. None of my friends knew anything about him and none of his knew about me.

'We're the world's best-kept secret,' he'd say.

He was right; it was much more romantic that way.

37

Gemma

I stayed on the staircase for a moment after David went into Rachel's flat. I didn't know what to do. The late-afternoon sun shone through the hallway window upstairs and I stood, my face and body hot and sweating, as I strained to hear him in the flat below. If I leaned over the banisters, I could hear the deep rumble of his voice as he talked on the phone.

Silently I tiptoed into Zoe's flat. I hesitated in the doorway, wondering whether to shut the door so that she'd have to use her key, but I worried that she'd forget I was meant to be there and be startled by me. Instead I left the door ajar and moved as quietly as I could through the living room and into the kitchen. I stood to one side of the kitchen window and looked out into the yard below. It had been a hot day; I saw that the back door to Rachel's flat was opened out onto her patio, and thought, *So he must be staying a while, then*.

I looked at my watch. It was five twenty. He'd said he was going to Liverpool for a night out with his friend. It would take him an hour or so to get there. I guessed he'd be having a shower before he went, but couldn't be sure. I was terrified of bumping into him as I left the building; just the thought of that was enough to make my heart race. And then I remembered

that the bathroom in this flat was above Rachel's; each flat was identical to the others in the block. I went into Zoe's bathroom and opened the window as wide as I could. Down in the yard below I could see steam coming from the drain. He was running the shower.

I grabbed the clipboard and my bag and left the flat, locking the door quietly behind me. I crept downstairs as fast as I could, then left the building, making sure that I went up the road away from Rachel's living room window, just in case he was looking out. At the end of the road I stopped and sent Zoe a quick text saying I'd been called away on an emergency but that everything looked fine. I'd get Brian to do the inventory. I had no intention of setting foot in that place again.

As I walked down the side street to get to my car, I tried to process what I'd seen. So Rachel was seeing David. When did that start? I knew she was single when she started work for me six months ago; we'd talked then about Liverpool and what it was like now, and she'd told me about being a caregiver for her mum and how it had been hard for her to go out at night. It sounded as though she hadn't had much of a life, and I'd felt really sorry for her. She'd said she was looking for somewhere to live and I'd asked her whether she had a partner; she'd said no, she hadn't, and she was quite happy that way. I hadn't thought anything of it; hadn't given it a second thought. I knew she'd made a few friends in the area and went to the same gym that Sophie went to, but I'd never heard her talk about a boyfriend.

Of course I'd never told them anything about what had happened to me in London two months before or anything that had happened since. She'd been in the office when David came in that day and definitely didn't seem to know him then. I remember her giggling with Sophie because he was a good-looking guy.

I frowned. We didn't have a rule about dating clients; there had never seemed the need, but we did have a rule about acting professionally around them. He was single and she was single. She wasn't dealing with his house purchase; she wasn't in a position to negotiate on his behalf.

Had he called her? How would he have known her name? Maybe he'd dropped in when I wasn't there, but why wouldn't she have said something? Or maybe they'd met on a night out. There wasn't really a reason why she couldn't date him – surely she would have told Sophie, at least? I thought about that. Sophie couldn't have known anything about it either. She would never have been able to keep that to herself. And yet Rachel and Sophie were good friends. Why would Rachel keep quiet about seeing a new man?

I felt responsible for Rachel, in a way. She had no family to talk to and she'd never mentioned any friends. I'd been surprised when she went on the hen weekend; she'd been so excited about that trip. I did remember that when she first started work she was always on her phone; I'd had to talk to her about that and she'd said it was just her university friends wondering how she was getting on.

I thought of the policewoman, Stella, then. I should tell her, I knew that, but I wanted to ask Rachel myself, speak to her face-to-face and give her the chance to tell me what she knew. And then I would call the police. I owed it to her to give her fair warning, though. I needed to tell her what her boyfriend had done to me.

The next morning I got to the office early and slipped the keys to Zoe's flat back in the key safe. When Brian and Sophie came in, I made a point of telling him that he needed to do the inventory for the flat, because I hadn't been able to go the night before.

'I thought you were going on your way home from work,'

said Sophie, who was looking worse for wear after her Friday night out.

'I was,' I lied, 'but Joe called and reminded me he had a doctor's appointment, so I had to go home to Rory.'

She accepted this without another thought and simply poured herself another coffee and hunted in her bag for more painkillers. But that morning I watched Sophie and wondered again what she knew. All the time she was photocopying house details and putting them on the racks in the window, I watched her and thought again about whether she knew about David and Rachel. Did everyone know?

And then I realized that if Sophie had known, she would also have known that Rachel wouldn't want me to find out. Surely she would have tried to put me off going there the night before?

When we stopped for coffee that afternoon and Brian had gone off to do the inventory at Zoe's flat, I said to Sophie, 'Did you have a good time last night?'

She smiled. 'A really good time! And I've got a date for tonight.' She whipped out her phone and showed us a photo of a young man who was beaming at the camera, his face flushed, his hair damp. He held a beer bottle; clearly it wasn't the first he'd had that night.

'Oh he's nice!' I said. 'Where did you meet him?'

She named a local club in the centre of Chester and told us how he'd singled her out from her friends and they'd talked all night.

'Is that where you usually go at weekends?' I asked casually.

'Yes, either on Friday or Saturday.'

'Does Rachel normally go with you?'

She shook her head. 'No, she doesn't like places like that. She likes to just go to the gym or to meet up for lunch or shopping. I go with my school friends or my sister.'

Lucy joined in. 'Maybe she's seeing someone.'

'No, she's not,' said Sophie. 'We were setting up dating profiles the other day.' A shifty expression crossed her face. 'Not at work, obviously.'

'And when you had that barbecue at Easter, she came on her own,' said Lucy.

I'd forgotten the barbecue. The weather at Easter had been great, so one Sunday evening I'd invited all the staff round to my house for a couple of hours. Lucy and I had watched Sophie chase Rory round the garden with a little bucket of water from his paddling pool, threatening to drench him with it. Both of them were almost crying with laughter.

'She's just a kid, isn't she?' Lucy had said. 'She seems so glamorous at times, but look at her now. This is the real Sophie.'

Rachel had arrived later than the others. She stood in the kitchen talking to Joe for a while, and Lucy had looked over at them and said, 'They're getting along well, aren't they?' I'd laughed. Joe got along with everyone. I don't think I'd met anyone who had a bad word to say about him. His Irish charm was obviously working on Rachel, though; I could see her laughing, her face pink and excited, as she talked to him.

'I think she's said more to Joe today than she has to us since we've known her,' Lucy had said that day. 'He's obviously charmed her.'

'He does have that gift,' I'd replied. 'It worked on me, anyway. Or it did.'

Lucy had looked at me sympathetically. 'It's always like that when you have a little child,' she said. 'You'll get back to normal soon.'

I'd nodded. I hoped so.

'Rachel seems to have settled in well, doesn't she?' Lucy asked now. 'I noticed you've been giving her more responsibilities lately.'

I said, 'Yes, she's been fine,' but I was too distracted to chat.

I couldn't stop thinking about David. Had he called in one day when Rachel was there alone? Had he liked her from the moment he saw her, that day he came to the office? Try as I might, I couldn't think of a spark between them. She'd blushed when she gave him coffee, but she was a nervous person at times. She hated attention drawn to herself. And when I'd met him in London, he hadn't mentioned her.

Had he targeted her since then? Had he seen another way to get to me?

38

Gemma

By the time it was five P.M., I was determined to go to the police there and then. I just had to trust Stella to do her best to make sure Joe didn't find out. I could hardly bear to think of the lies I'd told him. There were so many now. At night, unable to sleep, I'd go through them, my face burning with shame.

In the car park I got into my car and sat wondering what to do. My phone beeped with a message, and as I reached into my bag to read it, my heart sank. What was this going to be now? I relaxed when I saw it was from Joe, but when I read his message, I panicked.

What time will you be home? We need to talk.

Had he been sent something? David clearly knew our address, but did he know Joe's name? Why would he want to send him something anyway? Wasn't he content with making my life miserable?

My fingers were damp on the screen as I answered.

Just setting off. What's up? X

There was no reply at first. I panicked and had to stop myself from sending another message that would incriminate me. I had just started up the car and had reached the gate of the car park when I heard another message arrive.

Just come home now. I've sent Rory to Sam's house
for a couple of hours.

I started to shake. What had happened? I sent a reply:

Don't just say that. Tell me what you're upset about.
I don't want to drive home panicking.

I reversed back into my parking space and waited. I thought
I was going to be sick with the tension and couldn't have
driven then even if I wanted to. It seemed ages before another
message came through:

I'm trying to think of a reason why you would stay
in a hotel in Chester when I was away in Ireland.

My heart flipped. How did he know that? How did anyone
know that? I'd left our house just before seven P.M. and I
knew nobody had seen me. I'd been on the lookout for that.
And yes, I'd driven up and down our street at midnight, just
to check that David hadn't tried to burn the house down, but
when I saw that everything was okay, I'd gone straight back
to the hotel. Nobody had been following me. I'd driven at
least two miles without anyone behind me at all. I'd never
been to that hotel before, never mentioned it to anyone.

And then I thought, maybe he knows because of our bank
statement? I took out my phone and went onto our online
banking service. It showed that the last time it had been
accessed was this afternoon, just an hour earlier. I scrolled
down the list of credits and debits and saw that the hotel's
charge was there.

I could have cried with relief. Nobody had told Joe, he'd
just figured it out for himself.

But what could I tell him? Why would I go to a hotel when
I could stay in my own house? There had to be a reason. I
hadn't even thought about the hotel bill at the time; I'd been
in such a state that I'd used our joint debit card to pay for it,
without thinking he'd see it.

Then I had a flash of inspiration and sent him another message:

There was a mouse in the kitchen and I couldn't stand the thought of sleeping at home. Why do you think I had to clean up the house? I'm on my way now.

I started the car feeling dreadful. How many more lies was I going to have to tell him? And how on earth would I have got rid of the mouse?

Joe was waiting for me when I got in. He looked so guilty that I felt even worse. He came over to me and hugged me. I put my head on his shoulder, glad of the comfort but feeling terrible that I'd got it under false pretences.

'I'm so sorry,' he said. 'I know how you feel about mice. Why didn't you tell me?'

'There was nothing you could do about it from Ireland,' I said, hating myself for making him feel so bad. 'At the time I couldn't even speak about it without getting hysterical.' I've always been like that about mice; Caitlin and I had had them in one of our student houses and I'd had to go home to my parents' until some of the braver students had sorted them out. 'I meant to tell you when you came home, but then I didn't want to tell you when Rory was there. By the time he'd gone to sleep, I didn't want to think about it.'

I'd no idea that I could be so convincing.

'I thought the worst,' he said, his mouth against my hair. 'I remembered your knickers in your dressing gown pocket, and I thought you'd been seeing someone else.'

I knew that in the past I would have laughed at that suggestion. The idea of me having an affair would have been outlandish. I tried to laugh now and hoped it didn't sound forced. 'There's nothing to worry about.'

I wanted to say, *I wouldn't do that to you*, but maybe I had

already. How could I know? The more I thought about that night, the less I knew.

'So where was the mouse?' he asked. 'And how did you get rid of it?' He paused. 'You did get rid of it, didn't you?'

'I got Neil to come round.' Neil was one of the handymen we used for the tenancies. 'He sorted it out. Don't ask me any more than that; all I know is it's gone. He put poison down, too, but that's under the floorboards; there's no need to worry about Rory finding it.'

'So that's why you cleaned the house? Oh God, Gemma, I'm so sorry. I know it was a mess.'

I did feel guilty about that, but you know what, it was his fault it was a mess. He and Rory lived like teenage boys; they had great fun but the house was always untidy.

'Forget it,' I said. 'It was nice to be in a hotel.'

'You're going to get used to that,' he said. 'That's twice in a couple of months you've stayed in a hotel.'

My cheeks flamed and he laughed. 'There's nothing to be embarrassed about. You deserve a break. You work far too hard.'

I just couldn't help it. 'But Joe, what's the alternative?'

'What do you mean?'

'I have to work hard,' I said. 'I don't have a choice, do I? I can't afford to pay for staff when I could do the job myself.'

He moved away, going over to the sink to fill the kettle. 'We agreed to do this,' he said. 'When you got pregnant we knew we couldn't both work. And you wanted to keep the agency going. That was important to you, remember?'

I couldn't speak. I knew that was what I'd said, but it was nearly four years ago, before Rory was born. How was I meant to know how I'd feel years later? I looked over at Joe; he was calmly making tea and he seemed so reasonable. It was as though I was at fault, as though I couldn't keep a promise. Tears filled my eyes. I knew I wouldn't say anything more.

I never did stand up to him. Not really. I'd shout sometimes and I'd get upset, but I never seemed able to sit down with him and talk about things honestly. Even now, I could feel myself backing off.

I muttered that I was going to fetch Rory and left the house. Rory was with Sam, a boy from nursery who lived nearby, and the walk there and the chat with Sam's mother helped me calm down.

Back home I changed into shorts and a T-shirt and we sat out on the patio to eat the dinner that Joe had made for us. Rory told me again all about Ireland and the lovely meals that Nanny had cooked for him and the adventures he'd had with Grandad and his cousins. It sounded as though Joe had hardly seen him all week; as though he'd reverted back to his childhood self. *No wonder he wants to move back there. No wonder he wants us to live with his parents.* I thought of how it would be if we did that, how I'd be the only one in the house getting up to go to work every day, while Joe and his retired parents and our child had a permanent holiday.

I had to get past this. I knew my resentment was poisoning our relationship, but I couldn't find the courage to stand up for what I wanted.

39

Rachel

Sunday, August 13

I know I'd told the girls in the office that I was coming back on Monday morning, but I actually flew back on Sunday night. David had persuaded me to tell a white lie so that I had more time to spend with him. He didn't have to be at work on Monday morning and he wanted me to be at home with him. I loved that about him. He always wanted us to be close, all the time.

So I drove back from Liverpool and parked in our residents' parking bay. I flicked on the car's interior light and took out my make-up bag. I looked okay, just needed to touch up my lipstick. I smoothed my hair, wanting to look my best, and sprayed perfume on my throat and wrists. When I was quite sure I looked good, I jumped out of the car. As I took my cabin bag from the boot, I saw Jennifer, the woman who lived in the other ground-floor flat, drive in. I waited for her to get out of her car and we walked towards the building together.

'Have you been away?' she asked. 'I noticed nobody was around this weekend.'

'I've just come back from Amsterdam,' I said. 'A hen weekend.'.

'Wow, lucky you. What about David? Was he away on the stag weekend?'

'No, he's been here.'

She gave me a puzzled look. 'Really? A couple of lads were outside ringing on all the bells last night. Well, this morning. It turned out they were looking for Zoe, but she's gone now. I didn't want to go out to them, so I ended up knocking on your door, to see whether David would tell them to get lost.'

'He mustn't have heard you, otherwise he would've gone out to them,' I said. 'What time was it?'

'Oh, about three o'clock. Maybe nearer four. I was so annoyed; I had to be at work early today. He must be able to sleep through anything if he could sleep through that, though. I ended up shouting out of the window at them. They wanted Zoe's new address. As if I was going to give it to them at that time of night!'

We parted company in the hallway and I opened the door to our flat. It was pretty small, but it was a temporary arrangement. We made all sorts of plans about what we'd do when we sold my mum's house, and sometimes I did wonder how we'd manage in a much bigger house. So much space would be wasted. David liked to be with me, to be near me always.

My mum had left the house and her money to me. Well, there wasn't anyone else to leave it to. I was surprised she had so much, really. She certainly didn't spend a lot when she was alive, though to be fair, she'd paid for my university fees without a question, and for the year before she died, when I was looking after her, she used to tell me to use her credit card to get whatever I needed. She never bought anything for herself, though. Except alcohol. She never went out for the last few years; they delivered it to the house after I refused to buy it for her. I think she grew afraid of running out of money

as she got older, though she would've been good for a long time.

David was a great help in sorting all that out for me. After she died I wasn't fit for much, really. On the one hand there was a sense of relief that that era of my life had ended, but on the other . . . well, she was my mum, and even if she hadn't prioritized me, it didn't mean the reverse was true.

When I opened the door to the flat, David was there waiting for me.

'Hey!' he said, jumping up from the sofa. 'I've just opened some wine.' He kissed me and I could tell he'd had a head start. 'Welcome back!'

I hugged him close. It was so good to come home to someone who loved me, and such a change to come into a house where there was warmth and fun. He'd lit candles in the hearth, and a bottle of white wine stood on the coffee table, wet with condensation. He poured me a glass, then went into the kitchen and came back with a tray of cheese and crackers and a bunch of plump, dewy grapes.

'Sit down, babe,' he said. 'I've missed you. Now tell me what you've done all weekend.'

We sat and chatted about Amsterdam. David had been there several times, but this was my first time. I hadn't really been to many places, but now that my mum's money had come through, I was determined to change that. I was going to live the life I knew she'd want for me, if only she'd been sane enough to know it.

'You're looking nice,' I said. 'New shirt? It looks great.'

'Yeah, I did a bit of shopping on Friday lunchtime,' he said. 'Got a few new things.'

'And you saw Danny on Friday night?' I asked. 'Where did you go?'

He told me about the bars in Liverpool that they'd been to, bars that he and I often visited, where he had a lot of friends.

'What about last night?' I asked. 'Did you do anything?'

'No,' he said. 'I was wasted from Friday night. I drank far too much.' He grinned at me. 'I was missing you! I need you to be the sober one when I go out.'

I laughed. That was always my role, to stay a few drinks behind him so that I could get him home when he'd had too much. He wasn't like my mum when he was drunk; where she'd just want to talk about the past, he liked to talk about the future: what we'd do, where we'd go. It was exhilarating hearing him discuss travelling around backpacking in Peru or bungee jumping in New Zealand. I'd never thought of doing these things before and, frankly, the thought of them scared the life out of me, but the prospect of doing them with him was exciting.

'So you stayed in?' I asked.

He looked up. 'What?'

'You stayed in last night? You poor thing. I'm sorry, baby,' I said. 'I hate to think of you staying in at the weekend.'

'No problem,' he said. 'I was too tired to go out. I had a takeaway and got an early night.'

I steeled myself, waiting for the body blow that I'd heard occurs when someone discovers their lover's lies, but it didn't happen. I realized then that I'd always known that he lied to me, that he'd probably been unfaithful, too, though this was the first time I had evidence of it.

I took a sip of my drink. I didn't know what to do. I couldn't ask him again, or mention what Jennifer had said. It would sound as though I didn't trust him, and I knew that wouldn't go down well. I thought for a second of her bumping into him and mentioning it; I just had to hope she wouldn't.

'But you're right,' he said. He took the glass from my hand. 'I've been lonely here on my own. Why don't you make up for it?' His eyes gleamed. 'Pay the price for your weekend away with the girls.'

I smiled and stood up. 'Good idea,' I said. 'I'll just put this food away and I'll be with you.'

'Great,' he said. 'I'll get a quick shower.' He started to take his shirt off, walking into the bedroom leaving a trail of clothes behind him. I quickly picked them up and put them into the laundry basket.

When I heard the shower start, I went into the bedroom. Quietly, I slid the wardrobe door open. A couple of new suits were on his side of the wardrobe. The labels were still on the cuffs: Paul Smith and Hugo Boss. Hanging next to them were several new shirts, and below, a couple of shoe boxes had been thrown in, as though they were nothing. They weren't nothing, though. In his lunchtime, in just one hour, he'd casually spent thousands of pounds of my mother's money, and there wasn't the slightest acknowledgement from him.

I closed the wardrobe door and went back to the living room. The tray of glasses and plates was still on the coffee table, and I picked it up and took it into the kitchen.

On Thursday night David had put the wheelie bin out, ready for collection on Friday morning. Just before I left for Amsterdam, I'd taken the bag from the bin in the kitchen and put it into the wheelie bin, then put a fresh plastic bag into the kitchen bin.

Now I held my breath as I pushed the bin's swing lid. There was nothing in there. No takeaway food cartons, nothing at all. It was completely empty. Quietly I opened the back door and lifted the lid of the wheelie bin, just in case he'd put it straight out there. Sometimes I did that if the food was very spicy, though I'd never known David to do it.

That, too, was empty.

I locked the back door and stood against it with my heart pounding. I knew it. He hadn't been here on Saturday night. I'd known from the moment Jennifer spoke to me that he hadn't.

I didn't let myself think about where he'd been or who he'd been with.

I couldn't. I couldn't afford to lose him. Not now.

I picked up the bottle of wine and filled my glass to the brim. I drank it straight down.

By the time David came out of the bathroom I had put on the lingerie he liked, sprayed the perfume he'd chosen for me, and put on the music he liked best.

'Come on, sweetheart,' I said. My throat was swollen with tears I knew I couldn't shed. 'Let me make it up to you.'

40

Gemma

Monday, August 14

I found it really stressful waiting for Rachel to return to work. I knew I was going to have to talk to her, but I couldn't think how I was going to say it and what she'd say in response. What if she denied knowing him? I had no right to go into her flat to prove he was there. And I had no evidence that David had actually done anything, apart from an e-mail that looked like spam.

And I was worried about her, too. What had she got herself into? She was so young and she had no family to help her. If he was taking advantage of her, would she be able to cope?

I knew that if I went to the police and this ended up in court, it was likely it would be in the newspapers. We were a small enough town that even minor events were written about as though they were global incidents. Our local newspaper certainly loved to report sexual misdemeanours; if they knew that a married businesswoman had been posing naked for her client, they'd be all over the story. And if it was in the newspapers, Joe would hear about it. I couldn't bear the thought of that.

198

Rachel arrived back at the office after lunch. Sophie was surreptitiously putting on nail varnish, blissfully unaware of the fact that the smell was giving her away. Brian was on the phone to a plumber who was due to put in a new bathroom at a student house I owned near the university, and I was at my desk, working on an expenses spreadsheet for the accountant. Everything was normal, and as I saw her standing in the doorway, a breeze slightly lifting her hair, I knew that she thought nobody knew her secret.

She was wrong.

Ever since I'd seen David at her home, I'd wondered about him and how she knew him. I'd worried about her, too. This was a man who seemed hell-bent on destroying me. As she stood there, looking so young and so happy, I thought of how she'd feel when I told her about the things he'd done to me. I swallowed. She'd be destroyed.

Mid-afternoon, I received a call from Bill Campbell, one of the landlords I'd dealt with over the years. He'd bought up some flats in a dockside block and wanted Brian to have a look at them before renting them.

'Brian's at an auction this afternoon,' I said. 'I'll do it for you. Is later on okay?'

'Can you be there for four o'clock? Park up by the entrance and I'll buzz you in.'

He gave me the address and I wrote it down, repeating it after him. When I looked up from my call, I saw that Rachel and Sophie were looking at me eagerly.

'Are you going to that new development down by the racecourse?' asked Sophie. 'I walked past it last weekend. It looks amazing.'

'Yes, Bill Campbell's bought three flats there. He told me about them when I saw him last week.'

'I'd love one of those,' said Rachel. 'Do you know how much they're going for?'

I looked at her. She looked so calm and serene, the polar opposite of me right now. In an instant, the decision was made. 'I don't know,' I said. 'Why don't you come along with me and have a look at them?'

Sophie turned away, disappointed. She'd be even more disappointed if she realized what she was actually missing this afternoon.

Now was my chance to talk to Rachel.

Bill pulled up in his car ten minutes after we arrived. Rachel and I were in separate cars, so that we could make our own way home afterwards, and I pretended to be on my phone so that she didn't come over. I couldn't stop thinking that she would be going back to him and wondered what she'd say to him. And what he'd say to her.

'Sorry,' said Bill, when we met him at the door to the block. 'I'm running late.'

He tapped the code to get into the building and we exchanged pleasantries as we went up in the lift to the fifth floor. When the doors opened he ushered us out onto a landing that had a row of doors, each leading to a self-contained flat.

'So, I've just bought these three here.' He indicated those nearest to us. 'Got them at auction last week. I'm planning to rent them out for now, then see how it goes.'

We went into the first one and he said, 'You'll be able to deal with this for me, won't you? I want them rented as soon as possible, so can you get an advert out tomorrow? I've got painters coming in early next week. Nothing else needs doing; they're in good condition as far as I can see, but let me know what you think.' He told me the price range he was looking at, but said he wanted us to check around to see if more was viable. 'I can't stop, I've got to get to the council offices before they shut. Can you get the keys back to me?'

'No problem. I'll send Brian round with them tomorrow and I'll get him to place an advert, too.'

'Great.'

With that, he was off. The flats were empty and clean, ready for the decorators to start work before they were let. Rachel and I measured the rooms and made a note of any work to be done. We moved from flat to flat, careful not to miss anything.

'So Brian would normally do this, wouldn't he?' asked Rachel.

'Yes, but if you're going to take over in my absence, you have to know exactly what's involved in every job in the office.' Not that I had the slightest intention of even keeping her in the job, never mind promoting her, if she was going to carry on seeing David.

'This is the one I'd like,' said Rachel. 'Imagine seeing that view every day.'

We were standing in the last flat, looking out through its huge windows at the Welsh hills. Beautiful as they were, I hardly noticed them. All I could think was that now was my chance. There was nobody around.

It was time.

My stomach was knotted tight as I turned to Rachel. 'This would be a bit big for you, though, wouldn't it?' I asked.

She gave a little smile. 'Oh, that's okay. I like a lot of space.'

'But living here on your own,' I said. 'It's a lovely flat, but it's more suitable for a couple, isn't it?'

The difference in her was minimal, but I saw it. She stayed still, looking out of the window, and it was only because I was so fired up that I could see that her hands, which were touching the windowsill, now gripped it.

I took one step closer to her and watched as the tiny blonde hairs on her arms prickled to attention.

'I know,' I said.

She jumped then and turned. 'Know what?' Her voice was brave and strong; there was no sign of the nerves that had hit her earlier. She moved away from the window and gathered up the clipboard and laser measure that we'd brought with us, holding them against her chest.

I moved closer to her. 'How long have you known him for?'

'Who?' Her voice was uncertain then, and she swallowed hard after she spoke.

'You know who.'

She said nothing. I could hear her breathing, short, shallow breaths that made her face pink and damp.

'David Sanderson.'

She looked at me, her face defiant. Cool, almost. 'I don't know anyone called David Sanderson.'

She was probably telling the truth. I'd realized a while ago that it was unlikely he'd used his real name.

'I think you do. I don't know what he's really called, but I know you know him.'

She stayed very still and so did I, both so aware of each other, aware of every move. I wasn't going to be the one who broke that silence.

She caved. 'How do you know?'

'I saw him going into your flat.' The tension hit me and I gave a huge sigh. 'Did you really think I wouldn't find out? We manage that property. The chances of my discovering that you knew him were always high.'

She opened her mouth to speak, but nothing came out. I waited. It had worked before and I knew it would work again.

'It's my business who I live with.'

My stomach lurched. So he *was* living there. Ever since I'd seen him, I'd tried to persuade myself that maybe it was all innocent, that she'd only just met him and had lent him her key for some reason. Even now, I tried to give her the benefit of the doubt.

'I'm really worried for you, Rachel.'

She looked scornful. 'Why?'

'I don't think you realize what you're involved with. Your boyfriend . . .'

She cut in. 'He's not my boyfriend.' She looked me straight in the face then, and it was clear he gave her courage. 'He's my husband. We're married.'

41

Rachel

Last year

I've known David for years; he was one of my brother's oldest friends, but I hadn't been expecting him to turn up at my mum's funeral.

It was held in late October on such a grey, bleak day. My mother had distanced herself from so many of her friends over the years, and I hadn't had the nerve to get in touch with them at the end. When I say 'distanced herself', I really mean she'd phoned them up and screamed at them in the middle of the night, so I was reluctant to call them then.

The end of her life dragged out for over a year. A year when I wasn't able to work, wasn't able to do anything except look after her. Not that she was grateful, mind. I'd take her to hospital appointments where I'd hear mums talking about their daughters. 'I couldn't have asked for a better daughter,' they'd say. 'She's been such a comfort to me.' I would sit stone-faced when they'd talk like that. My mother had enough sense of propriety to pay lip service at times, though. Once I'd heard her saying she wouldn't have been able to cope without me. I was amazed, both by the sentiment and the idea that she was coping.

So her funeral was poorly attended. My dad wasn't there; that would have been one way to get my mother back from the grave. There was just me and a couple of neighbours who'd seen the ambulance come to the house and who'd called round later, when they saw I was home. She'd died in the ambulance, exerting her will right to the end. She'd been determined not to go into a hospital or hospice, but to die at home. When I'd found her unconscious one morning I called for emergency help, thinking she'd be furious when she came to, but that didn't happen. Ten minutes into the journey to Arrowe Park, she gave up the fight altogether.

I sat in the front row of the chapel at the crematorium, and our neighbours came to sit with me. An elderly cousin of my mum's turned up; she gave me a sympathetic look and touched my arm, but she hadn't been there when I needed her, so I was polite, but that was it.

The short service had just started when I heard the door to the chapel open. I wasn't expecting anyone else, but then I didn't know what to expect. The only other funeral I'd been to had been quiet, too. I was torn between looking at the minister and turning around to see who was there. The latter instinct won.

David stood in the doorway. I knew him instantly, though I hadn't seen him for more than ten years. He was taller than I remembered, and broader now, his hair still black and wavy. He turned to close the door, then walked up the aisle towards me. For a moment I felt dizzy, as though my brother was there beside him, just as he always was.

When he saw me looking at him, he winked, and that seemed so inappropriate but such a welcome diversion in all that misery that I winked back. As I turned back I saw that the funeral director had noticed and looked shocked. As well he might. I think that was the first time I felt like laughing in over a year.

He was waiting for me outside, after the service ended. 'Poor Coco,' he said, and suddenly it was like the old days. David had been visiting our house one day when I was little; I think I was four years old and the boys must have been eleven or twelve. I'd been playing with my mum's make-up and had made a right mess of myself. They'd laughed so much when they saw me and called me Coco the Clown. The nickname had stuck. I hadn't been called that for years, and as soon as David said it, it was like I had my family back. 'You've had a tough time, haven't you?'

For the first time since I lost my mum, I felt tears prickling the back of my eyes. I'd done everything – all the legal stuff, arranging the funeral, sorting the bills – on my own and I'd known that if I started to cry I'd never stop. Now at this hint of kindness from someone who'd known me as I was before, I could feel myself well up.

'It's all over now,' I said. 'Finally she's at peace.'

The neighbours said goodbye then, and my mum's cousin promised to keep in touch, though I wasn't going to hold my breath on that. They kissed my cheek, told me I'd been a good daughter, the very best, and they were off.

I was staring after them thinking I'd have to go back to the empty house, with no clue what to do with myself, when David said, 'You know what you need, don't you, Coco?'

'To sleep for a year?'

'You need to get drunk,' he said.

I laughed. 'What?'

'We should have a wake for your mum.'

'Wakes are usually held before the funeral.'

He shrugged. 'And did you have one?'

I shook my head.

'Well, then. Better late than never.' He smiled at me then and I couldn't resist. 'Come on,' he said. 'My treat.'

So off we went into Liverpool on the train, both dressed in

our sober black suits, on a Tuesday morning, to have our wake. We hopped from bar to bar and with each drink we had to toast my mum and say something nice about her. I struggled a bit with that, but he did well. He had the best memories. And then he went up to the bar to get more cocktails and when he came back I asked what they were.

'Between the Sheets,' he said, and he leaned over the little bar table and kissed me.

We were married within a month.

42

Rachel

Present day

Gemma stared at me, so shocked that her mouth fell open. She was clearly struggling to process what I'd said.

'You're married?' she said. 'To David Sanderson?'

I started to speak, to tell her that that wasn't his name, but stopped myself just in time. 'I'm married, yes.' I could feel myself flush. I hadn't told another person that I was married and it felt weird, as though I was pretending to be grown up.

'Since when?' she asked.

I bristled. What did it have to do with her? David and I had agreed I wouldn't go into detail. *There's no need for her to know anything*, he'd said. *Keep it to yourself. When in doubt, keep quiet.* So I did keep quiet, but it seemed Gemma could keep quiet longer than I could, as eventually I heard myself saying, 'A while.'

'And yet you said you were single,' she said. 'When you came to the interview I asked you and you specifically said, "I'm single. Never been married. Don't particularly want to get married."'

It sounded as though she was mimicking me, and I scowled at her. 'You've got a good memory.'

'Damn right I have,' she said.

I had to figure out how to play this. I'd known she'd find out sometime – that was part of it, knowing she would – but I'd thought we had time. I hadn't dreamed it would be today. One glance at her told me she wasn't going to leave here until this was sorted.

Oh well. So it was time. I was ready for her.

'Did you know him when he came into the office?' she asked.

I couldn't help it. I laughed at the thought of that day when I had to pretend I didn't know him and ask him how he liked his coffee.

Gemma looked shocked. 'Were you *married* to him then?'

I just looked at her. I wasn't going to tell her anything. I'd been preparing for this for a long time. *Don't incriminate yourself,* David had said over and over again. *Don't give her anything, not one piece of information, that she can hang you with.* I turned away and counted to ten. *Keep calm,* I thought. *Keep calm. She has nothing on you.*

'Rachel,' she said, 'there's something I should tell you.'

I readied myself. 'What?'

'He's trouble. David is trouble.'

I laughed again. 'I don't think he's the one I should be worried about.'

'He is!' she said. 'He's trying to destroy me.'

I was trying to keep quiet, trying to remember David's instructions, but I couldn't help it. It had to be said. 'Come off it, Gemma,' I said. 'You're making it sound as though you're a complete innocent here.'

She blinked. 'What? I am!'

The heat was rising now; I'd felt it simmering for years and all the time I'd tried to control it, to keep a lid on my feelings, but faced with her innocent expression, I couldn't control myself. 'Little Miss Perfect, always doing the right thing. That's how you portray yourself, isn't it?'

She looked at me as though I'd gone mad. 'Rachel, I have done nothing wrong. Nothing at all.'

I hardly heard her. I felt that if I didn't tell her then, I didn't know what I'd do. 'But you and I both know you have, don't we?'

She was staring at me. I knew my cheeks were red, knew she was wary now. I could feel anticipation rising in me. It had been dampened down for so long and now I was going to set myself free.

'We both know exactly what you are,' I said. 'What you've done. The question is, who else knows? Does Joe know, I wonder?'

She stared at me, her eyes boggling. She took a step back and I realized I was frightening her. Well, good.

'Did you tell him, Gemma? Do you tell him everything? Did you tell him what happened that night?' I gave her a hard, contemptuous look. 'Or did you lie, just as you always do?'

She looked like she'd been slapped. 'Are you saying that was my fault?'

'You and I both know the truth. That's what you can't stand, isn't it? You can say what you like, but I know the truth.'

'The truth about what?' she yelled. 'What your pervert husband has been doing to me?'

I flinched.

'You really know all that and you've the nerve to stand here talking to me?' she asked. 'You realize I risk losing everything because of him?'

And then the heat was in my face and I couldn't stop myself. Tears filled my eyes and I dashed them away. 'It's time you knew what it felt like,' I said. I felt like my heart was bursting. 'To know what it feels like to lose everything.'

'Do you think I don't know that?' she said. 'You know nothing about me!'

She was such an idiot. 'Oh I do, Gemma. I know everything.'

'So you know that your husband – your own husband – has been blackmailing me?' she said. 'You know that?'

I shook my head. 'You had that coming to you,' I said. 'It's what you deserve.' I drew myself up then and pushed my shoulders back. 'And he hardly did anything anyway.' I moved away a little, my eyes still on hers. 'Unlike you.'

'Unlike me?' she shrieked, as though she were blameless. 'What have I done?'

I was cold now; the heat had left my face. Left my body. I could feel my hands shaking. 'You've no idea, have you?' I said.

'What?'

I took a deep breath. 'You've no idea who I am.'

'What?' she said again, and to be fair, she looked completely bewildered. 'Of course I know who you are!'

'No, you don't,' I said. 'I'd always wondered if you knew.' I drew my shoulders back and looked her straight in the eye. 'I'm Alex's sister.'

43

Gemma

Fifteen years ago

It's odd the dreams you have sometimes; they're so powerful, so vivid, and yet the second you wake up, they vanish, no matter how hard you try to cling on to them. How does that happen? And other times they morph into reality and you find you're no longer dreaming. You're living in a nightmare.

When I woke that night at the party, my body was heavy and exhausted. My face was buried deep in the pillows and the smell of laundry was so intense I had to lift my head up to breathe fresh air. As I opened my eyes all I could see was darkness, and for a drunken moment I didn't know where I was. Then I remembered. This was Alex's room. I'd fallen asleep here while the party was going on downstairs.

I thought I'd go and find Lauren and realized I couldn't. The heaviness on my body wasn't exhaustion. It wasn't that I was too tired to move.

I *couldn't* move.

Something was on top of me, weighing me down. Something heavy. I tried to take a breath and couldn't. Then my legs

were suddenly wide apart and something was moving inside me in hard, vicious stabs. I tried to turn but I couldn't. I wanted to shout but something was pressing down on my chest. I felt like I was being buried into the mattress, as though all the air in my lungs had been pushed out of me.

My arms were dead by my sides. I tried to move them, but couldn't.

And then I heard the breathing. A rasping breath, hot on the back of my neck, just beside my ear. I wrenched my head away and the weight lifted slightly.

This time when I tried to turn, the pressure lifted completely and I gasped in air. I struggled to sit up and a blanket was thrown over me, over my face. In the pitch black I heard someone moving around, then the sound of a zip. I tried to push the blanket off me but then another one was thrown on top of me and I was tangled up in them.

I was still drunk, still unable to think straight. Panicking, I tore at the blankets, but everything was dark and I couldn't find a way out. And then I heard the bedroom door open and the landing light shone briefly in the room. I turned towards the light, ripping the blankets away from my head. In the second it took for the door to quietly shut again, I saw someone tall and dark-haired, wearing a T-shirt with *The Coral* on the back, hurrying from the room.

I fell back onto the bed.

Alex?

After he closed the door, the room was back in darkness. Panicking, I tried to get off the bed, to work out what to do. I couldn't think clearly; couldn't see anything. What had happened? Why was Alex in here? I floundered around in the dark, then remembered there'd been a lamp on in the room when I first lay down; it was on the bedside table. I scrambled over the bed towards it and fumbled for the switch.

In the lamplight I looked at myself in disbelief. My dress was up around my waist and my knickers were on the floor beside the bed. My head was fuzzy from sleep and alcohol and I couldn't think straight.

And then I heard Tom calling from downstairs.

'Gemma? Gemma! The taxi's here!'

I scrambled off the bed and pulled on my knickers. My new sandals were on the floor by the window and quickly I slid them on. I looked around frantically. I hadn't left anything behind.

I ran to the door, wrenched it open, and ran downstairs as fast as I could, my blistered feet rubbing against my sandals.

Tom was waiting for me. 'Lauren's in the taxi,' he said. 'Where were you?'

I shook my head and said nothing. I just wanted to get out of there. Outside I got into the front passenger seat. Lauren was behind me, with Tom next to her. They talked about the party, about how strange it would be to not see people again until they got back from university at Christmas, about how it wasn't long now and how they'd visit each other every weekend. Everything they said was interspersed with kisses.

I leaned my head against the window, feeling it cold against my burning skin. I couldn't think about what had happened to me. I couldn't talk about it. What would I say? So when Lauren spoke to me, I closed my eyes and I heard Tom say, 'She's asleep.' Lauren laughed and said, 'Lightweight.'

The journey seemed to take hours. My face was pressed against the glass the whole time, each bump in the road punishing me. I didn't cry. I didn't think about what had happened. I couldn't. I didn't feel safe enough to let myself do that.

When we arrived at Lauren's house, Tom took the money her mum had left us in the hall and paid the taxi driver. I went straight into the spare room, where I'd slept so many times

before. I couldn't take off my clothes. I didn't want to look at myself. The curtains were drawn and the room was almost dark, with only the faint glimmer of the light from the lamppost outside shining through. I sat on the floor by the wall, rested my head on my knees and hugged my legs tightly.

Someone went into the bathroom across the landing from my room, and just the sound of them shutting the door was enough to make me leap up. I stood panting in the dark, ready to scream. And then I heard Lauren say, 'Sorry!' and realized she must have woken her mum. As my breathing slowed I realized that of course it was only Lauren. It wasn't anything to worry about.

I sat down by the wall again and stayed there until six, when the sun was rising. Then I picked up my bag, holding my house key tightly in my hand, and tiptoed downstairs. Once outside in the cool morning air, I ran the half-mile to my own house on the same estate, focusing only on my feet as the blisters rubbed and burst with each step I took.

Safely home, I ripped off all my clothes, put them into a plastic bag and buried them at the bottom of the bin outside. I wouldn't wear them again. Then I stood in the shower, scrubbing my body until it was raw, not daring to look down at the blood that coloured the water pink as it swirled down the drain.

I still didn't cry. Perhaps if I had, things would have been different.

44

Gemma

Present day

Monday, August 14

I took a step backwards, unable to believe what I'd heard.

'Alex's sister?'

'Yes, Alex Clarke's sister. You remember him, don't you?'

I nodded. 'Yes, of course I remember him.' How could I not? 'But you don't look anything like him. And your surname's Thomas. Is that your married name?'

'It's my mother's name. Her maiden name. When my parents divorced, she and I changed our names. We didn't want anything to do with my dad.'

'Why didn't you tell me you were his sister?'

She laughed. 'Like you would have given me the job!'

I thought back to the application she'd written. She'd seemed so enthusiastic and her qualifications were great. She hadn't used Alex's address, I knew that. I would never forget that address, even now, fifteen years later. 'Did you know who I was when you applied for the job?'

'Of course I did.' She gave me a scornful look. 'I'm not stupid.'

'But why? Why would you want to come and work for me?'

She said nothing, just stood staring at me, her knuckles white as she gripped the clipboard.

And then I realized just what was going on. 'Are you in on this with David Sanderson?' Her sneer only reminded me that I didn't know his name. 'Or whatever he's really called.'

'You needed to be taught a lesson,' she said.

'I did? Why? What have I done?'

'Did you really think,' she said, then stopped. I could see tears in her eyes. She began again. 'Did you really think that you could ruin my brother's life and get away with it?'

'But Rachel,' I said, 'I was raped. Alex raped me.'

Even though it happened years ago, I still struggled to say those words.

'Don't you dare say that! He wouldn't do that.' Her voice broke. 'You know what he was like – how could you think he'd rape someone?'

'I was there,' I said. 'I was the one it happened to.'

'Nothing happened!' she shrieked. 'You lied to the police and Alex was arrested. And then you said you wouldn't testify. After doing all that damage! You're the reason Alex died. You're the reason my dad left. And it's because of you that my mum died. Everything bad that's happened to my family has happened because of you.'

She stood in front of me, red-faced and triumphant, but all I could think about were those years after the party where I'd had no self-respect and had put myself in dodgy situations with men I didn't even know, stupidly thinking that initiating things with them would mean I was in control. It had taken a therapist to show me that I was no more in control with them than I'd been that night at the party. If I hadn't

had that help, I don't know what would have happened to me. And even now, I knew that my problems with Joe were because I couldn't assert myself. I couldn't do it that night at the party and I hadn't been able to do it since.

My mother was on my side – she had been every day of my life – but she'd worried that I wouldn't be believed. I refused to testify because of that, and now, fifteen years on, I could see that she was right.

45

Rachel

Last year

It was on the night of my mother's funeral that I decided to take revenge on Gemma.

After he kissed me, David said, 'Come on, Coco,' and we drank our cocktails in a hurry and left the bar. We were at the Albert Dock in Liverpool and there was a hotel facing us. I said, 'Serendipity,' and he laughed and kissed me again. Within minutes we were in bed. When he discovered it was my first time, he was so tender. So gentle. I hadn't dreamed it would be like that.

Much later, he rang room service for drinks and we sat out on the balcony overlooking the river, watching as the lights popped on along the dockside. The sky was growing dark, the breeze was fresh, and though it was chilly and there was the threat of rain in the air, there was nowhere I'd rather have been. Being with David felt like I'd been given the chance of a new life, as though I was reborn, not as something new, but as the girl I'd been before it all went wrong. Before I lost my family. Now it was like my family had returned to me. When he put his arms around me, I felt sheltered. Protected. Something I hadn't

experienced in such a long time. Like family, it didn't take long to catch up with what we'd done in the years since we'd last met.

I knew at the time that he'd gone to Bristol University when Alex went to Oxford, and my mum had heard from someone that he'd gone abroad to work after his degree. Philadelphia, she'd said. He'd married someone there. I hadn't known the marriage had ended until he told me that afternoon. He told me a bit about it then, though he seldom mentioned it later. He told me he hadn't known her well on their wedding day, that he was in love with her until they'd been married a few months, when he really got to know her. He said that was when he knew it was over.

Of course I didn't have much to contribute when it came to my past. I was so much younger than he was, but I'd hardly done anything anyway.

'So you had to be with your mum the whole time?' he asked in disbelief. 'But aren't you working?'

'I haven't worked for over a year,' I said. 'I'll be looking for jobs now, of course. When she became ill – well, when she admitted to being ill – I had to stay at home with her. At least she couldn't drink as much then.'

'She had a drink problem?' He frowned. 'I don't remember that. Alex never told me.'

You can't believe how good it was to have a conversation where Alex's name was dropped in as though he were still here. Ever since he'd died I'd wanted to share my memories of him with someone who knew him too. My mother talked about him incessantly. If I spoke, she just spoke louder. She wanted me to be there, but only as an audience for her monologue. If I talked about him, I could predict the time it would take for her to find a bottle to comfort her. It was her loss, that was made clear, not mine. She said I was too young to remember him properly and that only a mother knows true love. Friends

avoided talking about him, in case I got upset, and of course my dad went after a year or so, so there was nobody, until I met up with David again, to whom I could talk about Alex. Not about what happened, so much, not about his death, but just passing remarks about him, about what he liked to do, things he'd said.

'It started after Alex died. She hadn't really drunk that much before. I'd never noticed it, anyway, but then I was only young. But afterwards . . . She became a full-on alcoholic. Within a couple of years I couldn't ask anyone home. I couldn't go to sleepovers; I was too worried that she'd fall down the stairs or choke on her own vomit.'

He hugged me. 'That sounds really tough.'

'I think she'd known for years that she was ill. She kept it from me.' Tears sprang to my eyes. 'I think she just wanted to die. She didn't tell me anything was wrong until that last year. I'd noticed she'd lost weight, but then she'd been thin for years. She wasn't interested in eating.'

'I had so many meals at your house when I was a kid,' said David. 'She was a great cook.'

'All that went straight away,' I said. 'I can hardly remember it now.'

But I could. If I let myself, I could remember walking home with my friends that last year of junior school, the summer before Alex died. I'd say goodbye to them at the end of my road and run up to my house. I'd come panting into the kitchen, my face red, excited to see my mum, and I'd find her listening to the radio, our dinner in the oven. She'd look up when she heard me at the door and I'd run over to hug her. I can still remember my face against hers, feel the softness of her cheeks, smell her perfume. I'd sit with her and have a biscuit and some milk while we waited for my dad and Alex to come home. We wouldn't eat dinner until they were there. And when Alex came in, she'd leap up to greet him. I noticed that even as a child: I ran to her and she ran to him.

He grimaced. 'And your dad couldn't help?'

'He'd gone by then.' I think I made it clear I didn't want to talk about him again.

'That's terrible, Rachel. Really terrible.'

'I still miss Alex,' I said. 'Every day.'

'I know, babe. I do too.'

'And do you know what?' I said. 'There's one person to blame for this.' I jabbed my finger at his chest. 'Just. One. Person.'

'Your mum?'

'No,' I scoffed. 'She couldn't help it. She just had one long fourteen-year breakdown.'

'You don't mean Alex, do you?'

'No.' I drank some more wine. I'd had too much to drink but it was one of those days when it seemed I couldn't have enough. 'I mean Gemma Brogan.'

'Who? Not *that* Gemma?'

I saw his hand grip his glass and I knew he was thinking of her, the woman who'd ruined my brother's life.

'Yes, the one who accused Alex.'

'Don't worry,' he said. 'I haven't forgotten her. How could I? But I thought she was Gemma Taylor.'

'She was. Brogan is her married name. I've been keeping tabs on her. She's married now, with a little boy. She's got a business in Chester and she's doing very well for herself.' I poured myself another drink. 'Very well indeed. But not for much longer.'

He gave me a questioning look.

'I intend to do something about it,' I said.

He laughed. 'What? What are you planning?'

Full of bravado, I blurted out, 'I want to stop her happy little life in its tracks, just as she stopped Alex's.' I saw him looking at me and stopped, embarrassed. 'Sorry, you must think I'm mad.'

'Are you kidding?' he said. 'Alex died because of her lies. That bitch needs bringing down.' He raised his glass and clinked it against mine. 'Count me in, Coco.'

46

Gemma

Present day

For a moment neither of us said anything; her accusations rang in the air. I could hear our breathing, high and fast in the empty room. We were both panting, both furious.

Rachel's face was so pale. She was staring at me as though she couldn't believe what she'd said. I'd never really thought about the impact this had had on other people. Just one action, one accusation, and wham, everyone's life changes.

'You'll have to forgive me if I see things differently,' I said. 'I'm sorry Alex died.' For the first time since it happened I realized it was true. I wondered whether his death had been an accident, or whether he'd felt guilty because of what he'd done. Whether he was too ashamed to live. 'Whatever happened, for him to be in such a bad way that he took his own life is really awful.'

Her mouth twisted and I knew she couldn't speak. I wouldn't have been able to either. I took a new bottle of water from my bag and passed it to her. She hesitated and I thought she'd refuse, but she took it from me and drank some of it.

'I'm not sure he meant to do it,' she said heavily, 'but what

do I know? I was only eleven at the time. It was as though I didn't know anything any more. But my mum . . . well, she thinks . . . she *thought* he'd done it on purpose.' She glared at me. 'You have no idea what it was like for me after he died. It was all she could talk about. All she could think about.'

'You can't blame her,' I said quietly. 'He was her child.'

'And so was I! And I was alive and needed her. And she begrudged that. Hated me for it. Every single day I was made aware of the fact that I wasn't him.'

'Don't think that, Rachel,' I said. 'Of course she didn't hate you.'

'What do you know? You weren't there. I was, day after day, with all her memories.' She grimaced and I could tell she was trying not to cry. 'What about *my* memories? I learned to say nothing, though. There was no point.'

She took some tissues from her bag and scrubbed at her face. Rachel's make-up was usually perfect, her hair glossy and smooth. Now mascara was smeared over her face, her hair tangled where she'd knotted it with her hands. She clutched the tissues now and crouched down by the wall. Suddenly she looked exhausted.

'Why don't you just go? Leave the keys and I'll lock up,' she said. 'I need a few minutes.'

I shook my head, too scared to leave her like this. 'I'll wait with you.'

She started to speak but gave up. Her head on her knees, she started to cry in earnest. I sat down beside her. For a long time we said nothing. When her tears had stopped and her breathing was back to normal, I said, 'So all these things, these things that David's been doing . . . they were to punish me for Alex's death?'

'If you hadn't lied,' she said, 'if you hadn't said it was Alex, then he'd still be alive. He'd be in his thirties now, like you. He'd probably have a family. A good job. Like you.' She looked

at me, anger and guilt on her face. 'Why should you have those things when he doesn't?'

'And David? What kind of man would do those things to a woman he doesn't know?'

'A man who lost his friend. His best friend. He's Alex's best friend. Was. We became close last year, when my mum died. We married not long after that. He's the only one who understands.'

I frowned. 'Was he at school with us? I don't remember him.'

'No, he didn't go to the same school as Alex. He lived a few miles away; they'd always gone to different schools. They played sport together. Hockey. That's how they met.'

'Whose idea was it that he did those things?'

She gave me a proud, truculent look. 'Mine. I wanted to pay you back.'

I sighed. She clearly wasn't going to listen to me tell her how my life had changed because of Alex. How overnight I'd gone from a quiet, confident girl to someone who I couldn't recognize at times. I couldn't tell her how I still longed to be the girl I used to be, the girl who wasn't scared of shadows, who could sleep in the dark.

'You don't deserve the life you have,' she said.

That much was true. I didn't deserve any of the things that she and David had done to me.

'You realize you've both committed criminal offences?' I asked. 'I've spoken to the police. They've told me which laws you've broken.'

She looked at me, astonished. 'We haven't broken any laws!'

'Are you joking? You think threatening to post photos on a voyeur site is legal?'

She looked at me as though I'd gone mad. 'What are you talking about? A voyeur site? I don't even know what that is!'

'Neither did I until your husband sent me a link to it. It's a

site where men post photos and videos of women without the women knowing. Photos of them naked or asleep. Doing intimate things.' I swallowed. 'You wouldn't believe some of the things on that site. I don't know how it's not closed down.'

'Photos?' she said. 'You mean the photo of him kissing you outside your hotel room?'

So she knew about that. And then it dawned on me. I had a dim memory of turning when I reached my room and seeing someone standing at the far end of the corridor. 'You were there? At the hotel?'

She was pale but nodded. 'That's not against the law.'

'And was it you that photographed me outside my room?'

I could see shame in her face. 'I wanted your husband to think you were having an affair.'

'But you sent it to me.'

She said nothing, just stared out in front of her, and I knew she'd been prepared to send it to Joe.

'And so was it you, Rachel, who took the photos of me naked?'

Her head swung round. 'What? What are you talking about?'

You know sometimes you hear someone speak and you recognize the ring of truth. That was what happened then. I didn't want to believe her, but I had to.

'The naked photos,' I said again.

'Naked? You had your green dress on. Don't be stupid, you were in the corridor! How could you be naked?'

'I don't know,' I said. 'I don't remember.'

'I don't believe you! Where are they? Show me them!'

'They were on Instagram and he withdrew them. I don't have a copy of them and I've deleted my account now anyway.'

'That's convenient!' I could hear the cogs whirring in her head. 'Where were you when these photos were taken?'

'In my hotel room. On my bed.'

She was silent for a long time then. When she looked up at me, her face was pale and strained. 'Why did you let him do that?'

'Do what?'

'Go into your hotel room with you.' She was shaking. 'Take the photos.'

I stared at her. 'I didn't let him do anything! I didn't know anything about them until they were sent to me. I don't remember anything of that night after I got back to my room.'

'He wasn't meant to go into your room,' she said at last. 'I took the photo of you both outside your door and went back to our hotel and waited for him. He wasn't long after me, perhaps half an hour. He said he'd stopped to have a drink at the bar.'

'So you didn't know he'd changed my underwear?'

Her head shot up. 'What?'

'Or that he took my knickers home with him?'

She looked horrified.

'I woke up in different underwear from the ones I wore to bed,' I said. 'The underwear I was wearing that night had gone.'

'Gone?'

'He sent it to my home address a few days ago.'

I could see her mind racing, trying to make sense of it all.

'I don't remember anything after I got back to my hotel room,' I repeated. And then it dawned on me. Finally. What an idiot I'd been. 'He drugged me, didn't he?'

47

Gemma

'No,' said Rachel. 'No. You were drunk. Really, really drunk. I saw you, don't forget. You nearly fell over when you got out of the lift at the hotel.'

It was as though she wasn't there. 'He must have drugged me,' I said. 'I wondered why I couldn't remember anything.'

'Gemma, you walked up to your hotel room all right. You weren't drugged.' Her voice was desperate. 'You drank two bottles of wine!'

'No, I didn't! We ordered two bottles, but I didn't drink all that. I wouldn't be able to. I don't drink much, Rachel. I haven't drunk that much for years.' I couldn't look at her. 'The next morning I felt awful. And yes, I know I would have felt bad just from the alcohol. I would have expected a hangover. But I've never drunk so much that I couldn't remember what I'd done the night before. Never.'

'Except when you were eighteen,' she said spitefully. 'You did that night.'

'Do you really think I can't remember what happened that night?'

She flushed.

'But the night I was in London ... I can't remember

228

anything after I left the restaurant. I paid the bill, I remember that. David said his room was on the tenth floor. We went up in the lift and I nearly fell over getting out. And I remember when I got to my door he kissed me and I turned away and I saw someone there.' I paused, remembering. 'How did I not know that was you?' I knew the answer, though. I was completely out of it.

'You were drunk,' she said.

'I've told you; I don't drink like that. Or I haven't since my early twenties, anyway. I had a few years after . . . after I left school when I hated myself. I drank then, just to forget. But now, now I don't see the point. And I can't remember any of it. It's not as though I remember going into my room, brushing my teeth or anything like that. I can't remember a single thing until I woke up the next morning.'

We sat quietly. I was trying to recall what had happened that night; a glance at Rachel told me that she was wondering the same thing.

'So when did you get the photos?' she asked. 'The other ones.' She grimaced. 'Not the one through the post.'

I stood up and went to the door to fetch my bag. Inside was my mobile, and I sat back down next to Rachel and opened my e-mails.

'Last Saturday. Here's the e-mail with the voyeur address. I'll open the link.'

She quickly shook her head. 'No.'

I ignored her. 'You need to know what you're dealing with.'

I opened the link and showed it to her. She scrolled down past video stills of women in the shower, on the tube, at work. She paused at a photo of a woman who could be seen through the opaque glass of her bathroom window and closed the screen, a look of disgust on her face.

'I hope you don't think I had anything to do with that.'

229

I didn't know anything any more.

She looked down at the e-mail address that had been used to send the link. 'I don't recognize this.'

'I wrote back,' I said. 'It bounced. It must have been set up just to send that. And there's another, too, from a different address.' I opened the e-mail containing the timer gif and showed her. The counter had stopped at 00:00:00.

'I don't get it,' she said. 'What is it?'

'It was a timer.'

She looked startled. 'What do you mean?'

'It was ticking when I opened the e-mail. It was counting down to midnight.'

Realization dawned on her. 'What happened at midnight?' she whispered.

'I didn't stay to find out,' I said. 'It was the night before Joe and Rory came back and I was on my own in the house. I thought someone was going to break in. I went to a hotel.'

She winced. 'I didn't know anything about this.'

'Was he with you that night?'

'He's usually with me. Which night?'

'Last Tuesday.'

She nodded. 'He was at home with me.'

'Were you awake at midnight? Did he do anything? Was he using his phone or iPad or something?'

She looked away. 'No. He wasn't doing anything.'

One glance at her was all it took to know exactly what he was doing at midnight. I shuddered at the thought of him having sex with her while he knew I was terrified something was about to happen to me. He was getting a kick out of this.

'So you met David again after your mum died?'

She kept her eyes averted, but nodded. 'My mum never recovered from Alex's death,' she said. 'She'd always had a problem with depression, but this really tipped her over the edge.'

I thought of Rory and how it would feel to lose him. 'I'd be the same.'

'And nothing seemed to work. She had antidepressants, she had sleeping pills, the lot. None of it made a difference. The house was a shrine to Alex. Photos everywhere, videos running, candles burning. It brought her no comfort. Basically she spent all those years wanting to die, wanting to be with him. And in the end she had breast cancer. By the time she saw the doctor, it had spread to her liver. Apparently she'd found a lump years before and didn't say a word. By the time I realized something was wrong, it was too late.' Her eyes were wet with tears. 'Don't tell me that would have happened if Alex hadn't died.'

'Rachel, I'm really sorry Alex died. I'm sorry you lost your mum, too. But that doesn't change the fact that he raped me.'

'But you withdrew the charge,' she said. 'Why would you do that if you thought he'd done it?'

'I know,' I said. 'I did withdraw it. You know what it was like back then. Well, maybe you don't; you're younger than I am. I'd been to a party; I was drunk. My family were going on holiday the day after the party; we'd been looking forward to it all year. It was supposed to be a celebration. I'd got into university and my parents were so proud of me. I cried the whole holiday and my mum thought I just didn't want to leave home.' I sat for a few minutes, thinking of that holiday, how I'd stayed indoors in the baking heat, scrubbing and scrubbing myself in the shower. 'And then when I got back I told my friend Lauren and she took me to the police station. When my mum and dad found out I'd told the police, they begged me not to take it any further. My dad had been on a jury in a rape trial a few years before. There was a not guilty verdict; he was the only juror who disagreed with it. He was horrified at the way the woman was cross-examined, and he was frightened that would happen to me. He said Alex's defence lawyers would

pull me to pieces.' I met her eyes. 'They would have, too. I would have been destroyed.'

She was quiet, then she said, 'I was eleven when Alex went to Oxford. I remember that New Year, just a few months later. He came home for Christmas but he wouldn't leave the house. And then when he did, a couple of days before New Year, he came home crying. He never told us what happened.'

I turned away. I knew my friend, Lauren, had seen him while she and Tom were out in a pub in town. I hadn't asked what she'd said to him, but I guessed it was pretty brutal.

'The next day he went back to Oxford. The term hadn't started, of course, so I guess there weren't many people around.' She put her head on her knees and wrapped her arms around herself. I could barely hear her. 'On New Year's Eve he phoned my mum and said he was going down to the river. There would be fireworks there, he said. And the next day we got a visit from the police. His body was discovered in the river early the next morning.'

She was crying now and there was nothing I could do to comfort her. I wanted to tell her it wasn't my fault, but there was a dead brother between us. Whatever had happened to me, I hadn't died, though I'd wanted to at times. I made a move to hug her, but she wrenched herself away.

'Don't,' she said. 'Don't touch me.'

A shift in the light in the room made me look at my watch. I stood up. 'I'm sorry, Rachel,' I said. 'I'm going to have to go. Joe's got something on at the running club tonight.' I sent him a quick text telling him I'd be five minutes.

She scrambled up and picked up her bag off the breakfast bar, then hesitated. 'Gemma, what are you going to do?' I said nothing, and once again she broke the silence. 'Are you going to tell the police?'

'I have to. You know that.'

'Can you just give me some time? He wasn't meant to go

that far. It's just . . . if you do tell the police, will you let me know in advance, so I can be prepared?'

I laughed. 'What, you want me to give you both time to get your story straight?'

'No! I don't want to be with him when he's arrested. I know I need to speak to them. I know I shouldn't have done those things. It's just . . . I think he could be trouble if he's confronted. I don't want to be there.'

Something about the way she said that made me ask, 'Has he hurt you, Rachel?'

She shook her head, but I wasn't convinced.

'Don't say anything to him about this, will you?' I said. 'Keep yourself safe.'

She stared at me then, her eyes brimming with tears, then she turned, her shoulders hunched, and hurried to the lift.

48

Rachel

I checked my phone as soon as I left the building and saw that David had sent a text saying he'd be late coming home. He was waiting for a call from a client and couldn't leave the office until he'd spoken to them. I looked at the time of his message; he'd sent it three minutes before. Quickly I sent a reply, Will miss you, sweetheart xx, and breathed a sigh of relief. He hated it if I didn't reply quickly. I'd had a warning from Gemma about using my mobile in the office when I'd been working for her a few weeks, and after that I had to tell him I couldn't just answer the phone whenever he wanted. Actually it was a relief she'd warned me; I was finding it stressful having to respond when I was meant to be working.

'I'm always worried something's happened to you, Coco!' he'd say. 'I can't help it; I love you so much, and if you don't reply I think the worst.'

It was romantic, really, I knew that, but I wanted to be seen as a professional, and more than once in that first month at work I'd looked up from replying to see clients exchanging glances. I'd make up an excuse, but I knew it sounded pathetic. Once I'd been warned, though, he backed off. The last thing either of us wanted was for me to lose my job.

I was so glad he was going to be home late. When I glanced in the rearview mirror I realized how shocked he'd be to see me like that. My eyes were pink and all my make-up had gone. My skin was shiny and my hair looked damp and bedraggled. I winced. I'd have to get back quickly and get into the shower before David got home.

It was rush hour now and the traffic was congested on the route home. My mind was full of the things Gemma had told me. Voyeur sites. Her underwear. Naked photographs.

I wanted to disbelieve her. I wanted to be able to laugh at her and tell her she was mad. That if those things had actually happened to her – and after all, where was the proof? – David had nothing to do with it.

I couldn't.

None of this really surprised me. Not really. There was a dark side to David; I knew that. I hadn't been married to him for a year yet, but I knew what he was like. He liked control. He liked secrets.

He liked to mess with people's minds.

Once I was home, I got straight into the shower and washed my hair and face, to cover up the fact that I'd cried away my make-up. I'd just stepped out of the shower when I heard David come into the flat and call my name.

My body went into full alert then. I could tell, just from the way he'd spoken, that he wasn't happy about something.

'Hi, David,' I called.

He came into the bathroom and stood in the doorway, watching me.

'How come you're having a shower?' he asked.

'I was so hot today,' I said. 'I just couldn't cool down at work. And I've been stuck in traffic for ages.'

He said nothing and I knew he wasn't convinced.

'And Sophie had styled her hair in a different way,' I said. 'I thought I'd have a go at doing it myself.'

Sophie was always safe ground with David. He found her absolutely no threat at all.

'I would have thought you'd be cooking dinner,' he said. 'It's nearly seven o'clock.' He smiled at me, but it didn't reach his eyes. 'How long does a guy have to wait round here for something to eat?'

'We've got chicken and salad in the fridge,' I said. 'You said last night that that's what you wanted today. I went out to Tesco, remember?'

He stood watching while I put on my robe, then walked behind me into the kitchen.

'Are you okay?' he asked. 'Your eyes look pink. Has someone upset you?'

Yes, you have, I wanted to say, but instead I said, 'No, I squirted shampoo in them when I was washing my hair.' I smiled up at him. 'I'll put some make-up on after dinner, sweetheart. You won't notice it then.'

David was the sort of man who liked women to look immaculate. I think he thought it reflected on him somehow. When Gemma had taken him out to view the properties that day, he'd bitched about her all evening, talking about the state of her car – apparently Rory had left his mark on the back seat – and the fact that she looked tired and didn't have much make-up on. He kept saying how unprofessional she appeared, though really she just looked like any other working woman. Her flaws needled him; I never knew why.

Tonight he seemed on edge. I wondered whether there was a problem at work, but I didn't dare ask. He'd already fallen out with a female colleague who'd picked him up on a mistake he'd made. Apparently she'd been promoted beyond her capacity and would soon be found out for the charlatan she was.

I'd heard quite a bit about her for the last few weeks; I used to want to write to her and ask her to quit, just for my sake.

We sat and watched television – there was a film he'd been wanting to watch on Netflix – and I brought him a bottle of beer and then another. He asked me to get him some whisky while I was in the kitchen and refused to pause the film, so I missed a crucial scene. I knew that appeased him in some way and I wondered what I was meant to have done to him. When someone is like this, you spend all your time trying to second-guess them and it is really, really tiring. Yet I massaged the back of his neck when he complained it was sore from driving, and I laughed as he told me about a guy at work who'd made a fool of himself. All the while I knew something was wrong. I would probably never know what it was; I was used to that.

At ten o'clock I was ready for bed. David said he was going to stay up for a while; he was looking at something on his iPad, and he put it face down when I kissed him good night. I was used to this and normally never let myself think about what he was looking at, but that night as I pressed my lips against his cheek I thought of the website that Gemma had told me about. And though I smiled and said good night, all I felt was disgust. Disgust with him and disgust with myself for putting up with it.

49

Gemma

Once again I got home to find Joe fuming because he thought he was going to be late for his running group.

'You won't be late if you go now,' I said, tired of taking the blame for this all the time. There was an early-morning group he could run with, but in his mind the evening one was more convenient. It wasn't, and I was tired of explaining that every week.

'What's for dinner, Mummy?' asked Rory once Joe had left.

'Haven't you eaten yet, sweetheart? It's getting late.'

'I wasn't hungry before,' he said, sitting at the kitchen island with a hopeful look on his face. 'Can I have a buffet for my dinner?'

I laughed and hugged him. We'd been to a wedding a while ago and Rory couldn't believe his luck when he saw the buffet. He spent most of the afternoon going up there with his plate and choosing what he wanted to eat. I opened the fridge and was so glad I'd remembered to order an online shop to be delivered that morning.

Quickly I prepared a few snacks for Rory, and after he'd eaten I let him beat me in a dozen games of Snap, but all the while my mind was racing with what Rachel had told me.

I had believed her when she'd said she didn't know that David had been in my hotel room that night. She was married to him, so why would she want him to do that? And if she knew I was drugged, she would have been there, just to be sure of what he'd done.

I shuddered. Had she been there? Was she lying to me about that? But then I thought of the look on her face when she saw the voyeur website. She wasn't that good an actress; that was true disgust.

While Rory splashed around in the bath, in his own imaginary world, I sat on the bathroom floor and wondered whether she'd be able to act normal tonight, to pretend nothing had happened. I knew I wouldn't be able to do that.

I thought about what she'd done. She'd started work for me without explaining who she was. That wasn't a crime. She might have passed my home address to David, but it was available online anyway. I wondered about the phone calls I'd received at home, where all I could hear was silence. Was that him? Or even her? I'd given him my mobile number and my e-mail address myself, but everyone at work had my home landline number just in case. And then in London she'd taken my photo, but she hadn't done anything with it, though sending it to me might indicate blackmail was intended. I had a feeling Joe would have received a copy of it one day, but he hadn't so far. What had she done, exactly?

I wanted to talk to Joe, but I worried that instead of thinking about what Rachel had done, he'd think about what I'd done. I'd lied repeatedly to him. Did it matter that I was being set up? All he would think about were my lies. I thought of Caitlin and yearned to talk to her too, the way we used to back in the day. When I met and married Joe, I was so happy. It was as though my family was complete. I knew, though, that no matter how hard she tried, her allegiance would always be to him. In marrying Joe, I'd lost my best friend, in a way.

Of course it wasn't like that really. She'd come round and it would be just like the old days, and we could sprawl on the sofas and chat and everything would be fine. Great, even. She was happy for me to criticize Joe as long as it made her laugh, as long as it was gentle and said with love. But how could I talk to her about a man in my hotel room and the lies I'd told Joe over and over again? Just that day I'd had a text from her saying, Ugh, you saw a mouse? I can't believe you didn't call me! and I thought, *Well, that's because there was no mouse,* but what I actually wrote was It was awful. Don't make me talk about it. Lies upon lies.

After Rory was out of the bath and had been read to, I went downstairs for something to eat. I couldn't face cooking anything then, but I knew Joe would be starving when he came back from his run. I made up a plate of sandwiches and put together a fruit salad, then sat in the living room, thinking about Rachel and how she'd got on that night. Had she spoken to David about it? Lost her temper over him taking things too far? Or maybe he'd noticed a difference in her and wouldn't rest until he found out what was bothering her. And was she really innocent? Perhaps I'd been wrong to believe her when she'd said she knew nothing about the photos and the website.

I grabbed my laptop, went into Incognito mode, and checked the voyeur site, scrolling through it, trying to both see whether I was on it and not look at the other women. My phone beeped, startling me. It was Joe.

Hey Gem, mind if I go for a drink with the boys? xx

Immediately I replied, Of course not. If he stayed out, I could stay on the voyeur site without worrying about him noticing and thinking I was a pervert. I added, Have a great night xxx

After another ten minutes on that site, though, I felt disgusting, and on impulse I reactivated my Facebook account. For old times' sake, I looked up Lauren's page. She and I had

been Facebook friends for a long time, but I'd hidden her notifications after a while. She had twins a few years ago and would post on there hourly, updating the world on their achievements. But that night I was thinking about the past, thinking about Alex and the party, so I looked at her page to see what she was up to nowadays.

She must have noticed that I was online, because within ten minutes a message came up.

Hi Gemma! How are you? It's ages since we spoke x

Hi Lauren, I replied. Great to hear from you. I was just thinking about the old days.

Oh me too, she wrote. Especially after seeing Jack's photos. Can't believe how young we look!

Jack?

Jack Howard. Remember him? That geeky boy who took Business Studies in school. He's quite good-looking now – I should've gone out with him when I had the chance! He's put photos up of that trip to London we went on, remember?

I thought back. Jack Howard. That was a name from the past. He'd had a crush on Lauren, but she hadn't had time for anyone except Tom.

I hadn't kept in touch with anybody from school. Even my friendship with Lauren had faded pretty quickly. I'd wanted to put that part of my life behind me, to start again, and in those days, before social media was so popular, it was easy to lose touch. When I met Caitlin, she easily replaced the friendship I'd had with Lauren, and although I knew that was unfair, I think Lauren was relieved by it too. By the time she married Tom and they moved to Australia, our friendship was reduced to Christmas and birthday cards.

I searched for Jack on Facebook. His profile was locked down, so I sent a friend request and went back to chat to Lauren.

We talked for a while, but it was difficult, really. I hardly

241

knew her now. I didn't know her friends, had never met her children. In a way, though, she was living the life I'd thought I'd lead when I went to university. I'd thought I'd emigrate; go as far away from home as I could. The thought of bumping into people from school for the rest of my life had horrified me. Even though my name hadn't been in the press, everyone had known. I knew there had been reunions over the years and normally I would have loved that, loved to have gone back and reminisced with old friends, reliving our youth and celebrating new achievements. I doubted I could have done that even if Alex had lived, but once he'd died, he was deified.

50

Gemma

I'd gone to bed by the time Jack accepted my friend request on Facebook. Joe was still out, clearly making the most of his late pass.

As soon as I found he'd accepted me, I went to search his photos. He was surprisingly organized and his albums were clearly labelled. I opened *Term 1, School* and there we all were. I found Lauren with her long blonde hair standing next to me. That morning we'd both straightened our hair; it had taken us ages and we'd both burned ourselves. We were laughing at Tom. My heart thumped at the sight of myself then, aged sixteen. Contrary to everything I'd thought about myself, my skin looked smooth, my hair shone, and I was much, much thinner than I remembered.

Alex was in that first album. Unlike Lauren and me, he wasn't taking any notice of the camera at all. There were photos of him standing for class rep, of him playing football, and of him lying asleep along three chairs in the canteen, surrounded by hundreds of students. One photo was a close-up. He was doing an experiment in a science lab and the photo showed him looking at the results of a test tube, his

expression thoughtful and clever. The photo was used later for the school's prospectus and he was overheard saying he was actually thinking about what he'd have for lunch rather than the results of the experiment.

I lay back in bed and looked at the photos of him. He looked so young. There was nothing predatory about him in those images, yet he'd come into a room where I was sleeping and he'd shut the door and turned off the lamps and he'd raped me, before leaving like a thief in the night. He stole something that night. I was never the same again.

There must have been twenty or thirty albums there. I was just looking through the photos to see whether I recognized anyone when I heard the key turn in the front door. Joe was home.

It took him about half an hour to shower and get into bed and tell me all the exciting things that the running club were up to. Given that I didn't know many of the people he was talking about, I struggled at times to keep track of what he was on about, but I let him talk and talk until eventually his breathing slowed down and finally I knew he was asleep. I got out of bed to go to the bathroom and he didn't stir. He was lying on his side, facing away from me, so I was able to prop myself up on my pillows and open my iPad again.

I could see on Facebook that Jack was online. I looked at the time – it was after midnight. Quickly I typed a message:

Hi, sorry it's late, just wanted to say hello. I was at Wirral School with you – I was Gemma Taylor then. I was Lauren's friend, remember?

I was nervous about his response. He'd been a friend of Alex's – how would he react to me now, after everything that had happened? Just a couple of minutes later a response popped up.

Hi Gemma! Nice to hear from you.

How're things? I asked. Just looking through some of

the photos you've posted - brought back so many memories.

While I waited for him to reply, I flicked through more of them. There were so many people I hadn't thought about in years.

It must be tough for you to look back, he replied.

I stared at the screen. Did that mean he believed me? I'd always thought everyone would have been on Alex's side. Facebook hadn't been around then, thank God, but I knew there would have been a lot of speculation and guessed I wouldn't have come out of it well. He was far more popular than I was at school. That was why I'd rarely gone home in the years following the party; I felt protected from the gossip when I was hundreds of miles from home.

Jack hadn't waited for a reply. He sent another message: Time's gone so fast. You and Lauren look great in your photos. I was badly in need of a makeover!

I laughed, relieved. It seemed he didn't want to discuss it any more than I did. If you knew the effort we went to every single day. I sent that message, then steeled myself and asked: Jack, do you have photos from the party? The party when we got our results?

I held my breath.

Are you sure you want to look at them? I thought it was better I didn't put them up here.

I hesitated. I knew what he meant and didn't want to explain myself. It's OK. I do want to look at them. That was a great night until it all went wrong. I wanted to see what I could remember about it.

There was a five-minute wait then, and I thought maybe he'd gone to bed without logging off, but then he replied:

Yeah, I have loads from that night. I don't have time to go through them and sort out which you might want. I'll stick them on Dropbox if you like.

That would be great, I replied quickly, relieved that I wouldn't have to face comments from old friends who were there. Thanks so much.

I sent him my e-mail address and he replied, Thanks, doing it now.

True to his word, in just a short time I received an e-mail telling me I could view the photos. I had to steel myself to open the album once they were ready to view. I'd never seen any photos from the party. Photos from other events were always posted on the noticeboard in the common room at school, but of course we'd finished school by the time of the party. Besides, I didn't speak to anyone apart from Lauren in those weeks before we went to university. After a while I saw a therapist every week for a few months, but by the time I'd been with Joe for a while I'd dealt with that period of my life. I thought I'd been successful, but now when I opened the album it all came back to me.

The first photos showed everyone arriving at the party at about seven o'clock, when the sun was low. There was a driveway up to the house, with tall trees either side; the road beyond was hidden from the house. It had been a long, hot summer and we were all tanned from the break. I scrolled through the photos and once again realized how young we looked, and how happy and relaxed we were. We'd all been together for those last two years, though some people had come from other schools, and others, like Lauren and me, had been friends since we were very young. Most of us arrived at the party at the same time; when I got there with Lauren and Tom, there were dozens of cars and taxis dropping students off. Everyone carried bottles of wine or crates of beer. There were shouted warnings from parents as they left, but nobody thought the night would be anything other than a fantastic end to our school days.

The photos then moved into the house, where huge bowls

of punch and bottles of beer filled the kitchen table and countertops. There were photos of people I hadn't thought of for years, happy and animated, talking to friends and drinking. Everyone was drinking.

And then I scrolled down and saw a photo of myself, holding a huge glass that was half empty. I knew it would have been full just minutes earlier. That was the thing we all did, then. There was no finesse, no tasting what we were drinking. The goal was to get drunk.

Lauren was there, too, wearing her little white dress with pink flowers. Mine was identical, though the colours were reversed, with white flowers on a dark pink background. We looked like mirror images and were so pleased with ourselves. We'd been shopping that day for our clothes and had hit the shops early so that we had time to get ready all afternoon.

Scrolling through again, I saw my first photo of Alex at the party. He was in the kitchen and the clock was behind him. It was just after eight P.M. and through the window I could see it was dusk. His face was flushed, his eyes bright. He looked just as he had when I'd seen him play football or when we'd bump into him in a pub in town. We didn't know him, didn't know him to talk to, that is. We couldn't have said he was a friend, except that on that night, of course, everyone was our friend. It was the last time we'd see most of the people from school, and besides, we were drunk. But even on the night of the party we didn't talk to him, though we were happy to stand and listen if he was talking to his friends. We'd seen him as in a different league from us. Looking at the photos again, I could see how hard we were on ourselves.

The next photos were outside, where the fairy lights lit up the trees and the barbecue could be seen smoking in the distance. I don't remember eating anything that night, but every time I smelled a barbecue for years afterwards I'd feel ill. I'd

been able to smell it in the bedroom. As the night grew darker, you could see from our flushed cheeks and stupid grins that we were getting more and more drunk.

I paused and closed my eyes. There were only a few more albums to go. Soon I would see what was happening while I was upstairs. Asleep.

I heard Joe stir behind me and pushed my iPad under the quilt. He moved further into the middle of the bed, nudging me towards the edge. I tried to move him back, but he grunted and turned over. I held the iPad over the edge of the bed, hoping he wouldn't wake and see it, but the drink had seen to it he wouldn't. He flung his arm over mine, trapping me under it.

I clicked the Off button on the iPad and dropped it gently onto the floor. I was about to settle down to sleep, but a glance at the clock told me it was after one A.M. I groaned. I'd have to be up at seven. I snuggled down in bed, pressing my back against Joe. *Or maybe half past.* I reached for my phone to reset the alarm and changed my mind when I saw a text from Rachel.

I need to talk to you. Can you get to work at 8 tomorrow?

51

Gemma

Tuesday, August 15

I wasn't popular with Joe the next morning as I was up and ready to go to work at seven thirty A.M. I shook him awake just before I left.

'Rory will be up soon,' I said. 'I've put a carton of juice and a banana on my side of the bed so he can get in with you and have that, but don't go back to sleep, will you?'

He groaned. 'It's still early! Why are you going in now? The office doesn't open until nine.'

'I've got things I need to do,' I said. 'I couldn't get back to the office last night, so I have to get things ready for the meeting.'

He'd lost interest already.

Rory shot into our bedroom just before I left and I gave him a huge hug. 'Your drink's here, sweetheart, and you can have that banana if you can't wait for breakfast. Dad's still dozing. Don't let him sleep too long, will you?' I winked at him. 'But don't torture him!'

He laughed and I could see he was trying to think up punishments for a sleepy dad. 'Can I go on your iPad?'

'Just for half an hour,' I warned, and set the alarm on it. 'When the alarm goes off, it's time for breakfast.'

I closed down Facebook and deleted my history. The last thing I needed was Rory looking at voyeur sites or photos of me when I was young and drunk. He found the game he wanted to play, then opened his carton and accidentally spilled some of his juice down Joe's back.

When I reached the office at eight A.M., Rachel was waiting for me at her desk. Her face was pale and I wondered if she'd had as little sleep as I'd had that night. Her eyes were red-rimmed and her hands shook on her mug of coffee.

She saw me looking at her and flushed. 'I know, I look awful.'

'You're fine,' I said. 'Tell people you have a cold.'

'In August?'

'Hay fever, then.'

I picked up the coffee she'd made for me and sat down next to her.

'I have something to tell you,' she said. 'Last night.' She swallowed hard. 'Last night I didn't say anything to David, obviously.'

So his name *was* David.

I waited.

'We watched a film on Netflix and he had a few beers.' She grimaced. 'With whisky chasers.'

'Does he drink too much?'

She nodded. 'He does sometimes. There's always an excuse, you know? He's celebrating something or someone's annoyed him . . .'

I wondered what excuse he had for drinking the nights he was terrorizing me. Was that a time for celebration?

'Anyway, last night he was annoyed because I wouldn't have a drink. I was frightened of telling him I knew what had happened, so I wouldn't even have one.'

'Good idea.'

'Anyway, I went to bed before him. I had a shower, said I was tired. He was on his iPad and stayed up for a while. I don't know what he was doing.'

My heart sank. *We'll probably find out in the next day or two.*

'Anyway, I went to bed and fell asleep quite quickly.' She looked away from me and started to fiddle with a pen on my desk. 'Have you ever woken up suddenly when you hear something that you wouldn't pay any attention to when you were awake?' I sat quietly, waiting for her to go on. 'I used to have an alarm clock that made a tiny sound – a little click – a second before the alarm went off. I would always wake up when I heard it.'

I nodded. 'Yes, I know what you mean.'

'Last night I woke up like that. I jumped awake but I didn't know why. It was really hot when I went to bed, and when I woke up, David was getting into bed. He pulled the quilt up over us; I must have kicked it off.' Her face was red now. 'I wear a T-shirt to bed – one of David's. It comes down to here.' She gestured to her thighs. 'When I woke up, it was pulled up around my waist. I didn't think anything of it; I never sleep well when it's really hot, so I thought I must have been kicking around.'

I sat very still, suddenly terrified of what she'd say.

'The thing is, Gemma . . .' She stopped, then looked at the clock and started again, speaking faster this time. 'I began to think about why I'd woken up. I couldn't go back to sleep afterwards; I never can if I wake up really quickly like that. And as I was lying there I was trying to think what had woken me. I hadn't heard David in the bathroom; I can sleep through anything, normally, so even if he'd had a shower it wouldn't disturb me.'

'Maybe you heard your bedroom door open?'

'It wasn't closed. We never close it. No, it wasn't that.'

'The bathroom door?'

She shook her head. 'It wasn't that, either. It doesn't click shut. And we leave the hall light on overnight, so it wasn't as though I heard him switch that off, either.'

Outside the window a bus stopped and I saw Sophie get off and cross the road to go into the corner shop. She'd be here any minute. I could hardly complain about her being early, but I knew we needed more time.

'Sophie will be here in a minute,' I said urgently. 'What do you think it was?'

Her eyes filled with tears. 'I think he was taking photos of me,' she said. 'While I was asleep. I heard the click and that's what woke me. Then he got into bed. He's got one of those lamps that charges up a phone. He plugged his phone into that, then kissed me good night and went to sleep.' She looked really miserable. 'I couldn't sleep.'

'Has he ever taken photos of you before?'

She shook her head. 'No, nothing like that.' There was a pause, and she said, 'Or at least not as far as I'm aware. How would I know, though?'

52

Rachel

Sophie came up to us then and I had to busy myself with the voicemail messages and e-mails, and get ready for the morning meeting. It was hard to concentrate and I could tell from the expression on Gemma's face that she was finding it equally difficult. Brian was back at work and I noticed she passed on the keys from the flats we'd viewed the day before, asking him to take them back to Bill later that day. My face smarted at the memory of that conversation.

I could tell that Gemma wanted to speak to me. She kept looking over and checking where Sophie was, as though she was going to come and talk to me if she got the chance. I kept my eyes averted. I couldn't focus on work and think of everything we'd talked about. I needed to keep my mind off David's activities last night, but now that I'd seen the voyeur site I was terrified that photos of me would end up there. I desperately wanted to check it, and I think that was when I realized what it had been like for Gemma. She'd said that she'd been obsessive about viewing it every day, looking at the new pictures that appeared there hourly, trying to work out if she was on there. I felt sick at the thought of David

doing that to either of us, and I had to force myself to be friendly to him when he sent his regular texts.

Eventually Gemma sent me an e-mail.

Are you feeling OK? Do you need to go home?

I gave a quick look around the office. A young couple were looking at the details of some first-time-buyer properties; otherwise only Sophie was there and she was preoccupied with the coffee machine.

No, I don't want to go home. He's working from home today and I'll end up saying something to him.

Sophie clattered in, bringing drinks for all of us and the biscuit tin.

'What were those flats like yesterday?' she asked me.

I didn't dare meet Gemma's eye. 'They were great, yeah.'

'Ask Brian to take you next time he goes,' Gemma told her. 'Have a good look around before we get tenants in.'

As soon as Sophie was back at her desk, Gemma sent me another message.

You need to say something. Those photos could be anywhere.

Instantly my face became hot. I know.

The clients came over to speak to Gemma then, and I heard them ask whether they could view a house that evening. She called the vendors to arrange it, and then when they'd left the office she took her purse from her bag. 'Sophie, would you do me a huge favour? It's Lucy's daughter's birthday next week. Would you pop out and get her a card and a present? Oh, and some wrapping paper, too.'

Sophie looked delighted. Time out of the office and shopping with someone else's money! She took the money and was gone before Gemma could change her mind.

As soon as the office was empty, Gemma pulled up a chair next to my desk.

'We need to go to the police.' She spoke in a low voice,

even though nobody was around. 'He took those photos of me and now he's taken photos of you. He could be sending them anywhere. It's illegal; you know it is. We need to do something. We need to stop him.'

'I know,' I said. 'But you know it'll get into the press, don't you? It's the sort of thing they love. Especially with him doing it to both of us. I read about a court case a while ago where a man was filming his wife at home and it was all over the newspapers. Aren't you worried about that?'

'Of course I am. Legally they can't print our names, but it doesn't stop people talking. They kept my name out of the paper before, but it didn't make much difference. Everyone knew about it before too long. It was awful.'

I couldn't help it. I snapped, 'What do you think it was like for us? At least you're still alive.'

She stood up, her face pale and strained. She leaned over and whispered, 'You think there wasn't a cost to me, too? I was raped!' Her voice shook. 'And now your husband is abusing me.'

I watched as she went back to her desk and put the files and stationery into her drawer. She locked the drawer and logged out of her computer. I couldn't take my eyes off her; she didn't give me a second glance.

Without another word to me she walked out of the office.

53

Gemma

I drove round aimlessly for a while, too shaken to go home. I parked the car in the car park overlooking the River Dee and paid for an hour so that I could sit and think.

I felt the bite of Rachel's words more than she probably expected. She loved her brother, clearly, and when he died she was only young. No matter what I thought of him, the idea of her seeing the police arrive at their house at New Year with such terrible news was truly awful. I didn't hear about it until a few weeks later. My parents had read about it in the local newspapers, but they didn't tell me, and by then, just months after leaving school, I wasn't really in touch with anyone any more. We were all away at different universities and it was too easy to slip away from the group. I'd refused to go home that Christmas and so we all went to my grandparents' in Staffordshire instead. I went back to London from there.

I do remember the shock of hearing about Alex's death, though. I'd been invited to Lauren's nineteenth birthday party at her place in Nottingham, where she was studying

256

English. Her birthday was at the end of January and I hadn't seen her since we'd started university the previous September, so I got the train from London and went to stay with her for the weekend.

As soon as I saw her, I knew something had happened. Her eyes were red and swollen and at first I thought she and Tom had broken up. She linked her arm through mine, just as she used to on the way to school, and we walked out of the station and into the cold night and she told me then that Alex had died.

I was really shocked at my reaction. I couldn't stop sobbing and she was trying to tell me it wasn't my fault and I knew it wasn't, of course it wasn't, but it felt like one big burden on top of the rest of it. I think what got to me was that I'd suddenly remembered him as the boy who dressed up as a girl for the school play. There was a moment where he was so clearly enjoying himself and everyone had laughed. I remember leaning forward to watch him, loving his confidence and the way his smile lit up his face when the audience laughed with him.

Rachel was probably at the school that night. It was odd to think we'd shared that experience, so many years before we met. I pictured her as an eleven-year-old girl, and in that instant I didn't know how I hadn't seen the resemblance between her and Alex. They had different colouring and he was six feet tall and built for the rugby pitch, which had made his acting debut even funnier. Now when I thought about it, I remember seeing him in the middle of our summer exams, looking as though he was really trying hard to think of the right way to say something in an essay, and I knew I'd seen that look on Rachel's face at work.

I winced. I wished I hadn't thought of that resemblance now. It would make it so hard to see her again.

Suddenly I felt overwhelmed. I couldn't go on like this, working with someone who hated me. Being destroyed by her husband. I picked up my phone.

'Mum? Can we come up and stay with you for a few days?'

54

Gemma

I went back to the office then and luckily Sophie was there, so I focused on work and avoided speaking to Rachel on my own. I knew I'd have to talk to her again about David, to persuade her to go to the police, but I couldn't summon up the courage to do it just then. I sent them both home ten minutes before closing time and phoned Lucy to tell her that I wasn't feeling well and that I would be taking some time off. She was great, offering to work every day for the next week.

'I'll ask my mum to take Maisie to school and back,' she said. 'She won't mind. I can be there nine to five.'

'I'll drop the keys off at your house on my way home,' I said. 'All my appointments are in the diary. But Lucy, you're in charge, okay?'

'Not Rachel? You said you were promoting her.'

'You're in charge,' I said again. 'I'll let the others know.'

She was quiet, then said, 'Is something the matter?'

My eyes filled with tears and I started to speak, but I couldn't go on.

'It's okay,' she said. 'Talk to me about it when you get back. And don't worry. I'll keep an eye on everything. I'm really

glad of the work and if you need to stay off a bit longer, then that's fine.'

Within a couple of hours I was driving to my parents' house with Rory. Joe hadn't been keen on coming up and offered to do some work on the living room and kitchen while we were away.

'There's no point us all going,' he said. 'It's not like I'd have much to do there. I might as well stay behind and get some jobs done in the house. It's impossible to do anything like that while Rory's around. I could paint the kitchen if you like? Freshen it up a bit.'

Part of me wanted him to come with me, but I knew I wouldn't be able to talk properly to my mum with him there. And I needed to. There was too much for me to deal with now.

It's only about thirty miles from my house to my mum's, but we tend to meet up in Chester to do some shopping and then she comes back to my house for dinner, rather than us going to visit them. It had been the same since I left home at eighteen. Every month my parents would come down to London for the day. My room there had been so small it was impossible for us to stay in it together, so we'd walk for miles, talking about my course and my new friends, and my mum and dad would talk about their jobs and the holidays they planned. We never spoke about what had happened.

That day, travelling up with Rory for company in the car, I found myself yearning to be back home, as I still saw it, despite everything.

Rory had been delighted to be visiting them with me.

'Just you and me, Mum?' he'd asked. 'No Dad?'

'Daddy will stay behind and do some painting.'

Rory had looked bemused, and I guessed he was thinking of Joe using his watercolours.

We'd packed our bags and set off on our little trip. He was

excited to be sleeping in my old bedroom and chatted constantly throughout the journey, telling me all the things he was going to do with his grandparents. I felt guilty then that he didn't see them more often; they'd been really excited to have us visit too, though I knew my mum had been concerned when I called her.

'Everything's okay with you and Joe?' she'd asked nervously. 'You'd tell me if there was a problem, wouldn't you?'

I pictured myself telling her everything that had happened. She would have had a heart attack before I'd finished.

'Everything's fine,' I'd said instead, but she didn't seem convinced.

We parked in their driveway and Rory jumped out, eager to ring their doorbell. This was the game they always had to play, to be amazed we were there.

As soon as my mum opened the door and shouted, 'Grandad, we've got surprise visitors!' Rory ran through the house to find him. I must have been looking a real state because my mum took one look at me and hugged me tightly.

We went into the house to find my dad. The game was that he would hide and Rory would have to find him. Although my dad was over six feet tall, this took longer than you might think.

Eventually, after finding him in the garden shed, where he was actually oblivious to our arrival, Rory and I sat at the patio table while my mum brought us some dinner and my dad made drinks.

It was so peaceful sitting there with them. The garden was enclosed and private, giving an aura of safety and security that I badly needed. Rory chattered away to them about all the things he and Joe had got up to in Ireland and I was able to sit back and relax.

'You've been working too hard,' said my mum. 'You'll stay for a few days?'

'I'm having a week off,' I said. 'I'm going to sort something out with Lucy, too.' I hadn't even thought of that until now. 'I'm going to ask her to work every weekday for a while, just for a few hours, so that I can have a break.'

'When did you last manage a day off work?'

'I took a day when Joe and Rory came back from Ireland.'

'And before that?'

'When Rory wasn't well.'

'It's not right, Gemma,' said my mum softly. 'And it's not fair, either, that you're taking on the whole burden. I thought Joe would go back to work soon, but you need to have a think about the way you want to live your life. It's not fair that you're the one working all the time.'

I was glad Joe wasn't there; she would have said the same thing even if he had been. It always caused problems when she complained about the way we lived.

'I know,' I said. 'I need to reconsider things. But Joe wants us to go and live in Ireland. His brother Brendan is moving there.'

'What will he do over there? Is there work?'

'He seems to think I could set up my business over there.'

'And he'll stay home with Rory?' Her mouth tightened. 'But surely you couldn't just start up in another country?'

Luckily Rory interrupted us to ask if he could have a bath. They'd had a Jacuzzi put in when they had their bathroom refitted the year before and it was always the highlight of his day. Mum's attention was on him then; she took him upstairs while my dad cleared the table and tidied up the kitchen.

'No, sit down,' he said, when I tried to help. 'Have a rest.'

I closed my eyes and tried to blank my mind but couldn't. I had so many thoughts racing around my head. Joe was the least of my problems right then, though of course my main concern

was stopping him from finding out what had happened. I knew I should go to the police. I knew now where David lived, and as long as Rachel hadn't warned him, it would be easy for them to question him. I was furious that he thought he could get away with it, but I was terrified, too, at what he might do next. I knew I needed to act before he could do anything more.

At seven o'clock I heard my phone beep from my handbag in the living room. My dad passed me my bag. 'It might be Joe,' he said. I knew he thought I was there because we'd fallen out.

It was a text from Rachel.

I'm really sorry. I shouldn't have shouted at you.

Relief surged through me.

It's OK, I replied. He's your brother. I know you loved him.

I sat in the sun a minute longer, then sent another message: You know you have to delete these texts?

Immediately she replied: I will. I'm deleting them straight away.

I had to know. What are you going to do?

This answer took longer. I need to get away from him. I might go abroad and put all this behind me. I thought I'd better warn you because of work.

Don't worry about that, I replied. As long as you're safe.

She asked: What are you going to do? You should tell the police now. Please, just tell me before you do.

She was right on both counts. She needed to get away. I needed to tell the police.

A second later she sent another message: We should go to the police together.

But Rachel, I wrote, if I talk to the police then you are implicated.

I know, she replied. I'll admit everything. I can't

believe the way I've acted. I've told David I overheard you on the phone saying you were thinking of going to the police, so he shouldn't do anything for a while. I said you wouldn't tell me what was going on.

Then another message popped up: He's back.

55

Gemma

Upstairs, my mum was sitting on a chair in the bathroom, watching Rory in the bath. It was a huge corner whirlpool bath and he would happily spend hours in there with all his toy fish and dolphins. I stood in the doorway and watched my mum as she chatted to him. Her face was soft and happy, and she smiled when she saw me there.

'It's like looking at you all over again,' she said. 'It's just wonderful, like a glimpse into the past.'

I knelt down by the side of the bath and tipped some water over Rory's hair. He laughed and splashed me, drenching me.

'Will you tell me what's troubling you, sweetheart?' she whispered. 'What's on your mind?'

Rory's ears pricked up at this. 'What's on your mind, Mum?'

I gave my mum an exasperated look.

'She's trying to guess what's for supper.' She stood up and reached for a warm, soft towel. 'Can you guess what it is?'

Rory stood up so quickly he almost slipped over. He clambered out of the bath and let my mum wrap the towel around him. 'And put one round my head,' he said. 'Like in the spa.'

My mum raised her eyebrows at me.

'We play spas, sometimes,' I admitted. 'He has cucumber on his eyes and I have to paint his toenails.'

'And does Daddy do that, too?' she asked Rory.

'No, but we did it to him when he was asleep on the sofa.' He laughed. 'Show her the photos, Mum.' He hugged me and just for that moment I forgot all my worries.

Later, while Rory was in bed and my dad was at a quiz night at their local pub, my mum and I sat on the patio. They have a fire pit, which my dad had lit before he went, to take the chill off the evening. She'd poured me a gin and tonic and I guessed she was trying to get me to open up to her.

'Is there something wrong at home? Have you and Joe been arguing?'

'No. Well, in a way. He's got himself all excited, thinking we could move to Ireland. But I couldn't do that. I've got the office and I wouldn't be able to operate over there. As you said, I don't know the area and I'm not qualified to work in a different country. It's just a pipe dream for him, really.'

'Does he accept that?'

I sighed. 'He and Brendan seem to think it could work.'

'Well, why doesn't he find work over there and let you take a few years off with Rory and get qualified then? You could keep the office open here and take on a manager. It's doable, isn't it? You could even come back every month or so. Flights are very cheap from Liverpool to Ireland.'

I kept quiet. I couldn't say to her that Joe had no intention of getting work. I knew what my mum thought of that. She'd been wary ever since he gave up his job to look after Rory.

'That's not the problem, though,' I said. 'I can deal with him.' I wanted to tell her what the problem was, but how could I? And then I thought, if I couldn't speak to her, I couldn't speak to anyone, so I said, tentatively, 'You remember what happened to me when I was eighteen? At that party?'

She stiffened. 'Of course I do, pet.'

'I've been thinking about it. I should have let the police take it to court. It wasn't fair, what I did.'

'What *you* did wasn't fair?'

'No. Alex was arrested but then let go without being charged, and people thought he was guilty just because he was arrested.'

'But he *was* guilty, Gemma! You mustn't feel bad about that.'

'I know, but he didn't have the chance to put his case forward, did he? Going to court would have been horrible, but at least he would have had an opportunity to have his say.'

'What could he say?' she asked angrily. 'He'd either say you agreed to it – and how could you prove you hadn't? – or that he hadn't done anything. There was no evidence by then. If you'd gone to the police at the time, it would have been different, but two weeks later? You think he would've just admitted it?'

'I had no choice,' I said, trying to keep my temper. 'We went on holiday the next day. By the time I was ready to tell the police, I was in another country.'

'I know, pet,' she said. 'I'm sorry. I wasn't blaming you. I just meant that after two weeks there was no evidence. His lawyers would have made things really difficult for you.'

'I know,' I said. 'I know. But . . . I don't know. I just think he should have had a voice. If he had, he might not have . . . Well, he might still be alive.'

'It was terrible what happened to him,' she said. 'It was. But that's not your fault, Gemma. And his death may well have been an accident anyway. There was nothing to show he'd done it on purpose.'

I knew he had, though. Even though we weren't friends, I'd seen him most days for two years and I'd got an idea of the

sort of person he was. He was proud and ambitious; he lost his reputation and his dreams when he was arrested. It couldn't be a coincidence that he drowned at New Year, just four months later.

'He'd always wanted to go to Oxford, you know,' I said after a pause. 'I remember on our induction day when we were sixteen, we had to say what we wanted to achieve by the end of the course. I could tell from the way he talked about it that he'd succeed.'

My mum said nothing, her lips tight.

'And I don't think the arrest would have stopped him practising law,' I said. 'I rang the Law Society a few years ago to ask them.'

She looked sharply at me. 'What did you do that for?'

'I needed to know. I phoned a long time after I heard that he'd died. Years. Of course I thought he'd killed himself and then Caitlin said maybe he'd done it because he couldn't have the future he'd wanted.'

My mother made a sound, then, a kind of *Well, he should have thought of that* kind of noise.

'But when I spoke to them, they said that as the charge had been dropped, it would be possible for him to practise. He'd have to declare the charge, but they thought it would be okay.'

'And you're thinking you would have done better taking it to court, to let him have his say? Gemma, sweetheart, you did the right thing. The only thing,' said my mum. 'What would that have done to you? And they could have paid for the best lawyers; you know that.' Her voice wobbled and I could see she was holding back tears. 'Think how you would have felt if they'd found him not guilty.'

I knew that would have crushed me, and I knew, too, that that was exactly how I would feel if I were accused and couldn't have my say, too.

And I thought of the ripples from that one night in August, when everything changed forever for Alex and for me, and for our families, too. We'd all suffered the after-effects of that night. The pain didn't just belong to me.

I spoke without thinking. 'I met his sister the other day.'

'Alex's sister? I didn't know you knew her.'

'I didn't even know he had a sister until recently,' I said. 'I didn't know anything about him.'

'I only knew because Lauren's mum told me,' said my mum. 'She came round to see me after you and Lauren had moved away.' She grimaced. 'I think she wanted to gossip about it. I had to avoid her for a while.'

I knew how she felt. After I'd reported the rape, a few girls from school wanted to talk to me, and I'd felt there was something almost indecent about their interest. After a while I wouldn't answer the door to them and would get my brother to say I was out when they phoned.

'Their mother died last year,' I said.

My mum was quiet, and then said, 'She must have been young. What was the matter with her?'

'She had cancer.'

'Oh, the poor woman. That on top of everything else.'

I wanted to tell her what Rachel had told me, about their mother's dependency on her, the fact that she'd wanted to die. I couldn't. Though I wasn't to blame, I was involved. I would have given anything for that not to be the case. My mum, though, didn't need to be. She didn't deserve to hear those things.

'How did you meet her?'

Just then my dad came back and spared me from having to answer that. We chatted then about the quiz and the team that had won, and we didn't go back to talking about Rachel and her family, though my mum kept looking at me all evening, and I knew the question was preying on her mind.

56

Gemma

Wednesday, August 16

The next morning I waited until the office was open, then sent Rachel an e-mail through the work system. It was the only safe means of communicating as there was no way David could intercept the messages.

    Everything OK last night?

She must have been on her own at her desk, because she replied quite quickly:

    I think so. I'm not sure. Who can tell, though?

I winced. Surely she should be able to go to sleep without worrying about someone taking explicit photos of her. And then I thought of myself, in my hotel room in London, and became fired up. I started to type an e-mail, saying:

    I'm going to talk to the police when I come back to
    Chester. You can come with me if you want to but I'm
    going anyway.

Before I clicked Send, I stopped. David was her husband. Was she really going to wait for the police to come round? Surely she would tell him – or he would guess. That would be

worse. Much worse. I shuddered. What would he do if he discovered she knew and hadn't told him?

I deleted my message. Instead, I wrote: You shouldn't have to live like that, and she replied, I know.

There the conversation ended. I went out with my mum and dad to take Rory on the ferry over to Liverpool and spent the day at the museums. Later we went for afternoon tea at a hotel, before going back to our car on the underground train. That was the thing that impressed Rory the most; he hadn't been on an underground train before and was beside himself. The fact that he was carrying a box of cakes from the hotel only added to his happiness.

Later in the afternoon, back at my parents' home, we borrowed the paddling pool from the next-door neighbour and she kindly sent her little girl, Evie, in to play, too. I don't know what it is about Rory, but if you want to keep him amused, just give him some water and he'll be happy for hours. So I sat outside to make sure the children were safe while my mum and dad napped on their garden chairs. Clearly the day had taken it out of them.

I pulled out my iPad and went back to look at the photos that Jack had put on Facebook, the photos of us throughout the two years we'd all spent together. I'd meant to tell Rachel to send Jack a friend request so that she could look at them, but I wasn't sure whether they would upset her too much. From the comments under the photos it was clear Jack had only recently put them up, and name after name of friends I'd had in school popped up to make fun of us all. I wondered if any of them remembered how that summer term had ended, though they would have known at the time, of course.

'Who was that girl . . .' I imagined them saying. 'That scruffy little redhead . . . Didn't something happen to her?

I can't remember now what it was ... Did she die or something?'

I blinked hard to stop the tears falling.

And then I gathered my courage and looked at the photos from the party that Jack had put on Dropbox.

I turned the iPad away from the sun. I could see which albums I'd viewed, and clicked on the next one. It was clear that Jack had run out of steam, or maybe even just run out of film, because of course it wasn't a digital camera that he was using then. The last fifty or so photos were random ones rather than several at a scene. So there was a group of girls doing karaoke, then a photo of the fire pit with all the smokers sitting around with bottles of beer. Then there was Lauren, sitting in the hammock with Tom. I stopped at that one, remembering that I'd wanted to go home at that point, but Lauren had avoided my eyes. I could just about see the love bite on her neck; it looked at first like one of the pink flowers on her dress.

I steeled myself. Now I was about to see what happened while I was upstairs. There were people dancing on the patio, though I think they were just doing it for a laugh. Or at least I hoped so. The next scene was the kitchen. Jack must have been making his way back into the house. Lauren was there now.

I remembered her telling me in the taxi going home that night that someone had tipped them out of the hammock and she'd got mud on her dress. I didn't reply, didn't say a word. I'd pretended to be asleep.

In the first shot she was at the kitchen sink, splashing her face with water. Tom was holding her hair up and for a second I saw how much Jack had liked her, as the droplets of water splashed her face, her hair held aloft giving her an air of grace that the love bite completely destroyed.

In the next shot she was sitting on Tom's knee, her arm casually around his neck. How much had it hurt Jack to take

that photo? And behind her, just about to walk out of the kitchen door into the hallway beyond was a young man. Not a boy. You could never have called him a boy.

This man was dressed in jeans and a Coral T-shirt. It was a T-shirt that was on sale at Glastonbury that summer. The same T-shirt that Alex had been wearing all evening.

It wasn't Alex, though, who was leaving the room unnoticed by the crowd.

It was David.

57

Gemma

My reaction was so physical it was as though someone had thumped me in the chest. For a second or two, no matter how wide I opened my mouth, I couldn't breathe. I put my head between my legs and tried to breathe, just as I had in the days and months, even, after that party. My parents were napping on their chairs on the deck and I could hear the distant sounds of Rory and his little friend as they splashed around.

And then it was as though the air burst out of me and with one huge gasp I started to hyperventilate.

'Mum!' Rory ran over to me and shook my arm. 'Mum! What's wrong?' He screamed. 'Granny! Granny!'

I heard my mother gasp, then shout my dad's name. She came running over to me, but all I could see was a blur.

'What is it, Gemma? What's the matter?'

I was struggling to breathe again. My chest was tight and felt like a balloon was about to explode, but I just couldn't get the air out.

I heard my dad in the kitchen, pulling open drawers, swearing under his breath, and then he was uncurling my fists and I could feel the rough rasp of a paper bag in my hands. He knelt in front of me, his eyes fixed on mine.

'Breathe into it, pet,' he said, and then I remembered him saying that all those years before and tears streamed down my cheeks. 'Breathe in and let's count. One, two, three, four. That's right. Now breathe out. Come on, blow hard. As hard as you can. And look at me. Look at me!' He counted again and I watched his face intently. 'You can do it. Come on, let's count again.'

My mum was hovering in the background, trying to reassure Rory and Evie that I was okay. She made Rory pull out the plug of the paddling pool with the promise of a spa night later if he was good now, then sent him off to find the biscuit tin for both of them.

'I knew we shouldn't have talked about it,' she kept saying. 'It's my fault. You never get over that sort of thing. I shouldn't have asked her questions.'

I could see my dad didn't know what she was talking about, but then something in him recalled doing this in the past, when he'd had to help me to breathe to cope with what happened. There was anger in his eyes, not at my mum or me, but fury that something that had happened to me, his only daughter, was still hurting me even fifteen years later.

Slowly, my eyes fixed on my dad's, my breathing returned to normal. My mum was inside now with Rory, having packed Evie off home. When the panic attack was finally over, my dad got up and pulled a chair over next to mine.

'We'll talk about it, Gem,' he said, 'but not now. Have a rest and we'll get Rory to bed. And if you're not up to it tonight, don't worry. You're here for a few days. There's plenty of time.'

My iPad had turned itself off while I was away from it. I couldn't bear the thought of seeing that picture again, but at the same time I panicked in case I might lose it. I asked my dad to go and check that Rory was okay, and in the couple of minutes he was gone, I sent it to myself on my private e-mail.

When my e-mail alert sounded, I knew it was safe.

*   *   *

That night I went to bed early, exhausted from the day. The tiredness I felt then seemed like the result of having to hold myself in for fifteen years.

I couldn't risk looking at the photo again. There was no one I could speak to except Rachel, and she was running her own gauntlet at the moment. I heard my mum downstairs, talking to Joe on the phone. She'd told him I was having an early night, but I'd made her promise not to tell him about my panic attack.

Why was David at the party? This thought raced around my mind for hours. What was he doing there? Rachel had said he and Alex were best friends, but that party had only been for people from school. I remember him saying that when a girl asked him if she could bring a friend.

'It's just for us,' he'd said. 'I don't want anyone else there, just us lot. It's the last time we'll all get together.'

I'd been there from the beginning and I hadn't seen David. I would have noticed him simply because he wasn't someone I'd met before. Everywhere I'd looked that night there were people I'd known for two years. Even if someone took completely different subjects, I had still seen them in the canteen or in the library or on the school bus. And he was a good-looking man, too, but that was the thing – all of the other students, well, they were more like boys to me. We called them boys, not men. David looked older than us and would have stuck out a mile.

I picked up my phone and sent a Facebook message to Jack Howard, the guy who'd taken the photos, asking him to call me whenever he was free for a quick chat. Within a few minutes, my phone rang.

'Hi,' I said. 'Sorry it's late.'

'Don't worry,' he said. 'What is it?' His voice was deeper than I remembered, but I knew I would have recognized it. He sounded friendly and I realized again how cut off I'd been from my old school friends.

'Thanks for sending the photos,' I said. 'There's one that I wanted to ask you about. It's a photo of Lauren.'

'Which one?' he said drily. 'I took tons of her.'

I laughed. 'You liked her, didn't you?'

'I was crazy about her. Took me a while to get over her. Still, that's a long time ago.'

I remembered his Facebook status. 'You're married now?'

'Yes; we're having a baby in a few months.'

'Oh that's lovely,' I said. 'Congratulations.'

'Thanks. So the photo – which one was it?'

'It's the one where Lauren's in the kitchen, sitting on Tom's knee.'

'Just a second, I'll have a look at it on my laptop.' I waited a few seconds, then he said, 'Oh that one. Yeah, I was a bit of a masochist, wasn't I?'

'You see that guy in the background? Do you know him?'

'That's weird. I never noticed him standing there. He wasn't at our school, was he?'

'No, he wasn't.'

'What was he doing there?' he said. 'It was just meant to be us, wasn't it? I remember I had to tell some guys they couldn't bring their girlfriends because they weren't from Wirral. Alex's mum and dad were really strict about that.'

'I heard Alex tell someone that too,' I said.

'I have seen him before, though. He looks older than the rest of us, doesn't he?' He was quiet for a while, and then he said, 'Oh yeah, I know who he is.'

I held my breath.

'I met him once or twice when he played hockey for All Saints School. We'd play against him sometimes. Alex went to All Saints until he was sixteen, before he came to Wirral.' There was a pause. 'I remember now. He went to Glastonbury with Alex.'

'Are you sure?'

277

'Yes, just the two of them went. The rest of us couldn't afford it. I heard all about it when Alex got back. He'd had a great time.'

'Do you know his name?' I asked.

'I don't know. I would have known it then. I'll get back to you if I remember.'

'Thanks. You've been a great help.'

'Gemma, is this something to do with what happened that night?' he asked.

'I don't know,' I said. 'I really don't know.'

'I just couldn't believe Alex had done that. I thought I knew him pretty well.' I said nothing and he went on. 'I'm not saying you were lying. Honestly I'm not. It's just . . . well, he was one of the last people I would've thought was capable of rape.'

I ended the call without another word and found that my face was drenched with tears. I wanted Joe. I wanted him to hug me and tell me everything would be all right. I knew he'd be out with Mike but sent him a message:

I love you, Joe. I miss you. I'll be home soon xx

Immediately my phone beeped.

I miss you too, sweetheart. It's not the same without you here. I love you. I'll call tomorrow xx

I smiled and sent him a photo that my mum had taken in the garden. I had my arms around Rory, my face next to his.

When I heard my phone beep a second later I expected it to be a quick reply from Joe, but it was a message from Jack.

I'm sorry if I upset you, he wrote. I feel awful about that. It's just that Alex was one of my best friends. About that guy – I've just found my old hockey fixtures. His name is David Henderson.

I felt a flash of victory at discovering David's real name. I replied immediately: Did you see him at the party? I know he's in the photo, but did you notice him there?

No, he replied. I didn't notice him at all. I would have wondered why he was there and said something to Alex.

If he had, none of this might have happened.

Desperate to speak to Rachel, but knowing she couldn't receive a call from me at home, I sent her an e-mail she'd get at work the next day.

Rachel, I need to talk to you. Can you call me as soon as you get this? Make sure nobody can over-hear you.

58

Gemma

I didn't sleep that night. How could I? I had a long bath to try to calm myself down, but hours later, my heart was still pounding.

I didn't get out of bed until nine A.M. the following morning. I was expecting Rachel to call me, but my phone was quiet. I had a quick shower, taking my phone into the bathroom with me, but she still didn't call. I tried to rationalize it: She'd call when things were quiet. They'd be having the morning meeting, and then she'd say she was going out to view a property and she'd call me from her car, I knew it.

I looked terrible that morning and my mum wanted me to stay in bed, but I was too agitated for that. Instead she said she and my dad would take Rory out for the day.

'Unless you want us to stay with you?' she asked. 'I think one of us should. What do you think?'

I needed to have that conversation with Rachel in private, so I refused.

'It's okay. I'll be fine. I'll catch up on a box set or something and just stay on the sofa all day.'

Eventually they left, with worried glances at me as they drove off. I breathed a sigh of relief. As soon as their car had disappeared, I was on the phone to the office.

'Hey, Gemma,' said Lucy. 'How're you feeling?'

'Okay, thanks. It's nice to be with my mum and dad.'

'I bet. It's good for you to have a rest. But you're missing out on something here,' she said. 'That postman – you know, the surfer guy – has only gone and asked Sophie on a date.'

Despite myself, I laughed. 'Oh, I wish I'd been there. I bet she's bouncing off the ceiling, isn't she?'

'She hasn't shut up about it,' she said. 'He only asked her half an hour ago and I've already got a headache.' She lowered her voice. 'Are you all right? You sounded upset the other day.'

'I'm fine, thanks. I just got so tired and I thought if I went to my mum's she'd look after me.'

She laughed. 'I bet she's thrilled you're there.'

'Yes, she is. Lucy, I need to talk to Rachel. Is she there?'

'She's chasing a mortgage offer for Mrs Davies at the moment, but I'll get her to call you as soon as she's free.'

It was half an hour later before Rachel called back. She sounded subdued. I could hear traffic in the background and guessed she was in the car park, out of sight of the office.

'It's me,' she said. 'Is everything okay?'

'I need to talk to you. Do you have time now?'

'Not really,' she said. 'I've got Mrs Johnson coming by in ten minutes and I need to make a phone call before then.'

I couldn't tell her then. I just couldn't. I dithered, not knowing what to do. She needed to know David was at the party, but how was I going to tell her when she was either at work or at home with him?

'Is everything all right?' I asked.

'I've decided to sell my mum's house. I can't use our office to sell it, though. I hope you understand.'

'Of course. Of *course* you can't do that. Don't even think about it. I didn't realize you hadn't sold it.' I hesitated. 'How long has it been empty?'

'About ten months. My mum died last October. I've not been there since. I went away to France with David for a month after she died – it was our honeymoon – and then I moved to Chester.'

'It'll be a lot of work, won't it, sorting everything out? We can help you, Rachel,' I said. 'Me and the girls in the office. You don't have to deal with it on your own.'

She gave a strangled 'Thanks,' then said, 'I have to go,' and the call ended.

Later that morning I got an e-mail from Rachel.

Sorry. Mrs Johnson was walking towards me so I had to go.

Instantly I replied:

I need to talk to you. Something's come up. It's really important.

Within ten minutes my mobile rang.

'It's me, Rachel. I'm having an early lunch break. What's happened?'

'You might be better going outside to talk about this,' I said. 'Can you do that?'

'It's okay,' she said. 'I'm in the car and I've parked somewhere quiet. What is it?'

'I should be telling you this face to face, Rachel. I'm sorry.'

'What?' she said. 'What's up? You're frightening me.'

'David was at the party.'

There was silence, and then she said, 'What did you say?'

'The party. Where . . .'

'Yes, I know which party. But he wasn't there. It was just for people from Alex's school. David was at All Saints.'

'I know that's what it was meant to be, but he *was* there. I have a photo of him. Hold on a second.' I pulled my iPad to me and sent her the photo. 'Check your messages.'

There was silence as she opened my message, and then she gasped.

'But how do you know this was the party?'

'See that girl in front of him? She was my best friend.' I didn't say Lauren's name, not wanting Rachel to realize she was the one who'd yelled at Alex in the pub, the one who made him go back to Oxford a couple of days before he died. 'We went to the party together. She bought that dress the same day. I was with her when she bought it.'

'Yes, but . . .' She was flailing around now. 'But it might have been another night.'

'There was another party in your house after that one?'

There was silence.

'He never told me he was there. And his name wasn't on the guest list. Alex had to write it up for the police. He had to ask the school for a list of all the students in his year and use that as a guide.' Her voice faltered. 'I've seen it. It's still at my mum's house. David's name isn't on it.'

'Maybe he just heard about the party and thought he'd turn up. Who knows? But Rachel, he was there.'

'Alex didn't know he was there,' she said, sounding puzzled. 'He couldn't have known.'

'Maybe he was in the garden when David arrived. A lot of people were outside. It was a really hot night.' I paused; I had something to tell her and I was scared to say it. 'You know I identified Alex because of his T-shirt.'

'Yes, the Glastonbury T-shirt. The Coral.'

I said nothing. I closed my eyes and waited for it to dawn on her.

When it did, her voice was unsteady. 'David's wearing a Coral T-shirt in the photo.'

And I waited again for her to make that connection.

'Does ... Oh God. Does this mean it might have been David who ...' I could hear the tears and the fury in her voice. 'Are you telling me now that it was David who raped you?'

59

Gemma

I couldn't speak. What could I say? I'd accused her brother of rape. He'd died as a result of my accusation, and her mother had died because she'd lost her son. Now I was saying it was her husband who'd done it.

'So you were lying?' she screamed. 'If you weren't sure, why didn't you say so?'

I couldn't answer. I sat with my head bowed, my phone clamped to my ear, listening to her outrage.

'Say something!' she yelled. 'All this has happened because of you!'

And suddenly I was sick of it. Sick of taking the blame for something that had been done to me so many years before. 'It hasn't happened because of me,' I shouted back. 'I was asleep on Alex's bed and someone raped me. I looked up and saw someone of Alex's height, Alex's build, with Alex's T-shirt on leaving the room. What was I meant to think?'

'I don't know. I don't know.'

We sat in silence for a while, both too upset to speak. I could hear her crying, then blowing her nose. She said, 'Where did you get the photo from?'

'Jack Howard. He was a boy from school who was there that night.'

'I used to know him. He was one of Alex's friends,' she said. 'He played hockey with him. We gave him a lift to matches sometimes.'

'He's the one who took the photo,' I said. 'He took hundreds of photos that night and David was only in this one. He knew David. Well, he'd met him a few times. He was taking a photo of my friend – he was crazy about her – and he didn't notice anyone in the background. But I talked to him last night. I asked him if he recognized the person behind Lauren and he said it was David.' I hesitated. 'David Henderson. That's his name?'

'Yes, it is.' She was quiet for a few moments, then said, 'I remember Alex and David going to Glastonbury. They loved The Coral. Even now . . . even now David plays their songs. I don't like it; it reminds me of that summer when Alex would play them and he'd dance with me.' She started to laugh but I could hear the tears there. 'And you're sure this is the night of the party? Absolutely certain?'

'Yes. There's no doubt, Rachel.'

'So Alex *didn't* do it,' she said. 'I knew he didn't.'

We said nothing for a minute or two. I was looking at the photo on my iPad and I knew she was looking at it too.

'I think we should go to the police,' I said. 'We should both go to the police together.'

'I thought that too,' she said. 'But do you know what, Gemma?'

'What?'

'I'd rather tackle him ourselves.'

I started to say, 'We can't do that,' but the line was dead.

60

Gemma

I was exhausted after that conversation with Rachel. I wanted to just go to the police and tell them everything, but I knew I had to get her to agree to that for her own sake. She'd been so powerless for so long; she needed to have some control now.

While I waited for Rory and my parents to come home, I went back to look at the rest of the photos from the party. David wasn't in any of them, and after a flurry of early photos, neither was Alex. There was one photo of Lauren on her own; Jack must have wanted to take a last shot of her before she left. She was standing in the hallway at the foot of the stairs looking impatient, and I realized she must have been calling my name. I felt sick at the thought of what had just happened to me. The front door was wide open and I wondered whether David had run out just a minute before Lauren got there or whether he'd waited upstairs until he'd heard me leave.

I made myself go through the albums again. I saved each photo in sequence to a new album I set up on my iPad. There were hundreds and I knew I wouldn't need them all, but I kept them anyway. I couldn't take the risk of Jack taking them down again or, worse, deleting them. Quite why he'd do that, I had no idea, but the thought of it made me panic.

By the time my parents arrived back with Rory I was desperate for him. I didn't want them to go off with him again; I wanted to spend time with him. But I knew, too, that I had to get this sorted and that would involve time away from him. I vowed things would change after that.

While I played with Rory and cooked him some dinner and listened to his stories of what he'd done that day, all I could think was: what did Rachel mean that she wanted us to tackle David ourselves? When I knew things would be quiet at work, I sent her an e-mail.

What did you mean?

Quick as a flash, she replied:

I think we should talk to him first. See what he has to say. Catch him off guard.

He'd just deny it, I replied.

A minute later she sent another e-mail with a link to a website. I clicked on it, and when the site opened I stared in disbelief. It was a site that sold covert recording devices and on the screen was a button that operated as a camera. A button that you could sew onto a shirt or jacket. It looked just like any button you'd have on a shirt and the set came with extra ones so that all your buttons would match. I looked at it closely. I couldn't tell the camera was there! And then the description stated it was a video recorder, too.

I replied: What is this?

He had it on his shirt when you had dinner.

How do you know? I asked. Did he tell you?

It was several minutes later that she replied, and when I saw her answer, I guessed she hadn't wanted to reply at all.

I sewed them on. I'm so sorry, Gemma.

I felt fury then, that they'd done that to me. And she'd known about it. I'd talked and talked that night and all the

time he was recording me. And of course he was in my room, too, and all that would be recorded, as well.

Was there anything else? I asked.

I don't know. I don't think so.

I need to go, I replied, and switched off my phone. I couldn't stand to talk to her right then.

61

Gemma

That evening, after Rory had gone to bed, I sat with my parents and watched a film on television. I could see them eyeing me cautiously. They knew that I had something on my mind, I could tell. When the film ended, there was an awkward pause where my dad opened his mouth to speak and my mum shook her head. I pretended not to notice, but stood up and yawned, saying I was ready for bed.

I called Joe from my bed that night, but when he answered the phone all I could hear was background noise.

'Sorry, sweetheart,' he said when he called me back a few minutes later. 'I was watching football at The Crown. I've missed you, Gem. It's lonely here without you and Rory.'

'Lonely in the pub?' I teased. 'Sounds like you're having a good time.'

'I was the first night,' he admitted. 'It was great. I'm never in the house on my own usually.'

I hadn't thought of that. He had plenty of chances to go out, what with running and football and seeing his friends, but of course if he was in the house, Rory was there with him.

'Did you like it?'

He laughed. 'Last night was really weird. The daytime was

fine. I finished the kitchen and it was so much easier without Rory there. But . . . it made me think of how different my life is now compared to how it was. And it was nice going out when I wanted and staying out late. But then when I got home the house seemed so quiet. I didn't like it!'

'I know. I didn't like it when you were away, either.' He was quiet and immediately I felt guilty. 'I'm sorry,' I said. 'I don't want to get into point-scoring.'

'Me neither. I thought you'd enjoy it, though.'

'I like the idea of it more than the reality.'

'Me too,' he said. 'When will you be back?'

'Not long,' I said. 'A couple of days.' And then suddenly I found the courage to be open with him. 'But Joe, we need to talk. I'm not happy with the way things are.'

There was a strained silence. 'You're not happy with us?'

'Of course I am. It's just work. It's not working out, the way it is. Not for me. I can't do it much longer.'

'What? You can't work?'

'I can. Of course I can. But it's not how I want to live.' I struggled to stay calm. 'I miss Rory. I'm . . . I'm jealous of you.' I could hear that he was about to speak and hurried on. 'I feel outside the family. As though I'm just there to bring in the money.'

'Oh, now . . .'

'Don't. Let me say this. Sometimes I feel it's like you and he are the family. That's what I see. He turns to you first. You always know what's best for him. I hardly see him some weeks. I'm up before him a lot of the time and I have to work most nights after he's gone to bed. I'm so tired.' I couldn't stop the tears. 'And I love the way you are with him. It's great. But I love being with him too. I want to do things for him.'

'But you do! He looks forward to you coming home all day.'

'But when he cries now, he goes to you. I'm his mum! He should be coming to me!'

'Gemma, sweetheart, don't be daft. We're both his parents.'

'I know. I'm just saying I want things to change. I don't want to work nonstop. I want to be part of his life. I'm happy to work, but . . .' He said nothing. I had no idea what I was even thinking, but then I blurted out, 'Why should it always be you at home and me at work? Why shouldn't I be at home some of the time? Why can't you go out to work as well?' I knew this would hurt him. I knew he'd think that I was criticizing him. But once the floodgates were open I couldn't stop. 'Sometimes you make out like I don't know my own child! I feel like a spare part in the family.'

And then I couldn't stop crying. I heard a knock on my bedroom door and my mum looked in.

I grabbed some tissues from the box on the bedside table. 'I'm on the phone to Joe,' I said.

She gave a quick sympathetic nod and quietly closed the door. And then I realized that she thought I was talking to him about the night of the party and that made me cry even harder, that I couldn't talk to him about that. Not now. That would have to be done face to face.

'Just a second, I need to go to the bathroom,' I said to Joe.

'I'll wait.'

In the bathroom I tried to calm down. I rinsed a flannel in cold water and pressed it against my burning eyes. I was glad I'd told him. He needed to know.

Back in my room, Joe said, 'Gem, we need to talk about this. Talk about it properly. I knew you were tired. I'm really sorry. I hadn't thought about it.' He was quiet, and then he said, 'You must hate me.'

'Of course I don't. I love you. I've always loved you.' I lay

down and it was as though he were next to me. 'Right from the moment I saw you. You saved me.'

'I love you too.' I could almost hear his mind racing. I knew he'd be going over what I'd said. I should have said it before. 'And I'm sorry. I'm really sorry. I should have noticed you weren't happy. We'll sort something out.'

I felt then that we would, but of course there was a whole other story that he knew nothing about. That I'd have to admit to. I couldn't do it that night. I just couldn't. I knew the time was coming when I'd tell him everything. I just hoped he'd be able to forgive me.

62

Gemma

Friday, August 18

I woke late the next morning and found Rory and my dad having breakfast in the garden.

'This is my second breakfast!' said Rory. 'I had one with Granny when she got up, then one with Grandad when he got up.'

He came over to me and sat on my lap, leaning back until his body was aligned with mine. He stroked my arm with his hand while he told my mum and dad in great detail what he had planned for the day, and then he wriggled round until he was facing me and whispered in my ear, 'Are you coming with us, Mum?'

I whispered back, 'Do you want me to?'

He nodded vigorously.

'Of course I will.'

As we got ready for the day ahead, packing up a picnic and spare clothes for Rory, I thought of Rachel in her flat with David last night. Had she challenged him? Was she safe? Despite everything, I wanted to contact her but I didn't know

whether David would be with her. I couldn't risk that, for her or for me.

And while we sat in the car and sang songs with Rory, and as we walked on the beach and built a sandcastle with him and raced down to the waves and ate ice cream and chased the gulls, I thought of her again. She'd married David thinking she'd have a new family, but yet again, she was alone. I didn't know whether she had any cousins or other relatives who could help her get through this, but it seemed as though her role as caregiver to her mum had meant she was pretty isolated.

When my parents offered to take Rory for a long walk along the beach, I agreed quickly. I sat on the sand and thought about what had happened. If David was the one who'd raped me that night, then Alex had died because of him. But he'd died because of me, too.

Why had I thought it was Alex? But try as I might, when I thought of that figure as he hurried from the room that night, I could see why I'd thought it was him. He was the same height, a similar build. It was the T-shirt, though, that had convinced me.

The Glastonbury festival had been on after our exams had ended. I'd known he was going. I don't even know who had told me, but it was probably Lauren.

And then on the day of the party, we'd picked up our exam results in the morning and he was wearing that T-shirt then. I'd stood behind him in the queue and I'd heard him talking about it, about The Coral, and how brilliant they were. For those ten minutes or so I was in that queue I was standing just inches from his back and I knew the image well by the time I saw it on the back of the man leaving Alex's bedroom.

I didn't see David at the party. I certainly would have

noticed someone wearing the same T-shirt. The photos that Jack had taken were pretty thorough. I couldn't think of anyone he'd missed out. And David was only in one of them, one that was taken just before I went upstairs. I'd looked through them again and again, and he wasn't there.

Rachel had told me about the list that Alex had written: a list of those at the party. He hadn't written David's name down. He mustn't have seen him there.

And Jack knew him and hadn't noticed he was there. I wondered then whether that had been deliberate on David's part. I remembered what the therapist I'd seen when I was living in London had said about rape, about how it wasn't caused by the desire for sex but for domination. Control. It was driven by anger, she'd said. Anger and hatred. It had confused me so much. I could never link those emotions to the Alex I'd known in school.

My phone beeped, startling me. It was a text from Rachel.

I'm so sorry I did those things to you.

63

Gemma

As soon as I saw Rachel's message, my anger towards her vanished. We both needed to focus on the person who'd done this to us, not on each other. I was about to call the office to see whether she was there when she called me.

'Rachel,' I said quickly, 'I'm sorry too.'

'It's not your fault,' she said. 'Neither of us is to blame.'

'I know,' I said. 'But are you all right? What about last night?'

'It was okay,' she said. 'Nothing happened. We just watched a couple of films and went to bed early. He had to be in Newcastle today for a meeting, so he set off at about five this morning.'

'Where does he work?'

'Andrews and Fitch,' she said. 'They're in Warrington, a big engineering company.'

'He's in sales there?'

'No, he works in their legal department.'

So everything he'd told me was a lie. Of course it was. And then I thought about it. 'He studied law at university?'

'Yes,' she said. 'At Bristol. Why?'

She started to say something else, but I interrupted her. 'Did he apply to Oxford?'

She stopped in her tracks. 'Yes, he did. He didn't get in, though. He missed out on an A grade in one subject.' She paused. 'Why? Why does it matter where he went to university?'

I shrugged. 'He told me he'd studied in London. Maths.' She was quiet and I guessed she already knew he'd told me that. I shook my head. I had to get over her involvement in this. So he lied about studying in London. Presumably he was trying to give us something in common. 'He must have been angry that Alex got into Oxford and he didn't.'

'I've never thought of that,' she said slowly. 'He would have been angry with himself, too. He sets really high standards for himself. Actually I don't think he would have been able to keep up the friendship with Alex long-term. It would always be a reminder of his own failure.'

I thought of David turning up at the party, furious and jealous. There must have been six or seven students from my year that had got into Oxford, and I wondered how he'd felt as he hovered on the edge of groups that were excited about a future he was denied. I wondered whether that was what led him upstairs to me, the desire to punish. To take revenge.

How had he felt when Alex was arrested? Was that when he really started to celebrate his own success?

'I know I said I wanted to confront him,' said Rachel, 'but I'm terrified.'

'So am I.' Just the thought of being in the same room as him made my heart pound. 'I can't do it. I'm too frightened of him.'

In the distance I saw my parents walking with Rory. Each of them was holding one of his hands and he was swinging between them. When he saw me looking at him, he started to run towards me. I felt awful for Rachel but I really couldn't talk to her. All I had time to say was 'Sorry, I have to go. Call me later,' before Rory bounded on top of me, pinning me to the

ground with hugs and kisses. I wrapped my arms around him and breathed in the summer smells of suntan lotion and ice cream, but my pulse was still racing at the thought of what we had to do.

Rachel called again later that day. We were all out in the garden when my phone rang.

'Is that Joe?' asked my mum. I could tell from her face that she was worried about my marriage, that it would all end in tears.

'It's work.'

'You're meant to be having a break from work!'

I could hear my dad hushing her as I took the phone upstairs to my bedroom.

'I think we're right not to confront him ourselves,' Rachel said as soon as I was able to talk. 'Shall we go to the police in the morning, while he's away? I'm not expecting him back until tomorrow evening.'

'Yes. Let's do it.' I felt a huge sense of relief that this would soon be over. 'I'll drive down early. I can be at the police station near the office at eight o'clock.'

'I'll be there,' she said. 'I'm going up to my mum's house after work tonight. There are some things I don't want David to get hold of. Papers, financial stuff. Will you be able to keep them for me, until it's all over?'

'Yes, of course. You can put them in the safe at work if you like.'

She hesitated. 'Gemma, you wouldn't come with me, would you?'

'What, to your mum's house?'

'Just for a few minutes.' Her voice was strained. 'I don't want to be there on my own.'

'No!' I said, horrified at the thought of being back in that house. 'I'm sorry, Rachel. I can't do that.'

'It's okay.' She sounded resigned. 'I didn't think you would.'

'Why do you need to go there now and not after you've told the police?'

'I need to make sure everything's safe,' she said. 'Just in case I have to get away quickly.'

'How come you didn't take all your mum's documents to your flat when you moved in?'

'I don't know,' she said slowly. 'I think I knew early on that I shouldn't let him know about all my mum's finances. She had a lot more money than I realized, and once we were married there was something about the way he thought he was entitled to it that I didn't like. I didn't tell him about her stocks and shares, though he asked several times whether she had any. If I don't get them now and he has the chance, he'll be all over that house.' Her voice broke. 'I just don't want to go in there on my own.'

I thought about her going back into her mother's house after everything that had happened there. She'd had to deal with so much. I summoned up all my courage. 'And you'll only be a few minutes?'

She breathed a huge sigh of relief. 'I know where the papers are. That's all I want, to just run in and get them, then get out again.'

I looked out of the window at Rory. He glanced up and waved at me. 'I promised Rory I'd spend all day with him,' I said. 'I could be there for seven o'clock, if you like.'

'Thanks so much. I know I don't deserve it, after everything I've done.'

'Forget it,' I said. 'Let's just get this over with.'

'I'll text you the address.'

'There's no need.' Even fifteen years later, I could still remember her family home.

* * *

My parents agreed to put Rory to bed that night. I took a while getting ready, and when I came downstairs my mum was waiting for me.

'You look nice,' she said. 'New top?' She gestured towards my blue cotton shirt.

'I bought it yesterday. It was in the package that arrived in the post this afternoon.'

'Oh, I saw you had a couple of parcels. What else did you buy?'

I held my wrist out to her and she smelled my perfume.

'Oh that's lovely. Isn't it similar to the one you had at Christmas, though?'

I ignored her and looked at my watch. 'I'd better run. I won't be late back.' I fastened her house key onto my car key fob. 'Don't wait up.'

But still she hung around the hallway. 'So you're just meeting a friend? Anyone I know?'

I was prepared for this. 'She's called Helen,' I said. 'I went to university with her. She's in Liverpool with work and asked if I wanted to meet up for a drink.'

'Helen,' she mused. 'Did I know her?'

'No, I don't think so. She studied languages. French and Spanish, I think.'

'Oh, okay.' My mum didn't sound convinced. 'I don't remember you mentioning her.'

I didn't reply, but just opened my shoulder bag and checked that I had my phone and purse. Once out of the house I breathed a sigh of relief. I loved my mother but she really had missed out on her true vocation; she would have been a fantastic detective. If she'd had any idea where I was going tonight, though, I knew she wouldn't have gone back into the house with a wave and a smile.

It took thirty minutes to drive from my parents' home to Rachel's. On the way I passed Lauren's old house. A different

family lived there now; they'd been there for years. There were lights on in the bedroom windows at the front of the house and my mind flashed back to the last night I was there: the night of the party.

Tonight I took the same route that the taxi driver had taken then. Unlike that night, there was no music playing, no excitement, and no breeze rushing through my hair. I wasn't with my friend, looking forward to the night ahead. Where last time I felt free, as though my life was beginning, tonight I was dreading going into the house again.

I slowed down as I approached Rachel's house. It was so much easier to think of it as her house, rather than Alex's. The front garden was surrounded by high hedges and I started to shake as I drove past them. I'd intended to park on her driveway but my palms were sweating and at the last moment I overshot the entrance and parked further down the road, just after the bend. There was a little shop there with a car park for customers and I pulled into an empty space. I was feeling dizzy with tension just at the thought of going into their house.

My phone beeped on the dashboard. It was Rachel.

Just saw you drive past. I'm here now.

I thought of her there in her mother's house, a house that had seen nothing but sadness in all those years. She seemed friendless, lonely, and it was only the pity I had for her that made me go there that night.

I climbed out of the car, then took my phone from my bag and left the bag in the locked boot. It would just be in the way if I had to carry boxes of papers. I slid my phone into the pocket of my jeans and put my key fob into the other pocket, pushing it right down.

I had to gather all my courage to walk towards the house. Rachel's car was parked on the gravel driveway and she

was waiting for me by the front door. As I approached her she waved then turned and pushed the door wide open.

'Hi, come on in,' she said, and all I could think was that was exactly what Alex had said when we arrived at the party that night.

64

Gemma

In the hallway I tried to keep a lid on the panic that rose in me. I hadn't been here since that night, fifteen years ago, but I remembered it well. Then, though, it looked well tended and loved. The oak floor had been polished and glossy; the Persian rug in the centre of the large hallway had been thick and expensive, its colours rich and vivid. I remember when Lauren and I had first arrived we'd looked around and she'd whispered, 'This is exactly what I thought Alex's house would be like.'

Now, though it was exactly the same inside, everything was dull, untended. There were marks on the rug, scratches on the floor. It was clear nobody had redecorated since I was last here. The curtains lay heavy and dusty and lifeless and I saw cobwebs draped over the chandelier that hung unlit from the ceiling. Everything was drab and I knew then that when Alex had died, the light had gone out of their lives.

I shuddered.

I saw Rachel watching me and my face flamed. This was her house, after all.

'It must be hard for you, being here,' she said. 'Thanks for coming.'

'It's okay.' I felt far from okay, though. My stomach was tight with nerves and I couldn't stop thinking how stupid I was to come here. Rachel looked so expectant, though, so trusting and so young that I smiled at her to reassure her. 'Where are the documents?'

'They're in my mum's room,' she said. 'Can you give me a hand?'

I hesitated.

'What?' she asked.

'I don't want to go upstairs.'

'I won't be able to carry them on my own,' she said. 'It'll just be one trip if we both do it.'

I took a deep breath. 'Okay.'

She took my arm and we walked upstairs. I clung onto the banister, wishing I hadn't come, wishing I were at home with Joe. Why hadn't I told him? He could have come with me, helped us do this.

My heart thumped as we reached the top of the stairs. The bathroom was ahead, just as I remembered. Its door stood open and I recognized the black-and-white tiles in a diamond pattern on the floor. Though I hadn't thought of it in all those years, in that one glance I remembered kicking a towel that was on the floor that night, knowing I was so drunk that if I bent to pick it up I would have fallen and hurt myself. I wished now I had picked it up. Wished I'd hurt myself and called for help and gone home. None of this would have happened.

We paused at the top of the stairs. I glanced to the right. The door to Alex's room stood ajar. Immediately I averted my eyes.

'Mum's room is here,' said Rachel. She led me past Alex's door and to a room at the front of the house. There were windows overlooking the front garden and the room was lined with photos of Alex. You wouldn't know she had another child. At the foot of her bed she had a large flat-screen television on a stand, with a DVD player underneath it. It seemed

to jar with the rest of the room, which was old-fashioned and dreary.

'She had all our old family videos put onto DVD,' explained Rachel. She wouldn't meet my eyes and I wondered whether she was embarrassed or ashamed. 'She would play them all the time.' She winced. 'Constantly. Wherever I was in the house, I'd hear them. And she'd fast-forward through the bits I was in, or my dad. She'd replay the parts with Alex in again and again. All his old rugby matches. Every time he won a prize. Every party and every holiday.'

I thought of Rachel living there with that running commentary of her dead brother's life playing on and on while she gave up the chance of her own life to care for their mother. She must have experienced such mixed emotions when her mother died.

She put her shoulder bag on the floor and crouched down to look under the bed. 'Oh thank God, they're still here.' She reached under it and dragged out several box files. They had stickers on them: *Maths*, *English*, *French*, *Psychology*.

'They look like your old school files.'

'That's what I wanted them to look like,' she said, 'in case he saw them.'

I was desperate to get out of there. 'Do you want us to pack all this up while we're here?' I picked up a pile of her family DVDs and looked around for something to put them in. 'Have you got a box? A suitcase?'

'Until the other day,' she said, 'I didn't want to see any of it again. And now . . . now I don't know what to do.' She turned away, but not before I saw that her cheeks were flushed. After a few seconds she said, 'Gemma, you have no idea what it was like.'

A photo of Alex with his arm around his mum caught my eye. It looked like they were on holiday; a bright blue pool was behind them and a white towel lay on the edge of a sun

lounger. He was about sixteen, tanned, his dark hair wavy and wet. His mother stood beside him, looking so proud. She was inches shorter than her son; even at that age he towered above her.

I turned away. I couldn't look at him. I felt such a complicated mix of shame and pity and anger.

'Rachel, there are no photos of you here.'

She tried to laugh but didn't quite make it. 'Well, no. He was the one, wasn't he? He always was.'

My heart ached for her. 'What, always? Even before he died?'

She shrugged. 'Look at her room, Gemma. You decide.'

'And yet you and he got on so well.'

'Oh I loved him,' she said. 'Absolutely loved him. My mum used to say, "He was the light of my life," and I'd agree. He was the light of mine, too. But he'd gone and she and I were the only ones left.'

I closed my eyes as I thought of them both losing that one person who meant more to them than anyone else. How could either of them go on?

Then the tension in the room changed. I noticed it even with my eyes closed. I turned to Rachel. She was at the window, looking out at the driveway.

'Oh no,' she said. 'He's here.'

'What?' For a wild moment I thought she meant Alex. Who?'

'It's David. He's here!'

dropped the DVDs onto her mother's bed and flattened myself against the bedroom wall. My heart banged in my chest. 'David?' I felt dizzy at the thought of seeing him. What's he doing here?'

Rachel's face was white with shock. 'I don't know! What should I do?'

'Don't let him in. Pretend you're not here.'

'But my car's in the drive. I'll have to go down.'

'Put him off. If you have to go with him, don't worry about me. Try to get him away from here.'

'Okay, okay,' she whispered. 'But you'll have to hide.' She backed away from the window and quickly shoved the box files back under her mother's bed. 'Have you got your phone? Mute it, just in case.'

Quickly I did as she said, and then his car door slammed and we both jumped. Rachel grabbed my arm and pushed me out of the room. I was willing to go; I wanted to run out of the house. 'Don't stay in here!' she hissed. 'He might come in.' She hurried me along the corridor and pushed open the door to Alex's room. 'Wait in there. Quick!'

I found myself flung into the room, and then she pulled the door so that it was open just a few inches. 'Don't make a sound,' she whispered.

I stood behind the door, staring at a room I'd last seen fifteen years before.

Everything was as it was then. His bed was made, the quilt cover and pillows just the same. Two blankets lay folded on a chair by the window; I remembered blankets had been thrown over my head as he left the room. I'd had nightmares about that for years, where I'd relived the struggle to break free of them. In the corner were his drums and guitar, beside me the large chest of drawers. His desk overlooked the rear garden, and books and cardboard files were piled up high. swallowed. He'd died after a term at Oxford. I thought of his mum – and Rachel, probably, too – going there to his room to collect his things and knew how broken-hearted they would have been.

And then I heard the doorbell ring and David call Rachel's name. My heart pounded. He was here, within reach of me.

65

Rachel

I've never been as frightened in my life as I was then, going downstairs to let David into the house.

'Hey,' he said, when I opened the door. He came into the house and put his arms around me. I reached around and squeezed him tightly and kissed his cheek. The last thing I wanted was for him to notice any difference in me.

'What are you doing here?' I said. 'I thought you were staying over in Newcastle?'

'Yeah, the last meeting was cancelled and I couldn't be bothered hanging around for the guys to finish work,' he said. 'I'll see them next time I'm up there.'

'How did you know I'd be here?'

'Oh, I was coming through Liverpool and thought I'd see what you were up to. Find My Phone showed you were here, so I thought I'd turn up and surprise you.' He spoke as though this were completely normal behaviour. I didn't know anyone else whose partner tracked them like that, but he always said he liked to know where I was. It was hard to believe I'd thought it was romantic when he first did it.

'I had nothing to do so I thought I'd come up and check that everything was okay here,' I said.

He walked around the hallway, pushing the doors to the kitchen and living room open and looking inside. 'Everything seems all right, doesn't it?'

'Yes, it's fine. I was just about to leave, actually,' I said. 'I'm starving. Fancy a takeaway? Chinese?'

I was really struggling to sound normal. David could pick up anything different about me from a mile away; my heart raced at the thought of him noticing anything now.

'Are you okay, darling?' he asked. 'Are you tired?'

'I'm fine,' I said. 'I just hate being here. It makes me feel really weird.' I put my hand in his and he kissed my knuckles. 'I want to be back home.'

'Come on, then,' he said. 'Pity we're in separate cars. Fancy going for a meal somewhere near here instead?'

'If you like.' It was always important that I gave him the choice, let him make the decisions. 'Though I'd like to get into a hot bath and have a glass of wine.'

He gave a soft laugh and said, 'I'll join you.' My skin prickled with disgust. 'Got your keys?'

In a flash I remembered that my handbag was in my mother's room. I cursed the fact that I hadn't just let him take me home in his car.

'My bag's upstairs,' I said. 'I won't be a second. You go and get the car started.'

'Don't worry,' he said. 'I'll fetch it.'

He took the stairs two at a time and I hurried after him.

'It's in my mum's room,' I said.

'Is there anything you want me to bring back now? Have you decided what you'll keep?'

I thought of the boxes of papers under the bed and hoped he wouldn't notice them. He would never believe that I knew nothing about them. 'Honestly?' I said. 'I never want to see any of it again.'

'Oh, sweetheart.'

We went into my mum's room. I wanted to shut the door, to give Gemma the chance to escape, but I didn't have the nerve. He'd know something was up immediately if I did that. And then he'd see her from the window. I nearly collapsed at the thought of him chasing her.

I picked up my handbag. 'Come on,' I said. 'Let's go. I'll call around some charities tomorrow and ask them to take the whole lot. They can sell whatever they want and chuck the rest.'

'But there'll be things you want, surely?' He stood in the doorway. 'What about the television? It's fairly new, isn't it? We could have it in our bedroom.'

'No,' I said. 'I don't want it. They can take it all.'

I was just about to say that I could afford a new television if I wanted one. I could afford a new house to put the new television in, if it came to that, and then I realized that in his mind, the money belonged to him. Not that it belonged to both of us, even, but that it was his. I knew if I wanted to buy something, whether it was a television or a house, he'd have to approve, and if he said no, it wouldn't happen. The rage I'd felt since I realized what he'd done nearly overwhelmed me: he'd caused my brother to commit suicide and my mother to die young and yet he thought her money was his.

And it was then that the courage to say something struck me. I knew Gemma was in Alex's room and she'd hear everything I said. I hoped she had her phone out, ready to call the police if he turned nasty. So quick as anything, before I could think about the sheer lunacy of what I was doing, I stopped dead in the hallway, just outside Alex's room.

'I'm glad you're here,' I said. 'I wanted to have a chat with you about Alex's party.'

66

Rachel

I felt as though my lungs were only half full of air; my voice sounded completely different. Higher-pitched. Breathless.

He stared at me for a couple of seconds. I could feel my chest heaving. He glanced down, then at my face. He sounded bewildered. 'What? What about it?'

'I didn't realize you were there,' I said. I tried to sound matter-of-fact, but my heart was racing. 'You weren't on Alex's guest list. I saw it, after he died. My mum used to go through everything. She phoned everyone on it several times, checking again and again. Well, you know that. I've told you often enough. But she didn't phone you, did she?'

'Why would she?' he said, slowly. 'I wasn't there. I wasn't invited. It was just for his friends from school.'

Now that I had started I had to go on, even though I felt like a lemming running towards a cliff. 'Well, yes, that was the idea. My mum and dad made him promise that. But you were there anyway. And Alex didn't know.' I stepped back a couple of feet. 'Why was that?'

'I wasn't *at* the party,' he said again, his voice louder now. He sounded confident; I would have believed him if I hadn't

known otherwise. 'I don't know what you're talking about.' There was a silence, and then he went on, 'Look, this must be upsetting for you, coming back here. I wish you'd let me sort it out with you at the weekend. We could have got the house emptied.'

'It's not upsetting at all,' I said. It was as though I could hear my voice from elsewhere. I thought of Gemma behind that door and hoped to God she was texting someone who'd help us. 'Hearing that my brother had committed suicide was upsetting. Sitting next to my mother in the ambulance as she *died* was upsetting. This is nothing in comparison.'

Irritation flitted across his face. 'I know, babe,' he said. 'You've been through such a lot. Come on, let's get you back home.' He reached out to hug me. 'You need a good sleep.'

And then I couldn't help it. I laughed, though nothing about it was funny. 'I don't think so.' I didn't dare look at him. He was standing between me and the staircase and I realized too late there was no other way out. The silence was thick and frightening, and I couldn't stop myself from breaking it. 'Do you really think I sleep well in my bed? With you beside me?'

'What?'

The memory of that night flashed before me and I shouted, 'You with your phone, taking photos in the dark? You must think I'm stupid.'

'I don't know what you're talking about,' he said again. 'Come on, sweetie, let's get back home.' The floorboard creaked as he took a step towards me. I took a step back and banged into the wall next to Alex's door. 'You're just upset because you're back here.'

'I'm not. I hate being here, but this is nothing to do with that.' He reached out and put his arms around me. 'David, you were at the party and . . .' His hands were all over my body now, stroking me as though he owned me. As though

he could do whatever he wanted with me. 'Get off me! Keep away from me!'

Now his voice changed. He sounded hesitant. Confused. 'You're not wearing perfume, are you?'

My stomach tilted. 'What?'

'When you opened the door, you kissed me,' he said. 'When I hugged you, I noticed that you weren't wearing perfume. You know I love it when you do.' He stared at me as though he couldn't recognize me and he sounded perplexed, as though he was trying to figure something out. 'But when I walked upstairs with you I thought I could smell it. I can smell it now.' He took a step back. 'And I think I recognize it.'

67

Gemma

There was such a long, tense silence that I thought I would collapse. When Rachel spoke, her voice was further away, back towards her mother's room.

'My mum had some perfume in her room. I sprayed it. It reminds me of her.' She was a good liar. Very convincing. But then she'd convinced me for months that she hadn't known who I was.

David had stayed in the same place, just beside the bathroom, outside Alex's room. Inches from me. 'I don't think so.' I didn't dare breathe. 'I think you're lying to me, Rachel,' he said. 'Why would you do that?'

Terrified, I leaned back against the wall. My hip touched something. Something hard. I slid my hand behind my back and felt around.

It was a hockey stick. Alex's hockey stick.

And I thought of the only time I'd spoken to Alex in school, right at the start of our course, when we were sixteen. He was getting onto a coach to go on a sports trip and he was carrying too much kit and dropped his hockey stick. I'd handed it to him and he'd smiled and said, 'Thanks, Gemma.' I hadn't realized he'd known my name.

Now, with my hands around that stick, I felt he'd passed it to me, just when I needed it.

And then the door to Alex's room opened wider and David walked in. His back was to me. He walked over to the window, past the lamp he'd switched off that night so many years before, past the bed where he'd raped me and the blankets he'd thrown over my head so that I wouldn't see him. I could hear him breathing in the stale air. My body was coiled like a spring.

Then he turned and my legs buckled.

'Well, well, well,' he said. 'Look who's here.'

He stood in the darkening room, looking straight at me. He was shocked, I could tell, but confident in his strength. Now, as then, I was no threat to him.

I stood motionless, my hands behind my back, gripping Alex's hockey stick so hard that my skin felt raw. I stared at David, not wanting to show any fear. My stomach had plummeted, though. I was scared, and in the instant I looked at his face, I knew that he knew that too. From a movement near me, I realized Rachel was standing in the doorway; the open door stood between us.

'What's going on?' he said. He glanced over at Rachel. 'What's she doing here?'

'Gemma and I have been talking,' said Rachel. She was trying to sound strong, but I could hear a slight tremor in her voice and I knew that of course he would have heard that too. He'd recognize it as a weakness. I knew he'd be good at spotting those. 'Talking about the party.'

'What about it?' he said. 'You've talked about it a million times. I've told you I wasn't there.'

I took a deep breath. 'But you *were* there.' My voice was shaky. 'You *were* at the party.'

'Oh, and how would you know about that?' he said.

'There's a photo of you there in the kitchen that night.' From the tightening of his jaw I guessed he hadn't expected that. 'You were wearing the Coral T-shirt.'

'The Coral? I don't have a T-shirt like that. You're mistaking me for someone else. For Alex.'

'You do,' said Rachel from the doorway. 'Or you did. Alex had photos of you both at Glastonbury that summer, wearing the same T-shirt. I've seen them.'

'Yeah, I had one then. It got ripped there, the night they played, and I left it behind.'

He was a good liar. His voice was steady. Reasonable. If I hadn't seen that photo, if I hadn't seen him wearing that T-shirt, I probably would have believed him.

'I don't think so.' Rachel was agitated now. 'You were at the party and you were wearing the T-shirt. There's proof of it.' She gave a mocking laugh, designed to make anyone angry. 'You're just making a fool of yourself if you deny it.'

He stared at her for ages then, the realization that she was on my side, not his, dawning on him. Then he looked back at me.

My legs began to shake. He was still the same man I'd taken to view properties in Chester, the man who'd charmed me at dinner in the hotel in London. He was still as tall, as dark and as handsome as he had been, but something had changed. He was now under threat. His body was tense, ready for battle, and in that moment I knew he'd do anything to win.

'So,' he said. 'You two are in this together? That's interesting.' There was a pause and I knew neither Rachel nor I dared to break it. 'After all the things you said about her, Rachel. I'm surprised.'

Her face was crimson.

'So all those nights you told me about how you wanted to

317

pay her back for ruining your life, for your brother dying . . . you were lying then? Were you lying when you told me how much you hate her?'

'That was before I knew what really happened.'

'You *know* what happened, babe. I've told you. I wasn't there. You were mistaken.' His voice went soft. 'I've always been honest with you, Coco.'

Coco? I thought. I saw Rachel hesitate and guessed it was an affectionate name he used for her. My stomach tightened. Was she going to be taken in by that? Where would that leave me, if she was?

'Remember what you said about her husband and son?' He mimicked her again. 'Why should she have a happy marriage? Why should she have a good job? Alex didn't have any of that.'

'He didn't,' she said. 'And I'm wondering why, now.'

He carried on, speaking as though he were her, in a high, breathless voice. 'And that poor son. He's being brought up by his father. I bet he wouldn't even recognize his mother!'

'Shut up!' she yelled. 'Ignore him, Gemma! I didn't say that.'

But she had. I knew she had. I thought of Rory in his pyjamas that evening, fresh and damp from his bath. He'd hugged me before I left, holding his toy rabbit to his face, rubbing it across his cheek as he always did when he was tired. My eyes prickled. He was my reason for working so hard, and I just wasn't spending enough time with him. The thought of someone criticizing my relationship with my son made the fear inside me turn to strength.

'Why are you focusing on what she said rather than what you've done?' I said softly. 'The night of the party, you came in here and you raped me.'

'I did what?' He sounded so shocked I almost believed him.

'You raped me.'

68

Gemma

His eyes flickered towards Rachel. 'What's she talking about?'

When she spoke, I knew she was crying. 'You did it, David. And you let Alex take the blame.'

He flinched, then. 'What? I didn't! I wouldn't do that!'

I wanted to get out of there. He was going to keep on denying it and I couldn't stand to hear him. But Rachel was blocking the doorway and she was shouting.

'You did do it! I *knew* Alex hadn't done it! And you let him . . .' She almost choked on her tears. 'You let Alex take the blame and then he killed himself. And you came round night after night and sympathized with my mum when it was you that had done it all along!'

'I wasn't here,' he insisted. 'I've told you!'

And then Rachel turned to me and said, 'Gemma, were you wearing a hair bobble, the night of the party?'

I stared at her, confused at the change of subject. 'What?'

Her voice was strange. It was as though she was thinking something over and couldn't quite believe it. 'Can you remember?'

'I can remember everything,' I said. 'And no, I wasn't wearing a hair bobble.'

I heard David take a step or two back. I glanced at him; his eyes were fixed on Rachel and he held himself very still.

'What about lip gloss?' she said. 'When you were at the party, when you were eighteen, did you wear lip gloss?'

'What the hell are you talking about?' said David.

'Yes, I wore lip gloss,' I said. 'Why?'

'Did you take it with you to the party?'

I nodded.

'Did you take it home with you?'

I stared at her. 'No. I didn't. I must have lost it.'

Her face was pale and her hair was spiked with sweat. 'Was it raspberry ripple? Or blackberry? Or maybe vanilla fudge?'

At her words, I felt a kaleidoscope of memories form into shape. I remembered dipping my finger into the little pot of raspberry ripple lip gloss as our taxi approached Alex's house. Lauren had dipped her finger into it too, and we'd smeared it over our lips and giggled, before going into the party. I'd slipped it into my pocket and hadn't thought of it from that day to this.

'It was raspberry ripple,' I whispered. 'How did you know?'

'I found it, didn't I?' she said to David in a conversational tone. 'There was a pile of stuff in an old bag of yours. It looked like a load of junk. That's what you told me it was, didn't you? You said an ex-girlfriend had borrowed your bag and left it all behind. You said you'd throw it away, but you didn't, did you? Didn't you think I'd check?' Her face was pink with strain, but she looked him straight in the eye.

David was breathing hard and fast and staring at her so fiercely I took a step back. I knew something was going to happen.

'You've done this before, haven't you?' she said. 'Those things . . . what are they, something from each girl?'

A muscle moved in his jaw. I was on high alert now.

'They looked like trash, but they were precious to you

weren't they? They were significant. Did you keep them to remember your victims by?'

'You're insane,' he said. 'I don't know what you're talking about.'

'Funny,' she said. 'Because you made enough effort to hide them the second time.' He stared at her and she said, 'You really need to think twice before you let your wife borrow your car. You lent it to me last night without even thinking. You were so keen that I should go out and buy you some whisky that you completely fell for it when I said my car was out of petrol.'

His jaw was tight, his eyes on her.

'Did you really think I wouldn't look in the boot?' There was a tense silence and she said, 'Underneath the spare tyre? Odd place to put things that mean nothing to you.' She glanced at me. 'Gemma, there were *loads* of them.'

And then he broke. He reared back and suddenly he was taller. Broader. I steeled myself and faced him head-on.

Here it comes. Here it comes.

'You stupid bitch,' he said to Rachel. 'She wasn't even awake. All that fuss, calling the police, when she was asleep the whole time.'

I nodded, once, and moved into his view. 'And how do you know that?'

'You,' he sneered. I steeled myself. 'You were so drunk. Lying there with your skirt up round your waist. Anyone could have had you. You pathetic bitch. If you didn't want it, you shouldn't have flaunted it.'

And there it was. The last fifteen years of my life had been a lie.

69

Rachel

For a moment I don't think either Gemma or I could speak. The sound of him admitting what he'd done resonated in the air, and for that moment all was still. And then my body responded.

I pushed the door wide open.

David stood, poised for action, in the middle of the room. He was staring at Gemma – I think he thought she was his main threat.

He was wrong.

I leaped into the air and slapped him hard across the face. He swore and swung away from me. He'd taken his eyes off Gemma and I could see her standing still, staring at him.

He turned back towards her.

Big mistake.

I hit him again. A loud slap resonated in the room. At the same time, Gemma shouted, 'You bastard!'

My eyes met hers and in that moment we were united. His reign over us was about to end; I didn't know how and neither did she, I think, but that look between us decided it.

We had had enough.

'It was so long ago, Rachel,' he said, attempting a beseeching look. He put his hand out to me. I think he intended to caress me. 'It meant nothing.'

I relaxed and he saw it and smiled. Then I leaped onto Alex's bed, using the wooden frame as a lever to push myself off again, just as I used to when Alex and I played Pirates when we were kids, that game where we weren't allowed to touch the ground. My body must have kept the memory of that move he taught me all those years ago just for this moment, as I kicked and spun around and threw myself as hard as I could against David.

He staggered, and just as he started to right himself, I kicked out again, catching his shoulder. He crashed to the ground and I leaped on top of him, hitting him over and over again.

All I could think of was Alex and my mother and the way my dad had left, without even saying goodbye. I thought of the house, full of memories of them all. And now this memory would override it: my own husband had raped Gemma and made everyone think his friend, my brother, had done it.

And I thought, just for a second, of the girl I used to be, the girl who played chase around the house with Alex, who taught him to dance. The girl who lay on the floor next to his bed night after night after he was accused of rape, listening to him cry.

I was thinking all those things, and more, when I saw, out of the corner of my eye, David's fist coming towards my face.

70

Gemma

Rachel crashed to the ground like someone in a cartoon. I blinked, thinking she'd bounce back up, but she lay still, her head against the wooden leg of the bed. Almost immediately there was a swelling the size of an egg on her temple and for one mad moment I thought she was dead.

'So,' said David. He was breathing hard and took no notice of his wife's body lying on the floor. He stepped over her: one step nearer to me. 'It's just you and me now, Gemma.'

I stumbled back until I banged into the door. I could feel my phone in my jeans pocket and I was desperate to take it out and call for help. I needed to get out of the room, to run away from him.

He clearly knew what I wanted to do. He reached out, his hand almost brushing my face, and I flinched. He touched my hair then and it felt like an assault. My eyes met his; I saw excitement there. He let go of my hair and reached out beyond me to slam the door shut.

I jumped.

He smiled at me. 'Not quite what you were expecting?'

I couldn't say a word. It was like being in a room with an

animal, one you can't take your eyes off. One that you're terrified of.

'So, who thought we'd meet up again here?' he said. 'This is where it all started between us, isn't it?'

I froze.

'Remember that bed?' he asked, his voice soft, almost a caress. 'How much do you recall? I'd love to know that. When did you become aware of me, Gemma? What woke you? Do you remember the first touch? I've always wondered.' His tongue flicked out to wet his lips. 'I liked to think of that, afterwards.'

Acid rose at the back of my throat. I tried to make myself not listen, to plan instead what I should do. I could feel Alex's hockey stick behind me and I tried desperately to gather strength from it.

'You were always my special one,' he said. His eyes were bright and I saw beads of spittle foaming at the corners of his mouth. I couldn't take my eyes off him. 'You were the first, you see.' For a moment he looked proud. 'I did pretty well, didn't I? It took you fifteen years to figure out it was me. In a way I would have liked more of a challenge, but you know, if you'd been a bit brighter, I wouldn't have had the chance to do the others. And not all of them were quite as acquiescent as you, Gemma. I wouldn't have missed out on that for anything. So in a way I should thank you.' His eyes glittered. 'You gave me the idea, the opportunity. You gave me everything.' He smiled at me. 'You made me what I am.'

I shuddered. His eyes were fixed on me, and while my mind raced as it thought of escape routes, I knew I had to distract him.

'America didn't work out for you, then?' I said.

'Let's just say my time was up there,' he said, and smiled at me.

I knew that Rachel had been right about the other women.

My body shook at the thought of what he'd done, and I had to gather all my strength to talk to him when what I wanted was to run as fast as I could.

'Funny you turned up at the funeral,' I said. 'Paying your respects, were you?'

He shrugged. 'Well, yeah, in one way you could say that. She was always good to me.'

And look how he'd repaid her.

'Then you fell in love with Rachel. Bit convenient, wasn't it?'

He laughed. 'She called it serendipity. To be honest, I'd forgotten all about her until I saw her standing there, crying by the coffin. It's amazing how a bit of money can make someone so much more attractive.'

'So when she said she wanted to get revenge,' I said, conversationally, 'you just thought you'd go along with it? Bit of excitement for you, was it?' Out of the corner of my eye I saw something move behind him. Rachel's hand lifted, just an inch. My stomach tightened. I had to keep his attention away from her. 'Or was it your idea all along?'

'Nah,' he said. 'That was her idea.' He laughed again. 'One of her better ones. And of course I didn't exactly object. It was fun getting to know you better the second time around.'

Anger burned inside my stomach. 'Shame you had to drug me to do that.'

He shrugged. 'Sometimes I like to take the easy way. I couldn't risk you turning me down at the last minute, could I? Well, I could . . .' He smiled at me and I knew that he would have loved that challenge. 'But Rachel was waiting for me back at our hotel, and I didn't give you that much anyway.' His eyes gleamed. 'I saved the rest for her.'

I tried so hard not to express disgust at this. 'What, so that you could take photos of her without her knowing? Just as you did with me?'

'Well, I do like my souvenirs.'

I know it was stupid, but I had to ask. 'What have you done with those photos?'

He grinned. He knew this was my weak spot, the thing I'd worry about for years. 'You'll never know, sweetheart.' He glanced over at Rachel. 'And neither will she.' He moved a step closer. I stepped back and the hockey stick rubbed against me. I couldn't swing it from that angle, I knew, and I didn't want it to fall to the ground. I knew he hadn't noticed it was there. I needed him to move away. My mind was working frantically when he added, 'Speaking of which, that photo from the night we met . . .'

I frowned, unable to understand for a minute. 'What, in London?'

'No.' He laughed. 'The night of the party.'

'We didn't meet! You raped me when I was asleep.'

He shrugged. 'Same difference. Where is that photo? I'd like to see it.'

'Jack Howard has it,' I said.

'Who?'

'One of Alex's friends.'

'So how did you see it?'

'He showed it to me.'

'And you showed Rachel?'

I hesitated.

'One of you has a copy of it. Come on, Gemma. I just want to see it.' He winked at me. 'Add it to my collection. Where is it?'

'My phone's in my handbag,' I lied. 'Downstairs in the kitchen. The photo's in an e-mail to Rachel.' I needed to get him out of the room, to call the police.

I could see him trying to work out what to do. He couldn't let me go downstairs alone. He looked at Rachel. She was still on the floor, her eyes shut. Purple bruises were blooming on the side of her face.

He glanced around the room. There was a wooden chair next to Alex's desk, over by the window. 'Sit there,' he said.

I tried to buy some time. 'What?'

He grabbed my arm and pushed me over to the chair. There were files on it and I recognized them from school. It was the work Alex had done there; the work that had got him into Oxford. David tipped the chair and the files scattered across the floor. He kicked a couple out of the way, then opened the wardrobe. Inside the door were Alex's school ties. With such ease I knew he'd done this before, he grabbed one and tied me to the chair. I could see Rachel on the floor; his back was to her as he wrenched my arms behind my back. I saw her eyelids flicker, just once. I had to alert her and I had to cover up any noise she'd make.

So I started to yell. It took him by surprise, I could tell. He slapped my face hard, so that my head whipped to one side, but I carried on screaming. He reached over to the wardrobe for another tie and stood in front of me, trying to tie it around my mouth. I was wriggling and shrieking and in all the commotion he just didn't hear her.

But I did.

71

Rachel

I'd never thought for a minute that Gemma could yell like that. She was really going for it, screaming and shouting and swearing. It was the best thing she could have done.

David was frantic, trying to tie her up and shut her up at the same time. He was used to more passive victims. He was used to me.

He'd never seen me as a threat, more of an opportunity. He'd walked into that chapel at the crematorium last year and he'd winked at me – who winks at a bereaved daughter at a funeral? And when I winked back, he knew I'd be putty in his hands.

Well, you know what they say: pride comes before a fall.

There was no need for me to be quiet because Gemma was making enough noise to cover me, but still I slid my feet up slowly and waited a second. He hit her again – a punch in the jaw this time – and I knew she'd be as bruised as me soon. She screamed as though she were being murdered and I felt a surge of admiration for her.

And then I knew I was going to do this for her, as well as for Alex.

Within a second I was standing. David didn't notice a

329

thing, but I knew Gemma had. She'd leaned forward and grabbed his hair in her mouth and was pulling it so hard he couldn't turn to look in my direction. Now he was shouting too, calling her names that made me feel sick. In two steps I reached the door and grabbed Alex's hockey stick. I'd sat with him before he went to Oxford and we'd wound new binding tape around the handle so that he could grip it better, and written his initials, *A.C.*, on the tape. He hadn't played hockey in Oxford; the tape was pristine.

Now with both hands on the stick, I stood behind David. Gemma looked up at me and I mouthed, *Let go*.

She gave one more vicious tug that made him scream, then spat hair onto the floor.

I said, 'David?' in the sweetest voice I could muster.

In the split second between him hearing me and turning around, he let go of Gemma and I brought the stick down on his head, as hard as I could.

He fell to the ground, stunned. I hit him again and again and in the silence between blows I heard the sound of bone cracking.

Gemma shouted, 'Rachel!'

I turned, thinking she was telling me to stop, but she said, 'Quick, untie me!'

I twisted her chair away from David. 'You watch him,' I whispered, and she turned to look at him while I struggled with the knots. I gave up and pulled open the drawer to Alex's desk and grabbed the scissors that had always been there. I cut the ties and put the scissors in my back pocket in case I needed them later. Gemma stood, rubbing her legs.

Then David stirred.

She and I stood frozen to the spot as we watched him kneel, preparing to stand. He turned to look at us and I panicked.

Gemma didn't panic, though. She picked up that hockey

stick and she raised it high in the air. With a grim look on her face, she brought it crashing down on David's back.

He swore and fell back, landing heavily on his shoulder. I held my breath, but he started to push himself up again.

Gemma was panting and her knuckles were white where she gripped the stick. She looked terrified. I was, too, but more than that, I was exhilarated.

'Here,' I said. I stood behind her and put my arms around her, her back to my chest. I could feel her body shaking, and mine was, too. I grabbed hold of the stick so we were both holding it. Alex had stood like this with me when he was teaching me to play hockey in our garden the summer before he died.

David was about to rise when I felt Gemma lift her arms. I pressed against her, my body touching hers, my hands right next to hers on the hockey stick, and it was as though Alex were with us too, as though he were behind me, guiding me. Protecting me. As though the three of us were one.

David's eyes flicked from me to her and back again. I don't think he could believe we were sticking up for ourselves.

'This one's for you, *babe*,' I said to him.

We lifted our arms higher still and Gemma shouted, 'It's from all of us, you bastard.'

And then with our bodies together, united, we brought Alex's hockey stick down with full force on David's head.

This time he lay still.

72

Gemma

Saturday, August 19

Joe was waiting for me in the reception area of the police station when I was finally allowed to leave. It was after two A.M. by then. He looked as exhausted as I felt, and he held me to him for so long that I thought I'd go to sleep in his arms.

'Where's Rachel?' he asked. 'Is she coming with us?'

'They've taken her to hospital,' I said. 'They want her to stay in overnight, because she lost consciousness.'

He winced. 'And are you all right, sweetheart?' He put his arms around me again and held me to him. 'I've been so worried.'

'I'm fine,' I said. 'Let's just get out of here.' Poor Joe, he'd been sitting there for hours waiting for me, not knowing what was going on. The police had told him I was being questioned about an incident that had occurred in Rachel's house; that was all he knew up till then. 'It was to do with Rachel's husband. Long, long story.'

He raised his eyebrows at that, because of course he hadn't known she was married. I hadn't even known myself until recently. It was good now to have him sitting beside me,

one hand on my leg as he drove. I said I'd tell him everything when we got back to my parents' house, and though I
closed my eyes and pretended to sleep, I knew he wasn't
fooled.

'My mum's going to be worried,' I said as Joe parked the car.

'I called her. I told her I was with you and we'd be back
late.'

'You didn't tell her anything?'

'I didn't *know* anything,' he said. 'I said we'd talk to them
in the morning.'

I could only imagine the self-restraint my mother had had
to show then. My dad must have had his work cut out calming her down, but as we entered the house, all was quiet from
their bedroom.

As soon as we were in the living room, Joe opened his
mouth to speak, but I said, 'I need to shower,' and ran upstairs
to the bathroom and closed the door.

I kept my eyes shut while I showered. All I could think of
was David saying, *You made me what I am.* I scoured my skin,
and the heat of the shower and the tears on my face and that
scrubbing motion reminded me of the shower I'd taken after
the party where I'd tried to wash away my shame.

Fifteen years later, it had finally ended.

Back downstairs in my dressing gown, I sat in the living
room while Joe made a pot of tea and some toast. Although I
hadn't thought I could eat a thing, I found I was ravenous and
sat at the kitchen table while he toasted more bread. He sat
quietly with me while I ate; I knew he was bursting with
questions but he didn't say a word.

When I'd finished eating, he tidied away the plates and
mugs, and we sat on the sofa, his arms around me, a blanket
covering us.

'I want you to tell me everything,' he said. 'Don't miss
anything out. Don't try to spare my feelings, or think you're

333

doing me a favour by leaving things out.' He stroked my face and kissed me. 'I love you, Gemma. I'll love you no matter what you say. But please don't lie to me.'

And so I told him.

It was an hour before I finished. He kept quiet throughout, though he did prompt me occasionally.

'And then we ran out of the room and Rachel remembered there was a key to the bedroom. They hadn't used it since Alex died; it was by the front door on a hook. I held the door shut and she ran downstairs to find it. Once she'd locked him in, I called the police and we waited outside, in the driveway. They were there within minutes.'

Joe's face was pale and drawn by the time I'd finished. 'The same man,' he said at last. 'I've hated him for so long, Gem. You know that. When I think of what he did to you all those years ago, I want to kill him. But now. The things he's done since.' He put his arms around me and buried his head in my neck. 'You must have been terrified.'

'You wouldn't believe it. When Rachel was downstairs and I was holding the door shut . . . It was an old door handle and if he'd been fit he would have been able to get out of there easily.' I shuddered. 'I knew he wouldn't be able to get up. I knew we had a few minutes, at least. But that thought, that he'd pull open the door . . . I was so frightened.'

'I wish you'd told me you were going there. I wish I could have helped you.'

'But we weren't expecting him to turn up,' I said. 'I was just going to be with her to pick up some documents. She didn't want him to find them.'

'Even so,' he said. 'I hate to think of you going through that.' We were quiet for a while, then he said, 'So what's happened to him now?'

'I'm not sure. Apparently he was coming to just as the

police arrived. They carted him off to hospital and he's under guard now.' I winced. 'We hit him pretty hard.'

Joe shrugged. 'Shame. But when the police got there and found him unconscious and locked in a room, did they just believe what you said? You both clearly had something to do with it.'

'We were taken to the police station.' We'd been glad to go. We *asked* to go. At least we were safe there. 'And I gave them my shirt.'

'What? Why did you do that?'

'That night at the hotel in London, David was recording me while we had our meal. He'd planned it all, known what he wanted to do.'

'Recorded you with his phone? Didn't you notice?'

'No, he had a video camera that was in a button that Rachel had sewn onto his shirt,' I said.

'A button?'

'I know. I couldn't believe it. Rachel told me about it; she sent me a link to it just the other day. I thought that two could play at that game, so I sent off for a shirt with buttons and I ordered the same recorder he'd bought, and I sewed the buttons on before I went out. Everything that happened in her house last night was recorded.'

He looked at me as if I'd grown another head. 'Sound as well?'

I nodded. 'It was clear as a bell. You could hear that we broke a bone when we hit him.' I swallowed hard, remembering also the clarity of the video he'd made of me criticizing Joe. That was the only thing I hadn't told him. I hoped he'd never hear about it.

He winced. 'But why were you wearing the shirt? You thought you were just going to help Rachel, didn't you?'

'I was testing it,' I said. 'I knew that Rachel would have seen the buttons before, on David's shirt; she'd sewn them

on. I wanted to see if she noticed them. If she didn't, I figured he wouldn't either. Before I had a chance to tell her, he'd turned up. The police wouldn't touch the button as it was evidence, but I gave them the login to the website where the footage was stored and they could see everything.'

He sat quietly, holding me to him. I knew it was going to take a long time for him to grasp what had been happening over the last couple of months. 'I just don't understand why you didn't go to the police straight away, as soon as you saw him going into Rachel's flat.'

'I wanted to talk to her first,' I said. 'I was worried about her. I knew that if I told the police before speaking to her, I'd never get the chance to ask her why she was with him. And then when I spoke to her she asked me not to go just yet. At first she said she wanted us to confront him together, but we were too scared to do that. We were going to go to the police tomorrow – today, now – and make a statement. And then he pre-empted us.'

'What do you think she'll do now?'

'She'll probably go abroad. She needs to get away.' We were quiet for a while; Joe's hands gripped mine as if he'd never let me go.

When he spoke next, he sounded so sad and confused. 'I just wish you'd told me, right from the beginning. When you came back from London, if you'd told me then, none of this would have happened.'

'I think it would, just in a different way. She was still determined to get revenge, and of course he loved having the chance to do whatever he wanted. And how could I have said to you, weeks later, "Oh, you remember that conference I went to a month ago? Remember I said I'd had dinner in my room and went to sleep early? Well, I didn't. I lied about that. And remember I texted you to say I was in bed, about to go to sleep? I wasn't. I was in a restaurant having dinner with a

client instead and we got drunk and then I think he kissed me, but I don't remember. Nothing else happened, though. I don't remember but I know nothing happened." '

He grimaced. 'I wouldn't have believed you. I know it. And it's my fault, too. You looked awful when I picked you up off the London train and I still went out. I knew you wanted me to stay home, but I didn't. I'm so sorry, Gem.' He gave me a tentative look. 'Do you think him being arrested will help bring some peace to you now?'

I thought for a while about all that had happened and how Rachel and I had united to overcome him. 'I think so,' I said. 'I hope so. Rachel will have a bigger problem, though. She's lost everything.'

'Not quite everything,' Joe said quietly. 'You've been a really good friend to her.'

'And she has to me, too.'

We sat in silence for a while, and then he said, 'About your job. How do you fancy taking on someone new?'

I closed my eyes, exhausted. 'I've already advertised. I told you.'

'No,' he said. 'How about if I come in with you? I could train up for Brian's job and take over the lettings when he retires. We could work it so that one of us was always at home with Rory.'

'You'd do that? You've never wanted to work with me before.'

'All this,' he said, 'not David, but all the rest . . . You're out at work all the time and I know you want to spend time with Rory. You've done so well, building up the business, and it's as though you're being punished for that now. I want your business to thrive. I want to be part of that, Gemma. I want both of us to do it.'

I hardly dared ask. 'What about Ireland?'

'Can we think about that as something for the future?' he asked. 'In a few years' time, maybe?'

'What, not by Christmas?'

He laughed. 'I'm sorry. I was an idiot.'

I was exhausted. 'Let's talk about it tomorrow,' I said. 'I need to go to bed.'

Outside the sky was still dark. We had a few hours until Rory would wake. He was sprawled in the centre of my bed; before I'd left the evening before, I'd promised him he could sleep with me that night. He lay on his back, legs and arms spread wide, Buffy buried in the crook of his neck. Carefully Joe and I got into bed either side of him and Joe reached over to hold me in his arms. Rory lay between us, his chest slowly rising and falling. In his sleep he seemed to know we were there, and snuggled between us.

It was all over.

I held Rory and Joe close to me. They were my future, but they weren't the only ones I had to consider now.

I thought of Rachel in her hospital bed and hoped she was sleeping and not thinking about the man she'd married who'd destroyed her family. I hoped she could move past the tragedy of her childhood, knowing she'd overcome the worst things life could throw at her. I knew she'd always be part of my life, the way she had been for so many years without my realizing it.

And Alex, too. I thought of the boy he used to be and how at last he was vindicated. There'd been a moment when I'd stood in his bedroom where I'd felt connected to him. I'd sensed his presence there, not just in the way his hockey stick stood behind me, as though it had waited fifteen years to be put into my hands again, but in the way his sister and I had moved as one to bring David down. Alex was there with us in that moment, rooting for us, giving us strength.

Rachel and I had to live our lives for him, now.

Acknowledgements

Thank you so much to Toby Jones at Headline and to Danielle Perez at Berkley for your invaluable editorial advice and support. It's been such a pleasure working with you both.

Thanks to my writer friends, Fiona Collins and Sam Gough, who made the experience of writing this novel such fun. I'm so grateful for your support and your tact when I went off piste!

Thanks to Anne-Marie Thomson for your advice about what an estate agent does all day. It was so kind of you to answer all my questions.

Thank you to Graham Bartlett, author and ex–Chief Superintendent of Brighton and Hove, for your advice and for talking me through what would happen to a woman in Gemma's position.

Finally, thanks so much to Daisy Ambrose for your social media advice.

Reading Group Questions

1. Do you think Gemma's parents were right to persuade her to drop the charge against Alex? Was it really in her best interest?

2. Given the seriousness of the accusation against him, do you think Alex should have had the right to defend himself in court?

3. If the case had gone to court at the time, do you think Alex would have been found guilty?

4. Gemma met Caitlin at university and they were best friends for years before Gemma met Joe. Gemma assumed that if she confided in Caitlin, her loyalties would be to her brother rather than her friend. Do you think she was right?

5. How much do you think David's rejection from Oxford – and Alex's acceptance – was the reason for his behaviour that night?

6. Gemma is terrified that, if her marriage ended, she would no longer live with Rory. Do you think this fear prevents some women from fulfilling their career potential and encouraging their partner to be a stay-at-home dad?

7. In the final scene, Joe says he wishes Gemma had talked to him, but there were occasions throughout the book where he clearly knew she was unhappy. Do you think the responsibility also lay with him to talk to her and to try to discover the cause of her unhappiness?

8. Alex's father responded to his son's death by running away and starting a new family, whereas his mother responded by breaking down and refusing to leave the family home. Why do you think Rachel blamed her mother rather than her father for her subsequent lack of a healthy childhood? Why do you think people can react so differently to a tragedy?

9. What difference do you think it would have made to Alex's mother's physical and mental health if she'd known what really happened at the party?

10. Rachel has grown up believing Gemma was responsible for the destruction of her family. After everything they've been through in this book, do you think they have the chance of becoming true friends?

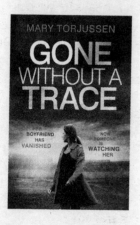

First published in paperback in 2018 by
HEADLINE PUBLISHING GROUP

1

Cataloguing in Publication Data is available from the British Library

ISBN 978 1 4722 4081 1

Typeset in Meridien by Jouve (UK), Milton Keynes

Printed and bound in Great Britain by CPI Group (UK) Ltd, Croydon, CR0 4YY

Headline's policy is to use papers that are natural, renewable and
recyclable products and made from wood grown in sustainable forests.
The logging and manufacturing processes are expected to conform to
the environmental regulations of the country of origin.

HEADLINE PUBLISHING GROUP
An Hachette UK Company
Carmelite House
50 Victoria Embankment
London EC4Y 0DZ

www.headline.co.uk
www.hachette.co.uk

THE
GIRL
I USED
TO BE

MARY TORJUSSEN

HEADLINE

'Divorce.' She posed shoulders back, right hip cocked like an Angelina Jolie wannabe. 'It does a body good.'

As did a competent plastic surgeon, I'd wager.

'Well, that's great. Good for you.' Pavlik's eyes did a fly-by up the woman's leg to her waist and past her cleavage, before landing innocently on her face.

Like many people in law enforcement, Pavlik had the uncanny ability to enter a room and take in everything without seeming to. Though, in the current example, a pair of bodacious D-cups was admittedly hard for anybody to miss.

The clerk was signaling for us to approach the desk and since everyone appeared to have forgotten I was there, I cleared my throat. 'Umm, Pavlik?' I'd started calling the sheriff 'Pavlik' when he'd suspected me of murder – not as unusual a circumstance as that might sound – and had never gotten out of the habit.

It had become our little joke, but now, with this beautiful woman spidering all over him, my use of his last name seemed less . . . cute. I mean, how was I supposed to mark my territory when I didn't even call said territory by its first name?

'I'm sorry?' Pavlik was still ogling Zoe.

'Jake, the desk clerk is ready for us.' I stuck my hand out to the other woman. 'Hi, I'm Maggy Thorsen.'

'Zoe Scarlett.' We shook professionally. Kind of.

'Zoe was with the Chicago Convention Bureau when I was the sheriff's office liaison to the bureau.' Pavlik, having put his eyes back in his head, seemed to realize an explanation was called for. 'We worked together a couple of times and when Zoe moved to Fort Lauderdale and became the conference organizer for Mystery 101 a couple of years back, she asked me here to speak.'

'And we're very glad to have you back.' Zoe was bouncing up and down. Or parts of her were.

'How nice,' I said lamely, thinking, Scarlett? Like Miss Scarlett in *Clue*?

The woman in question turned to Pavlik. 'Are you two . . . together?'

Apparently she'd missed our clinch, or maybe that sort of thing was common behavior between strangers in a Florida hotel line. Either way, the conference organizer recognized the way the question sounded and actually blushed. 'I mean, I'm not sure a double room was specified.'

I glanced at Pavlik. Hadn't he told her I was coming?

'I'm sorry,' the sheriff said, 'I—'

'Missy?' Zoe called to one of her minions in the milling mass near the elevators, the millers seeming to have regrouped. 'We'll check with my assistant, but I'm sure it's just a matter of making sure there are enough towels and the like. Missy Hudson!' Zoe Scarlett put a command edge in her voice this time. 'I swear that girl just pretends not to hear me when—'

'Excuse me, ma'am,' interrupted one of a foursome of golfers that had fallen into line behind us, toting bags of clubs that could have stocked a Cro-Magnon arsenal. 'If you aren't quite ready to check-in, would you mind if we play through?'

'Oh, no. Not at all.' Zoe waved for us to step out of the line. 'We may need to handle our situation with the hotel's event coordinator anyway. You just go ahead.'

The men hefted their golf bags as a young woman of about twenty-five with hair just on the blonde side of brown reached us. 'I'm sorry, Zoe. Did you need something?'

'Missy, this is the featured speaker for our forensic track, Sheriff Jacob Pavlik. I don't believe you were on the committee the last time he spoke at Mystery 101.'

'Good to meet you, Sheriff Pavlik. I'm Missy Hudson.'

'Jake, please, Missy,' he said, shaking the young woman's hand. 'And this is Maggy Thorsen.'

'Oh, of course.' Missy flashed a smile at me. 'I received your email saying Ms Thorsen was accompanying you, which was no trouble at all, given that Zoe had already requested a suite for you.'

Again, Zoe flushed. 'Well, good. Not to worry, then.'

It didn't take a mind-reader to realize that Zoe Scarlett – and could that be her *real* name? – had designs on something more than putting on a kick-ass conference this weekend.

'Is that Larry? Thank God.' Zoe was looking past her assistant and toward the front entrance of the hotel.

I turned, following her gaze through the floor-to-ceiling windows to a lanky man who was stubbing out a cigarette as a curly-haired younger guy spoke to him. As we watched, Smoker held up a hand to Curly-top that seemed more stop-sign than farewell and stepped into the revolving door.

If 'Larry' was trying to get away from the kid, he didn't succeed. Curly-top followed him in.

'Missy, can you handle this?' Zoe asked, already moving away.

'This' presumably being Pavlik and me. 'Not to worry, we can just get back in line,' I said to Zoe's retreating back.

Then I noticed the dozen or so people who'd queued up since we'd moved aside. The way things were going, it would be hours before Pavlik and I were alone in his reserved suite.

'No need to do that,' Missy said. 'I have an inside track.'

Stepping to one side of the desk, she stuck her head through an archway. 'Excuse me, Louis, but we're getting backed up out here?'

A man came out, struggling into a red-and-gold uniform tunic. 'I'm so sorry, Missy. We'll bring out two more clerks immediately.'

'That would be wonderful. The people arriving now will be anxious to get checked in – and changed, of course – before tonight's event. And could you also give me the welcome packet for the Flagler Suite?'

'Of course.'

The young woman certainly got things done. And pleasantly. My oft-irascible if not downright cantankerous business partner, Sarah Kingston, could take lessons from the mouths of babes.

Age-wise, I mean.

Raised voices drew my attention back to the entrance. Curly-top was nowhere in sight, but Larry the Lanky Smoker was talking to Zoe. He had a shaved head and handlebar mustache above a dress shirt and sports jacket, dark slacks and a pair of mated wingtips below. I recognized the style of shoes because it was one many of my former colleagues in the financial industry had favored while conducting business in the office or – in a more colorful version – on the golf course.

None of those shoes, though, had quite the panache of this pair. With strategically-placed patches of soft tan, dark brown, pale yellow and forest green, these wingtips didn't look so much like golf shoes as what golf shoes aspire to be when they grow up. The man wearing them expected to be recognized. To the point of demanding to be.

But I'd be damned if I could place him.

'If I must, I must,' he was saying to Zoe as he fussed with his mustache. 'But prior notice would have been appreciated.'

'I'm certain you were sent—'

'Here we go.' Missy, apparently not noticing the dust-up involving her boss, handed Pavlik an envelope. 'Everything should be in here, including your tickets for tonight's event. Since it's just barely six, you'll have time to freshen up and change before we meet in the lobby at seven-fifteen.'

'The lobby?' Pavlik echoed, as I saw any hopes of an intimate evening in the hotel suite circle the drain. But then Pavlik had been invited as an honored guest and being on the conference's dime would mean that he also had to be on the conference's time, not my own.

Bright side, this was his show and maybe they were taking us out to dinner. A nice seafood restaurant on the well-tended waterfront would—

'Yes, here,' Missy confirmed. 'And, please, by seven-fifteen for the bus to the station. Oh, and you did bring costumes, I hope?'

I perked up. 'Costumes?'

Pavlik glanced at me.

Wings, I mouthed.

The sheriff suppressed a grin. 'Nobody said anything about an event tonight, Missy, but you're paying me and comping us. The where and when are all we need to know.'

I admired the sentiment, if not the resulting postponement of nookie time.

'I'm so sorry.' Missy threw a concerned look at her boss, who was still deep in conversation with Larry the Smoker. 'Zoe didn't email you about our murder train?'

'No, but that's fine,' Pavlik said. 'By "murder train," do you mean like a mystery dinner theater, but on a railroad car?'

A similar train ran on weekends between downtown Milwaukee and Chicago's Union Station.

'Yes, though it's more "cars," plural, and we're just offering a mystery-themed cake and coffee. Not only is it cheaper and easier than full dinner service or even hors d'oeuvres on a train, but it gave me a great theme to build the event around.' Missy pointed to a sign.

'"Murder on the Orient Espresso,"' I read aloud, wondering why I, a public relations person turned coffeehouse owner – said coffeehouse even being in a historic train depot – had never thought of mounting an event based on Agatha Christie's classic 1934 mystery novel.

Though I wasn't above stealing the idea and smuggling it back to Wisconsin. 'What fun. Are you actually having espresso?'

'Yes. In addition to a full bar, of course.' She gestured toward the coffee cart. 'Boyce, the hotel's coffee vendor, will be onboard providing coffee and cake.'

I didn't point out that coffee – which could be easily brewed by the large pot – and espresso, brewed by the shot, were two entirely different efforts. Especially when dealing with a crowd. 'How many people will there be?'

'Fewer than twenty for tonight, which is a separate, ticketed event.' Missy frowned. 'I'd hoped for more, but then this is the first year we've done something on the eve of the conference.'

'That sounds like a very respectable turnout, and it'll give you a chance to get the bugs out for next year.' One of the 'bugs,' perhaps, being espresso for twenty. 'I own a coffeehouse in Wisconsin, so let me know if your vendor needs help.'

'Oh, that is *so* nice of you.' Missy gave me an enthusiastic if unexpected hug. 'This train event was my idea and I really do want to make it a huge success.'

The girl seemed to be starving for approval, something she probably didn't get a lot of from her boss – especially if Missy was trying to spread her wings a bit. Zoe, as mother bird, seemed more like the type to knock impertinent chicks out of the nest prematurely than to nurture them.

'Missy?' Zoe, as if she'd heard, came over with the lanky, bald man in tow. 'You and I discussed for weeks that Larry would play the role of our detective, Hercule Poirot, tonight. *Yet* he says you never even asked him to take part.'

Missy's eyes went wide. 'But Zoe, you said that *you'd* take care of . . .' Then, probably not wanting to argue the point publicly, 'I don't know what could have happened. Sheriff Pavl— I mean, Jake didn't receive an email, either.'

'Email!' Larry actually snorted. 'I don't respond to *e*mail.'

Even Zoe, trying as she was to calm the waters, seemed

surprised by that. 'But your "PotShots" is an online book review site. How can you not—'

'Precisely,' the man interrupted. 'Which is why I don't open my email. Do you really think I want to hear all the belly-aching from authors – whether newbies or established franchises – who seem to think I *owe* them a good review?'

PotShots rang a bell. 'Why, you're Laurence Potter.'

I felt Pavlik's surprise as Potter turned toward me. 'I am, indeed. And you are?'

'Maggy Thorsen,' I said, holding out my right hand. 'I enjoy your reviews.'

'Then you certainly can't be an author yourself.' Potter enveloped my fingers and drew their knuckles to his lips, a glint in his eye. 'How refreshing.'

'As refreshing as your critiques.' I took my hand back, willing myself not to reflexively wipe it on my pants. A rumored womanizer and sleazeball, Potter might be a nasty piece of work – as were his reviews – but he was also borderline charming and certainly entertaining. 'You sure don't pull any punches.'

A modest shrug, though I had a feeling that nothing Potter did was modest, and that what he did to appear modest was nothing like unrehearsed. 'Too many critics simply don't bother to review books that are dreadful. Personally, I don't subscribe to the old saw, "If you can't say something nice, don't say anything at all." In fact, I don't know why words uttered by some rabbit in a children's animated feature would be so revered in the first place.'

The words were 'uttered by' Thumper in *Bambi*. And it was 'say *nothing* at all,' not 'say anything at all.' Sheesh, if you can't trust a reviewer to get it right . . .

'What about the old saw, "those who can't do, teach"?' a voice from behind me contributed. 'Do you "subscribe" to that one, Larry?'

I turned to see a chic woman with short, choppy black hair. She wore a deceptively simple white blouse over designer jeans – and not the department store kind. I'm talking denims that command upwards of a thousand dollars. And have waiting lists.

'Laurence,' Potter snapped, his eyes narrowing.

The new addition to our group smiled icily. 'Oh, Larry, I've known you for years. Why so formal?'

'I've grown tired of correcting the hearing-impaired morons who insist on confusing my name with that of JK Rowling's detestable four-eyed wizard.'

Ah, Harry Potter.

'Be glad your name's not Dumbledore,' I said under my breath, winning me a warning look from Pavlik, who knew I liked to stir a cauldron myself now and then.

Meanwhile, the smile was etched on the chilly face of the elegant woman. 'So now you only need to inform them that Laurence is spelled with a "U" and not the more pedestrian "W."'

'As is the case with Olivier and Fishburne, so I'm in rather good company,' Potter said. 'And speaking of the company we keep, how nice it is to see you again, Rosemary.'

'And me, you,' the woman said. They air-kissed, each of them careful not to engage in any actual flesh-to-flesh contact.

It was obvious both of them were lying respectively through their tightly clenched teeth and suddenly I realized why. 'Rosemary Darlington. I've been reading about your new book, *Breaking and Entering*.'

And I had, on PotShots. The first book from the legendary lady of romantic suspense in years and Laurence Potter had absolutely eviscerated it. Called it smut, even. Apparently the 'Breaking' part referred to hearts. And the 'Entering' . . . well, as Potter had written on PotShots, *Do I have to spell it out for you?*

Rosemary Darlington had reportedly done just that, explicitly and with quite a few redundant – and occasionally imaginative – variations over the four hundred pages of her erotic suspense novel.

I had the feeling that this *was* going to be a fun weekend – both in and out of the hotel's Flagler Suite.

TWO

'So, if you knew Rosemary's book would be a sore point,' Pavlik said as he squeezed shaving cream into his palm, 'why bring it up?'

'Potter's review was obviously the elephant in the room – or lobby,' I said, inspecting our digs. 'Best to trot the thing out and let it take a few laps – dissipate the sting.'

'Mixer of metaphors.' Pavlik's reflection in the mirror looked past me to the oversized numbers on the bedside radio alarm clock. 'We have to be downstairs in thirty minutes.'

'Don't worry, I'll be ready. What's this?' I pointed at a box that had been on the coffee table when we arrived. 'A welcome gift from your friend Zoe?'

'Afraid not,' he said. 'And Zoe and I *are* just friends, while we're trotting out the elephants in the room.'

'Hey,' I said, raising my hands in utter innocence. 'Did I ask?'

'Of course not. That would be admitting you cared.'

'But I do care,' I protested. 'You know that. I just don't get jealous.'

An outright lie, of course. But showing jealousy only gives the other person – or persons – power. And, besides, as my now defunct marriage proved, if two people are meant to be together they will be.

Or not.

'So what is this?' I asked again, tapping on the box.

'I shipped a few things ahead for my panel.'

I should have known. 'Welcome gifts' rarely arrive in hotel rooms via UPS. And this one was addressed to Pavlik care of the hotel in the sheriff's own handwriting. Though a forward-thinking man might have shipped a few romantic . . . toys to surprise his lady friend. Perhaps flavored whipped cream or—

My stomach rumbled. 'Did Missy say they'll just have dessert on the train?'

'Cake, I think. Maybe we can grab a packaged sandwich or granola bar from the hotel's newsstand on the way out.'

Too much to hope the newsstand carried grilled snapper with lemon butter and capers to-go.

I picked up a glossy hardcover to the right of the UPS box. The cover of the book showed a steam train chugging over a narrow trestle, water on both sides of it.

'Flagler's Railroad,' I read aloud.

'Henry Flagler is a legend down here,' Pavlik said, apparently satisfied with the lathering of his face as he reached for his razor. 'Flagler's dream was to build an "Overseas Railroad" extending out from Miami over more than a hundred miles of mostly open water to Key West. And he lived to see it realized, too, but in nineteen thirty-five a hurricane destroyed large parts of it and killed a lot of workers. You can still see long sections of his railbed – mostly elevated – as you drive down the Keys.'

'He never rebuilt it?' I was flipping through the book.

'By then Flagler was dead, the railroad hadn't paid for itself and people had taken to calling the project "Flagler's Folly."'

'That's sad.' A grainy black-and-white picture showed the wooden trestle topped with thick crossties. The metal rail on one side of the track was completely missing. The other was curled like bits of ribbon, I imagined from the hurricane or its aftermath. The photographer must have been standing on one of the ties, shooting down the length. In the distance the trestle just disappeared into the water.

Had a train been on that trestle when the storm hit it? And if so, would we know it or would all traces of it – of *them*, the poor workers – simply have been swept away?

'Don't feel sorry for Flagler,' Pavlik said, nearly finished with his razor. 'The man was a highly successful industrialist and lived to see his dream come true. How many people do we know who can say that?'

'Very few.' I flipped to the title page of the book. Published by Florida History & Tourism and written by . . . 'Zoe Scarlett,' I said aloud.

'Zoe?' Pavlik repeated. 'I'm not sure she has dreams.'

I wasn't going to touch that one. I put the tourist book down, thinking it explained what Zoe did for the remainder of the year.

The man of *my* dreams set down his razor and inspected the closeness of his shave in the mirror. 'Not bad.'

'Not bad at all,' I agreed, unzipping my jeans. It was a shame we wouldn't be staying in tonight.

Based on my inspection, the Flagler Suite was large and luxurious, featuring a king-sized bed, ocean-view whirlpool and granite-countered kitchenette, should one need to grab sustenance traversing between the two.

Still, I told myself, if the room had romance written all over it, tonight's event promised more in the way of melodrama. Apparently the plan for the evening's loose re-enactment of Agatha Christie's *Murder on the Orient Express* featured Rosemary Darlington and Laurence Potter in the lead roles.

'I think you'd make a much better Poirot than Potter,' I said. 'Except for the mustache, of course.'

'Laurence Potter – and Rosemary Darlington – are the guests of honor. I'm just the lead forensics guy. Sort of the . . .' Pavlik's eyes followed me as I stepped out of my pants, '. . . working stiff.'

Thankfully, more like stiffy. Thus encouraged, I started to take my time, doing a bit of a striptease, unbuttoning my blouse to expose what I thought of as my 'good' red bra. Though, truth to tell, I intended it for no-good. 'Appropriate, then, that you're playing Ratchett.'

I slipped off the shirt and tossed it onto the bed, which had been turned down to expose the gazillion thread-count linens. 'You know, the *stiff*. So to speak.'

'So to speak.' The eyes in the mirror caught mine. 'I'm hoping we can get back here early.'

It wasn't so much Pavlik's words as the way he said them. Experiencing a little thrill down my spine, I sidled up behind him and wrapped myself around his bare torso, resting the palms of my hands on his flat abs. I'd forgotten how good he felt. 'Early would be great for me, too.'

Pavlik's eyes, usually blue against his tanned face and dark, wavy hair, could change to slate gray – nearly black – when he was . . . well, let's say 'agitated.' We should also acknowledge that this color transformation could come from anger as well as lust, and I had unfortunately seen more of the former than the latter.

Not tonight, though.

His mood-ring eyes were deliciously dark as he turned and tipped my chin up so my mouth met his.

'We're going to be late,' I said in a 'convince-me' kind of voice, tasting the lovely combination of residual soap and current sheriff.

'They'll wait,' he said, edging me toward the bed. 'The Orient Espresso isn't going anywhere fast. At least not without a corpse.'

As it turned out, Jake Pavlik was right.

In – oh, so many ways.

THREE

Luckily for our breach of punctuality, it turned out that wrangling mystery writers was akin to herding the proverbial flock of cats. When we arrived outside the lobby door ten minutes late, people were still milling about on the sidewalk.

It was dark, landscape lights illuminating the hotel's palm trees and tropical plantings. A tiny, nearly transparent gecko scurried past my foot and up the trunk of a— 'Whoa, what's that?'

The tree I referred to was shaped like a gigantic bunch of asparagus, thick multiple stalks topped by a wide green canopy.

'Impressive, isn't it?' Pavlik said. 'I asked about it the last time I was here for Mystery 101.'

'Impressive' was an understatement. The thing looked like it had been there for decades, if not centuries, a hunch borne out by the fact the tree seemed to have earned a spotlight and plaque of its very own. 'Incredible. And very southern-looking. Is it a mangrove?' I asked, pulling out the only tree name I could remember from the Florida guidebook.

'No, this is a banyan,' Pavlik said. 'You'll see mangroves mostly in coastal areas like the Bay of Florida and also in the sawgrass marsh of the Everglades. Mangroves can grow in salt water – even form islands. They're amaz—'

'And the banyans?' I reminded my own personal Mr Wizard.

'Glad you asked,' Pavlik said, grinning. He took my arm and hooked it around his to stroll closer to the tree. 'Banyans, *too*, are amazing. A type of fig or ficus, they're actually epiphytes.'

'Gosh,' I said, running my hand up and down his bicep. 'That *is* amazing. What's an epiflight?'

'Epiphyte,' he corrected. 'And it's a plant that lives off another plant.'

'A parasite.' If so, this was the Tyrannosaurus Rex of parasites. The canopy looked to be able to fill a city block and the gnarled trunk had to be eight feet across at the base.

'Technically, yes. Birds drop the banyan seeds, which germin-ate and grow in the cracks and crevices of other trees. As the banyan grows, its limbs drop these supporting roots you see and they eventually become the multiple trunks that wind around and envelope the entire original host tree.'

We were under the wide branches now, and I squinted up, trying to differentiate the leaves. 'So you're saying there's another tree in there?'

'Most likely just a hollow core where it once was. A banyan this old probably strangled the poor host tree long ago.'

'So the "guest" repays the host by smothering it to death and then taking its place like the poor host was never there in the first place.' I stepped back. 'Nice.'

'Don't worry,' Pavlik said, slipping his arm around my waist. 'I'll protect you from the mean old—'

'Excuse me,' a voice called. 'Can we *please* get everybody on the bus?'

Zoe Scarlett was standing under the hotel's marquis with a clipboard. She was showing even more cleavage than earlier, which I judged to be her idea of transitioning the look from daytime to nighttime.

'Thank God I can depend on you at least, Jacob.' Her gaze passed right over me to Pavlik in his black dress shirt, open at the neck, and black pants. 'Perfect.'

'I was afraid it telegraphed bad guy,' Pavlik said, flashing her a smile.

'*Stiff* bad guy,' I reminded him. Pavlik's smile grew broader.

Zoe swiveled to survey the floral sundress I'd chosen for its vintage feel. Besides, it was quick. Not a small consideration since Pavlik, bless him, was not. 'Megan, you're going to freeze in that.'

'It's "Maggy,"' I corrected. 'And as for freezing, the sun is down and the temperature still has to be close to eighty degrees.' I'd heard Floridians' bodily thermostats were set a bit differently, but Zoe's prediction was borderline crazy.

'Only for now.' Missy Hudson had come up behind us. 'A cold front is coming through tonight bringing storms, wouldn't you know it? An unfortunate last hurrah for our hurricane season.'

'Hurricane season?' I repeated, thinking of Flagler's ill-fated railroad.

Missy waved her hand. 'Hurricane season, wet season, rainy season – it's all pretty much the same. May through to October, typically, though, Mother Nature doesn't always observe the calendar. November first, and we'll be lucky to reach seventy-five tomorrow.'

Brr, seventy-five degrees Fahrenheit. Fifty-five was considered balmy in Brookhills this time of year.

'Besides, it will undoubtedly be cold on the train. Everything in South Florida is way over air-conditioned.' Missy was pawing through a bag of clothing. She pulled out a black shawl. 'Here, take this.'

'Thanks,' I said, taking the lacy wrap, though I doubted the train could be air-conditioned to the point that this Wisconsinite would feel a chill. 'But won't you need it?'

'Oh, not to worry – I have my fur.' She struck a pose. 'Can you guess who I am?'

Not surprisingly, Missy had gotten into the spirit of her event and the role she was to play. A wide-brimmed hat sat on care-fully finger-waved hair and a white fur coat partially covered a long silver dress that pulled a bit over surprisingly voluptuous hips before stopping just short of her glittery silver shoes.

'Well, I . . .'

'Mrs Hubbard,' Missy continued, sparing me the need to answer. 'Though I have to admit, I opted for Lauren Bacall's version from the movie rather than the plainer "American Lady" in the book. Such fun to get really dressed up, don't you think?'

'Well, you do look wonderf—'

I was interrupted by a wolf whistle as two men in suits – one double-breasted navy pinstripe, the other cream-colored – passed by to board the bus. 'Looking good, Missy,' Pinstripe called.

'Oh, thank you,' she nearly squealed in delight, and then lowered her voice to address me. 'When I saw this at Sally's – that's what my friends call the Salvation Army store here – I knew it would be perfect.'

The girl was glowing. I had a feeling Missy Hudson didn't get the opportunity to be the center of attention very often.

'Missy?' Zoe's voice. 'Did you find Larry and Rosemary?'

Missy nodded toward the bus standing ready at the curb, its headlights glowing in the dark. 'Laurence is already onboard,

Zoe. But Rosemary isn't feeling well. She suffers from motion sickness and is afraid the bus—'

Zoe interrupted. 'Tell the diva she can lie down in the sleeping car once she plays her part. But, until then, Rosemary needs to be on that train and mingling with our paying customers.'

'Oh, she will,' Missy said quickly. 'But I . . . well, I told her that if she prefers, I'd drive her to the station.'

Uh-oh, I thought. Our favorite little people-pleaser might have to clone herself to keep both her boss and guest of honor happy. But, to my surprise, Zoe relented.

'Fine. So long as the two of you are on the train and everything is ready when we leave. This event was your idea and I have no intention of saving it by dealing with the train people myself.'

Having won the battle, Missy now seemed appalled at the idea of her boss dealing with the 'train people.' Or any people at all, especially ones Zoe might consider underlings. 'Oh, no, you needn't talk to anyone at the station. I've arranged it all.'

'I certainly hope so.'

Missy was going through a small stack of cards and pulled one out for Zoe. 'Here's your event name badge.'

Zoe looked at it. 'Why do I need that? We'll have everyone's conference tags at registration tomorrow.'

'Well, yes,' Missy said, still holding it out tentatively, 'but these are for tonight's Murder on the Orient Espresso. See? They have our train-ride roles on them.'

The badge read 'Zoe' in big letters and, below it in smaller type, 'Woman in the Red Kimono.'

Zoe still didn't take the thing. 'What – no last name?'

'Well, no.' Missy pulled back her hand like she thought Ms Scarlett was going to bite it off. 'There wasn't room for that and the roles, if we wanted them to be readable. Besides,' Missy appealed to Pavlik and me, 'first names are so much friendlier, don't you think?'

'Well, it's for certain the only thing that *I'll* remem—' I started.

Zoe cut me off. 'Friendly, schmiendly. Without the full names, how can attendees know who's important?'

'You mean for sucking up?' I asked.

'Of course. Literary agents, publishing house editors, established authors. How's one supposed to know?' Zoe demanded.

'The name badges for tomorrow will have full names and be color-coded with all that information,' Missy gamely assured her. 'But for tonight I thought it would be fun—'

'Fine, fine.' Zoe Scarlett turned her eyes to the list she held, her hand trembling in excitement or anxiety, I wasn't sure which.

Missy Hudson – or 'Mrs Hubbard,' I suppose – tried to appear unfazed by the tsunami of criticism, but I could see her fighting the tears in her eyes as she handed Pavlik and me our own badges for the night.

'"Maggy/Narrator,"' I read from mine. 'But will I really be doing any narrating?'

'Oh, no. Not to worry.' Missy seemed more apologetic than defensive. 'I just didn't have a role for you and didn't want you to feel left out.'

'That's so nice. Thank you.' I peeled the backing off the badge and stuck it to my dress, then went to help Pavlik, who was having trouble with his.

'Jacob/Ratchett,' I said, affixing it to the shoulder of his shirt.

'I'm so sorry Jacob and Ratchett don't alliterate,' Missy said. 'Zoe decided which roles the sheriff and the guests of honor were playing.'

More special treatment for Pavlik, courtesy of our buxom conference organizer. But, hey, I rationalized, it had scored us a suite so far. As long as the woman kept her hands to herself . . .

Missy was leafing through the short stack of badges in her hand again. 'I chose the players and their respective roles so people could put them together easily either through alliteration or word association.'

'Which is why Zoe *Scarlett* is the Woman in the *Red* Kimono? Very clever.'

'Thank you. And then there's the fact that Agatha Christie never properly reveals who's wearing the kimono. Zoe didn't want to play a role.'

That figured. Nothing could top 'Countess of the Conference.'

The girl was pulling out another badge. 'See? I'm Missy/Mrs Hubbard.'

'Huh,' I said, looking. 'Missy, Mrs. And even your last names, when you think of it, alliterate. "Hudson" and "Hubbard," very neatly done.'

'Says the woman who attempted to assign seats in her coffee-house,' I heard Pavlik say under his breath.

'They don't all,' Missy was saying. 'The last names, I mean. That's why,' she lowered her voice and snuck a glance toward Zoe, 'I didn't put them on.'

I knuckle-bumped with her. 'Good for you.'

Zoe, who'd been running her finger down the clipboard, suddenly looked up. 'Good for who?'

'You and Missy,' I said with a smile. 'Are we all here?'

'Looks like it.' Zoe swept her hand toward the door of the bus, inviting Pavlik and me to climb on.

I went first, happy to see that most of the people who'd already boarded were wearing outfits that fit the 1930s, when Dame Agatha had set her *Murder on the Orient Express*. I loved old movies and though it had been a while since I'd read Agatha Christie's book, I'd coincidentally seen the 1974 movie version just a few weeks prior. It would be fun seeing who was who. Or was it 'whom'?

'Looking for a seat?' a pleasant African-American man on the aisle about halfway back asked. He was wearing navy pinstripes and I recognized him and the man next to him as the pair who had complimented Missy. He finished slapping on his nametag and stuck out his hand. 'I'm Markus, playing MacQueen, the victim's secretary.'

Markus/MacQueen. I was finding Missy's system helpful already. And the use of first names only simplified things even further for a newcomer like me. 'Nice to meet you, Markus, I'm Maggy. I'm actually looking for two se—'

'Larry'll always make room for a good-looking woman.' A slightly-built older lady diagonally across the aisle nodded toward Laurence Potter in the aisle seat behind her. Potter's face was buried behind a *Publishers Weekly* magazine, his briefcase on the window seat next to him.

Typical commuter ploy to discouraging sharing, but I was busy studying the elderly woman, who was wearing a dark dress with layers of pearls around her neck. Even without the nametag, I thought I had this one. 'Princess Dragomiroff, I presume?'

'Very good,' the princess said. 'And this is—'

'Greta Ohlsson, who gives evidence in part two, chapter six.'

The bespectacled middle-aged woman seated next to the princess wore a plaid blouse and tweed skirt like the 'Swedish Lady' of the book she held in her hand. The part had been played by Ingrid Bergman in the movie.

'A pleasure.' I pointed to my nametag. 'I'm not really narrating. In fact, I'm not even sure there is a narrator in the book.'

'The book was written third-person, so there would be a narrative voice,' Markus/MacQueen said. 'Will you be speaking at the conference?'

'Heavens, no. My friend,' I nodded toward Pavlik, who was still at the front of the bus engaged in conversation with Zoe, 'is, though, and we didn't know—'

'Ooh, you're with that good-looking sheriff,' Greta piped up in a soft, mincing voice. Tucking the copy of *Murder on the Orient Express* into her handbag, she turned to her companion. 'You do remember him from our conference two years back, don't you, Prudence? Zoe's "friend" from Chicago?'

The quotation marks around 'friend' were about as subtle as sky-writing.

On cue, the slinky redhead in question trilled out in response to something Pavlik had said. The laughter sounded more siren song than genuine amusement. Let's just hope the 'good-looking sheriff' could resist the lure of her silicone-rocky shores.

As if Pavlik sensed us all looking, he waved to me. 'Did you find two seats back there?'

I shook my head. 'Only one.'

'Go ahead and take that. I'll sit here.' As Pavlik said it, he slid into the seat next to Zoe.

My reasonable self told my other self that I didn't mind. After all, wasn't 'Maggy the Narrator' the one who had just gotten frisky with Pavlik in the very suite Zoe had booked for him?

Or . . . *them*?

The conference organizer whispered something into Pavlik's ear and then put her hand on his shoulder, hitching herself up with a smile to do a headcount.

It was a very thorough count, her breasts bouncing up/down and swinging back/forth next to Pavlik.

Game on, baby. I amped up my smile and said loudly, 'Excuse me, Laurence. Is this seat taken?'

Did I imagine it or had Zoe's smile slipped a bit? I glanced down at Potter, bald head buried in his magazine. Maybe Zoe, greedy girl, had designs on the guest of honor as well as Pavlik.

I cleared my throat.

Potter looked up. 'Sorry?'

Though we'd met just over an hour ago, he seemed to already have forgotten me. So much for Maggy Thorsen, femme fatale.

But Zoe could still be watching, so I kept smiling. 'I said, is that seat taken?'

'What she's too polite to say, Larry,' the aging-to-aged princess snapped, 'is you need to move your crap onto the floor.'

'Oh, I was simply and totally immersed in this article.' As Potter spoke, he lifted his briefcase and slid over to the window. 'Please. Sit.'

'You weren't saving it for someone?' As I sat down, I saw Zoe swivel back around toward Pavlik.

'More likely saving it *from* someone,' the princess said. 'I'm Prudence, by the way, and my seatmate is Grace.'

Prudence/Princess Dragomiroff and Grace/Greta Ohlsson. Missy deserved a gold star in my alliteration/memory-trick book.

I shook the princess's ring-covered hand. 'Maggy,' I said, before turning to Grace. 'Are you both writers?'

'Aspiring writers,' Grace said.

'Some of us aspire more than others,' the princess said sourly. 'Grace hasn't written a word since the last Mystery 101.'

'I teach kindergarten in Detroit,' Grace explained, unruffled. 'I'm afraid the little ones take up all my—'

'A word of advice, Maggy?' Prudence interrupted. 'Watch out for Zoe.'

'Zoe? What do you mean?' I knew exactly what she meant, but I wanted to hear it from her.

'She means,' Laurence Potter said dryly, 'that the woman is a venal fly trap.'

Venal, not venus. 'As in—'

'*As in* a mercenary snare of male privates,' Potter provided. 'Or must I spell it out for you?'

He pretty much had. But since 'innocent' had gotten me this far: 'I thought Zoe was married, at least until recently.'

A snort from Prudence/Princess, but it was Grace/Greta next to her who answered. 'Ignore these two, Maggy. We all owe Zoe – and Missy, too, as of last year – a debt of gratitude for spearheading this conference.'

'Ah, yes,' Potter said, lifting up his magazine to eye level again. 'Though the job does come with certain . . . benefits.'

Grace spread her hands. 'I'd like to know who amongst us doesn't come to these events partly to meet legends like Rosemary Darlington.'

'Legends.' The word came from behind the magazine.

'Whatever you think of the new book, Larry,' Grace said, 'you must admit Rosemary has written nearly fifty novels over the years, most of them very good. And now she's reinvented herself for a new generation. That makes Rosemary Darlington a legend in my mind.'

'And her own, if nowhere else.' Potter lowered his copy of *Publishers Weekly* and shook his head sadly. 'There was a time I thought Rosemary Darlington had genuine talent, but that woman could never have written this current pile of excrement.'

'Just because you don't like the romance genre,' Prudence snapped again, 'doesn't make it "excrement."'

'Absolutely right.' The magazine came down and the gloves, apparently, off. 'I've been unfair to excrement.'

Whoa, boy. This was getting fun. 'You're so knowledgeable,' I said as naively as a bedazzled fourth grader to Potter. 'Do you write, yourself? Novels, I mean.'

'Yes, Larry,' Prudence said, sticking out her neck like an elderly, but remarkably aristocratic, chicken. 'Do tell us what *you've* authored.'

'Happily,' Potter said as the bus lurched away from the curb. 'In fact, I have a book in the works right now.'

'Are you—' I started, but the bus driver slammed on his brakes, sending me flying forward. Potter put his arm out to keep my head from hitting the back of Markus's seat, managing to buff my breasts thoroughly with the back of his forearm in the process.

'Thank you,' I said automatically as I righted myself and slid the spaghetti strap of my dress back onto my shoulder.

'He should be thanking *you*,' I heard the princess mutter.

'What the bloody hell is this idiot driver doing?' Laurence Potter demanded as the door of the bus opened.

'Sorry, sorry.' The curly-haired young man I'd seen outside the hotel earlier that day climbed aboard.

'Oh, that's just swell,' I heard Potter mutter. 'The merely excruciating has managed to become the intolerable.'

FOUR

'**D**o you know him?' I asked Potter, ignoring the fact I'd seen the two of them together.

'Just another sycophant.'

'Better honey than vinegar,' the man next to Markus said. Sporting a small mustache, blonde hair slicked back, he looked a bit like the actor Michael York in his cream-colored three-piece suit. His hands nervously circled the brim of a matching hat in his lap.

'But they *said* at the registration desk that the event wasn't filled to capacity.' Potter's 'sycophant' was arguing his case to the bus driver.

Zoe stood up. 'Are you a conference attendee?'

'I just signed up.' He held up a nametag. The big letters read 'Danny' but I couldn't see the rest.

'The lady said I could be . . .' Danny turned the tag around so he could read it, 'Colonel Arbuthnot?'

Sean Connery played the role of the British Indian Army Officer in the movie. And this kid was no Sean Connery. Nor, I might add, did his real and assigned names alliterate.

But talk, he certainly could. '. . . so I was late. But I did pay for the conference.'

'And this event?' Zoe asked.

Danny nodded.

The conference organizer gestured toward the back. 'Well, then, welcome aboard. You'll have to stand for the time being, but there will be plenty of room on the train.'

'Great, thanks.' The kid made his way back as the bus began inching forward again.

'So, Larry,' Markus said from across the aisle. 'This book you're writing. Is it a novel?'

'Mr Potter – *you're* writing a novel, too?' Danny/Col. Arbuthnot had stopped next to us. A studious-looking kid, his eyes were the color of unwrapped Hershey's Kisses and about as readable. They were focused on Potter.

'Perhaps,' said the Great One, irritably. 'But you'd be better served by my book on writing from a few years back.'

Potter's tone was downright nasty, but you had to hand it to Danny, he seemed unfazed. In fact, the young man hunkered down in the aisle to talk earnestly across me to Potter. 'I'd love to read your book. It would be tit-for-tat, since I already sent you mine.'

I could practically feel the steam coming off Potter. 'What you sent, Master Danny, is a "manuscript." Not a "novel." If and when you get it published by a reputable trade house, I will be overjoyed to peruse it and tell the world exactly what I think.'

'Gee, that would be really great,' said the young man, either not getting or, at least, not reacting to Potter's sarcasm. Danny straightened up and extended his hand past my face to Potter. 'I'm going to hold you to that, sir.'

The reviewer looked at the hand before reluctantly shaking it. Then, with a guttural sound of disgust, he returned to his magazine.

Having apparently secured what he'd come for, Danny turned to me. 'Are you an author, too?'

'Nope. Coffeehouse owner.'

Weighing that, he must have decided there was no advantage to chatting up someone who couldn't help him in his intended career. Mumbling, 'Good to meet you,' Danny rose and moved on to a man in a blue, yellow and red checkered sports jacket sitting behind me.

The boy introduced himself and the two chatted in low tones. So quiet, in fact, that I couldn't hear them from just one row away, despite my best efforts. As I started to swivel back forward, I saw the seated man nod toward Potter's back.

'The kid's got balls, I'll give him that,' Prudence said as the boy stood up and continued on, working his way toward the back of the bus. Every few seats he stopped to introduce himself. 'And sending an unpublished manuscript to a reviewer? Talk about a death wish.'

'I assume that's not done?' I asked.

The princess shrugged. 'What's the point? Unless, of course, you're the type who gets a kick out of having your unborn child torn apart by jackals.' She turned and glanced at the magazine held by the jackal in question. 'No offense, Larry.'

'None taken,' Potter said mildly from behind it, seeming pleased by the comparison.

'Please leave the boy – is it Danny? – alone.' Grace, kindergarten teacher and apparent defender of the young, spoke up. 'Who amongst us hasn't deluded ourselves into thinking we're the next Hemingway or Christie, just waiting to be discovered?'

A collective sigh – or maybe it was a whimper – came from the assorted aspiring writers seated around me.

I repressed a grin. 'I suppose it would be logical to think that someone like Mr Potter would be just the person – in fact, that he could feel honored – to do just that.'

'Not if you knew him,' a voice behind us muttered.

'So is the kid's stuff any good, Larry?' Prudence asked.

I saw Potter roll his eyes behind the magazine before he finally lowered it to address the question. 'And how would I know that?'

'This Danny sent you a manuscript, or so he said.'

'And perhaps he truly did, but you can't honestly begin to believe that I open and read what the vast unwashed mail me *un*solicited, do you?'

In these days of electronic bills and bill paying, I barely got any postal mail. What I did get were obvious solicitations which I had no trouble discarding. I couldn't imagine, though, not opening something that was obviously personally addressed to me from one human being to another.

'Really?' I asked with the innocence of the uninformed. 'What do you do with it?'

'Either write "return to sender" on the envelope and give it back to the postal worker, or simply toss the thing, unopened.'

'Michael York' leaned forward to address us. 'In truth, since September 11, 2001, and the anthrax scare, publishers don't open mail unless it's from a reputable literary agent.'

'Are you a publisher?' I asked.

'No. A "reputable literary agent."' The man cracked a small smile, but didn't extend his hand. 'I hope you'll forgive me for not shaking hands, but I fear contagion.'

'Oh, I'm sorry,' I said, though he hadn't shown any symptoms. 'You're not feeling well?'

'No, no. I'm just fine,' the agent said, hands still rotating his hat like the steering wheel of a car doing perpetual doughnuts. 'Now.'

'Our Carson is not only a renowned agent, but a renowned germaphobe,' Potter said dryly.

Ahh, I got it. Not being contagious, the agent really *did* 'fear contagion.'

'I haven't shaken hands with anyone for over ten years,' Carson said proudly.

'Truly?' I was trying to imagine the business meetings and conferences, parties and receptions the agent must have been invited to during the span of more than a decade. 'Isn't that a little awkward in your line of work?'

'My clients understand,' the literary agent said, now with a genuine smile.

'They understand he's a nut job,' Prudence cracked out of the corner of her mouth.

'One that negotiates some of the biggest advances in our industry,' Potter countered.

I glanced at my seat companion in surprise. It was the first time I'd heard Laurence Potter say anything positive about anyone.

Except himself, of course.

'Well, it's a pleasure to meet you,' I said to the agent. 'And your costume is wonderful. Count Andrenyi, the Hungarian diplomat.'

'Costume?' He looked down at the hat in his hand.

Uh-oh. I got a sick feeling in the pit of my stomach. 'I'm sorry. I just thought . . . umm, I mean, you look so much like Michael York, who played the role in the, umm . . .'

The man exploded with laughter. 'I'm sorry, my dear, but I couldn't help myself.' He held up a badge encased in a plastic sandwich bag. It read, 'Carson/Count Andrenyi.'

Oh, thank the Lord. At least the germaphobe had a sense of humor. 'So you *are* playing the count tonight.'

'I am, and apparently I've nailed the role.' Carson the agent/ count was pleased with himself.

'Carson was originally on Broadway,' the man in the checkered sports jacket said from behind me. 'In fact, we worked together way back when. Rosemary Darlington was in theater, as well.'

'What interesting career paths,' I said, meaning it. 'Actor, agent, writer—'

'A lot of young people come to New York to study theater,' Carson said. 'Just as they flock to Los Angeles for the movie industry. Most of us end up doing other things. Only a very few can make a living at acting and even fewer become famous.'

'That's not so different to writing,' Markus said. 'How many writers give up their day jobs?'

'More than should,' Potter observed acerbically.

'That's true,' Carson agreed, whether because the reviewer had bolstered the agent a minute before or not. 'Writing fiction is, at best, project work. You start one book and hope you have a contract to publish another by the time the first is finished. And that the successor sells once it, too, is published. Nothing like a twice-monthly, automatically deposited payroll check, by any means.'

'Even the best writers have gaps between books,' Grace contributed. 'Look at our Rosemary. *Breaking and Entering* came out nearly five years after her last book.'

'Is she one of your clients?' I asked the agent. The more I learned about these bizarre people, God help me, the more I wanted to know.

'No, but she's represented by another agent at my firm, Natanya Sorensen, who was supposed to be here and play countess to my count.' He directed a smile toward me.

I returned it. 'You're . . . countess-less, then?'

'Natanya had the sniffles, and I insisted she stay home and take care of herself.'

'Good thing the woman listened,' I heard Prudence mutter. 'Or he'd have sealed her up inside a Baggie, too.'

Undaunted by the jibe, Carson continued his train of thought. 'I'm afraid Missy was very disappointed.'

'That's because she's a control freak,' Prudence said.

'That's unfair,' Grace protested. 'Missy's worked very hard to put this together for us.'

'I managed events for a large corporation up north,' I said, 'and I would've loved to include someone with Missy's initiative on my staff. Did you know she's driving Rosemary Darlington to the train station because the guest of honor didn't want to ride the bus?'

'Oh, dear,' our other guest of honor said, eyebrows knitting theatrically as he looked up from his magazine. 'I do hope it wasn't anything I said.'

What an ass. 'Didn't you realize you'd be doing this event together when you wrote that review of her book?'

'Of course,' Potter said. 'What would that matter?'

I shrugged. 'I assumed it would be just . . . awkward.'

Prudence snorted. 'As you can see, Larry's not the sensitive type.'

'If authors can't take criticism,' Potter said, 'they shouldn't be putting their work out there for everyone to read. The same for so-called authorities writing on their subjects. Am I right, Markus?'

Markus shifted uncomfortably. 'Well, yes. Reviews are certainly a recognized part of the industry.'

'Are you a published author?' I asked.

'More of a fan.'

'Fan?'

'Oh, don't listen to his self-deprecating bullshit.' Prudence the Princess confirmed her potty-mouth. 'Markus is a librarian, as well as a writer in his own right.'

Markus glanced uneasily at Potter, once again engrossed in his magazine. 'Just non-fiction. Readers guides and the like.'

'Writers don't exist without readers,' Grace pointed out.

'Your attention, please!' Zoe was standing up in the front of the bus, her hand on Pavlik's shoulder. Just for balance, *I'm sure*. 'We're approaching the station and since we're running late, I'd appreciate everyone exiting the bus quickly and moving to the train.'

She broke off and leaned down to look out the window, her breasts practically fwopping against Pavlik's cheeks.

'Oh, thank God,' Zoe said, straightening up and tucking a boob back in. 'Rosemary has just arrived.'

'Oh, thank God,' Laurence Potter echoed, gathering up his briefcase. Then a sigh before the words: 'That woman will be the death of me yet.'

FIVE

'So what's the deal?' I asked Pavlik when I joined him outside the bus.

'How do you mean?' The sheriff seemed uneasy, like a man who feared he was walking into a trap. 'I guess this must be a tourist train. You know, like the wine one in the Napa Valley or that Tootsie railroad in North Carolina's High Country.'

I waved away the fact that we were standing in front of something that looked more like a movie set than a train station that actually transported people who needed to reach somewhere. 'In North Carolina, it's "Tweetsie," not "Tootsie," but I didn't mean that. I was talking about the obvious friction.'

'Friction? Between who?' Pavlik looked even more uncomfortable. And why? After all, I hadn't asked what you get when you rub a sheriff and a conference organizer together.

Instead, I said, 'It's "between whom," I think. Around writers, better get that stuff right. And the "friction" I meant is between Laurence Potter and Rosemary Darlington, of course.'

'Oh.' Pavlik's face relaxed. 'I don't have a clue.'

'It seems to go beyond professional. Larry seems to take Rosemary's new book as a personal affront.'

Pavlik was smiling now. '"Larry"? Are you going to call him that the entire time, just to provoke the man?'

Of course. And Zoe Scarlett will continue to call you 'Jacob' in that possessively arch way just to provoke me. It's what we do.

I shrugged. 'It seems to be what everybody calls Potter. And besides, from what we've seen so far, it doesn't look like much is required to provoke him.'

We were following Zoe through the deserted train station. It was then the light dawned on me. 'Ah, the dragon kimono. I get it.'

'Kimono?'

'In *Murder on the Orient Express*. Zoe's wrap dress has a

dragon design on the back, see? It's a more modern' – and slut-
tier – 'version of the red kimono Christie gave to one of her
characters.' I looked at Pavlik. 'You *have* seen the movie, right?'

'No, but I read the book, which will probably endear me to
more people at a writers' conference.'

'Movies are written, too,' I pointed out. 'And I have to believe
that every aspiring writer here would also love a movie deal – oh,
this must be our train.'

Not much of a stretch, since there was but one. Missy, having
delivered her charge safely to the station, was squatting down in
her furs and evening dress, teetering precariously on her high
heels as she tried to tape a banner to one of the cars.

'You go on,' I said to Pavlik. 'I might as well earn my keep
by seeing if Missy needs help.'

'I'll save you a seat this time.' Pavlik gave me a quick kiss
on the lips.

'I'd like that.' I felt rewarded for not making a big deal – or
any deal at all, in fact – about Zoe and the seating arrangement
on the bus.

As Pavlik continued on to the rest of the group milling around
on the platform, I skirted the crowd, noticing Danny the supposed
sycophant talking again with the sports-jacketed former actor
from the bus. The two were standing on the fringe of the herd,
the plaid of the older man's jacket even gaudier in the lights of
the station. He seemed to be pointing out people of interest – or
more likely, of note – to the newcomer.

'Oh, dear!'

I reached Missy just in time to catch a corner she had just
secured – or tried, with duct tape, to secure – before it peeled
away and brushed the railbed. 'Can I give you a hand?'

'Oh, thank you,' Missy said gratefully. 'I'd planned to have
this all done before your bus arrived, but the traffic on my
"shortcut" was heavier than I expected.'

'It was good of you to drive Rosemary Darlington,' I said,
smoothing the banner. 'Given what I've seen, the farther apart
you keep her and Laurence Potter, the better.'

Though admittedly not nearly as much fun for onlookers like
me, who always appreciated being witness to a train wreck.

Not that I wanted to jinx the poor young woman's project.

'I didn't mind driving.' Missy swept her hat off and swiped her forehead with the back of the same hand. Wearing a fur coat in eighty degrees Fahrenheit must have been taking its toll, even on a Floridian. 'Rosemary suffers from motion sickness and buses are the worst. I hope she'll be all right on our trip tonight.'

'Eric – that's my son – gets car sick, but he's fine on trains as long as he's facing forward.' Which made me recall that passenger cars often had half the seats facing rearward.

'I suggested that to Rosemary,' Missy said, replacing her hat. 'Facing forward and, as you say, as far away from Laurence Potter as possible.'

The last was said under her breath and she glanced over at me, just seeming to realize it'd been said aloud. 'They . . .' Missy hesitated, '. . . have a history.'

Hmm. An affair gone wrong would certainly explain the venom with which Potter had criticized Darlington's literary side-trip to the erotic. Maybe I'd read the book just to see if one of the characters was a tall, bald man. 'So Larry Potter and Rosemary Darlington had a personal relationship?'

But Missy had colored up. And, apparently, decided to clam up as well. 'Conference rumors, I'm sure. Please don't say you heard anything from me, Maggy.'

'Of course not.' I was thinking about my dentist husband and the years of conferences he and his hygienist had attended so the office could 'stay current.' Undoubtedly there'd been 'rumors' in the dental community back then. I only wish somebody had bothered to share them with me. 'What happens in Fort Lauderdale, stays in Fort Lauderdale, right?' I said, echoing my earlier words to Pavlik in the hotel lobby.

Missy's eyes went wide. 'What do you mean?'

My turn to blush. I had no business inflicting my hard-earned cynicism on the next generation. Besides, if Laurence Potter – or anybody else – was playing musical beds, it was none of my business. I changed the subject. 'Are you a writer yourself, Missy?'

'No, not really. More a researcher.'

'That must be interesting. For authors?'

Missy moved the scissors aside with her toe and bent down to pick up the roll of duct tape while still holding up her end of the banner. 'Almost exclusively now. At first, I didn't get paid or anything, I just helped authors whose work I enjoyed.'

'That was certainly nice of you.'

'I was having a tough time getting a job in library science, what with all the budget cuts, and this gave me something to do – something I loved.'

'Library science,' I repeated. 'So how did you end up in event management?'

'You mean helping with the conference?' Missy looked surprised. 'Oh, that's just a volunteer post. It's not what I do for a living.'

'You don't get paid?'

'I get my hotel room comped, and I don't pay for the conference, of course. Plus, I meet such interesting people.'

An increase in the chatter coming from the 'interesting people' milling about on the platform drew my attention. The natives were getting restless. And Zoe Scarlett, of course, was nowhere to be seen to settle them down. 'You couldn't pay me enough to take orders from that woman.'

'Zoe?' Missy shot me a smile. 'She's not so bad, truly, though I think her divorce has left her a bit off balance.'

Not surprising, given the size of the woman's new breasts. I refocused my attention on Missy. '. . . has contacts everywhere, which is crucial,' she was saying. 'She really put this conference together.'

'If you say so.' I'd had experience with 'idea' people who were only too happy to hand off their ideas to other people – like Missy – to implement. And guess who'd take all the credit? 'But you seem to be the one who gets things done.'

'It's mainly logistics. Which is why, between you and me, I'm so excited about tonight.' She lowered her voice. 'I want to show everyone, including our guests of honor, that I'm capable of more creative things. Who knows where that might lead?'

Probably to Zoe dumping even more work onto her unpaid assistant. 'But how do you pay the bills? You said you didn't get paid for the research either.'

'That's changed, happily. A girl has to earn a living.' Missy tried a longer piece of tape, this time attempting to wrap it around a rope attached to the top of the banner.

Well, that was good, at least. 'Can you say who your clients are, or is that kept confidential?'

'I always ask about the confidentiality issues, because it varies from writer to writer. Everyone here, though, knows I've worked for Rosemary Darlington.' Missy took her hands away from the precariously hung banner. 'That's why she agreed to come to Mystery 101.'

'Wow, that's impressive. Zoe apparently isn't the only one with contacts.'

The girl looked pleased and not only because the banner seemed to be holding. 'Oh, it was nothing, really.'

'Not true. As you said regarding Zoe, contacts are crucial in event planning.' But I wanted to hear more about the research, especially in regard to Rosemary Darlington. 'Did you work on *Breaking and Entering?*'

A quick sidelong look. Missy seeming uncertain about my motives for asking. I held up my hands. 'Hey, I haven't read the book. I'm not judging.'

'Oh, not *that* kind of research,' Missy said with a slightly embarrassed smile. 'Heavens, I'm sure Rosemary . . . well, I don't mean to say she has more experience, but . . . Oh, dear, I'm still making a mess of this.'

The banner took another dive and I made a grab for it. 'I'm not sure even duct tape is up to this job.'

But I was also fairly certain the banner-hanging wasn't what Missy thought she'd messed up. Or, at least, not the only thing.

She was happy to follow my differing lead, though. 'You're right. I didn't ask the banner company to attach these ropes and they make it ever so much heavier. Maybe I should cut them off.' She was eyeing the scissors.

'Uh-uh.' I scooped up the scissors before she could and stepped back to look at our options for securing the signage to the side of the train. 'How secure does the banner have to be?'

'What do you mean?'

'Are we moving or staying right here in the station?'

'Oh, no, we'll be leaving in a few minutes. It's very exciting. I've managed to get us a sneak preview of a brand-new excursion into the Everglades.'

I surveyed the 'excursion' train. There were four cars and
. . . 'We have a locomotive on each end.' And facing opposite
ways.

'Of course. The west one,' Missy pointed at the locomotive
to our left, 'will take us into the Everglades. The east one will
bring us back to Fort Lauderdale.'

Seemed like kind of a waste to me. 'Don't they usually have
just one locomotive and then circle it around to the other end at
the station so it can go back in the direction it came?'

'Yes, if there *was* a station. We'll be stopping on the single
track in the Everglades and simply reversing back the other
direction.' A gust of wind ruffled the banner. 'I hope the storms
will hold off until after our three-hour tour.'

'Three-hour tour,' I repeated, the theme from *Gilligan's Island*
dancing through my head. Not to mention the photograph of
what was left of Flagler's Railroad after the 1935 hurricane. 'Isn't
the route through the Everglades called Alligator Alley?'

'Well, the driving one, anyway. However, we'll be on a railroad
bed that has just been completed – or almost completed – quite
a bit north of the highway. We won't even see Alligator Alley.
And besides,' Missy picked up one of the banner ropes and eyed
it with evil intent, 'you don't see quite as many alligators anymore.
The pythons are eating them.'

I reflexively glanced west toward the Everglades, imagining
ominous clouds building in the dark. Despite the Florida heat, I
felt a chill. 'Pythons? As in . . . snakes?'

'Yes, of course,' Missy said. 'Burmese pythons.'

She said it as casually as Wisconsinites would say 'Canada
geese.' But geese don't eat alligators. The worst they could do
is poop all over them. '*Burmese* pythons? How in the world—'

'—did they get to Florida?' Missy was trying to unstick the
tape she'd attached to her edge of the banner. 'Until a couple of
years ago it was legal to have them as pets.'

'Pet snakes.' Snakes in their natural habitat scare me enough,
but in the house? Brr. And what did you do with them? Take
Fido out for a slither? Play fetch the squirrel? A snake didn't
even have ears to scratch.

'. . . ball pythons,' Missy was saying. 'People who had
Burmese pythons before the law was changed are grandfathered

in and can keep the one – or more – they already have, assuming they get a "reptile of concern" permit.'

One or *more* 'reptiles of concern'?

'Unfortunately,' Missy continued, 'permitted or not, if the snakes get so big they're not cute anymore, people tend to dump them into the Everglades.'

I was kind of stuck on her choice of 'cute' when describing snakes in general, but especially those that could realistically consider alligators 'snack-size.'

'Isn't that like . . . I don't know, biological littering?'

'I suppose. And, maybe even worse, Hurricane Andrew back in 'ninety-two destroyed animal and reptile "breeding greenhouses" and pet stores, freeing their inhabitants. I've even heard there were panthers and monkeys and gazelles running free for a while. The panthers are encouraged – they're a native species and quite rare – but the rest of the animals were rounded up, supposedly.'

Supposedly. I knew where this was leading, unfortunately. 'But the pythons are still out there.'

'Yes, a nearly eight-foot female was caught recently and she had eighty-seven eggs inside her, can you believe that? I've heard that we could have tens of thousands – even a hundred thousand – pythons slithering around the Everglades these days.'

Missy looked west as I had, but kind of wistfully, I thought. 'It's very hard to be sure. What they do know is that reported sightings of white-tail deer have dropped by ninety-four percent, and the entire population of rabbits in the Everglades has been wiped out.'

Jesus. 'The pythons are eating them, too?'

'Yes, which you'd think would be good news for the alligators.'

'But it's not? Good news, I mean.'

'No. Alligators eat rabbits and deer – in addition to birds, turtles and fish, of course – so both the alligators themselves and their food supply have been affected by the pythons.'

Missy looked up from her work. 'Did you know that nearly sixteen-hundred people signed up to hunt Burmese pythons last year to bring down their numbers? But all those hunters managed to kill only sixty-eight in a month. Apparently pythons are slippery devils.'

Or their hunters didn't have enough incentive. 'Maybe they should send Fendi and Jimmy Choo in there after them,' I said.

'For designer handbags and such?' Missy looked thoughtful. 'In fact, a couple of local places are paying fifty or a hundred dollars a snake. After processing and all, a custom-made python purse can bring, like, twelve hundred dollars, shoes easily a thousand, and jackets nearly five thousand.'

Maybe I should go into the snake-catching business – or better yet, processing. 'Word gets out and the pythons will be wiped out in no time.'

'That would be a very good thing,' Missy said absently, her attention seemingly back on the banner.

'I'm sure the alligators would appreciate it.' Not to mention Thumper. And Bambi.

'I'm sure they would,' Missy said, looking up, 'but I don't want you to think there aren't consequences for the pythons, too.'

'Beyond being turned into Giorgio Armani stilettos?'

'No, no,' Missy said, a little impatient with me. 'I was talking about the snakes eating alligators, especially after they've had a big meal of their own. If you go on YouTube you can probably pull up photos and even a video or two of some pythons that have exploded during the digestive process.'

Oh, my. In my head, I'd been visiting the designer shoe floor of Barney's – and actually being able to afford something – and here was Missy yanking me back to the smorgasbord that the Everglades had become.

And with thoughts of rabbit, inside alligator, inside python, no less. The concept of turducken – a de-boned chicken, stuffed into a de-boned duck, in turn stuffed into a de-boned turkey and baked – had always seemed exotic enough, without imagining the Everglades own sushi version of the same. The one remaining comfort being that human beings weren't on the menu.

At least until the pythons ran out of rabbits, deer and alligators.

SIX

'If you want to get technical,' Missy Hudson snapped me out of my snake-themed reverie, 'pythons don't really eat their prey so much as crush it so they can swallow it whole and digest it.'

Lovely. 'And this differs from "eating" in what way?'

Missy looked up, apparently startled by the edge in my tone. 'Well, no chewing, of course.'

'Oh.'

'That's nothing, though. You want to know something really scary?'

I hadn't realized that what we'd already been talking about didn't qualify. 'Sure.'

'They've found a number of African rock pythons in the Everglades. Including a pregnant one.'

'And that's worse than a Burmese python?' Or tens or hundreds of thousands of them?

'Oh, yes. The rock pythons are Africa's largest snake – over twenty feet long. And the fact one was pregnant means they're reproducing here.'

'And not-too-tightly-wrapped people kept those things as pets, too?'

'Yes, can you believe it? The herpetologist at the Florida Museum of Natural History in Gainesville said the species is so aggressive they come out of the egg striking. His theory is that breeders didn't expect them to be so vicious – and hence so unmarketable to consumers – that they released them into the wild, too. The fear is the African rocks will mate with the Burmese and spawn a large and powerful population of hybrids – like a kind of Super Python.'

Just gets better and better. 'You sure seem to know a lot about these creepy-crawlies.'

'Well, most Floridians who live near the Everglades have heard the news reports, or at least should have. Knowledge is power.

Besides,' Missy was back to picking at the tape, 'I needed to research them for *Breaking and Entering*.'

'There's a snake in the book?' Other than the trouser variety, I meant.

'Well, yes. Rosemary wanted Kat, the umm, heroine to have an, umm . . . encounter with one. Or was it two?' The corner of the tape came loose. 'Damn.'

The subject of our conversation had gone from bad to worse. It was one thing to exchange views with someone my own age, but Missy couldn't be more than six years older than my son Eric, who was in his second year of college.

'Why don't I hop up into the train and open the window?' I suggested. 'You can hand me the rope and I'll secure it to something.'

'That's a wonderful idea! This is the passenger car, so—'

In my haste to get away from the images in my own mind, I didn't wait to hear the rest of Missy's instructions.

Entering the train, I turned right and nearly ran into a broad-shouldered man. He was wearing a boxy three-piece suit with a gold watch chain, presumably leading to a pocket watch in the vest. 'Can I help you?' he said, holding open a sliding door into the next car.

'Oh, I'm sorry,' I said. 'I was just looking for the passenger car.'

'This is the club car,' he said, hiking a thumb behind him. 'I'll be serving coffee and espresso drinks in a few minutes.'

'So our Orient Espresso will really have espresso?' I asked, spotting a brewer on one of the bars.

'That's the plan. Though it's not ready yet.'

'Oh, not a problem. I'm actually working on setting up myself.' I glanced out the window and saw that Missy was sorting out the ropes on the banner. 'I'm Maggy, by the way.'

The big guy wiped his hand and shook mine. 'Boyce. Or,' he pointed to his badge, 'M Bouc – the head of the railroad.'

Ah, Boyce/Bouc. 'I understand you run the coffee concession at the hotel. I own a coffeehouse in Wisconsin and there's no way I'd have the nerve to try to serve espresso to this many people at once. I'm impressed.'

'Don't be. I'll have brewed coffee, but I sure can't do hot

espresso to order, given the space restrictions and the fact there's also a full bar next to me.'

'So, the espresso machine is just a prop?'

'Not at all, though I have to admit I considered it,' Boyce/Bouc said with a wry smile. 'But Missy was so excited about the *Murder on the Orient Espresso* theme she came up with that I knew I had to work something out. My plan is to pull shots ahead and let them cool down for espresso martinis.'

'Pulling a shot' was our trade expression for grinding espresso, tamping it into a small filter and then brewing the shot.

Boyce was looking a bit embarrassed. 'Not ideal, I know, quality-wise. But . . .'

'Hey,' I said, waving off his professional discomfort. 'I think it's brilliant.'

'Thank you. Where did you say your coffeehouse was?'

'Brookhills, Wisconsin. It's near Milwaukee.'

'Oh, sure, I know the area. I went to college in Madison,' he said, referring to the University of Wisconsin's flagship campus in the state's capitol. 'And my parents still live in Milwaukee. Maybe I've seen your place. Where is it, exactly?'

'Originally in Benson Plaza on the corner of Brookhill and Civic. These days we're in the old train depot.'

'Brookhills Junction? Great area, but I remember it being pretty much abandoned.'

'It was, but we've rehabbed the station, which is the western-most stop for the new commuter train to Milwaukee.'

'Sweet,' Boyce said, recognizing the value of being able to serve five-dollar cups of coffee to bleary-eyed workers before they were fully awake. 'How long have you been open?'

'About two years.'

'Two locations in two years? I can't imagine having that kind of energy.'

'Believe me, it wasn't by choice. Our first place kind of collapsed.'

'Collapsed?'

'Yes, but we already knew we needed to relocate. Our landlord had decided not to renew our lease. That was before he had the run-in with the snow blower.'

'Snow blower?' Boyce repeated. 'What did he run into it with?'

'His head. But we think he was already dead.'

Boyce's eyes narrowed. 'Wait a second. Don't tell me you own Uncommon Grounds.'

'Oh,' I said, surprised. 'So you *do* know it.'

'Only through my parents. Wasn't one of the owners found dead in a pool of skim milk the morning you opened your first place?'

'Well, yes, but—'

'And, just recently, a body in the basement of the new location?'

'Under the boarding platform, technically, but—'

I was interrupted by tapping from outside the train.

'I'm sorry,' I said, grateful for the interruption. 'I promised to help Missy hang the banner. Do let me know, though, if I can pitch in later with your espresso brewing or anything.'

'You bet.' He said it automatically, though his expression was more in the vein of, *Right about when hell freezes over.*

'Great.' I was all too aware that trying to explain would only make matters worse. The truth was that Uncommon Grounds had more skeletons in its closet – and other environs – than Boyce had already mentioned.

The coffee man cleared his throat, probably eager to get rid of me. 'Did you say you were going to the passenger car?'

I nodded.

'Dining is next,' he said, pointing toward the sliding door opposite the one he was standing in, 'and the passenger car beyond that.'

We were standing in a vestibule, kind of an airlock with a metal floor and a sliding door on each of the four walls. Two of the doors – the one Boyce was standing in and the slider he'd indicated I should use – led to the adjacent train cars. The other two were exits to the platform on both sides of the train.

The dining car was through the slider, just as Boyce had promised. Eight white-clothed tables with C-shaped banquettes faced the aisle, four on each side. At the far end of the car, another table held a sheet cake frosted to look like a man sleeping. A knife protruded from his chest and red decorating gel with sparkles had been used to simulate other slashes.

I paused to admire the effect. The knife was real and had a brown staghorn handle, reminding me of a three-piece set that my grandmother had passed down to me. I pulled the knife up a bit and, sure enough, there was the same 'Hollow Ground Stainless Steel' stamp as the blade of my set. I'd managed to trace those knives back to the fifties. Well after the era of the book, certainly, but nonetheless, I thought it was a nice touch.

More tapping, increasing in insistence. I replaced the knife, but then turned back to swipe my finger across the cake frosting on the culinary victim's foot, where nobody would notice. I plopped the sweet icing in my mouth. It had been hours since Pavlik had bought me lunch and I was starving. Needless to say, with our last-minute hanky-panky under the blankie, we hadn't had time to grab a snack from the newsstand as he'd suggested.

Believe me, I wasn't regretting it. I'd take Pavlik over a granola bar anytime. Even a sandwich.

Through the next vestibule, I found a regular passenger car with rows of seats. At the end of that car was a restroom. Stopping just short of it, I slid open the window.

'Sorry,' I called out to Missy. 'I stopped to introduce myself to Boyce.'

She passed me the rope. 'No need to apologize. You're helping, after all. And as a guest, you should be relaxing. I'm sorry I got a little impatient with you before.'

The girl obviously had no idea of the heights – or depths – I'd seen true impatience reach.

I caught a glimpse of Pavlik walking toward the platform with Zoe, each carrying something in one hand. Behind them was a gaggle of what I guessed to be writers, probably eager to pick the sheriff's brains about gore and mayhem. I told myself that wasn't the part of Pavlik I was most interested in.

At least not this weekend.

'It's nice to have something to do, since I'm a little out of my element here.' I opened the next window and tied the rope around the post between them with a double knot. It wouldn't get me a merit badge, but it should hold. 'How's that?'

'Genius,' Missy said. 'Will you be able to close the window, or at least nearly so? I'd hate for it to get too hot in there.'

What a difference a few hours and fifteen hundred miles can make. In Wisconsin on the first day of November, you'd slam the window to keep out the cold air. Here it was the opposite.

'Good idea. That way the rope will be more secure anyway.' I slid down one of the windows to prove it. 'Is that far enough?'

'Perfect,' Missy said.

I moved a few rows forward and tied the other end of the banner the same way. By the time we had the banner secure people were already boarding the train, which made the point moot, when you thought about it. I mean, once everybody was on the train and we were in the Everglades, nobody would be able to appreciate the legend on the banner. And I didn't think the alligators and pythons – whether they were Burmese or African rock – would need help identifying us as boxed-car lunches. Or dinners, adjusting for the time of day.

'I have to take tickets,' Missy was saying through the open window, 'and hand these out.'

She held up a playbill, sepia-toned, so as to seem older. 'See? The cast of characters is on this side and,' flipping it, 'here's the diagram of the train.'

I took the playbill through the window. 'Very clever. If I remember right, the book had a diagram, too.'

'Correct. I'm not sure how readers could have kept the plot straight without a cheat sheet. Our diagram shows this little train, of course, not Christie's Orient Express. I've put "Murder on the Orient Espresso" here, see? I think the playbill will make a nice keepsake, don't you?'

'I do,' I said honestly. Missy had pulled out all the stops to make tonight a success. I hoped, for her sake, people took notice. I offered the playbill back to her.

'No, no – you can have the very first one.'

'Thank you.' I smiled and tucked the souvenir in my non-python skin handbag. For the first time in a long while, I had a hankering to do events again. Even if you're not on Broadway, opening night of anything presented to the public is a rush. 'But can I help you with the tickets and all?'

'Oh, no, I'll be fine.' Missy said, waving me off. 'But thank you so much and please – after you close this window – do mingle and enjoy yourself. These are fun people. And, who knows? Maybe by the end of the weekend you'll decide to kill someone.'

My face must have betrayed my thought.

Missy Hudson giggled, suddenly realizing. 'Fictionally, of course!'

SEVEN

Making my way up to the front of the train, I found Pavlik already in the dining car, sitting in one of the C-shaped booths. Zoe, naturally, was butt-to-buns next to him.

'Join us,' he said, waving me to slide in on his other side.

I was about to when I noticed that they both had drinks in front of them. 'Wait, where'd you get the wine?'

'There's a bar next door to the station,' Pavlik said. 'I'm sorry – did you want a glass?'

Did I want a glass of wine? Exactly how long had this man known me?

'Not a problem,' I fibbed. 'Do I still have time to hop off and get myself one?'

'Certainly,' Zoe said, before turning back to Pavlik and ignoring me. 'That's fascinating. As county sheriff—'

I didn't bother to hear more, despite my fascination with her sucking up. Instead I tried to thread my way to the nearest exit through the gaggle of people still boarding.

'You're not helping things, swimming against the tide like that,' Princess Dragomiroff, aka Prudence said. She was pushing up the bracelets on her sleeves like she wanted to sock someone. I hoped it wasn't me.

'I'm sorry.' I gave up and allowed myself to go with the flow. 'I just wanted to jump off and grab a glass of wine before we leave.'

'I wouldn't chance it if I were you,' Prudence said. 'Zoe told me we were leaving at precisely eight p.m. and it's just past that now. Once they fire up this baby, anyone not onboard will be left behind.'

'But she's the one who told me I had time,' I protested.

'I'll bet she did.' Prudence nodded toward the booth where Pavlik and Zoe still sat, heads together. 'The bar in the club car just opened and if I were you, I'd get whatever crap they're serving and hightail it back before our host inhales that sheriff of yours alive.'

I decided to take Prudence's advice. It required me to push my way past the exit to the front car, but at least I wouldn't risk getting off and being left behind.

Unfortunately, I wasn't the only one in search of libations. In fact, the line for the lone bartender was past Boyce/Bouc's espresso bar and out onto the platform. This seemed a problem in light of both Prudence's warning and the 'All aboard!' that somebody was shouting.

As I moved to the end of the line, a crack of thunder echoed. 'That bitch would have left me here in the rain,' I muttered under my breath.

'I'm sorry?' Markus/MacQueen stood on the platform.

'I just said "the . . . weather's a bitch."'

'Sure you did.' With a grin he stepped back and waved for me to get in line in front of him.

'Thank you, but there's no need. I'll just get a coffee for now.'

'All aboard!' again.

I beckoned. 'We'd better get on before the train starts to move.'

'You think the bitch will leave us in the rain?' Markus flashed me a grin.

I smiled sheepishly as he and I both part pushed and part edged our way into the train vestibule.

With multiple apologies and explanations, I continued on, bypassing the queue for the bar to get to the espresso station where there was no line at all.

I hesitated, not sure how welcome I'd be given our earlier conversation, but Boyce greeted me like an old friend – a sure sign he was bored. 'I'm afraid it's going to be a long night. Pete's doing gangbuster business, though. I'm thinking I should give him a hand rather than standing here twiddling my thumbs.'

'Pete is the bartender?' I asked, taking in the dark blue uniform the good-looking young man was wearing.

'Not really, but that's what Missy is calling him. He's also the conductor.'

'What?' I didn't get it.

Boyce laughed. 'Missy needed a bartender who could play "Pierre Michel," conductor of the Orient Express. Tomorrow,

Pete/Pierre Michel goes back to being Brandon, a server at the Olive Garden.'

Pete, it was. 'Do you want to help him while I staff the coffee bar for you?'

'I think I will, but there's no need for you to stay. If somebody does show up, I can always slide over and handle it.'

Old friend, perhaps, but this man had no intention of letting me get near his equipment.

Which was fine, I reminded myself. This was my vacation, after all. 'I'm sure there'll be a stampede for coffee once the cake is cut.'

'That's not going to be until after the program,' Boyce said. 'In the meantime, can I get you liquored up on an espresso martini and you can show these people what they're missing?'

'Gladly. And better make it a double.'

'Yes, ma'am. Double espresso or double vodka?'

'Both, please,' I said as Boyce tipped the espresso shot into the plastic martini glass. 'Do you know what kind of program is planned? Are we going to get clues and skulk around questioning suspects?'

A shake of the head. 'I'm not sure how elaborate it's going to be,' Boyce said, adding the clear alcohol. 'Missy told me her boss was willing to go along with the theme, but pointed out that the majority of the people – who are repeat attendees – would want to have a drink and catch up with each other on the first night.'

'Well, she's certainly right about the drink part,' I said as the train lurched away from the station. I was relieved to see that, though the exit door was still open, nobody was marooned on the platform. 'Let's hope the engineer goes slowly enough that we don't lose anyone.'

'I believe "slow" is part of the arrangement, given the train route isn't officially open yet. I have my fingers crossed we don't run into something unexpected.'

'You've heard about the pythons?' Apparently Missy wasn't overblowing this, either.

'Oh, yes. It's a real problem. Whipped cream?' Boyce held the spray can poised over my incipient drink.

'Load me up,' I said, sliding over a twenty. 'I hate snakes.'

He laughed, stuck a swizzle stick in my drink and slid the twenty back. 'My treat. One professional to another. And don't worry about the wildlife. They're out there and we're safe in here.'

'Thanks, for both the drink and the reassurance,' I said, raising the former. 'Let me know if you need help.'

'Will do,' Boyce said, sounding like he actually meant it this time. 'And have fun.'

'Hey, gigantic reptiles that eat each other, an untested train track, and a storm raging toward us?' I turned with my double-double, finishing over my shoulder with, 'If that doesn't spell fun, what does?'

EIGHT

Getting back to the dining car, I stepped inside its door. Zoe Scarlett was still to Pavlik's left on the banquette, but Rosemary Darlington and Laurence Potter had joined them. Potter was seated next to Zoe and Rosemary was on the other side of Pavlik, effectively putting her diagonally as far away from Potter as possible.

Bookended by the two most important men at her conference, Zoe was understandably incandescent. I wanted to smack her one upside the head.

This despite knowing full well I should be more threatened by Rosemary Darlington. As the author of the most erotic work of popular fiction since *Fifty Shades of Grey*, she'd certainly know all the moves. Still, the woman managed to come across as a class act.

As the 'Mary Debenham' of the book, Rosemary was wearing a light gray coatdress. The vintage garment crossed over at the front, forming a 'V,' like Zoe's, but in contrast to the red wrap Rosemary's dress was entirely risqué-free. A row of demure buttons fastened the panels of the dress, supported from below by a belt at her waist. The fullish sleeves of the dress ended in bands just below the elbow and, on her head, she wore a matching beret.

As I drew even with the banquette, Potter was talking. 'I'm not saying, Rosemary, that you haven't done all of us a service by . . . shall we say, enlivening our sex lives? I have to admit that even I learned a trick or two from your book.'

'How lovely,' Rosemary said with a tight smile. 'Shall I expect a thank-you note from your wife?'

Good deal. I may have missed the preliminary bouts, but it appeared I was still in time for the main event. Setting my espresso martini on the table, I slid in next to our female guest of honor.

'Big enough for you?' Pavlik was nodding at my drink.

'No, but it was as much as the glass would hold.' I clamped on the plastic stem as the train swayed and picked up speed.

'What *is* that?' Rosemary Darlington asked. Her tone didn't convey disdain so much as envy. Rosemary didn't have a glass in front of her, but looked like she could use one. Our female guest of honor was a tad green.

The way the tables and banquettes were set up – in that 'C' shape with the open ends facing the aisle – Pavlik was sitting dead center and therefore sideways to the motion of the train, with Zoe and Potter facing forward on one side of the semicircle and Rosemary and myself facing backward.

'This?' I said, gesturing toward my glass. 'An espresso martini.' Then, lowering my voice, 'Do you think if you sit on the other side, the motion of the train will be easier to tolerate?' I nodded toward the patch of unoccupied bench next to Potter.

'Thank you,' Rosemary said, matching my tone. 'But I'd rather projectile vomit.'

I laughed and took a sip of my drink.

Just then Missy came by. 'Oh, our signature cocktail! I love how you're embracing the theme, Maggy.'

If all it took to 'embrace the theme' was to imbibe caffeine and alcohol, I was her poster girl. I flicked my tongue to lick cream off my upper lip.

'Speaking of *Murder on the Orient Express* – or *Espresso*, I should say,' Missy continued, virtually chirping like a bluebird and tentatively settling on the very edge of the bench to Potter's left, 'can we talk about our program?'

'Excuse me, my dear,' Laurence Potter interrupted, 'but would you mind standing? I find my left knee aches if I can't extend it.'

Looking mortified, Missy jumped up and tugged at her evening dress. 'Oh, I'm sorry. I just—'

'No harm done, I'm sure.' Potter flexed his legs and extended them into the aisle, the multicolored toes of his wing-tip shoes ducking under the white cloth of the table across from us.

'Somebody's going to trip over Gumby's legs and sue,' I murmured automatically. One of the reasons I'd been happy to leave my role as events manager behind and open a coffeehouse was to escape the stress of being responsible for the safety and well-being of people who couldn't be trusted to behave responsibly.

Rosemary giggled. 'Gumby. Good one.' She had my martini in her hands.

I thought about reclaiming the drink but figured our female guest of honor needed it more than I did.

'Pardon me?' As if the vodka gods had heard me, Boyce, our onboard barista, was in the doorway behind me. But before I could order an espresso martini to replace the one Rosemary had commandeered, he said, 'Missy? There's someone who needs to speak with you.'

Missy, who'd been awkwardly standing in the aisle downstream of Potter's long, ungainly legs, looked grateful for the interruption. 'Of course.'

She stepped over Potter's wheels and kept right on going, Boyce on her silvery heels.

As the vestibule door to the club car slid closed, I caught a glimpse of Potter's 'sycophant,' Danny/Col. Arbuthnot, talking to a blonde woman I'd not seen earlier.

'Damnation,' Potter said, both hands reaching into his jacket, one pulling out a pack of cigarettes and the other a striking black and silver book of matches.

'No smoking,' I snapped as Potter knocked a coffin nail out of the pack. If I wasn't going to get my drink, he sure as hell wasn't going to enjoy *his* vice at our second-hand expense.

'What?'

'I said, no smoking is allowed inside the train cars.' Technically, I didn't know if that was true. But if not, it should be.

'Fine.' Laurence Potter dropped the loose cigarette and its pack back into his pocket, leaving the matchbook on the table's surface. 'I can't smoke and there's nothing to eat but that ridiculous cake. And even that, only after,' – air quotes – '"the crime is solved." What, pray tell, am I supposed to do until then?'

'Chat with attendees and be pleasant?' This from Rosemary Darlington. 'Seems the least you can do, given we are both being paid a fee for being here.'

Potter turned on her. 'And exactly who would you have me "chat" with? You?'

'Heavens, no. But perhaps that hero-worshipping mop-haired boy you seem to be avoiding.'

'Ridiculous,' Potter said. 'And I'll thank you to mind your own business, Rosemary.' He turned away from us.

If they *had* been lovers, they'd certainly perfected the 'quarrel' part.

'You seem to have struck a nerve with him,' I whispered to Darlington, who had simply smiled and gone back to her – or *my* – drink.

'I did, didn't I?' Rosemary was obviously pleased with herself. 'To be honest, I'm not sure what Larry has against the kid, but I'm happy to needle him, regardless.'

I resisted the urge to probe further into the Potter/Darlington milieu. 'So you've never seen Danny before?'

'Danny? Oh, the kid himself? No.' Rosemary was absently swirling what was left of my martini in its picnic-quality glass, like it was crystal from the Reidel collection. 'Maybe Larry's planning on stealing his book and foisting it off as his own. You know, like Agatha Christie's play, *Mousetrap*.'

'I think you mean Sidney Lumet's film, *Deathtrap*.'

She drained my glass and set it down. 'Christopher Reeve, Dyan Cannon, Michael Caine?'

'Yes, that's *Deathtrap*. I can understand your confusion, though, given the title and the fact that Lumet also directed Christie's *Murder on the Orient Express*. That was 1974, though, and *Deathtrap* was 1984, based on Ira Levin's play by the same name.'

Rosemary waggled her finger. 'Washed-up playwright decides to kill aspiring writer and stage his play as his own?'

'That's the one,' I said. 'Though the twists and—'

'Excuse me.' Missy was standing in the aisle behind my shoulder.

I turned.

'Surprise!' A blonde woman in a fur jacket nearly identical to Missy's – except this one looked more fox than faux – jumped out theatrically from behind her. I was fairly certain it was the same blonde I'd glimpsed through the door when Missy had answered Boyce's summons.

Laurence Potter's feet retracted like the Wicked Witch of the

West's after Dorothy squibs the ruby slippers. 'Audra! Uh – my dear! Whatever are you doing here?'

I swiveled my head to Rosemary. 'Don't tell me.'

'You got it.' Rosemary lifted and tipped my glass before tapping on the base to dredge the dregs. Then, 'All passengers, fasten your seat belts for Act Two. Wifey's here.'

NINE

'**Y**ou didn't really think I'd miss your 'guest of honor' stint, did you?' The new arrival kissed Laurence Potter on the cheek and perched awkwardly on the sliver of bench Missy had vacated earlier. 'Do slog over, my love, so I have some room.'

His face capturing the concepts of gloom and doom in one portrait, Potter obliged, starting a chain reaction counterclockwise, which ended with me. I stuck out my hand. 'I'm Maggy Thorsen. And you must be Mrs Potter?'

I got an icy look and a cold hand for my efforts. '*Mrs* Potter is Larry's mother. I'm his wife, Audra Edmonds.'

'A pleasure.' I'm sure.

'Hello, Audra – this really *is* a surprise,' Zoe said. 'Wherever have you been hiding?'

'Do you mean in general? I do have a job, you know, so I'm not free to travel to *all* of Larry's book events. Though I have to admit I learn something new each time I do.' She gave our other guest of honor a significant look.

Rosemary, my double-down martini probably making serious inroads on her consciousness, just shrugged.

From the exchange, I assumed Audra knew about whatever relationship Rosemary and Potter had enjoyed in the past. And maybe 'surprising' her husband was Audra's way of staying abreast of any new potential dalliances.

As if she'd read my thoughts, Zoe pulled her gaping wrap dress demurely together over her own breasts.

Audra idly picked up the pack of matches Potter had left on the table. 'But if you're asking, Zoe, where I was hiding, literally? The bartender – a lovely young hard-body named Pete or Pierre or something on his nametag – was kind enough to let me stow away to surprise Larry.'

She gave her husband a rather over-the-top adoring look. 'And you *were* surprised, weren't you, my love?'

There was something about the woman that reminded me of an early Katherine Hepburn. Even when Hepburn played a softer role, you sensed her strength.

'I certainly was,' Potter said, putting an arm around her shoulder and giving it a squeeze. 'You are my rock, and I must say you've gotten into the spirit of the occasion beautifully.'

'My outfit, you mean? Well, thank you. Even if you don't read your emails,' she surveyed her husband's lack of costume, 'I do. Though apparently,' she gestured toward Missy, who hadn't moved, 'is it . . .'

'Missy.' The girl nodded.

'Yes, well, apparently Missy and I had the same idea.' Audra shrugged out of her coat, revealing a period dress of deep blue silk chiffon, the waist cinched in and defined by crisscrossed ribbons. The skirt fell from a low inverted 'V' into what we now call a handkerchief bottom, but I had a feeling this was, like Rosemary's, a genuinely vintage dress. 'Coming as the fabulous Mrs Hubbard, that is.'

Missy gulped. 'I . . . we did. Can I make you a nametag?'

'No need,' Audra said. 'I won't be mixing much, and the only people I care to know of my presence have already been informed.'

'All right.' Missy drew herself up. 'Zoe? Would this be a good time to talk about the program?'

'Program?' Zoe, on Potter's right, looked a bit adrift.

For his part, I wondered how Potter felt about being sandwiched between his 'rock' and a potential new 'hard place.'

'Yes.' Missy seemed undeterred by her boss's marked lack of enthusiasm. 'I know you'll want to welcome everyone. You can use that intercom.'

She pointed toward the vestibule at the front of our car. 'After that, Markus – *not* as 'MacQueen' – will give a short talk on Agatha Christie's body of work and loads of lore. Once everybody's absorbed that, Mr Pavlik – sorry, I mean, Jake – Zoe will give you a signal. That's your cue to sneak into the first roomette on the left in the sleeping car at the back of the train. Oh, and assume the position of corpse.'

She giggled and I joined in to support the events woman, since you could cut the tension – or maybe bored disinterest was more accurate – with a blunter instrument than Missy's cake knife.

My stomach chose that moment to growl and Rosemary Darlington helped out by dropping her head on my shoulder. As the beret fell off her head and into my lap, our female guest of honor let out a snore.

'Oh, dear,' Missy said. 'It must be the Dramamine.'

'With a booster shot of my espresso martini.' I was craning my neck to confirm, indeed, that the illustrious author was drooling on my sundress.

'Perhaps Rosemary should take a little nap,' Missy suggested.

'Perhaps Rosemary already *is* taking a little nap,' Laurence Potter mimicked.

'Now, now, Larry. Be nice,' Audra Edmonds scolded her husband. Then, to Missy: 'Is there anything we can do?'

'Not really,' Missy said. 'If Maggy will just help me with Rosemary?'

'Of course.' I picked up Rosemary's hat and slid out, careful not to let her topple face-first into the banquette seat.

Our female guest of honor roused. 'Huh?'

'Dramamine and vodka apparently don't mix,' I said to her. 'Why don't we go and let you sleep it off?'

'Okey-dokey.' The woman slid out and stood up, albeit swaying. As I clamped on her left arm, a gust of wind hit the side of the train, driving rain against the windows.

'Storm's here,' I said, stating the obvious while trying to stabilize Rosemary.

'Oh, dear.' Missy had grabbed Rosemary's right arm. 'Laurence, if you could just lead everyone back to the sleeping car after Jake has been gone five minutes?'

'Why would I do that?'

Missy blinked. 'Well, because you're Hercule Poirot. You don't need to do much – just stroke your mustache as you solve the crime. I brought a fake one,' she dropped what looked like a woolly caterpillar on the table, 'but you don't—'

'Solve the crime?' the critic repeated. 'Who among us hasn't read the novel, after all? We certainly don't need to reenact it. Don't you think that's a little childish . . . is it Melissa?'

For the second time on the trip so far, Missy looked like she was going to cry.

I slid the mustache toward Pavlik. 'It's Missy, Larry. And if you'd prefer – and it's all right with Missy, of course – I'm sure Sheriff Pavlik would be happy to play the part of Poirot. You might prefer the role of Ratchett.'

Potter's eyes narrowed. 'The victim? I think not. Besides, I'm happy to pay homage to Dame Christie. She stood the test of time without prostituting herself. Unlike some writers any of us could mention.'

I felt Rosemary Darlington stiffen. 'And what do you mean by that?' was what I thought she said, though it came out more 'Mmmmoooomeeedat.'

'I'm sure Laurence didn't mean anything, Rosemary,' Missy said quickly. 'He—'

'I'm perfectly capable of speaking for myself,' Potter overrode her. 'Your new book, Rosemary, is not only pornography, but badly written, ineptly imagined pornography at that.'

'Larry!' This from his wife, of all people. I wondered how much of Potter's outburst was to convince Audra that he was no longer interested in Rosemary Darlington.

'I can't help it, my dear,' Potter said. 'This woman has – or *had* – talent, and she's gone and flushed it down the toilet.'

Rosemary shook off Missy and me, grabbed her beret and replaced it on her head. Almost.

'You know what happened to me, Larry? *You* did. Your criticism destroyed my confidence. I won't ever let anyone – and especially *you* – do that to me again.'

And with that, Rosemary Darlington stalked alone, and unsteadily, toward the back of the train.

TEN

Missy Hudson, cheeks flaming, followed Darlington.

Zoe Scarlett cleared her throat. 'Well, well. If you can let me out, Larry and Audra, I need to welcome our attendees and introduce the players.'

Whatever she was taking to stay so calm, I wanted some. I eyed my martini glass, which only served to remind me that it had been drained earlier by our female guest of honor in absentia.

Audra Edmonds stood up in the aisle, followed by Potter, who snagged the matchbook as he did so. Our hostess emerged and went to the front, where she slid open the vestibule door, amplifying the track noise, and appeared to push a button on the wall.

'Hello, mystery writers!' came through the sound system as I retook my seat and Audra Edmonds slid back in across from us. 'I'm Zoe Scarlett and I am so pleased to welcome you all to the first event of our glorious weekend, "Murder on the Orient Espresso."'

Applause, though sparse and, to my ear, jaded.

'As those of you who are Floridians may already have noticed, we are *not* heading north to Palm Beach nor south to Miami, but *west* on the new excursion spur into the Everglades. So much spookier, don't you think?'

As if the heavens had heard, there was a crack of thunder. Everyone applauded again, this time more enthusiastically, except for me. I shivered.

'Of course, the extra bonus,' Zoe continued, 'is that we won't be sharing our route with the Tri-Rail commuter train and Amtrak. No, no, we have these tracks all to ourselves. That's important, you see, because we have a *murder* to solve.'

Cue dramatic music, literally. The guy in the checkered jacket who had been seated behind us in the bus piped up with the Dragnet '*Bmmmm, bmp-bmp-bmp*' from the table next to Zoe.

'Thank you for the accompaniment,' she managed with a forced smile. 'I'd like to introduce our featured players for the evening, which you'll also find on your playbill.' She held up Missy's sepia-toned handout. 'And do feel free to ask participants to sign them as a remembrance of tonight's inaugural event.'

Heads nodded in approval of what I suspected was Missy's good idea. I feared, though, that given the number of people attending and the players listed, there weren't many fans/audience members on the train beyond the cast itself.

'First,' Zoe continued, 'as Mary Debenham, our guest of honor, Rosemary Darlington.'

Genuine applause, even though Rosemary Darlington was nowhere to be seen. Wherever she was, though, I trusted she was snoring and drooling blissfully.

Zoe plunged on. And not a bad strategy, since people listening to her in the other cars would assume Rosemary was in ours and vice versa.

'And, as Hercule Poirot, our second guest of honor, mystery reviewer and critic extraordinaire, Laurence . . . Potter.'

Applause, this time more tepid.

Not that it mattered. Potter/Poirot was nowhere to be seen, either.

'This is going well,' I whispered to Pavlik. I kept my voice down so Audra, the un-Mrs Potter across our booth, couldn't hear. I probably didn't need to worry, since Edmonds was pushing buttons on her phone and looking frustrated. I hoped she'd forgotten to charge it.

'What do you expect?' Pavlik asked in my ear. 'This isn't a "Maggy Thorsen" production.'

'For which I'm very grateful, since this threatens to become a train wreck.' Maybe I really *had* jinxed Missy's event with my earlier thoughts on enjoying train wrecks. 'Not literally, of course,' I added, hoping to undo any psychic damage.

Pavlik gave my shoulder a squeeze. 'Don't lose hope. The evening's young yet.'

At 'yet,' we hit a dip, sending me bouncing up off the banquette.

Zoe Scarlett droned on. '. . . our other players. As MacQueen, please welcome our Agatha Christie expert, Markus, um . . .'

A roar went up and Markus waved from the table next to us. Zoe went on to introduce, sans last names, Grace as Greta Ohlsson, the Swedish Lady, germaphobic literary agent Carson as Count Andrenyi, Prudence as Princess Dragomiroff, somebody named Big Fred as Foscarelli, and Harvey – the guy in the loud sports jacket – as Hardman.

I noticed that besides not knowing her longtime conference attendees' last names without the aid of the badges she'd harangued Missy about, Zoe didn't bother introducing the help: Boyce as Bouc, the director of the railroad, and Pete the bartender as Pierre Michel, the conductor depicted in Christie's *Murder on the Orient Express.*

Missy slid into the seat next to me, wiping her hands on a paper towel. She also looked like she'd put on lipstick and combed her hair for the occasion.

'Is Rosemary all right?' I asked.

'Sleeping like a baby,' Missy said, head directed toward the towel in her hands. 'It's probably for the best.'

'The best for your event. No question.'

'And now,' Zoe was saying, 'a special and heartfelt thank you to someone who has gone above and beyond for us. As Mrs Hubbard, played so elegantly by Lauren Bacall in the movie, I give you . . .'

Missy's head jerked up, her face shining. She slid over to the aisle and dropped the paper towel on the table, preparing to be introduced.

'Audra Edmonds!'

'You had to have seen that coming,' Pavlik said as I nursed the new espresso martini he'd brought me as Markus took over for his talk on Agatha Christie. 'Nothing has gone right for poor Missy.'

'Through no fault of her own,' I pointed out. 'And what did go well will be ignored anyway. That's the plight of the special event planner.' I sighed and gazed into my whipped cream.

'Poor baby,' Pavlik commiserated. 'Good thing you've left behind the drudgery for the exciting new world of coffee.' He nodded toward my martini. 'How is that, by the way?'

'Delicious, thank you. And your wine?'

'Awful, but if I switch I'll be sleeping it off next to Rosemary Darlington.'

'Ah, no, you won't, actually,' I said, swiping a finger into the whipped cream and offering it to Pavlik. 'That woman knows too many moves.'

'So I hear.' Pavlik licked the cream off my finger. Engagingly slowly.

I gave a little shiver. And, happily, not because I was either cold or scared. In fact, it might be raining cats and dogs, alligators and pythons outside, but inside the train it was comfortable and I was here beside my sheriff.

Life was good. I sighed.

'Something wrong?' Pavlik asked.

I laid my head on his shoulder and closed my eyes. 'Not a thing.'

I should have known it couldn't last.

ELEVEN

'Excuse me,' a voice said.

I opened my eyes to see Danny/Col. Arbuthnot's name badge sidle into sight. Tilting my head, I saw the tousled dark head.

'Danny.' I sat up and self-consciously slid the spaghetti straps of my sundress back onto my shoulder like we'd just been caught making out in the back seat of a Chevy. 'Have you met Sheriff Pavlik?'

'Jake, please,' Pavlik corrected.

'Jake,' I repeated. I wasn't used to all this first-name stuff. In fact, given Pavlik's position as Brookhills County Sheriff, I made a real effort to use his title when addressing him in front of others, especially his deputies.

'Thank you, Jake.' Close up, the young man looked older than I'd thought earlier, maybe mid-twenties. 'And please, call me Danny.'

'Danny it is.' Pavlik turned to me. 'And, obviously, you two have already met?'

'I don't believe so.' Danny's matte brown eyes showed no recognition.

'The coffeehouse owner?' I reminded him.

He squinted at me.

'I told you I wasn't a writer?' I tried.

'Oh, yes.' Danny turned back to Pavlik. 'Well, it's a real honor to meet you, sir. I'm looking forward to your workshop tomorrow on "How to Kill Realistically with Guns, Knives and Bare Hands."'

'That's the name of your panel?' I asked Pavlik.

'They edited it. My title was longer.'

Figured. So many weapons, so little time.

'And it's a workshop, not a panel,' Danny corrected, this time. '"Hands-on," the program says.'

'I'll be calling up volunteers and demonstrating some techniques,' Pavlik said, looking pleased by the younger man's enthusiasm.

For my part, I was imagining myself – a convenient 'volunteer' – being tossed around like a crash-test dummy. Maybe I'd sleep in tomorrow morning. Catch Pavlik's second panel. 'What's the other one you're doing?'

'"The Ins and Outs of Firearms,"' Danny supplied eagerly. 'All about guns and ammunition. And entrance and exit wounds, of course.'

Even better. The hotel probably had a nice pool. I'd hide there.

'You'd be surprised,' Pavlik said, 'at the number of mistakes in books – or in television and even movies, too. And it's not complicated stuff. Simple terminology, or the difference between a semi-automatic and a revolver.'

Danny was nodding. 'The protagonist of the last book I read – or tried to read, I should say – put a silencer on a revolver.'

Pavlik looked skyward. 'See what I mean? That's as bad as a having a revolver that ejects brass.'

'Everybody knows that it's semi-automatics not revolvers that eject casings.'

'And, of course, that revolvers can't be silenced.'

The two men – and I bestow that mantle of maturity loosely – cackled at the stupidity of it all.

'I understand you've written a book,' I said to Danny, trying to participate in the conversation. 'What's it about?'

'I'm afraid it's much too complicated to describe at a gathering like this,' he said, dismissing me again.

'Well, then it's much "too complicated" to sell, as well.' Zoe Scarlett slid onto the bench Audra Edmonds had abandoned after her introduction. 'If you can't describe your book, how do you expect publishers to categorize it and wholesalers and booksellers to display and sell it?'

'Then I'll publish it myself,' Danny said. 'Ebooks and on-demand publishing have changed the world for authors.'

'You're absolutely right,' Zoe said. 'But with something like a quarter of a million books being self-published a year, how is anyone going to find yours?'

'Because I'm good.' Danny's face was sullen, like a five-year-old who's been told he can't have a cookie before dinner.

'Yeah, you and two-hundred and forty-nine thousand, nine

hundred and ninety-nine other authors who think the same thing.'

Disheartening words, I thought, from someone whose own conference was dedicated toward teaching people to write and, presumably, get published.

'But there obviously are success stories,' I pointed out. 'I've seen books on the *New York Times* bestsellers list that are obviously self-published. The authors' names and the publishers' names are the same.'

'Sure, it can happen,' Zoe said. 'But lightning has to strike. Even today, with all this opportunity, books become bestsellers the same way they always have. One person likes a book and tells somebody else. The only thing that has changed is the medium used to have the conversation.'

Pavlik grinned. 'Zoe does a panel on changes in the publishing industry.'

'And another thing,' she continued her rant. 'Even if you self-publish, you need to come up with a pithy hook. One sentence that sells your book in the time it takes us to scroll on by. What's yours?' She stabbed a finger at Danny.

The boy's eyes widened. 'Well, I—'

'*That's* what you'll learn this weekend,' Zoe finished triumphantly. 'Now, go do your homework.'

'You've got a tough-love approach to promoting your conference,' I said, watching Danny slink, chastened, toward the passenger car.

'Can't coddle these writers.' Her head was swiveling like a lighthouse beacon. 'If you want something, you have to go out and get it.'

Which, of course, raised the question of what something – or *somebody* – she wanted.

I slid my hand off the table and onto Pavlik's thigh slowly, so Zoe would notice.

He glanced at me before asking, 'Umm, are you looking for somebody, Zoe?

'Larry,' she said. 'I *told* him I was going to introduce our players.'

Which was most likely why the man had disappeared.

'The last I saw of Potter was when he got up and stepped

back to let you out,' Pavlik said, laying his hand on top of mine. 'He didn't pass us to go forward to the club car, so he must have headed toward the back of the train.'

'Well, we'd better find him before Missy's "program" starts. Thank God Markus can be counted on to drone on and on.'

The librarian was still at the intercom, presenting his talk.

'Larry's probably in the bathroom,' I suggested. 'Has Audra seen him?'

'No,' Zoe said. 'And he's been gone for half an hour.'

I shrugged. 'Maybe he took his magazine in there with him. He's obviously quite the reader.'

'Huh.' Zoe seemed to be thinking it over. 'Perhaps I should go tap on the door.'

Pavlik watched her leave. 'Was that a thinly-veiled knock on male bathroom habits?'

'Hey,' I said, smiling, 'if the stool fits.'

Pavlik laughed and raised my hand to kiss the palm. 'You're one twisted woman, Maggy Thorsen.'

'Not as "twisted" as I'd like to be,' I said, sliding even closer. 'Bet even Rosemary doesn't have any wings in her boo—'

'Have you seen Zoe?' Prudence was standing at our table now, fingers twisting in the ropes of princess pearls around her neck. 'Missy is going batshit because she can't find Larry.'

And these people called themselves *mystery* writers? The train was four cars long, not counting the locomotives – first and last – so how tough could it be to find someone?

I had a thought. 'Maybe Larry's standing in one of the vestibules between cars smoking. I saw him grab the matches when he got up from our table.'

'Great,' Prudence said. 'Markus is done with his soliloquy and we're all supposed to gather here in the dining car before trooping back to solve the crime. Wait a minute.' She squinted at Pavlik's nametag. '"Ratchett." Aren't you supposed to be dead?'

'Zoe didn't give me the—'

'Well she *should* have,' Prudence said, looking more like the imperious Princess Dragomiroff. 'How are we supposed to view the body in the sleeping car if you're out here, obviously still alive?'

'Well, I don't know. I—'

Raucous laughter erupted from across the way. Grace/Greta was trying to climb up onto the table in a manner not befitting her role. In fact, the blouse and skirt somehow invoked more Naughty School Girl than Swedish Lady.

'Damn it,' Prudence said. 'We need to get some food into these people.'

'There's cake,' I said, watching Grace gain her footing and release her hair from its bun, shaking out the wild curls like Raquel Welch in *One Million Years B.C.*

'To be served when the crime is solved, from what I understand,' Pavlik said. 'Though maybe if you ask Missy—'

'Any sign of Laurence?' It was Missy herself, magically appearing but looking concerned.

'No, but Zoe went to check the bathroom,' I said.

'I've already done that.' Tears were welling up in Missy's eyes again. I couldn't help feeling sorry for her. 'Twice.'

'OK, let's look at this logically,' Pavlik said. 'He has to be in one of these cars. You're just missing him because people are milling around.'

A whoop came from the unincorporated mob as Grace slid butt-first off the table.

'We're coming to a stop already,' Missy said as Prudence shook her head in disgust. 'Now the rear locomotive will pull us back the same direction we came from.'

Since there were no lights outside to judge our speed by, I had to take her word for it.

'So, are there two engineers, or does the guy in front have to come through the train to get to the other locomotive?'

'Oh, dear,' Missy said, putting her hand to her face. 'There *is* no interior connection. Our engineer is a lovely older man – retired, in fact, and a bit eccentric. He'll have to go out in this rain and wind. We didn't think of that.'

'Would you like me to go out and check on him?' Pavlik asked.

'That's so kind of you.' Missy was trying to peer out the window. 'I'd be afraid, though, that you'd miss him somehow and accidentally be left behind. The Everglades is a dangerous enough place in the daytime. At night, and in this weather?' She shivered.

I was right there with her. Meaning inside the train was safe and sound, which is where I wanted Pavlik to stay.

But I knew the sheriff wouldn't be deterred by concern for his own safety, especially when somebody else might be in danger. It wasn't in his DNA. I wasn't sure I had that kind of grit myself – to run toward disaster, rather than away – but I was very grateful there were people like Pavlik who did.

So, I tried another tack. 'You're right, Missy. We certainly can't chance losing your main forensics speaker. There would be no one to teach the panels – or workshops – tomorrow.'

Pavlik looked at me.

'Imagine the disappointment if you didn't show up,' I said to him. 'You know, to teach killing and guns and bullets and such.'

'Oooh, that reminds me.' Missy turned away from the window to address Pavlik. 'Did you bring your own weapons or do you need mine?'

'You have . . . weapons?' I asked.

'Of course,' the two of them chorused.

'I meant Missy.' When it came to Pavlik, personal experience had taught me that asking Mae West's come-hither question, 'Is that a pistol in your pocket or are you just glad to see me?' wouldn't get me the answer I'd hoped for.

'Oh, yes,' the young woman said. 'But only props for the workshop. Rubber knives and the like.'

That was a relief, at least. Maybe I would attend, after all.

'. . . shipped everything I needed, along with my handouts,' Pavlik was saying.

That explained what was in the UPS box that had been waiting for us in the hotel room.

'My Glock Forty semi-automatic,' he continued, 'and a Colt Detective Special, a revolver designed for a six-chamber cylinder. I also have a variety of cartridges – standard, hollow-point, Hydra-shok, the Glaser Safety Slug—'

Suddenly the Flagler Suite wasn't looking quite so romantic.

'You *will* talk about caliber versus millimeter, won't you?' This from Prudence, whom I'd forgotten about. 'That always confuses people and we really need to know those things in order to write intelligently.'

'I'll have thirty-eight, forty and forty-five caliber cartridges as well as nine millimeter, to illustrate,' Pavlik assured Prudence, then turned to me. 'What we're talking about, Maggy, is the diameter of the ammunition. A forty-five caliber bullet or cartridge – the same thing, for our purposes – is forty-five one hundreds of an inch in diameter, or nearly half an inch across. A nine millimeter is, as you might guess, nine millimeters across.'

'And nearly equal to the size of a thirty-eight caliber,' Missy contributed brightly. 'If you do the conversion from metric, I mean.'

'A nine is a bit smaller than a thirty-eight,' Pavlik said with an approving nod. 'But very close.'

Obviously gratified, Missy asked, 'And did you bring – or ship – a variety of knives as well?'

'I have a rubber knife with a five-inch blade to use in the hands-on demonstration, of course. For show-and-tell, I shipped a switch blade, and gravity, pocket and buck knives.'

What, I thought, no death by butter knife?

'Oh, and my assassin's dagger, of course.'

So I *would* hang out at the pool tomorrow. Or maybe go to the beach. There was an original thought, given I was in South Florida. From rainforest tonight to sand castles tomorrow. And I'd thought Wisconsin was diverse.

'Gravity,' Prudence said. 'Is that the one with the button on the handle?'

'Exactly,' my personal weapons expert said. 'When that's pushed and you flick out to the side with your wrist, the weight of the blade opens the knife.'

'But isn't that a switchblade?' Missy seemed puzzled.

I, for my part, was completely lost.

'Not at all,' Pavlik said. 'When you thumb the button – or 'switch' – on a switchblade, the blade flicks out automatically.'

'So no gravity needed.' Prudence was nodding.

'Correct,' Pavlik said. 'The pocket knife, on the other—'

'We're moving,' I interrupted, feeling the train hiccup in the other direction. *And* with Pavlik still safely inside. My delaying tactic had worked.

'Oh, thank goodness.' Missy was back to the window. 'The engineer has already moved to the other locomotive. We must be starting back toward Fort Lauderdale.'

'Spry old fellow,' Prudence said.

'The engineer? Oh, he's quite the character.' Missy checked her watch. 'I do worry that we'll get back to the station too early, though. You know, before the crime is solved?'

'Maybe someone should make an announcement,' I suggested. 'Requesting that Potter and the rest of the "cast" come to this car.'

There was a flaw, of course, in my plan: Laurence Potter obviously didn't want to appear. Missy, however, didn't seem to see it. 'That's a wonderful idea, Maggy. Zoe should—'

'Zoe? Why not you?' Prudence prodded. 'You do most of the work, anyway. Why let her take all the credit?'

Missy blushed, tugging down her dress. 'Oh, no, I prefer to work behind the scenes. I couldn't.'

'You couldn't what?' Zoe, perhaps instinctively, had magically turned up, too.

'Maggy suggested that we make an announcement . . .'

'Maggy?' Zoe repeated.

I raised my hand. The woman was either stupid or trying to rile me. I was betting on the latter.

'Oh, right,' Zoe said distractedly, her attention drawn to the commotion in the corner, where a huge man dressed in a zoot suit was trying to climb onto the table.

Pavlik, having been thwarted in his effort to save the day by venturing into the Everglades, slid out of the booth. 'You!' he said in a thundering voice. 'Down! Now!'

The big man ignored him. With the train's swaying movement he looked like an overweight, overdressed mob surfer trying to position his feet for one last Big Kahuna of a wave. Worse, he was a decade off in his costume. The high-waisted trousers and long coats with wide lapels and padded shoulders were popular in the forties, not the thirties.

'Off the table, Fred!' Zoe bellowed.

'Fred' got off. Pavlik shrugged and returned to our table.

'Zoe, we think you should cut the cake,' Prudence suggested. 'Sop up some of the alcohol.'

'Too late,' Missy said mournfully.

'Too late to sop up the alcohol or too late to cut the cake?' One more Orient Espresso martini on an empty stomach and *I'd* be up on a table. Or under it.

'Maybe both.' Missy was agitatedly tip-tapping her foot. 'But what I mean is that someone took a big hunk out of our cake and made off with the knife. Can you believe that? What are we going to use to cut the rest of it?'

I looked down at my swizzle stick, hungry enough to give it a good-faith try.

'I'm sure we can come up with something,' Pavlik said. 'If all else fails, I have my trusty Swiss Army knife.' He reached into his pocket and pulled out yet another knife in addition to the ones that apparently awaited us in the Flagler Suite.

'But the original cake knife was also meant to be the murder weapon. We need it for the "reveal."' Missy was near inconsolable. 'Somebody has ruined everything!'

'Oh, for God's sake, don't be such a child,' Zoe snapped, adjusting her dress. 'It's not the end of the world.'

By this point I desperately wanted to do something to assist poor Missy, and if it got me closer to food then all the better. 'Show me the cake, Missy. Maybe the knife just fell off the table after someone messed with it. If not, we'll come up with a substitute.'

'Good idea.' Zoe seemed to be glad to be rid of her overly emotional assistant. And, perhaps, me. 'In the meantime, we can't wait any longer to solve our little crime. I was going to have you go back to the sleeping car, Jacob, but without Larry I wonder—'

I wanted to hear more about Zoe Scarlett's plans for Pavlik, but Missy had my arm and was pulling me toward the cake at the far end of the car.

TWELVE

'Hmm,' I said, looking at the hacked-up corpse that had been part of the cake. 'Somebody amputated the left foot.' Including the big toe, where I'd swiped the bit of frosting earlier, resulting at least in my tracks being covered there.

Missy looked forlorn. 'Didn't I tell you?'

'He or she might have taken the knife blade to carry the piece of cake on,' I glanced around. 'I don't see any plates.'

'I didn't put them out yet. So no one would get ideas of cutting it early, for all the good that did.'

'The best-laid plans,' I commiserated. 'By the way, I loved that knife – what a loss. My grandmother left me a carving set that contained one just like it.'

I was thinking about the gift, which I only brought out for special occasions like Christmas and Thanksgiving. The hinged brown box contained two large knives and a serving fork. One, with an eight-inch blade, was a twin of the missing knife.

'That's so nice,' Missy said. 'I got this one on eBay for four-teen ninety-five.'

$14.95. Apparently, I wouldn't be retiring on the proceeds from the sale of my family heirloom. But then if it *were* a collectible, Missy would hardly have put it in the cake. Unless . . . 'Maybe somebody *did* think it was valuable and stole it. I believe the handle is staghorn and—'

'Your attention, please.' Zoe Scarlett's voice came over the speakers.

The sudden lurch of the train coupled with a metallic grinding made me grab for a pole. Apparently the new tracks were adding a few more kinks for the return voyage.

'Hercule Poirot requests that all guests assemble,' Zoe continued, 'in the forward dining car. It seems there's been a murder.'

At the words, most of the costumed guests started to head in from the next car.

A clap of thunder was followed almost immediately by a searing flash of lightning outside the window. Although we'd been traveling through the blackness for more than an hour and a half, this was my first glimpse behind that curtain of darkness.

'My God,' I said, leaning down to peer out the window. 'There's nothing out there except low brush and the occasional clump of trees.'

'And sawgrass, as far as the eye can see. The Everglades is a "slow-moving river of grass,"' Missy quoted, seeming to relax a little. 'Over three million acres originally. It really is striking when you fly into Fort Lauderdale at night. You'd swear you're soaring above the clouds or over the ocean because you can't see anything and then, suddenly, the lights of South Florida pop up beneath you.'

Then Missy tensed again as people continued to file past us. 'I still don't see Laurence. Would you help me search while the rest of the group is occupied?'

My eyes lingered longingly at the cake, but I said, 'Of course.'

Missy turned, and I managed a last swipe at the frosting before following. 'Aren't you going the wrong way? You said the sleeping car is the last one, right?'

'Yes.' Missy stopped. 'Except that we've reversed direction, so it's the first car after the locomotive, which used to bring up the rear of the train, but now is the front.'

I think my eyes must have crossed, because Missy waved for me to come along. 'I'll show you.'

We passed from the dining car into the vestibule, where the noise of the track passing below the metal plates beneath our feet made conversation difficult until we opened the next door into the passenger car. It was empty except for Danny and Audra Edmonds. They were seated side by side, curly dark hair and blonde waves close as they chatted in low tones.

'Excuse me,' Missy interrupted. 'But we seem to have lost track of Mr Potter.'

Audra looked up. 'Have you checked with Rosemary?'

'She's not feeling well,' Missy said. 'She's lying down in the sleeping car.'

Danny's eyes flickered. 'Rosemary Darlington? I saw you go by with her before. I'd love to meet her.'

I bet he would. I'd also bet that if I quizzed the star-chaser he'd have no memory of meeting me once, much less twice.

'I'm afraid she's unavailable at the moment,' Missy said in the voice of an experienced gatekeeper. 'But I'd be happy to introduce you sometime during the conference,' she glanced at his badge, her nose crinkling, 'Danny.'

I caught the sign of displeasure, probably at Danny/Col. Arbuthnot's lack of alliteration.

'He signed up late and barely caught the bus,' I told her. 'You and Rosemary had already left, so I assume the conference registration person just assigned a character to him randomly.'

Danny glanced down at the badge self-consciously. 'Is there a problem? Like I told Zoe, I did pay.'

'No, no – it's fine,' Missy said and, to my surprise, smiled brightly at the young man. 'We're happy to have you.'

The two were probably close in age. Could love be in the air?

'Thank you,' Danny said. 'Are you an author?'

Before Missy could answer that she was 'just a researcher,' and thereby render herself invisible, I jumped in. 'Missy is one of the conference organizers. She knows everyone.'

That piqued his interest. 'A pleasure to meet you, Missy. You must have a very interesting job.'

Missy blushed. 'I suppose so. I—'

'Missy works closely with all sorts of famous authors,' I said encouragingly. 'And publishers, too, I'm sure. Right, Missy?'

'Well, I . . . No—'

'All guests to the dining car,' Zoe's voice thundered over the intercom again.

'Oh, dear,' Missy said. 'If we don't find Laurence, who's to solve the crime?'

'If it helps, Mr Potter passed through here not long after you and Ms Darlington did,' Danny said. 'He had a pack of cigarettes and was headed the same way.'

Toward the sleeping car. Having walked a mile in the cheated-upon spouse's shoes myself, Danny's statement would have raised a red flag for me. It apparently did for Audra as well.

'"The same way,"' she repeated, not seeming at all surprised. 'What a coincidence.'

'He may have gone out on the landing – or whatever you call

it, between cars – for a smoke.' Danny seemed to sense he'd said something to upset her. Why he cared, I didn't know.

'It's called a vestibule,' Missy said. 'And there's no smoking on the train, anywhere.'

So I'd been right.

'Like I said,' Danny continued, 'I wasn't sure where he was going, only that he had his cigarettes. I was going to follow, see if we could talk, but I saw Mrs . . . um, Audra, and thought I'd introduce myself.'

I frowned. Something wasn't right. 'I'm sorry, but didn't I see the two of you speaking in the club car before Audra surprised everyone?'

'Just for a second,' Danny said. 'I didn't know who she was then.'

Well, that explained it. I had to admit Zoe Scarlett was right. It *is* hard to know who to suck up to without a scorecard – or, at least, last names and titles on nametags. I was curious about this kid. Hell, about *all* these people. 'You sent your manuscript to Larry Potter, why—'

Missy tugged on my arm. 'We really need to find Laurence, Maggy.'

'Oh, of course,' I said and then to Danny, 'I'm sorry. We can talk later.'

'Umm, sure. Anytime,' he said distractedly. Then to Missy: 'I'd love to hear more about you. Maybe you and I can get together for a drink.'

Missy giggled and tugged at her dress. 'Maybe.'

As we pressed on toward the restroom at the end of the car, Missy was walking taller, with a sexy little wiggle that threatened to send her careening off her shiny spiked heels as the train chugged along the track.

Ahh, amour. And ambition. And always the twain shall meet.

Which brought me back to our guests of honor. Missy had said that Rosemary Darlington and Laurence Potter had a 'history.'

I took that to mean an affair and Audra Edmonds's reaction to Rosemary seemed to bear that out. But was this affair truly 'history' or more current events? As in, the two of them shacked up in the sleeping car at this very moment.

If so, I had to give both Potter and Darlington props for acting ability. The disdain he professed for her – and her new writing endeavor – seemed very genuine. Ditto, our female guest of honor's feelings toward the reviewer, not to mention her own reaction to the motion of the train, her medication and my espresso martini. If Rosemary Darlington was faking, I'd eat her beret.

As Missy and I reached the back of the car, wind was whistling through the opening in the windows I'd been forced to leave in order to secure her banner.

For all the good the thing was doing. Not only, as I expected, was there no one out there to see it except for the denizens of the Everglades, but the vinyl banner was slapping rhythmically against the side of the train, occasionally being lifted by a gust to cover the windows.

The sign might not survive the trip. I just hoped the windows would.

Hesitating at the restroom door, I said to Missy, 'I suppose it won't hurt to check again.'

She shrugged. 'Sure, maybe third time's the charm.'

'Speaking of charm,' I said casually, as I tapped on the restroom door, 'Danny is kind of cute.'

'You think?' She cocked her head. 'He seems awfully young to me.' She must have seen the surprise on my face. 'Oh, don't get me wrong, Maggy. What girl doesn't like a little male attention, but . . .'

'But?' I gave another knock.

'But he's really not my type. I don't like users.'

'Losers?' Still no answer from inside, I tentatively slid the restroom door open.

'No, *user*. Somebody who uses other people to get what they want. True love should be more than that.'

Not wanting to get into a discussion of 'true love' with the starry-eyed girl, I stepped my jaded self into the empty restroom. 'Huh, this is larger than I expected.'

Missy came in after me. 'Do you think so?'

'Well, bigger than an airplane restroom, certainly. I mean, we're both standing in here, not exactly comfortably and it smells like a flaming bag of dog poop, but—'

The door slid closed.

'Hey,' I said, grabbing the handle and giving it a shove. 'That's not funny.'

'Oh, I'm sure nobody did it on purpose, Maggy. It was probably just the motion of the train.'

We did seem to be slowing. 'The door is stuck.'

'I think you locked it.' She pushed the handle the other way and yanked open the door. 'Here we go.'

We stepped out into the hall and I let out the breath I'd apparently been holding. 'Thank God for South Florida's insistence on over air-conditioning.'

'It *was* a little stuffy in there. Now, where were we?'

'Heading that way,' I pointed, proud that I was getting the hang of this front-is-now-back, back-is-now-front reorientation. At least I had a sense of which way we were going, which was more than I could say of my one and only cruise. I'd spent the entire four days wandering the halls and punching up information on the computerized 'You are here' maps. And eating, of course.

My stomach growled again.

Beyond the restroom was the vestibule leading to the sleeping car. I had a hard time seeing why someone would come here to smoke. The exit doors on both sides of the vestibule had no outside platforms, the floor was a rumbling metal ramp and the space was noisy and smelled.

Come to think of it, it probably wasn't unlike a lot of places smokers had been banished to.

'What's that?' Missy said, pointing to something in the corner to my left.

'An empty book of matches.' I picked up the black and silver pack. 'Potter's, do you think?'

Missy took them and read, 'Titanium.'

'What's that?'

She looked embarrassed and handed them back to me. 'A . . . gentlemen's club?'

'Ah, then definitely Potter's.' I slipped the match book into the pocket of my sundress.

Missy looked around the cramped space again. 'He came this way, then.'

'But probably not to smoke,' I said, looking around myself.

'Unless he did it in the restroom. Maybe that's why it smelled like that.'

'I think that was just train smell and toilet. There are a lot of us onboard and we've all been using that restroom. I think the other is at the far end of the sleeping car.'

'So if Potter isn't in this bathroom, maybe he's in that one. The only other option is . . .'

'Oh, dear. Do you think he's with Rosemary? I wondered if that's what his wife was insinuating.'

'Insinuating' was putting it mildly. 'Could Potter have snuck in there after you left?'

She shrugged. 'I hate to think he'd do that, but, well, I'm starting to believe no one is what they seem to be.'

As far as I was concerned, Laurence Potter was exactly what he seemed – a pompous sleazeball, but then I tend to be judgmental. 'Where is Rosemary sleeping it off?'

'The farthest roomette – that's what the train company calls the little sleeping compartments – from where we are. On the left. I knew we'd be using the nearest one to the passenger car for solving our program's crime, so I wanted Rosemary to be as far away as possible so she wouldn't be disturbed.'

'Good idea,' I said, not bothering to add that it was also the room where, like the last one on a hotel corridor, two people could fool around with less likelihood of being discovered. 'We know Potter came through here, because of the matchbook. Is there an outside platform anywhere that he could smoke?'

'You mean like on the back of an old-time campaign train? I doubt it, though I suppose he could open an exit door.'

Yikes. 'Haven't you seen the news stories about people disappearing from trains?' I asked. 'Granted, many of them were older or ill but the authorities suspect they got confused and thought the door led to the bathroom or the next car. Once opened, with the velocity of the train, they—'

'Oh, dear. But then why aren't the exits kept locked?'

'Because there are also safety issues arguing against that. People need to be able to get out quickly in case of an emergency.'

Could Potter have opened the exit door to have a smoke and somehow, perhaps when the train hit a rough section of track, tumbled out?

Leaving the question and the vestibule behind, I opened the first roomette door on the left and peered in. All I saw was blackness and all I felt was warmth. Someone had opened the window. 'Hello? Is anybody in here?'

Missy reached past me and felt for a light. 'I think—'

As I took a step forward, she screamed and grabbed my arm.

At first I thought the scream was because my sandal had landed in the mutilated left foot from the cake left lying on the floor, grinding buttercream into the carpet.

But then I saw the body, knife protruding prominently from the chest.

THIRTEEN

'We have to get the sheriff,' I said, backing-pedaling and pulling Missy with me. 'He'll know—'

The body sat up, and Missy's scream nearly deafened me. But the corpse wasn't the critic, of course. It was Pavlik in the fake mustache.

'Damn it, Pavlik.' Deafened but not mute, I stomped my foot into a second smear of cake icing on the floor. 'You scared the living hell out of us.'

Missy was crying. 'How did you get past . . . ohhh.' Realization dawned on her tear-streaked face. 'Did you shut us in that bathroom?'

'I'm sorry.' The sheriff was smiling and didn't appear a bit apologetic. Perversely desirable, though. Made me want to jump right in that bunk with him.

Missy, however, was not as easily mollified. 'That was cruel.'

Pavlik held up his hands. 'Truly, I am sorry. I couldn't resist, but it was a childish thing to do. Please forgive me?'

Now it was Missy who was smiling, her toe doing little coy circles. 'Well, I suppose so. If you promise not to do it again.'

With luck, the opportunity to shut two women in a train bathroom in order to scare them by playing a fictional murdered villain come-to-life wouldn't pop up on a regular basis.

'Promise.' Pavlik crossed his heart.

Oh, please.

The sounds of a crowd and sliding doors opening and closing were getting closer.

'Can I hope those are the frenzied villagers, coming to burn you at the stake?' I asked pleasantly.

'Merely to solve my heinous – or not so heinous, given my character's own crime – murder.' Pavlik lay back and repositioned the knife.

'Is that my cake knife? You took it?' Missy demanded, eyes narrowed.

'Uh-uh.' The sheriff held it up. 'My Swiss Army knife. With the blade closed, of course.'

'Ohhh.' All appeared forgiven again.

'Did you send that with the rest of your "weapons"?' I asked. 'I didn't think you'd opened the UPS box.'

'This?' Pavlik held it up. 'It's more tool than weapon. I brought it with me. In my luggage, of course.'

In truth, the thing did look like some gadget you'd see on an infomercial. 'But wait!' I said, mimicking the medium's pitchmen.

Missy teetered on her heels. 'I wasn't going anywhere.'

'No, I meant . . . never mind. Does that thing have a cork-screw?' I asked Pavlik, thinking we might snare a bottle of wine for the room on the way back to the hotel.

'Of course not. This is a *classic* Swiss Army knife. Not one of those fru-fru all-in-ones.' Pavlik closed his eyes. 'Now get out, you two, before you blow my cover.'

'Will do, Sheriff.' I went to follow Missy into the corridor, but as she reached to slide the door closed behind us, I held up my hand.

I stuck my head back into the roomette. 'By the way, did you open the window?'

'Me?' He opened one eye. 'No, it was open when I came in, though I'm grateful for the warmth. Dead men don't shiver.'

The eye closed.

'He's so funny,' Missy said as we made our way down the corridor, quickly checking each roomette as we went. Behind us the participants were gathered around the door to Pavlik's chamber. 'And nice.'

'He is,' I agreed, closing the second to last door. 'Most of the time.'

Missy stopped and looked at me, disbelieving. 'Please don't tell me he's a louse, too.'

Louse. Great word, and probably fitting of the era we were supposed to be in. 'Oh, no. Pavlik is a very honorable man.' Which I'd found to be a problem at times. Like when he suspected yours truly of murder.

'Well, that's good.' Missy stopped at the door to the last compartment. 'This is where I left Rosemary. Shall I rap?'

Another genteel turn of phrase. 'Probably a good idea.'

She did, using just the tips of her fingernails.

'Huh?' we heard from inside.

I tried the door, which slid ajar. So the thing hadn't been locked from the inside. 'Rosemary? We're just checking to make sure you're OK.' And alone.

'Who's there?'

'Missy and Maggy,' my fellow quester said, flipping on the light.

Rosemary was on the bunk alone, arm up over her eyes. 'Jesus, are you trying to blind me?'

'Sorry, it's because the Everglades are so dark. You can even see the stars at night.' Missy leaned down to point out the window.

'I don't see any stars,' Rosemary said. 'In fact, isn't that rain streaming down the glass?'

'I'm afraid it is,' Missy said, looking again. 'Oh, dear. It's coming down in torrents.'

Oh, dear, was right. 'Well, we're on the way back, at least.'

'The train seems to be going quite slowly, though,' Missy said worriedly. 'I hope there's no flooding on the tracks.'

Flooding? In the Everglades at the end of their so-called 'wet season'? Who would have thunk it, as my son Eric would say. But then he was a smart-aleck teenager and I, his more mature parent. Or I should be. 'Flooding? In the Everglades? Might we have foreseen that possibility?'

'Oh, don't be a worry-wart, Maggy,' Missy said a little sharply, which indicated to me that she herself was worried. Or, perhaps, didn't appreciate being criticized in front of an important client like Rosemary Darlington. 'We've already *had* record rains this year.'

I wasn't sure why her latest little factoid was supposed to reassure me.

Nonetheless, I kept quiet as Missy continued. 'The Murder on the Orient Espresso is being solved as we speak and our event is a success!'

Her statement made me think. 'But what about Poirot? Who's playing him?'

'Potter, of course,' Rosemary said.

Missy and I exchanged looks. Rosemary was out of the loop

when it came to his vanishing act, but I wasn't going to be the one to fill her in if I could help it.

'I suppose it's possible he's been up front the whole time,' Missy said slowly. 'After all, Audra was able to stay hidden until she sprung herself on Laurence.'

'Audra,' Rosemary sniffed. 'That woman is hateful to me.'

'To be fair, she apparently has reason,' I countered. 'To hate you, I mean.' You can take the cheated-upon woman out of the state, but you can't take the state of being cheated upon out of the woman.

Rosemary, for her part, looked genuinely bewildered. 'Me? Why?'

'The affair?' I knew I should drop it, but my list of things I should do had probably filled three volumes by then.

Still a blank look, then changing to comprehension. 'Oh, you mean between her husband and me? There was never any affair.'

'But why would people say it if it weren't true?' Missy, trusting girl that she was, seemed sick at the thought. 'And his wife, even.'

'It's probably the percentage bet with Larry, though not in this case.' Rosemary looked at her researcher. 'Don't worry, Missy. I know there are rumors about an affair and I truly don't care. In fact, at the time I preferred that people thought that than the truth.'

'Which was?' I asked.

'That my career was floundering and he offered to mentor me. I was supposed to be the "Next Great American Novelist," with his help. And for a percentage.' Rosemary was sitting on the bunk cross-legged, dress hitched up to her waist. 'Instead he nearly ruined me.'

'How?' I was remembering what Rosemary had said earlier about Potter destroying her self-confidence. I'd assumed she'd meant more personally than professionally.

'Oh, nothing horrible.' With her short cropped hair, Rosemary looked like a little boy. 'But Larry was relentless about my writing the book he had in mind, exactly the way he imagined it.'

'Why didn't he just write the thing himself?'

'That's what I asked him after the fourteenth or fifteenth draft. You know what he said?'

Missy and I both shook our heads.

'He said, "Happily. And I'll give you half the proceeds if you'll allow me to publish it under your name."'

'Rather than his own?'

'I'm a brand.' Rosemary shrugged. 'Or was, back in the day.'

'You still are,' Missy said staunchly.

'What do you mean by "brand"?' I asked.

'As with products – or authors – that are "brand names," in and of themselves,' Missy said. 'Like maybe James Patterson or Janet Evanovich. The public has a nearly insatiable appetite for anything they write. It's hard for the author to keep up with the demand.'

'Sounds like a good problem to have,' I said.

'I suppose it is – or would be,' Rosemary said. 'Not that I would know. Back in my day, ebooks hadn't mainstreamed, so just the publishing and printing processes made it necessary—'

'In your day?' Missy scolded. 'Your last novel was only five years ago.'

'Might as well be five decades, given the pace at which publishing is changing.' The 'legendary lady of romantic suspense' sounded tired.

'I understand *Breaking and Entering* is doing very well,' I said, although I had no idea whether that was true or not. The book was certainly being talked about.

'That's right,' Missy said, with an approving glance toward me. 'Before you know it, Rosemary Darlington will top the *New York Times* bestseller list again.'

Rosemary smiled. 'Thank you. At the very least, I'm hoping it gives me a running start at it.'

Missy looked pleased that she'd been able to raise the woman's spirits.

Me, I just wanted more dirt. 'So you decided to end it with Potter? The collaboration, I mean.' I'd taken Rosemary at her word about the affair. Or lack of one.

'Yes, and none too soon. My work needs to be more . . . organic? It morphs as I go on and that gives me great pleasure – it's what keeps me writing. Things fall into place and every day brings a new "aha!" moment. Larry, on the other hand, is the ultimate planner. Or maybe a better word would be controller.

Pages and pages of outline. It felt like an unavoidable school assignment and nothing I did seemed to please the teacher. By the time he approved the outline, I hated the book. Worse, I hated writing, period.'

'How long did you work that way with him?' I was thinking the story might explain why there had been such a gap between books by Rosemary Darlington.

'Nearly a year.' She shivered and put a hand up to the air-conditioning unit by her head. 'Happily, that's all in the past.'

'Absolutely,' Missy said. 'Water under the bridge.'

Another quaint expression, but I was examining what looked like an airplane tray table 'in the upright and locked position' on the wall inside the compartment next to the bunk. 'Hey,' I said. 'This flips down into a sink.'

Missy pointed. 'And below that is a toilet.'

'Huh.' I lifted the lid to see the blue water. 'So, each roomette has its own toilet and sink?'

'Apparently so, though I'm sure I saw . . .' She stepped into the corridor. 'Oh, yes – there are more facilities off the corridor, just like I thought.'

I followed her out. 'Seems like the sleeping car has cornered the market on restrooms. They couldn't have spared one or two more for the rest of the train?'

'Good point,' Missy said. 'We'll have to remind people they can use the lavatories back here. After the crime is solved, of course.'

'And by Potter, let's hope.' I slid open one of the 'lavatory' doors she'd indicated. 'There's no toilet in here, just a shower, sink and dressing area.'

Missy pulled open the matching door on the other side of the corridor and looked inside. 'This one, too. I guess that makes sense, given what you said about each room having its own toilet facilities. The only thing the sleeping car passengers would need is a shower and somewhere to dress before venturing out into the corridor again.'

Scattered applause came from the group down the hall, and they started to troop away from us and toward the dining car. 'Is it time to cut the cake?' I asked.

'Did someone say cake?' came from the roomette. Rosemary

had slipped back under the blanket. 'Can you bring me a piece?'

'Certainly,' Missy said. 'Back in a flash.'

'Let's hope there's something left of it when we get there,' I said to Missy.

'We still don't have a knife,' she said as we approached the room Pavlik had used for his portrayal of the victim, Ratchett.

'True, but the sheriff does have his "classic" Swiss Army knife.'

'Oh, dear,' Missy said. 'We should have cleaned that up.'

The crowd had finished the job I'd inadvertently started, stomping the cake in the hallway to an unrecognizable blue and white mish-mash.

'Now it'll be tracked all over the train,' the event planner lamented.

I guiltily rubbed the edge of my own shoe against the carpet.

The door of the roomette had been left open and I stepped in. 'Just let me see something.'

'What's wrong? Did Jake forget to close the window?'

I noticed that using Pavlik's first name was no longer a problem for the girl.

'No, it's closed.' And a good thing too, since the wind was pummeling rain against the glass. I went to where the sink was located in the other roomette and, sure enough, it seemed to be standard equipment. I let the thing down, then re-secured it in its original position.

Next I lifted the lid over the toilet.

A cigarette butt floated in the blue water.

FOURTEEN

'I don't get it,' Missy was saying as I slid the door closed. 'How did you know that Laurence had been smoking in that room?'

'Easy.' I was feeling smug. 'The cake in the doorway, for one thing. He must have dropped it opening the door. And then there was the open window. Potter must have been worried about setting off any smoke detectors.'

'Wow,' Missy said. 'You really should write mysteries. How did you know Laurence wouldn't flush the toilet?'

'He's a man. I'm surprised he didn't leave the seat up, too.'

In truth, the floating cigarette butt had been a lucky break. Not that I was going to admit it.

Missy screwed up her face. 'But if Laurence was smoking in the roomette, he wouldn't have needed to open the exit door. So, what was the matchbook doing on the floor next to it?'

'Beats me. But since the book was empty, we know Potter dropped it *after* he had his smoke,' I said as we passed the spot in question.

'And on his way to rejoin the rest of the group in the dining car?'

'Exactly.'

'That's wonderful reasoning, Maggy,' Missy said, nearly walking between my heels like my sheepdog, Frank. 'You're a genius.'

'Not really,' I said modestly, stopping to look around in the passenger car. No sign of Potter, nor of Audra Edmonds and Danny, but Prudence and Grace were sitting in adjacent seats, talking to Markus. Fred, the table-dancing behemoth, was nearby, as was Harvey/Hardman in his checkered sports jacket. All five of them had hunks of cake in their hands and a trail of crumbs leading from the dining car and ending in their respective laps.

I couldn't tell if the commemorative cake had been cut with Pavlik's Swiss Army knife or just gnawed off.

'Oh, dear,' said Missy. 'I never did put the plates and forks out.'

Oh, dear, indeed. 'I hope the cleaning team has a vacuum.' Or a sheepdog. My Frank would make quick work snuffling up the leavings. Hell, at this point *I* was nearly hungry enough to do it myself.

'We lose our deposit if we don't return the train spic-and-span, so I'm afraid that little task falls to me,' Missy said unhappily.

I knew I should offer to help, but the truth was I was downright exhausted. It had been a very full day since we stepped onto our plane at Mitchell International in Milwaukee. 'Shouldn't the train be pulling into the station soon?'

'Yes, but I fear the rain has slowed us down. Haven't you noticed we're barely creeping along?'

Honestly, no. But now that she said it – and I'd become accustomed to the train motion – it did seem as though the critters in the Everglades could probably have outpaced us.

Missy stopped at the cake to rectify the plate situation, though I wasn't sure why she bothered. The crumbs that were left in the flat box required a thimble at most.

Resigning myself to a not unpleasant – if perhaps ill-advised – liquid diet, I continued on to what had been the first car on the train and now was the last: the club car. There I found Pavlik, Zoe and Audra standing at a high table with Carson. The agent stood a little apart, as if his need for personal space was greater than everyone else's and they were happy to cooperate.

At the adjacent bar, Boyce was serving coffee. I waved to him and sidled in next to Pavlik. 'I see the murder has been solved and all is right with the world.'

'It is now,' Pavlik said, sliding an arm around my waist. 'Would you like something?'

I weighed my options, trying to be an adult. Though I truly wanted a drink, another martini or even a glass of wine might send me over the top.

'I'll just grab a cup of coffee when Boyce has a moment. I heard the applause,' I said, turning to the others in the group. 'Did things go well?'

'Jacob was a marvelously villainous victim,' Zoe said. 'And we're very grateful to Carson for stepping in as Poirot.'

I turned to Audra. 'Wait. Your husband never showed up?'

Her eyebrows shot skyward. 'We all assumed you'd found him and he declined to participate.'

'It wouldn't be the first time.' Carson took a sip of what looked like bourbon in a small clear plastic cup. I wondered if he'd brought both himself. In a Baggie. 'Your husband – and my client – is a very stubborn man.'

Another wrinkle. 'You represent Larry Potter?'

'And Audra.' Carson nodded to the woman next to him. 'My very first husband-and-wife writing duo.'

Pavlik leaned down to whisper in my ear. 'You didn't see any sign of Potter?'

'Signs, yes.' I beckoned the sheriff away from the group. 'I think he went back for a smoke. We found his matches on the floor near an exit and a cigarette butt in the toilet of the room where you were playing dead.'

Pavlik looked surprised. 'Toilet? I didn't even see a bathroom.'

'Not a full one, just a sink that flipped out from the wall and a toilet. You might have thought the cover was a shelf.'

'Huh – some observer I am. I didn't smell cigarette smoke when I entered, but Potter would have opened the window to let it vent into the fresh air.'

'Exactly. We assumed he'd snuck in there to bolster his nicotine level,' I was saying as Missy joined us from the next car. 'Did you give up?' I asked her.

'On what?' asked Pavlik.

She waved her hand. 'Oh, nothing. Just all the cake crumbs.'

'There's no housekeeping service,' I explained, 'so Missy feels responsible for returning the train in the condition it was when we boarded. Meaning, mostly clean.'

'Well that's absolutely ridiculous,' the sheriff said.

'It is?' Missy was wide-eyed.

'Of course. We can't let you do that alone. We'll be glad to help, won't we, Maggy?'

I nearly groaned, but the fact was that despite my worst intentions, I wouldn't have left the girl to clean the train alone.

If Pavlik and I were scrubbing and vacuuming, however, I was going to make damn sure Zoe Scarlett did, as well.

Which reminded me. 'When Zoe announced the solving of the crime—'

'What are you saying about me?' Apparently feeling left out, the woman in question had pivoted in place, effectively abandoning Audra and Carson for our party without having to take a step.

'I was just saying that Missy and I assumed Potter had surfaced while we were at the back of the train.'

'I'm afraid not,' Pavlik said. 'Are you sure—'

A squeal of metal on metal, followed by a thud. I was thrown into Missy and the two of us slid down the wall. Zoe grabbed onto Pavlik, who struggled to keep his own balance as the train tilted precariously and shuddered to a halt.

The lights flickered, but managed to stay on. 'Everybody OK?' Pavlik asked in his command voice, putting out a hand to help me up.

I, in turn, pulled up Missy. 'Think so.'

'Did we derail?' Missy was rubbing her butt, probably where she'd landed.

'Is there any place to derail to?' I asked, thinking of Flagler's railroad trestle. 'I mean, without being at least partially submerged?'

'Is everyone all right?' Pavlik called out again.

Boyce was getting to his feet. 'I'm fine, although I'm not as sure about the espresso machine.'

'We've lost a few bottles from the bar,' Pete the bartender reported, 'but I'm OK.'

Both Audra Edmonds and her agent appeared shaken but also unhurt. Carson was holding his hands out like a skater trying to keep from falling or, more likely in his case, touching anything.

'I'll check on the others,' I said to Pavlik. I crossed the eerily quiet vestibule to stick my head into the dining car. 'Any injuries in here?'

'Just bounced around a bit,' Prudence said. She was braced in the aisle, pearls askew and her dress ripped at the hem, as if she'd stepped on it while trying to steady herself.

Markus and the rest of the group that had been chowing down in the passenger car were filing in behind her. Greta had a smudge of icing on her nose.

'What happened?' a sleepy-looking Rosemary Darlington appeared and, behind her, Danny.

'We're not sure,' I said. 'But—'

The vestibule door opened behind me, admitting Pavlik. Now everybody started firing questions. Or comments.

'Did something blow up? I thought I heard an explosion.'

'Don't be silly. We must have run into something.'

'Or, perhaps, might the engineer have had a heart attack, thereby rendering him unconscious and leaving us hopelessly stranded in the Everglades?'

This last soliloquy was delivered by Harvey, whose palm was dramatically placed over his checkered heart.

Sheesh. No wonder Broadway had spit him back out.

Pavlik held his hands up in twin stop signs. 'I'm going forward to the locomotive to investigate. In the meantime, everybody please stay where you are.'

I touched Pavlik's arm. 'Speaking of the engineer, are you at all surprised he didn't come to check on his passengers?'

'I am. Though maybe he already has his hands full.' My sheriff looked grim as he continued on toward what was now the front – or east-facing – end of the train.

I went back the other direction, retreating to the club car, where Boyce was hoisting his espresso brewer back into place.

I helped him settle it on the bar and then leaned down to pick up the metal frothing pitcher. 'You didn't get burned, did you?'

'Not a bit, thank you. I'd finished brewing the last of the espresso and was letting things cool down. You need a hand there, Pete?' he called over to the young bartender.

Pete turned around from the closet behind his bar, a bottle in each hand. 'No, I'm good. Luckily, we have reinforcements.' He raised the liquor over his head.

'Something tells me we're going to need it,' I said. 'Or at least some people will.' God forbid anyone think that would include me.

'What happened?' the bartender asked. 'Did one of the passengers pull the brake?'

'The brake?' I repeated. The thought had never occurred to me.

'Right here. I saw the thing when I boarded and asked about

it.' Pete pointed to a cord dangling from the ceiling. At the end of it was a red ball and on the wall next to it a sign warned, 'For emergency use only.'

'Each car has one,' Pete explained. 'But you're only supposed to pull it if someone gets caught in a door or dragged or something. The train stops right where you are – in its tracks.' He smiled at his railroad joke. Cute kid.

'As we just did,' I said.

'Correct.' Pete was straightening the bottles on the back bar. 'So if the guy next to you is having a heart attack or something, it's the last thing you want to do because it could take even longer for help to come.'

I looked at the guy next to me, who happened to be Boyce. 'I suppose that could be what happened.'

'We'll find out.' He gestured toward the direction Pavlik had disappeared. 'We're lucky to have some law enforcement with us, regardless.'

'Amen,' I said. 'Usually I have to deal with these things myself. Until the police or sheriff's department arrives, of course.'

Boyce shook his head. 'So you've been in a lot of train derailments, too?'

I felt myself blush. 'No, not really. Just the other . . . emergencies.'

'Uh-huh.' Boyce glanced at Pete and apparently decided not to pursue the subject. At least for the time being. 'Is everyone up front safe?'

'So far as we can tell.' In truth, everyone I'd *seen* was all right. I couldn't be certain that all of the passengers were accounted for. Maybe it would make sense to take a roll call just to be sure.

'Pavlik is going to check on the engineer,' I continued. Then I frowned.

'What's wrong?' Boyce asked. 'I mean, beyond the obvious.'

'According to Missy,' I was already heading for the vestibule, 'there's no inner connection between the locomotive and the passenger cars. The sheriff is going to have to go outside.'

'Do you want—'

I didn't wait to hear the rest, letting the connecting door close behind me.

The dining car was empty, the rest of the group still congregated in the passenger car, chattering. Pavlik must have been delayed by further questions, because I was just in time to see him slip into the vestibule beyond.

Before I could catch up, he'd slid open the exit door and disappeared.

FIFTEEN

'**W**ait!'

Pavlik was standing on the gravel bed beneath and sloping away from the tracks. 'What?'

The bed was narrow, but it was there, which was a relief. I'd imagined we were traveling on some sort of elevated trestle like that in the photograph of Flagler's ill-fated railroad. In actuality, though, our tracks were mere inches above the swamp.

This was good news because we needn't fear falling. Bad, because we were within serving distance of whatever creatures were making dinner plans.

At least, though, I thought as I jumped down after Pavlik, the warm rain had slackened to a steamy sprinkle. 'Do you have your knife or, even better, your gun?'

'Knife, yes. Gun, no. Why?'

'There are alligators and pythons and, umm . . . lions.'

'Lions?' Pavlik looked skeptical.

'I may have that part wrong.' I was frowning again. 'But definitely the rest.'

'Well, then, stay close.' Pavlik was walking along the outside of the sleeping car toward the locomotive. 'That way, if something drags me away, you can properly identify it for the local authorities.'

I scurried along behind. 'Is it my imagination, or is that pitched down?'

'You mean the front of the locomotive? Sure looks like it to me, too.' He grasped a vertical bar and swung himself up and into the already open door of the engine car.

'You know,' I called up, 'there are emergency cords in every car that can stop the train, if they're pulled. Maybe that's what happened.'

'I noticed the cords,' the sheriff's voice came from inside the cab.

I shouldn't have been surprised. The man was aware of everything. And revealed nothing, damn it.

A hoarse *sqwaaak* pierced the air and hung there, followed by a series of raspy *wok, wok, woks*.

'Shit!' I edged closer to the train. 'It's like we're in a Tarzan movie.'

'Funny you should say that.' His head appeared. 'Apparently at least a couple of Johnny Weissmuller's Tarzan movies of the thirties and forties were filmed somewhere in Florida. Legend has it that some of the rhesus monkeys used in the movies escaped. Supposedly it's their descendants that run wild here today.' Pavlik jumped down from the cab. 'Cool, huh?'

Well, I certainly had goose bumps, if that confirmed his opinion.

The big front headlight of the train illuminated the Everglades in front of us, which was a good way to capture a black hole of nothingness. Oh, I could see water, scrub grass – sawgrass, presumably – and some sort of foliage, but nothing else except low, shapeless shadows as far as the light could pierce the gloom.

'Holy mother of God,' a male voice said.

Startled, I saw the figure of a man standing next to the nose of the locomotive. I didn't remember noticing him earlier.

'Oh, dear,' I said, sounding like Missy, even to my own ears.

Pavlik and I strode toward the man. Well, Pavlik strode. I scurried fearfully in his wake.

'Jake Pavlik,' the sheriff said, sticking out his hand to the other man. 'I assume you're the engineer. Nobody onboard seems to be hurt. What happened?'

The engineer turned. His name was 'Theodore B. Hertel, Jr,' according to the embroidery that covered nearly the full width of the pocket on his bib overalls. It probably didn't improve my first impression of our train pilot that he shared a first name with my ex-husband, but his appearance didn't fill me with confidence either. The man looked close to eighty, and if the denim overalls had been striped and matched with a hat and red bandana, I'd have said he was in costume for the event. I only hoped he wasn't as 'fictitious' as our bartender/Wagon Lit conductor, Pete. Or whatever his name was.

'Did we derail?' I asked anxiously. 'Or someone pull the emergency brake?'

Hertel shook Pavlik's hand, but virtually ignored me. 'Well, sir, I certainly did pull on that brake my own self. Have to say, I'm glad to hear the people *in*side the train are OK.'

A shiver crawled up my back. I didn't like the way the engineer had said that, given that Pavlik and I were standing *out*side.

Was that banjo music I heard? In addition, I mean, to the feral monkeys and God knew what else.

Pavlik seemed unconcerned. 'Looks like the track is flooded.'

The nose of the engine was tilted down and the tracks in front of it gone. Or at least submerged under water blacker than a crow's wing.

'You're right about that, for sure,' Hertel said, rubbing his chin. 'But I'm thinking that might be the least of somebody's worries.'

I put my hand on Pavlik's sleeve, trying to pull him away from the engineer who even *Missy* thought was 'eccentric.'

'What?' Pavlik glanced over at me. Hertel was watching me, too.

'DoodooDOOdoo—' I tried shakily.

'Maggy, use your mother tongue, please?' Pavlik went to shake off my hand.

'Dueling banjos,' I hissed, hanging on. 'Ned Beatty. Squeal like a pig?'

The engineer was eyeing me suspiciously. Hertel had abnormally long earlobes, like he'd been hanging heavy earrings on them for years and years. He pulled at one lobe, a more likely cause of the droop. 'No, ma'am. That just ain't right.'

'It's not?' I was backing away. Pavlik could fend for himself.

'No, ma'am. It weren't *Dueling Banjos*. That was the name of the music. The movie was *Deliverance*. But I'm scratching my head wondering why you're trying to sing about anything when we've got this mess on our hands.'

Pavlik cocked his head, probably wondering which of his two companions was crazier. Then he turned to the engineer. 'I'm a county sheriff up north, but I don't know a whole lot about trains or the Everglades. I assume from your exclamation that we're stuck pretty good?'

'My "exclamation"?'

'"Holy mother of God"?' I was trying to be helpful.

'Oh, that. No, it weren't the flooded track got me down. I seen worse. It's that what sort of took me by surprise.' He pointed.

Pavlik and I both followed Hertel's index finger. On the other side of the dip in the tracks and not ten feet away from us was the biggest fucking snake I'd ever seen.

With a pair of custom-made wingtips protruding from its jaws, the knees and shoes flicking up and down in a primeval two-step.

SIXTEEN

'Holy mother of God!' I screamed, echoing the engineer's sentiments. Except I had more information to add: 'It's Potter!'

Pavlik and Hertel just looked at me.

'Those are Potter's legs sticking out of that thing.' Even as I said it, I was backing-pedaling as far and as fast as I could.

The snakes I was accustomed to sunned themselves in my flower bed. They were maybe two feet long and an inch thick and *they* scared the bejeebers out of me. This one . . . this one, it could be a whole different species. Not a snake at all. This monster was big enough to devour—

The limbs sticking out of the thing did a scissor-kick. 'Oh-my-god, oh-my-god,' I said, as my back slammed into the locomotive. 'He's still alive!'

'Well, ma'am,' Hertel said, 'I suppose that's possible. I didn't spot the snake until I climbed down to examine the tracks, but I think we've got us some kind of python. They like to squeeze their victims mostly to death and then swallow 'em whole to digest later. Sort of nature's doggy bag.'

I think I liked the guy better when I thought he was going to murder us. 'Enough with the nature lesson!' I screamed. 'Do something!'

Pavlik was already pulling the knife out of his pocket. He flipped out the blade and started forward. Then, over his shoulder, 'Maggy, go get help from the train.'

I screamed 'Help!' at the top of my lungs and forced myself to move away from the relative protection of the train's engine. I might be shaking like a leaf, but there was no way I was leaving Pavlik with only Euell Gibbons for back-up.

'Can you tell how deep the water is?' I asked the sheriff as he waded in, knife in his hand.

'To the bottom? I'm not sure. But I can feel the ties seven or eight inches below the water. I'm standing – and staying – on what's left of them.'

'I'm coming with you.' What was I thinking? Clearly, I wasn't. The words were out of my mouth before I *could* think.

'I appreciate the offer, but you're afraid of snakes, remember?'

I was, but then I used to be scared of spiders and mice too – things that my then-husband dealt with at home when we were married. If divorce has taught me anything, it's that a person is as brave as she needs to be.

I puffed out my chest. 'Not anymore,' I said, hoping that saying it would make it true. I turned to Hertel. 'You have anything I can hit this thing with?'

The engineer pulled a long flashlight from a loop on his belt. 'This do?'

I took it, my hand sagging under the unexpected weight. 'Geez, yeah. This should be good.' I was imagining hitting the snake with the flashlight and having it bounce off like a rubber mallet on a concrete block. 'Listen, can you call for help?'

'Happy to, though it'll likely just be coming from the train. Cell communication's down.'

Lovely. I had started to follow Pavlik, wondering what the hell we were going to do once we got there, when I heard Hertel again. 'They say to stay away from the pointy end.' He chuckled. 'I hear tell these big fellers don't like to be disturbed during supper.'

I'd been noticing that the snake wasn't moving much, other than sort of gulping. And keeping a wary eye on Pavlik and me.

The good news for us, if not for Potter, was that there really wasn't a 'pointy end.' The snake's mouth was full – stretched impossibly like the thing had dislocated its jaw not only into two parts, top and bottom, but into four quarters in the effort to swallow a human being.

'I've got this friend who brags he can eat a steak as big as his empty head, but these critters are the only things I've ever seen that are actually capable of doing it.' Hertel was just chock-jolly-full of culinary lore.

My foot had found the first wooden crosspiece under water and I stepped unsteadily out onto it. 'Could you please get help from the train? Let them know that it's Lar . . . Laurence

Potter.' The least I could do was to call the man by the name he preferred, given the indignity of his current circumstances.

'Hey, isn't that the big-shot reviewer we had onboard?'

I forced myself to look more at the wingtips than the snake. It wasn't much of an improvement. 'We think so.'

'Now how in the hell do you figure he got out here?'

'That is a very good question,' Pavlik said, not looking around. His tone indicated that messing with him would be even worse than messing with the snake at this point. 'One we'll try to answer once we get him out of *that*.'

He hiked his thumb at the snake and, as if on cue, I swear the monster burped.

Potter's leg slid in to the ankle.

I gagged.

'One down,' I heard Hertel say. 'One—'

Ignoring the rest of it, I waded anxiously over to Pavlik. 'Can you cut him out of there?'

'I think so. With so much of Potter inside of this thing, I'm betting it can't constrict anything else.' A glance my way. 'Like me or you.'

He looked at my flashlight. 'Any part of that snake gets near you, wallop it hard with the business end and run.'

'Gotcha.' Now that I was closer, I realized what I had imagined was Potter's movement was the snake's mouth and head absorbing the actually still body. Almost like a curtain being worked onto a rod – the snake the curtain and Potter as rod. 'Please, God, he can't be alive in there, can he?'

'Don't know, but I'm sure not leaving even a corpse inside that thing's digestive system.' Pavlik was not eighteen inches from the snake, stepping up on the wooden crosspieces that looked like the rungs of a macabre ladder with one end submerged in the water.

The snake did a kind of shimmy, assuming the shimmier was the length and girth of an I-beam. I splashed back into the water. 'Be careful!' I called to Pavlik, who was trying to circle behind the snake as best he could, given the narrowness of the railroad bed.

Hertel began talking again. 'I hear tell that these fellers tire easy. Or at least the Burmese do, though this beauty looks to be one of those bigger devils.'

'You mean an African rock python?' I was trying to steady my nerves, though conversing with the engineer might not be the best way to do it.

Pavlik gave a backwards glance at my question, probably wondering how I'd know anything about snake species in the Everglades.

'The very ones,' Hertel said. 'Surprised you've even heard of them, cuz we ain't seen many around here yet. But to my eye, this queen bitch looks pregnant, so I have a hunch that's going to change.'

Wonderful. If the snake in front of us wasn't, in itself, a super hybrid between the Burmese and Rock pythons, we were messing with the mother ship.

'Don't touch it!' I yelled at Pavlik, panic rising. 'Did you hear what he said? If you cut the thing open they'll all come crawling out.'

'No, no, no.' Hertel was practically chortling, like he'd been yanked back to his days of reading The Hardy Boys and Tom Swift. 'This ain't no *Aliens* movie, you know. Snakes lay eggs. All you gonna find inside that one is what looks like the floor of a hen house.'

'Chicken eggs,' I managed in a squeaky voice.

Pavlik turned around and put a hand down to help me. His words, though, were more for my psyche than physical well-being. 'Steady, girl.'

'You know what you might say?' Hertel went on. And on. 'You might say this snake's done bitten off more'n she can chew.'

Honest to God, if I were within batting distance of the man, I'd have beaten him to death him with his own flashlight.

Hertel laughed at his own sick joke and rubbed his chin thoughtfully. 'Last year, I spent some time with guys that went out on that python hunt. Which is how come I know so much, case you've been wondering.'

Slowly the snake stretched and then seemed to coil back on itself, the one leg and both multicolored shoes still protruding. I had a flash of my Uncle Gus after a huge Thanksgiving dinner, sucking on a festive toothpick.

And contemplating dessert.

Pavlik jumped back.

Hertel said, 'If I was you, I wouldn't be practicing my dance steps on that—'

'If you know something that will help, tell us!' I screamed at Hertel. 'Otherwise, just . . . shut . . . up!'

Instead of being hurt or incensed, the engineer seemed gratified, even complimented. 'Well, Sheriff, appears to me you've got yourself a feisty one there. But yes, ma'am. I guess I will leave you to it. Though they do tell me that these snakes – well, the Burmese, at least, and like I said, I don't know if this one—'

'*Now!*'

Honest to God, it was like I was talking dirty to Hertel in bed. The nastier I got, the more he seemed to like it.

'Yes, ma'am.' Now he was smiling widely. 'Well, like I said, these snakes get tired out easy. In fact, the trappers treadmill 'em.'

'"Treadmill"?' Pavlik asked, coincidentally saving my sanity.

'Yup, they hold the tail of the snake and run their hands up along, under its belly. Makes the python think it's the one moving – escaping – so it tuckers itself out trying. Once that snake's exhausted, you can grab 'em by the base of the head and dump them in a pillow case.'

I looked at the snake. 'Would have to be a big pillowcase.'

'I don't intend to capture this one, so I wouldn't worry.' Pavlik had positioned himself behind the snake once more. Or, more precisely, behind the snake's head. If he was fully behind the snake he'd be standing another twenty feet down the railroad track. 'Maggy, try and get his attention.'

I wondered if snakes could smell fear. If so, I figured I already had the python's undivided attention.

Heart thudding, my legs like jelly, I tried to get a grip of myself and moved to the front of the serpent's head, but as far away as I could get without stepping back into the water and inadvertently becoming some other critter's quarry. You know, like the goofball who steps into the street to evade a pickpocket only to be mown down by a truck.

'Oh, and the other thing I found real interesting.' Hertel kept spewing his grisly little *bon mots*. 'Snakes go dormant when they're digesting.'

Pavlik was watching me. 'Ready, Maggy?'

I met his gaze and nodded. Since one eye was on each side of the creature's head, I had to pick left or right. Choosing the former, I waved at it. The snake turned the other way and looked at Pavlik, as if to say, *Is this broad serious?*

Meanwhile, Hertel was still compulsively sharing. 'Feller told me if you scare 'em right after a big meal, they—'

'Try making noise,' Pavlik said out of the corner of his mouth. He was stone still, the knife unwavering in his hand.

'Hey!' I yelled, jumping up and down. 'Anaconda. Over here!'

The snake reared its head like the cobra in Kipling's *Rikki-Tikki-Tavi*. Even though my brain told me this wasn't a venomous snake, my feet didn't believe it.

In fact, they had recovered impressively from their previous jelly-like state and were now backpedaling rapidly into the water, demanding to know why we believed Hertel's claim that this was a python at all. After all, we'd just met the man, and—

'Blaaaaaaaah!' An explosion in front of me.

A full lower-third of Potter was now hanging out of the snake's mouth.

'Holy shit,' I said, taking another half-step back. 'What's—'

'Blaaaaah!'

Now I could see Potter's belt.

'Kill it, kill it!' I screamed in horror as I fell backwards onto the bank. 'It's spitting out Larry Potter so it can eat me!'

'Blaaaaah-blaaaaah.' The snake's eyes were huge and it looked . . . well, concerned?

'Like I was saying,' Hertel had come from behind to help me up, 'I hear tell you scare one of these things after a big meal and—'

'Blaaah! . . . Blaaah . . . Blaaaah!'

Pavlik had the knife poised, but was holding fast. 'Sounds like it's got something stuck in its throat.'

Under the circumstances, I couldn't think of anything to say other than, 'the whole damn monster *is* its throat,' and anyway, speech had momentarily left me. I kept my mouth shut.

'Yup,' Hertel said, 'kind of like he's hockin' up a loogie. Or a "Larry" maybe?' The ancient engineer was laughing as he offered me his hand.

I pushed his helping hand away and got up under my own steam. 'That's in poor taste.'

'Taste,' Hertel was still chuckling. 'Now there's another good one.'

I weighed the flashlight in my hand, considering which critter I should knock senseless – or more senseless, in Hertel's case – with it.

'Blaaah – blaaah! . . . Blaaaah . . . BLAAAAAAH!'

I turned around in time to see the entire body of Laurence Potter erupt from the snake's mouth and land in the water, face-down, not two feet away from me.

'Holy shit.' My stomach was heaving and I pleaded with whatever was in it – a little cake icing and a lot of espresso martini, probably – to stay down there.

'No wonder the poor bitch had trouble getting your reviewer in. And out,' Hertel said, coming up beside me. 'That thing there had to get hung up somewhere along her gut.' He pointed.

'That thing there' was a staghorn handle, buried past the base of the blade in Laurence Potter's back.

SEVENTEEN

'I guess we can eliminate "accident" as the cause of death.'

The statement was my weak attempt at bravado as the python – Burmese or African rock, with my money on the latter – shuddered its last on the opposite bank.

With me refusing to touch any part of Potter that had been inside the snake, the sheriff and I managed to drag Potter's body onto what passed for dry ground on the railway bed near the locomotive. We stood and watched while Hertel – finally, and mercifully – left us to climb onto the train in search of help, Pavlik instructing him not to provide any details to even the hoped-for helpers.

'Unless that snake managed to hop up into the train and steal the knife from the cake,' Pavlik said, 'I think we can assume Potter was stabbed and either fell or was tossed off well before it got hold of him.'

I shivered and glanced toward the gaping snake carcass. The python had split its sides – and not in the good way – during the final effort to urp up the reviewer.

Pavlik, who'd been crouched down examining Potter's body, rose to his feet. 'The knife is plunged in so deeply a good portion of the handle isn't even visible. We won't know for sure until the autopsy, but I can't imagine a person being strong enough to do that.'

I lifted my eyebrows. 'So we're back to the snake as cause of death?'

'Not necessarily.' Pavlik waved toward the road bed. 'If our decedent, knife already in his back, hit the ground a certain way, his own weight might have punched the blade deeper. Or, as you say, the snake's constriction might have forced the knife farther into the body.'

I felt sick again. 'And that's what killed him?'

'We don't know that yet.' Pavlik put his hand on my shoulder. 'Potter might have already been dead from the wound. Or from drowning.'

You know you're in a bad place when the thought of somebody dying sooner rather than later cheers you.

But here we were. Welcome to the Everglades.

'What's that?' I asked, moving closer to Pavlik.

'The water dripping off the leaves and grass, probably,'

'I hear that, as well, but this is kind of a tick, tick, tick.'

'You mean like a clock? Inside a crocodile perhaps?'

Captain Hook's crocodile. My sheriff was channeling Peter Pan. 'I know it's silly, but – there! There it is again.'

Pavlik listened. 'Probably some kind of night bird. They have a lot of species down here that we've never heard or seen.'

'And, of course, alligators, not crocodiles,' I said with a self-deprecating laugh.

'No, they have crocodiles, too.' Pavlik was crossing the flooded breach back to our friend the python. 'Just not as many as they do alligators.'

More great news. With a nervous look around, I followed him.

'Did you get a good look at this thing's teeth?' I pointed a cautious toe at a portion of the snake's head. 'They tilt backwards like those one-way exit spikes in parking lots. You know – the ones that cause "severe tire damage" if you back over them.'

'A very efficient creation of nature. And from the looks of the maternity ward, Hertel was right about one thing: she was eating for about eighty.'

I looked into the belly of the beast and could swear that some of her eggs were rolling against each other. 'We're not going to leave them here, are we?'

Pavlik eyed me. 'Please tell me you're not that hungry. Or maternal.'

Ugh. 'No, thank you very much, on the former. As to the latter, just the opposite. I know everybody down here is concerned about the population of pythons in the Everglades, and I think the 'ticking' noise might be coming from inside the eggs. Maybe we – or better, *you* – should smash them or something.'

Pavlik shook his head. 'I get your point, but outside of what Hertel told us, I have no proof that's a python. Nor that it's legal to kill whatever it is or its eggs.'

'Pavlik, it was eating another member of our species, and you're going to risk letting its offspring grow up to slither in Mommy's footsteps? Not to mention following her dietary habits?'

The whole thing was starting to feel surreal. Whatever were we doing stuck *here*, talking about *this*, while standing next to . . . *that*? I averted my eyes.

'I get it, Maggy. And if the creature hadn't ruptured, I would have happily slit the thing's throat if I could find it. As it is, though, I'm not sure I feel right about smashing the eggs. We'll let the authorities decide on that when they arrive.'

'Unless the eggs hatch first, overrun the cars and *Murder on the Orient Espresso* gets made into a sequel to *Snakes on a Plane*,' I muttered. 'Then all the "authorities" will find of us is our shoes. Maybe.'

'Good flick,' Pavlik observed as the rain started to fall heavier again. 'A classic, in fact. But I have to say, if these eggs can hatch themselves, make their way up and into the train and then kill us all, we deserve what we get.'

Terrific. Now Pavlik was Charles Darwin.

On the opposite side of the breach, the engineer came around the locomotive's corner. 'I tapped the first two I saw. Will they do?' He hooked a finger toward Boyce, the coffeehouse owner, and Markus, the librarian.

'Jesus,' Markus said. He was looking at the flooded track. 'What do we do?'

'I didn't tell them nothing,' Hertel said to Pavlik. 'Like you said.'

Pavlik nodded. 'Sadly, the track's not our biggest problem.' He gestured toward Potter's body in the shadow of the locomotive.

Boyce stepped forward. 'Isn't this one of our passengers?'

I realized the coffee man wouldn't necessarily know Laurence Potter by face.

'How in the hell did Potter get out here?' Markus asked, not seeming to know what to make of it all.

He could join the club.

'Apparently he fell off the train and,' Pavlik waved toward the python in front of us, 'was attacked by a snake.'

It was true as far as it went, but it didn't fool Boyce, who had begun to circle the body. 'A snake carrying a knife?'

Pavlik's eyes narrowed, as if he was appraising Boyce. 'Time on the job?'

'Military police, two hitches, one tour in Iraq.'

I didn't quite see why it took a specialized background to notice a knife in a man's back, but I'd grown accustomed to the fact that people who've served in the military or law enforcement seem able to recognize each other. Pavlik had explained it to me as an awareness, displayed by a way of carrying oneself and cold calmness in being ready for anything.

My opinion? This was a *big* anything.

'That's a python – African rock, I think,' Markus said, coming to join us on the opposite bank. 'Did he explode?'

'She,' Hertel corrected. 'But "explode" is a fair description. Full of eggs, I might add.'

Since Markus seemed to know something about pythons, I was hoping he was willing to share the facts, sans Engineer Hertel's colorful embroidery. 'Can those eggs hatch?'

'You mean right this second?' Markus pursed his lips, squatting down to get a better view of the snake. 'The female would need to lay them first and then coil her own body into a nest to keep them warm.'

'Doesn't look like that'll happen,' Boyce said.

'A good thing, too,' Hertel said. 'You don't want to be around a Mama Python protecting her eggs, 'specially if you and me are right and this is one of those African rock jobbies.'

'Bigger and meaner,' Markus concurred. 'Do you think Potter was protecting himself with the knife and somehow got it in the back during the struggle?'

For a second I thought Pavlik might go along with the theory for expediency, but then he seemed to reconsider. 'Pretty unlikely, I'd say. He—'

'What in the world are you all doing out here?' Zoe Scarlett had rounded the locomotive and come up behind the engineer and Boyce. She stopped short and Missy, following on her boss's heels, nearly rear-ended her.

Then both of them looked down at Laurence Potter.

'Oh, dear,' Missy Hudson, the mistress of understatement said. 'Is he . . .?'

'Dead,' Hertel said, flatly. 'Stabbed and squeezed, then swallered and *ree*-gurgi-*tated* for good measure.'

Missy turned green, but it was Zoe who fainted dead away.

EIGHTEEN

I registered a benefit of the train having already reversed on the tracks so it now pointed east and back toward the station in Fort Lauderdale: the sleeping car, where Pavlik wanted to stash Larry Potter's body, was the closest one to us.

Leaving Missy, Markus and the recovering Zoe to continue on to the club car entrance at the rear of the train, Pavlik and Boyce had carried Potter's body to the exit where I'd found the matchbook. They stood waiting while I slid open the door.

'You may just have to count to three and sling 'im up there,' Hertel said from behind them. 'This train doesn't have no steps to pull down, because the station's got high platforms and that's the only place people will get on and off.'

We all looked down at Potter. Pavlik had hold of the reviewer under his arms and Boyce had hold of the feet. I couldn't see how they were going to "sling" him – one-two-three, heave! – and have him land inside the train as opposed to splattered up against it.

'Fireman's carry is the best,' Boyce said, setting down his end. 'I'll get him.'

'You sure?' Pavlik asked. 'We can—'

'Yup.' Boyce leaned over, wrapped his arms around Potter's waist and levered him up onto his shoulder. 'Gotta keep in shape.'

Straightening up, the coffee man swung himself and his burden up and into the train, seemingly effortlessly.

'Your tongue is hanging out,' Pavlik growled to me. 'Put it back where it belongs and climb in.'

'Yessir,' I said, swinging myself up ahead of him. Zoe's swoon at the sight of Potter's body, while understandable, had made me feel absolutely plucky by comparison.

'Don't you want a . . . pristine room?' I asked, as Pavlik slid past me to open the first door on the left for Boyce, who was waiting patiently. 'This is where you – and Potter, if my theory is right – were earlier.'

'Which makes it the perfect place now,' Pavlik said. 'Any evidence was already trampled over during our little play and this way we don't chance contaminating another possible scene.'

'Murder scene?' I asked, as Boyce went to deposit his load.

'He was stabbed somewhere,' Pavlik pointed out. 'There must—'

'Oops,' Boyce said as Potter slipped off his shoulder and onto the bunk. 'He's kind of slippery.'

'Probably python tummy juices,' Hertel said from the doorway. 'Not to mention the rain. It's coming down cats and dogs again out there.'

As if the Everglades themselves were writing our stage directions, lightning flashed through the window, illuminating the body.

'Let's keep him up on his side,' Pavlik said, assisting. 'We don't want to jam the knife any deeper into his back.'

'Not going to matter much now,' Hertel opined, clicking on the roomette light.

We ignored him as the two other men settled Potter onto the bunk, facing away from us toward the window.

I suppressed a shiver. Given my new-found 'pluck,' I attributed the reaction to the fact that my sundress was rain-damp. With the window closed and air conditioning on, the sleeping space felt like an icebox. And it smelled none too sweet, as well. 'What do we do now?'

'I asked Markus, Missy, and Zoe to keep this to themselves, but have everyone convene in the passenger car.' Pavlik hooked a finger in the direction of the next car. 'We'll need to explain the situation and outline our options, assuming there are any.'

Then, to Hertel, 'I assume, since the track is underwater, we're stuck here?'

'You're plumb right about that. We can plow through a little water, but it looks to me like the railroad bed might've washed away under the tracks and sunk 'em, which is why we have that gulley between us and where the snake had ahold of him.' He nodded at Potter.

I looked at the dead man, who could easily have been curled up in bed 'with his trousers on,' as the old nursery rhyme goes. *One shoe off and one shoe on. Diddle, diddle, dumpling, my son John.* 'Should we cover him or something?'

'I'd rather not,' said Pavlik. 'The less we tinker, the happier the crime-scene people are going to be when they get here. In fact, we should clear this car and post a guard to keep everyone out.'

He looked at Boyce. 'Will you take first watch?'

The coffee man née military policeman nodded.

I was relieved Pavlik had found a comrade-in-arms in Boyce, especially since his next choice probably would have been me. Much as I appreciated the trust, being left alone guarding a dead body – especially one that had been headfirst in the digestive tract of a very pregnant nightmare – was beyond creepy, even bordering on sci-fi.

Besides, I told myself, much better that I be present when the sheriff briefed the rest of the passengers. That way I'd know what he had and hadn't told them and, therefore, what I was free to say. That was the kind of judgment – or lack of judgment – call that had gotten me into trouble before.

Moving to the warmer corridor, Pavlik waited for the rest of us to follow him out before sliding the door closed behind us. Then he and Boyce went room to room – one opening the door, the other entering, then alternating for the next one just like you would see in the movies.

Satisfied no one was in the sleeping car besides us, Boyce asked, 'Do you want me posted here in the hall?'

'Let's go through to the next car,' Pavlik said, leading the way into the vestibule.

'Wait a second,' I said, backtracking. 'I don't think we closed this exit door completely when we brought the body in. That's probably why it's so toasty warm in the hallway.'

'Stop!' Pavlik barked, but I'd already grabbed the handle and went to slide the door closed.

My hand came away, sticky.

NINETEEN

The rumble of voices could be heard as Pavlik slid open the door of the passenger car.

'It *must* be blood,' I whispered to Pavlik as I slipped past him into the restroom to wash my hands. 'That's also the area where I found Potter's matches.'

'Time and forensics will tell us just what the substance is,' the sheriff said, maddeningly reassured. 'As for the matches, are you sure they're his?'

'Yes.' I dried my hands on a paper towel before plunging one of them into the pockets of my sundress to retrieve the empty matchbook. I held it up. 'See? These were the matches he had at the table in the dining car. At first, Missy and I thought he might have opened the door to smoke and fallen out.'

Pavlik took the matchbook. '"Titanium"?'

'Apparently it's a "gentleman's club," or at least that's what Missy called it. Knowing her gift for sugar-coating, it could be a brothel, or even an S&M dungeon, for all we know.'

'I think we'll position you in here for now,' he called back to Boyce, who was still in the vestibule talking with Engineer Hertel.

The two men joined us. 'I assume people can use the restroom here in the passenger car?' Boyce asked.

'Yes, but nobody goes through the vestibule into the sleeping car.' Pavlik nodded toward the door that had just closed behind the engineer. 'I'll see if I can find you a chair so you can sit with your back up against the door to the vestibule, facing into the rest of the passenger car.'

'Yes, sir,' Boyce said, taking up the position. This time even I could see the military in his bearing. I felt, rather than saw, his hand itching to rise in a salute.

Guard stationed, Pavlik, Hertel and I paused. I could hear the buzz of speculation coming from the rows of seats beyond the restroom.

'After we settle down the passengers,' Pavlik told the engineer, 'you and I will go to the locomotive, where we'll call the authorities. You'd have a better idea than I do which jurisdic—'

But Hertel was shaking his head. 'Sorry, but as I told your girl here,' he hooked a thumb back to me, 'we're purely in-commun-i-cado out here.'

'What do you use?' Pavlik asked. 'Radio?'

'Well, now, this being a new line and our being a little off the grid, official-wise, I have this.' He held up a cell phone, and not even a very smart one.

I was still trying to translate 'off the grid, official-wise' to plain English. 'What exactly—'

We were interrupted by Missy, who had added the wringing of hands to her repertoire. 'We're doing our best, but people are getting very impatient for answers. We . . . we haven't told Audra.' Missy's voice broke. I could see tears.

Pavlik squeezed her shoulder. 'I'm sorry – this shouldn't all fall back on you.'

'He's just wonderful,' she whispered to me as Pavlik strode to the front of the car.

While I couldn't echo the worshipful tone, I did the sentiment.

'Excuse me,' Pavlik said, standing in the aisle at the front of the car. Zoe was seated in the first window seat, twisted around to Markus behind her. I wondered how much help either had been to Missy in keeping a lid on things.

At least they'd herded the group as instructed into the passenger car. There were just a few seats to spare, including the one next to Zoe. I took it, feeling charitable. 'How are you?'

'Better,' she said, looking surprised that I'd asked. 'Though I'm not sure why. We're in a terrible fix.'

'What's happened?' Prudence called from a few rows back. She was sitting next to Rosemary Darlington. 'Why have we stopped?'

'According to our engineer,' Pavlik pointed at Hertel, but didn't give him an opportunity to speak, 'a portion of the railroad bed has been washed away by the storm, temporarily stranding us here.'

'Isn't Jacob going to tell them about Larry?' Zoe whispered to me.

'Got me,' I said. 'All I know is that *we* shouldn't.'

'Where is he? I mean . . . Larry?'

'In the sleeping room where the "crime" was solved.' I used my index fingers to fashion air quotes.

'But what happens if someone goes in there to lie down or something?' Zoe persisted. 'Or he starts to smell?'

I was afraid that ship had sailed, but didn't see how my answer could give her any comfort. 'Don't worry. Pavlik will handle it.'

Zoe was looking at me quizzically. 'Why do you do that?'

'Do what?'

'Call Jacob by his last name?'

'I don't know,' I snapped, charity out the window. 'Why do you call him "Jacob"?'

Zoe shrugged. 'He was listed as "Jacob Pavlik" the first time he spoke here. I was in charge of the nametags and program materials and I guess it just . . . stuck.'

It could be the truth, I supposed. Zoe was looking for an explanation in return, so I obliged. 'He suspected me of murder. Believe me, "Pavlik" was the nicest thing I called him.'

Zoe's eyes flew open and she managed a weak, 'Oh.'

'So,' I said brightly. 'How long have you known Larry?'

'I, uh . . . about five years, perhaps?' She was edging away from me as best she could, given the constraints of the side-by-side seats.

'You needn't worry about me,' I told her, feeling a little hurt. 'I didn't commit the crime then and I certainly didn't have any reason to kill Potter now. But somebody must have.'

'Must have what?' Zoe was looking a lot like she did before she passed out. Happily, if she toppled, she couldn't go far.

'A reason to kill Larry Potter, of course.' I slid closer and in a confidential tone whispered, 'So who do you think it was?'

'How would I know?' The conference organizer was back to the window.

'But you *know* these people. For example,' I nodded toward Rosemary Darlington, 'could the legendary author have finally snapped when her rumored former lover trashed her new book? Or maybe,' I hooked a thumb over my shoulder at Danny, 'it's the aspiring young writer who's the killer. He's practically been stalking the victim, after all, since the critic refused to read his work.'

'Then there's the literary agent.' A head tilt toward Carson, seated with Markus across from us. 'Could he have had a reason to kill his client? Or what about the librarian? I'm pretty sure he was one of Potter's "victims" in the past. And what about the long-suffering wife?' I couldn't see Audra Edmonds, but plunged on anyway, still keeping my voice down. I was on a roll. 'Might Don't-Call-Me-Mrs-Potter have done away with her cheating mister?'

'I . . . I don't know.'

'Of course not. How could you?' I turned back full-face to Zoe. 'The only person who *does* isn't talking.'

'You mean Larry?' Zoe's voice was raspy, as if she couldn't draw in enough air.

'And the killer, of course.' I swept my hand to encompass the entire assemblage. I couldn't help myself. 'Or killers.'

Zoe was surveying our fellow passengers warily, so I left her to it and turned my attention back to Pavlik's question-and-answer session, chewing things over in my mind.

'. . . say, we're stuck here,' Carson was saying. 'But for how long?'

'Has someone called for help?' came from Grace, who looked a little worse for wear. Hopefully she hadn't been dancing on top of a table when we'd come to our abrupt stop, but her body language did project an aching head.

'Unfortunately, it appears the only communication is by cell.' I noticed that Pavlik didn't elaborate. 'And there seems to be no service here.'

Cell phones magically appeared in hands.

'Huh,' Markus said, looking at his. 'Not a single bar.'

'We're still deep in the Everglades.' I tried to look out the window, but all I could see was my own reflection against the black backdrop of rain riveting down the glass.

'There are no cell towers. Or at least not many.' Zoe slipped her phone back into her pocket. 'And I'm sure the storm didn't help matters any.'

'I hear the Everglades is like twice the size of Rhode Island,' Danny contributed. 'Some hunter got separated from his friends a while back and they didn't find him for four days.'

Prudence sniffed. 'Must have been decades ago. Now—'

'You'd think,' Danny interrupted, 'but this was like three years ago. And just this past spring a whole family got lost. They were found a day later, but the newspaper story I Googled said they got lucky. They could have been out here a week.'

'A week?' Missy's voice squeaked from somewhere in the back of the car. The assistant event coordinator was probably keeping a low profile.

'Please,' Pavlik said, holding up both hands. 'I'm not familiar with the area. But once it's light, we'll have a better idea of what we're dealing with. For tonight, stay in this car and the two behind it – the dining and club cars. The forward one is off limits.'

'The sleeping car?' Rosemary asked. 'Why?'

'See?' Zoe hissed, elbowing me. 'I knew they'd ask.'

'At least a few of us should be allowed to catch some zzz's in there,' Prudence contributed in support of our surviving guest of honor.

'I'm afraid that's not possible,' Pavlik said flatly. No explanations, no apologies.

I dug an 'I told you so' elbow into my seatmate's ribs.

'Oh, yeah?' demanded the big guy who'd followed Grace onto the table earlier. 'Who says?'

'Can it, Fred,' Zoe said, rubbing her side. 'The sheriff is in charge.'

'Some cop from Hicksville, Wisconsin?' The guy surfed table-tops – I guess it figured he had more nerve than brains. 'That doesn't give him any authority here.'

'And you are . . .?' asked Markus.

Fred got up and unsuccessfully tried to hike up his belted pants over his enormous paunch. 'I'm in South Florida law enforcement. I should be in charge.'

Geez, just what were we being treated to, '*Lord of the Flies: Their Boomer Years*'?

Though in truth, I'd prefer that classic over the Donner Party experience in the Sierra Nevadas, given that this guy looked like he could give the python a run for its money at an all-you-can-eat buffet.

'You're a gate guard at a senior housing complex,' Zoe said, cutting him off at the knees. The woman still had some fight in her. 'When was the last time someone was stabbed to death there, huh?'

Uh-oh.

'Stabbed to death?' someone echoed, sounding more than a little horrified.

'And,' a firm, also female, voice from the back, 'just *where* is my husband?'

TWENTY

I wouldn't say the writers with us on the Orient Espresso were ghouls exactly, but they did seem loathe to let a forensic learning opportunity pass by unexploited. However impromptu and even if the corpse was, in a vertically integrated sense, one of their own.

'I don't see how it would hurt,' Prudence was saying. 'I mean, you said the man is already dead.'

'And, outside a funeral home, I've never seen a dead body,' Grace whined. 'This may be my only chance.'

'You said he was stabbed?' Harvey – the man playing Hardman, the American detective disguised as a 'flamboyant American' in Christie's book – was taking notes. 'How many times?'

Obviously thinking about the number and variety of blade wounds in Christie's original, he winked at me.

I'd been bombarded with nonstop questions since Pavlik had taken Potter's wife away to break – or, thanks to Zoe – elaborate and maybe soften the news for Audra.

I wished the sheriff good luck on the last, especially since at least one paragraph of his explanation would have to include the expressions 'cake knife' and 'exploding python.'

I was twisted around in my seat to face the crowd, one knee tucked under me and my patience wearing thin. 'I told you. I can't—'

'So the cause of death is a stab wound or wounds, plural?' from Danny, who seemed to be tapping notes into his iPhone.

'The knife was stuck in his back,' Missy piped up. She was still a little green around the gills, but determined to be helpful. 'Though the python—'

'Python?' Prudence interrupted. 'Nobody mentioned a python.'

'There's a snake on the train?' Grace was glancing around like the thing was going to slither down the aisle.

'No, no,' Missy said, seeming to realize the firestorm she'd just sparked. 'And I didn't say it was the cause—'

'There *is* no python – or snake of any type – on this train.' Pavlik had entered from the dining car, shooting a dark look at the young woman. 'You have my word on that.'

I knew the drill all too well, but Missy looked like the sheriff had slapped her. The bottom lip trembled and I knew she was seconds from another round of tears.

'Oh, look,' I said, holding up my cell phone to distract the group. 'I have service!'

A dozen phones promptly reappeared and then disappeared as their owners realized I was mistaken. Or lying.

'Sorry, phantom bar,' I said, tucking my prop away. 'Anyway, you're welcome to ask the sheriff, but I can't imagine that the authorities in any state would want us traipsing in and out of that sleeping car before they have a chance to examine it.'

A surge of muttering waved down by Big Fred, of all people. 'Folks, the sheriff's tootsie has it right. The crime scene must be preserved.'

'It's in all the books,' someone else said. 'And TV shows, too.'

A third piped up. 'But we could go one by one. Or just send a representative to take a few photos we can share.'

OK, maybe they *were* ghouls.

'It'd be like a press pool,' Prudence said. 'Back in the day—'

Pavlik held up his hands. 'I appreciate your *concern*,' I had to hand it to him, he managed to sound more commanding than sarcastic, 'but I think your – and our – time here is better spent trying to figure out how Mr Potter spent his last hour or so on this train.'

I shot Pavlik a look of disbelief and, since he was standing in the aisle next to me, I tugged on his pants leg.

He held up his finger to the assemblage and leaned down. 'What?'

'You're encouraging witnesses to discuss the things they saw?' I whispered.

'You really think we can stop them?' He shrugged. 'At least this will keep them busy and away from the body. We can make a record of what they claim to have seen and done before their memories are further compromised.'

Hmm. My 'tootsie' was a smart cookie, too. God knew when
the local authorities would arrive and by then this group would
have written their own storylines and rearranged their memories
to match. Not to mention using their cell phones as we drew
sufficiently near civilization to sew up book and movie deals
before we left rail for pavement at the station.

'Maggy, I have to ask you to serve as secretary,' Pavlik said,
raising his voice so the rest of the group could hear and pulling
a notebook out of his pocket. 'I'll conduct the interviews and
record them on my smart phone.'

Even without the ability to make a call, we could do that.
'Good idea.'

'Oooh,' Grace squealed. 'This is just like *Murder on the
Orient Express*. Do you want to interrogate us in the dining
car?'

Pavlik said, 'I think that will do nicely. Just give us a few
minutes to set up.'

A tired-looking Zoe Scarlett stood and tugged closed her
perpetually gaping dress. She was looking less like a bombshell
and more like its crater. 'What would you like me to do,
Jacob?'

'Stay in this car and Maggy will let you know who to send
in next.'

The woman, who an hour ago would have thrown me a scathing
look, just nodded resignedly and turned away. 'I can't believe
this,' I thought I heard her say. 'I just can't believe this is happening
to me.'

'Do you think it's odd there was just one real railroad employee
on the train?' I asked Pavlik as we prepared the same table
in the dining car where we'd sat earlier in the evening. It was
just past midnight. 'Shouldn't there have been a conductor
and . . . I don't know, a brakeman or steward or
something?'

'Got me,' Pavlik said, sliding into the booth. 'We'll ask Zoe
and Missy when they're in here, but it sounds to me like corners
were cut, probably because of budget limitations.'

'Missy did say she'd hoped more people would attend.'

'And now there's one fewer.' He handed me his smart phone.

'I thought you wanted me to take notes.' I held up the cell. 'What do I do with this?'

'Changed my mind.' Pavlik took back his pad and flipped it open. 'You video and I'll take notes. I need to be looking at their faces directly, not paying attention to a screen.'

Made sense. My ex, Ted, had been a camera bug and I swore the man never experienced any place that we went except afterwards on video and photos. Always had his eyes glued to a lens, following the strategy of 'make camp and break camp: we'll look at the pictures when we get home.'

'Did you bring a charger?' I slid the control on the phone to 'video.' 'I'm afraid this could take all night.'

'Yes, I did, and I hope it will. Take all night, I mean.' Pavlik was jotting down a list of buzzwords toward his questions. 'The longer we can keep these people engaged the better.'

'You mean the less trouble they'll be to us?'

'That's exactly what I mean. You saw it. Their imaginations are already running away with them.'

I found it hard to believe that the imaginations of even a bunch of mystery writers could measure up to the reality of what we'd just witnessed.

'The minute Missy mentioned pythons,' Pavlik continued, 'they started fabricating. That's what I want to avoid.'

'That's not really fair,' I protested. 'There was a python. A big one. And eggs, filled with little bitsy pythons. Remember?'

'But not on the train.' Pavlik spaced each word as though it were a separate sentence.

'True.' As far as it went.

'Remember, Maggy: we obtain information, not provide it. The detail of the python's involvement is better kept among those of us who are already privy to it.'

The detail of the python's 'involvement'? I was starting to feel like I'd fallen down the rabbit hole with Alice. 'You've reminded Missy, Zoe, Boyce, Markus and Engineer Hertel to keep mum?' Our privy wasn't very private.

'I have.'

'Then consider the snake off the table,' I said. 'What's next?'

'Any chance you remember the order of the witnesses called in *Murder on the Orient Express*?'

'No, but we do have access to a crib sheet.'

Pavlik, for nearly the first time since I'd known him, let a look of confusion cross his face.

TWENTY-ONE

Grace/Greta's copy of *Murder on the Orient Express* in front of us, we surveyed the chapter headings of 'PART II – THE EVIDENCE.'

'Let's see, first witness.' I looked at Pavlik. 'Pete the bartender is playing the role of Pierre Michel, the fictional "Wagon Lit conductor."'

'I can't imagine he has anything to tell us,' Pavlik said. 'He's been behind the bar in the club car most of the time. Besides, he's not one of the people we want to keep occupied.'

'Good point. What about Engineer Hertel? Should we call him to the stand?'

'I'm not sure we can keep the natives from getting restless out there while we get an encyclopedic lowdown on Wild Kingdom – The Everglades Franchise.'

Another good point. Hertel was probably more a bizarre Marlin Perkins than a carnivore's Euell Gibbons.

'Still,' the sheriff said. 'I do have one thing I need to clarify with him before we talk to anyone else. So yes, bailiff, please bring in the first witness.'

I grinned and got up.

Pavlik's hand stopped me before I could get any farther. 'I know this hasn't been exactly what you expected when I asked you to come along.'

I smiled. 'You mean when I invited myself?'

'Yeah, since you mention it.' His blue eyes flashed. 'But I'm glad you did. Even now, and maybe especially now, given what's happened. You were truly stand-up brave following me off the train when I know you were scared.'

'Try terrified.'

A grin. 'Yet when we confronted that goliath of a snake, you were nigh-on to heroic.'

'Just "nigh-on"?' I teased, giving him a quick kiss on the lips.

'And there's no one else *I'd* rather be with, either. Especially stuck in the Everglades with a murderer onboard.'

His hand stopped me again. 'That person *is* still here somewhere, Maggy. The only other possibility was that he – or she – bailed into the Everglades.'

I remembered what I'd been thinking earlier. 'Do you want me to take a head count and compare my tally to Zoe's passenger list?'

'Already done.'

'By whom?'

'By me, just now, when everyone was seated in the passenger car arguing with you. Nobody's missing.'

I shook my head. 'What a mess.'

'You're telling me. And God knows whose jurisdiction we're in. We could be on federal park land, the Seminole Indian Reservation or just county, state or private land.'

'Aren't you going to get in trouble with whoever the authorities are?' I blushed. 'I mean, you've scolded me often enough for sticking my nose in and mucking things up and now you've . . .'

'Become functionally you?'

'A civilian,' I tried.

'Technically, but I'm still law enforcement. And I'm the best we've got or will have until we can contact someone both official and local. I'd like to get what we can down on the record before people start swapping – and blending, and embroidering – their individual stories.'

'Like they probably are, as we speak.'

'Which suggests . . .' He gestured toward the door.

Got it: bring on the engineer.

'Well, golly, that's a real good question.' Engineer Theodore B. Hertel, Jr was sitting across from us, pulling on his earlobe. I hoped, for symmetry's sake, not the one he'd been dragging down out on the railbed with Potter and the python.

He stopped and then went to his chin. 'What's this?'

I set down the camera/phone and leaned across the table. 'Looks like you missed a spot,' or three, 'when you shaved.'

'That's a relief,' he said. 'Thought it was a hairy mole. Those puppies can turn into cancer, you know?'

I didn't know. And I didn't want to know. Not now and preferably not ever, especially from this master of disaster.

'Back to the question,' the sheriff prompted.

'Which was?'

A trained interrogator, Pavlik didn't roll his eyes, though I feared I might be rolling enough for the both of us. 'Given that we found Laurence Potter's body on the opposite side of the flooded track from where we sit now, can you tell me when we passed through that area on the way out into the Everglades?'

I thought I knew where Pavlik was going with this.

'Before we reversed direction to go back east, you mean?' He was back to tugging on the lobe, but the one on the other side of his head.

'Correct.' Pavlik waited.

'Well, now. That's hard to say. You see, I'm not quite sure just where we are.'

'I can understand that,' Pavlik said mildly. My brain, on the other hand, was screaming in all capital letters, 'WHAT THE HELL DO YOU *MEAN* YOU DON'T KNOW WHERE WE ARE IN THE MIDDLE OF THIS—?'

'Let's start with the "when," then,' Pavlik continued, giving my nervously vibrating thigh a reassuring squeeze under the table. 'We know that tonight's event was to be a three-hour-long round trip. That would mean you turned the train around halfway through that time or ninety minutes after we departed the station, right?'

'Well, technically we don't turn around. Just stop and I take her back the other way.'

I could have smacked the man, but the sheriff apparently thought we were making progress. 'So you confirm that you "took her back the other way" ninety minutes after we left the station?'

'Probably that, like you say, give or take. This isn't an exact science, you know.'

Seemed like a hell of a way to run a railroad.

'And how many miles into the Everglades would that have taken us?' Pavlik was writing again.

'No way of telling.'

Pavlik looked up from his notes. 'You didn't glance at your odometer?'

Hertel looked puzzled. 'Odometer? Ain't got one. Leastways

that's any use to the engineer. No, we just chug from one assigned stop to 'nother along the same track. What would I do with an odometer?'

I suppressed a grin as Pavlik seemed to ponder what Hertel could do with his odometer. 'So you don't know how far we traveled before we reversed directions.'

'No sir, that I don't.' Hertel shifted on the banquette. 'Not quite sure why it matters, tell you the truth.'

I saw Pavlik's knuckles whitening as he gripped his pen, so I took over before he decided to bayonet the guy's eye. 'Let's forget distance for now. If we know what time we reversed, and how long after that we came to a stop because of the damaged track, we'll know approximately when we passed this spot on the way into the Everglades.'

'Meaning that's when this Potter became snake-bait, huh? Well, that's real good reasoning, I have to say. Not sure it'll hold water, though.' Hertel was grinning.

'And why is that?' I asked between my own clenched teeth.

Mercifully, my tag team partner stepped in. 'We left the station a little after eight?'

'Correct-o-mundo. Eight-oh-four, to be exact.'

'And we've agreed we reversed ninety minutes after we left the station, so as to be back within the three-hour timeframe. That means, of course, nine thirty-four.'

'Give or take,' I added before Hertel could.

Pavlik's pen hovered over a sheet of paper he'd torn from his pad. 'And the train travels how fast?'

Hertel worried the errant patch of chin hair. 'We averaged about forty on our way out.'

'Good, good.' The sheriff wrote it down. 'So at forty miles an hour, we'd cover sixty miles in an hour and a half.'

I gave Pavlik an admiring glance. He'd get his gold star later.

The sheriff began chewing on the eraser end of his pen, giving me a glimpse of little Jacob Pavlik in grade school. 'We still need to know what time we were stopped here by the flooding. With all the commotion, I didn't think to look.'

'Maybe Missy or Zoe noticed,' I suggested.

'Well, now, I can tell you that,' Hertel said.

'You can?' Pavlik and I looked at him. 'Why didn't you say so?'

'You asked how far we chugged into the Everglades, which I didn't know, and what time we left the station, which I did. You never did ask when we stopped out here.'

'I'm asking it now.' Pavlik's eyes were narrow slits. 'When?'

This time I patted his thigh.

'Why, a mite before ten p.m.'

I threw a smile at Pavlik. 'That means that Potter went off the train here about nine.'

'And "here" is approximately forty miles west of the station.' Pavlik leaned back against the banquette and stretched.

'And how do you figure that?' from Hertel.

'Easy.' I pushed Pavlik's paper in the middle of the tabletop so the engineer could see the sheriff's notes. 'We reached the place we reversed at nine-thirty and, according to you, our current position at ten. That's a half hour after reversal, meaning we must have passed this spot a half hour *before* reversal or nine p.m. That also means that at forty miles an hour we would have covered – you guessed it – forty miles between eight and nine p.m.' I sat back now, too, pleased with our paired reasoning.

But Hertel frowned. 'Sounds simple enough, but the problem is we weren't traveling at the same speed coming back east as going out west. In fact, I was keeping the throttle at near crawl because the track was flooding. And good thing, too, or I wouldn't have been able to stop before that wash-out.'

The engineer pulled the paper toward him and dug a stub of a pencil out of his bib pocket. Touching it to his tongue, he started to work. 'Now if a train's heading one direction at forty miles an hour, and another at, say, twen—'

I let my forehead hit the table and took the self-inflicted pain without whimpering.

TWENTY-TWO

Pavlik's eyes were glazed over the instant Theodore B. Hertel, Jr closed the door behind him. 'So the long and the short of it is that the later it got, the more the rain slowed us down.'

'There is no short, when it comes to our engineer.' I was holding my head in my hands. 'Only long. Really, really long.'

'Did you understand all that?' Pavlik asked. 'I feel like we just lost more ground than the road bed in front of the locomotive's nose.'

We had Hertel's chicken scratchings in front of us, but given that we hadn't maintained a steady speed, even he hadn't been able to calculate our location with any degree of reliability. And I wasn't sure we'd have understood if he had. The man had the presentational skills of your average batty theoretical physicist.

'Well, we have to start somewhere.' Pavlik drew himself up. 'We know we reversed around nine-thirty and got stuck here at ten.'

'Correct. What we don't know is where "here" is.' I checked my cell. One a.m.

The 'Dark Side of Midnight,' as legendary Milwaukee jazz DJ Ron Cuzner had dubbed his late-night show way back when. Ron had kept me company through countless hours spent rocking Eric when he was a colicky baby. And today . . .

I shook myself back into the present.

'. . . try to bracket the time of death,' Pavlik was saying. 'We know Potter was alive as Zoe got up to welcome people. Hopefully she'll be able to tell us exactly what time that was.'

Or, more likely, Missy would. 'So that time, whatever it is, will be the early end of our bracket. The latest has to be well before we reversed directions at nine-thirty.'

'Why "well before"?'

I chewed on my lip. 'I see your point. Since we don't know how slowly we've traveled since the turn-around – or "reversal," as Hertel insists – let's just say Potter went off the train before nine-thirty.'

'Why not after?'

'Because you said he'd fallen or been pushed—'

'Let's use "exited," since we don't know. It'll be more consistent.'

Honest to God, Pavlik was nearly as maddening as the engineer. 'You said he'd *exited* when we came past this point on the way into the Everglades.'

'Actually, I didn't. You did.'

I tried to think back to the conversation with the engineer and who had said what.

'See?' Pavlik pointed at his notes. 'You took over questioning here and made the statement to Hertel.'

Son of a bitch, but the sheriff was right. 'Only that has to be how it happened. We're on *one* side of the break in the tracks—'

Pavlik interrupted. 'Let's call what lies in front of the train – to the east of the locomotive – the flooded track. We don't know there's an actual break or that the tracks are washed away, rather than merely covered.'

'So stipulated,' I said, though if I clenched my teeth any harder, I'd need to wear a mouth guard to spare my molars. 'But my point is that Potter's body was on the opposite side of *the flooded track* from where we sit right now. Remember? We had to wade through water to get there?'

Pavlik was writing. 'The *snake* was encountered on the opposite side, east of the flooded track.'

'With Potter's body *in* him.'

'Mostly.'

'Thank you.' I was one heartbeat away from—

'Maggy, you think I'm nitpicking, but this kind of detail is important.' Pavlik read from his notes: 'The snake was encountered on the east side of the flooded track, opposite the train's stopped position. The lower portion of the victim's body was protruding from its mouth.'

'The *African rock python* was encountered,' I corrected. Two could play this game.

'We have only the engineer's opinion that it was a python,

and only,' the notes again, 'Markus's belief that it was, indeed, a rock python.'

I threw up my hands. 'Hey, maybe it isn't even a snake. Why don't you just say a really big worm with teeth dwarfing a great white shark's? Want me to go out and count them?'

'Sarcasm rarely becomes you, Maggy.' Pavlik was writing again.

'I was going for "facetious."'

'Well, you missed the target.' He still didn't look up.

I sighed. 'OK, I'm sorry. Obviously, this detecting is more complicated than I realized.'

'The record-keeping is tedious and using the same terminology to identify something may seem repetitive, but believe me, it reduces ambiguity and makes the detecting, as you call it, easier and conviction much more likely.' He raised his head and smiled. 'Apology accepted.'

I cocked my head. 'Aren't you going to tell me what word I should use instead of "detecting"?'

Head down again. 'I'm trying hard not to.' A beat. 'But "investigating" might be a good choice.'

Pavlik was just too cute and I laughed, genuinely. '"Investigating" it is, Sheriff. Now tell me what difference it makes to the investigation to say that both the snake and Laurence Potter's body were on the east side of the flooded track, versus the *snake* was on the east side of the flooded track with Laurence Potter's body inside it. Mostly.'

'Happily.' Sheriff Jake Pavlik, out of his jurisdiction or not, made steady eye contact. 'The difference is how Potter got there.'

TWENTY-THREE

'**A**re you saying Larry Potter didn't necessarily exit the train as we passed this spot on our way west?'

'Exactly,' Pavlik said. 'The—'

I interrupted. 'Do you know if pythons eat . . . dead things?'

'Carrion? If you're asking whether they're scavengers or consume only what they've killed themselves, I don't have a clue.'

'We'll have to ask somebody.' My kingdom for Google. 'I'm sorry, I interrupted. You were saying?'

'Just that the snake could have retrieved the body – or Potter, still alive, if that's the way it went down – from another location.'

'Retrieved?' The word made the thing sound more like a loyal hunting dog than a repulsive, slithering man-eater. But then foxes probably weren't so fond of hounds, either.

'Yes. Retrieved the body and conveyed it to where we found them both on the east side of the flooded track. That means Potter needn't have exited the train on the *east* side of the flooded track, but anywhere in the vicinity.'

'And the time?'

'According to the engineer, he didn't see the snake – and Potter – until he'd brought the train, now eastbound, to a stop and climbed down to investigate,' notes again, '"a mite before ten."'

'So, this "mite before ten" would be the latest Potter could have exited one of the cars, and the start of Zoe's speech the earliest.'

'Agreed.' Pavlik wrote it down and gestured toward Grace's tattered copy of *Murder on the Orient Express*. 'Who's next?'

'"The secretary, MacQueen,"' I read. 'That would be Markus.'

'Have Zoe send him in,' Pavlik ordered. 'But first, and I should have thought of this earlier, grab some bottled water and a rack of clean glasses.' He hooked his finger to the club car behind us.

I stood up, too tired to question. 'Will do, boss.'

'Oh, and Maggy?'

I stopped and turned around. 'Yes?'

'Glass glasses, not plastic. And use a towel when you take them out of the rack.'

I got the glasses and, on Pavlik's orders, poured the water into three of them. One for him, one for me and one prepared for our next witness. And that witness's fingerprints. Then I went to the far-end door and slid it to access the vestibule.

The train was eerily still without the clatter of the tracks passing below. I pulled open the door of the passenger car, half-hoping the whole lot of them would be asleep. If so, Pavlik and I could follow suit. It had been a long day.

But alas, Zoe was still awake and seated in the front row, with Prudence now next to her. The latter looked up.

I stepped in. 'Is Markus—'

'Here,' a voice said, and he stood up.

'See?' Grace popped up from the seat behind Prudence and Zoe. 'I told you we'd be called in the same sequence as the characters in the book were.'

'That means I'll be very nearly last,' Rosemary Darlington, aka Mary Debenham said. 'Wouldn't you rather go alphabetical? Perhaps start with "A" for Arbuthnot?' She hooked a finger toward the young man seated next to her. Danny had finally snagged an audience with the great lady.

'Andrenyi comes before Arbuthnot,' Carson, aka Count Andrenyi, pointed out. 'I should go first.'

'I think we'll stick with the book's order.' I turned to Zoe. 'Is the only railroad staff on the train the engineer?'

She shrugged, as if it didn't matter, and called out, 'Missy?'

The first Mrs Hubbard half-rose from a seat next to Pete the bartender about three-quarters of the way back. I had to hand it to Missy, she certainly was being sought out by the young men on the train. But then we only had three passengers under the age of thirty – it shouldn't be surprising that they'd seek each other out.

Even from this distance, I saw Missy blush. 'Maggy, we had a very tight budget, you know.'

Which had managed to put us in a very tight spot. 'And . . .'

'And, well, the train people said we had to have a conductor and I told them we did.'

'Don't tell me,' I said. 'Pierre Michel?'

The line between fact and fiction was quickly blurring. Although for these people maybe they were the same thing.

'Yes.' She plopped back down in her seat and added miserably, 'They wouldn't let us go otherwise.'

'With good reason, Missy,' Markus said, not unkindly. 'The conductor is the person in charge.'

'Really?' I asked. 'I always thought they just took tickets.'

'Uh-uh.' Markus was shaking his head. 'My mother worked at Amtrak's headquarters in Washington, and my brother Kevin is an engineer. The engineer runs the locomotive and reports to the conductor, who communicates with dispatchers and oversees the train and its passengers.'

And *our* 'conductor' was a kid whose real name was Brandon and worked at an Olive Garden. Lovely.

'Then you're it, MacQueen,' I said to Markus, gesturing for him to go ahead of me.

As we entered the dining car, Pavlik looked up from his notepad and stuck out his hand. 'Thanks for your help out there. And for keeping the particulars of the situation to yourself.'

Markus shook and slid in on the opposite side of the semicircular booth. 'Not a problem. Zoe came to almost as soon as Missy and I began helping her back to the train. None of us was eager to spend more time out there with that Jules Verne creature split open on the opposite bank.'

Pavlik shifted over so I could sit next to him and passed the smart phone to me. 'Do you mind if Maggy tapes us? It'll help the investigators if we can get everyone's initial impression.'

'Not at all,' Markus said, his open face curious. 'Are you going to read me my rights?'

'You're not a suspect.' Pavlik gave him a friendly smile. 'At least, so far as I know.'

I raised the phone and through it, saw Markus's gaze waver. 'Well, no. Of course not. But I'm happy to answer any questions you might have. Not that I necessarily can.'

Pavlik raised his hands. 'Understood. First off, could you state your full name and home address for me?'

Markus complied, giving an address in Washington, D.C.

'Just for the record,' Pavlik continued, 'could you detail your movements after you boarded the train?'

'Let me think.' Markus picked up the glass of water in front of him, then set it down again. 'I saw Maggy here,' he nodded at the camera/phone, 'when I was in line for a drink. From there I made my way back through the train, stopping to talk to people here and there until I reached the passenger car.'

Pavlik, who had been studying his notes, looked up. 'We do know that Mr Potter was in the dining car until Zoe Scarlett welcomed everyone over the speaker system. Would you know about what time that was?'

Markus pulled out a handkerchief – not the dainty square of initialed cambric in *Murder on the Orient Express*, but a big honkin' one – and mopped his brow. 'I remember thinking it was later than I'd expected. When Missy asked me to speak after Zoe welcomed everyone, I assumed it would be right after we left the station, which was just past eight, as you'll recall.'

This last was directed to me and I nodded encouragement.

'I remember checking the time at nearly nine and thinking they thought it best to let people chat and get liquored up before they had to sit and listen to me talk.' A self-deprecating smile.

'From what I recall from the previous time I was at this conference,' Pavlik said, 'people come from all over and may not have seen each other for quite a while during the interim.'

'Exactly.' Markus was nodding. 'Everyone wants to catch up. Find out who got published. Who found an agent. Or even was lottery-blessed by receiving a film option.'

'So you looked at the time and it was nearly nine, you said. What time exactly?'

'Eight fifty-five, maybe?'

'What did you do then?' Pavlik asked.

'It suddenly hit me that perhaps the sound system could only be heard in the dining car and, for all I knew, the program had begun and they were looking for me.'

'Not true, though.'

'Correct. As I went forward to check, I heard Zoe greet the gathering.'

'Did you see Laurence Potter?' I asked from behind the phone/camera.

'Come to think of it, we did cross paths in the dining car. He was going toward the back of the train as I was moving to the front.'

'Did you pass him before the cake?' I asked.

Finally, a roll of the eyes from Pavlik. Unfortunately directed at me.

Markus looked confused. 'Are you asking if I saw Larry before I went past the table with the cake on it?'

I glanced at Pavlik. When there was no response, I nodded at Markus.

'We were coming from opposite directions,' the librarian said, 'but as I recall we crossed paths about halfway through the dining car.'

'So you'd already passed the cake, but he hadn't reached it yet,' I summarized.

'Correct.'

'Did you notice the cake as you went by?' Pavlik followed up.

'I did.'

My turn. 'Was the knife still in it?'

This time I got a glare before Pavlik turned to Markus. 'Can you describe the cake?'

It was only then I remembered that Pavlik had been seated on the banquette at the front of the dining car for most of our ride. Except for going to the club car – the opposite direction – to get my second espresso martini, he hadn't left the table and therefore hadn't seen the cake before it was hacked apart. Nor the knife, until we discovered it in Potter's body.

'Umm,' Markus glanced nervously at me and then back at Pavlik before answering. 'I don't know . . . shaped like a sleeping man? Blanket pulled up to the neck. Covered with icing, of course.'

'Of course.' This time Pavlik seemed to purposely not look my way. 'And did you see the knife?'

'Sure. Stuck in his chest.'

Pavlik did a double-take. 'You saw the knife in Potter's *chest*?'

Markus's eyes grew wide. 'Oh, no. No, no. It was in the cake's – I mean the "man" depicted in the cake's – chest.' He looked back and forth between us. 'You saw it, right?'

I turned to Pavlik. 'The cake knife was stuck in the frosted body's chest.'

'Explains the white goo,' Pavlik said to himself. 'Any idea where Potter was headed when he passed you?'

Markus shook his head. 'Since the bar was the other way, I assumed he was going to the bathroom or to see someone in the passenger car. Tell you the truth, I didn't even realize the sleeping car was there.'

'You've told us you knew you were to speak next. Did you also know Potter was about to be introduced?'

'Are you asking why I didn't stop him?' Markus asked. 'Believe me, Potter did pretty much whatever he wanted and no one had the nerve to mess with him. Or they'd pay.'

Pavlik's eyes rose. 'First-hand experience?'

'Me?'

'You're a writer, aren't you?'

'Markus writes—' I started, and slapped my mouth shut. 'Sorry. Go ahead.'

'I write non-fiction,' Markus supplied. 'Books on classics, mystery compendiums, readers' guides, like that.'

'So you've never had the pleasure of being reviewed by Potter?'

'No. Well, yes. Once.' Markus looked miserable. 'Maybe.'

'Maybe?'

'Umm, well, he did review a . . . well, sort of an encyclopedia I did of crime writers.'

'Sounds impressive,' Pavlik said. 'Did Potter like it?'

'Not exactly,' Markus directed the words toward his clasped hands on the table.

'Excuse me?'

'I said,' the man looked up, 'that while he praised the "effort," Potter found a bit of fault with it. Not at all unusual in a work of this length.'

'How long was it?'

'Three volumes.'

'And how many errors did Potter find?'

'One . . .' Markus, just murmuring, stammered anyway. 'One hundred and forty-eight.'

I remembered the interchange between the two men on the bus. I'd known something wasn't quite right there. Potter had seemed to take great pleasure spreading salt into that wound.

I said, 'It would take forever to read all three volumes cover-to-cover and fact check each page.' Being a lover of old movies, I had a couple of reference books on that subject that sounded like what Markus was talking about. Listing upon listing upon listing.

'It's what PotShots does,' Markus said simply.

'Apparently.' Pavlik made a note. 'Do reviews like the one Potter gave you affect sales?'

A throaty laugh. 'Any review is better than no review.'

Like any publicity is good publicity, but I wasn't buying it. 'Assuming libraries and schools use your books as reference material, wouldn't the inaccuracies present a real problem for them?'

This time it was Markus directing annoyed looks my way. 'Maybe sales weren't what they could have been, but this happened more than a year ago. I certainly wouldn't murder a man over it, if that's what you're implying.'

'Good to know,' Pavlik said as he tapped me on the shoulder so he could stand. 'Could you send in whoever it is who's playing the next person on the list . . .'

'Ratchett's valet, Masterman,' I supplied. 'If there is one.'

'Will do.' Markus slid out of the booth, too, but then stood his ground. 'You have no doubt in your mind that Potter was murdered?'

'If you can come up with another plausible explanation for the knife on this train winding up in his back, I'd be glad to entertain it,' Pavlik said.

'Now that you say it was the cake knife in his back, I'm at a loss. He sure didn't jump off the train with it between his teeth to fight pythons.'

'Agreed.' Pavlik swept his hand toward the door.

Taking the hint, Markus moved to the door and slid it open. 'Though that leaves us with what seems like an even more unlikely scenario.'

'What's that?' I asked.

Markus stepped through into the vestibule. 'That one of my friends is a murderer.'

The door slapped shut.

TWENTY-FOUR

'Do you think whoever stabbed Larry Potter is a threat to kill again?' I asked Pavlik as we waited for our next witness. While I'd been happy to point out to Zoe Scarlett that we were *all* murder suspects, I really hoped this crime was a one-off. So to speak.

'We have to assume that anyone who crosses that line has the potential to cross it again.' Spreading his fingers inside Markus's glass to lift it without compromising the fingerprints on the outside, Pavlik leaned over to place it carefully on the table behind us.

'But why?' I asked. 'This has to have been a personal attack against Potter. Someone followed him to the sleeping car.'

'And grabbed a hunk of cake en route?'

'Potter probably did that. Remember? He was complaining not only that he couldn't smoke, but there was nothing to eat onboard except the cake. I wouldn't put it past the man to take matters in his own hands and cut the cake.' I had sublimated my own swipe at the frosting into relative irrelevance.

'Potter certainly struck me as somebody who believed rules – of etiquette, in this instance – didn't apply to him.'

'So you think Potter was a . . . sociopath?' I heard the far door of the vestibule open.

Pavlik was regarding me with a wry grin. 'Honey, I'm not sure there isn't a little sociopath in all of us – you and me, included.

'What? I—'

Before I could inquire further, the near door slid open.

The man who'd been taking notes earlier entered. Harvey/ Hardman's checkered sports jacket might be loud, but his voice was even louder.

'Hope you folks don't mind,' he said, every bit the blustering American of Christie's novel. 'But I have things to do and people to see. I took a poll and nobody minded that I went next.'

I minded. With a sigh, I skipped over Missy as Mrs Hubbard, Grace the Swedish Lady, Prudence the Russian Princess, Carson as Count Andrenyi and Danny as Col. Arbuthnot on my neat list and put a grudging checkmark next to Mr Hardman the American. Then I checked the time. Nearly 2:30 a.m.

'Things to do and people to see at this hour, Mr . . .?'

'Hardman.' We all shook hands.

Before I could tell Pavlik that 'Hardman' was the man's fictional identity, Harvey blustered on. 'I know what you're going to say. Maybe it's *people* I should be doing and leave the seeing to others.' Cue hardy laugh.

You had to give it to the man – he raised the bar of 'Ugly American' to new levels, stereotype-wise.

'Have a seat. Maggy, would you mind getting Mr Hardman a glass of water?'

'Not necessary,' Harvey said, waving me to sit back down.

I ignored him, poured the water and handed it to him.

'His name really is Harvey,' I told Pavlik. 'He's just playing the part of Christie's "Hardman."'

Harvey accepted the glass, but set it down immediately. He glanced back toward the closed connecting door to make sure we couldn't be heard, then leaned in anyway. 'You do know the Hardman character is just a blind. I'm a private detective.'

'And *you* do know,' Pavlik said, 'that you're only a fictional character, right?'

Harvey sat back like Pavlik had punched him, a look of astonishment on his face. 'But this is just part of the show, right? The whole crazy man-eating snake story?'

'Take my word for it, Harvey,' I said. 'The python was real, Potter is dead and neither incident was in the script.'

Harvey cocked his head. 'Listen, you don't have to worry about me. I'm not part of this group – just an actor. I've been playing these kinds of parts for years, and—'

'For the last time,' Pavlik said, honing an edge in his voice that made me fear for all mankind. 'This is *not* a show. A man has been stabbed to death, more than half devoured by a snake the length of a fishing pier, and this train is stranded in the Everglades with no current means of communicating to the outside world.'

'Oh.' Harvey seemed to deflate beneath his flashy sports jacket. 'Well, that's not good.'

'No, it's not,' said Pavlik. 'Your real name, please, as well as your profession and address?'

Harvey wiped his forehead on a cocktail napkin and scribbled his answers on another.

'Thank you,' Pavlik said, after reviewing the details. 'How many of the people on this train did you know prior to boarding?'

'Know personally, you mean?'

'Personally, or via telephone, telegraph, carrier pigeon, email, Facebook, Twitter.' Pavlik was getting wound up. 'I really don't give a shit, Harvey. Just tell me if you know any of these people.'

'And therefore have a motive, huh?' Harvey leaned back. 'Well, let's see. Zoe Scarlett. And Missy Hudson, of course, was the one who invited me.'

'Who else?' asked Pavlik.

'Well . . . no one,' Harvey said, trying to smooth down the independent-minded lapels of his God-awful sports jacket. 'I mean, not really.'

Even I could see that Harvey was prevaricating.

'How about Potter, Harvey?' the sheriff asked.

'What about Potter?'

Pavlik's eyes darkened. 'Cut the crap. Did you know anything about Laurence Potter before you boarded the train?'

'Well, well,' Harvey said. 'If you put it like that, of course I'd *heard* of Potter. What writer hasn't?'

'Then you're a writer as well?' I asked.

'As well as what?'

'As well as an actor.'

'Oh, yes.' Harvey dipped his head. 'I've tried my hand at the occasional screenplay or two, here and there.'

'And that's how you knew Potter?'

I could tell that Pavlik wasn't going to let go of his bone.

'I didn't say I knew him *personally*. A friend offered to show him one of my screenplays, but I ultimately decided against it.'

'Why?'

'A different friend warned me off. Said Potter had a reputation for . . .'

Pavlik growled, 'Giving unkind reviews?'

'Well, yes, that too, but my second friend was talking more about Potter stealing other people's ideas.'

'Like whose?' I asked.

'Rosemary Darlington, for one,' Harvey said. 'Word has it he was mentoring her a few years ago – professionally *and* personally, if you get my drift.'

I didn't bother to correct him. I was too busy thinking about Rosemary's slightly drunken suggestion that Danny was dogging Potter because the young man suspected the uber-reviewer had stolen his manuscript. Not to mention that I'd seen Danny whispering with Harvey on the bus.

'And that kid, Danny,' Harvey continued, like he'd read my mind. 'He's been pumping me for information on Pott—'

Two doors slid open in rapid succession and then Missy was standing there. 'I think you'd better come. And quick.'

'Why?' Pavlik and I answered in duet.

'Well, Audra has a gun and, oh, dear, she's going to shoot Boyce.'

TWENTY-FIVE

'I want to see my husband.' Audra Edmonds was, indeed, pointing some kind of pistol at Boyce, not three feet in front of her, Danny the Sycophant just to her side.

Boyce didn't look too worried. He was sitting on the stool we'd found for him, leaning against the door of the vestibule leading to the sleeping car, arms crossed. 'I'm afraid not.'

'Are you blind?' She waggled the barrel to prove her point. 'I have a gun.'

'And a permit for it?' Pavlik asked quietly from behind her.

Audra turned, startled, which is when Boyce stood and pushed down her wrist so the muzzle was pointing to the floor before he pried it from her hand.

'Of course I have a permit,' Audra said to the sheriff, rubbing her forearm and seeming dazed by his question. 'This is South Florida. Santa and his reindeer can carry concealed weapons.'

'Unfortunately, that's true,' Boyce said, handing Pavlik the gun, butt first. 'It's easier to get a CCW permit down here than a driver's license.'

'Or a Resident Beach Parking permit,' contributed Danny.

Absently, I wondered how he hyperlinked to that connection. And which of the two permits Danny had attempted to get.

The young man stepped past me to take hold of Audra's non-shooting arm. 'She's really upset,' he told Pavlik. 'Can we go to the club car, maybe find her something to drink?'

'As long as she doesn't expect to get this back anytime soon.' The sheriff held up the gun and we watched Danny and Audra shuffle/stumble off.

'Interesting,' I said under my breath. 'A variation on the *Deathtrap* twist, perhaps?'

'What?' Pavlik asked.

'Never mind,' I said, linking my arm with his. 'We'll watch it together some time. What's next?'

'Excuse me, Sheriff.' Carson/Count Andrenyi was standing in front of us.

'Yes?'

I couldn't remember if Pavlik knew who the man was. 'This is Carson, the lit—'

'Of course,' the sheriff said. 'I saw you in the club car earlier. You're Mr Potter's and Ms Edmond's agent.'

But when Pavlik extended his hand, Carson leaped back like a two-legged gazelle.

'He doesn't shake,' I whispered to my lover.

The sheriff lowered his hand. Slowly, I thought, so as not to embarrass Carson any more than the man had himself. 'What can I do for you?'

'I do understand that you're interviewing people in order and I should wait my turn.'

'He's Count Andrenyi,' I said to Pavlik. 'In Christie's sequence, the second to last.'

The sheriff shrugged. 'It sounded like a good idea at the time, but I think that moment has passed. Why don't you follow us?'

I led the way and got Carson a glass of water while Pavlik settled in across from him and opened his notebook. 'Do you have something you'd like to tell us?'

I tried to hand Carson the water, but he just waved me off, refusing to touch the glass.

I set it down and picked up the smart phone. 'Do you mind if I video our conversation?'

'No, I suppose not,' Carson said. 'Though I'd appreciate both of you keeping this confidential unless it has a bearing on Larry's death.'

'I'll do my best,' Pavlik said, 'but you have to understand that I don't have jurisdiction here. We'll need to answer the authorities' questions when they arrive, just like everyone else on this train will.'

Carson thought about that for a second. 'Understood.' He leaned forward. 'I'm a little concerned about Audra and that young man.'

Pavlik rocked three inches backward. 'That "young" . . .?'

'Danny,' I interjected. 'The one who was so interested in your workshops and who just escorted Audra to the club car.'

Mystery 101's principal forensics speaker shook his head. 'I'm starting to think you know more people here than I do.'

I shrugged. 'I get around. You've been . . . monopolized.'

'And I'm sorry about that,' Pavlik said. 'When we get—'

Carson cleared his throat.

'Sorry.' Pavlik shook his head again. 'It's been a long day. And night.'

'I understand,' Carson said. 'I just want to get this off my chest before I have time to think better of it.'

'Shoot.' The sheriff raised his pen. 'Uh, Danny?'

'Correct. The young man saw a trade announcement about a novel that Larry and Audra are working on. Danny got it in his head that Larry stole the idea from him and sent me an email outlining his accusations literally chapter and verse.'

So Rosemary, even under the influence, seemed to have been right.

'How is Potter supposed to have come across this "idea"?' Pavlik asked.

'Danny apparently sent him the manuscript originally, hoping to get Larry's endorsement or perhaps a referral to an agent, like myself, or an editor. Larry says . . . said that he didn't even open the package.'

'Did you believe him?' Pavlik asked.

'Of course. He's my client, after all.' An embarrassed smile. 'Or was.'

'So why has Danny been cozying up to Audra,' I asked, 'if he thinks she might have been in on this?'

'I have no idea. Perhaps he hopes Audra will confide the plot of their new novel, and therefore prove Danny right about the plagiarism.'

Or, I thought, maybe the two already *were* acquainted and had hatched a plot of their own. One that didn't include Laurence Potter lasting until the final chapter.

'So what's the book about?' Pavlik was asking.

'I can't really tell you that.'

'Carson, I'm certainly not going to steal Potter's plot,' Pavlik said. 'And even if I considered the possibility, I can't write.'

'It's true,' I told Carson as we heard the sound of the far vestibule door opening. 'The sheriff is addicted to redundancy.'

We all looked toward the door, but nobody entered.

Pavlik turned back to Carson. 'The plot?'

'The reason I can't tell you is because, well, there really isn't much of one.'

I mulled that over. 'So . . . Potter couldn't have stolen it?'

Carson shifted uncomfortably. 'From what I could tell from Danny's email, his manuscript doesn't have much of a plot, either.'

I felt like banging my forehead on the tabletop. Again. 'I don't understand.'

'You've read Rosemary Darlington's most recent book?'

'No,' Pavlik said.

'I haven't either,' I said, 'but I understand it's very steamy. Erotic. Is that what you're talking about?'

'Pretty much.'

'And that's what Potter's new book was to be like as well?' Sounded to me like Rosemary had more of a case against the recently deceased than Danny did.

'Everyone's doing it,' Carson said, 'which is part of the problem. Larry and Audra's had the twist of being written by a man and a woman. The reader sees the scenes from two different viewpoints.'

'Top and bottom?' I guessed.

Pavlik stifled a laugh. 'And what about Danny's . . . uh, "plot"?'

'From a man's point of view only.'

'Gay or straight?' I asked.

Carson cocked his head. 'You know, I'm not sure. But that might be a great twist for—'

This time Pavlik interrupted. 'Do you believe that Danny could have killed Potter over any of this?'

Carson shrugged. 'I wish I knew. These aspiring writers take everything so seriously. They don't understand that there are only a handful of basic plots with shoulders broad enough to carry the three-to-four hundred pages of a novel, and what we're all doing is re-imagining – no, more *spinning* – them. And even if someone did steal a concept, no two writers would come up with the same book.'

A gust of wind rattled the window next to us, making even our stationary train car sway.

Carson stood up. 'I've had my say, and thank you for the opportunity. Do with the information as you will.'

Pavlik stuck out his hand reflexively and then retracted it nearly as so. 'Thanks very much.'

After Carson left, Pavlik looked at me. 'Well, what do you make of his story?'

'Could be true, I suppose. According to Rosemary Darlington, Potter once tried to browbeat her into writing a novel to his specifications, with the further conditions being she'd publish it under her own name and split the proceeds fifty-fifty with him. Rosemary, smart woman, finally told him where to stick his book, but maybe Potter saw a brand-new opportunity when Danny's material landed on his doorstep. Except this time he had no intention of splitting the money or credit with anyone. Or at least not anyone but his wife.'

Pavlik nodded approvingly. 'Anything else?'

'Everybody seems to be writing dirty books.' I'd slid around to the back of the booth and was peering out the window.

'Makes you wonder where they're getting all their ideas, doesn't it?' Pavlik dug in his jacket pocket and produced the matchbook. 'Here, perhaps?'

'Here where?' I had my cheek close to the glass, a hand cupping my eyes in an effort to cut down on the glare of the interior lights so I might see into the natural gloom.

'You spot something out there?' Pavlik asked. 'Maybe a gremlin on the wing?'

'*Twilight Zone*, season five, *Nightmare at Twenty-Thousand Feet*, starring William Shatner,' I recited, still looking out. 'And, if you think about it, trains don't have wings. Though current events have persuaded me that fins mightn't be a bad idea.'

'The rain's coming down hard again?'

'Not really. In fact, I can see the moon. But there sure is a lot of water out—'

A rumble beneath us sent my face crashing against the glass.

TWENTY-SIX

'**A**re you all right, Maggy?'

'I think so.' Trying to sit up, I groaned. Apparently when the train shifted, I'd slammed my head and then shunted onto the floor beneath our table.

Pavlik, crouched in the aisle, extended his hand toward wending me out. Once emerged, I saw that the dining car was cockeyed, the side where we had been sitting noticeably about six inches lower than the other.

Engineer Hertel came lurching up, much like his train. 'Sorry, folks. Seems like all that rain we've gotten has undercut even these tracks we've just been sitting on. The ballast might be washing away and I'm starting to fear we're on the ground. Or will be soon.'

He fears we're on the ground? Ballast? I rubbed my temple where I could feel an unsightly egg already forming. I'd been thinking about airplanes before the crash, but . . .

I looked around. Nope, definitely a train, not a plane. Nor a submarine. 'I hate to ask this, but do we need to get to higher ground?'

Hertel scratched his nose. 'Well now, that wouldn't be a bad idea. If we had some, I mean. Not much in the way of elevation in these parts, although you might want to stay away from the lowest parts of the train so combined weight don't go flipping us over.'

My sheriff's head was swiveling. 'The club car behind us looks like it's at more of an angle than even this one. Any idea if the locomotive we're towing beyond is still on solid ground?'

'Well, sir,' Hertel said, hitching his fingers behind his overall straps. 'You gotta be careful when you're talking with a railroad man. Being "on the ground" is our way of saying derailment.'

'Derail . . .?' I echoed. 'Why—'

'Because a train's place is on the tracks, you see. Our wheels touch the ground and we're in real trouble.'

Ahh, now his earlier statement made sense. 'You said you feared we might be "on the ground." So you do think the train's derailed?'

'Not a clue, pardon my pun around you folks. Like I said, the ballast – that's the rocks in the train bed – might not be laid down proper. If that's so, there could be more problems coming.'

More problems?

Pavlik seemed to think about that. 'Is there anything we can do to head them off? I'm just thinking that if something as heavy as our rear locomotive tipped, it might be putting extra strain on the rest of the cars.'

I thought I saw what he was getting at. 'You mean like a Slinky, with the locomotive being the first coil starting down the stairs and the rest of us following?'

'Well, now.' Hertel pulled on his left earlobe as he considered that. 'I'd say it depends on how much of the track is washed away. I hate to speculate, you understand, but I'm startin' to wonder if, when they were running out of money, a few corners mightn't have been cut.'

'You mean a few *more* corners, right?' I asked. 'In addition to our not having a conductor?'

'Aw. Little lady, we don't need no conductor. All's they do is boss everybody around. Those FRA guys just want to provide work. Not that there's anything wrong with that.'

'FRA – Federal Railroad Administration?' Pavlik looked at me. 'I assume you spoke to Zoe or Missy about the train staffing?'

'Missy,' I confirmed. 'Somehow she managed to slide by the authorities – whatever they are for an "off-the-grid" operation like this – with a fictional conductor-backslash-bartender.'

'Well, now, that's not fair,' Hertel protested. 'Everything is fiction, when you think about it.'

I wasn't sure if he was talking about the mystery train or whether we were about to take a detour into Hertel's vision of metaphysics and the meaning of life.

I was inclined to pursue the subject, but Pavlik retook control of the conversation. Probably a good thing, since my mother always said if you're afraid of the answers, then you shouldn't be asking the questions.

'Assuming some of the cars are still . . . stable,' Pavlik said, 'would it make sense for us to uncouple any that might do us damage?'

'If you was Superman, maybe,' the engineer said.

'I take it that's a no?' Pavlik kept his tone even.

'You ever seen two train cars being coupled, Sheriff? They bang 'em one right into the other, like two big ol' Indian elephants doing the dirty. Sorry, ma'am.' A wink at me. 'These huge C-clamps, they hook together. Knuckle, we call it. You can't undo that with no screwdriver and pair of tweezers, I'm here to tell you. But aren't you getting ahead of yourselves?'

I looked at Pavlik, a little dazed by this outpouring of train lore. 'Umm . . .'

'Engineer Hertel's right,' Pavlik said. 'We need to know what we're dealing with and I'd like to leave Boyce here. Are you willing to be heroic again and come out with me to reconnoiter, Maggy?'

'"Nigh-on" to heroic, I believe was your term,' I said, smiling. 'But, of course, I'll go with you.'

In truth, my head was hurting where I'd bumped it, and the second last thing I wanted to do was to go outside with *any*one. The *very* last thing, though, was to let Pavlik do it alone. 'Should we check on the passenger car first?'

As I said it, the vestibule door from that direction slid open and Zoe stuck her head in. 'You OK in here?'

'We are,' Pavlik said.

'Thanks for asking,' I said, a little snippy. We could have been lying dead on the floor for all they knew, yet it was only now our comrades had thought to check on us?

'Assuming all is well in the passenger car, Zoe,' Pavlik said, 'Maggy and I are going to go out and take a look.'

'We're fine.' Zoe had one of Missy's shawls around her shoulders and, despite her words, seemed shaken. 'You go ahead.'

Pavlik was studying her. 'I should update Boyce first.'

Zoe held up her hand, palm out, and seemed to pull herself together. 'That's the least I can do, given everything you've already done for us.'

'We shouldn't be long.' Pavlik seemed reluctant to leave. 'You sure you're all right?'

'I am, Jacob.' Zoe smiled. 'But thank you.'

Enough of their lovefest. The egg on my temple was throbbing, and I wanted to get our second expedition in the books.

'I think you'll be just fine goin' out that way.' The engineer had the vestibule door between the dining and club cars open. 'She seems to be holding steady.'

Yippee. I pulled on Pavlik's sleeve. 'The sooner we go, the sooner we'll be back. You can brief everybody then.'

'She's right.' Zoe was pulling off her shawl. 'Would you like this, Maggy?'

Even I was getting suspicious. The woman was being too courteous, but, unlike Pavlik, I didn't give a shit why. 'Thanks, but I think I'll be fine.'

'You might wanna go while it's clear and you can see by the moon,' Hertel said, cocking his head toward the windows. 'Down here, storms come on as fast as they go.'

Pavlik was watching Zoe as she opened the door and stepped back through the vestibule. 'We will, but would you mind checking on the passenger car?'

Hertel looked surprised. 'Me? I thought I'd stand by right here. Make sure you get back safe?'

'That's not a bad idea,' I said to Pavlik. 'Whatever they're doing in there, we'll find out soon enough. Besides, we may need his help.'

Pavlik hesitated, then nodded. 'You're right.'

Back in the Flagler Suite, I would have asked the sheriff to repeat that, maybe teased him that he said it so seldom I wanted to hear it again.

But now, I just nudged one of our 'fingerprint' glasses out of the aisle with my toe. Another 'good idea at the time.' Too bad, but I assumed we'd each be fingerprinted officially when help finally arrived. After all, a man had been killed.

But as the three of us moved into the vestibule of the precariously tilted club car, a murderer amongst us seemed – however irrationally – to be the least of our problems.

TWENTY-SEVEN

'**C**areful,' Hertel called to us as I took the sheriff's hand and jumped down to join him on the railroad bed. 'That water's gotten mighty close in.'

The engineer was right. The good news was that the cant of the club car meant the distance from the exit door to the tracks was reduced. And the moon was bright enough for us to see, at least a ways. The bad news was that it allowed us to see that the tracks were nearly submerged.

'Hope those are old shoes,' Pavlik said, looking at my kitten-heel sandals.

'They are now, or at least they have been since our last foray out here.' I held up one foot. 'I think the cork platforms are coming unglued.'

'They're not the only thing here coming unglued.' The sheriff started to slosh east alongside the tracks. 'Did you notice Zoe was acting oddly?'

'Must be the stress,' I said, following him. Or maybe I'd scared her half to death with my talk of murderers everywhere. But it was true. Someone had killed Potter and right now it could be almost anybody, including Zoe herself.

Maybe that was why she was coming unhinged.

Pavlik was squinting up the line. 'Looks like the passenger and sleeping cars are still high and dry.'

'Well, that's good, at least.' I rubbed the bump on my head. The pounding was starting to lessen as we reached the front locomotive, still in place, nose down facing the flooded tracks.

'This seems pretty much the way it was earlier,' Pavlik said.

Earlier, as in the fight to reclaim Potter's body. Pavlik and I might have won the battle, but the python had certainly won the war. At least until the thing had explo— 'It's gone.'

'What's gone?' The sheriff had stepped up into the locomotive to look around and now stuck his head out.

'Our python.' A chill ran up my back as I pointed across the gulley to where the remains of the pregnant python had been strewn on the railbed. 'And its eggs.'

'Maybe it's the tide, if there is one. Or I suppose an alligator could have claimed it,' Pavlik said, jumping down from the cab. 'Poetic justice, given what we've heard about the balance of nature out here.'

'Too bad there aren't enough Bambis and Thumpers left in the Glades to rise up, unite, and exact revenge on the lot of them.'

'By Bambis, I assume you mean deer, though I suppose it could just as easily be a hot woman from a personal ad. But what are Thumpers?'

Poor boy. Yet another classic I'd force him to watch with me.

'Thumper is a bunny.' Then, fearing he'd think I was referring to the Playboy kind, 'You know, like Bugs?'

'Bugs?' Pavlik still seemed confused. 'Even in the Everglades, I don't think they have insects big enough to consume a snake's body in just a few hours.'

'No, no. Bugs! As in Bunny—' I interrupted myself as the sheriff waded into the water at an angle away from the train bed. 'Where are you going?'

'I'm just trying to get a better view of the trailing locomotive.'

'Oh.' Now that the rain had stopped, the nocturnal creatures seemed to be out in force. And in good voice. On a Wisconsin night you'd hear crickets and toads, maybe the occasional owl.

But the sounds of the Everglades were far more exotic. Rising from everywhere and nowhere – at least nowhere I could pinpoint. They seemed to have a physical presence and, of course, they did. We just couldn't see it.

'Hey, Pavlik, what is that?' I was looking at a mound rising from the water. Amazing I hadn't noticed it earlier, since it had to be a city block in width, or so it seemed in the low light. Directly opposite the sleeping car, the berm had a tangle of trees on it. 'Is it one of those mangrove islands you were talking about?'

'Maybe.' But he was gazing the other way.

I took a step closer to the water to get a better look. Away from civilization and its ambient light, the sky was hazy with stars. 'I think I see fireflies. But they're . . . I think they're red.'

'Fireflies aren't red.' Pavlik still wasn't paying attention.

'True. At least I've never seen any this color.' I waded in a cautious foot or two and squinted. 'I think there are two of them, but they're not flitting around like you usually see. Maybe sitting on something.'

'Two? How far apart?'

'Six or seven inches?' Another step. 'It's hard to judge from here.'

'Probably an alligator.'

I turned, though, in retrospect, that might not have been the smartest move of my life. 'Alligator?'

'Its eyes, to be precise. According to the pilot of the airboat ride we took the last time I was down here, their retinas reflect red in the dark.'

We took? Who was the 'we'? But something more immediate – and considerably less catty – also struck me as I splashed hastily back to dry land. 'Did you say airboat?'

'Airboat or fan boat, so-called because the flat-bottomed vessel has a giant fan up top that propels it over marshes and shallow water.'

Like the Everglades. 'I don't suppose the transit powers-that-be thought to equip the train with one.'

'An airboat that we'd stow and deploy like a life raft? Somehow I doubt it.' Pavlik returned to the track. 'Are you staying to explore, Marco Polo, or coming with me?'

I snuck a glance across the way to where I'd seen the red 'fireflies,' but they'd disappeared. Or, more likely from what Pavlik had said, crawled away on its belly like a reptile. 'With you. Definitely with you.'

As I trailed after him, the night animals shifted into high gear. *Chk, chk, chk, OWoo, Wwaahk, Wwaak. . . Quock! Quock, quock!*

'That last was a night heron, I think,' Pavlik said as we retraced our steps west along the railbed toward the exit door.

'We're probably disturbing them.' Happily, we'd be out of their hair – and feathers or scales or jaws – soon. As in, safe in the train.

'Most likely.' Pavlik passed the dining car and the entrance where Hertel waited and kept right on going.

'Aren't we going back onto the train?' I asked, hanging back.

'I have to check something out first. I'm hoping my eyes deceived me.'

I hesitated before following. Whither he goest, I will go. Whither I wanted to or not.

Hurrying to catch up, I nearly ran up the sheriff's back when he reached the rear of the club car and stopped.

'What is it?' I asked, pulling up short.

Pavlik pointed.

Our now trailing locomotive, the one that had earlier led us west, was illuminated by moonlight reflecting on the water.

The water on all *four* sides of the tipped locomotive.

'I guess there's no point worrying about uncoupling anything,' I said.

TWENTY-EIGHT

'**W**ell, I'll say I'm not surprised,' our engineer, Theodore B. Hertel, Jr, said after we filled him in. 'You *expected* us to get stuck out here?' I asked sourly. We were inspecting the club car, walking sideways in the aisle so we could grab hold of the counters and tables along the way to keep our balance. Boyce's espresso machine had bitten the dust again. I hefted the thing onto the bar and it slid right back off. This time I left it.

'No, ma'am. Not that. It's just that once the track started to wash out, what with the rain continuing and all, like I said, the ballast . . .' Hertel shrugged his shoulders, the denim straps of his overalls almost touching his earlobes.

I stopped short, causing Pavlik to run into me this time. 'Are you saying we could lose these cars, too?'

'I sure am hoping not,' the engineer said, opening the vestibule door to go into the dining car. 'The rain's stopped, which is always a good sign.'

This from the man who just an hour ago told us storms roared up quickly here.

Pavlik picked up his cell phone from the table we'd been sitting at when the car tipped. 'It's nearly four a.m.'

I said, 'What are we going to do?'

'I'm not sure there's anything we can do until the sun comes up.' Pavlik was pushing buttons on his smart phone. 'When it gets light, we'll decide our next move.'

'Do you have a signal?' I asked, my futile triumph of hope over experience.

'Afraid not.' Pavlik looked up from his miniature screen. 'I tried to send a text message last night, knowing they require less bandwidth than a call, but it wasn't delivered. I was checking now to see if we might have had intermittent service and the thing sent itself. No soap.'

The thought of soap made me feel my head where the bump was, to see if it needed cleaning.

'Still hurting?' Pavlik asked as we followed the engineer to the next car.

'A little, but I was just checking to see if the skin was broken. It's not, though.'

'I could have told you that.'

'You checked?' I asked, pleased he'd been concerned.

'Of course. If you'd been dripping blood out there, we would have been alligator bait. Or at least python nuggets.'

'Or both.' I punched him in the shoulder and then turned the other cheek, literally. 'Truly, can you take a peek? How do I look?'

Pavlik grinned and pulled me against him as we waited for Hertel to slide open the door. 'Lovely, as always.'

'Lie, Pinocchio, lie,' I chanted, parroting the old joke.

Entering the passenger car, I was surprised to see that people seemed unconcerned. In fact, they seemed to be having a fine time.

'Everything all right out there?' Prudence asked, pearls askew and her voice a little more airy than I'd previously heard it.

'Just ducky.' Pavlik put his hand on the back of the first seat and surveyed the scene. Then nearly under his breath, 'Jesus, Maggy. I think they're all drunk.'

The passenger car was, indeed, as high as it was barely dry. Zoe Scarlett was making her way to an empty seat, but instead of simply sitting down in it, she scarfed a bottle of what appeared to be Kahlua before moving on.

Pavlik shook his head. 'Well, that explains it. I'm going to check with Boyce.'

I followed the sheriff, stopping at the row Zoe had. There had to be fifteen bottles there, some on the seat, some in a box on the floor. Pete the bartender was snoring next to them, head tilted against the window.

'How'd you get the entire contents of the bar in here?' I asked Markus, who was slouching across the aisle.

'The bartender helped Audra and that kid Danny bring it to us.' He nodded about halfway back in the car, to where Audra Edmonds sat beside Rosemary Darlington.

Now *there* were curious seatmates. The widow and the woman she suspected her husband had been cheating with?

'And good thing, too.' Zoe was a few rows farther down with the Kahlua bottle. 'Since I'm not sure we'd want to go up there now.' She took a swig. 'Should have gotten glasses, though. This is unsanitary, even given the alcohol content as anti*slept*ic.'

She giggled, then stopped. Then resumed and couldn't stop.

Given the situation, it might not be the worst thing in the world if they all got drunk and fell asleep – or passed out – until help arrived, even if by boat.

Assuming it ever did.

Trying to remain positive, I continued on past Harvey/Hardman, who had his plaid jacket reversed and tucked under his chin. He probably meant it as a blanket but the effect was a really gaudy bib. Then again, you'd never see the food stains on it.

Pavlik was at the back of the car, talking to Boyce.

'You wouldn't have seen the three of them,' Boyce was saying. 'They bypassed the dining car where you were, coming back in this exit.' He pointed to the vestibule.

No wonder we'd heard opening and closing with no one actually entering the dining car itself. The threesome had risked going out into the Everglades to smuggle the booze without our noticing.

We should have asked *them* to be the scouting party.

I put my hand on the bathroom door handle, intending to check out the bump on my head, when it slid open and Missy appeared.

'Oh, I'm sorry, Maggy,' she said, stepping out. 'Go ahead, but be warned. It's pretty disgusting with all of us using just this one.'

I looked at Pavlik, thinking of all the toilets and sinks in the sleeping roomettes. 'Do you think we—'

He shook his head. 'Sorry, but we've already made things difficult enough for the crime-scene people. The least I can do is keep that car reasonably untainted.'

I sensed his frustration and put my hand out. 'Hey, you've done a great job of keeping everybody calm during a horrible situation.'

Harvey let out a snort and began to snore.

'Not, apparently, as effectively as the booze did,' Pavlik said. 'You want to take a break, Boyce? I can take over.'

'I don't mind if I do,' the other man said. 'This is one of those times I wish I still smoked, but maybe I'll just go answer the call of nature.'

I stepped aside to let him go into the bathroom, but he shook his head. 'Given the sheriff saying the rain has stopped, I think I'll venture out.'

Boyce continued on to the exit.

'Guys are so lucky,' I said. 'You can go anywhere.'

'One of our many charms,' Pavlik said. 'Why don't you get some sleep? Once the sun comes up, a couple of us will probably have to hike out of here and get help. I'd like you to be fresh.'

I sniffed my armpit. 'I'm not sure that's possible, but I'll do my best.'

Pavlik laughed.

But I put my hand on his forearm. 'Are you sure we should venture off our little . . . island instead of just waiting for help?'

'I'm not sure we have a choice, but we'll talk about it before I decide. For now, though, sleep. OK?'

As if I'd sleep. So I did the next best thing – found two open seats right behind Audra Edmonds and Rosemary Darlington.

'Hello, ladies,' I said, slipping into the window seat behind Audra. 'Don't let me bother you, I'm just taking a nap.'

'No bother,' Rosemary said, getting up. 'I'm grateful for the reprieve.'

'Bitch,' Audra said to her back as the author retreated.

'I take it Ms Darlington and you have some sort of . . . history?' I asked innocently, using Missy's word.

'No,' Audra said pointedly, 'but Rosemary and my husband did, much as she denies it.'

'I know that Mr Potter mentored her,' I was using last names to create distance from the participants, 'but are you saying they had something more?'

'That's exactly what I'm saying.' Audra turned and put her back against the wall of the train, stretching her legs out across the seats before smoothing the handkerchief hem of her vintage dress. 'The man is – was – the most calculating of cheaters.'

Edmonds managed to look bored. Amazing, given the subject and the fact that her philandering husband had rather recently also become her dead one. 'You know that book of hers? That fount of smut?'

'*Breaking and Entering*? I read Mr Potter's review of it on PotShots.'

Audra laughed. 'Review, my ass. The man was just covering his.'

'His ass, you mean?' I was confused. Again.

'Of course. You know all those things the couple does in her book? Those are the very same things Larry had been suggesting we do.'

'You mean in bed.'

'No, in the grocery store.'

And Pavlik thought *I* was sarcastic. 'You think he learned these . . . techniques from her?'

'Where else? Let me tell you, a husband suddenly comes home with new ideas to spice up the spousal love life, you better believe he's probably learned it through recent extramarital experience. Larry, in particular, wasn't the type to read and follow self-help books. More the help-yourself category.'

I wasn't sure I could argue with Audra's logic, and I had to give her credit for a nice turn-of-phrase. 'But weren't you and Mr Potter working on a book of your own?'

She snorted. 'Larry's idea. Both Rosemary and he must have had so much fun, they couldn't wait to write about it afterward. He was just ticked that she dumped him and then got to it first.'

'Hence the horrible review?'

'What do you think?'

I wasn't sure what I thought. 'Yet you and he were still intending to go ahead with your own . . . romantic novel?'

'The only reason he wanted my name on the book was for the hook. It would be sort of a he-said, she-said. Or *did*, in this case.'

I suppressed a smile. 'And did *you*?'

'Do those things?' Audra exploded. 'Of course not. Which

is how I know the old dog learned those new tricks from a different bitch. And probably by going to that horrible club, as well.'

'Titanium?'

She blinked. 'Yes. But how did you know?'

'The matches your husband was using.'

'So you saw them, too?'

I didn't tell her I'd also found the empty matchbook on the floor near the door where he might have made his final exit. 'I did. What kind of club is it?'

'Leather. S&M. Swingers. All of the above, and mostly mixed together.'

'You've been—?' I started to ask, but the look on her face was a conversation-stopper. 'On another subject, I know Mr Potter seemed to be having some sort of dispute with that young man, Danny. Has he been bothering you, as well?'

'You mean earlier tonight? Or I guess it would be last night, now.'

I nodded.

'Honestly? Yes. He wanted to know when Larry came up with the concept for the book.'

I didn't want to mention Carson, so I said, 'I heard Danny ask Mr Potter about the manuscript he sent him. Does he think your husband somehow stole his idea?'

'Of course. As if "boy meets girl, boy does girl and then both do everybody else in sight" is a ground-breaking development in human sexuality.'

'So you saw his manuscript?'

'Whose?'

'Danny's.'

'No, of course not. How would I do that?'

'I thought your husband might have showed it to you.'

'Larry and I share very little these days, including a bed. And by my choice, before you ask.'

Interesting. Yet the woman had taken the trouble to 'surprise' her guest-of-honor husband and seemed to have a considerable number of jealous bones in her body. A case of 'if I can't have him, nobody will'?

I said, 'You mentioned "boy meets girl," et cetera as the idea

Danny thought your husband stole. How did you know what his manuscript was about if you didn't see it?'

'The naive boy told me about it, of course. In return for this stunning revelation, I assured him his ground-breaking concept was safe.' Audra Edmonds shrugged and closed her eyes, seeming to lose steam. 'Believe me, Larry's book died with him.'

TWENTY-NINE

When Boyce returned from outside, he insisted on re-taking the watch from Pavlik. The sheriff slipped into the aisle seat and put his arm around me. I laid my head on his shoulder. 'Did Boyce see anything out there when he drained the lizard?'

'How you talk.' The sheriff nuzzled the side of my neck.

'So, I've been thinking.' I pushed myself up to see over the back of Audra Edmonds' seat. The woman was snoring softly, mouth open. 'Audra seems to be the most likely suspect in her husband's death, either alone or allied with Danny or even Carson.'

'Danny I can wrap my head round, but Carson? What would his motive be?'

I'd thought about that. 'He's in love with Audra and wanted Potter out of the way? Maybe there's a financial incentive for Audra to do away with Potter, rather than divorce him.'

'There's always a financial incentive. Believe me, no one comes away from a divorce in better shape than they went into it.'

I could sure attest to that. Happily, other considerations – things like human decency and the law – kept us from knocking off our spouses. For the most part.

'Audra just informed me that she's scrapping what she called "Larry's book,"' I told Pavlik. 'But who knows? Maybe she's lying and fully intends to finish and publish it. Plus, Potter's dramatic "exit" will mean lots of publicity, with only the grieving widow and Carson left to rake in the profits.'

The sheriff opened his mouth to comment, but I was on a roll. 'Audra and personal motives aside, maybe Carson had a pure business reason to knock off Potter – something to do with Danny's manuscript. Carson says Danny emailed him accusing Potter of stealing it, but perhaps he already knew what was going on. Larry could even have let him see the manuscript.'

'So Carson killed Potter, his client and perhaps co-conspirator? Why? Better that they take Danny off the board.'

'We know Potter turned to Rosemary to write for him once. Perhaps he wasn't a very good writer, but Carson got him the publishing deal thanks to his notoriety and profile. Then Carson read Danny's work and saw a promising young talent that could boost a literary agent's reputation and make him more money over time than Potter ever would have.'

'Why not just represent both?'

'I don't know enough about the book business to speculate.' Not that it stopped me, of course. 'Some kind of conflict of interest? Threat of lawsuits because of . . . creative jealousy? Writers rage?'

Pavlik ignored that. 'I honestly don't see Carson stabbing somebody to death, no matter which somebody. The man doesn't like to get his hands dirty, remember.'

'Maybe that's just a front. I mean, he refused to touch the water glass so we couldn't get his fingerprints and we thought nothing of it. Convenient, don't you think?'

'And he's nurtured this faux phobia all these years just for this moment?'

Suddenly exhausted, I scooched myself back against the sheriff and snuggled in, wrapping his arms around me like a blanket. 'You have a good point, not to mention a nifty way with words. The writers must be rubbing off on you.'

'They aren't the only ones rubbing on me.' Pavlik's breath tickled my ear. 'You'd better behave or I'm going to have to do you right here and now.'

'Threat or promise?'

Pavlik's arms tightened. 'Listen, Maggy. Boyce and I have been talking. Unless cell service improves now that the storm has stopped, we may have to hike out of here.'

I couldn't imagine convincing the other passengers to step into the water just to cross the flooded track, much less hike along the tracks once they reached the other side. Unless, of course, a booze bar or a giant bottle of aspirin was at the end of the rainbow, in which case all bets were off.

I turned to face him. 'It could be fifty miles back to Fort Lauderdale. And that's assuming, given the flooding, that there's a railway bed to walk on.'

'We'd take cell phones and call for help as soon as we reached an area where there was service.'

'That makes some sense. But you're not thinking everyone would go with us, are you? Plus, what about the alligators, snakes and all?' I fought the shiver that threatened to climb down my spine.

'Actually,' Pavlik said, seeming to tread carefully. 'I was thinking Boyce would come with me, given we don't know what we may find. Not only does he have some training, but he's an outsider to this group.'

I should have been relieved but, in truth, I was a little hurt. I might not be Linda Hamilton in *Terminator 2*, but hadn't Pavlik just complimented me on how well I'd accounted for myself under dire circumstances? 'So you trust *him*.'

'Yes. And I trust you, too.'

I brightened. 'So I *am* coming with you.'

'Honestly, I was hoping you'd take over Boyce's post and keep everyone else out of the sleeping car.'

I saw the reasoning, though I didn't like it much. But then how logical was it for me to be disappointed that I couldn't again become one with the denizens of the Everglades?

'Sure you want a sociopath minding the store?'

Pavlik smiled. 'Struck a nerve, did I?'

I shifted uncomfortably. 'My roommate in college called me a sociopath once. I guess ever since I've wondered if she was right.'

'What was her reasoning?'

'You mean besides her being a psych major? I found the apartment, so I took the bigger bedroom.' I shrugged. 'It seemed only fair to me.'

'Well, cheer up.' Pavlik gave me a squeeze. 'You're probably just self-centered.'

'Thank you. Coming from you, that means a lot.'

Pavlik looked past me out the window. 'There's a glow on the horizon. The sun is starting to come up.'

So it was. I could actually see the water and scrubby grasses across from us.

'And still not raining.' I sighed. 'When will you go?'

'Soon. But not until I've kissed you properly.'

And he did.

*   *   *

'But the dispatchers must have missed us by now,' Markus was saying. 'We haven't knocked the next signal down. They'll know exactly what block to find us in.'

'His family is in railroad,' I told Pavlik. I knew it sounded like 'my uncle sells insurance,' but even at this short acquaintance, I trusted Markus and his information.

Despite the 148 errors in his books.

Pavlik had briefed the passengers – now sober in more ways than the obvious – on our current situation, as well as his plan.

'What do you mean by knocking the signals down?' he asked Markus.

'There are electrical circuits on the track,' Markus explained. 'When a train passes through it breaks a connection – a signal – giving the train's location. That's what causes the gates to go down at railroad crossings and stop automobile traffic. A knocked-down signal also informs dispatchers that a train has crossed into another section or "block." Or not, in our case. It may take a while, but eventually someone will come looking for us.'

'We're saved!' Grace said, clapping her hands. Everyone was sitting up a little straighter, hangovers be damned.

Pavlik turned to Engineer Hertel. 'You couldn't have told me about this?'

'I would've if they'd been working,' the old man said, pulling at an ear. 'Same with the radios, which somebody neglected to equip with batteries before we left.'

Somebody. I wondered who. Or whom.

I was starting to wonder if the engineer was, in reality, an evil genius who'd hatched a plan to not only murder Potter and feed him to a giant python, but strand us here in the Everglades 'purely in-commun-i-cado' so he could make his escape.

If only he *would* make his escape.

The whole car had slumped again.

Pavlik just shook his head. 'Since I don't know how far we'll have to walk to find cell service and call for help, it may be a while before we get back. Hopefully not too long.'

'Are we talking hours or days here?' Harvey asked.

'Hours, I hope.' Pavlik turned back to the engineer. 'I assume we're most likely to find civilization by heading east.'

'You are. Besides the track not being finished all the way west anyway.'

'Good point,' Pavlik said lightly. 'Though I'm hoping we wouldn't have had to walk all the way to Naples anyway.'

'If you're not back by, say, tomorrow morning, what should we do?' Prudence asked. 'Send out a search party?'

Pavlik and Boyce were standing at the door by the dining car – the exit The Raiders of the Last Car had used to sneak back the booze. I was on the opposite end of the passenger car, keeping an eye on the door the coffee man had been guarding earlier.

'What do you think?' Pavlik said to his new sidekick. 'Noon tomorrow?'

Boyce nodded. 'Don't send anybody out alone, though. At least two people.'

A hand went up. 'But what about snakes? And alligators?' Missy asked in a shaky voice.

'We'll take my knife and Ms Edmonds' pistol.' Pavlik held it up, index finger carefully outside the trigger guard. 'If anyone else happens to have a—'

With that, a dozen handguns appeared from holsters and handbags, fanny packs and pockets.

Pavlik shrugged. 'How could I forget we're in South Florida?'

'Don't leave home without 'em,' Harvey said. 'I think you'll like my Glock Forty.'

'I have a forty-five Colt,' Prudence said. 'Great stopping power . . .'

Vaguely relieved that none of The (unofficial) Untouchables had sub-machine guns, I left the group to debate the relative pros and cons of our available weapons and sat down on the stool by the door, feeling adrift. Pavlik was the only one of these people I'd known for more than twenty-four hours, and now he was leaving me here alone with them.

And one of 'them' was a murderer.

Yes, it was for a good reason. And, of course, he was taking far more risk than—

'You OK?' Missy asked quietly. I hadn't noticed her come back.

I gave her a smile. 'Yeah, just a little—'

'Scared?' She sat down on the edge of the seat nearest me, legs swiveled into the aisle so we could talk. 'Me, too. This was all my idea and it's my fault that we're stranded here. And, and . . .' She gestured toward the door leading to Larry Potter's body and a sob escaped from her throat.

I tried to reassure the girl. 'You had no way of knowing a severe storm was going to hit or that the track bed would become unstable.'

'But that's the point,' she said. 'The mystery train which I wanted us to take wasn't up and running yet, so I, I . . . kind of cobbled things together.'

Hence, Theodore B. Hertel, Jr, the aged-out engineer, Pete the 'pretend' conductor/bartender and the incomplete and perhaps improperly built track. All to save face – and her event.

But no good would be served by reminding Missy of that now.

'Fine mess you got us into here,' a different voice snapped. Zoe Scarlett was standing over Missy. 'Stuck here without any food and now we're even running out of things to drink.'

I was thinking cause and effect. Zoe looked like she had one howler of a hangover.

'I'm so sorry,' the girl said tearfully. 'If you want, I'll go with the sheriff and Mr Boyce.'

'You'll do no such thing,' I said. 'We may need you here.'

Pavlik came up behind Zoe's right shoulder. 'You two ladies mind if I have a word alone with Maggy?'

Missy sniffled and shook her head, disappearing into the stinky bathroom. Zoe pivoted and went a few seats back and collapsed, palm to her forehead.

Pavlik held out a smallish gun to me, and I took it from him carefully. It was a semi-automatic, but that's about all I could tell you. Nor, believe me, did I know or care whether the diameter of the ammunition was measured by caliber or in millimeters. 'Loaded?'

'It is. Plus the safety is off and I've chambered the first round, so if you pull the trigger, a slug flies out of the muzzle and toward whatever you're aiming at.'

'How many bullets in this?'

'Seven. Just level on bad guy-or-girl's belt buckle and fire 'til they fall. Oh, and here's some extra ammunition.' He handed me something the size and shape – if ten times the heft – of an old kitchen matchbox.

If I couldn't stop the killer with seven, I somehow didn't envision having the time, or even know-how, to reload, but I accepted the extra rounds from him. Their 'box' reminded me of the match*book* I'd found. 'I know this doesn't have any bearing on our most immediate problem, but Audra Edmonds says Titanium is a sex club her husband spent time at. Pointedly without her.'

'A woman scorned?' Pavlik suggested.

'A woman cheated upon,' I said. 'Believe me, we're capable of anything.'

'Thanks for the warning.' He put his hand on my shoulder. 'You going to be all right here?'

I wanted to say, 'No. Take me with you. Leave a bigger, stronger, actually *trained* Boyce here with these strangers, one of whom is a killer.'

Instead, I stood up. Setting the gun and ammunition carefully on the stool, I wrapped my arms around Pavlik and rested my head on his chest. 'I'll be fine.'

He caressed my hair. 'Take the stool and sit on the sleeping-car side of the door. Don't worry about touching things, the police can always take and then exclude your prints. If anybody tries to come through this door, warn them you'll shoot. They keep coming, blow them away.'

'Gotcha.'

Pavlik tilted my face up toward his. 'I'm serious.'

'I know you are. I won't let anybody in.'

'It's not protecting the crime scene I'm worried about. It's your being hurt.' Pavlik's eyes were about as dark as I'd ever seen them.

I pulled his head down to my lips and kissed him. 'Please come back soon. And safe. I'll be OK, but just . . . please come back.'

'You got it.' He was smiling. 'Believe me, the last thing I want to tour is the inside of a python's gut.'

'Which *would* be the last thing you ever toured. Promise me if you come across any predators, you'll shoot first and worry about environmental protection later.'

'Promise.' He crossed his heart with his fingertips and then touched them to my lips.

I smiled and stepped back. 'Got your cell phone? And is it all charged?'

'Yup, and Boyce is AT&T and I'm Verizon, so we've got at least those two carriers covered.'

'Would you like to take mine, too, just in case?' I dug it out of my pocket. 'It's not doing me any good here.'

'I could, but then how would you count the minutes until my return?'

'Huh. That's very true.' I slipped the phone back into my pocket. 'Now get the hell out of here and save us.'

THIRTY

When Pavlik and Boyce left the train at 8 a.m., I waved goodbye through the window.

Happily, the day had dawned bright and sunny. Locals said that sunset would be around 6:30 p.m. this time of year, so that would give the two men more than ten hours of daylight. I hoped that was enough.

In fact, I was kind of hoping they'd walk about 100 feet, raise the cell phones over their heads like I always did when I was looking for service and, bingo, there it would be.

Once they'd been gone a half hour, though, I decided to do as Pavlik suggested.

'I'm going to move into the next car,' I told Missy. 'Would you make sure people know it's still off limits? Pavlik told me I should shoot to kill.'

Missy's eyes grew wide. 'You know how to fire a gun?'

'Pavlik taught me,' I said. 'But what about you? I keep hearing how everybody here has a permit to carry.'

'Oh, I do, too,' Missy said, 'but I barely know which end of my gun to hold. They only have you fire three bullets to qualify at the gun range.'

South Florida sure did seem to make it easy, but given the wildlife, I wasn't sure I blamed the authorities. If an alligator or python walked or slithered into my backyard, I might want some way to protect myself and any kids or pets.

Leaving Missy behind, I went through the door into the vestibule, where I'd found the matchbook, and then on to the sleeping car. The interior of it was very quiet.

Setting down the gun and the box of extra bullets by the door to the roomette where Potter's body lay, I returned to the passenger car to retrieve the stool.

'Am I in your way?'

I turned to see Danny sitting across the last two seats on the right, back against the window, feet poking into the aisle.

'No, you're fine,' I said, folding up the stool. 'I just need to take this back. If you're going to be sitting here, could you let people know the sleeping car is still off limits?'

'Sure.' He swung his legs off the seat and leaned forward. 'Missy already told me that, though. I think she went to get cardboard and markers to tape something up on the door.'

The girl was a natural event-planner. When in doubt, make a sign.

'Missy's great,' I said, figuring it couldn't hurt to build her up in his eyes. Maybe something good could come of this trip. 'She's very . . . efficient.'

Way to go Maggy. Every guy is looking for a woman who's . . . 'efficient.'

'Yeah, and kind of sexy, too.' I brightened momentarily, but he finished with, 'Too bad she's not my style.'

I wondered who was. Audra Edmonds, perhaps?

I perched on the edge of the seat across from him, thinking that with Pavlik off on his mission to find help and get us out of here, this might be my last opportunity to grill Danny. Or at least I hoped it would be. 'Bet you didn't expect all this when you signed up for the conference.'

'You've got that right. I really lucked into it.'

'There's a dead man in the next car and we're stranded in the Everglades. You call that "luck"?'

'But look who the dead man is. And who I'm stranded with. I hear people bond for life over experiences like this. You can ask them for favors years later and they'll come through.'

'You remind me of my son,' I said, lying through my teeth. Eric was five years younger and an actual human being.

'Oh, yeah?' Danny said. 'Does he write?'

'No, but he texts regularly.' I smiled. 'Now tell me about your book – or is it called a manuscript at this stage?'

'Getting closer to becoming a book with every minute we're here.' He lowered his voice confidingly. 'I've snagged an agent.'

'Congratulatons!' I said. 'Who is it?'

'Carson – that guy who doesn't shake hands. Audra introduced us.'

How accommodating of the widow. And the agent. Maybe my

speculation about Carson wasn't as farfetched as Pavlik seemed to think. 'But isn't that a little awkward?'

'Awkward? Why?'

'I understand your book is very much like Mr Potter and Ms Edmonds' projected novel.'

'Projected, maybe. But it's not going to happen.' The kid might be sitting down, but there was a definite swagger in his voice.

'Really?' I asked innocently. 'Have you and Ms Edmonds decided to collaborate on *your* book, instead?'

'My book?' He seemed genuinely shocked.

'Yes, of course. Since Audra introduced you to her agent, I thought she might have a new partnership in mind. Assuming,' a thought had struck me, 'this all happened after her husband was dead.'

The young man's eyes narrowed. 'What do you mean by that?'

I shrugged. 'Seems clear to me. Did Audra introduce you to Carson before or after the sheriff and I returned to the train with Potter's body?'

I could see the wheels turning in the young man's head. 'After, definitely after. I remember because I figured Audra agreed to introduce me because she was grateful for my help.'

'Your help?'

'Sure. We bonded when I took her to the club car after she nearly shot that guy.'

Boyce, standing guard over Potter's already cold body.

On the other hand, sweat was beading on Danny's upper lip. 'Shit. I hope she didn't get that idea. I mean, Audra's awfully old and this is a sex book.'

I opened my mouth to inform the little twerp that even a woman of Audra's advanced age, which I judged to be early forties, still had sex.

And then I remembered she apparently didn't. At least, not with her husband.

Back in the sleeping car, I unfolded the stool and situated it across from the door of the roomette where Potter's body lay. Sitting down, I tried to figure out what to do with the pistol. On the floor, it was too far away from me to easily reach. Maybe I'd just sit on the floor next to it.

Though I'd wasted ten minutes of my life going back to get the stool, at least my conversation with Danny had been enlightening. If the kid was to be believed, he'd achieved everything he'd wanted when he'd set foot on the bus: not only was there no book forthcoming from Potter and Edmonds, but he'd secured a literary agent.

According to Danny, the initial contact with Carson had been via email – almost certainly the accusatory message Carson had mentioned. Then, in gratitude for Danny's aid during this so-called bonding opportunity he had 'lucked into,' Audra had introduced aspiring writer to agent.

Carson hadn't yet been approached by Danny when Pavlik and I met with the literary agent in the dining car but, given his suspicions of the kid, wouldn't it have made sense to inform us of this new development?

Maybe the germaphobe's hands *weren't* quite as clean as he'd like people to believe.

I shivered, suddenly very glad Pavlik had suggested I camp out in the sleeping car, even if its only other occupant was a corpse. Or maybe because of that.

Moving the stool out of the way, I decided the best place to sit was with my back against the wall of the roomette across the narrow corridor from Potter's – this despite the nasty smells not quite contained inside. But this way, at least, I could comfortably keep a peripheral eye on that door as well as the outside exit and the doors leading to the passenger car.

But first . . .

Gun ready in my hand, I slid open the door across from Potter's, clearing that roomette as Pavlik and Boyce had.

The space was empty, of course. Once I checked that one, though, I felt like I had to do the others, just to be sure. I went down one side of the car and into both shower rooms, my still-damp sandals echoing on the tiles. Then I worked my way back up to the space where Potter's body lay.

I slid open the door and, holding my breath, stepped over the two frosting smudges and into the room. Potter was on the bunk, of course, faced away from me like he was still just napping.

I tiptoed nearer, still trying not to breathe, and—

'Maggy?'

I jumped back and turned, raising the gun, which was now moving in sync with my shaking hand. 'Holy shit, Missy! You scared me to death. What are you doing in here?'

Missy looked hurt. 'Well, I knocked on the door to give you this, but I didn't hear any answer.'

She was holding out an e-reader. 'I've got a ton of books loaded on it and I figured it would help you pass the time. Oh, and I also put a "Keep Out" sign on the other side of the door.'

My heart-rate descended toward quasi-normality. 'Thanks, Missy – that's very nice of you.' I took the reader. 'And I'm sorry I yelled. And, well, almost shot you. I must have been at the other end of the car checking the showers when you knocked.'

'No, I'm the one who should be sorry,' Missy said, her eyes welling up. 'But when you didn't answer, I was worried.'

'I appreciate that. I was just making sure everything was secure.'

She glanced over at the bunk, her nose wrinkling and her next words a little strangled. 'Can we get out of here?'

'With pleasure.' I let her precede me out the door. 'And thank you again.' I held up the e-reader.

Missy smiled. 'You're welcome. Come to the door and call out if you need anything.'

'I will. Thanks.' As she turned away, I couldn't resist saying, 'I noticed you talking with Pete. He seems like a nice guy.' Unlike Danny. 'And really good-looking.'

'I suppose, but too young. And a waiter.'

My, my, but the younger generation was picky. 'Everyone has to start somewhere.'

Missy sniffed. 'His real name is Brandon. I saw him at the restaurant last week and asked if he'd like to earn some extra money.'

'That was smart.'

'You're telling me. You know how much it costs to hire a professional bartender? And I bought all the liquor at Costco.'

You had to give the woman credit. She knew how to stretch a dollar. I hoped it wouldn't come back to bite her in the form of lawsuits by the passengers on the train and even the train company itself.

Which was another reason I'd wanted out of event planning:

the liability if something went awry. At least I'd been bonded and had a corporation standing behind me. If I were Missy, I wouldn't expect a whole lot of support from Zoe.

After the young woman left, I settled onto the floor. Propping the gun against my right thigh, I picked up her e-reader.

She wasn't kidding about the books. A ton of them and, in the mix, some of Rosemary Darlington's.

Including . . . I scrolled down. Yes, *Breaking and Entering*.

Leaning my back against the wall, I punched up the book cover. Steamy, in itself. A woman in red leather, a dog collar around her neck and a whip in her hand. A man's naked body was half-hidden in shadows, the glass of a broken window on the floor nearby.

I looked around guiltily, like I was twelve and reading the early scene in Mario Puzo's *The Godfather*, where Sonny and the bridesmaid . . . well, you know. I clicked to the next page. These e-readers were great – convenience, discretion, *and* they couldn't accidentally fall open to the spicy pages you've read. And reread.

The first chapter was a lot of set-up. I yawned, resisting the urge to peek ahead.

Kat opened the door, knowing what she wanted but not if she had the nerve to take it. He was lying on the bed facing the window, his skin glistening in the moonlight. The edge of the white sheet revealed his firm, naked glutes. Kat wanted – she desperately needed – to run her fingers along the curve of them.

As Kat reached out, the man roused. Stepping back, she watched from the shadows as he rolled onto his back, sending the sheet slipping to the floor.

Kat nearly gasped aloud. She moved forward, waiting for him to settle before she let her nails barely touch, tracing his mustache and lips. The curve of the neck cords to his throat.

Thud-thud, thud-thud, thud . . .

The pulse suddenly stopped under her fingertips.

Panicked, Kat laid her hand flat against his chest. She was praying now, to feel something, anything inside.

A flutter. Not quite a beat, more a . . . twitch? Once, twice, three times. It grew stronger and then stronger again, settling into a rhythm before seeming to coil back on itself, regrouping to race faster, heading toward a seemingly inevitable crescendo. Then, just as Kat thought her own chest would burst, his did. Bits of tissue and cartilage splattered onto the window pane, seeming to mingle with the rain streaking down the outside of the glass.

Kat held her hand up in front of her, trying to understand what had just happened. Blood and something thick and white covered her fingers.

A movement caught Kat's eye. She looked down into the man's open chest and . . . it looked back at her.

A python. Where Larry Potter's heart should be.

THIRTY-ONE

'Stay away from the pointy end!' I yelled, my head falling back against the wall, waking me.

Looking around, I waited for my own heart to settle back into my chest. Sunshine poured in from the windows by the vestibule door and I could hear voices – if not cheerful, at least reassuringly alive – in the passenger car beyond.

Apparently, I'd nodded off and managed to combine our current situation and Rosemary's book into one hell of a dream. Getting to my feet, I retrieved the pistol and, holding my breath, crossed the aisle to Potter's roomette and opened the sliding door. Still there, chest intact, no snakes in sight. Check, check, check.

My cell phone told me it was 10:20 a.m.

I slid Potter's door closed. Some guard I was. Not only had I fallen asleep for two hours, but I'd awakened with a full-blown case of the heebie-jeebies.

As I turned from the corpse I was responsible for guarding, my stomach growled. I wasn't sure what that said about me, but I feared it wasn't good.

I also needed to use the bathroom, preferably not the one in what I'd come to think of as Potter's room. I also didn't want to return to the passenger car or dirty an unused roomette's facilities.

That left the compartment Rosemary had napped in. It was at the end of the hall, but I could leave the door open so I'd hear anyone coming through from the passenger car, as Missy had.

As I flipped open the toilet, I thought about the one in Potter's room. I'd touched it when we'd found the cigarette butt and I hoped that wouldn't cause problems with the police. Potter obviously hadn't been stabbed in there anyway, because there was no blood.

In fact, come to think of it, I hadn't seen blood anywhere when I'd inspected earlier.

How could that be?

After washing my hands, I sat down on Rosemary's bed to think. Had Laurence Potter been killed when the train stopped because of the flooding? It had seemed an outside chance when Pavlik and I first talked about it, but if the victim had been stabbed outside, it would explain why there was no blood found on the floors inside the train.

But stabbed by whom? And where had Potter been up to that point? We knew he'd visited the sleeping car, as evidenced by the cigarette butt in the toilet. The possibility he'd been tucked away with Rosemary in this roomette had certainly occurred to me, as it had to Audra, Potter's wife.

Could Rosemary have faked the motion sickness to have an excuse to lie down? Perhaps she'd invited Potter to steal away for a little early evening delight and, when he'd arrived, killed him. Perfect timing and apparent alibi. The female guest of honor was drunk and sleeping it off.

Then there was Audra. She'd said she wasn't sleeping with Potter and that it was by her own choice. Was that the truth? Or the words of a woman determined to save face with people who might know more about her husband's peccadillos than she did? If I'd gotten wind of Ted's extracurricular activities would I have shown up at one of his conferences, as Audra had?

I thought so. The only thing worse than *knowing* is suspecting. Always wondering if you're being made the fool. That suspicion, in and of itself, could make you act foolishly.

Could it also make you a killer?

Audra had been with us in the dining car when her husband had disappeared, but she certainly could have slipped out later and killed him. Ditto pretty much anyone else on the train, given the one-hour window of opportunity from nine to ten p.m. that Pavlik and I had settled on. Even Zoe Scarlett, once she'd finished her welcome speech. Much as I'd love to pin the murder on the woman, though, I couldn't see why Zoe would kill her guest of honor. Sure, she might have had the unrequited hots for Potter, but the same was true for Pavlik and he was still alive, right?

Please, God.

I twisted to look out the window, blinking back unexpected tears. But there was no Pavlik to the rescue, no anybody. A train full of people and I'd never felt more alone.

Wah-wah-wah. I wasn't the one tramping about in the Everglades with snakes and alligators.

Ignoring the inner voice that said, *No, you're the one sitting on a train with a corpse and a killer,* I stood up. Time to man my post. And man up, period. Tucking the bunk's pillow and blanket under my arm, I returned to the corridor outside Potter's room and settled onto the floor.

Pillow stuffed comfortably behind my back, I tried to think. Specifically, *not* about Pavlik.

So how about Danny? Without Audra as co-conspirator, I didn't see what he would gain by killing Potter rather than suing him for stealing his work. In fact, it suddenly occurred to me, wouldn't the kid be best off waiting until Potter's book was published, so he could jump on the bandwagon (if there was one) and really benefit from its success?

I supposed it could have been in the heat of the moment – Potter being his supercilious self and the kid just having enough – or a bit too much – of it.

When you thought it through, though, anybody who killed Potter must have done it without premeditation, since we assumed it was Potter who had carried both the hunk of cake and the knife – the eventual murder weapon – back here.

Kind of blew my original theory that Audra had been working in tandem with Carson or Danny. So where did that leave me?

In a word? Nowhere, just like Hercule Poirot in the original *Murder on the Orient Express.* And since Potter had but a single knife wound, I couldn't even fall back on Agatha Christie's multiple killer solution for my 'aha' moment.

I eyed the two frosting smudges on the floor. One marked where I'd stepped on the cake. Could the other have been where the knife lay before the killer picked it up and plunged it into Potter?

But, again then: where was the victim's blood?

I got up and scanned the walls and the carpet. Nothing was exactly clean, but I was fairly certain I'd be able to spot a blotch of blood. No, the only blood in this car was what I'd felt on the exit door handle and gotten on my hand like the fictional Kat in my dream.

Blood, in that case, and thick white . . . what?

I jumped up and went to the exit. Because the sun was shining in from the window across the way, I could get a better look than I had the night before. There was certainly something dark there, but what I'd felt had been sticky, meaning the blood hadn't completely dried yet, I supposed. How long would that take, given the natural humidity of the Everglades and the artificial air conditioning on the train?

Trusting Pavlik that my prints could be excluded – and figuring I'd already touched the thing anyway, so whatever potential damage was really damage done – I gingerly touched the door handle. No longer sticky, but dry and crusty. Crouching down, I saw something else – something glistening. I touched it with my finger and this time it did come away sticky. And red, almost gelatinous.

Wait a second. First warily sniffing it and then touching it to my tongue, I realized it was cake decorating gel. The stuff that had been used to represent blood on the cake.

Returning to Rosemary's bathroom, I washed my hands in the pull-down sink, taking a paper towel out of the wall dispenser to dry them as I walked back.

The piece of cake Potter had taken – the foot – hadn't had any of the fake blood on it. That decorative touch was concentrated around the knife 'wounds.' That meant whoever had touched the door handle had also held the knife.

Potter? And . . . his killer?

I settled back down onto the floor of the sleeping car and picked up Missy's e-reader. I didn't expect to get any more reading done, even if the story had intrigued me. Of course, what I'd actually read and what I'd dreamed might be two entirely different things.

I pushed the toggle on the reader and the John Steinbeck screensaver morphed into words. Curious to see what the last paragraph I'd read was, I saw:

Kat opened the door, knowing what she wanted but not if she had the nerve to take it. He was lying on the bed facing the window, his skin glistening in the moonlight. The edge of the white sheet revealing his firm, naked glutes. Kat wanted – she desperately needed – to run her fingers along the curves of them.

As Kat reached out, the man roused. Stepping back, she watched from the shadows as he turned onto his back, sending the sheet slipping to the floor.

'Oh, dear,' Kat nearly gasped aloud.

I laughed, recognizing Missy's pet expression. I'd forgotten that Missy had worked with Rosemary on the book, though apparently my subconscious hadn't. It had even inserted snakes, though that vignette might have had to do more with our current situation than my conversation with Missy about researching them for *Breaking and Entering.*

Regardless of Rosemary's writing and my imagination, though, it was very nice of her to insert a piece of Missy in the book. I'd bet the girl was thrilled.

Then I shifted, intending to do a search for 'snake' in the text and see if Rosemary had been more imaginative in its use than I had. I had a feeling my dream had been much tamer than the real thing – or the real *fictional* thing, to be precise.

I slid over the pistol to get comfortable, in the process accidentally setting it on the damp paper towel I'd brought back.

'Better not do that,' I said to myself, a little punchy despite my nap. 'Guns are metal and some metals rust.'

Pulling the towel out from under the firearm, I leaned forward, intending to dab at the frosting on the carpet in front of me.

At the last moment, I pulled back. If I was right about the cake and the knife lying there, I'd be an idiot to mess with the evidence. Not that it would be the first time.

The paper towel and the cake reminded me of something, though. What was it?

The towel wasn't unusual. From what I'd seen, the same ones were used in the bathrooms throughout the train. In fact, Missy had left one on the table in the dining car when she'd thought Zoe was going to introduce her as Mrs Hubbard.

Instead the woman had introduced Audra Edmonds, Larry Potter's wife.

But why would that be significant? By then Potter was

already missing. Whether he was dead, we didn't know. Missy had gone out even earlier, taking Rosemary Darlington to the sleeping car. Could our event planner have seen Potter on her way back?

Had – and I couldn't even believe I was thinking this – had the two of them quarrelled and Missy stabbed him, then stopped to wash the blood off her hands, brush her hair, apply lipstick and return to the table?

Ridiculous. And even if it were possible, why? What possible connection could there be between the slightly awkward young woman and the great Laurence Potter?

The e-reader was still in my lap. I toggled the switch and the page came up, the words 'Oh, dear,' leaping out at me.

Missy was a researcher and worked for Rosemary Darlington on this book.

Missy, the seeming innocent, knew what 'Titanium' was when I showed her the matchbook.

Breaking and Entering was a complete departure from anything Rosemary had ever written.

Potter had said the woman he'd known 'could never have written this current pile of excrement.' Were the words an overstatement, made for effect, or did the reviewer actually believe Rosemary Darlington didn't write *Breaking and Entering*? And if so, how would Potter be in a position to know that?

'Position,' I said out loud. Audra thought her husband had 'learned things' from Rosemary. What if, instead, both of them had learned them from Missy. Rosemary Darlington, literarily, to use in her book and Potter . . . literally?

Could Potter and *Missy* have been involved in an affair? She certainly wouldn't be the first insecure young woman to fall victim to an older man who's more interested in punching her ticket than validating it.

Missy would see Potter as a famous, interesting, and therefore powerful figure in the industry. Very different than Danny and Pete, who were too young and unsuccessful for her taste. But if Laurence Potter wanted her, that was different. It would mean *she* was different.

So what had happened? Had Potter been angry after reading

Rosemary's book? Had he recognized Missy as the true writer and threatened to expose Rosemary?

If so, both Rosemary and Missy might have a reason to kill him. Could they have teamed up on the guy? Only if all three of them – the two women and Potter – were here in the sleeping car together.

I got up and went back to the vestibule and the exit, taking the paper towel with me. First, I examined the surface of the door as well as the walls to its sides. I didn't see any signs of blood or even frosting, but the lab would know for sure. Since I'd already done enough preservation-of-crime-scene damage, I used the towel to carefully open the door.

It slid without difficulty. Certainly easily enough for even a small woman to yank it open and let somebody with a knife in his back 'exit the train' with no one the wiser.

I jumped down onto the railway bed.

The water seemed to be receding. At least three feet of gravel stretched from each side of the track before the bed sloped away into the wetland. A big improvement over what Pavlik and I had dealt with during our trips outside.

Across the way, I saw that the 'island' I'd spotted on our last excursion was, indeed, a rise of land supporting the growth of sawgrass, tangled shrubs and even some scrubby-looking trees. I wished Pavlik was here to tell me if they were mangroves or not.

The sun was nearly straight-up noon. The sheriff and Boyce had been gone for four hours, and it could be many more before they returned. In fact, they'd told us to wait a full twenty-four before even sending out another scouting party. I wasn't sure I could stand by and do nothing for that long.

Turning back to the train, I stood on my tiptoes to reach the top of the vertical grab bar next to the door. Running my hand along the bar, I knew I was searching for some kind of confirmation.

If Potter had been stabbed outside the train after we'd stopped, his assailant would have gotten gunk on the railing or outside door handle as he – or, more and more likely, she – had swung back in. And then again on the inside door handle, where I'd already found it, when the killer closed the door.

But . . . nothing. No stickiness on the grab bar or on the outside door handle, which I checked next. I supposed the driving rain could have—

A shadow shifted on the opposite bank, just twenty feet away.

'Alligator,' I said out loud, if in a slightly ragged tone.

'Oh, dear.'

THIRTY-TWO

Missy's voice had come from behind me.
I turned. The girl must have circled the end of the sleeping car and was standing about as far away from my position as the shadow had been across the water in the other direction.

'You scared me,' I said for the second time that day.

'Sorry, Maggy. We're all going stir crazy in there, so I thought I'd come out for a stroll in what passes for fresh air this time of day.'

Missy was right about the 'passes' part. You could nearly see the steam rising off the plants in the midday sun.

'Is it safe to be wandering?' I glanced toward the alligator. Or the void where it had been. Suddenly an alligator you couldn't see was worse than one you could.

'Don't worry.' Missy lifted up a revolver with a short but stout barrel, her hand holding the 'right' end. 'I have a gun.'

Oh, I was worried, all right. Mostly because I did *not* have one. I'd left the semi-automatic Pavlik had given me on the floor of the train when I'd jumped down, thinking I'd quickly finish what I needed to do and be back inside. Like they say, though – the first step was a doozy.

And so here I was.

Missy raised the muzzle of her gun on a line with my belly button, then stepped toward me. 'What were you doing?'

'What do you mean?' I was trying to keep my voice casual.

'You were polishing that railing or whatever it is. Did you find something wrong?'

'Nope,' I said. 'I'm just a little ditzy. I fell asleep reading a passage on the device you so kindly loaned to me, and I had a dream about snakes. I came out here to reassure myself that none were poking around the train and, umm . . . dried off the rail so I wouldn't slip getting back in.'

It was a little weak, but then so was I at the moment.

'Oh, were you reading *Breaking and Entering*? I'm surprised you got to the snake part so fast. Were you skipping ahead?' Missy looked so proud I decided to go with it.

'Couldn't resist. I also noticed the use of your catchphrase. That was so nice.'

Her face darkened. 'What do you mean?'

'The "oh, dear." You say it all the time. I thought it was a great compliment to you that Rosemary had Kat using it.'

'Oh, yes,' Missy said, lowering the gun's muzzle. 'That *was* nice. Sort of a . . . a—'

'Tribute,' I finished for her. It was apparent to me that Missy hadn't even realized until this moment that, as a writer, she'd given her main character her own subliminal signature. 'In gratitude for all the hard work you did, researching and all.'

'Yes.' Missy tried to smile. 'That was . . . nice.'

Allrighty then. 'Well, I'd better get to my post. Good talking to you.'

'You, too.'

As I grabbed the bar to pull myself up, I heard the sounds of Missy starting to move away, the staccato of the glittery heels on the gravel, the swish of the evening gown in the abominable humidity. Then stillness.

'You know.'

I debated whether I should continue my swing up onto the train and slam the door closed.

In that second of deliberation, I lost that option.

When I looked back, Missy was still there, gun levelled at my waist. 'I said *you know*, don't you?'

I let go of the bar and dropped back down to the railroad bed. 'I don't know anything, Missy.'

She smiled, but unhappily. 'No, I'm the one who doesn't know anything. Not even what I put in my own book. Or Rosemary's, I should say.'

'So you ghost-wrote the novel. That's perfectly legitimate. And you did a good job. Rosemary must be very pleased.'

'She is,' Missy said. 'Or at least she was, until Laurence wrote his review. I couldn't understand why he would rip it apart like that.'

'Did he know you wrote *Breaking and Entering*?'

Missy gnawed on her lower lip. 'I think he guessed. There were scenes he,' she flushed, 'might have recognized.'

'He was planning on writing a book of his own, using those kind of . . . "scenes."'

Had I actually read the book instead of falling asleep for two hours, I might have known exactly what we were referring to. I believed, however, that Missy's manner gave me the gist of it.

As my allusion to Potter's projected novel seemed to sink in, Missy looked genuinely astonished. 'But Laurence hated *Breaking and Entering*. He called it smut. And he honestly wasn't very good at . . .' she blushed again, 'most of the scenes anyway. He didn't even like going to Titanium.'

'So, you went to Titanium?'

Missy must have heard the surprise in my voice. 'Why shouldn't I?' she said defensively. 'It's the perfect place to meet people.'

Yikes. 'Is that where you and Potter met?'

'Of course not.' She seemed shocked at the very idea. 'We met at Mystery 101. I knew it was . . . kismet. Laurence was so different than any man I'd met before.'

Might have something to do with 'meeting' them at a sex club.

'He wasn't a user, like the others,' Missy continued. 'I did everything they wanted and more and it still wasn't good enough. Laurence thought I was special. He called me "Melissa," and taught me things. I taught him other things in return.'

'That was very . . . reciprocal of you,' I said lamely.

Missy's brow furrowed. 'But like I said, Laurence just wasn't very good at sex. Why would he want to write a book about it?'

'To make money, I suppose. All I know is that it was supposed to be a he-said, she-said, authored by Audra and him.'

'Audra? But he didn't *love* her.'

'That's what they all—' I stopped myself.

But not in time. Missy waggled the gun barrel toward me the way a kindergarten teacher might her index finger at a misbehaving child. 'You were going to say, "That's what they all say." But Laurence wasn't like that.'

This time I had the smarts not to even open my mouth.

'He told me he loved me.' Missy's eyes welled up and overflowed. 'And now he's gone.'

She started to sob. I moved close enough that I could have put my arm around her. But first, I needed a little clarity. 'I'm sure you're right, Missy. But what did you mean before when you said that I – Maggy – "know"? Know what?'

Missy lifted her head. 'About Laurence and me. I felt you look right into my soul when you said what happens in Fort Lauderdale, stays in Fort Lauderdale because that's where we first met. In fact, it was at this very conference last year.'

Ohhh. 'To be honest, I believe I was talking about Potter and Rosemary. I really wasn't thinking about you.'

'Oh, I'm glad.' Missy shuddered, but now was nearly glowing again. 'We worked very hard to be circumspect. Laurence would even be . . . well, nasty and condescending to me in public. We would laugh about it later.'

Ha-ha-ha. Me? I would have smacked him one. 'Well, you two had me fooled. In fact, I was sure we'd find him with Rosemary when you and I first went back into the sleeping car.'

'Laurence was incapable of doing something like that.' The gun in one hand, Missy swiped across her eyes with the back of the other.

'Of course he was,' I said hastily. 'At the time, though, I didn't know about your relationship.'

'Relationship?' Missy scrunched up more than wrinkled her nose. 'That's not why it was impossible, Maggy.'

'Then . . .?'

'Why? Because Laurence wasn't on the train anymore.'

THIRTY-THREE

Maybe Theodore B. Hertel, Jr was right. Maybe, in the end, everything *is* fiction.

Because this sure felt like make-believe.

The sun was shining brightly, the alligators and snakes off on frolicks of their own. I was wearing a flowered sundress and kitten-heel sandals, albeit a little worse for wear. Missy, the leading lady, was in a silver evening gown and spike heels. The revolver that completed her ensemble could have been a prop.

I cleared my throat, trying to choose my words carefully. If I played it straight – treated Missy like a co-investigator rather than the killer I feared she was – maybe she'd let her guard down. 'So Potter wasn't on the train when you and I went to check on Rosemary. Can you be sure of that?'

'Yes, but it's a long story,' Missy said, waggling the gun toward the door of the train. 'Would you mind if I sat down? These heels are killing me.'

I felt myself relax a bit, thinking my half-baked plan might be working. Or maybe, even, that I was wrong in my suspicions. 'Be my guest.'

Missy, casual as could be, handed me her gun, grabbed the rail and pulled herself up, settling on the floor of the doorway through which Boyce had carried Laurence Potter's body.

'I hate to get this dress dirty,' Potter's lover said, tugging it down, 'but I'll have it thoroughly cleaned before I donate it back to the Salvation Army.'

'Good idea.' I was looking at the gun in my hand, trying to put together what the hell was going on.

'So, shall I continue?' Missy was swinging her legs like a first-grader on a jungle gym.

'Please.'

'As you know, I took Rosemary to the sleeping car and settled her in. As I started back, do you know what I saw?'

'No.'

'The piece of cake you stepped on, along with my staghorn knife. Both on the floor. Can you believe that?'

'No.' I figured the shorter my responses, the less likely I'd screw up.

'I was so angry somebody had not only *cut* a piece of cake without asking, but then dropped it right there and didn't even bother to pick it up. How would that look when Sheriff Pav— I mean, Jake, was pretending to be Ratchett?' Missy looked like she was going to cry again. 'And that's not even counting that the knife was supposed to be the murder weapon!'

'Inexcusable.'

'Exactly what I thought. I picked up the knife so nobody would step on it and opened the door to check on the room. Imagine my surprise to find Laurence there. Not only had he filched the cake – unsuccessfully, I might add – but he was smoking.'

'Smoking?'

'Yes, and we all know that's not allowed on the train. We could even be fined for it.'

'Gosh.' Even if I had wanted to say something stronger I wasn't sure what it would be.

'The window was open and the air conditioning was woofing right out into the Everglades. Cake in the hallway, and Laurence just sitting there. Do you know why?'

'Uh, no.'

'He said he was having a smoke.'

'And . . . he wasn't?'

Missy looked at me like I was the one who was nuts. 'Of course he was. I just told you that.'

'Right, sorry. So what happened next?'

'I asked about his wife showing up. I wasn't mad, Maggy. I just thought it was a good opportunity for us to confront her together.'

'About . . .?'

Another Maggy-you-stupid-idiot look. 'About *us*, of course.'

'Do you mean he was leaving his wife?' At least this time I didn't add, 'That's what they all say.' Just my luck, I'd been married to the only cheater who'd actually meant it.

'As it turns out, no. But apparently Laurence was nothing but a hypocrite anyway. Writing scathing reviews of our book when you say he intended to publish one just like it. Assuring me he was leaving Audra when he clearly had no intention of doing so. Laurence said,' Missy elongated her neck like a chicken in an imitation of Potter, '"your ardent desires aside, Melissa, I have no desire to make an honest woman of you."'

Melissa. I'd corrected Potter when he'd called her that, but it hadn't been a mistake – probably more a signal between them. Potter had made his young mistress feel special. Maybe he was the only one who ever had, despite the fact that she tried so very hard. 'I'm sorry, Missy.'

'Oh, Laurence didn't stop there.' Missy's feet were still dangling and she was kicking her heels against the train's side as she talked. 'He told me I was pathetic and should just grow up. That he thought "Murder on the Orient Espresso" was a juvenile idea, and he wouldn't be part of it.'

A five-minute conversation, and the man had managed to undercut the woman in every area of her life. 'What did you say?'

'I didn't get the chance. Laurence just scooped up his cigarettes and matches, turned his back on me and stalked off.'

One of the shoes flew off with enough force that I flinched and nearly had to duck.

'I couldn't believe it.' Missy was sobbing outright now. 'He stomped right past that cake he'd dropped, with me following. I said he had no right to treat me like this.'

I held the gun ready.

'Laurence wouldn't even turn around!' Missy looked past me, as if she were watching the scene unfold. 'Just opened the door into that vestibule, intending to go right on into the passenger car. He was shoving his stupid cigarettes into his pocket and dropped his matches by the exit door. I called to him, but he didn't hear me. Maybe because of the noise of the train or maybe because he just didn't want to.'

The second shoe went flying, also barely missing me. 'What did you do then?'

Missy seemed surprised at the question. 'I picked the match-book up, of course. But when I tried to hand it to Laurence, he knocked it right back out of my hand. Said the thing was empty and nothing but trash. That he had no further use for it.'

She braced a hand on each side of the doorway and leaned forward. 'He wasn't just talking about those matches, you know, Maggy.'

'No?'

'No.' Her eyes were staring at something I couldn't see. 'The cake knife was in my hand and when he made to leave again, I . . . I stopped him.'

'With the knife?' I asked in a hoarse whisper.

Missy nodded up and down, up and down, like she was in a marching band and had to perfectly synchronize with its other members. 'He fell against the door, bleeding. I had it on my hand already, but before it got all over I just . . . just slid the door open.' The last words were barely a whisper.

'It' being her lover's blood. Missy took 'tidy' to new heights.

I was trying to understand, or at least appear like I understood. 'Listen, I know you didn't mean to—'

But before I could finish my sentence, Missy Hudson launched herself from the doorway where she was sitting, toppling us both into the shallow water of the Everglades.

THIRTY-FOUR

I held the revolver high, thinking Missy was going to fight me for it. Instead, though, she put her hands on my chest and shoved me under the eight inches or so of swamp water and kept right on going, as if we were playing a soggy game of reverse leapfrog.

Scrambling back up, I coughed and gave chase.

Missy was already slogging toward the berm/island on the other side. I followed, trying to keep the gun from getting wet.

I didn't call for help, which was probably dumb, but I was the one waving the firearm and chasing someone. Who would the citizens' militia behind me choose to shoot?

Missy had made it across to the other bank, the one with the mangroves growing on it. She'd taken about three feet into the sawgrass when she froze and said, 'Don't move.'

'Me?' I looked at the revolver in my hand. 'I have the gun. *You* don't move.'

Over her shoulder she whispered, 'It's a python.'

'Good,' I said, much more calmly than I felt. 'How about you and me retreat slowly back to the train and leave the monster alone.'

'I don't think she'll let us.'

I crept up behind her and peered over a shoulder. A mottled nest of white eggs was not four feet in front of Missy's bare feet. The nest had a head. A pointy head.

'Is this the kind that's pretty protective?' I asked, backing up. I was remembering the old joke about not having to outrun the bear, just the person with you.

'*Really* protective,' Missy said, grabbing my arm so I couldn't move without startling the snake. 'Don't leave me here.'

'I won't.' I was feeling ashamed of myself. Murderer or not, Missy didn't deserve to end up as snake food, despite the fact she'd turned her lover into it. 'Don't worry.'

'I won't.' And with that, she gave a brutal yank on my arm, sending the gun flying and me staggering into the snake's nest.

THIRTY-FIVE

The female python and I were eye-to-eye. I tried to get back up, reminding myself that they didn't bite so much as squeeze you to death.

And then eat you.

The thing started to uncoil almost casually, like a cross-armed street punk, breaking away from his gang with a, 'Wait here, dudes. This won't take me long.'

Only this reptilian thug intended not only to put the squeeze on me, but have me for dinner. And not in a Welcome Wagon kind of way.

I managed to get to my feet and take a step, only to be tripped. While I was busy watching the head, the coils had snuck up on me from behind, launching me back nose first into the sawgrass.

Frozen in fear, I felt something thick glide over and then around my leg. The monster would envelope me like the banyan tree did its 'host,' first strangling the life out and then enveloping me as if I'd never been there at all.

I pushed up on my elbows hoping to scrabble away, but the coils had continued to climb, reaching my waist. I wanted to scream, but couldn't seem to get my breath, whether from fear or the creature's evolving death hug.

Yanked back, I fell off my elbows, my face grinding into the ground. When I turned my head, the python's head slid into view. A split-tongue lashed out, nearly touching my nose. I tried to evade it, but the rows of backward-pointing teeth drew—

An explosion. And then nothing.

No sound. No light. Nor could I feel the painful, suffocating clamp of the python any longer.

Was this how it felt to die?

If so . . . hey, not so bad.

Sure, I could use a little music or maybe a pearly gate or two. But I'd settle for a simple dazzling light to move toward. It was awfully da—

'Maggy?'

I opened my eyes.

Missy was standing straddled over the python. The creature's head had been blown apart.

Before I could open my mouth to thank her, the girl turned the gun in my direction. 'I'm so sorry, Maggy.' She seemed dazed.

'It's all right, Missy.' I was holding up both hands as best I could. 'I know you didn't want to hurt anyone.'

But she was shaking her head, back-and-forth, back-and-forth. 'That's just it. I think in a way I did. After—' She swiped at a string of snot hanging from her nose. 'Afterwards I was glad Laurence was gone. Dropped into the Everglades to be dealt with by animals like him. It seemed . . . right.'

No muss, no fuss. I hoped I wasn't her next recycling project.

'But you—' She gestured toward me with the gun. 'You don't deserve to die.'

I didn't know what else to say but, 'Thank you.'

'You've been nothing but nice to me, Maggy. And I almost killed you. Or, at least, let the snake kill you.'

'But you *didn't*,' I insisted, hoping it was a self-fulfilling prophesy.

'Thing is, with you gone no one would need to know. They might not even find your body. It would be so . . . neat, so orderly. Life *should* be orderly.' The gun was shaking.

'Hello?' Markus's voice called from the direction of the train. 'Who's out there?'

Pushing myself up on my hands and knees, I lunged upward just as Melissa 'Missy' Hudson put the muzzle of the gun in her mouth and pulled the trigger.

THIRTY-SIX

The shots brought people running from the train at a gallop, Markus in the lead. 'Oh, my God. What happened?'

I was sitting next to Missy's body on the ground. She still held the gun in her hand, the back of her head horribly . . . just not there.

'Missy killed herself and,' I hesitated, 'Potter.'

'Are you sure?' Zoe Scarlett had arrived, quickly followed by Prudence and Theodore B. Hertel, Jr. 'I mean, you're the one who's alive and she's not.'

'The girl still has the gun in her hand,' Markus pointed out before I could answer.

'And why would Maggy kill Potter?' Prudence demanded. 'She didn't even know him.'

'Why would *Missy* kill him?'

A new voice. 'Because she loved him and he was an asshole.' The crowd parted, revealing Audra Edmonds. 'I don't know why I didn't do it myself, years ago.'

'Well, will you look at that snake in the grass.' Engineer Hertel didn't seem to take any notice of Audra or even Missy or me. He was ogling the python. 'This here's gotta be another of those rock pythons – look at how broad she is. And them eggs! They're about to pop and I hear tell they come out striking.'

I got up and took two steps back. 'We need to get Missy out of here,' I said. 'Markus, maybe you and,' I saw the literary agent coming toward us, 'Carson can carry her back to the train?'

The germaphobe in his white suit looked down at Missy, covered in swamp water and snake remnants, the back of her skull gone, but he nodded. 'Of course.'

The two men picked up the pathetic little rag doll, all dressed up with literally no place to go. I followed after them as they conveyed Missy across the shallow water to the train. As I went, I stopped to retrieve first one glittery shoe and then the other.

When we got to the door, Markus climbed into the train.

Carson handed the girl up to him and then the rest of us hoisted ourselves in.

'Wait,' I said, awkwardly retrieving the semi-automatic and Missy's e-reader which I'd left on the floor. I kicked my pillow aside and opened the door of the roomette across from Potter's. 'Put her in there.'

When they'd placed Missy on the bunk, I covered her with a blanket and put the e-reader next to a hand. Then I picked up her shoes from the floor and we left, softly closing the door as if we didn't want to awaken her.

The rest of the group continued on to the passenger car, but Carson was standing in the corridor, staring at his filthy hands.

'Why didn't you tell Pavlik or me you were representing Danny?' It didn't matter now, but I still wanted to know.

'Danny?' Carson was holding up both hands like a surgeon who'd scrubbed for an operation, and was impatiently awaiting sterile gloves.

'Your new client? The one whose sexy book will now take the place of the novel Potter was writing?'

Carson had the grace to look embarrassed. 'I told him to send me the manuscript. I was intrigued. I didn't say I'd represent him.'

Given the agent's personality and, more importantly, Danny's, that made sense. The kid had gotten carried away – just assumed the agent would take him on.

'If you want to wash your hands . . .' I opened the door of the roomette next to where we'd just left Missy and flipped down the sink. 'And thank you for helping out there. I know it couldn't have been easy for you.'

'You're welcome,' Carson said, trying to operate the faucet with his elbow. 'I've found I can do these things if necessary. Or . . . appropriate.'

'Me, too.' I leaned in, turned on the water and left him.

Since there was nothing left to guard or anybody to guard it from, I returned to the passenger car, sinking wearily down into a window seat.

'Here, drink this.' Zoe Scarlett gave me a plastic cup with about an inch of brown liquid in it.

Adoption Undone

A tale of two sisters

KAREN CARR

Published by
British Association for Adoption & Fostering
(BAAF)
Saffron House
6–10 Kirby Street
London EC1N 8TS
www.baaf.org.uk

Charity registration 275689

© Karen Carr, 2007

Reprinted 2008

British Library Cataloguing in Publication Data
A catalogue record for this book is available from the
British Library

ISBN 978 1 905664 24 5

Project management by Shaila Shah,
Director of Publications, BAAF
Cover design by Helen Joubert
Designed by Andrew Haig & Associates
Typeset by Fravashi Aga
Printed in Great Britain by T J International
Trade distribution by Turnaround Publisher Services, Unit 3,
Olympia Trading Estate, Coburg Road, London N22 6TZ

BAAF is the leading UK-wide membership organisation for all
those concerned with adoption, fostering and child care issues.

The paper used for the text pages of this book is FSC certified.
FSC (The Forest Stewardship Council) is an international network
to promote responsible management of the world's forests.

Printed on totally chlorine-free paper.

FSC
Mixed Sources
Product group from well-managed
forests and other controlled sources

Cert no. SGS-COC-2482
www.fsc.org
© 1996 Forest Stewardship Council

Acknowledgements

There are so many things I am grateful to Jon for: his undying love and faith in me, his support and his strength. His unfailing honesty and thoughtful comments have given me much to think about and made the process of writing this book more interesting and challenging; his ability to entertain the children and to allow me the space and time to write is a rare but much welcomed talent and worthy of thanks in itself.

The same is true of my longest standing and closest friend, Annie, who has read and "red penned" my work in a kind and honest way. She has always listened with apparent interest, enabling me to rant or reminisce freely depending on my mood.

I have to give an enormous thank you to our good friends Andrew and Flick who supported us during the darkest moments of the adoption breakdown. Flick was by my side the whole time. The book doesn't do justice to the practical and emotional support they gave when it was so very much needed.

I would also like to thank Sharon from After Adoption whose work is a lifeline for adopted children and their families.

I am grateful to Irene Machin who read and commented on my final draft. She has successfully adopted two children herself, and the fact that I am still a practising social worker is in no small part due to Irene's professional support. Finally my thanks go to Hedi Argent, the series editor, for saying, 'yes, I think we can work together', and then patiently steering me through the process of writing our story.

The names in this book have been changed to preserve anonymity.

About the author
Karen Carr is a Senior Social Worker in a Children In Need Team in the North West of England. She is looking for a new challenge now that this book is complete.

The Our Story series
This book is part of BAAF's Our Story series, which explores adoption experiences as told by adoptive parents.

Also available in this series: *An Adoption Diary* by Maria James, *Flying Solo* by Julia Wise and *In Black and White* by Nathalie Seymour.

The series editor
Hedi Argent is an independent family placement consultant, trainer and freelance writer. She is the author of *Find me a Family* (Souvenir Press, 1984), *Whatever Happened to Adam?* (BAAF, 1998), *Related by Adoption* (BAAF, 2004), *Ten Top Tips for Placing Children in Families* (BAAF, 2006), and *Josh and Jaz have Three Mums* (2007), the co-author of *Taking Extra Care* (BAAF, 1997, with Ailee Kerrane), and *Dealing with Disruption* (BAAF, 2006, with Jeffrey Coleman), and the editor of *Keeping the Doors Open* (BAAF, 1988), *See You Soon* (BAAF, 1995), *Staying Connected* (BAAF, 2002), and *Models of Adoption Support* (BAAF, 2003). She has also written five illustrated booklets in the children's series published by BAAF: *What Happens in Court?* (2003, with Mary Lane), *What is Contact?* (2004), *What is a Disability?* (2004), *Life Story Work* (2005, with Shaila Shah) and *Kinship Care* (2007).

For Lucy and Hannah

Remember

Remember me when I am gone away,
Gone far away into the silent land;
When you can no more hold me by the hand,
Nor I half turn to go yet turning stay.
Remember me when no more day by day
You tell me of the future that you planned:
Only remember me; you understand
It will be late to counsel then or pray.
Yet if you should forget me for a while
And afterwards remember, do not grieve:
For if the darkness and corruption leave
A vestige of the thoughts that I once had,
Better by far you should forget and smile
Than that you should remember and be sad.

Christina G. Rossetti

Contents

Foreword

This is the true story of an adoption – and of an adoption breakdown. Although adoption is the only way to secure a legal alternative family for children who cannot remain in their birth families, adoption cannot guarantee permanence any more than other children can be guaranteed that their family will be there for them for ever. But an adoption undone is not an adoption legally ended – there is no possibility of an annulment or dissolution. Children belong to their adoptive families even if they have to leave them; only another adoption order can change their legal status. While the success rate for infant adoptions has always been high, the disruption rate for adoptions of children aged four and over is generally put at around three out of ten.

However hard the family and older child try to fit together, however well families and children are prepared for the transition, the match cannot work every time because each child is unique and each family is unique, and no one can foretell exactly how this child and this family will impact upon each other. If the preparation for adoption of the child and the new family is not careful,

i

skilled and thorough, if assessments are inaccurate, if support is inadequate or unavailable, and if problems are not addressed when they emerge, then the risks of breakdown inevitably increase.

It strikes a more hopeful note to call an adoption breakdown a "disruption"; it is a disruption, not an ending, of the family placement process for the child. We can learn from what went wrong and try to do better next time. Many children who have experienced the upheaval of disruption have eventually been successfully adopted. And families who were unable to parent one child have gone on to build a thriving adoptive family.

But when disruption happens, there is pain for everyone: for a bewildered child who has to move again, for a family who feel they have failed, and for social workers who have to pick up the pieces. It is important not to apportion blame or to allow distress to turn into anger. Disruption is rarely the result of what one party has done or left undone; it is usually a combination of unidentified, misunderstood and unpredictable circumstances.

Karen Carr's brave story of Lucy's adoption and the disruption four years later is a rich illustration of how high hopes and the best of intentions could not keep a much wanted child in the family. It is a tale of endeavour and loss and unfulfilled love.

Hedi Argent
Series Editor
July 2007

1

2 December 2004

Miss Pickering turned our attention to the "threshold criteria": 'Right, let's have a look at this again and see what we are prepared to accept.'

It began: 'Mr and Mrs Carr adopted Lucy in February 2001 after she had been living with them since July 1999.' Miss Pickering looked up. 'That was a long time...did you foster her first?'

'No, we were never her foster parents. We knew we wanted to adopt a little girl, a sister for Hannah, relatively close to her in age, playmates and confidantes for each other as they grew up. The reason it took us so long to get around to applying for the Adoption Order was because we were having problems and we were never sure what to do for the best.'

* * *

Stories often start with phrases like "today was no ordinary day". But for us today *really* was not like any other day. The chances were that we would never have a day like it again for the rest of our lives; at least, that was what we were hoping. It was just over five years ago that we met Lucy for the very first time, but today, on 2 December 2004, we were closing the last chapter of her life with us.

Annie, my closest friend, turned up at 8.15am, as promised, to look after our seven-month-old baby daughter. The weather was quite mild for the time of year, but it was drizzly and dull. She had driven some 30 miles in rush hour traffic to get to us on time.

Hannah, our eleven-year-old daughter, had already left for school by the time Annie arrived. We had taken her to the breakfast club early because we wanted to protect her from more upset and worry. But it was no use; she had guessed that something was happening. It was nothing out of the ordinary to see her father and me dressed up in suits. Jon always wears a suit and I frequently do if I have an important meeting planned, but I was still on maternity leave from work and it wasn't just the clothes that gave it away. We were both full of nervous energy; we were too lively and talkative for first thing in the morning.

Eventually she had asked, 'What's going on, Mummy, is it something to do with Lucy?' We had stopped trying to hide the truth from Hannah a while ago. We sat her down and explained that we were in court again today and that this was the final hearing in the care proceedings relating to Lucy, our adopted daughter, and Hannah's sister.

'Will we be able to get on with our lives then?' she asked.

'I hope so, Hannah, I really do.'

'Will you not always be on the computer writing letters and stuff?'

'I won't be doing it so often,' I said.

When the time came for her to leave for school, she looked up at us both with big, anxious brown eyes and said, 'Good luck for today. You tell that Judge that we always looked after Lucy as best as we could.'

'Don't worry, Hannah,' I said, as I thought to myself that the days of running and hiding in shame were definitely over.

Annie made us all a cup of tea and then gave us her

verdict on our chosen attire. 'Karen, you look very business-like, but not over the top. The suit is smart, makes you look taller but it's also very feminine.' Annie spends much of her time describing what she sees. If something were light blue, she would have to say powder blue, or baby blue, or sky blue.

'I just think you need to put some lipstick on.'

'Why?' I asked.

'You look much prettier with lipstick on,' she said. I didn't bother to explain that my thoughts were completely focused on trying to be strong and assertive and that something as trivial as lipstick would have been a distraction.

'I'm not in the mood for lipstick,' I said.

'Jon, you look smart, very business-like, just right,' Annie offered. The usual banter that characterised Annie and Jon's relationship was non-existent today; normally neither of them can resist the odd quip and "put down". Today, a sense of austerity prevailed.

We set off for the court at 9am. It was at least an hour's drive away and we needed to speak with our barrister before the hearing, which was scheduled for 10.30am. Jon drove and the time flew as we dissected the latest social worker's statement yet again. We went over our response to it. Was it strong enough? Had we made our point clearly enough?

These questions were purely academic anyway, because the local authority agreed with us that the adoption had broken down and that they needed to take "parental responsibility" for Lucy, although we would still be her legal parents.

(The only way a local authority can get parental responsibility for a child is to apply to the court for a Care Order. The court has to be satisfied that the "threshold criteria" are met. The threshold criteria are the reasons the local authority has to give for needing a Care Order.)

Why, if we were all agreed that a Care Order was

3

necessary, were we still in court several hearings and ten months later? It was because the local authority had tried to claim that we had emotionally abused Lucy. Although we were agreed on the ultimate objective, we could not accept the wording of the "threshold criteria". Our stance was: either prove it or change it.

That's why we were here again.

What was exceptional about today, was that this was the first hearing that I was attending. Until now, Jon had braved it alone. I have been amazed at his strength of character since the "disruption" – the generally accepted word to describe the breakdown of an adoption and which is described in the Foreword. He has done everything in his power to protect me from further suffering. I can imagine how difficult it must have been for him, all those people thinking that he had abused Lucy, but he still went there, trying his best to hold his head up high. Even our own solicitor was unsupportive and was persuaded by the social worker's statements.

Before today I had not felt emotionally strong enough to go to court with Jon. I could not face the people who had distorted our intentions and actions and misrepresented us in their statements. I had such intense feelings of loss, grief and failure that I feared that, if I saw them in court, I might either attack them physically or crumple in a blubbering heap of self-pity and cry out 'it's not fair!' Neither of those options was appealing to either of us.

Thankfully, I had finally moved on from that stage and felt an overwhelming sense of injustice that gave me the confidence to be vocal and assert myself appropriately, or possibly, slightly aggressively.

While Jon parked the car, I walked into the courthouse and noticed Lucy's social worker in the small café, sitting alone with a cup on the table in front of her. She looked me up and down and continued to sip her drink. Obviously she didn't recognise me. Why would she? The last time we had met, she had come to the house to discuss Lucy and future contact arrangements. At that time, I had been looking like a slob, wearing extremely baggy tracksuit bottoms and a long yellow T-shirt that in the past I used to wear for bed. I had only recently given birth and I had gained over a stone in weight from my pre-pregnant size. I had let my hair grow into a state, my roots were about an inch and a half long, which is never attractive on dyed-blonde hair, and my eyes were permanently puffy and red because I was spending large parts of every day crying.

My mind drifted to the last time I had been in this building; I was filled with a deep sense of mourning for what might have been. Just over three years ago, in February 2001, we had received the Adoption Order for Lucy in this same court from the same Judge.

I could recall the day clearly. By then, Lucy had already been living with us for 19 months. Lucy, then five, and Hannah, aged eight, were wearing similar dresses, bought from Laura Ashley especially for the occasion. At the time I was at university studying for a Diploma in Social Work, and with only Jon's income we had no money to spare but I had managed to get both dresses in the New Year sales. Lucy's was royal blue, Hannah's was navy blue; they were mid-calf length with an attached underskirt and little delicate roses in the same colour sewn across the front. Hannah wore her long mousy brown hair down, with a clip holding it off her face. Lucy had her ever so slightly darker hair in two high little pigtails. Lucy was always very specific about how she wanted her hair and from a very early age could do more or less any style by herself.

I recall Hannah being very loving towards Lucy on that day, telling her not to worry, and wanting to take care of her and hug her and hold her hand. She was glad that Lucy would now be her 'forever sister and that nothing and no one could ever do anything to change that'. This is what we all had truly believed.

But Lucy was nervous and possibly even a little scared and said she was upset because she would not see her social worker any more. This was Lucy's way of making us realise that adoption meant something very different for her. For Lucy the relief of feeling more like one of the family was offset by yet another loss and she was trying to make sense of what it all meant. Lucy always stayed close to me when we were all together, but that day she made an extra effort to make sure she didn't lose her tight little grip on my hand. She told us that she wanted her social worker and the Judge to think that she was 'a very sensible girl'.

Our moods, Jon's and mine, had been somewhat subdued. We had been arguing the whole weekend again...

My thoughts were brought back to the present by feeling Jon's arm around my waist.

'You feeling okay?' he asked.

'Why couldn't we make it work, Jon, she was just one little girl...How on earth did it come to this?'

Our barrister had still not arrived, so we took a seat on a row of red plastic chairs joined together by metal bars and fixed to the floor. Jon joked that they had been screwed down the night before to stop me from throwing one at an unsuspecting social worker.

A few moments later, the Guardian ad litem arrived and sat facing us. Guardians ad litem (now called Children's Guardians) are appointed by the court; they are supposed to be independent, and provide the court with a view of what is in the best interests of the child. We greeted one another and she asked how Hannah was.

The Guardian's name was Marjorie; she always had a quizzical look as though she was trying to work something out. She was a short woman with a stocky build and a strong North West regional accent. She had an air of 'I say it like it is and I call a spade a spade' about her.

'Fine,' I said, 'Hannah is doing really well'. We spent a few more moments in uncomfortable conversation; she asked about the baby and whether or not I had returned to work.

'Mr and Mrs Carr?' It was a relief to all of us when our

barrister approached. 'Yes, hello!' We rose to meet her, and shook hands. She introduced herself as Miss Pickering and invited us into a small side office.

Miss Pickering was a tall, slim young woman with slightly pointed features; she had very straight, fine, collar-length hair. She came across as rather nervous. I got the impression that in the past she had possibly been uncomfortable with her height, as she seemed unwilling to sit up straight. However, she was articulate and supportive, although I felt that she could lack the assertiveness to really put a strong case forward. She carried a large dark leather bag bursting with papers, and carried more files in her hands.

We explained our difficulty to her: just about everybody, including our own solicitor, thought that we were making a fuss about nothing, that we were arguing against the wording of the "threshold criteria" just for the hell of it. It did not seem to occur to anyone that the local authority was equally determined to blame us for the breakdown of the adoption. Furthermore, what the social workers had written in the "threshold criteria" was just untrue. 'What is wrong with these people!' we would repeatedly bleat to one another with indignation.

The local authority claimed, amongst other things, that we were only self-interested. They resorted to a popular overused phrase in social work: that '(we) could not prioritise Lucy's needs over our own'. My instinct was to fight against what the social workers had written about us even amidst the grief we were all feeling. I had qualified to become a social worker myself in 2002, three years after Lucy came to live with us, so that I could learn more about children adopted from the care system.

Jon had just wanted to let them get on with it. We both wanted to protect Hannah and to rebuild our lives as a family unit again. For Jon, this meant letting the local authority do and say as they pleased; we had taken the decision to let Lucy go, we had failed her as her parents and we had to accept anything that was said about us and take the consequences.

But I could recall the many moments I had shared with Lucy, all the effort and energy we had all put into our relationships to make it work. I still felt the overwhelming pain of losing her. I once heard an African-American activist describe loss and injustice as 'a pain that goes as deep as the marrow'. At the time, I had been struck by what appeared to me to be his poetic ability to communicate to someone like me the depth of human suffering caused by racism. His words stayed with me, they altered my world view. But after we had let Lucy go I felt I truly understood what he meant: some emotions are so deep that they strip you and run right through you, to the core, or "the marrow".

I was willing to accept the pain of the loss we would feel, and the guilt, but there was no way I was going to allow anyone to re-invent the past four-and-a-half years of our life with Lucy.

Miss Pickering listened attentively, with a timely "mmm" now and then and an occasional understanding nod. She was apologetic because she wasn't that familiar with our case. She had been appointed at the last minute and she confessed to looking over the case notes only the previous evening. She was surprised that there was 'an awful lot of paperwork'.

She had only been talking with us for about ten minutes but, unlike our previous legal representatives, she picked up on my fervent passion and our sense of injustice. I appreciated Miss Pickering's attempts to appear genuinely concerned. She adopted an almost counselling-type approach.

'It is a dreadful state of affairs that Lucy was ever placed for adoption in the first place,' said Miss Pickering. 'It seems to me you were used almost like guinea pigs.' Her raised eyebrows now almost met in the middle. With the best will and effort in the world, the odds had been stacked heavily against us.

I always remember a piece of research about children born into poverty called *Born to fail*. In retrospect, after reading papers from the original court proceedings, when Lucy first came into public care, I believe it was true of Lucy's adoption, that it was *Bound to fail*. We discovered that two psychologists and an independent social worker had given evidence and argued, at the time, that Lucy should not be placed for adoption. They had predicted a high probability of adoption breakdown if contact with her birth family continued, but at the same time had warned of the risks to an adoption if the attachments between Lucy and her birth family were completely severed. These predictions turned out to be entirely accurate.

'And were you told any of this?' asked Miss Pickering.

We told her that we had been informed that there was a psychologist who had argued in support of the birth mother but that he was 'as mad as her'.

'So what did you know about the circumstances before you went ahead with the adoption?'

And that takes us back to the beginning of our story.

2

Lucy and her birth family

Miss Pickering referred to her papers. 'What a tragic set of circumstances,' she said.

* * *

Lucy's mother, Fiona, had suffered from mental health problems for much of her adult life and was diagnosed as having a personality disorder. She was 42 years old when Lucy was born; her older daughter, Jade, was already six at the time. We were told that the family had come to the attention of social services because Jade was displaying serious problems in school. She was openly self-harming, making sexually explicit remarks, and she was under-achieving and disrupting the class with constant attention-seeking behaviour. A number of referrals were made to social services by the school, but others came from the general public. Apparently the home was practically uninhabitable, and there was frequent mention of neglect and one of physical abuse when an anonymous caller reported seeing Fiona hit Jade repeatedly in public. Social services offered support and the family moved into a mother and baby unit for a while. But things did not work out, and the girls were finally removed after the NSPCC became involved and forced the hand of the local authority. Lucy was almost eighteen months old and Jade was seven-and-a-half.

The social workers disclosed that Fiona herself had been adopted as a baby and had never met her biological parents. They believed that she had been sexually abused by her adoptive father but admitted that she had never said that, it was just a feeling they had.

The social worker said there was never any doubt that Fiona loved both her children dearly. After they were removed, Fiona worked with psychiatrists, psychologists and social workers in an attempt to have her children returned to her. For some considerable time, the local authority provided intensive parent training sessions twice-weekly for Fiona with both of the girls. The social workers told us they believed that Fiona suffered from a form of Munchausen's Syndrome, because she seemed never to tire of demanding attention from a variety of professionals. She would turn up at the social services' office and telephoned them several times a day; she wrote both children lengthy cards and letters daily, and put in formal complaints about their foster placement every week. During contact visits she would ask Jade questions and then make complaints about her answers. She would also tell Jade to run away, believing that if she did it often enough, the local authority would send the girls back home.

Hearing all this made me feel for Fiona. I could not help putting myself in her shoes. If somebody tried to take Hannah from me, I would do anything to prevent it.

We explained to Miss Pickering that we never questioned what we were told, and that it didn't occur to us to ask if there was anything else we should know. 'Of course not,' said Miss Pickering with a shrug, 'why would you?'

The strain of all the complaints was too much for the foster carer and she decided that she could not keep both sisters. The local authority placed Jade in a children's home temporarily while they looked for an alternative long-term foster home for her.

I know that hindsight is 20:20 vision, but maybe the local authority should have applied to court for an Order to restrict Jade's contact with her mother as Fiona had clearly caused her placement to disrupt. It was the first of many times that this was to happen. But the consensus was that Jade's attachment to her mother was too strong to take this action. Fiona's influence over Jade continues to affect her foster placements even today.

The problem faced by the professionals involved with the family at the time was how to plan for two sisters with a six-year age gap. Fiona could not accept adoption for either of her children and contested the plan until she was not allowed to contest it any more.

Despite all the experts' recommendations, the local authority social worker and the Guardian ad litem proved to be more influential in the final decision-making.

The court ruled that Lucy should be placed for adoption and have continuing contact with Jade and indirect contact with her mother; Jade was to be placed in long-term foster care and continue to see both her mother and her sister.

We were told by social workers that we needn't worry as there was very little attachment between Jade and Lucy; they said that Jade would not want to go on seeing her sister. They also believed that Jade was learning to deal with her mother's behaviour and would not jeopardise Lucy's adoption by passing on information to or from their mother – they were wrong on both counts.

So now they needed prospective adoptive parents who were willing to have a type of open adoption. Enter Mr and Mrs Carr…

* * *

Miss Pickering gently steered the conversation back to the

present situation and the matter at hand. 'Look, we need to be clear and precise about any changes we wish to make to the "threshold criteria". At this stage you cannot really go altering too much,' she said. 'I'm very conscious about the time. The Judge will be calling us to Chambers soon and will expect us to have reached an agreement.' She looked over the amended copy. 'Right, I will go and discuss this with the other side, fingers crossed and I will be back shortly.'

Jon and I mused over the amended draft: 'Mr and Mrs Carr adopted Lucy in February 2001 after she had been living with them since July 1999.' 'Talk about summarising,' said Jon, 'that makes the whole process sound a lot easier. Remind me to thank them later for such a compelling and comprehensive account of those years.' It is true that the sentence says nothing about the process of adoption or of the people who are involved. We adopted Lucy in 2001 but the idea had sort of come to us many years earlier when Jon and I first met in 1989.

3

Who we are

Miss Pickering was gone for a considerable time. We sat waiting for her return in the 10 x 10 foot sparsely furnished, blandly decorated room. Having other people discussing our private affairs and the enforced revisiting of our relationship history allowed the mind to drift easily into reminiscence.

* * *

Jon and I met in 1989 at a dinner party arranged by mutual friends. I was living alone in a small rented bed-sit at the time and Jon still lived at home with his parents. The friends who invited us had recently become foster parents. They had a teenage boy placed with them and were struggling to manage his behaviour. The placement very quickly broke down and our friends decided that fostering was much harder than they had anticipated and it wasn't for them.

Jon and I would discuss this boy frequently. We felt he had been given a raw deal, not by our friends, but by what life had handed to him. At the start of our relationship, we felt fostering was something we would like to do. In fact, we had only been together for a couple of years when we applied to become foster carers. A social worker visited us at home but thought our partnership was still quite new and asked us to apply again in a year or so if we were still interested.

If we had been successful in our initial attempt at fostering, we may have realised, as our friends did, that it was not for us. Maybe then Lucy could at least have been spared the weaving in and out of our family. Hannah would never have suffered the trauma of having a sister who was ultimately too difficult for her to love, and Jon and I would not have ended up in court.

The fostering idea fell by the wayside as we got on with the routine of normal living, whatever that is. For us it was working hard and trying to improve our income and environment. Both Jon and I had some way to go in terms of developing a career. I worked in a variety of low-paid, low-skilled occupations, such as shop assistant, or waitress, or bar-work; I had also worked in factories. When Jon left school, he qualified as a mechanic but then decided that manual work wasn't for him and he became a trainer of apprentices. That gave him the experience to apply for a post to work with teenagers on government training schemes. This is what he was doing when we met.

We both went to night school, where I gained qualifications in Social Science, Government and Politics and Counselling. Jon completed his membership for the Institute of Personnel Development.

We had to scrimp and scrape to make ends meet, as many young couples do, but we were in love and we wanted to start a family. In 1993, Hannah was born and we were both instantly besotted with her; we were truly a happy family. Jon and I discussed my going to university full time. Getting an education was something I had failed miserably at as a child due to excessive truanting with Annie and other wayward children. We had no money to spare, but the university grant in 1994 was as much as I had been earning in my low paid jobs; it made sense to get a degree so that my earning potential would increase.

Neither Jon nor I liked where we were living, it was not ideal for raising children. We had a two-up two-down mid-terrace house in the North West of England, many miles from where either of us had lived before. The cost of housing was affordable but there was a high population of minority ethnic communities in the neighbourhood and racism was rife. Then one day it was announced in the local newspaper that there were plans to close the local swimming baths and convert the building into a mosque. The whole community took up positions for and against and became divided by race and religion as class and other distinctions fell by the wayside. The white British locals united to stop the plans. Jon and I became ostracised by our neighbours because we refused to sign a petition against the proposal.

We were concerned that the hostilities and resulting racist language could influence Hannah if we remained where we were, so we decided to move to a different town. This may appear to be a drastic step, but racist language was very much a part of the everyday conversation of the people of this town. One memorable example was shortly after we had moved to the area and I was shopping in the local market looking for some material. I was having a friendly chat with a stallholder when suddenly she said, 'Wait a minute, love'. She nodded towards a potential customer, an Asian woman, and gave me a knowing look as though we shared a common belief. Then she proceeded to follow the customer as though pulled by a magnetic force until the woman left. When she returned to me she said, 'You have to watch 'em, otherwise they'll fill their pockets.' I remember thinking that I could have filled my own bag in the time that she had followed the woman. I believe this kind of language is insidious and permeates the soul, moulding a personality of irrationality and fear; I didn't want that for Hannah.

Jon's parents gave us some money to help towards the

deposit, and so we moved in August 1996 some 40 miles away to another town, still in the North West of England.

The years seemed to fly by and, before we knew it, Hannah was four-and-a-half years old and had started school.

I was extremely protective of Hannah. I am one of five children, four girls and a boy. With the exception of my brother we were all sexually abused as small children. Also, after my mother gave birth to our youngest sister she became very ill, and for approximately ten months we were placed in local authority care, again with the exception of my brother who remained with our father. We were poor, my mother worked as a cleaner and my father was in and out of work; his trade was painting and decorating but ill health limited the amount of work he could do. Once, when we were really young, I asked my mum why we'd gone on a holiday without them to a strange place called St Anne's. All she said was that underprivileged children go on free holidays.

As an adult and as a mother I am driven by the need not to repeat the history of my childhood. This is not to blame my parents for anything; we are all victims of victims and this is certainly true of my parents.

Jon is the younger of two children; his sister is four years older. When he was five, his parents built their own large detached bungalow. Jon feels that during his childhood he was overshadowed by his sister. He constantly strove to gain the approval of his parents. He believed they felt his mistakes were part of some inherent defect in his personality rather than the normal behaviour of adolescent boys and young adults.

Having first-hand experience of being abused as a child certainly shaped me as a mother and I struggled to trust almost any adult with Hannah. I began to think that she would be safer if she had a sister or brother. We realised that if we decided to have another baby now, Hannah could be almost seven before the baby was born, possibly even older. Also, Hannah was turning into a very sociable little girl; she loved the company of other children, especially if we invited friends from school over for tea. She was lonely on her own. We wanted her to have a sister she would be close to in age.

Jon and I had always considered ourselves to be open-minded, tolerant of difference and with a lot of love to give. If only life were that simple; at the time we had naïvely believed that adoption was the best way forward...

* * *

We could hear hustle and bustle outside the door. Miss Pickering rushed in, choosing not to sit down. 'They are refusing to make the changes,' she said, 'but we have to go in now, we are likely to be called back after lunch.'

We walked in to a very large courtroom. Mounted on the wall, above where the Judge would sit, was a large coat of arms. There was a large long wooden bench facing the rest of the room; this was raised so that the incumbent Judge was elevated above his audience, who would sit on a row of less imposing benches opposite him. In between were the single desks where the Clerk to the Court would sit and a pedestal or platform for witnesses. The décor gave the impression of failed grandiosity. I think it is supposed to appear as a great bastion of "Britishness", with all the pomp, tradition and pretension that these occasions call for. And although all the "actors" played their parts, the place had all the ambience of the local social security office.

All the barristers were already sitting in the first row facing the Judge when we entered. We sat with the Guardian to our right on the next bench; the social worker came in behind us and sat to our left.

The Guardian managed to attract my attention and before I knew it we were in the middle of a heated conversation. She was saying that the adoption had not broken down because of Hannah.

Trying to convince those who are already convinced of their own view is not an easy task. Ordinarily, if someone were to call me a liar, I would, without a doubt, challenge them with passion, but my emotions had been battered, so I just said that what happened with Hannah was the straw that broke the camel's back; this is the truth, of course.

The Judge arrived. He seemed some distance away but I still noticed that his grey suit was covered in dandruff all over the shoulders. Deference prevailed as we all rose to pay our respects to an age-old tradition, inner frustrations momentarily forgotten while we waited for the Judge to position himself and sit down.

The Judge addressed the barrister for the council. 'Have you all reached an agreement?'

'No, your Honour, Mr and Mrs Carr have produced some evidence from the Child and Adolescent Mental Health Services Team confirming that Hannah attended for an appointment as they have suggested, but we believe that this is self-reporting from Mrs Carr.'

Miss Pickering stood up. 'Your Honour, the local authority has referred Lucy to this same CAMHS team. Why does the local authority accept its assessment in relation to Lucy but not in relation to Hannah?'

I felt the urge to speak and although out of order, I did not stop myself. I stood up and said, 'Your Honour, Miss Pickering has done a fine job trying to represent us. Nevertheless, she has only very recently picked up our case and cannot be in possession of all the facts. The reason we have provided this piece of evidence is because the local authority has written in the "threshold criteria" that "Mr and Mrs Carr claimed that Hannah had begun to suffer but there was no evidence from education, health or from the social workers to support this". This prompted me to see if there was any evidence, and I found that the facts had been recorded in the CAMHS case file.'

The local authority barrister struggled to respond. 'We are unsure of this piece of evidence,' she said.

19

The Judge appeared impatient. 'There is no blame being apportioned in this case, am I right?'

'Yes, your Honour, but Mr and Mrs Carr are wanting to change the thresh...'

The Judge interrupted. 'Then all that needs to be included in the "threshold criteria" is that the Carrs adopted Lucy, they had these difficulties and were then unable to continue to care for her, and by that very fact the "threshold" has been reached. That is the case, isn't it, or am I missing something?'

'Yes, your Honour, that is true,' replied the barrister.

The Judge ordered us to come back after lunch, having reached an agreement.

4

Meeting Lucy

The same Judge had issued the first Care Orders in respect of Lucy and her sister Jade in July 1999. He had also ratified the Care Plan for Lucy to move in with us just weeks later, and had granted the Adoption Order in February 2001. Being in front of this Judge again felt odd. It was almost shameful, as though we had let him down, yet we had deliberately engineered for the case to come before him because he knew Lucy's family history.

We were here today some five years later to acknowledge defeat. The thought crossed my mind that he might also feel some sense of failure, as he had made all the Orders leading to the adoption. In fact, at a previous hearing, when Jon had attended alone, the Judge acknowledged that he remembered the case well, as it was such a difficult case and he had felt for Fiona, the girls' birth mother.

* * *

In July 1999, Lucy had been living in her foster home for almost two years. She had a foster sister called Shahida who was two years older than her. Their foster carer, Tracy, had decided to adopt Shahida whilst Lucy was living with them. We were led to believe that the relationship between Shahida and Lucy was competitive.

We had just come back from a camping holiday in the South of France; as usual we had taken Rebecca, our niece, with us so that Hannah would have someone to play with. During this trip we had made the decision that if the local authority did not have some good news on our return, we would forget about adoption and have another child of our own.

As soon as we got home from holiday, Valerie, the social worker who had assessed our suitability for adoption, contacted us. We had got to know her quite well as the assessment for adoption is a lengthy and intrusive process. She came to our home eight times; the assessment took over six months to complete. She also visited our friends to obtain references.

Valerie was softly spoken with a friendly face. Her appearance defied the stereotypical image of a professional woman. She looked like she might spend hours with her grandchildren baking biscuits and cakes and put out saucers of milk for all the cats in the neighbourhood. Her personality matched her kindly appearance. She came across as understanding and genuine. Later, she was to become involved in the breakdown of the adoption and my opinion of her did not alter.

Valerie told us that a child had been identified who matched our hopes: a little girl aged around four. Valerie wanted us to meet the little girl's social worker. We were both excited and nervous in equal measure by the news that we might soon have a second daughter and a sister for Hannah.

Within a matter of days two social workers were sitting in our living room drinking tea, eating biscuits and discussing Lucy and her history; at least those bits that they wanted us to know. They told us that Lucy was a bright child and that our situation was ideal because our family replicated her two previous homes, that is, Lucy being the younger of two sisters.

We had no reason to doubt this logic and accepted what the social workers told us. However, perhaps a deeper analysis of Lucy's behaviour and position in her previous homes would have indicated that this family composition was far from ideal and in fact eroded her self-esteem; Lucy was used to competing for attention and feeling less valued or worthy than the person she was competing with.

Since the disruption we have seen Lucy's previous social work files. It was recorded on numerous occasions that the relationship between Lucy and Jade, her birth sister, was troubled. Lucy would compete for their mother's attention constantly during contact sessions: 'Lucy refused to leave her mother's knee, Fiona could not get anything else done and she could not manage to put her down.' That or something similar was observed over and over again.

It was also felt that Jade had been parenting Lucy to a large degree before they were removed from their mother's care. But at the same time Jade used to steal Lucy's food, and there was evidence that Fiona favoured Jade when they were both still in contact with their mother. Also, of course, after Lucy was adopted Jade continued to have contact with their mother while Lucy couldn't.

In her foster home Lucy once again found herself competing against an older foster sister for attention. Shahida was in the process of being adopted, while Lucy was having to leave. Shahida went to ballet lessons but Lucy didn't. On our first visit we noted that Shahida was all dressed up in very pretty clothes, with her hair in a bun. Lucy was dressed in what presumably were her best clothes, given that she was meeting her new parents for the first time. Although adequate, her clothes were not in the same league as Shahida's. As our relationship with the foster carer grew, she admitted that a lady up the road who had a son a few years older than Lucy used to pass his old clothes on to her.

Lucy was nearly four years of age when she came to live

with us, and she had not been special for anyone so far. Without doubt any child would be emotionally damaged in these circumstances. Trying to get Lucy to understand that it was OK for Hannah to have hugs and kisses was to be a massive hurdle for us as a family; Lucy took any show of affection towards others, especially Hannah, as a rejection of herself.

Lucy's social workers seemed to be very excited about our family. We were told that one couple had already withdrawn their application for Lucy, but we were never given too much detail about why. The social workers gave us a photograph of Lucy from when she was about two years old and sent a video of her at around the same age, in the post.

From then on, the introductions had to be done in haste because Lucy's foster carer was going into hospital for surgery the following Monday. It was Tuesday now and we arranged that we would visit the foster home on Friday with Hannah, and that the social worker would meet us at the house; on Saturday we would visit again and take Lucy out for a picnic; then on Sunday I would collect Tracy and Lucy and bring them to our home for tea; Jon would take Tracy home later the same evening, leaving Lucy with us.

Even after our adoption training, we had a rather romantic notion of what a child who was coming up for adoption would be like, although we had never discussed this with each other or even consciously thought about it. Nevertheless, lurking somewhere in our minds, was the image of a waif-like figure who, finding love, would be just the same as Hannah, that is, one of us!

One of our stated reasons for wanting to adopt was for Hannah's sake; yes, we wanted another child, but we chose adoption so that the child would be close in age to Hannah. Not long after Lucy came to live with us I read a book on adoption breakdown: it said that wanting to adopt a child to provide a "friend" for an existing biological child was doomed to failure. At the time this did not make sense to me but it does now. I would not agree that it is "doomed to failure", but there are obvious inherent problems. That is, what happens to the adopted child if the biological child becomes too distressed? To take it further, what happens to the adopted child if the biological child develops real mental health problems? Had these questions been put to us in our assessment, we might have fallen at the first hurdle.

Friday came around very quickly, and there we were, knocking on the door of where our daughter-to-be had lived for the last two years. The door opened and before us stood a nervous and chubby little girl. She wore glasses and her dark mousy brown hair fell forward over her face, her fringe needed cutting and half-covered her glasses. She was clearly self-conscious and any attempt at communicating with her resulted in her staring out front just above her own eye level and never making any eye contact at all. She had very pretty features with clear bright blue eyes and a scattering of freckles over her nose and cheeks. I did not hear her utter a single word on this first visit.

Tracy was a single woman. She had a much older teenage son and had separated from his father when the boy was still a baby; they lived in a council property with gardens at the front and back. Tracy was a large, jolly, shiny-faced woman who had fixed ideas in regard to childrearing. She told us that she did not think Lucy had any real attachment to herself or to Shahida, the foster child she was adopting, or even to her older sister Jade. She believed that Lucy would not be particularly bothered by the move from her home.

As I write that paragraph, it is remarkable that we believed it. Of course, I am a social worker myself now, so it is easy to have a better understanding with hindsight. But the social workers then also accepted Tracy's view. So we were led to believe that a child of almost four years had no real attachments to any of the significant people in her life. What is even more astonishing is that this was not perceived as a problem.

During that first visit, although Lucy didn't talk directly to us, she made her presence known. She continually climbed onto the settee and then jumped off the side, almost hurting herself in the process, but Tracy made no attempt to stop her.

Knowing Lucy as we very soon did, she would almost certainly have ignored any attempt to get her to behave. Maybe Tracy was concerned that we wouldn't want to adopt Lucy if we saw her being defiant. Or perhaps Tracy was concerned that any attempt to correct her behaviour could create an embarrassing situation. Whatever the reason, Lucy was left pretty much to get on with it, while Tracy tried her best to talk to us.

Lucy pushed the boundaries further: she went into the kitchen and came back with half a loaf of Sunblest bread in her hands. Tracy made light of the episode by saying that Lucy would eat anything you put in front of her. Lucy sat down on the carpet and proceeded to eat the bread. She came to me and offered me a piece. I thanked her for it; it looked like a gesture of acceptance and I felt warm towards her. I did my best to eat some of it.

There was a park near Tracy's home and somebody suggested that it might offer more opportunity for some interaction between Lucy and ourselves. So we all walked to the park; Tracy came along as well but Lucy walked independently and pretty much stayed alone. She was clearly aware of our presence but chose to do her own thing even when we were in the park. Hannah remained close to Jon and me most of the time, but she kept trying to join in play with Lucy, who didn't seem to notice. Lucy enthusiastically tried out the slide and roundabout and appeared to enjoy herself despite the lack of interaction.

On the journey home Jon and I discussed the visit. 'She seemed to be watching us,' I said, 'what do you think?'

'I don't know,' said Jon. 'I'll feel better when we take her out on our own tomorrow, it will feel less contrived then.'

Hannah was excited about going for a picnic the following day and she asked lots and lots of questions about Lucy, most of which we couldn't answer.

We arrived to take Lucy to the picnic, in two cars. I worked near where Lucy lived, some 30 miles away from our home, and I had been at work that morning. We left Jon's car at Tracy's house and drove to a local country park in my car. It was a large park with swings and squirrels and had loads of quiet spots ideal for picnicking; the weather was warm but overcast.

Lucy seemed different that day. She was just as self-conscious but a bit more talkative and we were surprised that she referred to me as "mummy". Her body posture was not the same: she didn't stand up straight or walk properly – she would lollop from one foot to the other. Jon made a joke saying she had turned into "Galon" overnight, a character from *Planet of the Apes*. We had our video camera with us so that we could catch the first moments of being together as a family. Lucy momentarily came out of her shell as she was running along shouting 'watch me skip, Mummy!'

In time, this video made quite painful viewing because it is clear that as Lucy is skipping and shouting to me, Hannah is running after Lucy and shouting 'chase me, Lucy', but Lucy doesn't. She is only interested in me. We were not concerned at all at the time and we reassured Hannah that Lucy had a lot going on, but in actual fact it turned out to be a problem that we never managed to fully work through.

When we sat to eat our picnic, Lucy withdrew back into her self-conscious shell and reverted to staring directly in front and not focusing on anything. Although she did not appear to be listening, she was. If she was asked which sandwich she would like, or asked to throw some food to the pigeons that were surrounding us, she immediately answered or responded. But she spoke in a mechanical monotone voice, which made her sound almost robotic.

We didn't think too much about it at the time, but later when I was a student social worker, I read a book about separation and loss and the impact it can have on a child's physiology: losing a parent can produce a diminished body awareness in children and they can appear inattentive or clumsy. It would have really helped to know about these effects on a child at the start of the placement, as we would have been better prepared. Instead, we just thought it odd that she was different from the way she'd been the previous day at the foster carers'.

Jon and I didn't have huge expectations after the first visit but we were hopeful that Lucy and Hannah would get along. Hannah's expectations were similar to our own, that she would have someone to play with. Lucy's expectation, I imagine, was to be liked and wanted by us all. It never occurred to Hannah or to us that they would not just naturally get along like children do. We were not aware that, in effect, we were including Lucy, but on condition, right from the very start.

Of course, we did not really appreciate the position Lucy was in: she was desperate for a mother figure, she had only ever known female carers, she was about to lose everything that was familiar to her. Everyone around her, including the social workers, were "selling" her the idea of a new family and expecting her to be happy about it. It must all have been very frightening and confusing for her.

We finished the picnic and set off back to Tracy's house but as we reached the car we could see it had been broken into. My handbag had been stolen with all our money, Jon's car keys, the house keys, driving licence and other items of sentimental value. They had also stolen a huge fluffy toy dog of Hannah's which her auntie had bought for her after she trapped her thumb in a door at school. Hannah absolutely loved that dog and was as angry as any small child could be that someone had just taken it from her.

We had parked close to a huge skip, rather like the ones you see at a refuse tip, and as we looked inside the boot to see what else was missing, we spotted a woman and a man who had clearly just finished having sex, we may have even interrupted them. She was pulling down her skirt and he was cleaning himself up. Their embarrassed faces stared at us as we disapprovingly redirected the children's attention and set off to look for a police station. The man got into a car and drove off as the woman walked away alone.

We had to arrange to have all the locks on our house changed and had to get hold of another set of keys for Jon's car. Nevertheless, we eventually returned Lucy to Tracy's house and she immediately informed her that 'Mummy had her bag stolen'. She seemed to be very worried about my bag in particular. Hannah continued to be angry about the loss of her fluffy dog.

Over a glass of wine that evening, Jon confided that he felt that having the car broken into, the bag stolen and seeing the couple were bad omens and he was concerned that "something out there" was trying to warn us not to go ahead. But I felt differently. I remembered the day when I returned home from hospital after giving birth to Hannah. Jon had parked the car outside on the public road for easy access. On that day the car had also been broken into and the radio and other things stolen but we have never been happier than since Hannah was born. I managed to reassure Jon that there was nothing to worry about. Besides, Lucy was coming to live with us the following day!

I had arranged to pick up Lucy and Tracy after I finished work. We had already taken some of her belongings so there wasn't much left to pack before we set off for Lucy's new home.

Jon and Hannah were getting things ready at home. Jon had prepared a meal and Hannah had got all her toys out that she thought would be suitable for two to play with. On the face of it, we were all getting what we wanted. But was Lucy? At only almost four years of age, she was too young to fully grasp what was happening. She really wanted to live with her mother, and if she could not be with her, did she want to stay where she was?

There is a saying, that *to a worm in horseradish the whole world is horseradish*. This was Hannah's reality, her "horseradish" was having doting parents who clapped with delight at any achievement no matter how slight; her world was to be loved, cherished, and made to feel special; she was number one. Lucy had never been a worm in horseradish. That state of blissful certainty and ignorance that we shared had been denied her. After two abrupt placement moves and the loss of her sister and mother at crucial stages in her development, Lucy's only certainties were, in fact, uncertainties.

Jon had made a Sunday roast and Hannah had erected her *Barbie* playhouse. The conversation batted around trivial matters of total irrelevance to the circumstances. Tracy stayed for about an hour after we had finished eating. Then it was time to say goodbyes. Tracy was convinced that Lucy would be fine after she'd gone, and for a while it looked like she might be right. They said goodbye with a kiss and a hug and everything appeared to be fine.

Hannah's friendly overtures seemed to pay off and the girls played a little, then it was time to put them to bed. They would have to share a bedroom; we had not had time to get our spare room ready or any money to buy new furniture. We did manage to buy a bed, but nothing else. So the girls had to share all their space, including the wardrobe and chest of drawers.

Lucy wore a pair of Hannah's dalmatian dog pyjamas. Although there was a three-year age gap between the girls, they were roughly the same height, and Lucy was stockier than Hannah, so they were a good fit. We knew nothing of Lucy's bedtime routine so we tried to do with her as we had always done with Hannah. That is, teeth brushed and a story. At some point Lucy began to cry and became increasingly distressed. I guessed that the change from her usual routine had brought home to her that things were going to be different from now on; she had had very little preparation or time to get used to the idea. Hannah also became tearful and said, 'Please, Mum, if she wants to go back to Tracy's then let's take her'. It really upset Hannah that Lucy did not seem to be happy to be with us. We hadn't warned her that this might happen because we were not prepared for it ourselves. Lucy sat on my knee and continued to sob for a considerable time. This happened for a few nights before she began to settle down.

In the very early days of Lucy's time with us, I began to realise that her place in the family was being seen in terms of how her presence affected Hannah. Although unintentionally, we were not truly seeing her as an individual with the same rights to happiness, love and security as we all enjoyed. I do not want to appear too self-critical because I think it was probably a natural response. We idolised Hannah and would do anything for her. We had embarked on this journey with her in mind and had been completely honest with professionals about our expectations. I shared my thoughts with Jon. I was concerned about the potential long-term damage to Lucy's sense of self-worth if we continued as we were. On an intellectual level he understood and he committed to considering Lucy in her own right. But on an emotional level he struggled more and more to accept her as equal to Hannah, and he felt almost as if getting too close to Lucy was tantamount to a betrayal of Hannah.

5

Holding onto the past

'Do you feel guilty?' Marjorie, the Guardian, asked when we returned to the court after lunch.

'It isn't as simple as that,' I tried to explain. But she repeated, 'Do you feel guilty?' She persisted with the question until I answered, 'I don't know what I feel'. I was frustrated with her questioning.

Later that day I had time to reflect on Marjorie's words. Her question was too simplistic; any brief answer in a courtroom seconds before the judge was due to arrive could never do justice to the situation. This little girl had been so much a part of all of our lives for such a long time. It is really an insult to ask such a question, as if some definitive conclusion could have been drawn from my answer.

* * *

Lucy lived with us for four-and-a-half years and I can clearly recall the way she looked on her first morning in our home. Even though she had a disturbed night, she came downstairs in the morning wearing the red dalmatian pyjamas, and very confidently walked past us, straight into the kitchen, clearly expecting her breakfast. She was tiny and looked different with her hair all messy and hanging down. We were all pleased that Lucy appeared to feel comfortable with us. A small thing like expecting her breakfast and eating what she was given felt like some kind of acceptance.

As adoptive parents, you instinctively find ways to claim your child. You look for similarities to yourselves, as you do with your own children. Lucy wore glasses; she had blue eyes and was on the plump side. Jon also wears glasses, has blue eyes and is on the plump side. Looking back, it was as though we were trying to create a biological link. Relatives and friends all did the same. 'Oh, Lucy takes after Jon,' people would say, 'and Hannah takes after Karen.' This was also a way of making Lucy feel less different. Is this a good thing? I still don't know.

In reality Lucy has a completely different bone structure to Jon, and Hannah actually looks a lot like her dad. Hannah and Lucy have similar colour hair, but Hannah, aged seven, was slight and small and Lucy, aged four, was well built and fairly tall. Initially these differences were swept aside, as we concentrated on the similarities. It was important to Lucy that she looked like us and did not stand out; it must also have been important to me, as I would do Hannah's and Lucy's hair in similar styles and buy them similar clothes. Nevertheless, we were all delighted when we met biologically related sisters who did not look like each other. 'See,' Jon and I would say to the girls, 'you two look more alike than they do.'

The social workers had asked for photographs of Jon, Hannah and myself and compiled a little life story book about us just prior to Lucy moving in. On the last page it reads, 'Karen will be your forever mummy, Jon will be your forever daddy and Hannah will be your forever sister,' with pictures of us all smiling.

I cannot imagine what all this must have meant to Lucy. She had only found out that she was leaving her current foster home a couple of days previously and suddenly she had a different family all grinning from ear to ear, and unbeknown to her, with not much understanding of a child's needs in these circumstances.

Our training, well over twelve months ago, had informed us that children who are looked after by the local authority are often subject to frequent moves. I recall their use of visual imagery to get their point across. They showed us a large drawing of a street with several houses on it. They then told a story of a child who'd had so many placement breakdowns that he could have lived in each house in the last two years.

They demonstrated how we metaphorically build a wall as we develop and grow. If all of our needs are met throughout life, we will have a complete wall. Children who are looked after by the local authority will often not have had even their basic needs met. If they have not formed a strong relationship with one specific person, they will lose some bricks; if they have suffered neglect, they will lose more; and even more if they have been physically, sexually or emotionally abused. If enough needs are not met, and if too many bricks are missing, the wall cannot stay up at all and will crumble to the floor.

We were also told that children who have been sexually abused often display sexualised behaviour. Even very young children can behave provocatively. This obviously makes these children vulnerable to further sexual abuse.

The training was successful in getting us to feel very sorry for children who end up in the care system. However, it did nothing to prepare us for dealing with this little girl we brought to our home. Feeling sorry for a child is not the same as having some idea of what she might be going through or understanding how this could impact upon her behaviour and relationships. Feeling sorry does not give you the skills and knowledge to respond appropriately. But what feeling sorry can do is mislead you into believing that you do know all you need to know.

We agreed with the social workers that the introduction

to our home, which should have taken place prior to Lucy coming to live with us, could in effect take place afterwards. In other words, we would keep in close touch with the foster carers to enable Lucy to make the transition to our family more gradually. She could telephone Tracy and Shahida and we would visit them.

On the second day, I suggested that we telephone to let them know that everything was alright. I had telephoned Tracy the evening before to warn her that Lucy was going to ring, so that she could prepare Shahida.

When Lucy first came to live with us, she had a strange speech difficulty. She put an "s" on the end of each and every word. It is actually difficult to do if you try. On the phone, Tracy asked Lucy if she'd had her tea and Lucy said yes, she asked her what she had eaten and Lucy told her. When it was time to say goodbye, Lucy said to Tracy, 'mes loves yous Tracys'.

Tracy was clearly surprised by Lucy's emotional expression. 'Oh Lucy,' she said, 'you're funny.'

We had been told that Lucy would not really be fazed by the move to our home, but she was clearly attached to Tracy and to her birth sister Jade. She never showed any feeling for her foster sister Shahida. However, Tracy told us that the morning following Lucy's departure, Shahida had become really distressed, and no amount of comforting could console her.

Of course Shahida could freely express her emotions. She was in a safe environment with her adoptive mother with whom she had lived for most of her life. While there was a void where Lucy used to be, her routine remained the same as always. But Lucy was in an unfamiliar environment, with lots of new people to occupy her. For a sensitive shy child like Lucy, that is almost like an assault on the mind and body.

Lucy named all the fluffy toys we bought her either Tracy or Jade, after her foster carer and her birth sister. Very occasionally she would call them Fiona after her birth mother. If I am being honest, this created an early problem in the home. I am not suggesting that how we reacted was "right", but we wanted Lucy to feel a part of our family. Hannah was only just seven years old, and she would get cross as she felt that Lucy was deliberately trying to hurt her. Jon became irritated because he felt that Lucy was being disloyal, and I would try to get her to rename some of her toys, by saying 'they can't all be called Tracy or Jade'.

The only way I can justify this is to say that emotions are emotive, emotions are what move people into action or reaction. People will often say in all sorts of circumstances, 'you must remain objective' as if this were an easy task. Our perception of objectivity is entirely based on our personal beliefs, which are, in turn, coloured by our emotions. I believe that emotions transcend logical thinking. The use of propaganda during times of war shows the degree to which people react to their emotions. They may never have encountered "the enemy" but, armed with enough emotive language created for the sole purpose of demonising the enemy, people can literally go and kill complete strangers.

We were not armed with enough information to enable us to make sense of what we were encountering. We had very little preparation for this particular child, called Lucy, and as a consequence our emotions were very immature, and we had too little knowledge, so all we could do was follow our instincts. After a few years of reading and learning, it seems obvious that Lucy was getting comfort from calling her toys by the names of the people who were familiar to her, and maybe it was a way of holding on to her past. She created her own continuity in her own way, by making them part of her "new family". It was probably the best way of surviving for a little child living in an alien environment. I know that when she left our home, she made the decision that she wanted to be a social worker, like me. Perhaps this is a more grown-up form of the toy naming behaviour.

Those early weeks at home were peculiar as we were all

unused to the situation we found ourselves in. At first Lucy tried to mould her personality to her environment. Indeed, at an initial review meeting with the social workers, Jon and I can remember saying that 'Lucy fits right in' and that 'it is as though she had always been here'. At the time we were told that it is usual for children when first placed to have a "honeymoon period". We weren't completely naïve, we did expect to have problems, and we guessed that as Lucy became more trusting she would be bound to test our commitment to her.

Lucy did not start to speak until she was two years old. The social workers told us that this was due to a lack of early stimulation and that in any case her sister used to speak for her. Lucy's unusual speech problem very quickly cleared up while living with us, even though she'd had it since beginning to talk. This may have been due to the high degree of one-to-one input she was getting as I reduced my working hours. When Lucy went for an adoption medical a few months after she came to live with us, we were delighted that the doctor felt that Lucy had progressed in every area since moving into our home.

Previously, the doctor had recorded that she was difficult to assess, that she was lacking in confidence and presented as unhappy. She was a child who needed speech therapy, avoided eye contact and had behavioural problems. It was now no longer felt that a referral for speech therapy was necessary; her awkward gait and her social skills had improved, and she presented as sociable and engaging. Even though it was sometimes very difficult to manage some of Lucy's behaviour at home, we definitely felt we were on the right track and had no hesitation in congratulating ourselves.

Lucy was home alone with me for much of the time, as Hannah went to school and Jon was at work. I used the same parenting techniques with Lucy that I had used with Hannah, and slowly Lucy responded.

To bring Lucy's early personality to life is not easy, as

her character was complex and full of ambiguities. For example, when Lucy met someone for the first time who might be important or significant for her in the future, such as people in nursery or school or neighbours or visiting family, she would be incredibly shy, and it was difficult, if not impossible, to get a word out of her. Conversely, if we were in a crowded room where everybody was anonymous, like in a restaurant, or a lift or a doctor's waiting room, Lucy would do everything to get attention. She would sing or laugh loudly or ask strangers questions, jump up and down, decide to play roly-poly and skip around. I am not entirely sure how we were perceived, but most of the time I think people were indulgent. Lucy was engaging and sweet, not irritating or destructive.

Lucy was also fiercely independent. When she first arrived she wanted to do everything for herself; it would get to a stage where we would have to force her to let us help. One day she was trying to get her coat on, but it was upside down. She was getting frustrated but still would not let us help and would not listen or turn it around. She ended up getting really cross and she began to cry out of frustration because we were laughing, not to be mean, but it was genuinely funny. Nevertheless, she still continued to struggle and shrugged us off until she had completely exhausted all ideas of how to do it for herself. She eventually allowed me to do it for her.

In the early days she also struggled to get her socks on, do her hair, brush her teeth, put pyjamas on or anything else that needed to be done. It made my heart open out to Lucy. She needed someone to love her, and to look after her, even while she was as determined as she could be to look after herself.

But she was as defiant as she was endearing. When Lucy succeeded in doing something for herself after refusing to let us help, she would be victorious, strutting around as if to say, 'I don't need you, ha!'

As we all began to know each other, we realised that

Lucy was an extremely astute little girl. She had a distinct ability, or skill, to engage adults in conversation.

She would say things like 'I like your hair', or 'that's a pretty top, where did you get it?' or she'd ask people where they had been, had they been there before, would they go again? She could always think of relevant questions that people would want to answer. It was interesting to watch a four-year-old be so absorbed in grown-up talk.

In virtually no time at all Lucy had gone from being quite poorly developed to knowing her colours, learning the alphabet, being able to count and write her name. She was incredibly quick to grasp information, in particular anything to do with numbers. Yet she used to worry that she wasn't as good at maths as she could be.

Lucy had an absolute need to know how her day was going to be set out. She had to have her breakfast the second she woke up, then she would ask what was going to happen until 12 o'clock, which was lunchtime. Lucy was very particular that lunch had to be at 12 o'clock; this was easy in the early days before she could tell the time, but even pre-school she knew where the hands of the clock had to be at noon. Eventually she did learn to accept that lunch could be at a different time. After lunch she would question what we were doing until teatime. Her need to have this structure to her day led to her being able to tell the time at an early age.

Although this sounds quite charming, it was actually very draining. Every day for a long, long time after she arrived, the questions would start as soon as she'd had her breakfast.

She'd say, 'What are we doing next, Mummy?'

I'd answer, 'We're going shopping, Lucy'.

'To buy some food, Mummy?'

'Yes, and maybe some other bits and pieces.'

Lucy would think for a second and then say, 'What else do you want, Mummy?'

'I don't know. We'll see when we get there.'

You could see her mind computing the information and then searching for the next question. 'Where are we going to, Mummy?'

'The shops.'

'Which shops?'

'I'm not sure yet, Lucy.'

'What are we going to do after that?'

'We'll go back home, or maybe to the park.'

'Will we go home first or to the park first?'

In the end I'd say something like, 'You know, Lucy, you don't need to know exactly what you're going to do all the time. Sometimes people don't know what they are going to do for the rest of the day or even the whole week.' But Lucy would carry on with, 'What are we going to do after that?'

To which I'd reply, 'We'll have lunch.'

'Will it be 12 o'clock, Mummy?'

'About that, yes.'

She'd think for a moment, and then, 'What are we having for lunch, Mummy?'

I'd think and say 'a sandwich.'

'Just a sandwich, Mummy, that won't be enough.'

'Well, you'll have a yoghurt and biscuit or an apple or crisps like you usually do.'

'What will we be having today, Mummy?'

'I'm not sure what we've got, Lucy,' beginning to get irritated, 'we'll see when we get home.'

'I think we've got some crisps, Mummy.'

'Then you can have some crisps.'

'What are we going to do after that?'

The questioning would not end until it was time for her to go to bed.

There is a day that stands out as memorable when our relationship reached a new level of understanding. But it was not by any means the only day when things had been difficult.

Lucy and I had gone into town shopping; there were a few things I wanted to buy, including a birthday card. Lucy had been relentlessly asking questions one after the other. Usually when Lucy asked these questions continuously, she did it as though she wasn't really paying attention: she would skip or clap her hands or play with something at the same time. On this particular day I was in a shop looking for a birthday card and I wanted to concentrate on reading the messages. Lucy was persistently asking what was going on, why we were in the shop and so on. We then got into what can only be described as a quick-fire control battle. I was answering her questions at lightning speed, but she was throwing them back even quicker. It was exhausting, so I decided to ignore her. Then Lucy began pulling all the cards out of the shelves and throwing them on the floor. Needless to say, I told her very firmly to stop it, but she continued to throw the cards, then she began laughing hysterically and running around the small shop before throwing herself to the floor.

That was it – I grabbed her and lifted her off the floor by one arm. Lucy then began to scream as loudly as she possibly could. 'Please Mummy no, I'm sorry, please Mummy no, I'm really, really sorry, no Mummy don't, don't hurt me Mummy, Mummy please don't hurt me, I'm sorry!' She was shouting these words at the top of her voice. She grabbed hold of the shelves so I couldn't get her out of the shop. I lost my grip of her so that she fell to the floor. She went like a dead weight. The shop assistants and customers just stared at us as I desperately tried to drag Lucy out of the shop. When we got outside she just stopped screaming as if nothing had happened.

I walked – dragged her to the car and put her inside. Lucy then calmly asked, 'What are we doing next, Mummy?' I placed my face about two inches from hers and shouted at the top of my voice, 'Don't you EVER do that again and shut up – now!'

As we got nearer to home, she started to ask again what we were doing next. I could not believe her doggedness. The questions went on. When we got home I sat her on a tall bar stool in the middle of the kitchen, so that she could not distract herself with anything else. She seemed to understand the situation when I began to fire question after question at her.

'What are you doing now, Lucy?'

'I'm sitting on a stool.'

'What are you doing after that?'

'I'm having my dinner.'

'Then what are you going to do?'

'I'm going to play.'

'What are you going to play?'

'Doing hair.'

Unlike me, Lucy was able to answer any question I gave her; this went on until Lucy began to laugh.

'I am not laughing, Lucy. WHAT are you doing after that?'

By now Lucy could barely get her answers out, she was giggling that much. I couldn't help myself and started to laugh too. After this we had our first real, emotionally charged talk about her feelings of insecurity and needing to know everything that was going to happen, her place in the home and her fear that nothing was permanent. I learnt that she was not being deliberately demanding, irritating or frustrating and that, in fact, she was a scared little girl trying to make sense of her world.

This was not the end of Lucy's questioning, but when she did have the urge to ask the same questions – and she did, out of habit probably – she would realise, look at me and then laugh, so it was the beginning of the end.

Soon after her arrival it gradually dawned on us that Lucy had a definite preference to be with me at all times. This came as a surprise to Jon and me, as we had expected Lucy and Hannah to develop a relationship first. We felt that they would naturally incline towards one another because of their age. This really shows how ignorant we were about the dynamics of adoption.

Lucy would have to sit directly behind me in the car. It

took us a while to notice, because it didn't occur to anyone why she was so determined to sit in a particular seat until Hannah finally realised after another battle about who was sitting where. 'That's what it is,' she exclaimed, 'you want to sit behind Mum!'

From then on we designated them both a permanent seat. Lucy would always sit behind the driver's seat and Hannah behind the passenger's. I was driving most of the time, but if we went out and Jon drove, Lucy would have to sit behind him, so she wasn't getting what she wanted all of the time. If we were in Jon's car she would also have to sit behind the driver's seat. It took Lucy a long time, probably as long as twelve months, to fully accept these arrangements without resentment when she had to sit behind Jon.

We went out to eat as often as we could afford to, and again, Lucy would always sit herself next to me. If she were not allowed to, she would be disruptive – talking or shouting over other conversation. So more often than not we allowed her to sit next to me, just so we could enjoy the meal.

Lucy got her own way in this respect most of the time. It did not appear to be a problem for Hannah and, by and large, I don't think it was, until much later on in their relationship. Lucy also loved to play with other children, including Hannah. But she played like a much younger child. She would physically be with the others, but would mostly be doing her own thing. She and Hannah made friends with two sisters, Chloe and Louise, who lived around the corner. The sisters were the same age as Lucy and Hannah and we soon became close friends with their parents Flick and Andrew. We needed good friends in the times to come.

* * *

Marjorie, the Guardian, was still asking, 'Do you feel guilty?' in a way that implied that I should be. It seemed that the Guardian was placing herself as judge of a situation that she clearly did not understand. This is not intended to be a personal criticism but a criticism of the lack of adoption expertise of professionals in generic Children's Services. They are appointed because of their qualifications, skills, and knowledge. They cannot, and will not be, specialists in all areas. Nevertheless, they are asked to provide an "expert opinion" on adoption matters, and they do not hesitate to give it. Society would never ask psychiatrists to perform brain surgery because they are not qualified to do so. They understand how the brain works, but they would be horrified if we then expected them to operate to prevent epileptic seizures. I am absolutely certain that our social workers, during and after the disruption, and the Guardian had no, or little, experience of adoption. The social workers came from a "child protection" background and tried to fit an adoption breakdown into that framework. That is, they tried to fit a round peg into a square hole and, like a baby, they had no idea that what they were trying to do was impossible.

I was frustrated by the Guardian's ignorance that day in court and when I got home I wrote her a letter. At the time I was still very much grieving for the loss of Lucy, and I did not have the benefit of hindsight that I have now as I write this book. But these are extracts from the letter that I wrote.

> *Dear Marjorie,*
>
> *I feel compelled to write to you following completion of your report in relation to Lucy, because I want to explain certain things to you. You have written about my family, including Lucy, and I want to respond to you.*
>
> *I am writing this because I do feel that you have tried hard to understand the truth. I am also speaking from the heart. This is not for court reports and cannot do me*

any good whatsoever, so I hope you accept it as true.
Firstly, I would like to thank you for placing Lucy in
the centre of your thinking throughout your report. You
quite rightly indicate that both the local authority and
ourselves appeared to lose sight of the purpose of our
statements.

Lucy has lost a family, and Hannah has too. We all
have. There is a feeling that something is missing
almost constantly; it has been like a bereavement. Since
Lucy left I have asked Hannah on numerous occasions
whether she wants to see Lucy and whether we can't
work something out, but Hannah is adamant that she
does not want to. She says she misses Lucy sometimes
and she feels sorry for her, but she is clear that she does
not want to see her.

In court you asked me if I felt guilty and I said 'yes'.

I don't know if I feel guilty, but I do feel a deep and
constant sense of loss. Initially I was in shock. But I feel
hurt for Lucy; I can imagine a lot of what I believe she
is thinking and feeling. I hope with all my heart that
Lucy has peace and love in her life and I pray that she
is able to find a home where she can stay and feel secure
enough to get over all that has happened to her. I am
the person who supported Lucy through thick and thin,
who helped her through her sadness, who kissed her
every day, who loved her every day, whom she loved
back, who taught her to read and write, who helped her
make sense of her past, who tried to fill the void caused
by her early childhood experiences, to whom Lucy
confided all her deepest fears. So I believe I feel her pain
to a degree that I have never experienced before and
hope never to experience again. I feel the fear that I
imagine she is experiencing at this moment of going
through more change in her short little life, and I feel
that I want to bring Lucy home and say everything will
be alright, that is what I feel.

45

But I think guilt is an emotion attached to wrongdoing, and my belief really is that in the end we acted to protect Hannah.

I have no idea if Marjorie read or even received the letter; she never gave any acknowledgement.

6

Keeping in touch

We were called back before the Judge in the afternoon; presumably he had by now read over more of the paperwork in relation to the proceedings. He peered over his half-moon spectacles and, shaking his head in slow motion, looking from one solicitor to the next, he said, 'Lucy has a half-sister, Jade. What arrangements are being made for contact between these two?'

Our barrister, Miss Pickering, spoke. 'Your Honour, my clients are clear that Lucy should continue to have contact with Jade, as this relationship has been the one constant in Lucy's life. They believe it will be detrimental to them both if the relationship is not maintained.'

* * *

On 15 July 1999, Lucy was living with Tracy and Shahida; she was completely immersed in their family, albeit as a temporary member. Her day, her routine and her activities were entrenched in the culture of their household. Lucy referred to Tracy's relations as her aunties and grandma. She saw her birth mother, Fiona, and Jade, her sister, every fortnight. She attended nursery five half-days a week; she played almost daily with a little boy who lived a couple of doors away on the same street. On 15 July, Lucy was unaware that any changes were afoot. Nevertheless, by 20 July, her life had changed immeasurably and would never be the same again.

Lucy was moved 30 miles away to live with people she did not know, she would only see her birth mother one more final time, and her contact with Jade was cut to between four and six times a year. In future she would only visit her foster family, and what had been her home for almost two years, at her new family's convenience.

When Lucy moved in with us, we agreed to what social services call "indirect contact" with Fiona. We were told we would need to update her on Lucy's progress once a year and Fiona would send Lucy a card with a simple message on her birthday and at Christmas. Jade continued to have weekly direct contact and frequent telephone calls to her mother.

We agreed to direct contact with Jade and I can recall some of the discussions we had with the social workers about it at the time. We were to arrange and manage it ourselves together with Jade's foster carers. Jade and Lucy's social workers were sure we wouldn't experience any problems – they didn't envisage that the contact would continue much beyond a couple of years. They told us that the age gap between the two girls was too great for them to maintain a proper relationship; Jade would soon be approaching her teenage years and would be more interested in spending time with friends and boyfriends. This concerned us; we thought that it might be traumatic for Lucy to develop this relationship further if we were all expecting Jade to stop wanting to see Lucy in a couple of years. The social workers assured us that the contact was not frequent enough for them to get to know each other in any real sense, and that Lucy's attachment to Jade was weak anyway. They told us that the purpose of contact was to help Lucy's sense of identity and she would not be harmed unduly if it stopped abruptly. We weren't knowledgeable enough to question this at that time.

The social workers explained that Jade had a lot going on in terms of contact because she also saw her dad once a month. They believed that Jade was able to keep all these different aspects of her life and her relationship with each family member separate. In other words, the social workers were not concerned that Jade would pass any information on to their mother about Lucy's situation or whereabouts, or let anything that their mother said influence her interaction or behaviour with Lucy.

It saddens me now that not only did we not question things enough, but even when we did, the social workers truly believed what they were telling us. In a way the children were lucky because, unusually, the same social workers had been involved with Lucy, Jade and Fiona from the first referral right through to their permanent placements. I'm in no doubt that they wanted the best for the girls. But even a stable and secure adult would have difficulty compartmentalising close personal relationships without being influenced by someone they loved dearly. Jade was just ten years old, it was an exceptionally tall order for an emotionally damaged and neglected child, and in time, Jade would not be able to pull it off.

We were also told that Lucy's relationship with Hannah would rapidly develop and she would soon become the more important sister in Lucy's life. This seemed a reasonable assumption to make. After all, Lucy would be spending most of her time with Hannah from now on, and living as sisters would surely create the bond!

We were fed opinions and accepted them as facts. We didn't consider the issues in enough depth. If we had, we might have realised that when you are dealing with children who have already had a number of abrupt separations, we don't know how they will behave or react when they are placed in a new family. There is research and experience, and sometimes we can predict, but there are no objective facts. This is social science, not physics or chemistry.

It was agreed that the first contact between Jade and Lucy would take place at our home so that the social workers could bring Jade with them and hold Lucy's "Looked After Children" review at the same time. This was in August 1999, shortly after Lucy moved in with us. We were apprehensive, but we had learned that to deny contact with a child's family could be damaging in the longer term as it was almost like denying the child's history.

Jade was likeable and keen to make an impression on us; she was a tough-talking girl with a lot of street credibility. She was tall for her age with an athletic figure. There was some resemblance between the sisters in their skin tone, freckles, eye and hair colour. The second Lucy and Jade saw each other, they just smiled and held each other's gaze, shyly approaching one another for a hug. We could immediately see that Jade and Lucy had a comfortable affectionate bond; it instinctively felt right to sustain it.

Jade referred to Jon as "mate" and questioned me on my care of Lucy; I could sense that she needed to know whether or not Lucy was OK with us, and she gave us her approval. As they were leaving, we could see the relief in Jade's demeanour. She appeared happier than when she first arrived; perhaps she felt comfortable with us, and was pleased that Lucy was well looked after and had a nice home. The first visit passed without a hitch.

In the autumn of 1999 we telephoned Jade's foster carers, Sandra and Ken. They were very experienced and had been fostering children for years. They were an elderly couple and were already grandparents. I generally spoke with Sandra when I phoned and we got to know each other reasonably well over the following couple of years.

We agreed we would collect Jade then go out for the day with the three girls, Jade, Lucy and Hannah. We had high hopes for the meeting and were naïvely determined to have family days out like this every other month. In reality that proved to be very difficult.

Sandra and Ken lived over 40 miles away and it was a

strenuous journey, usually in heavy traffic. They lived in an area where there wasn't anything in the way of activities, entertainment, or even a park or gardens. For our first two visits we collected Jade and then travelled to the nearest city centre, where we would spend a couple of hours looking around, have lunch and then take Jade home. It felt as though we were spending the day in the car. Also, it was stifling for Lucy and Jade who weren't able to have time on their own, and it made us aware that Hannah was being left out.

Watching Hannah reminded me of when I was a very small child. Lots of the children at the primary school I attended used to bring in sweets that would be given to the teacher and then handed out again at playtime. I never had any sweets and I still remember the feeling of desperately wanting some and watching from the side as the other children lined up to get theirs. On one occasion I raised my hand for some sweet cigarettes, unwittingly the teacher gave them to me, I ate the lot and got into trouble.

Hannah listened to Lucy and Jade's conversation from the side, wanting desperately to be a part of it. It was apparent that, despite what the social workers had said, Lucy and Jade naturally inclined towards one another; they slipped into effortless uncomplicated chitchat that excluded the rest of us. We watched Hannah trying hard to join in. Jade would try to encourage her, but Hannah only wanted to be close to Lucy. She felt, and was, rejected by her. Lucy was just four years old at the time and it was quite natural for her to rejoice in the affections of her forcibly estranged sister. From the second Lucy saw Jade, her whole attention was on her.

How did we feel about this? We understood the need for the contact but Hannah was suffering. Up until this point she had been an only child for over six years and had been the centre of our world. Now suddenly she was dealing with feelings of rejection, she no longer had all our attention and she had to share her bedroom and her

51

clothes as well as her parents. I can see this now, but at the time we were very caught up with the changes for Lucy and simply tried to reassure both of our daughters.

Stopping contact with Jade was not an option, but the arrangements were not working, and we needed to talk things through with Sandra and Ken. They were amenable people and didn't mind sharing some of the responsibility. But there was a problem. Ken was disabled and used a wheelchair and he found it difficult to drive for long periods. Also, they were a generation older than us. Nevertheless, they offered to bring Jade to our home for some meetings, while they had a day out in a nearby seaside town. This would take some of the pressure off us and Hannah would be able to invite a friend of her own to play. Other times, we would go on as before. We did find a play activity centre near where Jade lived, so we didn't have to walk around the city streets. This wasn't ideal, as Jade was too old for it, but at least it gave Lucy and Jade some space to be alone.

I recall one time when we had picked up Jade and driven into the city. We all fancied lunch at McDonalds and stopped off for burgers. It was the last contact before Christmas in December 1999, Lucy's first Christmas with us. As soon as we had sat down with our food, Jade began to talk excitedly. 'Remember what our mum's like, Lucy?' she asked, not wanting or waiting for a reply. 'She gets us loads and loads of presents, you know,' she said opening up the conversation to include the rest of us, 'doesn't she, Lucy, you remember?' She went on to describe bags and bags of presents that Fiona had bought them both. Jade was always animated when she talked about Fiona, and she nearly always was talking about Fiona when she was with Lucy. Jade certainly idolised their mum and put her on a pedestal. She thought she was just perfect in every possible way. She constantly tried to remind Lucy of home life; she was much older than Lucy when they had been taken away, and she still spoke to their mum daily and saw her every week.

It was understandable that Jade felt very close to their mum, but it was uncomfortable listening to the adulation. We were not prepared for Lucy's birth mum to be so present in our lives. When Jade went to the toilet I decided to follow her to have a chat. I explained that Lucy didn't remember as much as she did about their mum because of her age. I also said that it was really important for Lucy to feel part of *our* family. Jade said, 'Oh yes, I'm sorry, I'm sorry, I wasn't thinking'. She seemed unsure of what was expected of her. 'Have I not to mention her anymore, should I call her Fiona?'

'No, no, that's OK,' I said, 'it's just that Lucy doesn't have the same memories as you and don't forget, she can't see your mum again, so you just need to tone it down a little. Maybe if Lucy asks questions about her, it's alright to answer, and you can talk about things that are important and part of your life now, that's fine too. Do you understand?'

Jade's response really took me by surprise. 'Can you adopt me?' she asked. 'I'll be good, I promise, I just know we'll get on well. Sandra and Ken are nice but they're too old, please, if you adopt me I don't mind not seeing our mum, I don't see her that much anyway and I could help you look after Lucy and Hannah.'

'Hey, hey, slow down, where's this come from, Jade?' I interrupted. 'We can't adopt you, Jade, you know that and anyway we were only approved for one child, I'm really sorry.' I put my arm around her, not really knowing what to do or say. I hugged her for a few minutes and tried to comfort her by telling her that she could have an overnight stay in the future. For my sake she pretended that this was almost as good a solution. We stayed and chatted for a while in the toilets, but I knew that she wasn't happy.

Jon and I were very fond of Jade and we did discuss the possibility of adopting her, but we didn't consider it in a serious way, mainly because of Hannah. We believed that it would make her feel even more of an outsider.

Frequently, we would arrive for contact to find Jade with bags of gifts and messages to pass on to Lucy from Fiona. At Easter 2001 we came home with literally a boot full of toys and memorabilia for Lucy and Hannah. She had bought Lucy books and videos with 'you're my ever-loving daughter' messages written on them. There were games and a moneybox for both children with money in them. She also sent a number of large framed portrait photographs of herself for Lucy, and some photographs of herself and Lucy that she'd had taken on a contact visit when Lucy was in foster care. She sent two Easter cards, one for Lucy and one for Jon and myself. In Lucy's she had written that she was Lucy's birth mum and there wasn't a day that went by when she didn't think about Lucy. She usually attached her full name, date of birth, address, landline and mobile telephone numbers. In her first card to Jon and me she made a number of requests. We had previously sent her a homemade video of Lucy playing and doing various things at home. She asked if we would make her another one, and if we would have some professional photographs taken of Lucy and send them to her via social services; she wanted us to arrange to have more photographs taken of Lucy and Jade together when they next had contact. On the inside of our card there was barely a millimetre of space left where she hadn't written something, with her writing getting smaller and smaller to squash as much in as she could. She was begging and pleading rather than making a simple request. It was always like this. I kept a few of the cards she sent to us in case Lucy might need to see them when she grew up. This is an extract from one dated 9 July 2003, just seven months before the adoption broke down for good.

> *I have heard nothing about Lucy for an extremely long period of time, Jade's social worker reckoned it is well over a year…I wrote before and asked you if it was ever*

going to be possible with both your agreement and most importantly with the child Lucy's agreement to see Lucy face to face? I never meant to get you Karen annoyed. I can well understand you wanting to protect Lucy from any kind of upset. I may seem extinct but as Lucy's ex-mother neither do I wish Lucy to suffer any remote distress. <u>Our minds think alike and we are both in agreement on the same matter here</u> (double underlined). *I am thrilled that Jade saw her sister last Sunday...Jade was definitely disappointed, disillusioned and angry before this...If I'd known before that Jade was seeing Lucy I could have given Jade a camera...Please, please write to me Karen via the social worker, I'd like some pictures and drawings that Lucy has done...absolutely anything to do with Lucy, school reports...please tell Lucy I still love and miss her and will until I'm dead. Please send an up to date photo so I can frame it, thanks, Fiona.*

In one of Lucy's birthday cards she wrote:

I will love you forever, have a nice happy time as I'm sure you will, from Miss Fiona Walton your birth mummy, I send you my endless love to you honey. Please can Karen and Jon Carr send me a negative of a recent picture of Lucy and some more photo's please and a new video if they would be so kind.

Every time I wrote an update I sent Fiona photos of Lucy and her friends, and I always pointed out who all the children were and who was Lucy's best friend. I also sent her videos of Lucy's birthday parties. Lucy always knew we were sending Fiona letters and as she got older she would add a very short message herself. She usually wrote something like 'I hope you are having a beautiful time'. There was never a formal mailbox arrangement – it was a matter of Jon and I remembering to do it.

However, it got too much when once, on Lucy's birthday, her last birthday with us, I noticed a Post Office van pull up outside. The driver got out and knocked on our door; he gave me a birthday card for Lucy that measured approximately 1 ft by 3 ft. Fortunately, Lucy and Hannah had gone out to play. The card was full of messages from Fiona, with elaborate hand-drawn figures of Lucy's age in gold pen. Had we displayed it with her other cards it would have stood out ridiculously, and I cannot imagine how Lucy would have interpreted it.

Once when Jade's social worker rang to ask me to write a letter to Fiona, I took the opportunity to discuss all the other letters and messages that were inappropriate. I explained that we were having serious difficulties and it was complicating things further. He told me that Fiona was a very demanding woman and that she telephoned him every day. He also said, 'Well, what do you expect, she is Lucy's mother!' He told me everything we had received had been vetted and approved by his line manager. Then he suggested that I put the cards and letters in the bin. I had already got rid of the large card, but felt it was immoral, and it should not have been my place to do that.

I put in an official complaint to the local authority regarding what I believed to be unsuitable mail from Fiona. I also wrote a letter to Fiona myself explaining that Lucy had been with us for some years now and her reference to us as Karen and Jon Carr in Lucy's cards was confusing and upsetting for her. I told her that some of her cards had not reached Lucy because of their inappropriate nature. (Until now I had replaced them, signing them myself from Fiona. However, Lucy was a clever girl, and had noticed that Fiona's writing was like mine.) I explained to Fiona why her messages needed to change or I would not pass them on. I was unaware when I wrote that letter that it would have unforeseen consequences that would affect Jade and Lucy and would, to some extent, become the first phase of the disruption.

By the time the complaint to the local authority was made, the contact arrangements with Jade had changed significantly. It happened probably around eighteen months after Lucy arrived. It was the evening before we were due to have another visit. Hannah had been unusually quiet all day but we could not get her to tell us what the problem was. Then after she had gone to bed we heard her creeping down the stairs and she slipped a little note under the door.

Both Hannah and Lucy often gave us notes like this: sometimes it was because we had had a good day and they wanted to tell us that they loved us, or just to draw us a nice picture, and sometimes it was because they had been naughty and wanted to say sorry.

This time Hannah had drawn a picture of Jon and me on one side.

The note read, 'Dear Mum and Dad, to the best parents in the world, you know Jade well, I don't know her that well. Love from Hannah.' We brought Hannah downstairs to talk it over. She told us that she hated these contact visits because it was boring and took up the whole day, and she felt completely left out by Lucy. She felt it had nothing to do with her because she had no relationship with Jade. From then on, one of us took Lucy to see Jade and the other stayed at home with Hannah. More often than not, Jon drove Lucy because he had an uneasy relationship with her and we hoped that it might help them bond with one another.

Friends and relatives frequently asked us why we continued with these contact sessions as it caused us distress on a regular basis. After I qualified as a social worker, even colleagues would advise us to stop. The truth was, we did want to stop because it was difficult, costly, time-consuming and it upset Hannah, even when she stopped going. She certainly had reason to be envious or jealous. Lucy was more loyal to Jade than to Hannah. Hannah would mimic Lucy by saying, 'Jade is fantastic,

Jade is the best.' Of course, like any little sister, Lucy knew which buttons to press to get a response from Hannah and then she would praise Jade even more. It caused a rift in the family and the strain began to affect the quality of our life. The reason we persisted with the contact was because we truly believed that it would be cruel to deny Lucy her sister, and we would be answerable to Lucy as an adult.

I can remember one particular visit when I had driven Lucy to see Jade. The weather was absolutely terrible. It was cold, wintry and dull. The sleet had turned the streets grey with splashes of muddy sludge from the constant flow of traffic. The motorway traffic was slow-moving with huge articulated lorries filling the two lanes that were still open. Driving is not one of my stronger points and I was finding the journey very stressful. 'This is the last time I'm driving to see Jade,' I complained, meaning I would get Jon to do it in the future. Lucy didn't answer or say anything. I complained some more. 'Oh my God, how long is this going to take?' It had already taken at least twice as long as it usually did. Then I began with a little road rage. 'Why don't you indicate? That's what it's there for, IDIOT!...'

I didn't realise how Lucy was taking all of this. The visit went well but when it was time to say goodbye, Lucy became upset; she was hugging Jade, she began crying and became clingy. This was very unusual, we had never had tears when it was time to go. On our way home Lucy began to cry again. 'Why can't I see Jade any more?' I was confused, Lucy's behaviour didn't make sense.

'What do you mean, what makes you think you can't see Jade again'?

'Because that's what you said, you're never going to go there again.'

As soon as I got the chance I pulled over and explained what I meant, that it was too far for me to drive and Jon would have to take her in future.

For Lucy's last twelve to eighteen months with us, we reached an agreement with Jade's foster carers that we would meet at an out of town shopping centre about half-way between where we both lived. From then on it was again mostly me who took Lucy. This was much easier, even enjoyable; occasionally Hannah wanted to come as well. Jade was a teenager now and had grown taller than me. She always tried to include and play with Hannah as much as with Lucy.

Jade and I always got on really well and she would tell me about her mum, dad and her foster placements, how she was doing at school, boyfriends, classmates and her hopes and dreams for the future. She had three placements break down while Lucy was with us and we met with three different sets of foster carers. During one contact visit Jade told me that if she had another placement breakdown she was going to go to court herself to see if she could go back to her mum. Jade's moves disturbed Lucy. She worried about Jade, and it made her more insecure regarding her future with us.

We always tried to allow Lucy and Jade some time alone together to talk. We managed like this for about three years. The contact had a purpose: they were sisters and had a shared history that was important. The idea that it was for identity reasons only was ridiculous; if that were the case a photograph would have sufficed.

Sometimes, after seeing Jade, Lucy would become a little sad, or she might want to go through her life story book. Once she asked us to drive to the area where she was born; she also wanted to have a look at where Hannah was born. So we spent a whole day just driving down memory lane. It was fun for all of us. I am sure that we would have done something similar even if she were not having contact with her birth family. As Lucy grew older she became more able to question and understand her situation. The contact always served as a reminder that her place in our family was different from Hannah's. It created uncertainties rather than upset.

Then out of the blue things suddenly changed. It was

shortly after a visit from Jade to our house, when she'd had a good few hours alone with Lucy. A day or two later Lucy became distressed, she appeared confused and asked lots of questions about her birth mum. She wanted to know what Fiona was doing and she wanted to see her. This went on for a few weeks. She also expressed concern about Fiona's heart and was worried that she wasn't well. This was not typical of Lucy. I promised her that when she was older I would definitely arrange for her to visit Fiona. I was able to reassure her that Fiona was well and healthy. We believed the change was probably connected in some way to Jade, but we weren't concerned that it was anything untoward. We put it down to her growing awareness.

Then about three weeks after Jade's visit, we received a telephone call from her foster carers. It was quite late at night and the foster carer struggled with what she had to say. She told me she had debated long and hard about whether or not she should ring us. She warned me to supervise all the contact between Lucy and Jade in future. She didn't want to tell me why, but I pressed her for more information. She said she had overheard Jade on the telephone. She was telling Fiona what she had said to Lucy. Apparently she had told Lucy that she and Fiona were her true family and that they would all be together again one day, that Hannah was not her sister, and that we didn't love her. The foster carer didn't want to tell me any more because she hadn't heard it clearly, but she assured me it had been a lengthy conversation.

I believe that this was Fiona getting at Lucy through Jade, because of the letter I had written to her about her inappropriate messages.

During the next meeting back at the shopping centre, I did my best to supervise but it was impossible. Lucy and Jade strolled ahead and I couldn't hear them properly anyway. Lucy was seven years old now and Jade thirteen; stopping the contact after three years wasn't an option.

Lucy's interest in Fiona became more intense. She

started to look at her life story book much more frequently. She moved it from under her bed to the side of her bed. She took out the photos which Fiona had sent a few years previously and placed them about her bedroom. And she wrote on some photos in her life story book: 'I love my birth mum Fiona, I also love Mummy, Daddy and Hannah'. Whenever we went into a shop or bank and somebody had a name badge with Fiona written on it Lucy would say, 'Look Mum, Fiona'; she would wonder if it was her birth mum.

After all this time Lucy confided in me that Fiona had cried the last time she saw her. She told me that she was worried as she thought Fiona was missing her. She had this idea that she had breathing problems and might die.

I sought advice from our counsellor at After Adoption, an organisation which offers ongoing support to adoptive families, as I usually did when we were struggling or had any problems. She was always helpful and supportive throughout the time Lucy was with us. She believed that as Lucy was worrying so much about Fiona, it would be of some benefit for her to have direct contact. I agreed with her. I thought the situation was very unfair on Lucy; she knew all about Fiona from Jade who still saw her mother on a regular basis, they talked mainly about Fiona when they were together, Jade just couldn't stop herself. For Lucy it was like having a jar of sweets in her bedroom but not being allowed to eat them.

Jon and I discussed meeting Fiona face-to-face many, many times. He believed that it would only exacerbate our problems, not relieve them. He felt it would add to Lucy's feeling of belonging elsewhere and be bad for us as a family.

The last time I took Lucy to meet Jade was about a month before the final disruption. We were having lunch and Lucy asked Jade nonchalantly, 'When you're older do you think you'll go back home?'

'Definitely yes,' Jade answered, 'but I won't stay long.

What about you Lucy, will you?'

Lucy copied what Jade had said, 'Yes definitely, but I won't stay long either'.

Contact was always emotionally draining for us and added to the many arguments that had become commonplace in our household. Lucy never got the chance to be our daughter in the true sense; we cared for her, loved her and did all we could for her. But in our case contact was disrupting the placement.

* * *

Back in the courtroom, the Judge continued, 'What is the attachment between the two girls? Are they having any contact at the moment?' The local authority barrister turned to her client sitting just behind her and they whispered for a moment or two. 'The local authority is in the process of assessing whether or not there is any attachment between the two girls, they have had no contact with each other since the adoption broke down...'

Twelve months later Jon and I were in court again on a matter indirectly involving the adoption breakdown. We were approached by a solicitor acting on behalf of Jade. She was taking the local authority to court herself to make an application for contact with Lucy.

7

Looking for help

The local authority report to the court initially said that we had refused any kind of support, and that we had only one meeting with After Adoption before we took the decision that the adoption was over and declined any further help.

To read that about yourself and your family in an official document, at a time when your lives have been turned upside down, evokes extraordinarily strong emotions. Especially when the information is made public and is untrue. Throughout all the social services' submissions there was a determination to paint a picture of a middle class family who had a quick change of mind about wanting to adopt and had decided to dispose of a child. In one report they even used the term "dispense with". Without directly saying so, they implied that the reason for the breakdown was because I was pregnant with our second biological child. What they did not know, of course, was that we could have had a baby at any time. The choice to have one now had been made by all four of us. That is, Jon and myself, Hannah and Lucy.

* * *

Our relationship with the organisation After Adoption

began in September 1999, only three months after Lucy moved in. I had contacted the social workers from the placing local authority, saying that we felt very much in at the deep end. At the time I believed that our problems stemmed from the speed at which Lucy had come to live with us. I felt we needed help with building Lucy's relationship with all family members, but in particular with Jon. We were advised to contact After Adoption.

A social worker from After Adoption visited us at home and we explained our difficulties. She was called Helena and she was really supportive, and it was helpful to be able to show our feelings. She always visited in the evening so the children were in bed and we could talk freely.

At the time After Adoption aimed to employ people who were personally connected with adoption. Helena and her partner had adopted three children with special needs. One of her children had Down's syndrome, one was deaf and had learning difficulties and the youngest had been diagnosed with a life-threatening condition. Helena's compassion blew our minds. She came across as dedicated not only to her own children, but also to helping others make their adoptions work. With no hint of 'you only have one child with very few problems, relatively speaking', she was easy to work with and talk to.

We worked with Helena from September 1999 until December 2000. She told us that Lucy's behaviour was pretty standard as the "honeymoon period" was now over and she was testing the boundaries and our commitment to her.

About six or seven months after being placed with us, Lucy's behaviour became very defiant. A battle of wills was a daily occurrence. Lucy expected to be picked on and she expected to be unfairly treated. If Hannah ate some sweets she shouldn't have eaten, and was discovered, she would accept that she was wrong and even expect to be told off, but Lucy's world was different. If she had taken sweets without asking, and was found out, she would be convinced that Hannah or anybody else would not have been told off for the same thing. She had an overwhelming sense of injustice and it would lead to raging tantrums.

I was always able to get through to Lucy though, and after her tantrum had subsided I would be able to sit with her and explain how and why something had happened. But it took a massive effort to enable her to understand that any other child behaving in such a way would also have been told off or lost their pocket money or been made to go to bed early or whatever. I would have to provide examples of when Hannah or even Lucy's own friends had got into trouble for similar misdemeanours.

Dealing with Lucy's tantrums became very much a part of our lives. I think she'd been living with us for about two years before we saw any real improvement. For instance, if we were watching a family film on TV and all Lucy's attempts at disrupting it by clicking, clapping, singing, and doing roly-poly had not worked, she would eventually go and turn it off manually. Then she'd get into trouble and be told to sit on the stairs for five minutes. But she'd kick and scream and getting her to sit on the stairs could take well over an hour. By then, of course, all our tempers were frayed, the moment gone and the film ruined.

But Lucy did make progress. In time, rather than going and turning the TV off, she would stand next to it with her finger about an inch from the switch, only threatening to switch it off. And once she was more able to control her anger, she learnt that getting into trouble wasn't the end of the world, and it was better just to sit on the stairs than to have a tantrum.

After one of these upsets, when we had all calmed down, I found it easy to hug Lucy and to explain that everything was fine, that it was normal for children to be naughty from time to time, and that it was a parent's job to show them how to behave better. I felt connected to Lucy on an emotional level. Maybe because of my own background I understood what it was like to feel out of control and to be misunderstood. I could help her to believe that even if she felt "bad" she was "good" inside.

But Jon didn't understand fears of being out of control; until the disruption, being out of control was something he had never experienced. Certainly the adults during his childhood had been stable, sober, secure and committed to one another. It is difficult to describe Jon's parenting of Lucy. He supported me as opposed to being a proactive parent himself, especially during the first few years. Lucy's preference for me, coupled with my reduced working hours, meant that I could spend more time with her to build up a significant emotional bond. I suppose I got to know the real Lucy. Whereas, when we were all together, her behaviour always seemed to dominate. Consequently, it was difficult for Jon to get as close to her.

Helena listened to our story and invited Jon to attend sessions with her after work to look at ways of developing his relationship with Lucy. He would arrive home feeling positive and eager to try out suggestions. But he expected quick results and changes in Lucy's behaviour without changing his own behaviour first. When things didn't work out Jon would feel rejected.

On the whole, Helena thought that we were dealing with Lucy's tantrums very well and believed that time would be the best healer. She also thought that it might be useful to speak to other families who had experienced similar difficulties. So we found ourselves being welcomed by a couple who had adopted a young girl. They also had one biological older daughter and the age difference was similar to that between Lucy and Hannah. But that is where the similarities ended.

This couple had adopted because the mother could not have any more children. It was touching listening to her account of their struggle. They were desperate to have another child and she talked and talked of the void that was filled the day their adopted daughter arrived. They had both felt this immediate attachment to their adopted child.

They said that their daughter was very destructive and exhibited some fairly disturbing behaviour. We felt that their problems were far worse than ours, although they didn't see it that way. They described her wrecking her bedroom and personal belongings. They told us that the school had complained about her because apparently she had deliberately ripped the sole off her shoes and she was generally disruptive in class. The parents thought the teachers were being insensitive and did not understand her difficulties as an adopted child.

They had built an enormous playhouse for their children that took up nearly all of the back garden. They wanted to spoil their adopted daughter to make up for her earlier traumas.

When we left this family we thought that comparatively speaking we were doing well and we realised that things could be a whole lot worse.

I visited another family who had overcome very similar problems to our own. This family had adopted three siblings, but the father and one of the children had a relationship very like that between Jon and Lucy. They had also contacted After Adoption and received a lot of support. At one point they had considered sending this child to boarding school, but then decided that they wanted to work on their relationship instead.

Unfortunately Jon didn't meet this family as he was at work when they were available during the day. I saw them over a couple of months and talked with the mother who gave me loads of encouragement and advice, but then she went into hospital for an operation and we ended up losing touch. Knowing and meeting with this family made me more positive about our situation and Jon and I were determined to try harder to make it work.

Yet despite our efforts and the support from After Adoption, Jon's relationship with Lucy continued to spiral downwards. But it was so gradual that it was hardly noticeable. Then we realised that Hannah was suddenly verbally and physically supporting Jon. She felt that Lucy rejected them both by her obvious preference to be with me, and so Hannah wanted to stick up for her dad.

Lucy's preference for me impacted on every area of our lives. If we were discussing what to watch on TV and there was a minor disagreement, we'd take a vote. Lucy would always say, 'I want to watch what Mum wants to watch.'

In any discussion about anything, she'd say, 'Mum's right'.

If one parent was going to the shop: 'I'll go with Mum' or 'I'll stay with Mum'.

When choosing food in a restaurant: 'I'll have what Mum has'.

At home, if I left the room for any reason, she would feel the need to follow me within minutes. Sometimes I would come out of the toilet to find her sitting outside. As time went on we all got used to it and we even joked about it.

It was more of an issue at bedtime. We had always taken it in turns to put Hannah to bed and this included Lucy when she arrived, but she would become upset if it wasn't my turn. Sometimes she would hold me in a vice to say goodnight, as though she was never going to see me again; occasionally she would have to be literally prised away from me. As time went on she got used to the routine but she could still become miserable if Jon was putting her to bed, and this went on right up until she left our home.

I found Lucy's behaviour exhausting; it felt as though she constantly required my attention, but more than that, Hannah was being pushed out. Hannah's relationship with me was becoming affected as she began to opt to be with Dad to make up for Lucy not wanting him. She would ask him to take her to bed, she'd want to go along with him if he went anywhere. When out walking or shopping Hannah began to walk with her dad as Lucy would immediately lay claim to me and make it difficult for Hannah to get near me. Lucy wasn't being selfish, she was just happier when she was with me. We were beginning to divide into two separate units despite our efforts to be a family.

They say that, in order to thrive, humans need warmth and physical contact with other human beings, but when Lucy first came to us she was uncomfortable and incredibly self-conscious about accepting meaningful affection. Her body would become stiff and rigid. Conversely, I would often arrive at school to pick her up to find her sitting casually on the teacher's knee.

In spite of monopolising me, it was a long time before Lucy appreciated my attempts at showing her physical affection. When we were cooking I would sometimes sit both Hannah and Lucy on the kitchen worktop so they could either join in or just watch. On one particular day it was just Lucy and me. As usual I had lifted her up, but today was different. I could feel her arms wrap tightly around my neck – she was deliberately holding me close as I lifted her. In effect, she was giving me a hug.

I found enough excuses to have to lift her up and down that day just to make sure I wasn't dreaming, and every time she held on tightly, sometimes leaving her hand lingering on my shoulder or arm even after I had sat her down. As on so many occasions, I thought we had made progress, and this gave me hope. I couldn't wait for Jon to come home to tell him about the day and he was equally pleased because it gave him hope too.

After Adoption continued to provide us with support and we were allocated a new worker named Sharon. She had a more theoretical approach than Helena. Sharon would offer very practical advice and assistance by giving us information, tips and techniques based on attachment theory. She asked us if we had ever heard of re-nurturing, and would we like to try it, she really believed it would help build attachment and bonding between us all. Yes, we were keen to try it out.

The idea behind re-nurturing is to simulate the early developmental shared experiences that occur naturally in birth parent and infant relationships. It is believed that the re-visiting of these earlier stages can heal old wounds.

Sharon provided us with tangible methods for re-nurturing, like wrapping Lucy up tightly in a soft shawl and cuddling and rocking her whilst making good eye contact. This is one experience that parents and babies frequently enjoy. The eye contact is specially important. The exercises can be varied if either you or your child feels silly doing this when the child is older.

Jon tried the re-nurturing strategies and relationships did improve. He varied some aspects of the technique. He took Lucy to the swings in the park and slowly pushed her from a face-to-face position whilst maintaining eye contact. We gave her a soft piece of cloth, sprayed with scent that she could always have in her pocket; the idea was that she could inconspicuously feel it at any time of the day and know that she was part of us and that we were thinking about her.

We also sang nursery rhymes when bathing, spoon-feeding, and nappy changing. Lucy wore a nappy at bedtime until she was quite old. We managed to do all this in a fun way and Lucy, for probably the first time, learnt to enjoy being dependent.

With me at least, Lucy particularly liked the rocking sensation. One day we were away from the rest of the family upstairs, and I asked her to come and sit on my lap. As she did, I lay her gently down so that she was looking up at me, and I swung her on my lap from side to side. This moment is engraved on my memory and will be forever; if I have ever had a "eureka" moment this was it. We just gazed into each other's eyes, smiling. I could read her face and feel her infant-like neediness. I really believed then, in fact I knew, that everything was going to be alright. Nothing and no one could have persuaded me otherwise.

But for all our success with re-nurturing, it still didn't lead to the changes we were hoping for in Jon and Lucy's relationship, partly because Jon felt foolish doing some of the exercises and didn't fully buy into the ideas of re-nurturing. He just wanted a "normal" family life; he didn't want to have to work so hard to have a relationship with his daughter. And he didn't like having to ask for advice and support from an outside agency, as good and well intentioned as it was. I suppose we all thought it would be easier than it turned out to be.

Prior to Lucy being placed with us Jon and I used to share a bottle of wine in the evenings at weekends. We would sit up until the early hours of the morning chatting and debating various issues. But now we began to drink much more heavily; we started having the odd drink during the week, and that steadily increased until we were drinking almost every night.

From the day Lucy arrived in our home she became the main topic of conversation after the children had gone to bed. In the early days, possibly for a year or so, we would generally discuss the situation, but from the start there were disagreements. Very gradually the discussions turned into arguments as I began to blame Jon for Lucy not getting close to him. I criticised every tiny little interaction he'd had with Lucy that day. If there was nothing I could pick on from that day, I would start on something from the past.

I would shout and tell Jon he wasn't trying hard enough; that he needed to make some real effort to engage Lucy; that if I could do it so should he. He would argue that he was doing all he could and how could he engage when she was happier without him. I would try to make him see that certain ways he had of dealing with Lucy were pushing her away. To me it appeared that he was hard on her and he frequently called her a nuisance; I accused him of picking on her or not being as good with her as he was with Hannah.

I would even say that we should end the placement because I could see that it wasn't going to work and the longer it went on the harder it would be for us all. Jon would argue vehemently against the idea of Lucy going back into local authority care. He was always absolutely convinced that he could and would make it work in the end. He could see I was right in some of the things I said, but he insisted that he only told Lucy off more than Hannah because she did more things wrong than Hannah did.

Then our arguments became more aggressive and angry. The children were being disturbed by the noise. Lucy clearly saw me as the aggressor. Hannah would complain that she could hear what we were saying, but Lucy would physically attack me if she was woken by our shouting. She would run at me and scream, 'You leave Dad alone, Mum!' It always stopped the arguing, as we then had to reassure Lucy because she became so distressed by the situation. These were the only occasions when she preferred Jon to settle her in bed.

We intermittently remained in contact with Sharon from After Adoption throughout the time that Lucy was with us. We felt she gave us appropriate support and guidance. She would have liked to meet with Lucy and Hannah but that never happened due to school and work priorities. Looking back, we think this was a big mistake on our part. We thought the problems were entirely the responsibility of the adults and didn't seek help for Lucy until just a few months before the adoption broke down completely. Most often I would contact Sharon when we were going through a particularly stressful time; then Jon and I would talk it over in the evening. We always took the advice she gave us seriously.

For much of the time we were not too concerned about Lucy and Hannah's relationship. Yes, they argued and fought, but don't all brothers and sisters? We believed that they also loved one another. We focused on the relationship between Jon and Lucy, and located the problem to be with Jon because he was the adult.

We went on a family holiday to Turkey in July 2003; Hannah was now ten years old and Lucy seven. In many ways it was the best and the worst holiday we ever had whilst Lucy was with us. It was good because for once we could afford a decent hotel and we had enough money – that was a first for us! But family holidays could be a hard time for Lucy. I think the packing of the bags and the physical move destabilised her and perhaps triggered more painful memories of packing and moving. She would become very demanding but she would settle after a day or two.

During this holiday Lucy and Hannah largely ignored each other; they didn't play together but instead did their own thing. Lucy was clamouring for our attention and Hannah resigned herself to the situation. When Hannah tried to show off her swimming, Lucy overshadowed her by taking her first swim unaided. Jon caught it on video. She was very proud of herself and so were we.

I didn't really notice what was happening until Jon pointed it out. Hannah was just very quiet, jumping in and out of the pool, swimming alone, not interacting with anyone in particular. Lucy, on the other hand, was loud and excited and could be heard, 'Watch me swim Mum, I can jump in, watch me Mum!' It was her nature to be that way.

About two-thirds of the way through the holiday, a large group of men came to stay at our hotel. They were rowdy and drinking heavily throughout the night, running up and down the hotel corridors and banging on doors. Jon had made a complaint and we were concerned that there could be repercussions when they were drunk, so we insisted that the travel company move us to a child-friendly hotel.

Moving to a different hotel completely threw Lucy and she became really upset. She couldn't explain why, but again we felt it had triggered memories from her past when she had to leave unexpectedly. For the rest of our stay her behaviour exhausted us. When we returned from the holiday, Jon and Lucy's relationship seemed to deteriorate further and so did Hannah and Lucy's.

Life at home became very difficult, almost intolerable. If Jon went out and left us on our own there appeared to be more harmony in the home. Almost the second he walked back in, the arguments would start again. I felt too much in demand and pulled in all ways emotionally; I started to go out by myself, either walking, or driving or to see family and friends, anything to get out of the house as often as I could. They all got along differently when I wasn't around and largely ignored one another. But even so, I would often come home to find Lucy in trouble for something or other.

First thing in the morning before leaving for work and school was a particularly stressful time. Lucy was always specific about what she would wear. She could have enormous tantrums if we tried to make her wear socks, shoes or clothes that she didn't like. Socks in particular were a big issue. She liked short socks, no matter what the weather. And they had to feel a particular way or she would refuse to put them on. Once we were in Asda and she tried on dozens of socks before she found what she wanted.

One morning Lucy said that she needed some new shoes as the ones she had were hurting her. I had nothing important on that morning and said I would take her to get some new shoes before going to work.

But Lucy didn't want to go. 'No, no,' she said, 'it's OK Mum, we can get them another time.'

'But Lucy, I have the time to go this morning. I'll take you and then drop you at school.'

Lucy was clear that she didn't want to go shoe shopping just then, but I insisted if her shoes were hurting her then she needed new ones. So I dropped Hannah off at school and took Lucy to buy new shoes.

Once in the shop we were looking at the various styles and Lucy spotted some she liked. 'OK then, let's try them on,' I said.

'Do I have to? I think they'll fit,' said Lucy, for some reason reluctant to try them on.

'Of course you've got to try them on...how will we

know if they fit you or not? Come on Lucy, stop messing around and try the shoes on, I've got to get to work,' I said, probably losing my patience a little.

'OK,' she said and tried to hide from me while she took her shoes off.

'What are you doing? Come here!' Then I discovered why she suddenly needed bigger shoes and why she had been reluctant to go shoe shopping that morning. She was wearing three pairs of socks!

'Why are you wearing three pairs of socks, Lucy?'

She put a big smile on her face as if really I knew why she was wearing so many socks.

'You'll have to tell me, Lucy, because I don't know.' No reply, she continued to smile. 'How long have you been wearing so many socks?' She started laughing. 'A few days,' she said.

I removed two pairs of socks and drove her back to school in her old shoes. The best answer I could get from her was that she was cold, but she was laughing her head off while she said it and so I still have no idea why she started to wear three pairs of socks.

She also liked her hair a particular way and sometimes she would want to leave the house with literally dozens of ponytails and clips in her hair. 'Oh Lucy no, you know you can't go to school looking like that,' I'd say crossly, because it was a conversation we would have at least two mornings of every week.

'But why not? You said yesterday that I couldn't wear the pink fluffy one and I haven't got the pink fluffy one in.' She'd be both crying and shouting at the same time. We would continue to argue until it was settled, but Jon would usually snap and say something like, 'You look stupid, Lucy, just take them out'. It would be comments like this that would cause an argument once the children were in bed.

We didn't have the patience or understanding to deal with what appeared to be trivial or even irrelevant issues first thing in the morning, every morning. We were reacting to each situation as though it was all down to bad behaviour; we were getting angry over really insignificant little things. We had got into a habit of going from nought to sixty in about two seconds.

In August 2003, Jon contacted Sharon from After Adoption himself; he arranged to go to her office for help with his feelings in relation to Lucy. Jon told me he was honest in these sessions with Sharon; he found her to be supportive and helpful. He asked her if it would be a good idea for Lucy and him to spend some time together alone, without the rest of us. Sharon thought it would help.

We had a touring caravan and it was easy for Jon and Lucy to go away for a few days. We were worried about telling Lucy that she was going away on her own with her dad. We expected tears, to say the least. We decided to make the reasons behind the trip explicit and tell Lucy the truth.

Jon said, 'You know how we don't always get along together?'

'Yes,' Lucy said.

'Mum and I think it might be a good idea for me and you to have a little holiday on our own, to get to know each other better.'

She couldn't have surprised us more! She was thrilled, animated and couldn't wait to go with him. 'Yes,' she said, and was soon gloating that she was going on a holiday with her dad.

So that Hannah wouldn't feel left out, we visited my sister and Hannah's cousins.

The caravan trip appeared to be a success as they had enjoyed each other's company. They had talked things through. Jon said that he asked her why she thought they didn't get along too well together. She told him that he shouted too much, and she gave him examples. She also said that he used affectionate names for Hannah, such as "OK kid!" but that he never did that with her. She talked about some of the things she did deliberately to provoke him. They both made a promise to each other that they would try harder when they got back home.

*   *   *

When we first read in the court reports that we had only had one session with After Adoption, we insisted that the local authority change it but, as with all the other statements which were incorrect, they refused to alter a word. So Sharon wrote a letter outlining our involvement with After Adoption over the past four-and-a-half years, and Miss Pickering now had the unenviable task of getting the wording amended.

One of the things Sharon said to me when I first rang her to let her know that the adoption had broken down was that out of all the people she has known who have struggled with their adopted children, she really thought we had tried our best to make it work.

Because we were having to prove every point we made, it really meant a lot to hear that at the time; in fact it still does, very much so.

8

Hannah and Lucy

'They're saying that the only reason you're disputing the threshold criteria is because you don't want to lose face and are driven by your need to look good to other people,' explained a weary Miss Pickering.

'What!' we snapped, much louder than necessary. 'Whenever we disagree on any issue, they try to shame us into silence.' Both Jon and I were outraged; my tone rose a few octaves.

Miss Pickering tried to calm us down. ' I know,' she said, 'infuriating, isn't it?' shaking her head, then nodding, then shaking it again. 'I don't know why they won't just change it.' She seemed genuinely perplexed. 'It's not as if they have any evidence. I could understand it if they did, but even when you have provided medical evidence showing how Hannah was suffering, they are still refusing to accept it, it really is very confusing,' she said, 'very confusing.'

* * *

My mind drifted back again to the first night Lucy was with us...I'd been sitting with Lucy sobbing on my knee, Hannah had been tearful, 'Please Mum, if she wants to go back to Tracy's then let's take her'. It shouldn't have been this way; this was not an emergency placement, it was an adoption but I was having to do my utmost to console a small child I barely knew. We weren't prepared for this. In fact, there was so much we weren't prepared for, including the impact on Hannah, who was not quite seven at the time. Our adoption training had not even mentioned any possible problem for birth siblings. The only advice I remember was from Valerie, the social worker who assessed us for adoption. I told her that every morning, without exception, Hannah would come into our bed for a kiss and a hug, and I thought this would have to stop when we had a child placed with us. Valerie said that we shouldn't alter Hannah's routines, as it could lead to resentment.

Because of the short notice, we had no time to go out and buy anything before Lucy's arrival. We had a bed, but that was all. The spare bedroom was full of junk and not properly decorated. So we had little choice but to move Lucy into Hannah's room where they shared toys, furniture and even clothes because most of Lucy's either didn't fit properly or were worn out. And the two girls were about the same size.

Looking back, it is remarkable that we didn't realise that it was a lot for Hannah to give up in one weekend.

We made it a priority to get more furniture for Lucy but getting a bedroom sorted out was not so easy. The third bedroom was at the bottom of the stairs and felt separate from the others. Nevertheless, Lucy wanted to move into it, so we bought her second-hand drawers and a cupboard and painted the room.

Lucy stayed in the room for a couple of months but didn't like being so far away from us. Then Hannah agreed to try it but, for the same reason, she didn't like it either; I don't think she lasted a whole week. So we converted Hannah's room to make it comfortable for them to share. Neither Hannah nor Lucy liked sharing a bedroom, but that was what they had to do for over three years until we could raise a loan on the property to build an extension, so that they could both have their own bedroom upstairs.

We realised that Hannah could become jealous of Lucy when, a few weeks after she moved in, I found a pin strategically placed in Lucy's bed. Hannah immediately admitted to putting it there but insisted she had done it for fun. We did our best to be attentive to both of them.

Hannah had lots of questions about Lucy's behaviour. We had prepared her to meet a child who would play up and test the boundaries. We hadn't prepared her for a child who played up, tested the boundaries and was also hurting. At times Lucy's hurt was so deep it felt tangible, nearly visible and raw. Sometimes trying to reach her was like almost losing grip of a life you were trying to save.

For adults, this was difficult to grapple with; for a seven-year-old it must have been completely unnerving. Hannah would try to advise Lucy on how to deal with a punishment from the grown-ups: 'Just sit on the stairs for one minute and that'll be it,' she'd plead. But Lucy rarely took her advice, although she watched Hannah being made to sit there and could see that it was all over in a few moments with very little fuss.

As a baby Hannah had been responsive and loving, and she grew to be funny, intelligent, pretty and was always adored. She has lots of her father's characteristics: he is quiet and unassuming; they are both silently strong people, with a clear sense of justice.

We were proud of Hannah's every little achievement, from her first steps to riding her first bike; from learning her alphabet to writing her first stories.

We have "bits" of her stored in the loft: her first cut baby curls, and a variety of teeth; the umbilical cord clamp from when she was born, and even the positive pregnancy test that told us she was on her way. We still have her first shoes, T-shirt and babygrow; we parted with her first dress, but only for her beloved Tiny Tears doll which also lives in the loft with an army of oddly named fluffy toys, including

Bogey Bear, so named by her cousin after Hannah had a particularly bad cold.

Prior to Lucy's placement with us we would invite cousins to sleepovers as company for Hannah. I recall one summer holiday, very shortly before Lucy came, Hannah was bored and so I said I'd ring her auntie and invite her cousin Anna-Rea to sleep. Anna-Rea was about ten months older than Hannah. I listened to them playing in Hannah's bedroom. 'OK, we'll play schools and I'll be Miss. Take out your reading book,' Hannah said with some determination.

'Schools is boring,' said Anna-Rea, 'I'm not playing that. I want to play pop stars.'

'My mum has brought you here to play with me,' I heard Hannah very sternly tell her older cousin with a clear air of "it's my way or the highway" in her tone – adult intervention was required. Hannah's expectation of a sister was always having someone to talk to, to play with, to fight with, to share secrets with.

We had bought Hannah a cat and a rabbit a couple of years earlier; maybe her perception of Lucy's arrival was that she was getting a new pet. The truth is that I don't know what Hannah's thoughts were at the time and her memory is fading now. Her main recollections of the early days are that it had felt weird having some other person in her room, and that Lucy had introduced her to having things like lemonade, coke, sweets and chocolate more frequently than she had been used to. Chocolate was something we very rarely gave Hannah. Not that we had anything against it, but we had a theory that she probably wouldn't develop a taste for it if she didn't have it as a young child. As theories go it wasn't that hot; at thirteen, Hannah is an out-and-out chocoholic.

If I ask Hannah today how she got on with Lucy, she answers that it's easy for young children to play together. She says, 'they make friends without making friends, if you know what I mean'. Her view is that young children are naturally attracted to one another and will instinctively play a game of hide-and-seek or tag rather than interact in any other way.

We have lots of video footage spanning the years Lucy was with us, and much of it shows Jon and me desperately trying either to encourage the girls to play together or making rather obvious attempts to be fair. It makes interesting viewing because you can see Lucy year-by-year growing in confidence, but some of it is quite uncomfortable to watch, because Lucy appears more on the periphery of activities than a part of them. It's clear she is feeling self-conscious and a little bit fazed by what's going on around her. There is one particular day where we were having a family celebration for Hannah's birthday. My sister, her husband and their children have come to visit. Hannah dances with her cousin – they are used to dancing and playing together. Then the music stops and Lucy wants to have a go, but the cousin doesn't know Lucy that well and she dances with her just long enough so as to not embarrass them both, and then Lucy once again moves away and becomes an observer. Jon says that I can't use a video to judge our family relationships, because people only film what they want to record. While I agree that this is true, body language can speak volumes, especially during celebrations.

On one of the videos, Lucy's demeanour on her fourth birthday is noteworthy. It is morning, she opens her presents as we sing "happy birthday" to her. Her posture is stiff and still, as though she doesn't like being the centre of attention when it is forced upon her. Her main present – a bike – is hidden behind the curtain.

'Lucy, just go and open the curtains in the dining room, please,' I say. We all follow her in to see her face when she finds her bike. She doesn't really respond; we have to tell her a few times that it is her bike before it seems to sink in.

We used to hide her main present every year and she fell for it every time. On her last Christmas with us we bought her a new bike again. But she was getting bigger and so were the bikes. So we hid it outside. 'Lucy, can you just go and put this rubbish outside in the bin, please,' I said. Poor Lucy, it was Christmas Day and raining! She put on her new teddy bear dressing gown with a hood and ears attached and her new slippers and set out to the bin crying. She didn't wonder why we were all following her. But this time when she saw her bike, at least she knew whose it was, and there was a big smile on her face.

If the video evidence is to be taken at face value, the best year we had was 2002, when Lucy had been with us for three years and we went camping in Devon. Lucy and Hannah are swimming with a huge inflatable crocodile. They are being competitive and pushing or throwing each other off into the water, but they are having fun and are engrossed in their game, apparently unaware we are there, let alone filming them.

Lucy and Hannah obviously had their fair share of squabbling and one-upmanship, just as any sisters would. They were always running to one of us, with a 'she's done this or that' and 'it's not fair'. But we believed that their relationship was healthy by and large even though Hannah felt insecure in relation to Lucy's birth family. She was jealous of Jade and often disheartened that Lucy's loyalties appeared to lie elsewhere and not with us.

Some problems were enduring and ran almost the length of the placement. Hannah remembers that, from the seat in the car designated to her, she couldn't see out of the window because there was a sunshade stuck on it. We weren't even aware of this at the time, and it seems such a tiny little thing, but I suppose we usually went in the car twice a day, or more, so it was enough to feed a young child's sense of injustice.

Another long-running dispute was also concerned with the seating arrangements in the car. This began approximately six months after Lucy came to live with us. On almost every journey I would hear Hannah shout, 'Stop it Lucy! Mu-u-um, she's pulling faces at me'. Like most parents, I'd tell Lucy to stop it. Lucy would vehemently deny that she had done anything wrong. When I say "vehemently", it is no exaggeration. She'd cry very loudly, 'I've done nothing wrong and I'm going to get into trouble now'. Then she'd get angry with Hannah, 'You're a liar Hannah, Mum she's lying, and it's not fair!' When I turned around to look directly at Lucy she would be sitting there all prim and proper. I could only see Hannah in my mirror because, of course, Lucy was always behind my seat. I would look at Hannah's angry-looking face peering at Lucy and I believed Lucy. The pin in Lucy's bed may have still been in my mind. It got to the stage where Hannah wouldn't bother to tell me, but I would still see her peering at Lucy in my driver's mirror and I would tell her off. One day, when I had unintentionally positioned my mirror so that I could see a large section of the back seat, I discovered that in fact it was Hannah who was telling the truth. I spotted Lucy leaning over silently and pulling faces at Hannah, and Hannah angrily looking on. This must have gone on for a long time, possibly over twelve months.

I now know that what made things worse was the way I dealt with Lucy's bad behaviour. I suppose I tried too hard to make Hannah understand Lucy. I'd tell Hannah that Lucy hadn't been in a proper family, that she didn't know how to be with people and wasn't used to being loved. I would tell Lucy off and talk to her about what she'd done, but invariably Lucy would be the one who sat on my knee while I explained why she shouldn't behave in this way or that.

The reader might be thinking: 'How could you be so dim-witted? Lucy was obviously being rewarded for bad behaviour.' And to say, 'You would have had to be there,' doesn't do the situation justice. On the one hand, we had a child who had had disrupted attachments, who had lost all she knew, who needed very careful loving yet firm nurturing. On the other hand, we had what appeared to be a secure, well-loved, emotionally strong and intelligent birth child. We did not appreciate what the arrival of Lucy had entailed for Hannah. We minimised the quarrels the girls had and attributed them to sibling rivalry; in fact, I bought a book on sibling rivalry and how to deal with it.

One midsummer, sunny, peaceful afternoon, nearly four years after Lucy had come to live with us, the girls had been playing upstairs and I was pottering about in the garden; Jon was at work. Suddenly the tranquillity was interrupted when Lucy came screaming down the stairs towards me. She had a red mark on her face, she was really distressed and crying, saying that Hannah had hit her.

We never used physical punishment as a means of correcting behaviour and always encouraged the children to resolve quarrels by other means. So it was a serious matter that Hannah had hit Lucy across the face. Hannah was right behind Lucy, she was equally distressed, but also very angry.

'OK, tell me exactly what happened.'

Lucy was the loudest. 'She hit me across the face because...'

I couldn't make out what either of them was saying.

'She ripped my book on purpose, I didn't hit her Mum, I didn't hit her...' Hannah cried.

Both girls were adamant that they were telling the truth.

I was in a real dilemma, Lucy was very upset, and looked as though she had been hit. She admitted ripping Hannah's book but Hannah had never hit or fought with anyone in her life. She had never witnessed violence and had not been even lightly smacked. My feeling was that it would be an unlikely response for Hannah to hit out, even if she was angry.

I became angry myself – obviously one of them was lying but I didn't know who. I began to shout at Hannah, out of frustration, but also because I thought I would be able to get the truth from her. 'Did you hit Lucy, Hannah? Tell me again exactly what happened,' I asked them both repeatedly. Hannah was crying and then said she was confused, she didn't know what had happened now and maybe she had hit Lucy.

'What do you mean, maybe you did hit Lucy?'

'I just don't know, I don't know any more, maybe I didn't realise that I hit her, but maybe I did.'

I really couldn't decide the best way of dealing with this, so I left it until Jon came home from work to discuss it with him. Jon was no wiser. But as I was telling him about it, I looked over at Lucy and saw she was smiling, and I just knew that she was not telling the truth. I decided not to broach the subject again until the following day. When I had the opportunity I took Lucy to one side. 'You weren't telling the truth yesterday, were you?' I asked her calmly. Lucy gave a familiar sheepish smile like she did whenever she was caught out.

Discovering the truth left us with another dilemma: does Lucy get into trouble for telling such a mean lie to begin with? Or would that teach her that it's not a good idea to tell the truth? Or should she get praised for being honest now? Well, what we did was to tell Lucy that it was a good thing that she had told the truth and thanked her; we then explained that she could have got Hannah into serious trouble and described the potential consequences. She had to apologise to Hannah and was sent to bed early.

From Hannah's perspective, was that good enough? I still don't know.

The fact is that we just assumed that Hannah was fine; she appeared to be so undemanding and secure that it was easy to overlook her needs.

Part of me is ashamed to admit that I dealt with the problem of Lucy telling lies by putting the responsibility onto Hannah's shoulders. I asked Hannah to promise me that she would always tell the truth, because Lucy still had not learned how to live in a family. I told Hannah that if she promised to tell me the truth, I would promise that I would always believe her. This seemed like a good idea at the time, but in retrospect it was too much pressure to expect a nine-year-old to always tell the truth. It's in their job description to tell white lies and to exaggerate. I believe now that this was the start of Hannah feeling overwhelmed by our circumstances. I am not denigrating myself here, as I did the best I could with the knowledge and skills I had at the time.

But the hurt to Hannah has been long lasting, and she still feels that I let her down. Her perception is that Lucy frequently got her into trouble for things she hadn't done.

Today Hannah is very clear that there were times when she and Lucy were close and, as she says, they were 'like proper sisters'. She has fond memories of when they used to play with Chloe and Louise, the two little girls from around the corner. There was another pair of sisters who had moved into the area and all six girls would play together. Hannah recalls that, when there were arguments, she and Lucy would separate into opposite camps. Each group of girls plotted and planned tricks on the other, but Lucy and Hannah confided in each other at night, so that neither of them would get too hurt, upset or into trouble. Hannah remembers that Lucy never held a grudge and although she was quick to lose her temper she would get over it fairly quickly too, especially if Hannah wanted to play a game with her. She also talks about Lucy's generosity, and laughs about one Christmas when she persuaded Lucy to swap all her new Christmas toys for Hannah's old ones. Fortunately we discovered this arrangement in time to put a stop to it.

Hurting herself and blaming others became part and parcel of who Lucy was. It was rare, but occasionally she would rub herself vigorously in a particular spot to make it go red and would then say somebody had hurt her. I never could believe that Lucy was doing this intentionally until I saw it with my own eyes. It was one day when Lucy was in trouble for some reason and I had told her to go to her room. She was in a stubborn mood and refused.

'You will go to your room, Lucy, if I have to put you

there myself,' I told her firmly.

'No I won't and you can't make me! You get lost you...you stupid idiot!' She shouted the last words to emphasise that she was really angry and I was going to have a battle on my hands.

'Right, come here you cheeky...' and she was off running around the living room to get away from me.

As usual, when I caught her she went like a dead weight; by now Lucy was a big girl and it wasn't easy to lift her like that. But I persevered and set off up the stairs with her. Once she realised that I was able to carry her she started kicking, screaming and trying her best to escape. After I got her to her room, instead of going downstairs, I stayed and watched her through the crack of her bedroom door. I was shaken to see her rubbing her head forcefully. She then ran to the door shouting at the top of her voice: 'Look what you've done to me,' pointing to her head.

I didn't have time to think up a measured response and so I reacted instinctively.

'I haven't done that to you, Lucy, you have done that to yourself.' My confident tone must have thrown her a little. She was confused and said haltingly, 'No, no I haven't'.

I was very calm at this point. 'Yes, you have, Lucy, and it's very naughty to say that somebody has hurt you when they haven't.' Lucy still didn't understand how I knew she wasn't telling the truth.

'Right, OK Lucy, go and get Lamby for me.' Lamby was her favourite fluffy toy that she slept with every night. I took Lamby and sat him where she had been, then I carried her to look through the crack of the door.

'If Lamby was rubbing his head now, would you be able to see him?' I asked.

She was still defiant, 'Well, you did hurt me,' but the fight had gone out of her and I could sense she was both remorseful and maybe a little ashamed.

Out of all the problems we ever had with Lucy, whether in relation to contact, or feelings of not belonging, or the worry of Hannah feeling excluded, or the inappropriate messages from Fiona, or the strained relationships between us all – her ability to convince us that she had been hurt or hit by one of us felt most threatening. Jon and I were concerned about the possibility that, as she grew older, and became more sexually aware, her child-like rubbing and saying someone had hurt her could turn into something much more damaging.

It didn't help that Lucy's social workers contacted us, after she'd been living with us for two years, to tell us that Jade had made an allegation that Tracy's older son had sexually abused her when she had lived there with Lucy. The social workers didn't believe Jade, but nevertheless Tracy's foster children had to be moved while the complaint was investigated. They told us that they might have to speak with Lucy at some point. We never heard anything again so assumed that the allegations remained unsubstantiated.

In the spring of 2003, when she was nine years old, we began to notice a change in Hannah's personality. Her once sunny playful nature became darker as she started to denigrate herself. When we first noticed we didn't pay a great deal of attention; she just appeared to be making comments to get a response, such as, 'I look like a boy, don't I?' Hannah is such a feminine little girl, that the question seemed ridiculous. 'Don't be so silly,' we'd say, and then leave it at that.

There was a gradual dawning that something was affecting Hannah as she continued to be self-critical and to distance herself more and more from the routine of family life. As the months rolled by, she became quite withdrawn and she complained a great deal, most often about her appearance.

By November that year she was like a totally different child, becoming upset over the most trivial of things, easily angry and oversensitive, believing that people were talking about her all the time. She was sulky and moody and was sure that she was ugly, fat, and that people didn't like her.

At a parents' evening before Christmas, we asked her teacher if Hannah had fallen out with anyone or if she was unhappy at school. He said he hadn't noticed anything at all and told us that Hannah was one of those children everybody liked and who got on with girls and boys equally. Academically she was in the top set for everything. We received a similar report about Lucy.

Having positive feedback from the school lulled us into a false sense of complacency. Despite the difficult relationship between Jon and Lucy, despite all Lucy's confusion about her birth mother and Hannah's apparent identity crisis, and despite the increasing tensions in the family, the girls were doing well in school!

Hannah's self-esteem received a little boost after the comments from her teacher but her general demeanour didn't improve. I drove myself crazy trying to puzzle out what was going on. Was she being bullied? Was a schoolteacher abusing her? Was nothing going on, was Hannah perhaps predisposed to mental illness? I talked endlessly to my sisters and friends about Hannah's personality change and Lucy's growing desire to see Fiona and her increased sense of belonging elsewhere.

I realised that something was seriously wrong with Hannah when she started to become obsessed about being overweight. She is and always has been a slim, petite little girl. She started to refuse food unless it was low in fat, she stopped eating chips, chocolate and sweets. She was also becoming so quiet that her presence was barely felt. At one stage, the school nurse wanted to see us to discuss Hannah being underweight, she wasn't too concerned but wanted to make us aware. It is literally only as I write this that the reality of it is fully clear to me: ten-year-old Hannah was successful in her efforts to lose weight.

Close family and friends began to worry about Hannah. Her friends Chloe and Louise were upset that she didn't want to play any more. Their parents, Flick and Andrew, commented on how anti-social she appeared to be; we spent many nights going over the possibilities with a few more bottles of wine.

One evening, Flick and I were out walking her dog, when she decided to confront me with a view that I didn't like too much at the time.

She said, 'Lucy takes up all of your time and you're always dealing with her problems and issues. Maybe this is Hannah's way of getting some real time from you.' That didn't ring true for me; it seemed to minimise the problem somehow. How could this sort of behaviour just be about getting attention?

I became defensive: 'Hannah gets plenty of attention. She knows how much we love her, every night before she goes to bed she has one-to-one quality time with us.'

Flick clearly didn't want to upset me, 'But does she, Karen? What was it Julia said to you after she had looked after them both?'

She was referring to Julia, a nanny I had once employed for a week, during a school half-term break. She had found Lucy exhausting to look after. At the end of the week she told me that she couldn't manage her, then she said of Hannah, 'Poor thing, she doesn't get a look in, does she?'

I was offended by her remark at the time and explained that Lucy did need firm handling and if you let her take all your attention she would do so, but I assured her that I didn't allow Lucy to monopolise my time and there was no need to pity Hannah. I decided not to use Julia anymore – convinced that she was incapable of looking after my children. Obviously I wasn't seeing what those close to me were seeing. Interestingly, Lucy really enjoyed Julia coming to the home whereas Hannah didn't.

One day I walked into Hannah's bedroom and saw her looking at herself sideways on in the mirror; she was bending over and pulling at the skin on her flat stomach.

'Hannah, what on earth are you doing?' I said. 'For God's sake, you'll hurt yourself, what's the matter?'

She came back at me in a rage and began punching herself in her stomach. 'I am fat and ugly,' she said, angrily hitting her stomach to the beat of her words.

No amount of reassurance could convince her that she was wrong about her body image. Jon and I committed to keeping a close eye on what and how much Hannah ate and how she was behaving, but it was a difficult situation. Although we knew very little about eating disorders, we knew enough to be aware that control issues were significant. Therefore, the last thing we wanted to do was to nag her at mealtimes. Also, on the face of it, the very early stages of eating disorders look like healthy eating. Choosing low fat, low calorie foods is actively encouraged these days, particularly in schools. It had become very difficult to discuss anything with Hannah, as she took everything the wrong way, and she was very defensive about any suggestion to talk to our family doctor.

In September 2003, Lucy moved from the infants up to the juniors, so that she and Hannah would see each other frequently throughout the day. Hannah was in Year Six and Lucy in Year Three. A number of incidents at school caused their relationship to deteriorate further.

Year Six pupils were given some extra responsibilities in school. It was their job to introduce the new reception class to the school and walk them up the hill for assembly and lunch. For some reason, one little girl took an instant dislike to Hannah and would say things like, 'I'm not holding her hand,' and 'I want to walk with someone else'.

Hannah couldn't accept this and tried to make the little girl like her, but it didn't work and she continued to avoid Hannah. We told her that small children do this sort of thing sometimes and it really wasn't anything to worry about. Then one day, when I was picking Lucy and Hannah up from the after school club, this little girl jumped up and pulled Hannah's hair. I was told by the assistant that this child was causing a lot of problems in school with this sort of behaviour. We took no further action but from then on

Hannah made no further effort to befriend her.

A few days later, I overheard Hannah asking Lucy why she was suddenly playing with this particular little girl. I asked Lucy not to play with her because sisters should support each other. Hannah said she didn't want to force Lucy to stop playing with her if that was what she wanted to do. At bedtime that evening I asked Lucy how she would feel if a child hurt her and Hannah made friends with that same girl afterwards. Lucy said she would probably be upset and that she wasn't going to play with her again anyway. 'Good girl,' I said, kissing her goodnight.

But there was more. Hannah had a friend called Janet when she was in Year Five. But Hannah felt that Janet was too bossy and she made other, closer friends. Hannah's view of Janet was that she was an extremely popular girl, she was good at sports, she was clever, she was pretty, confident, and Hannah believed that all the boys fancied her. She told me that Janet was a 'powerful girl', and although she no longer wanted to be her friend she didn't want to get on the wrong side of her either. Hannah would come home from school and say that she was happy that Janet was no longer her friend, 'She shows off to all the boys, she thinks she's the best at everything'. Then, one day, Janet came up to Hannah in the playground and accused her of saying things about her at home. That evening Hannah was upset about what Janet might say or do at school; she was also angry with Lucy. She said that other children always stuck up for their brothers and sisters as she had stuck up for Lucy many times. It was one thing for them to argue with each other, but it was wrong to get each other into trouble outside the home.

We talked at length with Lucy to make her understand why families should stick together. We tried to explain to Hannah that, because of her background, perhaps loyalty had less meaning for Lucy and she was still learning. Hannah didn't accept this explanation and argued that Lucy was always completely loyal to her sister Jade. She also insisted that if Lucy loved her she would not want to hurt her. Hannah continued to isolate herself from the rest of us, and was still preoccupied with her weight.

I had qualified as a social worker in 2002 and was now practising. I became good friends with a colleague who joined the organisation. She confided in me that when she was a child she used to suffer from both anorexia and bulimia and had spent time in an eating disorder unit. We discussed Hannah at length. At the time I believed that she was eating well enough, even though she was preoccupied with what she was eating. Based on her own experience, my colleague thought that she was possibly showing early signs of anorexia. One fact rang a bell: Hannah bending over and looking at her stomach scrunched up in the mirror. She gave me some information about organisations I could contact and recommended a book.

Shortly after the first incident with Janet, Hannah complained that Lucy was still playing with Janet in the playground, and that Janet was making fun of her in class. She was worried about what Lucy was telling Janet and said that Lucy had stopped playing with the children from her own class.

The situation was getting Hannah down. Her growing sadness was fuelled by the rejection she felt from Lucy. It was as though Hannah's whole personality was being sapped away, and we couldn't stop it happening. She needed support from her family, and I firmly told Lucy that she must not tell Janet what Hannah said at home. Lucy promised that she would not play with Janet anymore. I considered the possibility that Janet may have been bullying Lucy, but Lucy said not.

A couple of weeks later, Hannah and Lucy started squabbling when we were out shopping.

'Yes…and you've never stopped playing with Janet, have you?' Hannah was having a go at Lucy. I intervened to discover that Lucy had indeed never stopped playing with Janet. I really wasn't pleased with Lucy and I told her so.

Lucy immediately retorted with 'you all don't care about me anyway, and you don't love me'.

I knew where this had come from. Fiona was feeding ideas to Lucy through Jade, because of the letter I had written regarding the inappropriate messages she had sent.

I replied, 'Lucy, sometimes I don't think you want to be with us!' I noticed she had a really sad look on her face and as usual I couldn't go on being angry with her.

'Lucy, do you want to be with us'? She didn't answer but instead looked down at her feet.

'We'll talk when we get home,' I said.

When we arrived home Lucy sat on my knee and I asked her if she was happy. I'm ashamed to admit that I cannot recall where Hannah was, even though she was the one who had been so upset. Lucy said that what she really wanted was to see Fiona. She thought she would be OK if only she could see her again. She said that Jade saw her and it wasn't fair on her that she couldn't. I told her that I would talk to the social workers to find out what could be done, but I couldn't promise anything.

Later that evening, when we all sat down at the table to eat our evening meal, I recounted these events to Jon. Lucy promised again that she would stop playing with Janet and this time she apologised to Hannah. Hannah barely lifted her head throughout the meal and had nothing to say. After Lucy had gone to bed she popped a little note under the door to say she was sorry. I still have the letter; it reads:

> *Dear the best loving familly aspesilly Hannah, I'm sorry for making you sad and playing with Gannet I will stay away from them and get Rebecca not play with her instead. Lots of love sister Lucy.*

There were lots and lots of kisses and little pictures of hearts.

* * *

The social worker's statements to the court barely mention

Hannah, and when they do, it is only to imply that she was treated more favourably than Lucy. They dispute that Hannah had any kind of upset or worry whatsoever.

9

Social workers in the house again

It seemed that the social workers wanted to include something contentious in every paragraph of their reports. This left us having to prove that what we had said was true; consequently the care proceedings had dragged on, and here we still were, having to argue every point several court hearings and ten months after the disruption.

The threshold criteria had originally said that Mr and Mrs Carr had advised the local authority that Lucy's behaviour had become manipulative and was badly affecting Hannah. It stated that there was no evidence from health, education or social services to support this view.

The social workers had come to our home to speak with Hannah but they neither asked her any questions about her relationship with Lucy, nor tried to establish the state of her mental health. We told them that we were in the process of seeking professional medical help for Hannah, but they didn't ask how, when or from whom.

They went into school and discovered the girls had good attendance records, were always dressed appropriately, and yes, we always went to parents' evenings. We had made sure that both girls enjoyed the best the school had to offer in the way of extra-curricular activities and that they did all their homework. The teacher didn't tell them that Hannah had begun to self-harm and therefore, remarkably, it couldn't have happened!

Well, we were the ones who had been living with Hannah...

* * *

After Lucy's sincere apologies and little letter she sent to Hannah we were hoping to be able to start anew. Jon and Lucy had had their trip away together a couple of months earlier, and there was some improvement in their relationship.

I had contacted the social workers from the placing authority to tell them that we were having some problems with Lucy; that she seemed to have an overwhelming desire to see Fiona again. They agreed to come and see us.

We were just hoping that the old Hannah might begin to emerge as things improved.

In the autumn of 2003, Jon and I had every reason to be optimistic about our future. Both our careers were flourishing. We had reasonably well paid, secure, rewarding and even challenging work. We had two beautiful, healthy girls who were achieving at school. For the first time since Jon and I had met we were enjoying a disposable income. We owned a nice home in a pretty area, where crime was low. We had two cars and good friends – life could have been good.

I started to look forward to Christmas; being able to afford all the presents the girls had asked for made a huge difference to the shopping experience. I decided to get rid of all our tired old tacky Christmas decorations and spent a fortune on new classier ones; colour co-ordinated to match our newly-decorated, ultra modern, golden living room.

It was late November before the social workers

managed to come and see us. It felt odd having them in the house again. Valerie sat on our settee, she hadn't altered at all in the four-and-a-half years since we had last met. She was with her manager and the manager of the permanence team. We explained that Jade had been passing messages to Lucy from Fiona and described the impact we believed this was having on her, such as her concern that Fiona was unwell and her fears that she belonged elsewhere. Lucy had become preoccupied with her life story book and was struggling to understand why she couldn't see Fiona when Jade could. We told them about the difficulties that Jon and Lucy had always had, and how we tried to resolve them, and how new problems were emerging in Hannah and Lucy's relationship. I asked Valerie if she had discovered anything whatsoever during our assessment that made her feel we might have serious problems. Her response struck me. She said, 'I was surprised to hear that Jon has problems attaching with Lucy'. I regret that I never queried what she meant by that.

I told them that we had been supported by After Adoption since Lucy moved in almost four-and-a-half years ago, and had been advised that Lucy should see Fiona as it might ease some of her anxieties.

They listened and were sympathetic, but said that Fiona was still suffering from a substantial personality disorder and believed any direct contact would disturb Lucy further. They came up with two options to help us: one, to provide some respite care for Lucy. There was no way we would consider this; it would give us a break, but I couldn't see how it could be a positive experience for Lucy. We thought it would completely destabilise her. The second option was family therapy; this we took up.

During the weeks leading up to Christmas, Hannah's mood deteriorated further. A very clear indication of how she felt was the degree to which she cut herself off from her friends, even on special occasions. Hannah, Lucy, Chloe, Louise and other friends of theirs were in the Brownies and a day out at Cadbury's World had been arranged. Hannah was really excited; she has always wanted to go to Cadbury's World since her paternal grandparents had taken her cousins, and she had wanted to go but couldn't.

'Mum, Mum! Can we go on the trip to Cadbury's World? Please Mum, pleeease,' they both begged, 'Chloe and Louise are going, can we, can we?'

'When do I ever say no?' I asked.

They were both looking forward to it. But then a few weeks later Hannah abruptly declared she was no longer going, 'I don't want to go, I never really wanted to go in the first place'. Something wasn't right; we were waiting for the real reason she didn't want to go to emerge, but it never did.

As the time drew nearer, her friends were almost begging her to go with them. 'Oh come on Hannah, think of all the choc-o-late, choc-o-late, choc-o-late!'

Jon and I also tried our utmost to encourage her, and gave her the opportunity of going, right up to the last minute. But on the day we looked on as Lucy and their friends boarded the coach and Hannah watched from the car. Nothing could persuade her to go and so she didn't. She gave no explanation, other than that she didn't want to.

The first family therapy session came just five days before Christmas Day. It was to be only Jon and myself; the children would join us subsequently. We saw two women, a psychologist and a social worker. They immediately made us feel at ease and it was as though we hadn't been able to wait for this moment. Everything about our family circumstances was spewed out. It was a relief for both of us to sit in that room and completely unburden ourselves in such a non-threatening way. We mentioned that we were also having problems with Hannah, but the conversation was almost exclusively about Lucy. As we were leaving we made an appointment early in the New Year. Jon began to thank them for listening and they said that they really hoped that they could help us. The psychologist said, 'Just one final question before you go…what do you want at the end of this?' She turned to Jon. His words scared me as he clearly spoke from his heart, his brow furrowed, he looked directly at the psychologist and said, 'I just want to be able to end all this with the minimum amount of pain possible to all concerned.' Silence…

My nervous laugh broke through. 'Just wait a minute! We are not quite at that stage yet,' I said, strongly emphasising the word "not" and throwing Jon an angry glance. I hadn't heard him say this before and I was furious with him for saying it here. I was desperate to get out of the building. The psychologist looked at Jon with an interested smile as we left.

We bickered on the way home because I was as mad as hell that the first time I had heard Jon say this was in front of others; I had been unprepared for it. He defended his position by saying that they would not be able to help us unless they knew exactly how he was feeling and he hadn't planned to say it but didn't regret it now that he had!

On the last day of term before Christmas I picked up the children from the after school club. There was no hint of any of the recent tension between the girls. We were all going to be at home now for over a week. The house proudly boasted the poshest Christmas decorations we had ever owned. Putting them up was a joint effort as it always had been. I wanted to invite everyone I knew around to the house to marvel at our wonderfully tasteful glossy magazine arrangements. We had all shopped until we dropped this year; we were stocked up with beer, wine and we had enough food to feed the street for a month. It was freezing cold outside and we had a blazing fire inside. All the presents had been bought, wrapped and delivered. We were well prepared to let the festivities begin.

In the evening I was browsing the internet when Hannah came into the room and just stood beside me looking nervous. I stopped what I was doing and turned to her. 'What's the matter Hannah, you OK?' She didn't speak but shook her head from side to side. I could see tears welling up in her eyes.

'Hannah, you can tell me anything, you know that. What is it, darling?' I patted my lap for her to sit down. 'Come and sit on Mum's knee,' I said. She sat down and silently cried for a few minutes leaning her head on my chest.

'What's the matter, Hannah? I can't help you if you don't tell me what's wrong,' I said, stroking her hair. She sat up and turned to face me, her big brown eyes wet and scared, and then she lifted her top up to reveal her stomach. I could see a long scratch, it had broken the skin and had bled slightly. I didn't understand at first but then I did; she was telling me that she had deliberately hurt herself.

This knocked me for six, but nevertheless she had come to me, which was a good sign. This was clearly a cry for help and we would do anything we could to help her. We sat down and had a lengthy conversation, talking over what had been troubling her. She didn't say anything specific except that she got worried and angry, and that when she told me her problems she wasn't happy with the way I dealt with them. She didn't mention Lucy other than to say that she took a lot of my attention, and she best liked our time after Lucy had gone to bed. We tried to work out what the triggers might be to her feeling bad and angry and came up with some suggestions for venting her feelings in other ways than by hurting herself.

Later Jon and I discussed whether or not we should take her to see the doctor. We decided to leave it until after Christmas; we would give her as much attention as possible and think about it again then. Surprisingly perhaps, we had a relaxed Christmas, apparently enjoying each other's company.

One of Hannah's presents was a three-quarter length baby pink coat, with large buttons and a hood with white edging. They had only been back at school for a couple of days, when Hannah came home with her coat covered in mud at the back. She was upset.

'Oh, what's happened to your coat, Hannah?' I thought she must have sat down in something.

But she said, angrily, 'Lucy and two of her friends ran into me in the playground and knocked me over.'

Lucy immediately and convincingly jumped to her own defence. 'It was an accident, she's always trying to get me into trouble.'

Hannah was quick to reply, 'Well, if it was an accident, why were you laughing?'

'I wasn't laughing, you're a liar Hannah, she's lying Mum, I wasn't laughing. Why didn't she tell the teacher then?' She was scowling and stabbed her finger in the air.

'OK, that's enough,' I interrupted. I assured Hannah we would have her coat as good as new the following day for school and I gave Lucy the benefit of the doubt. With a child like Lucy I had to be sure she had done something wrong before I could take any action and I wasn't sure, it could have been an accident. It was only after Lucy had left that I reflected and realised that it was highly unlikely that Lucy had accidentally bumped into Hannah with enough force to knock her over in a playground full of children.

On 9 January 2004, I was tickling Hannah on the settee. We'd had a good evening and were all in high spirits, and Hannah was laughing and wriggling around enjoying the attention. Jon had taken Lucy to bed and was running a bath for me. When he came back to the living room and sat down, I said, 'Right, I'm going to get in the bath'.

Hannah ran past me laughing, 'Not if I get there first,' she said, throwing her clothes off as she ran upstairs. I ran up behind her doing the same thing. She was getting excited trying to get into the bath before me. As she climbed over the side of the bath something caught my eye. 'Oh, what's that Hannah? Did I scratch you when I was tickling you?'

Hannah's face changed, she looked thoroughly ashamed and ran out to her bedroom. I ran after her and insisted she show me. There were scratch marks on her stomach again. This time there were two distinct marks about six inches long. They were clearly a few days old and were scabbed over. I was too upset to know how I could deal with it. I suggested Hannah come into the bath with me so we could talk. I pleaded with her to tell me what on earth was going on.

Her words were, 'I can't hurt Lucy so I just hurt myself. If I go to you, then you tell me to be more tolerant and if I go to Dad then it starts arguments – so I just hurt myself.'

I asked her how she had made the scratches and she told me she had used the "feet" of her "bang on the door clock".

As I sat crying in the bath with Hannah, it all suddenly became clear. Despite the very best of intentions and hard work to create a family in which we could all flourish, we had reached a stage where Hannah was so distraught that she had resorted to turning her anger against herself.

Lucy had her own internal struggles about belonging to another family and was developing allegiances elsewhere.

Jon and I were drifting away from each other at a furious pace. I could see that our whole family life was in tatters. It was then that I knew the adoption was over.

I didn't want Hannah to carry the guilt of thinking it was because of her, so I told her that her dad and I had been going to family therapy in a last attempt at trying to sort things out. As it hadn't helped, we had decided to end the adoption, and that Lucy would have to leave. At first she looked horrified and said, 'She's not going into a children's home, is she?'

'No,' I said, 'definitely not.'

'Good,' she said, and smiled.

After Hannah had gone to bed I told Jon what had happened. His initial reaction was to say that there was no way Lucy could go back into care. But I was resolute. He said we should sleep on it and see how we felt in the morning.

I couldn't sleep that night and searched the internet for information on children who self harm; it made frightening reading. One article I read said that when children self-harm it is always a sign that something is seriously wrong. It is a way for young people to deal with very difficult feelings when they feel trapped and helpless. It said that when family life involves a lot of abuse, neglect or rejection, it can lead to young people self-harming. The article also made a link between self-harm and eating disorders and explained how the secretive nature of it makes it difficult to detect. I looked at many websites that night, and all of them without exception linked self-harm in young people with abuse of some sort and many made links with eating disorders.

It is difficult to describe my emotions at that time, as they overwhelmed me; I had let Hannah down. My will to protect, love and nurture her was uncompromising. I believed I had the power to make her better and I would have done anything, literally, to make her well again. Had Jon stuck to his guns and refused to let Lucy go back into care, I think I would have packed our bags and left with Hannah. It was as though suddenly I saw everything differently and realised how much I had overlooked her. I was so grateful to Jon for standing by Hannah; he may have saved her by being there for her.

But I was also furious with Jon for making me be the one who had to say enough is enough and insist that Lucy had to go, although he had been the first to suggest finding a way to end the adoption. I understand that we were all doing our best and trying to do the right thing, but I still struggle to forgive him for that. My need to protect Hannah overrode my need to care for Lucy and that is the regrettable truth.

* * *

Back in court I thought again about when I had first seen the social workers' comments. I realised that Hannah's meeting with the Child and Adolescent Mental Health Services (CAMHS) team was likely to have been recorded and to be on a file somewhere. I contacted the CAMHS team to ask if they had any official record of Hannah's appointment five months ago. Fortunately they did, and I was able to produce a copy of it for the final hearing I attended in December 2004. Below is an extract of the report we received from the CAMHS team.

> *...Hannah presented as a shy young lady who did not want to attend as the issues have now rectified themselves which, you may recall, were over her sister Lucy, the breakdown of the adoption and Hannah self-harming.*

> *...Hannah and her mother were saying that there have been definite improvements, especially with Hannah not saying she was ugly and she could be heard having more fun with her peers and becoming more outgoing...*

> *Regarding the self-harm issues, this happened on only a couple of occasions...She denies any recent intentions to carry out this behaviour...*

The social workers still didn't accept that it was true, but they finally had to change the wording of the threshold criteria!

10

Out in the cold

The final court hearing, which so bewildered Miss Pickering, took place on 2 December 2004, ten months after Lucy had left us. She had been with us for exactly four years, six months and twenty days, but the last month was the most painful we lived through.

It was on 9 January 2004 when I discovered that Hannah had been self-harming again. It was on 9 February 2004 when a social worker picked Lucy up and she left our home for the last time.

Assessments had to be completed before the local authority would agree to accommodate her and therefore we could not tell Lucy that the adoption was over until we knew for certain what was going to happen. It was very clear that we were under considerable stress and that the family was in crisis. We believed absolutely that we had done all we could, that the adoption had come to an end, and that for Hannah's sake it needed to end sooner rather than later. We asked for Lucy to be moved gradually in view of her traumatic experiences of previous abrupt and sudden separations.

I am not aiming to justify anybody's actions during that last month, but I think it is important to describe our behaviour and interactions at the time. I have always parented instinctively. I was able to get close to Lucy that way. I may have read a lot about attachment, loss, separation and re-nurturing but my driving force was my instinct. Finally, my instinct to save Hannah became dominant, and I have to use the word "save" because in my mind that is exactly what I was doing. I was scared that she might do something more serious to herself and I blamed myself for not recognising her suffering sooner, so that I was now frightened for her sanity. For months family and friends had warned us that they had noticed a change in Hannah. But I don't think anyone suspected it was as bad as it was.

Now I was by her side every waking moment when she wasn't in school. Jon was just as protective. We scrutinised every inch of her bedroom and belongings to determine whether or not anything could be used as a sharp instrument. She had collected badges since she was tiny and kept them in a sandwich box in her bedroom; we removed them and threw away her "bang on the door" clock.

We became scared of letting her get upset for fear that she would find a way to hurt herself again. It was as though she had a round-the-clock entertainment team, jumping to her every whim. I bought her a karaoke set, even though we had just had Christmas.

My aim was to get rid of this shell that now enclosed Hannah, and get back the happy and bright child she had been. And so, in some desperation, we smothered her with over-anxious attention. She occasionally asked if Lucy was still leaving. We told her that she was probably going but we didn't know when. We suggested she try not to think about it and as soon as we knew anything we would tell her – she never asked for Lucy to stay.

I had made the decision that Lucy was to leave, and I think as well as wanting to protect Hannah I was also distancing myself from Lucy, again instinctively. During those last four weeks Lucy must have felt left out in the cold. I had been her warmth, her comfort and her refuge from the outside world. What did she make of my sudden distance? Although a lot of that time is very hazy, I recall one evening when Hannah was sitting on my knee. Lucy wasn't trying to edge her way in so I suspect she must already have learnt that Hannah was flavour of the month. Lucy looked at me and said, 'God, Mum, you're getting as bad as Dad with Hannah,' and she had this hurt expression on her face. Normally, if she had made a comment like that, I would have reassured her like a shot, in fact I'd have been falling over myself to make sure she understood that she was every bit as valuable as anyone else, but not now. 'Don't be silly, Lucy,' was all I said.

Even if it's a bit of a cliché to say it, it breaks my heart now to know I didn't reach out to Lucy when she needed it, but it was a measure of my concern for Hannah that I couldn't. I still hugged and kissed Lucy, read her bedtime stories, and bought her favourite treats and foods, but in comparison to my usual self I was different, and she knew it.

Whereas I had become distant with Lucy, Jon seemed to completely detach himself. One day he frightened Lucy. It was a weekend and I had decided to take the girls out for the day to a working farm which also had a play centre and swings. Jon was going to his mother's. It was freezing cold outside and the ground was covered in ice. When the girls came down dressed to go, Lucy was wearing open-toed sandals, short white socks, a short skirt and T-shirt. She agreed to change and put some jeans on but refused to change her socks and sandals.

Rather than the usual negotiating or arguing, I simply said, 'You change or I go without you'. She didn't move. I gave her one last chance. She still didn't move and so Hannah and I went on our own.

When we came back, Lucy took me to one side to tell me that her dad had shouted at her at lunchtime and she had been scared. When I confronted Jon he said that he knew he had gone too far. He said that she was arguing over what she was going to eat and he had got frustrated. He said he had been trying to get through to her that she has to learn to do as she is told. He said he was worried that, wherever she was going next, no one would be as understanding as us and that could lead to a series of short-term placements for her. He said he had been shouting at her inches away from her face when he realised he was going over the top and had taken himself upstairs to calm down.

The following day, when the girls had gone to school, I telephoned social services, crying on the phone, saying it wasn't fair on Lucy that while the three of us were moving closer together, she was being left out and it was cruel. They said that we just needed support. They did not grasp the nature of the crisis in our home. Of course, we discovered later that they didn't believe what we had told them about Hannah, and they were convinced that Lucy was going only because I was pregnant.

That day, when I picked up the girls from school, Lucy said, 'You are going to want to go into school when I tell you what happened to me today, Mum.'

'Oh, I doubt that Lucy, but go on, tell me,' I said, not really in the mood to listen. I was distracted and walking so fast back to the car that both children had to run to keep up with me. Lucy began her story, and continued as we got in the car and drove off.

'I went into school this morning and I was a bit late because (something had happened to slow her down, I can't remember what) when I got into class they had all finished saying their prayers and so Miss said I had to stand up and say it on my own.' Her voice started to go as she tried to tell me what had happened. 'I was crying and trying to say my prayers but she wouldn't let me sit down until I had finished, and I couldn't speak because I was crying.' By now, tears were streaming down her face.

I was so angry; Lucy was going through enough at

home, and she didn't go to school to get bullied by the teacher. I turned the car around and drove back to school. 'Is Miss still there, do you know?'

'I think so,' came the happier reply, now that I was taking notice.

I marched into school looking for "Miss". Fortunately, I think for both of us, she wasn't there. The Deputy Head, who was also Hannah's form tutor, was there, so I told him what had happened. I also took the opportunity to tell him that the adoption was breaking down. I explained that Lucy was going through a really tough time at home at the moment. He was sympathetic and said he was unaware and surprised that Lucy was adopted. He excused the teacher's behaviour by saying that she was very young and still getting to grips with a whole class of children, and she frequently got it wrong. He said he would try to ensure that Lucy got some extra support and he would have a word with the teacher in question.

It was such a surreal time in our lives. The stress within the home was unbearable. Hannah remained my prime concern. I just wanted to be with her and to look after her; I wanted her to know how much she was loved. But Lucy was still my responsibility and my feelings of guilt were overwhelming; I couldn't be close to her when I knew what we were doing to her. I was still pregnant so I guess my hormones didn't help.

One evening, I am ashamed to admit, I was so stressed out that I bought myself a bottle of wine, and proceeded to get drunk. Once the girls were in bed I screamed irrationally at Jon. I blamed him for everything and said he needed to do something for once instead of leaving it all to me. Lucy needed to go, the adoption had broken down, I was trying to protect Hannah and why wasn't he doing something, and if anything happened to her I would hold him responsible. I really wasn't pleasant. That night Jon wrote a letter to the local authority saying that he would take Lucy to the social services office and leave her there if they didn't take some action. Very shortly after they agreed to accommodate Lucy.

On Friday 6 February 2004 we found out that Lucy would be leaving on the next Monday. Again, Lucy was going to be moved abruptly. I couldn't persuade them to plan gradual introductions. I was literally begging them on the telephone, but all they would say was that the decision had been made. I reminded them of what we had first asked for and told them how this move would damage Lucy, but they would not waver. So we had just the weekend to prepare her.

My friend Flick collected the girls from school and took them to her house. I called Jon to tell him the news. We arranged that he would pick up the children, bring Lucy home, then take Hannah for a drive and tell her while I would tell Lucy.

The second Lucy walked through the door she knew something was seriously wrong because of my bloodshot eyes and tear-stained face. 'What's the matter, Mum, is it the baby?' she said, concerned as ever.

'No, Lucy, please come and sit down. I need to talk to you.' Lucy sat beside me on the settee. I couldn't think of how to say the words and so I started with, 'I am so sorry, Lucy'. I couldn't stop the tears. 'I am so, so sorry.' I held my hands over my face.

Lucy hated to see me upset and she tried to put her arms around me as she said, 'Is it Dad?

And then she said it.

'Do I have to move?'

I answered straight away, 'Yes, Lucy, that's it. We have decided you have to move.' She took a sharp breath, her hands fell to her lap, she sat bolt upright and stared ahead.

'OK, OK. When do I have to move?' she asked.

I was surprised by her apparent strength and resilience. 'Monday,' I answered.

'How many days is that?' she counted using her fingers, 'Friday, Saturday, Sunday and Monday – four days,' she said.

Then, 'Where are Hannah and Daddy?' she asked.

'They have gone for a drive.'

She interrupted me, 'Is Daddy telling Hannah now?'

'Yes,' I said.

Lucy looked at me. 'Mum, we have to lock all the doors, close the curtains and turn all the lights on, and I want you all to put me to bed tonight.' So that's what we did. The last room we went in was her own bedroom. There were two windows, so we closed the curtains. Every light in the house was on.

We sat on her bed and decided to do some colouring and she said to me, 'Mum, I'll only remember the good times, I promise.' Then she said, 'I thought I was going to stop breathing and die when you said that'.

The memory of hearing those words truly haunts me even now.

Lucy was told that it was all about her dad's relationship with her. I didn't want Lucy blaming herself or hating Hannah. So it seemed easier to blame it all on Dad; we thought both she and Hannah would understand that.

While we sat on her bed, Lucy realised that she would lose her bed as well. She loved her bedroom. She hugged her pillow and said, 'My bed, I love my bed'. About twelve months previously when we had the extension built, both girls had chosen their own new bedroom furniture. Lucy had chosen a midi-sleeper bed; with extra bits of furniture; she had made a little den underneath it. The room was painted white and pink, with beech flooring and two round pink rugs. She had a flower-shaped bedside lamp. She was always happiest in her bedroom. With all her own belongings around her, she was snug and secure.

Suddenly she asked, 'Can Dad not go instead?'

'No Lucy, Dad can't go, I'm sorry.'

Then she said, 'Why do I always have to be the one to go?'

Keeping in touch with Jade, and witnessing all her placement breakdowns had, I think, served as a constant reminder to Lucy that she was adopted and that it could happen to her. She was still very much a product of the care system.

That last weekend I spent as much time with Lucy as I could. On the Saturday, we were driving into town and Lucy was working everything out in her mind. 'How long have you known that I was going to leave?' she wanted to know.

'A few weeks – why?'

'So when that social worker came to talk to me at school, did you know then?'

'That is when we decided, Lucy, yes.'

'Well, you haven't been sad all that time then, have you?'

'Sometimes we don't look sad even when we are, Lucy.'

She thought about it for a minute or two, then she said, 'Fiona couldn't look after me because she was ill, you're not ill.' She was both curious and accusing.

I tried to explain that all the shouting and arguing had been affecting us all, and that it was no way to live.

As I was explaining, I thought that we should have told Lucy the truth, she deserved to know the truth. We thought the reason we gave the children would make sense, but we were wrong. The relationship between Dad and Lucy had always been up and down, more down than up. But it was not particularly bad at that time, so it probably didn't make sense that she suddenly had to leave because of it.

We were very surprised when on Saturday afternoon Lucy asked if she could ring her friend Rebecca and go to her house and play. We wondered if she understood exactly what was happening.

When she came home she said, 'I'm going to miss you Mum – I am, but...' she paused and looked up to make sure I wasn't upset or offended, 'but in some ways it is quite exciting, they might have loads of money.' Perhaps she felt that material possessions were more reliable than people.

On Sunday Lucy was becoming concerned about where she was going. She was worried that they would give her food she didn't like and make her wear clothes she didn't like, or make her do her hair in ways she didn't like. She was worried that they wouldn't know her routines, for washing, bathing and bedtime. Lucy was very particular about these things; if she was made to do things differently, it made her thoroughly miserable.

Her biggest fear was about me coming to school to pick up Hannah and leaving her behind. Lucy was to stay in the same area, go to the same school and would still attend the after-school club. In the end we avoided the problem by bringing my maternity leave forward so that I could collect Hannah straight from school. I would wait at the end of the road and she would come out to meet me.

Given that we could not do proper introductions, the only thing I could think of was to write a letter to the carers explaining exactly who Lucy was and listing all the things she liked, her routines and idiosyncrasies and the telephone numbers of her friends and Jade, her sister.

We asked the girls if they wanted to stay at home on Monday. Lucy chose to stay but Hannah went to school. On that Monday we must have spent a great part of the day packing her belongings, but the day is a blur to me now. My only recollections are of Lucy sitting next to me on the settee and asking me the time frequently, and then asking, 'So how long have I got left?'

At four o'clock two social workers arrived to take Lucy away. Then she was gone.

* * *

Nothing in the court reports could convey the feelings of an adoption disruption to Miss Pickering. She would have to do the best she could with the recorded facts.

11

After Lucy left

Mr and Mrs Carr declined a plan for rehabilitation and stated that they wished contact to reduce until it ended completely.

This was the wording in the threshold criteria. Miss Pickering advised us against trying to alter this section and holding up proceedings further. We agreed with her. After all, when Lucy was first accommodated by the local authority, and we were at the height of the trauma, the statement was true.

* * *

After Lucy left, we found ourselves in a bizarre situation. Our circumstances had changed so quickly; we were in shock.

I was due to see Lucy the following Saturday. It was such an awful feeling. We had facilitated contact with Jade for the last four years; I never expected to be having "contact" with Lucy myself. I was extremely worried about seeing her. I tormented myself with images of what she was going through. I was preoccupied with thoughts that I had taken a mother away from her for the third time in her life.

I re-lived every time that I had told her she would be with us forever. I pored over photographs and couldn't get my head around why we couldn't make it work. I cried on the telephone to friends and family. I was particularly demanding of my younger sister, who came to stay with me later to help me cope emotionally.

Jon planned to have very little contact with Lucy. We thought it made more sense as we were saying that the adoption was ending because of him. We never had a word of advice about this. I can only assume that as I was a social worker they believed I would be in control, or knew exactly what we were doing or even should do. But the truth is that we were in such turmoil that we didn't know whether we were coming or going. We had been on an emotional rollercoaster for four-and-a-half years and it had all come to an abrupt end, with one of our children self-harming and on the verge of an eating disorder and the other being placed in local authority care – we were clueless.

I was scared about that first contact; I was unsure whether I would be able to handle my feelings if Lucy was too upset. Would I be able to return her to the foster carer? I just didn't know.

Then came Saturday. I met with Lucy alone at first; Jon would bring Hannah later if I telephoned to say it was all right. I was amazed to see that she was quite OK. She even said so to me, 'I'm fine, I'm with the kind of family I like, Mummy'. Part of me suspected that she was trying to protect me. Lucy has a real capacity to empathise with people when they are unhappy.

I telephoned Jon to ask him to bring Hannah as Lucy seemed fine and I took them both to a large soft play area. It was a very noisy place. I knew my sister was keen to know how Lucy was, and I wanted to put her mind at rest so I decided to text her, which was something I had never done before. My text message simply said, 'You know, sometimes life isn't as bad as it appears to be'.

For some reason, my sister thought that it was a kind of

parting message and that I was about to commit suicide. She couldn't get hold of anybody and I couldn't hear my phone ringing and so in a panic she set off down the M6 to get to me. Fortunately, once I left the play centre I noticed her missed calls and was able to reassure her.

To prevent Hannah witnessing too much possible distress, Jon came to pick her up about half an hour before I was due to take Lucy back to the foster carers. Lucy and I spent that time with her sitting on my knee and she asked about coming home. I couldn't stop myself from becoming upset, and Lucy kept saying, 'It's OK, Mummy'. I couldn't believe how strong she was. We sat hugging for what seemed like an eternity, without speaking. I managed to tell myself to get a grip! Lucy had been through enough without me making it worse for her. By the time we got to the foster home, we were both composed and dry-eyed.

The next visit initially went as smoothly as the first, but then, while driving back to the carers, Lucy was very quiet and the following conversation took place.

'You're very quiet Lucy, are you OK?' I asked.

After a moment she said, 'Do I have to stay at the foster carers'?'

'Why do you ask?' I wondered where this was going.

Lucy turned her head away and went on asking, 'Would you cry if you thought I wasn't happy?'

I knew that if I said, 'Yes, I would cry,' she would say no more. She never wanted to see me upset.

So I said, 'If you were unhappy I might be able to help you, and it would upset me if I thought there was something wrong but you hadn't told me about it.'

She listened, thought about it, then said, 'Would I have to move if I wasn't happy?'

I answered as honestly as I could do, 'That would depend on what it was you weren't happy about.'

She thought again before she said, 'If I wasn't happy and I moved to lots of different places, could I come back home in the end?'

'I'm so sorry, Lucy, but that's not possible.' I felt as though my heart was being ripped out so God only knows how Lucy felt.

'So what if there were no more foster places for me to go to, then would I have to come home?'

I asked Lucy if she wanted to go somewhere to have a talk and she said she did. We found a quiet spot and she told me all her worries about the placement. She didn't think they liked her, and she gave a list of reasons why she wasn't happy. Much of it amounted to different routines, not knowing the people, her shyness, and not being able to make her needs known. I was able to talk it through with her and make her understand that time would make it better. As hard as it was, I also had to be clear that she understood she couldn't come back to us. It would have been cruel to give her false hope and to destabilise the new placement. We both shed bucketloads of tears but managed to calm down by the time I returned her to the foster carers.

For the first few months there were lots of conversations like this, and twice I had to go to the foster home and calm her down when she became too distressed. Then somebody took the decision that Lucy's telephone calls to our home should be limited. I only found out because Lucy told me that the foster carers had not allowed her to telephone me. She thought I would have the power to reverse this new rule. I tried to, but to no avail.

There was one change in Lucy that surprised me; she started to deny the existence of Fiona, her birth mum. She pretended to the foster carer and to the teachers at school that I was her birth mum. When pressed by her social worker, she said she didn't want to see Fiona, and Lucy also told me that she had changed her mind, and she didn't want to see her any more. The social worker suspected that she was in some sort of denial. Lucy didn't appear comfortable talking about it so I dropped the subject, but I did ask her why she had told the foster carer and someone at school that I was her birth mum. She didn't answer but gave me that head down, eyes up, "caught out" smile that she did so well.

As time went on, I could tell Lucy was developing a positive relationship with her foster carers and the rest of their family. Lucy played the guitar and she taught her foster carer how to play; she became interested in church activities and started to enjoy football, things we didn't do at home. Unfortunately, they were not in a position to offer her a permanent place in the family.

The Children's Guardian, Marjorie, came to visit us at home, but her views had been influenced by the social workers. One of the questions she asked in relation to our unborn child was, 'So what's this baby all about then?' This was the first tangible indication that anyone thought we were giving up Lucy because I had finally conceived! Marjorie didn't try to hide her surprise when she learned that I could have chosen to have a baby at any time; I had no biological problems and all four of us had planned to have this baby at this time. It was clear that we did not match her preconceived idea of who we were, and as she was leaving she said, 'Well, my view of you has certainly changed – for the better.' Marjorie was of the opinion that it would be best for Lucy to reduce our contact until we stopped seeing her altogether. At the time we agreed, but I think now that it was the wrong thing to do, and I fear that it might have harmed Lucy even more than the disruption. Lucy had lived with us longer than with her birth family, but a tidy finish was considered to be more important than Lucy's right to continuity. Lucy had begun to ask for Jon, and I had been thinking along the lines of her coming to see us at home, perhaps once a week. If social services had supported us, and respected our concerns regarding Hannah, maybe home visits would have turned into weekend visits and, who knows, there might not have been an unhappy ending after all.

Instead, we took Marjorie's advice and reduced the

contact to once a fortnight, then to monthly, followed by a two-month gap. Hannah had a final visit in August 2004, six months after Lucy left us. Jon and I said goodbye to Lucy a week later at the foster carers'.

I wrote a final goodbye letter and got her many token gifts which I thought might mean something to her at a later stage: an angel of courage, an angel of faith and an angel of hope, and a cross with 'keep me safe' written on it. I know this may appear to be overly sentimental, even sloppy or gushy. I packed everything in her memory box along with all the "bits of Lucy" that we had stored in the loft.

We had a distrustful relationship with the social workers. They said in court reports, and told the Children's Guardian, that Lucy was not affected by the move from our home. Their reasons for saying this are unknown to us. They were secretive about their plans. They stopped Lucy telephoning me during the week of her birthday. We only knew what we saw during contact.

In November 2004, a psychological assessment of Lucy was completed; this was three months after contact had stopped. It concluded that Lucy's main attachment figure, in fact her only attachment figure, was me, but it reported Lucy as saying that she had found it much easier to cope after the contact with us had stopped.

Lucy was moved to a new permanent foster home after 15 months. Unfortunately, right from the start there were problems. Lucy's new social worker seemed to try hard to maintain the placement but I understand that it has broken down and they are hoping to find another "permanent" family for her.

The information we receive is limited. I don't think the local authority acknowledges us as Lucy's "real" parents because we do not have a biological link. Our parental responsibility comes by way of the adoption order, which made us Lucy's legal parents. We sent Lucy gifts on her birthdays and at Christmas until the local authority said this was sending her mixed messages. So after two years we had to stop. I insisted on sending her a final gift and a letter explaining the reasons why there would be no more in the future. We have no idea how Lucy reacted to this: I can only hope that after two years she didn't feel rejected even further.

Last Christmas we didn't have a card from Lucy, for the first time since she left. Her social worker tells me that she calls us Karen and Jon now, and I understand that she still speaks about us with affection. I am told that she continues to do very well in school, apparently much to everybody's surprise.

I always told Lucy that getting an education really helped me to be able to do what I wanted when I grew up. I impressed on her how important it was to take advantage of the education system, so I am really pleased that she is grasping those opportunities.

A section of the parting letter I wrote to Lucy says,

> *Something else that we often talked about, Lucy, is what a very clever girl you are, you always join in and try to do your best in school. Well, you must always try to do your best at school. Because being good at school is one of the best ways of being able to do whatever you want to when you grow up, so you must always remember to just keep doing what you have been doing, and try as hard as you can...*

Who knows, maybe she did remember that.

Hannah had been upset the night we discovered we only had the weekend left with Lucy, and she cried when Jon told her that Lucy would be leaving.

Nevertheless, from the day Lucy left, she began to get well again. She found it impossible to talk about the self-harm. For a long time, broaching the subject was like stepping on eggshells but other changes were immediately apparent. We were at Flick and Andrew's one night the following week, when Flick said, 'Just listen'. We could hear Hannah shouting and laughing. Being able to hear Hannah at all when she was in a group of three was rare these days. It was a clear signal that Hannah was improving.

Once she had gone, Hannah hardly mentioned Lucy and this concerned me, as I didn't know what was going on in her head. I decided to take her out for lunch so we could chat without distraction. When I raised the subject, Hannah said that she thought it was wrong that Lucy had had to leave. 'Well, if your brothers or sisters were really naughty, you'd never think it was OK for them to leave, would you?' she reasoned.

There were so many times when I had desperately wanted to pick Lucy up and bring her home. So when Hannah said this, I thought I would introduce the possibility of more contact at home. 'We don't have to keep doing what we have been doing, we could alter the contact, make it longer, or more frequent, maybe even have it at home.' As soon as it looked like this might be a possibility, Hannah had a change of heart.

'Well, I don't know how I would cope if I saw her any more than I do now,' she said.

'So you wouldn't like her to come home to see us then?' I pushed a little.

'I like it the way it is now,' she said.

I didn't want Hannah to feel responsible for making decisions that weren't hers to make so I didn't push any further.

Neither Jon nor Hannah ever wanted to increase the contact and both were relieved, I think, that it stopped. When discussing now how she felt about contact then, Hannah says it was 'awkward and a bit fake. We were both trying to be nice to each other because we knew it wasn't going to last long. We didn't want to argue but that's all Lucy and me knew, that's what we did – we argued!'

I believe that the decision to write this book has been cathartic for Hannah, as well as for me. Discussing it, she has been more open and able to express herself better than at any time since Lucy left. Hannah confesses that she was 'very glad when Lucy went'. She said, 'I felt free'. Then she asked, 'Have you ever played that game, "pile on?"'

'Well, er, no, I haven't actually Hannah, but go on.'

'It's where everybody lies on top of each other and the one at the bottom has to wriggle out to get on top.'

'Yes, go on.'

'When Lucy was here, I felt as though I was always at the bottom and I couldn't get out. When she left it was as though everybody just got off.'

Hannah says that she honestly doesn't understand why Lucy's presence brought her to the stage that it did. 'I just got so low,' she says, but when she left, 'I just stopped being sad, stopped hurting myself, I started feeling hungry, I started talking to my friends again and all the arguing stopped.' Then Hannah reminds me, as though I might forget, 'Do you remember when I didn't want to play with my friends?' She says of Lucy, 'I loved her and hated her at the same time, the sadness just happened. I still get sad now, but it's nothing like it was, I'd never hurt myself now.'

I put it to her one day that I thought she was on the verge of an eating disorder just before Lucy left.

'Mum,' she said bluntly, 'you have no idea.'

'Oh really? So tell me,' I said casually, as though I was barely interested. I didn't want to scare her out of telling me.

'Well, I never ate breakfast. I'd put only a tiny bit of cereal in my bowl, then swill the milk around so it just looked as though I hadn't finished it all. The only drink I would have was water and I stopped eating chocolate, sweets, crisps and chips.'

'So what did you eat at school?' I asked.

'Nothing. I just threw my lunch in the bin.'

'What, every day? Didn't your friends notice or say anything?'

'Nope, I'd just moan that it was rubbish, then I'd mess with it for a bit, then throw it.'

It's still worrying to hear all this. I knew that she had stopped eating obviously fattening and sugary things, and she had complained that she was fat, but I didn't realise that she had taken it as far as she had. It's striking how far a child can go with an eating disorder before parents become aware of it.

Had Lucy not left, Hannah would have undoubtedly continued with the eating disorder and self-harming. I am guessing that by the time I'd have been certain she needed help, she would have been well and truly in the grip of these life-destroying habits.

A lot has been said about the relationship between Lucy and Jon throughout this book, but is that really the whole story?

Jon was always committed to Lucy. Except in the family therapy session, he never said he wanted her to go. When I thought it wasn't working and that she might have to go, he insisted that he would try harder, that he could work it out. Even when I finally said she *had* to go, he still tried to persuade me otherwise.

On many occasions Jon defended or protected Lucy. Once when we were all out in the country together, near where we live, Lucy fell off her bike and cut her head. He picked her up and ran about a mile and a half home, so he could get her to hospital. Hannah and I had to meet them there because we couldn't keep up. It turned out to be not as bad as it looked but it needed gluing at the hospital.

Another time he had a bit of a run-in with a resident who lived close by because he went to retrieve a toy her child had taken away from Lucy. When she started school, he got involved every bit as much as I did, and he always put smiley faces on his comments in her reading record: Lucy loved that. He went to parents' evening, helped her prepare for school plays, was an active dad at her birthday parties and put effort into ensuring she had a social life with her friends. He drove the difficult journey on his own for a long time to maintain contact with her sister. He went for sessions at After Adoption alone to help build their relationship and he took Lucy away on his own.

Since she has gone, he has had a few tearful moments, but it didn't take him long to slip back into the lifestyle he had prior to her being here. He is saddened that it didn't work out but not heartbroken. He is clear that Hannah's cry for help had to be given priority in our lives, and that in the end we did the right thing. After Lucy left he wanted to support me because I was not doing so well; I was continually crying and was unable to attend meetings about Lucy or go to court. I was proud of the way Jon stood up to defend us; he had a strength about him that I didn't have at the time.

Jon is a doting father to Hannah and Macy, our little girl who was three years old in May 2007. My relationship with Macy has suffered because I just switched off from the pregnancy when the adoption broke down. I attended counselling sessions on the advice of the midwife as she was concerned I might succumb to post-natal depression. I didn't suffer from post-natal depression because my mind was completely full with thoughts of Hannah and Lucy.

I managed to care for Macy on a day-to-day basis. But that special connection or bonding was often missing. I remember looking at her and thinking what a sweet baby she was, but I almost couldn't recall how she got here, and sometimes I was shocked to realise that I had another baby. The only memory I have of Macy as a very tiny baby is the four days I was in hospital after she was born. I know that she is mine because I remember loving her for those four days. But as soon as I got back home I was again entirely preoccupied with Lucy and Hannah. While Hannah started to show very quick signs of recovery, the reality of the devastation to all four of us hit me. And there were ripple effects on our extended family members and also on Jade and their mother Fiona.

My mother reacted badly to the loss of Lucy, even though they didn't see each other more than a couple of times a year. I hadn't told my parents about all of the problems so I suppose it came as a shock. For a while I fell out with my mother because she didn't know about Hannah and she believed that Lucy should have stayed.

Fiona and Jade ended up losing what contact they had with Lucy. Eventually Jade had to take the local authority to court herself to obtain a Contact Order. I understand that Fiona has reverted to her previous behaviour of constantly telephoning the social worker to ask for direct contact.

I want it to be widely known that so many of our difficulties could have been avoided if child practice guidelines had been followed from the beginning. Lucy should never have moved in with us after we had spent no more than an hour-and-a-half alone with her. The inappropriate letterbox messages from Fiona and the risky contact with Jade should have been better managed, supported and monitored.

Although I hold some resentment towards the authority that dealt with us when our adoption was breaking down, the potential for learning lessons is my main concern and has nothing to do with a desire to point the finger or apportion blame. For the sake of all those children to be adopted in the future, who can be so very hurt if the adoption fails, I want at least to try to share what we have learnt the hard way. That is why I wanted to tell our story.

When we left the court on 2 December 2004, the threshold criteria had been agreed, but the final hearing was not the last. A further hearing was to be held in February 2005 because the local authority had not yet identified a permanent placement for Lucy.

It is hard to remember sometimes that we are still Lucy's parents, and that we will continue to hold legal parental responsibility for her unless she is adopted by another family. We have left a letter on her social work file to say that if she ever wants to contact us for any reason whatsoever, then we would like to hear from her. So who knows, perhaps the story has not finally ended after all.

12

The lessons learned

I searched the internet one evening and eventually came across a site where I posted a message asking if anyone had been affected by adoption breakdown. For the last year I have supported a few families who contacted me. I have no idea where they live as our correspondence has been entirely by email. The similarities in our stories are unnerving. That is, when adoptions are breaking down, local authorities do not always respond appropriately. I have personal knowledge of only four adoptions which have disrupted, but we all have a similar story to tell. That is in itself quite disconcerting.

After Lucy left, I telephoned the psychologist whom we had seen before Christmas to cancel subsequent appointments and to explain what had happened. She told me that she and her husband had had an adoption breakdown, and had a son whom they had placed back into care. She was very supportive and offered us counselling for as long as we needed it. She said that our circumstances were very similar to her own.

Our experience has highlighted some important points that I think would have helped our adoption to be more successful. None of it should come as a surprise to professionals in family placement and permanency teams. But that only makes it all the more alarming that these basic principles of good practice were disregarded in our case.

1. If there is a belief that a child has no significant attachments to anyone, then that child has attachment problems and some therapeutic work needs to be undertaken before placing the child for adoption. When Lucy moved in with us, she had an array of people involved in her life but, according to her foster carer and social worker, she would 'leave them all without a backward glance'. She had already left her birth mother and sister, she was abruptly leaving her foster family, which included aunties and a grandmother – and now there was us – how confusing!

2. The birth children of prospective adopters need to be involved in the whole adoption process (in England and Wales they can now be assessed for adoption support in their own right under the Adoption Support Regulations 2003). Hannah wanted a sister and we wanted a daughter who would be near enough in age to be Hannah's life-long companion. These were not the best reasons for adopting and should have been addressed during preparation and training.

3. It is important that prospective adopters and their children-to-be have some real understanding and knowledge of each other before they are joined together. Prospective parents must know everything about the child's routines and preferences prior to placement, as it's difficult, if not impossible, for a child to express their needs "on the day". And it can be distressing and bewildering for a child and a parent when both are unaware of what is expected of them. Simple tasks like getting ready for bed, or eating a

meal together (at a table or on your knee?) may become triggers for distress. Children can feel rejected if their routines are disregarded. Introductions should never be planned to fit in with an adult agenda. Lucy's introductions were arranged around her foster carer's admission to hospital.

4. Every measure should be taken to ensure that no inappropriate messages from a birth family member are getting through to an adopted child. Lucy suffered a lot of anxiety, fear and confusion that led to her not knowing where she belonged, because the contact with her birth mother and sister was not monitored or reviewed properly. Letterbox contact needs to be carefully managed – it is not an easy option.

5. Prospective adopters need to know everything about the children being placed with them. We only discovered from medical records after the disruption that we hadn't been told about Lucy's tantrums 'that can last for hours and hours' and that she was seeing a child psychologist prior to being placed with us. Those tantrums continued, when she was with us, for a considerable time. I understand that they have resurfaced in foster care. The positive note here is that Lucy's current social worker has referred her for further psychological assessments.

6. Action should be taken if there are signs of specific relationship difficulties in an adoption placement. We informed social services early on that there were problems with Jon and Lucy's relationship. They pointed us in the direction of After Adoption, but there was no follow-up even though Lucy was still on a Care Order to the local authority.

7. I strongly believe that the current method of

responding to the risk of adoption breakdown by many local authorities is inadequate. Dealing with disruption requires family placement and adoption expertise and should not be left to Initial Assessment and Child Protection teams, as it often is. These teams have little experience of adoption or knowledge of the law in relation to adoption. New legislation should go some way to ensure that expert advice and support is more readily available, as of right, until adopted children reach the age of 18.

8. Adoptive families should be trusted and treated as responsible parents unless there are concerns about safeguarding the children. Above all else, when adoptive families are in a state of crisis, they must be taken seriously. Their views need to be heard, their perceptions have to be taken into account and their pain has to be acknowledged. Lucy flourished with us for four years in spite of many problems. Letting her go was the hardest thing we have ever had to face.

9. When a family is saying that they have tried all they can and that the placement must end, the adopted child could be at risk of emotional abuse if action isn't taken to support the child. One of the families that I was in touch with by email ended up with the child isolated in his bedroom because he was not moved or worked with when the parents said the adoption had broken down. In our own case we all became emotionally distant from Lucy when we determined to end the adoption – but neither she nor we had anyone to help us with our feelings.

10. When an adoption does break down, a disruption meeting should be held with all concerned to explore what went wrong and why, and to inform future plans for the child, including

contact arrangements and other ways of maintaining continuity.

*   *   *

On 8 January 2004 we were a family of four with some vision of our future. We were soon to be a family of five, and we were all excited about that. We had spent the last twelve months completely renovating the house. We had decided to take a break from decorating until after Christmas – we'd get it finished early in the New Year.

It turned out to be two years before we got around to completing it.

Macy was almost eighteen months old before I felt able to make a good enough effort to really truly bond with her.

That's how long it took for the impact of Hannah's self-harming and Lucy's leaving to begin to subside, and for us to generate the enthusiasm to do normal things again.

Unfortunately, we don't know what the long-term impact will be on Lucy. She is still waiting for her "forever family" and she is still our absent daughter. We found and lost each other and we have all been damaged as well as enriched by the experience we shared.